DUNCTON RISING

Based on Mayweed's map found in Seven Barrows

WILLIAM HORWOOD

DUNCTON RISING

Volume Two of
THE BOOK OF SILENCE

HarperCollins*Publishers*

HarperCollins*Publishers*
77–85 Fulham Palace Road,
Hammersmith, London W6 8JB

Published by HarperCollins*Publishers* 1992
9 8 7 6 5 4 3 2 1

Copyright © William Horwood 1992

The Author asserts the moral right to
be identified as the author of this work

A catalogue record for this book is
available from the British Library

ISBN 0 00 223941 8

Set in Linotron Caledonia by
Rowland Phototypesetting Ltd
Bury St Edmunds, Suffolk

Printed in Great Britain by
HarperCollinsManufacturing Glasgow

Moles who appeared in *Duncton Tales*, Volume One of *The Book of Silence*

AVENS   A young and aimless would-be scholar from Avebury.

BANTAM   A Duncton female who becomes a Newborn. Sadistic and vindictive, and a friend of Snyde.

BARRE   Newborn Senior Brother Inquisitor, of a bullying sadistic kind.

CHAMFER   Drubbins' young brother and a keeper of the peace.

CHATER   A journeymole working for the Duncton Library, and mate of Fieldfare.

CHERVIL   A powerful and senior Newborn Brother.

COBBETT   Master Librarian of Beechenhill, and brother of Stour and Husk.

COMPLINE   Senior Delver of Compline Chamber of the Charnel.

DRUBBINS   Elder of Duncton Wood at the time of Privet's arrival, and a close friend of Stour.

DRUMLIN   Daughter of Gaunt and mother of Glee.

FETTER   A Newborn Senior Brother Inquisitor sent by Thripp to 'cleanse' the Duncton Library of blasphemous texts. He travels in company with his colleagues Law and Barre, among whom he is first among equals.

FEY   Kindly female who helped her mate Tarn care for Shire in Crowden.

FIELDFARE   Middle-aged female who befriends Privet on her arrival at Duncton. Resident of the Eastside and mate of Chater.

FIDDLER   A young warrior mole of the Rollright system.

FIRKIN   Copy Master of the Duncton Library.

GAUNT   The leader, known as Mentor, of the lost delvers of the Charnel Clough. Father of Drumlin.

GLEE   Albino female contemporary of Rooster in the Charnel Clough, close friend of Humlock.

HILBERT	Legendary last known medieval Master of the Delve. Founder of the Charnel Clough delving tradition.
HUME	A Senior Delver of the Charnel, and Rooster's mentor.
HUMLOCK	Blind, deaf-mute contemporary of Rooster in the Charnel Clough; close friend of Glee.
HUSK	Reclusive Keeper of Rolls, Rhymes and Tales, brother of Stour and Cobbett. Killed by the Newborns at the end of *Duncton Tales*.
LAVENDER	Drubbins' mate.
LAW	Newborn Senior Brother Inquisitor, in Duncton with Fetter and Barre.
LIME	Privet's spiteful sister by Shire, and the favoured one.
MAPLE	Nephew of Lavender, much respected for his strength and fighting knowledge; but essentially a gentle mole. Has not yet come into his own.
NONE	Female Senior Delver of the None Chamber of the Charnel.
PRIME	Dwarf Senior Delver in charge of Prime Chamber of the Charnel. Half sister of Gaunt.
PRIVET	Scribemole born at Crowden in the Moors. Daughter of Shire, granddaughter of the infamous Eldrene Wort. Is in search of the Book of Silence, the last of seven Books of Moledom. She is now middle-aged and once 'loved and lost' Rooster.
PUMPKIN	Library aide who works closely with Stour. Now elderly but fiercely loyal to his Master and entrusted with the task of helping to resist the Newborns.
RED RATCHER	Rapine leader of the Ratcher Clan of the Charnel Clough. He fathers Rooster by Samphire, the only one of his mates he cannot dominate.
ROOSTER	Son of Red Ratcher and Samphire, born in the obscure Charnel Clough high on the Saddleworth Moors. Believed to be a Modern Master of the Delve, the first in centuries, but a wild, massive, ugly, unpredictable mole. Once Privet's beloved.
SAMPHIRE	Rooster's mother. Originally abducted from Chieveley Dale by Red Ratcher.
SANS	Foster-mother of Shire, a cold disciplinarian.
SEDUM	Mother of Humlock.
SEXT	Senior Delver of the Sext Chamber of the Charnel.

SHIRE	Privet's mother, and herself daughter of Wort.
SNYDE	Unpleasant hunchbacked scholar and scribemole who has clawed his way up to be Deputy Master of the Library.
STOUR	Master Librarian of Duncton Wood and regarded as the greatest scholar and librarian in moledom. Now near the end of his days, and an outspoken enemy of the Newborns. He is in secret retreat in the Ancient System.
STURNE	Unsmiling librarian, one of the Keepers in the Library. Trusted before all others (but Pumpkin) by Stour, who has always appeared to reject him. He alone knows of Stour's final retreat, and its purpose. Nomole knows that his affiliation to the Newborns is a courageous pretence.
SWARD	Known as Sward the Scholar. A wandering scribemole of the Moors.
TARN	An aide in the Crowden Library, who befriended Shire. Mate to Fey.
TERCE	Senior Delver of the Terce Chamber of the Charnel.
THRIPP	Sinister but charismatic leader of the Newborns, originally of Blagrove Slide, now resident at Caer Caradoc. He is Chervil's father, but little else personal is known about him.
TURRELL	A grike mole living in seclusion on the Moors with his mate, Myrtle.
WESLEY	Scholarly Newborn who helped form Newborn cell in Duncton's Marsh End. His coming warned Stour how dangerous the Newborn sect might be.
WHILLAN	Parents unknown. Fostered by Privet after being mysteriously discovered by Stour at the cross-under into Duncton Wood, his newborn siblings dead, his unnamed mother dying. Trained in scribing by Privet and Pumpkin. As yet untried and untested.
WORTHING	A Newborn Brother who lives in the Marsh End.

Characters from *The Duncton Chronicles* referred to in *Duncton Tales*

BALLAGAN   Sometimes called the 'First Mole'. His story has not been told but he is thought to be the founder of the Seven Ancient Systems, and father of moledom.

BRACKEN   Duncton mole from the Westside who is hero and leader against Mandrake in *Duncton Wood*. Lover of Rebecca.

MAYWEED   A great route-finder and aide and friend to Tryfan and Spindle.

SPINDLE   Former aide at Uffington, befriended by Tryfan, to whom he became a brave and loyal assistant.

TRYFAN   Bracken's wise son, born at the end of Duncton Wood. He becomes leader of the followers against the moles of the Word.

WORT   The 'Eldrene' Wort was an evil ally of the moles of the Word in *Duncton Quest* and *Duncton Found* who caused much harm to the followers. She escaped to the Moors, sought the Stone's forgiveness, and gave birth to Shire.

CONTENTS

PROLOGUE

So, mole, you lost no time finding your way back to me here in the Clearing by the Duncton Stone!

Though from your appearance this early morning – the rough look to your fur, the bleariness in your eyes, the unsteadiness of your paws – it seems you have had little sleep.

No, no, tell me not about the revelries of last night, of the food eaten and the tales well told; least of all of the new friends you've made, whose company, no doubt, you'll go scurrying after just as soon as you've heard the tale I promised to tell you today.

It's not that I am not interested in life down in Barrow Vale, but rather that my mind is already filled with moles aplenty, and tales, and a time of special trial and tribulation in this system of ours when such triumphs as we had were so hard won.

You see, whilst you made yourself so busy through the night with living moles, I made myself busy too, remembering moles who though no longer here in body, are hereabout in spirit; and thinking how it is that their faith, their courage, and their loyalty to each other and the Stone have lived on through the days and years of time to imbue this Stone with something of its special Light.

That you make the effort despite so long a night to come in time to see the rising of the sun is most appropriate, in view of the nature of the tale that we are about to embark upon. For was it not at this very time of day – though it was a winter's morning, not a summer's – and in this very Clearing, that Duncton found its strength and pride again so long ago? It was! And that is what I wish to speak about.

But if you want to hear this new tale, find me food again, indulge my meanderings of thought, and scribe as you have never scribed before, imagining yourself to be not the scribemole taking down the text but the very text itself come into being as I speak.

Since our tale begins at dawn here by the Stone, and for all you may know will end here too, I suggest you call it 'Duncton Rising'. Yes, yes, scribe it down, mole, scribe that down . . .

1

Good. You have scribed it. It will be so then for ever more: *Duncton Rising*. Most suitable and apt.

Even better, you've got me some worms, and you're watching with a worried frown to see that I eat at least a few, almost as if you doubt that I can cling on to life much longer. Be of greater faith, mole, for I am a *Duncton* mole, and therefore I cling on until the rightful end, trusting that my faith in the Stone, and my love of mole, will see me through.

Let us be silent for a time; let us listen to the light wind in the trees and the rustling resonance of the High Wood about the Stone; let us wait here where we are, which is always the best place to begin a tale, for before long, if we have faith enough, my memory and your trust will surely bring to life a mole whose coming will begin our tale for us.

Aye, listen, mole! Can you not hear it now, the sound of somemole approaching? Stance down and be quiet, get your scribing paw ready again, for I do believe that our tale has found its own beginning, and whatmole can speak of the wonders to which it may yet take us!

See, *here* he comes, there, just by the Stone itself . . .

A timid, elderly, unassuming kind of mole, isn't he? With less fur than he once had to cover his worn body! But don't dismiss *him* – as brave moles go, he is among the very best and most courageous.

I might have known *he* would be the one! For what would Duncton's rising against the Newborn threat have been without him? See him, listen to him, pay him respect, for we might wait on a hundred years before we found a better beginning to our tale this morning than he will give us, as the sun rises beyond the Stone and we venture back to a great time, to the company of great moles, and seek to learn at last to hear with them the Silence of the Stone.

PART I

Prayers and Pilgrims

Chapter One

November, dawn, and a hurrying mole.

Dank malevolent flurries of wind harried the deserted reaches of the High Wood on Duncton Hill, rushing about the ancient beech trees and threatening at their roots before hurrying on; while overhead, between the leafless treetops, grey clouds dragged after each other across the sky and out of sight.

Dull, poor light as yet; of a dreary, wintry kind, that did nothing to cheer the heart of the humble mole who had made his way up out of his isolated tunnels, across the slopes and now reached the Stone Clearing itself.

Pumpkin, elderly Library Aide to the Duncton Library which had so recently fallen into the censoring paws of the Newborn Inquisitors, had come to say his prayers. It had long been his custom to do so daily, and these days he did so at dawn, for it was only then that he could be sure that the busybody Newborn guards and zealots would not be about, and he could make his way to the Stone unimpeded, free to say words and offer a faith whose daily ritual was his only strength in this time of doubt.

Having journeyed through this particular wintry dawn and arrived at the Stone Clearing, his mind as full as ever of history, self-doubt, and growing fears for others, the mole Pumpkin struggled to cast all thoughts aside and begin his prayers. He stared up at the Stone, he stared away from it, he fretted at the ground, he sighed and turned to face the Stone again.

'Harder, ever harder,' he whispered. 'But now . . .'

He began as he often did by asking the Stone to continue to offer its protection to all those engaged in the struggle against the Newborn moles, though doubts and small rebellions of faith were not far away. Indeed his petition for moles in general, sincere though it was, was usually but the prelude to matters that really concerned him more, and this particular dawn his thoughts turned to absent moles to whom, in better times, he might have turned for succour and support in his self-effacing way. Yet with the Stone, his courage fully summoned, his thoughts getting clearer by the moment, he dared be more direct.

'If I may be so bold, Stone, you might keep a special watch on the following *particular* moles for whom, as you know, I have especial fondness. I hope you will not think it presumptuous of me to remind you of whatmoles they are, and what they have done for your cause, though no doubt your memory is infinite and all-embracing; but the fact is that in troubled times like these an ordinary mole like me finds it all too easy to forget that you are on our side . . .'

He spoke in a puzzled, gentle voice, as if he did not quite like the rebellious direction in which his thoughts were taking him.

'I cannot truthfully say,' he continued, 'that you have showered the High Wood with what I might call hints or signs of encouragement in recent days. In fact a mole might even think that you had forgotten us altogether . . .'

A certain acerbity now came to Pumpkin's voice, and the semblance of a frown, though a weak one, marked his brow. Library Aide Pumpkin, it seemed, had grave doubts about the Stone and the unpleasant changes it had recently allowed (as it seemed to him) to occur in the state of moledom.

'I urge you, Stone, to try to see things from a mole's point of view and to appreciate that though we may have faith in your plans for the future, *we* have to put up with the present, and all the terrible things that are now going on in the Library, and in Duncton Wood as a whole. It makes even a cheerful mole like me feel dejected sometimes, and in need of encouragement which, lacking friends as I now do since they've all gone off in your name, I somewhat miss!'

The dawn wind flurried about him, the wet leaves shifted and trembled on the ground and Pumpkin essayed a smile as if to say 'I have moaned and whinged a bit, and feel better for doing so, but perhaps I should now get on with the important part of my prayer'.

'Now, let me see, there's quite a list of moles whom I wish to commend to your attention and care, beginning of course with the Master Librarian himself, Stour, who at this very moment is in retreat in the dangerous and forgotten tunnels of the Ancient System which lie here below the High Wood. I trust you're keeping an eye on him, and making sure he's not lonely or hurt in any way. Many's the time in the past days I've been inclined to go down into the tunnels myself to see if he needs me, for no Master Librarian could have been more kind nor more thoughtful to a Library Aide as *him*. No, none *could* have been . . .'

Tears came to kindly Pumpkin's eyes as he thought of the mole he

6

loved so well, who had taught him all he knew about books, their cataloguing, and their conservation.

'Well, Stone, I can tell you that if he hadn't given such very strict instructions that he was to be left alone I would have gone to him before now, or at least tried to. But if ever you think I should go to Master Stour – if he's in need, or needs support – you tell me in some way, for I'll do for him all that I can.

'Meanwhile, there's other moles to think of and worry about for whom these prayers will not go amiss. There's your old friend Drubbins for one, who's the only other apart from me of those whom Master Stour entrusted with his final thoughts and instructions before he went into retreat, who was ordered to stay in Duncton Wood. Now Drubbins isn't looking too well these days, which isn't surprising as he's having to deal with the Newborns, whom he doesn't like, all day long, and do his best not to betray his friends in the Wood. Give him strength, Stone, give him your love.

'Then there's the five good moles who left the Wood at Stour's bidding, to try to see what they could do to right matters, and find out something about the lost Book of Silence, and, if they could, bring it back to Duncton. There's not one of those five that I, Pumpkin, Library Aide, am not proud to call a friend, proud to know, and proud to think that on the glorious day when they come back home again they'll seek me out and say, "Pumpkin, we're glad to see you once more, and to see that some things in our beloved system don't change and are dependable!"'

Once more tears came to Pumpkin's eyes, indeed they trickled down his grey face-fur as he stared at the Stone, and visualized this reunion of moles who loved, trusted and respected each other, and might one day – if the Stone granted it – be all together once again.

'I'll say their names, Stone, if you don't mind, though I'm sure you're growing tired of my repeating them in my prayers to you. But in this time of trial and loneliness my prayers here in the Stone Clearing are what keep me going, and saying the names of my friends helps me believe that they're alive and well, and will come home again one day, safeguarded. There's Fieldfare and her beloved Chater, both commanded by the Master Stour to go in the direction of Avebury and muster support for the Stone, or at least remind moles of the dangers of the Newborn creed. There's Maple, strong Maple, who I've always thought had a destiny to lead moles in battle, for when he was a youngster didn't he come to me and ask to be shown texts about campaigning, battles and the like? Didn't I myself help him with the difficult words, and take him about this Wood and show him where the great battles of our own past were fought? I did! I ask you to look after him, and see that he fights justly and truly, as I told him great leaders do. And you see to it, too, that when the time comes, he knows when to pull in his talons and say "Enough is enough"!

'Then there's Whillan, who does not seem old enough to be gallivanting about moledom at a dangerous time like this – but that's what the Master ordered, and so it has to be. Now, Stone, I remember the day he was carried into the Library by the Master himself, who had found him down at the cross-under beneath the roaring owl way with his mother dying and his newborn siblings all killed by the rooks.

'Bless me, but I've never seen a sight like it, nor want to again, as when that poor pup, struggling for breath, shivering with cold, and bleating his little life away, lay on the Library floor with all those old books about him, and nervous aides wondering what the Master was about bringing him there. From that day I watched Whillan grow, and when, like Maple before him, he came to me to learn scribing and explore the Library, why, it was the nearest I ever got to having a pup of my own. Of course, I'd never admit this to anymole, but I feel I contributed something to Whillan's rearing, and I can't believe you would want him to come to harm in the wide world beyond this system of ours having, as it were, had such a hard and tragic time getting into it. But there's not a day goes by but I worry for him, and I hope you're watching over him, for he hadn't had time to grow up and find himself before the Newborns came and the Master ordered him off into moledom to do what he could for the Stone's cause. Protect Whillan well, Stone, for there was always a special light in his eyes, and a certain set to his snout that said to me that this was a mole among moles; one whose destiny would carry something of your Light, and honour your Silence.

'Lastly, there's Privet, *scholar* Privet, who you know well enough without me having to tell you that I learned to love and respect her more than any other of the scribemoles that came through the portals of the Library. She's a great mole, Stone, and all the greater since Stour insisted that it was she who reared and nurtured Whillan, despite her protests. That was a heart-warming thing that was, seeing a prim and proper scholar like her coming to grips with a mischievous pup such as Whillan was.

'Aye, you *do* work in mysterious ways, Stone, making moles grow and deepen in themselves, as if you're preparing them for tasks only you know are coming their way. I never in all my life worked for so

8

wise and modest a scholar as Privet, excepting the Master himself, of course. She could scribe Whernish as well as Mole, she could ken a mediaeval story as well as a modern one, and despite her chilly exterior she could make moles love her and be loyal to her – even journeymole Chater, who never had much time for scholars.

'But off she went as well, with Maple and Whillan to watch over her, the scribemole who I believe the Master knew would one day, somehow, find the lost Book of Silence and bring it back to Duncton Wood. All that will be very well, but all *I* ask on her behalf is that when her task is done you give her time and space to find the one thing that eludes moles unless they live right however good their scholarship: happiness. For *that* was something that was lacking in her eyes, and on her thin and troubled face, even when young Whillan was at his most endearing; even then she seemed to fear it could not last. But that's it, isn't it, Stone? She never feels, not ever, that happiness can last, or the friendship of another mole, and so fear of the future destroys her pleasures in the present.

'And we know the reason, don't we, Stone? Or part of it at any rate . . . Its name is a mole's – Rooster, Master of the Delve, a *most* mysterious mole, most striking. Not the kind of mole I would like to meet on a dark night, or down in a ruined chamber served by ancient tunnels. But there we are, there's no accounting for love, and it seems that *he*'s the mole she loved and lost. A mole, I fancy, she could do with finding once again to tell him . . . Well, an old mole like me who's never had a mate and never will, won't presume to put words into her mouth for what she should say to a mole such as Rooster, should she ever find him. But Stone, please an old mole, and bring those two together once again; if you do, I'll die happy, with my faith in your essential goodness fully restored!

'So there they are, the moles I wish to pray for this miserable dawn, and those on whom I believe a great deal may depend. Watch over them, Stone, guide them, help them, show them your Light and let them be touched by your Silence.'

Pumpkin was silent for a time, and seemed to have finished; the wind flurried on about him and the dawn's light brightened a little towards another morning. Yet he looked up once more at the grey Stone, so silent, so unyielding, so forbidding, and half opened his mouth to say something more. Then he seemed to have second thoughts, and shook his head and turned forlornly away, as lonely and isolated a mole as any who had ever come to the Duncton Stone for prayer and guidance.

9

Yet even as he headed east out of the Clearing, to cross the High Wood to begin another wretched day in thrall to the Newborn Inquisitors, he paused, and scuffed at the leaves a bit, and turned round to face the Stone once more. A watching mole would barely have seen him, for Pumpkin's grey and wizened form was almost lost in the huge shadows and shapes of the beech tree roots.

'There's another mole, isn't there, Stone? One I should pray for as well . . .'

Pumpkin looked reluctant, and grumpy. He frowned again, and pursed his mouth with distaste at having to even think about this other mole; then a look of annoyance came into his eyes and he found something different to say, something which justified avoiding adding to his prayers a mole for whom, it seemed, he felt rather less love than he felt for the others, but to whom he still had some kind of duty.

'Can't pray for ever without a bit of encouragement,' he said, his eyes dropping from the Stone to the damp beech leaves which covered the Clearing's floor. 'I need a sign to keep me going, a *hint* that something good is on the way. Nomole prays for *me*, you know. I mean, I know that Master Librarian Stour said it would be hard, but I didn't think it would be *this* hard. It's not that I'm blaming *you*, Stone, because of course allmole knows you're above blame, just as, if I may say so, you are above praise. You *are*, and we're the ones who have to struggle and strive, aren't we? Not that you should construe that as criticism, though I admit that if I had a choice between being a Stone or a mole I would, this particular dawn, choose to be a Stone.

'The simple fact is that I feel I am not up to the task you have set me. I feel I should remind you that I am a mere library *aide* whose position until now has demanded only that he fetches and carries for scholars and scribemoles, tendering advice when he is asked, and keeping order for those who have not time for such tedious work. Is it reasonable, this Library Aide humbly asks, that he should be required to fulfil some other task whose nature, whose beginning and ending, whose demands, remain unspecified and mysterious? It is not!'

Pumpkin, now thoroughly roused on his own behalf, even took a step or two back towards the Stone before he continued.

'Now, Stone, I do not wish to bargain with you, but if I may say so, this particular mole would be motivated rather better than he is if you could apply a small part of your infinite and eternal wisdom to finding a way to show me that I am on the right track. This would help. So, too, would some hint that I am not alone in my struggle and that there are other moles about who share the burden. Yes, that's it, that's my personal petition to you this dawn: send a sign!'

Pumpkin continued to stare boldly at the Stone for a moment or two longer before, his ire dying, he retreated back into the modest and kindly mole he truly was and looked meek and apologetic.

'Well,' he added feebly, 'that's about it. Well, all right, almost it.'

How forbidding the Stone was, how silent, how great the void into which a mole of faith, as Pumpkin was, must utter his prayers!

'As for that other mole, and you know the one I mean, it is *very* hard for me to add him to my prayers. Why, he came to the Library the same day I did so many decades ago, and as he's risen and gained seniority and honours I've stayed just an aide, and I don't begrudge it, I really don't. Sturne always had talents for study and scholarship that I did not have. And when he's come to my burrow, as he has from time to time at seasons of celebration because he and I have no other moles to share such occasions with, I've been pleased with his taciturn company, and I've been happy to hear his attempts at being merry. But, Stone, it's hard, it's so hard, now the Inquisitors have made him Master of the Library in the proper Master's place, and he's accepted all they say, and their ways, and he daily orders me to destroy text after text and never *once* shows any remorse or guilt.

'But, Stone, I feel that of them all he's the one who needs your help most, the one I should pray for above others. Therefore, Stone, give your help and guidance to Keeper Sturne, lead him back to thy good ways, and may the day come once more when he and I can share a worm or two in companionship, and look back at this time as a nightmare which is long gone and forgotten. Because you see, Stone, whenever others have said bad things about Sturne (and many have over the decades, I assure you, because he's not a mole who endears himself to others, or makes friends), I have never once let those comments pass without supporting him, and saying that there's something good in him, something solid, something *true*, and I say it again now, to you, Stone. Help him now in this time of trial, for even from our first day in the Library I felt that for all his talents with texts, *you* had given me something he did not have, which was a capacity for contentment, for happiness. Stone, Keeper Sturne has never given me or any other mole a reason to call him friend, but I count him among my friends, and pray for him now.'

Pumpkin bowed his wrinkled head towards the Stone, evidently

11

glad to have got over his reluctance and spoken out on behalf of Sturne. He paused a little, nodded with new-found ease and contentment, and turned for the last time from the Stone and was lost among the great trees of the High Wood, as modest, as good, as loving a mole as there could be. One well worthy, indeed, to represent the legendary qualities of the moles of Duncton Wood, who have stanced boldly by the Stone in times of doubt and faithlessness, and uttered their prayers, and raised their paws in defence of the Light, and the truth, and the Silence, which are of the Stone.

But it seemed that he was right, for as he went there was nomole to say a prayer for *him*. None to petition the Stone on his behalf, or to speak aloud of his qualities, and commending them to the Stone, ask it to guide him through the great shadows that now beset him on all sides, and bring *him* through safeguarded.

Yet perhaps there *was* something more, and perhaps though he knew it not, those dear lost friends he had prayed for uttered their prayers for him that same dawn. For as he turned his back and wended his way wearily through the High Wood, the light about the Stone grew bright, and a warm spirit met the flurries of the cold wind and turned them and chased them away, a spirit of grace which danced from the Clearing after Pumpkin. So that when it caught up with him, and he was all unawares, its Light seemed to shine on his old fur, and its Silence to accompany him, to catch up with him, and be with him.

So much so indeed that he stopped and stared about in wonder, as if he half sensed something was there. His mild eyes were caught by a Light he could not see, and his loving heart was comforted by a Silence he could not quite hear. But something was there, something . . .

'Send a sign!' he had prayed, and at least he now understood with the certainty of his great and simple faith that a sign *might* come.

Then Library Aide Pumpkin continued on his way, his step light for the first time in days, and a hum of pleasure mounting in his throat. For he realized that when all was said and done, and however grim things seemed, he was still what he most wished to be in the place he wished to be it; a library aide in what all his life had always been the greatest Library in moledom.

'And it will be again, it *will*!' he said to himself before resuming his cheerful humming, and thinking that even on a grey November dawn when there is as little hope among the trees as there are leaves, there was surely nowhere as beautiful in all moledom as the ancient High Wood of Duncton.

Pumpkin's doubts and concerns about the state of moledom and the safety of his friends, not to mention uneasiness at his own dangerously isolated position in Duncton Wood, were well justified by recent events.

The slow insidious build-up of the Newborn presence in Duncton Wood, which had begun twenty moleyears before with the arrival of a small cell of Caradocian moles preaching the creed as promulgated by the sinister Thripp of Blagrove Slide, had reached its culmination only shortly before Pumpkin spoke his long petitionary prayer before the Stone. Newborns had come up from the Marsh End one night, and though they may not originally have intended to go as far as they did, had killed old Husk, Keeper of Rolls, Rhymes and Tales, and had deliberately destroyed his great collection of texts.

But wise Stour, Master Librarian of Duncton Wood, had long since foreseen better than anymole what was coming. Having been raised in Duncton Wood, the system more dedicated than any in moledom to the rights and freedom implicit in worship of the Stone – which rights include the freedom *not* to worship the Stone – he foresaw the inevitable consequence of Thripp's self-righteous movement, which was increasingly quick to condemn those who were deemed not to subscribe to the strict Caradocian way, and even to punish them.

Master Librarian Stour had long believed that once the Newborns had gained power and felt confident that none could easily stance in their path, then they would inevitably begin to censor moledom's great libraries of any texts that might be construed as liberal, or in some way undermining the 'true' Caradocian way. It had been against such possibilities, which his study of history had shown repeated themselves with grim regularity, that Stour had advocated long before, and then brilliantly carried through, the policy of copying and disseminating texts to twelve different systems in moledom, believing that their general availability – indeed their continuing existence – would thereby be assured. This policy, for which he won agreement at the famous Conclave of Cannock, which was convened soon after his appointment as Duncton's Master Librarian over four decades before, was as much as moledom could have done to safeguard its texts, ancient and modern, but Stour can have little thought that its efficacy would have been tested in his own lifetime by such a censorious movement as that of the Newborns.

Yet finally the question had been, as the moles of Duncton had grown increasingly aware, exactly when Thripp and those close to him would decide to make a claim for control of moledom as a whole – in the name, naturally, of truth, justice and freedom. Stour had expected that when it came to Duncton Wood it would be in a form more subtle and less cruel than proved to be the case with the attack on Keeper Husk. But then, in the past, other more worldly Duncton leaders might have gathered intelligence from systems beyond Duncton Wood, guessing that the Newborns were unlikely to make a bid to control one of the greatest systems of moledom until long after they had secured their positions in other lesser systems.

But Stour was first and foremost a scholar and librarian, not a military or political mole. And yet . . . as those few moles who like Pumpkin were not yet intimidated by the Newborn presence reflected on such matters, they could not but admit the fact that the Master had *never* really been 'only' a librarian, and concede the possibility that his seeming indifference to the rise of the Newborns over the previous two decades might conceal a deep and thoughtful strategy.

Certainly Pumpkin himself now believed that the reason for the only other retreat the Master had made into the tunnels of the Ancient System (in the spring years prior to the present crisis) was his need to reflect on the best way for Duncton moles to respond to the Newborn move to take control when it came. Pumpkin was sure that Stour was not interested in wars – the decades of peace that followed the terrible war of Word and Stone a century before reflected moledom's general desire to avoid such conflicts again. Nor were there many systems in moledom that did not still harbour the bloody ghosts and shadows of the war of the Word, in tunnels that had been sealed up to hide the massacred dead from sight: such tragic tunnels, their corpses turned to skeletons, all intertwined with the roots and tendrils of trees and plants from the surface above, were found from time to time, a reminder to living moles of the dangers of war and religious strife. Few vales and rises, few quiet places in woods and by streams, had not heard the cries of the victims of the Word.

On these things Stour must have reflected long and hard as the shadows of strife lengthened once more. Having pondered the past, he had decided that so far as he could influence it future defenders of the Stone must seek a different solution for peace as the Newborns gained strength; and certainly, they must explore every peaceful means available before resorting to fighting.

Stour had said as much to those moles he had commanded to escape the system, whom Pumpkin had just prayed for; he had done so in the belief that the solution to a peaceful future lay in the discovery of the Book of Silence, popularly known to moles as the 'lost and last' Book, for it was the only one of the seven Books of Moledom which had not been recovered through the decades and brought to the care of successive Master Librarians of Duncton Wood. By the time Stour took up the Mastership six of the seven Books had 'come to ground' (as the ancient prophecy put it), and only the Book of Silence remained to be found and brought to Duncton to be reverently laid once more in its rightful place, which was with the other six beneath the Duncton Stone itself.

So Stour's answer to the rise of the Newborns had finally been not a counter-struggle by armies of Stone followers, but the sending of a single mole, Privet, supported by only a few others, to search for the 'lost Book'; and while she did that, he himself went into a final retreat in the eerie tunnels of the Ancient System beneath the High Wood, whose ways nomole knew, and whose Dark Sound nomole could surely long survive. Yet there he had gone, taking with him the six Books of Moledom already in the Library and, as Pumpkin and the others had discovered to their astonishment, a whole host of other texts which he had secreted away in the tunnels against such dire days of Inquisition and censorship as had now come about. His task was to hide these precious texts until better times came, and to be a living example in prayer and retreat of spiritual resistance to the new evil.

Of allies left in Duncton Wood, apart from Pumpkin himself, there seemed only one: Drubbins. He was Stour's contemporary and oldest friend, the mole who had led the system in all general matters which had nothing to do with the Library itself, but who was now too old to hope to travel. He had, in any case, preferred to stay, and, with Pumpkin, do what he might to bamboozle and hinder the Newborn Inquisitors – a thankless and probably hopeless task.

But the other mole who had stayed behind had not been revealed by Stour as an ally at all – indeed most of Stour's friends regarded him as a dour, unlikeable kind of mole – Keeper Sturne. Morose, silent, without the natural good grace and friendliness of a Drubbins or a Pumpkin, his career in the Library had long been overshadowed by other moles, notably Snyde, brilliant scholar, vindictive librarian, warped mole who had the odour of a deviance which had not yet fully emerged; the mole whom Stour had, unaccountably as it seemed, appointed Deputy Master in preference to Sturne.

Chapter Two

The escape of Privet and the others from Duncton Wood in the face of Newborn attack, guided by Chater, had gone unnoticed, and by the time dawn arose on the seventh day following their departure they were well away. They had lain low for several days somewhere in the flat flood plains of the Thames that lie to its south.

'Seeing as Fieldfare here has never ventured a single pawstep out of Duncton before, and you, Whillan, have but little experience of journeying, we're going to take things slowly at first,' said Chater purposefully, once it was plain that the Newborns had not followed them, and they had all recovered from the rigours of the previous days and nights. He was a solid, rough-furred journeymole, something past middle age, with a gravelly voice and direct manner that belied the good nature that made him so much beloved by Fieldfare, his lifelong mate.

'This is anonymous sort of ground to cover with a thousand different ways to go, and a mole would have to be unlucky or foolish for pursuers to find him here. Anyway, I think that the Master was right to say that if Snyde does set off to find you, Privet, and with others too no doubt, he'll go by the more obvious northern way, by Rollright – so he'll get further away with each day that passes until such time as your Caradoc route swings you north and towards him once again.

'Now I said we'll go slowly, but I didn't mean easy. Trouble is, as a journeymole I'm trained to feel responsible for you all and since Fieldfare and I are going to part company from you at Swinford I've only got until then to teach you what I can about the business of journeying. Of course, Keeper Privet here, as with much else, prob-ably knows a lot more than she lets on – must do, to have got down to Duncton from the north in safety all those years ago. But then maybe she'll have forgotten a bit, and won't mind—'

'I don't mind at all,' said Privet promptly, a little smile softening the natural severity of her face. 'You tell us all you think we need to know, and anything else besides.'

'Well, I'll address my remarks to young Whillan here,' said Chater

16

promptly, 'and if you others pay me the compliment of listening, so much the better. Now let's start the lessons right away . . .'

He looked ahead and wrinkled his eyes as he gazed keenly at the route they were to take. Then he raised his snout and scented at the air a bit before inclining his head and listening hard for good measure.

'Wakes a mole up to look about a bit before moving a paw,' he grunted, 'especially when there's something in the air that warns him to expect roaring owls to cross his path.'

'Already?' said Fieldfare uneasily. They had crossed under the roaring owl way to get out of Duncton Wood, and later passed under again to get on to their present route, but this was the first time they had to set paw on ground where roaring owls went.

'Already, my love? You've got to assume it's all the bloody time in an area like this! Yes, that sickly, oily smell is their fumes, and these ruts in our path big enough to drown a mole if they get muddy, are their tracks . . .'

There was a sudden roaring behind them from beyond the high hedge of a ploughed field, and the ground vibrated so much that Fieldfare nearly jumped out of her ample skin.

'Get in the grass and keep your snouts down while it goes by – and don't worry, it'll be a slow one,' called out Chater, making sure the others had dived for cover before he himself did. 'It's the fast ones that make no noise you've got to fear . . .' he continued indefatigably as it approached.

The great roaring owl, with its gyrating black paws and shiny glinting eyes rattled and roared past them and on down the path ahead, and peace came back to the countryside once more; Chater pulled himself out of hiding, ran back on to the path, and looked on the way it had gone.

'We're not going to follow it?' said Fieldfare, emerging from the grass more slowly, and smoothing her fur back down.

'It's the quickest route we'll find,' said Chater cheerfully, 'and journeymoles like making things easy for themselves. Now there are five kinds of roaring owls and that one was the most benign.'

'I would have thought a dead one is the best,' said Maple, as they continued on their way. He was large, strong, young-looking and alert and though he carried himself with natural authority he was easy with it, and able to be self-effacing and willing to learn from anymole who had something to offer, as Chater had.

'So you might, lad, so you might,' said Chater, 'but you'd be wrong.

17

Dead roaring owls have all kinds of holes and havens, tunnels and shelters which no self-respecting creature like a mole would go near, but which certain other living things, like adders for one, and foxes for another, not to mention screech owls and the like, are not slow to use. You've got to go carefully with a dead roaring owl, I can tell you . . .'

So Chater shared his experience and told them all he could in the few days they had together, condensing a lifetime of journeying as he told them how to watch the ways ahead, and to guard the rear, and showed them how to make a scrape-shelter safe for the night, and the best way to approach tunnels which might not be as deserted as they seemed.

'Chater has not yet mentioned another kind of roaring owl way, one altogether bigger than those he has so far led us across,' said Privet, who now she was clear of Duncton Wood was more willing than before to tell of her own experiences.

'Bigger and more dangerous than that which the cross-under out of Duncton Wood passed beneath?' asked Whillan.

'Bigger, certainly, more dangerous I'm not so sure. They are very wide you see, and can be heard a long way off, and sometimes at night the gazes of the roaring owls never seem to end, coming on and on. But I believe they are not so dangerous for a mole who knows how to climb their embankments and follow in the sterile concrete ways along their course. The danger is not the roaring owls, provided you can keep your snout clear of their fumes, but from diving kestrels, rooks, and even, so I have been told, rats.'

'Rats!' declared Whillan with a shudder, his eyes widening and his expression hardening. Rats were creatures he had only ever heard of, for though they had been known in the lower levels of the Pastures below Duncton, they had never come to Duncton Wood itself. But allmole had kenned, or been told, of Tryfan's famous passage through the tunnels of the Wen, where rats were prevalent and nearly killed him and his companions.

'An observant mole can usually smell a rat,' said Privet, adding with an ironic smile, 'and a wise mole always can. Now, I hope that Chater will not mind me referring also to the matter of temporary burrows; as he will know, these are an art unto themselves which a travelling mole will do well to master. You see, Whillan, most of the time we use tunnels and chambers whose suitability and security are long established – especially in Duncton Wood, a system blessedly free from pressures from other creatures and two-foots. But a travelling mole must make do with what she can find, and sometimes she can't find much that's suitable.'

Chater nodded ruefully, as if to indicate that he too could say a thing or two about unsuitable places in which he had at times been obliged to rest his weary body.

'There was an occasion—' continued Privet.

'You mean, concerning yourself?' interrupted Whillan impulsively, concerned as the young often are to make things clearer and more precise, not appreciating the subtlety of Privet's tale-telling, which sought to approach the past, even through the remembrance of a brief moment of a journey somewhere, sometime, as if it *was* elusive, just as a journeying should be.

'Myself?' said Privet with a gentle smile, remembering another, less happy self, a self less free than this one. 'Perhaps. Yes, perhaps it was me.' She frowned a little, enough to stop Whillan asking further questions, and perhaps to teach him to leave her to tell her own tales in her own way; and to listen, always listen, for the manner of a mole's speech is as important to the understanding of her heart, if not more so, than what she says.

'On that occasion, the end of a long day's journeying found that weary mole near a river which she could scent but not yet see. Now, Whillan, as you might expect, the ground was moist, and thereby wormful and it was the latter fact that made the area appealing as the site for a temporary burrow, and not the former, which warned her away from it; nor even the fact that there was no sign of other mole nor any burrowing creature.'

'I can guess!' said Chater.

'Ssh, dearest!' said Fieldfare, fed up with the interruptions. 'It's Privet who's speaking.'

Privet laughed. 'Chater *has* guessed,' she said. 'That mole was woken in the depth of night by a creature that had crept up silently and stealthily, a creature more dangerous than a hunting tawny owl: water. The mole woke up drowning in a swirling blackness of mud, with no way to go that was safe, even if she could have seen or scented or heard which path to take.'

'The river had flooded!' said Whillan, his eyes wide.

'It had surged,' said Privet. 'That mole, that tired and foolish mole, was lucky to escape only with a fright and very muddy fur indeed.'

'Aye, I've been in the same situation myself,' said Chater.

'Then there's the question of sound, which of course is lacking in any useful warning kind of way in a scrape made for the night, as

19

opposed to a properly delved tunnel. A mole is easily crept up on by predators in such a situation, and that's why unless she knows the area and its creatures very well she had best be on her guard, and choose a spot that not only offers some warning of light or sound, but is easily defended as well . . .'

By such tellings as this they were all pleased to discover that what they had long suspected was true – Privet knew a great deal about journeying, and much too about the history of moledom, mediaeval and modern, and in the days of travel that followed she proved willing to talk about such things, and only fell silent and reverted to her old reticence when pressed too closely about the details of her past after her departure from the High Peak. It was one thing for her to refer to some incident when she was 'on the way to Beechenhill', but quite another to answer any question about what she did when she got there.

'Let her tell things in her own way,' Maple counselled the impatient Whillan privately, 'and in time she'll tell you what you want to know, you see.'

One of the recurring themes in what she said – and her remarks were usually addressed to Whillan, just as Chater's were – was how anonymity and the adoption of a low snout is as good a way for moles to survive as shows of strength and dominance.

'That's true as far as it goes, Privet,' agreed Chater on the last night before they reached Swinford and the point of parting, 'but a mole must know when to show his strength as well as when to retreat, and that's only learnt by experience. There's many a tale I could tell you which would have ended bloodily for me if I had adopted a low snout, as you put it.'

'But isn't it a question of *spirit*?' said Whillan suddenly, frowning in the way he did when some problem or other worried him. 'I mean, all the great moles of the past, like Bracken and Tryfan, maybe even Lucerne—'

'He wasn't a *great* mole, Whillan!' declared Maple, who opposed all evil, all hypocrisy, whether in the present or the past.

'No, not a great mole, Maple,' said Whillan immediately, his eyes gleaming with the excitement of intelligent debate, 'but he was one who knew how to hold power for a time and therefore his history is worth studying. No, what I mean is that a mole who has sway over others, many others, can never maintain it by strength alone, though I suppose he may win ascendancy by tyranny at first. But to retain it, to use it, he must have something more, and that's what I mean by spirit. Belief. Faith. Isn't that what kept you going, Mother, through all the trials you've talked about? For anymole can see you don't have much physical strength and never will have!' It was one of Whillan's touching habits that in moments of animation he sometimes called her 'Mother'.

'Yes, my dear, you could call it spirit . . .' She stanced up and moved away from them a little to stare into the dull, dank November night. 'Others, wiser than I shall ever be, have called such spirit, *love*. As time overtook them, and the physical strength they had when young began to wane, it was love that gave them strength and authority, love for other moles before themselves, love for life. That is what the Stone Mole taught long ago, and it is what abides in the Stone's Silence and Light for those who have courage to contemplate it.

'And lack of such love is, perhaps, the Newborns' greatest weakness. I do not doubt their sincerity or sense of right purpose, but somehow, somewhere, they have lost their sense of love for those they see as weaker than themselves.'

She paused for a time, and a slight mist drifted upslope from the Thames valley below, which they would have to cross on the morrow.

'Now, Stour,' she whispered, '*he* has such love for mole. So many years others thought him severe and cold and yet . . . he has love for us. As the Stone Mole had. I have begun to pray for Stour in his dark and lonely struggle every day, and will until the day comes I see him alive again, or know for sure that he is safe and secure at last in the Stone's Silence.'

How hunched and small she seemed, and yet how strong the sense of thought and concern she gave out, the embodiment perhaps of something of the spirit she had talked to them about.

'My dear,' said Fieldfare, going to her in her motherly way, 'grand ideas are all very well, but as well as loving others a mole must be loved. Without my Chater here to live and strive for, to worry over, to hold through the dark nights, why, I'm not sure that I'd be able to love others at all. Love begins in the home burrow.'

'Yes, yes, of course it does, Fieldfare, and always will,' replied Privet. 'Some moles are blessed with a love as you and Chater are, whilst others . . . our opportunity comes and goes, as mine has gone . . .'

The others fell silent when she said this, hushed indeed, for they hoped she would continue to speak more personally. She did not disappoint them.

'I told you enough of Rooster, and of my time up in the High Peak with him, for you to know that I grew to love him, with a passion too great for one as innocent as I was then, and as shy, to know what to do with! Often have been the times when I wished I had behaved differently, and given myself up to that passion, in body, as well as heart and spirit. Don't look so surprised, Whillan! I'm not quite as inexperienced in such matters as my reluctance to talk about them, or my failure to mate in Duncton Wood, might lead you to think!'

'Er . . .' began Whillan, as embarrassed as he was surprised at this sudden revelation, 'um, yes!'

Privet laughed, and almost seemed to wink at Fieldfare, who of all of them seemed least surprised. But the moment passed, and to their general regret Privet revealed no more then about her 'experience'. Instead she thought a little and continued, 'I loved Rooster far more than I knew at the time, far more perhaps than I care to admit even now. It was as if he was my whole life, a part of me; and I know that despite all I was part of him. But love was not a word we knew or understood, and the dark winds that blew in our youth across the High Peak, which are part of the same winds that blow across moledom today, caught us up, and scattered us apart, like fruit that have grown together on the same high, forgotten branch and tumble in the autumn winds, and roll far asunder, their seeds dispersing to make new life which, perhaps, one distant day, will grow near once more . . .

'Yet we can still feed our love for others from the memory of what we once knew, and hope that our pups and wards – our seed – might fare better than we did in the search for individual love. Meanwhile, we must strive to learn that greater love for moles the Stone leads us towards . . . we must!'

This strange metaphor of love and quiet declaration of intent moved Whillan greatly, and increased his sense that he had been lucky indeed to have been cared for by such a mole as Privet; even if she only showed him love in undemonstrative ways which used words too often, and touch too little, the example she gave would be with him always, as he hoped would Chater's guidance in journeying.

'I'm tired,' he declared suddenly, daring to acknowledge what others felt, and winning nods of recognition that they should preserve their strength for the journeys yet to come, and get some sleep.

'I'll take the watch, Chater,' said Maple quietly, 'for I'm not tired yet, and want to think about things a bit by myself.'

'Aye, lad,' said Chater heavily, 'you take the watch, but if you get tired rouse me and I'll take over from you.'

So ended their last conversation together us a group, and they went below into the shelter of the temporary burrow they had organized earlier, while Maple stared at the drifting mist, and wondered in his own way if love, personal or divine, would ever come to a mole such as he. For love was . . . what?

Maple sighed and scratched himself, and watched the night bring out the stars and moon above, soft through the slight mist, as he listened to the rustles and calls of the creatures of the dark.

By next mid-morning, after a trek over low, drear, marshy ground, they had reached the cross-over of Swinford, where decades before the Stone Mole himself had crossed the Thames. How huge and inexorable the grey flow of the great river seemed, as unremitting as the tide of change that had brought them to this place to part. How reluctant they were to move, knowing that once they did their true journeys would begin, whose outcome none could guess, but all must doubt.

Fieldfare said her goodbyes on the near side of the cross-over, preferring to wait below the roaring owl way along which Chater had to lead the others. She had hoped that the weather might clear and that together they might all have a last glimpse of Duncton Wood, which rose somewhere north-east of them. But that was not to be, and their home system now seemed almost as far away as the places to which their different tasks were sending them.

'You have become my dearest friend,' whispered Fieldfare to Privet as they embraced a final time, 'and you brought new thoughts, new ambitions, to my life. Why, I'd not be bound for Avebury but for you!'

'Nor parted from the place you love!' replied Privet ruefully.

'"Tis moles that matter most, not places, though I daresay I'll miss Duncton almost as much as I'll miss you!' Fieldfare sniffed a bit, and held Privet closer, her generous paws warm and firm on Privet's thin back. 'A lot goes with you, my dear Privet, something of our future I think, so look after yourself well, and remember that this mole who holds you now loves you as sister, as mother, and as friend all at once! And you, Whillan, and you too, Maple' she said, pulling back from Privet and going to the others, 'you look after her for me and see she comes to no harm.'

'We will!' they said, as each in turn was enfolded in Fieldfare's embrace.

'And you look after Chater!' they said to her.

'Look after my beloved! Why, the Stone itself could not put us apart

23

now. Look after him? I'll not let my Chater suffer harm, and he'll never see me hurt! Will you, beloved?'

'Wouldn't dare!' said Chater with a grin, adding gruffly, 'now, come on, the time's marching on and we better get across.'

So up an embankment on to the roaring owl way they went, out of sight of Fieldfare, but never out of mind.

'Don't be long, my love!' called Fieldfare after them, for want of anything else to say, 'don't be long!'

And if she shed a tear or two as she dolefully watched the Thames flow by, and sniffled a bit, and frowned and looked cross, it was all gone when, but a short time later, her Chater came back.

'Well!' he said, 'that's safely done. Now it's just you and I, my love, on a journey into the unknown! Are you nervous?'

''Course I am,' sniffed Fieldfare, ''*course* I am, my dear. But remember when you and I first met, when we were no more than pups?'

'I do, my sweet,' said Chater.

'Well, I was nervous then. That was a journey we began then, wasn't it? We had adventures aplenty on the way, even if together we never set a paw out of Duncton Wood. There were our tunnels to make, our pups to raise, our friends to learn to know and love. We said at the start that if we had troubles our love would see us through.'

'Aye, we did,' said Chater quietly, his flank to Fieldfare's and the great river flowing silently below them.

'My dear, it's been our love that's seen us through, hasn't it? When you were away on your travels and I missed you, as I often did, I knew we had something stronger to keep us going than the strongest moles, born of the Stone itself. That Longest Night when you did not come home, why, the Stone sent Privet to our Wood and to my burrow, and she helped me take my mind off things, and told me you'd get back. Which, of course, you did.'

Chater nodded. 'There's not been a day, hardly an hour, when I've not thanked my stars that you're my love, my dear,' he said, his strong paw in hers. 'And when the going was hard, as it was in the early days of my journeying when the Master expected so much of us, I kept going because I knew that at the end of the journey you would always be waiting.'

'You were always there when the pups were there, and you always came back just when I was thinking I was neglected,' replied Fieldfare. 'When I felt like a shared moment in the Wood you always seemed to come along, and when I wanted to be silent you understood. Then, when I needed you down at the Marsh End, to save me from the Newborns, you were there; you were always there when I needed you most of all,' said Fieldfare.

'Always will be, *always*,' replied Chater passionately.

'Now a new journey is beginning, Chater, and we're making it together, just as we did when we were young. Yes, my dear, I'm nervous, but I'm not afraid, no more than I was the first time.'

'It's a long way, Fieldfare my love, a long way to Avebury for a mole who's never journeyed before. You'll get tired, and I will too.'

'Our love will never get tired, not ever!' said Fieldfare. 'Now, come on Chater, let's stop this dawdling!'

'Who's leading, you or me?' said Chater.

'*We* are!' declared Fieldfare, and paw to paw and flank to flank, like two young moles who had only just declared their love, they turned south and set off towards the ancient system of Avebury.

Chapter Three

'Patience,' purred Brother Chervil, 'is a virtue which I would have thought you had, living in Duncton among followers as you do, Brother Snyde. We must wait a little longer before we depart.'

'And with each passing day let that old fool Stour, and his friends, get ever further from us, ever nearer to Caer Caradoc?' said Snyde irritably, thinking, as he did, that Stour had left Duncton. 'Time knows nothing of the virtues and vices of moles, Brother Chervil; time waits for nomole, true or false, believer or false believer.'

Their voices echoed about the Main Chamber of the Library, and the aides, by now all well aware that Snyde had assumed control of the place, knew that an era had passed and change was on the way. Power had made Snyde quicker than ever to criticize those he thought his minions, and had made him pompous too. He considered himself and Chervil as equal in rank, and the two most powerful moles in Duncton; but astute observers, who knew Chervil, doubted *that*.

'Time, Brother Chervil, marches on,' continued Snyde emphatically, warming to his theme and as always irritated by the Newborn's continuing calm smile, 'like those moles whom Stour is misguidedly leading to Caer Caradoc. Privet, of all moles! To be given the honour of being a delegate, and she but a jumped-up mediaevalist with a northern accent! It will not do!'

Chervil smiled broadly. 'I doubt that the Master Librarian would march anywhere; he has neither the stamina nor the inclination. Even had a mole month passed, rather than but days, you and I would quickly catch up with him. But then, there will be no need for us to hurry. I have long since sent young Brothers out ahead on the fastest route to Caer Caradoc, and we will have news of Master Stour's party in good time to locate them, stop them, and join them. Meanwhile I would not concern yourself with any notion that a female will be allowed to be a delegate at Caradoc. Duncton's eccentricities regarding the qualities of females will not be tolerated by the Inquisitors at Caer Caradoc!'

Chervil's eyes narrowed and his voice, normally low and soft, suddenly sharpened as he looked to the shadows of some stacks beyond where Snyde stanced.

'You mole! Are you . . . spying on us?'

Snyde turned, stared, and laughed dismissively as the familiar form of Pumpkin emerged, carrying a text.

'That's only Pumpkin, just a library aide.'

'Only' Pumpkin came forward with the text that Snyde had ordered up, placed it down, looked as abject and apologetic as he could, and began to back away again.

'Are you Newborn of the Stone, mole?' asked Chervil, who rarely missed an opportunity to put others on the right spiritual path. 'Are you joyous in the Stone's knowledge? Does your spirit dance and your voice desire to sing?'

It must be said that unlike most Newborns, whose eyes were cold and who spoke such things as if they had learned them by rote, there was an infectious sincerity about Chervil as he asked these questions. He was also a mole with a menacing authority, and when he exercised it, genuine charm.

'Sing? Joyous? Newborn?' croaked Pumpkin, trying his best not to look Chervil in the eye, as much from a fear of being drawn into the over-earnest world of the spirit he represented, as from being identified as a mole who intended to resist conversion, real or pretended, for as long as he possibly could.

'Well, er, yes, I suppose I could, I mean I am or might be reborn,' he faltered. 'I certainly like the Stone, yes, that's for sure. But joyous? Now there's a thing!'

'Stop rambling, Aide Pumpkin, and go about your work,' said Snyde coldly.

'Yes, Deputy Master, sir, I will!' said Pumpkin thankfully.

'I am Master Librarian now, Pumpkin, and don't forget it!'

'No . . . Master,' said Pumpkin, almost feeling pain as he gave so august a title to so foul a mole.

Chervil chuckled. 'They certainly obey you, Brother Snyde, even if they don't like you. Impatience may be a problem for you, but authority is not. I am glad I am not one of your library aides.'

'And I am glad I am not merely one of your Marsh End followers, Chervil,' responded Snyde with a smile that was a touch too confident, a touch too arrogant, betokening a mole who had not yet learnt the useful art of seeming to be more modest than he felt; and, too, one who underestimated Chervil.

There was a momentary hard glitter to Chervil's eye before his customary smile returned, even warmer than usual.

'So you will feel it safe to leave Keeper Sturne in charge of the Library when you leave for Caer Caradoc with me?'

'Sturne is mediocre,' said Snyde shortly, 'and always will be. Frankly, he is little better than a library aide like that tedious mole Pumpkin, for he has no wider view of Library matters than he sees in front of his snout. Hard unimaginative work has got him where he is, and that perhaps has made him more ambitious than he has a right to be. In consequence he is a bitter mole because of the failure of his hopes. Master Librarian Stour certainly has no confidence in him. He never gave him much promotion. But I suppose he will deputize for me well enough while I'm gone, and stance down very willingly when I return – and when I do I hope I shall confirmed as Master Librarian of Duncton Wood and so be even more ready to be of service to the Newborn cause than is possible so long as Stour is alive.'

His eyes flicked round and looked up the ramp to the Master's now-deserted cell, and the high galleries that ran from it round the end of the Main Chamber. He had already been up there many times, stancing in the Master's cell as if it were his own, and peering and peeking from the dusty galleries to watch the aides at work, noting which were idle, which incompetent, which needed punishment.

He had observed – and reported as much to Chervil – that the galleries were so dusty that Stour could not have been into them for a very long time, and yet they were the perfect place from which to spy on moles working in the Main Chamber.

'Slack, you see, not interested in discipline. That will change when I take his place.'

'And censorship?'

'Much needed,' replied Snyde immediately, shifting his crooked body and opening his mouth as if almost hungry to begin such work. 'There is much that must go. Old blasphemous works which have no place here and should long since have been destroyed. I never could understand Stour's desire to see such texts copied and distributed to other libraries in moledom.'

'I believe he thought that by so doing they would have a better chance of being preserved,' said Chervil softly.

'Preserved? Against what?'

'Oh . . . revisionists like us. Moles who have enough confidence in their interpretation of the Stone's desires to be resolute and clear in what should and should not be allowed. Moles who believe there is no room for vague notions of "freedom" and the "liberty of ideas" and the "universality of scholarship", when such opinions are misused by unbelievers to undermine and destroy the very liberty of faith in the Stone for which our great ancestors of the past fought and died. Liberty carries responsibility, and that demands clear decisions. That is why the Elder Senior Brother Thripp has pronounced that the libraries of moledom must be cleansed of the taints and stains of adulterated texts.'

'I have said as much for many a year,' said Snyde smugly, 'but in this of all libraries, presided over by Stour himself, you would hardly expect . . .'

'Yet he has favoured you with advancement,' said Chervil, eyes narrowing as he pondered the implications of a thought that had just come to him.

'He could not deny my talents,' said Snyde. 'Stubborn unbeliever he may be, Brother Chervil, but I will admit that he promoted talent where he saw it. Now we must consider how to censor the Library.'

'You are willing to destroy all profane and impious texts?'

'Did I not direct your brothers to Rolls, Rhymes and Tales and tell them what to do?'

'True, you did. It is a pity the mole Husk died as a result. I have noted that you chose to remain in hiding while the deed was done. We Newborns like to stance up and be counted.'

'It would be unwise for me to be seen to be involved in the destruction of such texts, or to have harried Keeper Husk. Some moles harboured a liking for that has-been.'

'That "has-been" was found dead by the Stone,' said Chervil.

'The Stone has judged him then,' said Snyde indifferently.

'And the texts he collected all those years? All gone?'

'Not one remains. I checked through what was left after the storm and personally destroyed what little had survived.'

'Good,' said Chervil with an approving smile. 'You win our confidence.'

'I wish to take my rightful place as Master Librarian here,' said Snyde. 'My only interest is in a reformed Library.'

'And library aides like Pumpkin, of whom you were dismissive just now? Can you rely on them? He was the one who was with Keeper Husk when the brothers went to reform him, was he not?'

Snyde shrugged and then frowned, as if feeling suddenly that he must assert himself.

'You are well informed, Brother Chervil: Pumpkin was indeed

there. I interviewed him myself later, not letting him know of course why I did so, and expressing due sorrow that so many texts had gone. I am satisfied that the Master had sent him to Keeper Husk himself and in being there he was only doing his duty. You may not understand that humble though such moles as he are, library aides are not easily found – not good ones. They save time, they know their texts, our work could not be done without them. I made it clear to Pumpkin where his loyalties now lie: to me. We will need such workers while we cleanse the Library. After that . . . they will be dispensable.'

'Good, good,' said Chervil. 'But I trust you will not be so possessive of your new domain that you will not willingly make available moledom's greatest library and its holiest of texts to the scrutiny of the greatest Caradocian scholars and divines?'

'The Stone's will must be done,' said Snyde.

'And you trust this Sturne? You are satisfied that he can deputize for you in your absence?'

'I trust him to be for ever subordinate. In any case, he has expressed a willingness to be Newborn which appears genuine. He will do.'

Chervil blinked. 'A dangerous trust. Moledom is led, and always was, by moles who were once subordinate.'

'Like me!' said Snyde, confident again. 'I have bided my time and earned my place. Sturne is not made of such stuff as that.'

'And you think you will return as Master here because . . . ?'

'Because the Master Librarian cannot long survive his foolish venture. It is mere hubris, an attempt to live again the glories of his past when he alone summoned and carried the Conclave of Cannock. No, he cannot return to Duncton Wood as Master.'

'No,' said Chervil, 'no, I don't suppose he can. The Stone will pass judgement on him. He would have done better to stay in Duncton Wood. Elder senior Brother Thripp has made clear that the time of such moles as he is over. This place . . .' said Brother Chervil, looking about uneasily. For a brief moment he even looked vulnerable.

'Oh, a mole gets used to it,' said Snyde. 'Now tell me straight, when shall we depart? I *am* impatient.'

'Soon, I think. We are expecting certain of our brothers to return to Duncton Wood to begin their work of revision here.'

'Here?'

'In our great Library, the Library of which one day you will be Master.'

'What moles are these?'

'Some Brother Inquisitors of Caradoc, three in number I am told.

Trained moles, who will know what books to make more prominent, what books may stay, and what must be destroyed. They are on their way from Rollright, where they have been doing similar work, and they will direct Sturne in what to destroy and what to save. This will be the last major library in moledom to be revised.'

'They will surely need me . . . yet I trust I *will* be able to go to Caer Caradoc?'

'Initially their work will simply be to make a record of what they find here, and check what records you have. Librarians, particularly those of ambiguous faith like the Master Stour, have a habit of not listing texts which others might find objectionable. Why, there was that scandal at Beechenhill when a Brother Inquisitor proved beyond reasonable doubt that the Librarian there had inclinations towards the Word, and harboured many of their most corrupting texts.'

'Yes, I have heard something of that. The Librarian concerned was named Cobbett.'

'Yes,' said Chervil, adding with cold menace in his voice, 'and a substitute was found for him. No matter, the situation here in Duncton is rather different, and now the Master Stour has chosen to yield up his power to younger, more right-thinking moles, if only by default, I think that our Inquisitors will in the end, with your co-operation, make things satisfactory with the minimum of trouble.'

'Was there trouble at Beechenhill?' asked Snyde, his head twitching a little nervously, less out of fear – he was not a mole easily made afraid – than from the effort involved in attempting to weigh up the new situation he was in at the same time as protecting for himself what, no doubt, he hoped would soon be the domain in which he was officially in charge.

'Beechenhill has a reputation for resistance,' said Chervil curtly, 'and is not an easy system to control if its moles do not wish it.'

'The scholar Privet was at Beechenhill for a time, I believe,' said Snyde, hoping to sow a small seed of doubt in Chervil's mind about that mole.

'Yes,' said Chervil, 'I had heard.'

'You constantly surprise me by how well informed you are, Brother Chervil, for a mole—'

'For a mole as out of the way from the centre of Newborn affairs as this?' said Chervil. 'Yes, well . . . it is wise for a mole to be informed. But to present matters; the cataloguing of texts here will take some time and can be satisfactorily done while you are away in Caradoc provided you appoint a competent mole to deputize for you – and that you seem willing to do. After that you *will* be needed, Brother Snyde, but by then you will be back from Caradoc.'

'And you, Brother Chervil? Will you be coming back, or will your duties here have finished?'

'Elder Senior Brother Thripp will instruct me on my next task when we get to Caer Caradoc. I trust I will come back here in time. There is . . . something about Duncton that I like. It is a gentler place than Caradoc.'

His voice was almost wistful, but Snyde was never one to notice such subtleties, and did not seem to now, nor ponder what the implications of such wistfulness might be for himself.

'Yes, yes, it has its charms I suppose, but if it had no library it would be nothing at all and I would have long since gone elsewhere.'

'I suppose you would,' said Chervil, eyeing the chilling misshapen form before him and wondering how Duncton could have produced such a mole. Joy, supposed Chervil, was not a thing that had ever lightened Acting Master Snyde's narrow eyes.

'The Brother Inquisitors should be here soon,' said Chervil, wishing to bring the conversation to an end. 'When they finally come I shall brief them immediately, and we can go. You have definitely decided to appoint Sturne to work with them?'

'Keeper Sturne will do,' said Snyde.

'I am sure that Keeper Sturne will satisfy their needs,' agreed Chervil, 'and I suggest you make the mole Pumpkin their minion, for fetching and carrying and so on.'

'I would have suggested him myself,' said Snyde, 'no aide knows the place better than he. But I thought you doubted his loyalty to the Stone, or at least to the good news of the Newborn way?'

'Oh I do, I do. But the moles the Inquisitor will send are not mere aides, you know. They are trained to scent out those who seek to hide texts, or otherwise preserve them from the Stone's burning Light. Trained in conversion too. By the time you return from Caradoc I am sure that they will have not only seen through Pumpkin's vague support for us, but have converted it into a passionate loyalty to the cause. He will be a changed mole, and more tractable, and that will inspire other library aides here to be the same. Meanwhile, until they come, Brother Snyde, please try to remember that patience is a virtue.'

For four more days Snyde was forced to wait, and pace to and fro, and tap his talons and snarl at aides and Keepers alike, before the assistants to the Inquisitor came back. When they did, guarded by a group of strong, silent moles, they did not smile at all: three males, all middle-aged, all dark, all with the clipped accent of the Welsh Borderland. He was briefly introduced to them, and the first two spoke their names in the same chilly voices.

'Brother Fetter.'

'Brother Law.'

'And this is Brother Barre,' said Fetter, introducing the third and most silent of the three. A powerful-looking mole with tiny sharp eyes and a curved snout that had wrinkles at its sides, as if it had been forced at birth into an inquisitive position and had never got back into its proper shape.

Snyde introduced Keeper Sturne as briefly to them, and Library Aide Pumpkin as well. Then, feeling his position demanded it, he made a long briefing speech to them all, designed to make clear that happy though he was to have such Inquisitors in Duncton, their role was merely to record. Any decisions about how to dispose of dubious texts could wait until he got back.

The aides stared unblinking at him and said nothing.

'So,' said Snyde uneasily, 'we understand each other then!'

'May your journey be a safe one,' said Fetter coldly.

That done, Snyde and Brother Chervil, with guards to watch over them on the way, finally set off down the south-east slopes towards the cross-under that leads moles all ways from the system. Snyde did not even look back for a second as they passed under it, and out of sight of the Wood up beyond the pasture slopes. But Chervil paused, and looked back for a time on the system that had been his home in exile for so long. He said not a word, and the guards gathered respectfully round him while they waited.

'Duncton Wood,' he whispered at last, and from the way he said it a mole whose mind was open to such things, and knew well the ways of the Stone, might have thought Chervil was being rather more than merely wistful, and uttering two words that spoke of a liberty he had tasted for a time, had never known before, and now began to understand he might regret losing. A cold wind blew through the concrete tunnel of the cross-under and parted the fur on his haunches and back. For a moment he noticed it not, but saw only how the light of the winter sun, lost behind mists and November gloom for so many days, now broke through and caught the pale trunks of the leafless beeches of the High Wood. They seemed to shine and shimmer with the colours of life itself. Where he came from, to where he was now returning, leafless trees never seemed to shine as they shone here and now in Duncton Wood.

33

'We go!' he said sharply, turning and following Snyde out through the cross-under, and passing him without a word to take the lead as the guards hurried to keep up with him.

'Do we really need so many guards as this?' asked Snyde irritably of one of them. He had never travelled out of the system, and on the rare occasions he had imagined doing so he had thought he might be able to see the scenery without seeing what seemed a crowd of moles at the same time.

'There's trouble in moledom,' said the guard heavily, 'and we can't risk harm coming to *this* particular brother. The moles in the north are causing what the Senior Brother has called "difficulties".'

'Ah, yes . . .' said Snyde, who had no idea what the mole was talking about, but realized that he would not be likely to get more information if they saw he was ill-informed, and also that he had better make it his task to become informed as quickly as possible. 'I have heard something of this . . .'

'What have you heard, Brother?' asked the guard.

'That the recusants need to be brought into line,' he said smoothly.

The guard was suitably impressed by the unusual word but he in turn did not wish Snyde to know he had not fully understood.

'Yeh . . .' he agreed.

It was just the kind of conversation Snyde enjoyed and was good at. 'Tell me, Brother, what's the latest?' he asked confidentially. 'We have had our snouts rather too firmly into library matters these days past.'

The guard was glad to talk.

'Well, all I know is that our brothers are well on the track of the rebel Rooster, who as you know has proved elusive and troublesome until now. What's more . . .'

The mole rambled on obligingly and told much that Snyde did not know. He listened with interest, remembering all that was said, and only at the end, reviewing what he had heard, did a thought occur to him, and fill him with sudden alarm and apprehension. For the guards kept darting astonishingly respectful looks at Chervil, and fell over themselves to be obliging when he wanted anything. All of which seemed in excess of what might be due to a mole who had been merely the Senior Brother in a cell of Newborns in Duncton Wood.

It was then that with a start Snyde remembered that the guard had said, 'We can't risk harm coming to *this* particular brother'. No sooner had he remembered this than he recalled a remark by Master Stour himself, all that long time ago when Chervil had first come to the

34

system so unexpectedly: 'He seems a remarkably well-trained mole for what is surely a minor posting from Caradoc. There's more to his coming than there seems.'

The guard seemed to guess something of Snyde's thoughts. 'He's back in favour with the Elder Senior Brother Thripp,' he said. 'You'll know what that means.'

'I can't say that I do, exactly,' said Snyde with his usual ambiguity.

'But you surely know who Brother Chervil is?' said the guard incredulously.

Snyde stared, unsure whether or not to admit to ignorance of something else that perhaps he ought to know. Chervil was Senior Brother Chervil, that was all.

'Brother Chervil is Thripp's son,' whispered the guard, 'and now his period of punishment in exile is over. We're to take him home.'

Thripp's son? *Chervil?* His *son?*

Snyde scarcely blinked before he began to calculate, and when he did it was but a moment before the implications sank in. Then, with what growing pleasure could he contemplate that the Stone had put him in the right place at the right time with the right mole! Yes, it had!

'Truly, the Master did me a favour trying to leave me behind!' he gloated.

'Hurry up, Brother Snyde, you're lagging and we have a long long way to go!' called out Chervil.

'Yes, of course! I will!' said Snyde eagerly, seeking with each word he spoke to put the sound of respect into his nasal voice as he hobbled and hurried his hunched and crooked way along the path which Chervil led them on.

Chapter Four

Late November found Chater and Fieldfare set fair for their journey to Avebury, and it seemed that nothing more could now hinder them. Certainly something *had* hindered them thus far, and that was Fieldfare's slowness, for she was so long unused to journeying, so plump, so appreciative of pauses, rests, pleasing delays to admire the view, and downright stops (to catch her breath and declare, 'Bless me! I never knew moledom was so big and the ways so long!') that they spent more time stopping than starting.

Not that Chater had minded at first. He had so long wanted to have his love at his flank on a journey worth the making that it was as much pleasure for him to pause as it was for her. What was more, when they did so he was made to realize that he had spent all his working life as a journeymole travelling, yet not seeing what he travelled through, and so her slow pace suited his new-found mood of discovery and contemplation.

It must be said, however, that Chater was beginning to want to get on with the journey to Avebury, and had put his paw down about a diversion that Fieldfare had mooted, to visit the Fyfield System which lay a day's trek off to the south-east. He had not objected too loudly, but his protest was registered, as was Fieldfare's counter-protest.

Meanwhile, Chater would have been the first to admit that there was an exciting sense of rediscovering themselves together about the journey thus far, so that when they came to fabled places like peaceful Bablock Hythe, it seemed a positive affront to life itself to hurry on without stopping for a few days to enjoy the place, and meet the quiet moles who inhabited it.

It was the same further upriver – for they took a route along the River Thames – when they came to Appleton, a system which had a somewhat dark record in Woodruff's Chronicles since it was there that the Eldrene Wort first came to power and evil prominence. Not that there was much sign of darkness or evil when they were there, for the moles had put the sinister past of their system behind them, and gave a warm welcome to the two journeyers from Duncton.

Chater was naturally cautious about saying who they were until he was sure that the Newborns were not about and looking for them, but the Appleton moles reported merely that from time to time the Newborns passed their way, but no cell of Newborn faith had been established in their system.

'So where do they head for when they go south of here?' he asked.

'Buckland,' they told him, 'Buckland, and Avebury beyond that.'

'Hump!' mused Chater, 'at least we know where not to go!'

'Where are you off to then?' they asked.

'Uffington,' lied Chater immediately, glancing at Fieldfare to keep her quiet. She did not have his professional caution in replying to the questions of prying moles, and nor would she have necessarily realized that not all moles are what they say they are, especially if they are Newborns. He could not help it if others noted the coming and going of strangers – and he would not be at all surprised if moles passed on to the occasional Newborns who came by news of other travellers, so it was unwise to give too much away.

The news of the Newborns in Buckland did not surprise him, nor even dismay him. Buckland had a vile reputation anyway, having been made notorious by the moles of the Word as a centre of torture and cruelty, and it had been his misfortune to visit it once before. It was true it was on their route, but in the undulating terrain of the Vale of Uffington it was easy enough to avoid. As for the Newborns being at Avebury, he would have been surprised if they were not – and certainly Master Stour had expected them to be there. The question would be – how many and how entrenched? *That* they would only find out when they got there. Meanwhile . . . Appleton, and a few more pleasant days of dawdling.

'We must go, Fieldfare,' Chater kept urging.

'My love,' she would reply,' 'it is *so* pleasant doing not a lot after all those years in Duncton raising young.'

'But . . .'

But how could he deny her?

Yet on the fourth day of this unlooked-for delay, when once again he sought to urge her on, the new reason she gave for staying was startlingly different, and to him rather more annoying.

'No! I don't feel it's right to move today. There's a reason we should stay here and that's why the Stone has made it so alluring in Appleton.'

'Reason my mystical arse, beloved,' said Chater promptly. 'The only reason is because you're lazy. You're not a travelling mole. You're—'

'Chater! You will eat your words.'

And only hours later he almost did. For whatmole should come into Appleton from Fyfield way, but one who when he heard that Duncton moles were visiting the system sought them out and told them that if they were from Duncton then there were two moles across in the Fyfield system looking for guidance towards Duncton Wood.

'They were asking the way to Duncton and the state they were in they wouldn't have got further than the nearest stream into which, having tumbled, they would be too weak to get out again.'

'You mean they are ill?' said Fieldfare.

'Half dead, yes. They looked like vagrants to me and I told them to stay where they were and rest up a bit. To which they replied there wasn't time.'

'Chater of Duncton, we are going to Fyfield!' declared Fieldfare with sudden energy. 'This is the news I felt coming, and these must be the moles whom destiny has put in our way. That's why the Stone told us to wait here in Appleton – to hear about them.'

'My own sweet,' said Chater with considerable exasperation, 'the Stone told nomole anything. You've got it into your head—'

'Are you with me or against me?'

'With you, unfortunately,' said Chater.

'Then let's go!'

'Only if,' said Chater, not moving, 'you promise on your love of me that if these so-called moles in Fyfield aren't there we won't go chasing after them, and if they are, then when we've heard them out and helped them as best we can we continue with the task we've been set, which is to go to Avebury.'

'Dearest Chater,' said Fieldfare meekly, 'I will do whatever you think fit once we've talked to them. As for them being there, of *course* they will be, the Stone has already seen to it! Quite apart from which Fyfield is said to have been the birthplace of Privet's grandmother the Eldrene Wort, and I had intended going there anyway to pay our respects.'

'Yes, dear,' said Chater grimly, and still bickering in their gentle loving way, off the two moles went.

They set off from Appleton along the south-western slopes of the Thames valley until, reaching woods nearby in which Chater had rested his weary paws on previous journeys, they turned south towards Fyfield.

The weather was fine, the sky a luminescent pale blue, so bright that it gave the wings of flocking rooks that special sheen that makes even those dark carrion-feeders worth admiring. The woods thereabout were still, and the few leaves that remained on the branches were all russet and gold, and each seemed to try to represent the many that had already fallen, and put on a final show of autumn beauty before the winter came.

Yet, though glorious the day, as they approached Fyfield itself, which had for so many decades been unvisited by all but a few vagrant moles and the odd pilgrim from systems nearby, Fieldfare felt a curious despair, a haunting sadness, quite at odds with the weather and her previous mood. Then, as they drew near the Stone itself and could see it clearly not far off, she paused in her progress.

'I can't see moles nearby,' she said. 'Maybe if we wait they'll make themselves known. You know, in the old stories that my parents told me, Fyfield was once almost as great a system as Duncton itself. But . . . times change.'

'What happened to it?' asked Chater, who since their journey had begun had been surprised not only at Fieldfare's ability to enjoy the places and the moles they met, but at the fund of lore and stories she had – and which, now he came to think of it, he should have remembered she had, for she had so often repeated such tales to their pups when they were young.

'It became wormless,' said Fieldfare, 'and my mother said that when that happens to a system it's a sign that something dark and dreadful will take place there in the future.'

'I would have thought that being Wort's birthplace was a dreadful enough thing to happen to any system.'

Fieldfare paused and stared ahead, suddenly feeling quite flooded with a confusing mixture of despair and hope, of great darkness and great light.

'What is it, my dear?' asked Chater immediately, for he could see that his mate's breathing was suddenly fast and furious, and her eyes were pricking with unexpected tears.

'I . . . don't . . . know, Chater. It's just that when you said that, I remembered Privet's tale, and how Wort tried so hard to do the right thing at the end, and *did* it too, and how hard that must have been for her, giving up her only pup to save its life. And then I thought . . . I thought . . .'

'My love!' said Chater, putting his paws round her, for her silent tears had turned to open sobbing and she could hardly catch her breath for the emotion she felt.

'Well . . .' she continued in gulps and gasps, 'I just thought that we were lucky to *have* had young, and a happy life, and to be together still. And here we are at this deserted place and it feels as if it's waiting for mole to put things right again. The Stone feels *sad* here. And . . . and . . .'

'And . . . ? My cherub?' whispered Chater, doing his best to draw out whatever was distressing her.

'I'm going to lose some weight!'

'You're going to lose weight?' repeated poor Chater faintly, unable to keep pace with either her emotions or her thoughts.

'Yes, I'm going to eat less. I've been too self-indulgent all my life, I've had things too easy! When I think of moles like Wort and Privet, and Stour, and Husk, and *you*. Moles like you are not overweight. But me! I'm going to do something worthwhile with my life! I am!'

She pulled back from him, eyes sparkling, and a look of new-found purpose on her ample face.

'Well!' said Chater, unable to think of much to say. 'Well! That's good then! But . . .' and a grim thought occurred to him: a *thin* Fieldfare. 'I like you being plump,' he said.

But at that moment, with the new mood of resolve that had come to Fieldfare, it was quite the wrong thing to say.

'How you can say such a thing as that at such a time, Chater, I do not know! How you can even *think* it I can't imagine. Sex! My mother warned me that sex is all journeymoles think about and she was right. Plump indeed! Well, I shall become thin, undesirable, and worthwhile!'

'But, beloved,' said Chater, at once abashed and affronted, 'you are worthwhile as you are.'

'Yes, worthwhile for *that*!' his beloved snapped. 'I sometimes think . . .'

But whatever she sometimes thought had to wait, for their wrangling was brought to a sudden stop by the sight of two pairs of wide and frightened eyes staring at them from one of the ruined tunnel entrances near the Stone.

'Who's there?' said Chater sternly.

But the eyes only stared and blinked slowly, and the bright sunlight caught the shaking movement of a wan snout.

'Chater! Ssh!' said Fieldfare warningly, in a voice so determined that it seemed that she intended no delay in turning her resolve to be 'worthwhile' into action. 'Leave this to me. It's the moles we were told about, I'm sure of it!'

She put a firm paw on one of his to tell him to bide his tongue and stay where he was, and then slowly, and in as friendly a way as she

40

could, went towards where the moles had hidden themselves.

'They're hiding from *me*?' thought Fieldfare to herself, astonished, as she advanced on them, wondering in what circumstances anymole could ever regard *her* as so frightening they needed to hide.

'What is it?' she asked gently, speaking into the shadows in which the moles cowered, and watching helpless as they retreated yet further from her. 'What do you want? What's wrong? *I'll* not harm you.'

The eyes of the moles stayed wide and fixed upon her, one pair higher than the other; a male and a female, probably.

Fieldfare heard the female whisper to the male, '*Ask* them. It's all we can do.'

'I won't harm you, mole,' said Fieldfare, trying once again to reassure them, waving Chater further back because he still had an intimidating look about him in the expectation that it was all a trick.

The male poked his snout out a little into the air and said, 'Where are you from?'

'My name's Fieldfare of Duncton,' she replied. 'We're pilgrims, sort of. We heard there were two moles trying to get to Duncton and since we're of Duncton ourselves we thought we would come here and see if we could help. We wouldn't advise anymole to go to Duncton at the moment, unless they were Newborn of course!'

The snout came out further into the light, and a pair of diffident pale eyes stared at Fieldfare.

'You're not Newborn then?' the mole enquired doubtfully.

'Do I look Newborn?' said Fieldfare, not knowing whether to feel amused or slighted.

'Not very,' said the mole, adding, in a voice that could barely conceal his excitement, 'er, are you *really* of Duncton Wood?'

'We are.'

'Who's your friend? He looks fierce.'

'He's no friend,' said Fieldfare with a smile, 'he's my mate. His name's Chater. Chater, my love, come on over here and look less threatening and more pleasant. Smile or something, dearest. These moles think you may be a danger to them.'

Chater did as he was told, but it was only after he had patiently answered further questioning to affirm that he too was of Duncton, and benign, that the hiding mole said, 'Wait a moment, I will consult my better half.'

The snout retreated and much subterranean whispering ensued, and some pattering of paws beneath, and away, and around and about. Until suddenly, and to Fieldfare's and Chater's surprise, several moles emerged from various points around them as if they had indeed been preparing the kind of ambush that Chater had feared. Except that these moles were so ragged and motley, so starved and thin, so weak from disease and the strains of flight from danger, that Chater could have dealt with the whole lot of them with one paw.

But physically downcast though they were, a spirit of purpose and courage was in their eyes, and pride as well, and a touching disbelief that they had found two friendly moles, and both from Duncton Wood.

As they emerged into the light of day the one to whom they had been talking came forth, and after him the mole they guessed was his 'better half'. She was the weakest of them all, and needed help to clamber out of the entrance, which her partner gave her most gently and caringly. But he was little more fit than she, and neither seemed able to stance straight without helping the other somewhat, unless it was that in the place from which they had fled they felt safest if they leaned against each other. Yet the others, who Chater saw numbered six more, mostly male, looked to these two for leadership, and came and gathered about them now, staring in continuing disbelief at the Duncton moles.

One or two were sobbing mutely, it seemed in relief at having found friends. One sank down on his haunches, too weak to stance more proudly. Others shivered with fever, or fatigue, and one old one leaned on another and simply stared expressionlessly at the Stone that rose a little downslope.

Then, like the rising of the sun, there came to the face of the leading male a look of pride, as if he had been on the most terrible journey imaginable and had led his weaker partner and friends on with the promise that at the end of it there would be comfort to be found; and here, when all seemed lost and his promises and encouragements all come to naught, *here* was his vindication. While on the face of his thin partner, who clung to him tightly as he supported her, was nothing but tiredness, hopelessness, and a desire to sleep.

But nothing daunted, the male said, with what last vestiges of pride and strength he had left, 'We are followers of the Stone. We are *not* Newborn and never will be!'

There was a weak and ragged chorus of, 'No's' and 'Never-will-be's' at this declaration of intent.

From the way he said it, with a firm stare from which the fear had now gone, it was clear that he did not wish Fieldfare to remark upon the diseased appearance of himself and his partner – he wished to be treated as an equal.

So, though he was barely able to stance upright because of his own weakness and his companion's need of what faltering strength he had left to stay upright herself, Fieldfare instinctively knew she must not, as yet, offer them help. Chater must have thought the same, for though he had been in the act of going to assist some of the others he stopped still and listened as the mole spoke again.

'So, if you're followers like us, let us go to the Fyfield Stone all together, to pray and give thanks.' He looked at his fellow moles and said, 'Surely, we have been led here by the Stone and these two moles of Duncton are the answer to the moleyears of prayers we have made, and a vindication of the lives lost by our friends during the journey we have made to be here. Let us therefore give thanks before we do aught else!'

Then, tenderly supporting his companion, and turning his head to hers in the gentlest and most loving way, he said, 'We are joining these other pilgrims to go, as tradition demands, all together on this last short way of our journey. You can make it there, can't you, my dear?'

'Are these moles truly of Duncton?' the female whispered.

'They are of Duncton, my dear, the Stone has sent them in answer to our prayers. Now we will give thanks and then we will ask for their advice and assistance, for allmole knows that in moledom's hour of need, Duncton moles will help.'

'Aye!' cried the others as Fieldfare exchanged a glance with Chater which told him that *she* was not going to turn her back on these good moles even if it did mean delaying their journey to Avebury. While for his part, Chater's look said, 'Whatever promise I compelled you to make about going on after this is now cancelled. *I* am not going to be the Duncton mole who did not know where to give help when it was needed!'

The female slowly raised her gaunt head towards the Stone, surveying the very short distance which separated her from it; after a few moments, in which from the weariness in her eyes, and the shaking of her paws, it seemed she judged the distance to be great indeed in her present state, she eventually nodded briefly and looked down at the ground again.

'Well then,' said the male rather formally, surveying the ground ahead for bumps and pitfalls, 'well . . .'

Then, very slowly, in imminent danger of collapsing with each short and careful step he made, and with Fieldfare and Chater just behind, the two moles led the way to the Stone. Never before in her life had

43

Fieldfare been so grateful for her health and strength; and never had Chater felt so sombre and sensible of his own good fortune as flank to flank, and with more than one of the weak moles leaning on them for support, they all moved slowly forward. In those last few steps to the Fyfield Stone, shared as they were with moles who surely had travelled a much harder journey through life to be where they were, Fieldfare and Chater felt in the group a spiritual awe they had never shared before and a resolution to be or do something 'worthwhile' rose up in them together.

Indeed, as they reached the Stone and the stronger helped the weaker forward to touch it, Fieldfare and Chater instinctively reached out a paw to each other, and turned to look into each other's eyes, and their love deepened in this witness of it before the Stone, and they sensed that their journey to Avebury, begun so simply, continued so slowly, was now about to find in some unspoken way a deeper purpose than either of them could ever have conceived, and the beginnings of a different goal.

'Thank you, Stone, for bringing us in safety here,' the male whispered. 'Thank you for bringing us into the company of these moles of Duncton. Continue to help our friends and our kin who cannot be here, but who gave us the strength to dare leave on their behalf. Help us, through these moles you have sent now, to find a way to help allmole.'

His companion seemed to gain a little strength from these words and from touching the Stone, for she succeeded in letting go of him, and stancing on her own paws, though with great difficulty. She stared up at the Stone, a terrible faith in her eyes, and she whispered, 'Help them Stone, as you helped us come here. Help them.'

Then she could stance alone no more, and nor could her companion or their friends. As Chater helped some, Fieldfare helped others, so that there at the Stone's base, they lay down, with Chater stancing guard over them while Fieldfare hurried off to find some food, wondering who they were and where they were from, and what this meeting might mean for them all.

For Pumpkin, November and the first days of December was a hard and confusing time, and made much worse by the sudden and apparently inexplicable change in Sturne's attitude towards him. The library aide had always understood that it was hard for a mole like Sturne to be easy with others, or to know how to say a kindly or polite word to smooth some troubled moment away. He had realized too, though a little sadly, that as the years went by and Sturne rose up the Library's hierarchy, from scholar to Keeper, he would find it even harder to acknowledge either publicly or privately that through all these years, unspoken though it was, there was a special bond between the two, unequal though they were, which had been formed that very first day they came to dedicate their lives to Library work.

Pumpkin could bear all that, knowing as he did that each Midsummer, and each Longest Night, Sturne would come of his own accord to Pumpkin's untidy burrow and, with little said but much felt, would mark the occasion by consuming a juicy worm and, in his stiff cold way, tell some tale or other that seemed to him to have a dash of humour or spot of interest in it. This unbending of Sturne in his presence meant much to Pumpkin, and over the long years, the decades indeed, of their strange relationship, he liked to think that Sturne felt the same.

'The mole may find it hard to relax and enjoy life,' Pumpkin often said to himself, 'but I *know* he's a kind mole in his own way, and that he means no harm by the way he looks; it's simply the fact that the Stone forgot to show him how to grin and smile like other moles.'

If, sometimes, Pumpkin thought of Sturne affectionately in his wanderings and muttered such things as, 'This is something you'll enjoy hearing about come Longest Night,' and even mentioned him sometimes in his prayers, he did so in the real hope that one day, perhaps when Sturne was retired from the Library and able to spend more time at leisure, the Stone would grant him the peace to enjoy life a little more, and unbend, and smile.

'Why, Stone, I don't mind saying that if you have to take from me a whole year's smiling and being content to give Sturne a single day of real joy and happiness, because there's only so much to go round and some moles need more than others to get them going, then you take it away from me. I'd give anything to see that mole smile a whole day through!'

Such had been the thoughts that good Pumpkin entertained for Sturne, and this was why, unique among the library aides, he never ever said a bad word about Sturne, or willingly listened to another mole who did. Which being so, it is not surprising that poor Pumpkin was so distressed, faced as he now was by the terrible fact that Sturne's elevation to the exalted position of Acting Master Librarian had turned him into an autocratic monster whose strictness and ruthless authority seemed to know no bounds.

Knowing him as he thought he did, Pumpkin had expected at least some token of resistance to the demands the Newborn Inquisitors were making within hours of their arrival, that certain texts be removed, notably those scribed in pious memory of Holy Beechen of Duncton Wood as expositions of his 'Way'.

'There is only one true way, Acting Master Sturne, and that is the way to the Stone as promulgated by Elder Senior Brother Thripp, using the creeds and gospels of Holy Beechen himself, and dispensing with these soft and vapid accounts in your Library of what he was supposed to have said, and supposed to have meant!'

'Indeed,' Pumpkin had heard Sturne say obligingly, 'and it is right that the Library be reorganized to recognize the value of Thripp's texts.'

'*Elder Senior Brother* Thripp is the way he is formally known, and those of us who are dedicated to his mission prefer to call him by his full rank and title. But we are not so, shall we say, *dogmatic*, as to insist that others call him so, though we who have taken the vow prefer it. But, in courtesy, please call him *Brother*, if you will.'

'Of course, it was a slip of the tongue,' Pumpkin heard Sturne reply on that occasion. 'I am somewhat new to the Newborn way and am grateful for all the guidance I can get from moles as experienced as yourself, Brother Fetter.'

'Dear, oh dear!' muttered Pumpkin to himself when he heard this, and more of it, and still more as the days went by, 'it seems that Sturne has been turned finally their way. I fear I may have lost an ally here! Yes, indeed I have!'

When Sturne began to show that he had no patience at all with the grumbling of the library aides concerning the wholesale disposal of texts which until then had been kept most carefully, and in the driest places, to make way for modern texts which were carried up from the Marsh End of all places, all of them blathering on about the Newborn way, Pumpkin had no doubt that the Acting Master had been 'converted', or was well on the way to being.

Drubbins, the only mole Pumpkin dared confide in, confirmed the fact, saying that the Acting Master had been downright rude to him when he dared remonstrate about the matter of the texts.

'I never did like Sturne much, I must say, but I'm afraid his elevation to his present position is a blow for the cause Master Stour made such plans for. These Newborns certainly know how to get at a mole, for good or ill, and they seem to have won him to their dogmatic side.'

For all the vigour of Drubbins' comment, there was something

46

shaken about his voice that made Pumpkin look at him rather more closely. Why, if Pumpkin had not seen with his own eyes that there was not a mark, or scratch, or bruise on the venerable elder he might have thought he had been . . . assaulted. He had the same kind of distant and nervous vulnerability about him as he, Pumpkin, had displayed as a young mole when some large Westside youngsters had had a go at him.

'Are you quite all right, sir?' enquired Pumpkin, concerned.

'Me? All right? Of course, of course,' replied Drubbins unconvincingly. 'But what we can do . . . I . . . just don't know, Pumpkin. What's worse than all of this is that I'm not sure that you should be seen talking to me. The Newborns might draw the wrong conclusion.'

'You mean the *right* conclusion,' said Pumpkin flippantly.

But the cheerful smile on his face faded as Drubbins turned his pained eyes to him and said, 'Mole, these are dangerous times, more dangerous perhaps than any of us but wise Stour realized. They . . . questioned me yesterday. They asked me many things in confusing ways and their eyes were colder than any ice or blizzard wind. I was frightened, Pumpkin. I'm an old mole now, and my life has been lived through peaceful times. The fragile strength I have to offer bends and breaks before such winds as the Newborns bring.'

'Did they *hit* you, sir?' asked Pumpkin, scandalized.

'No, no, they are subtler than that, and nor are they yet sure of themselves. I do not think they know anything at all of Stour's plans and I did not say anything to arouse their suspicion. And yet, Pumpkin, when those moles surrounded me, and their eyes bored into me, and I grew confused, I felt it might be easier to tell the truth. Pumpkin, forgive me, I . . . am not strong.'

To Pumpkin's astonishment, old Drubbins, the most stable, balanced and wise elder he had ever known, or ever expected to know, suddenly lowered his head and wept in a frail and croaky way.

'Mole, you know the last thing I would ever do is say anything about the whereabouts or plans of my friend Stour.'

'Of course you wouldn't, sir.'

'But after they had finished with me yesterday I feared that I might not withstand their pressure for long if they do that sort of thing often. I fear I may prefer to kill myself than suffer their tortures again.'

'Sir, you mustn't say such a dreadful thing. Come and stay in my burrow for a time.'

'No, no, that's just what I must not do. I do not think they suspect you, for their minds are caught up in hierarchy and they would not

47

understand that Stour would have entrusted so much to you, a mere aide as they would see it.'

'No, sir,' said Pumpkin with a modest grin.

'So that may be your best protection. Be obedient, keep your snout low, and if you must pay lip service to the Newborn way then do so abjectly. I may not last much longer under their regime, and much may depend on you. Much. Now, leave me, and pray for me! And do not risk coming here again.'

'No, sir, I won't, sir, and try to perk up a bit because . . . because whatever we may be suffering, the Master's in retreat on our behalf, and those brave moles like Privet and the others are adventuring half across moledom to try to bring things to rights, or prevent them getting worse.'

How worried Pumpkin looked as he parted from Drubbins, and how hard it was to look cheerful for the old mole's sake.

'Pumpkin!' Drubbins called after him, 'good luck! The Stone be with you.'

'Good luck to *you*, sir!' cried out valiant Pumpkin, feeling most uneasy, as if Drubbins might really try to hurt himself. As he went through the Wood he felt that he was all alone now, without friendship or support. 'Except for the Stone!' he muttered to himself as he neared his burrows. 'Yes, that's with me, as it has always been.'

Then, the thought still lingering as he thankfully stanced down in his cosy chamber, he said to himself, 'And *you*, Rue, who once lived here, I know you're with me. And your friends, and all those good moles who went back and forth this way, better moles than me, and stronger too. They're with me, and they'll help me if I call to them, starting with great Bracken himself, first mole in modern times to understand that it is the Silence we must strive to reach. Why, I've got a whole army of support to see me through the time ahead until things change!'

A short time after this, after some days of irritability and tiredness, Pumpkin awoke one morning with a fever, a runny snout, and a painful throat. He struggled molefully into the Library, did his work feeling increasingly ill and full of aches and pains, had to bear a public chastizing from Sturne for some misdemeanour or other – he was not sure what, since his ears buzzed, his eyes felt all swollen, and just listening made him feel tired – and he had gone home and retired to his nest.

When he next woke it was night and he knew he was not well at all; his snout was blocked, and every joint and talon in his body ached.

'Oh dear,' he whispered to himself, 'I am not well. I am ill. I . . .'

and he felt tears come to his painful eyes, and self-pity overcame him, and a sense almost too much to bear that he was alone in Duncton Wood and not a single mole cared for him.

Next morning he knew he could not go to the Library, not even to tell them he was going straight back to his tunnels again. No, he *was* ill, and in his burrow he would stay. So he did, bunged up, tired, confused and feeling thoroughly miserable, getting steadily worse for several days before, weak as a new-born pup, he felt his condition level out to one of general and all-consuming misery.

That day, or a few days later perhaps – he was not sure, the time drifted by – Acting Master Librarian Sturne thought to send another aide to his tunnels to find out what was wrong and, most unsympathetically, to suggest he get better as soon as he could, as his help was needed for 'the reorganization'.

'Whad reoraniayshun?' asked Pumpkin as best he could.

'Of the Library, Pumpkin. They're clearing so much out you wouldn't believe it!'

'Argh!' said Pumpkin.

'It's quite shocking, in my view. Perfectly good texts, and not all of them copied so far as I know, are being disposed of.'

'Ergh!' declared Pumpkin, wishing the aide would go away. A nice enough mole, meant well, knew his job, but, oh dear, 'Attiishoo!' ejaculated Pumpkin.

'You're not well, old fellow,' said the aide.

'Aaargh!' gulped Pumpkin.

The visit seemed to Pumpkin to have lasted far too long, and the painful conversation to have lasted even longer, and he was utterly exhausted at the end of it. The Library texts, and all the aides, and the Newborns, and the Stone, and all moledom itself could go and lose themselves as far as he was concerned. He just wanted to sleep, and for his head to clear, and for the pain behind his eyes to go.

'Pleague league me alogue!' said Pumpkin.

'Only doing my job, unlike some,' said the mole and left.

Or had he left?

When Pumpkin awoke again he was aware that a mole was near, and there was the scent of food. A not entirely welcome scent but it made him nauseous. He opened his eyes and saw that time had passed and day was nearly done.

'Who's there?' he said, struggling to focus his aching eyes and see whatmole it was. For the first time in all the long years he had lived in those tunnels they felt . . . chill.

49

'Library Aide Pumpkin, I am sorry you are unwell.'

The voice was as acrid as the scent.

Pumpkin finally opened his eyes and stanced up on shaking paws, the chamber swimming about him. One mole? No, three moles. All close, all dark, all with shining eyes that stared at him and glittered and were cold as ice.

'We felt we should come to talk to you, Pumpkin,' said the mole.

'Wahd abow?' said Pumpkin, wincing at the ragged soreness of his throat.

'We were wondering,' said the mole, eyeing the worm and then taking a delicate nibble at it and speaking as he tasted and chewed, 'we were wondering . . .'

'Wammole are you?' asked Pumpkin, beginning to recover himself.

'. . . we were wondering what you know about the death last evening of the mole Drubbins?' said Brother Fetter, Newborn Inquisitor, smoothly.

Chapter Five

'The journey westward'. . . How those words reverberate now in the minds of moles who know Whillan's great text* describing how he, Privet and Maple made their trek from Duncton in time to take part in Thripp's infamous Convocation of Caer Caradoc.

It was the journey of three great moles into the final setting of the sun of innocence over a moledom much of which was already darkened by the advancing night of the Newborns. A journey which until its final part seems now almost miraculous in the way it avoided those coming shadows, so that those three moles might know, if only briefly, but remember for ever, a moledom where systems were welcoming to the traveller, and where faith and trust, openness and good humour, were the abiding qualities of the moles they met.

In telling her tale the night before they left, Privet had said truly that it is often only moleyears later that moles see that what they least understand and most resist is what in its wisdom the Stone knows is best for them. So now the Stone decreed that they had a time of quiet journeying to ready themselves for the harder times to come.

As Whillan himself later scribed, 'It seemed we wandered through a land of contentment and goodness, where moles had the old virtues of friendliness and welcome, of wholesome curiosity mixed with an innate sense of our need for privacy; in system after system we found moles old and young, male and female, who held the Stone in reverence and regard, and who felt sure that moles who came as we had done from Duncton Wood, and were on a mission to Caer Caradoc at which matters of importance would be discussed, must be moles worthy of their confidence. There is nothing like having moles believe in you to make you believe in yourself and wish to live by the precepts of the Stone.

---

* *The Journey Westward* is the first of Whillan of Duncton's now classic quartet of texts describing the journeys of his life. The other three are, of course, *The Long Way North, Eastward,* and the last text, only recently discovered, *The Journey Home.*

'When the darker times came, and come they eventually did, it was always of those modest moles, and simple, beautiful places in the Wolds, that I would think; and when I had to find courage to defend what I believed was right, or strength to conquer any weakness of mind or body that I felt, it was not theories that sustained me, but the memories I had of that journey among the moles of the High Wolds.'

That all this would be so could not have been at all obvious from the way the journey at first developed through the dull cold days that followed their parting from Fieldfare and Chater at the Swinford cross-over. It was long and hard, and each was lost in their own thoughts for days on end. But there came a new dawn when the day seemed warmer, and lighter, and they found they were ready to enjoy each other's company again.

From that moment on their journey became a blessed thing as day after day they trekked north-west, ever higher into the Wolds, where the rocks are soft and golden, and the soil is warm and good, and all seems to conspire to keep the worst of winter at bay, or, if unable to do that, to turn its chills and frosts to something beautiful in the hills and high vales, copses and little woods, streamlets and forgotten ways.

Feeling themselves now well clear of Duncton, and unlikely to be quickly discovered even if they made themselves known to moles they met, it was not long before they ventured to contact communities whose territories their obscure route took them across – which was not hard, for most were out and about and busy clearing their lower runs and burrows for the winter soon to come. Privet had already decided that once they met other moles they would make no attempt to hide who they were, where they were from, or where they were going – though both Maple and Whillan would have preferred to be less open, thinking that by being vague they might put back the day when, as seemed inevitable, the Newborns would catch up with them, but they deferred to Privet's wish.

'We are journeying in pursuit of truth, and to see that true words are spoken at Caradoc, and it does not help our cause, or the Stone's, if we lie about who we are,' she said.

Chater had taught the rudiments of safe journeying to Whillan well, and in concert with Maple he led Privet on through those bright days, cautiously at first, but with increasing speed and efficiency as their confidence increased.

It was not long after this upturn in their mood that their circuitous route swung them northwards into the valley of the River Windrush, whose cheerful waters flowed past them in a south-easterly direction and would, had they turned that way, have led them back towards Duncton Wood. Instead they turned upstream and began that part of their journey which led them to the forgotten heart of old moledom. By Burford they went, and Great Barrington; to Sherborne and then up and on to the little system of Broadmoor, whose moles tell a merry tale and keep visitors lingering. But Bourton beckoned, and on to it they went, to meet the moles whose sturdy independence and simple cunning a century before had kept moles of the Word from proceeding further than this point into the Wolds. Here Maple was much in his element, glad to exchange views with moles whose ancestors had fought a good fight against the Word, and who continued to the present day to post watchers, on the look-out for threats against their freedom and integrity.

Not surprisingly, it was in Bourton that the three moles gathered the clearest evidence that the Newborns were ready to advance from the major systems such as Duncton into areas which, like the Wolds, were off the main communal routes of moledom.

'Aye, they've been sending whipper-snapper missionaries up to turn our minds,' said Stow, Bourton's tough senior elder, 'but we've been giving them short shrift here, and sending them packing. A wheedly lot, the Newborns, but not to be underestimated. They've already taken over a couple of the bigger systems along the vales of the Cherwell and Evenlode, which lie east of us, and they'll be back again to tell us what to think before long. One of their strongholds is the Evesham system which lies beyond the Wolds, near which you'll have to go on your way to Caradoc. Perhaps you should have taken a tougher stance in Duncton Wood!'

'Maybe,' replied Maple, 'but I think not. Our tradition is one of tolerance, and until a mole or a sect shows their true colours we shouldn't deny them the right to express themselves. That's doing to them what we don't want them to do to us. The trouble is that the Newborns are well led by Thripp, and he's bided his time.'

'Aye, he may have judged it well . . .' said Stow, and several of the powerful Bourton moles about him nodded sombrely. Whillan and Privet noticed that in such company Maple seemed to gain in authority, and to command respect out of proportion to his proven experience, or even his age. He carried himself as a mole of integrity, the kind others would think twice about crossing.

'There's consolation for moles like us in the history of wars in moledom, both ancient and modern,' said Maple seriously, his words the

53

more authoritative because of the long study he had made of moledom's military history. 'We may seem late in getting started in opposition, because it's in our nature to give others a chance, even if we suspect them of malevolence and evil-doing, as some of us have long suspected the Newborns. But at least we know that when we do decide to resist them, and fight for what is right, the majority of moles whose voices are rarely heard will be behind us, and support us. It has always been so in moments of moledom's greatest darkness, for it's then the Stone sends forth a leader to show us all the way.'

'That's well thought, and well said!' declared Stow. 'You may rest assured, Maple of Duncton, that if ever a call goes out for support for just resistance to the Newborns, our moles here in Bourton will not be found wanting in courage or loyalty. As for others in the Wolds, especially those peaceable tradition-loving moles in the systems in the High Wolds west of us amongst whom you'll soon be travelling, I reckon that you can always count on their support as well.

'There's something dark and dingy about the Newborns, however reasonable and full of the Stone's praise their words may be. Well, we've not fallen for it here in Bourton and we never will – send the word, Maple, and we'll be alongflank you before you can say "Perish the Newborns!" Mind you, I expect you've heard that the Newborns aren't having it all their own way?'

'No?' said Maple. 'Some of your moles have crossed their path and had the better of it?'

'Oh, not *here*, not here. We've merely avoided trouble so far. No, I'm talking of that mole up north they call Rooster.'

The three Duncton moles were suddenly silent and attentive at this unexpected mention of Rooster's name, which Stow noticed and misinterpreted.

'You know something of him then? Where he is and what he's at?'

'No more than what we had heard before we left Duncton in October – that he had been taken by the Newborns and was held somewhere in captivity,' replied Maple evenly. 'It was something we hoped perhaps to hear more of at the Convocation in Caradoc.'

'Oh, no,' said Stow, 'we've heard something since then.'

'Aye,' said one of his colleagues eagerly, 'we've heard that the stories of Rooster being taken prisoner were put about by the Newborns, to put others off any idea of following or supporting him. He's said to be where he always was.'

'The Moors?' asked Privet quietly.

'The Moors?' repeated Stow, shaking his head. 'That's not a system

54

I know about, if it *is* a system. As far as we've heard it, Rooster's stronghold is Beechenhill, which is why the Newborns don't take kindly to him. That system was a centre for resistance against moles of the Word.'

'Where did you hear he was not held by them?' asked Whillan.

'From a mole you'll likely meet in the next few days as you climb up into the High Wolds. In fact, he's only been gone from us a couple of days, and as he's got a snout for news and interesting moles and the tales they tell, I'll warrant he'll make his way to you before long. His name is Weeth. He's a talkative bugger, but that's his way.'

'Whatmole is he?'

'A good question. He's from Evesham, but since that became Newborn through and through he's been wandering about looking for somewhere else to use his restless paws. He's well known up in the Wolds, mainly because he *is* restless, and always going here and there poking his snout in where he shouldn't and getting into trouble.'

'He's not a Newborn spy then?' asked Maple.

'The thought had crossed my mind,' said Stow, 'and he might very well be in a sense. Certainly he seems not to get caught by them. But we gave him a heavy going-over when he first appeared and came to the conclusion he's all right. He's too individual to be Newborn, if you see what I mean. And you *will* see what I mean! As for what he had to say about Rooster, he got *that* recently from the Newborns over in Evenlode Valley – said they were abuzz with it and that, in fact, the latest rumour is that Rooster's on his way to Caer Caradoc as part of a delegation of moles representing Beechenhill. Very confusing.'

At which startling news Privet must have been much shaken, but she contrived not to show it then, nor later did she want to talk about it. Rooster seemed so long ago in her past that rumours such as this, and the possibility of meeting him again, much beloved as he once had been by her, were too much for her to contemplate.

'Why did this Weeth go up into the High Wolds?' continued Maple.

Stow shrugged. 'Looking for what he calls "opportunity". That's his creed and watchword. Believes there's a mole will give him opportunity. Naturally he wouldn't say which mole, but then Weeth likes making a mystery of things. He'll tell us next time we see him.'

'When will that be?' asked Maple, thinking it might be worth lingering a few days more in the hope of meeting Weeth.

'You never know with a mole like that. Here today, gone tomorrow and back Stone knows when. Only one thing's certain: it's when you least expect it.'

'Well . . .' said another Bourton mole with a grin.

'Well?' said Maple.

'I've noticed that Weeth usually appears just when moles are settling down to eat. It's a knack he's got. I don't suppose he's gathered a worm for himself in months.'

'I like the sound of Weeth,' said Privet. 'Moledom *needs* individuals.'

'Answer me this if you can,' said Stow.

They looked at him expectantly.

'It's about this mole Rooster, and something Weeth said but couldn't explain. It's the sort of thing a Duncton mole might know, seeing as you're a learned, scribing lot.'

They waited.

'What exactly *is* a Master of the Delve?'

As the three travellers moved on up into the High Wolds other moles of Stow's tough kind seemed always to seek Maple out, and pledge him their support if ever they were needed – almost as if he intended them to, and was preparing the ground against the day when resistance might indeed need to be organized, and quickly too.

On they went then into regions where isolation had preserved the secret forgotten world of old values; quaintly delved systems, that lie in the upper reaches of the Windrush; through Naunton, past Guiting and on to the High Wold itself, where the Windrush is little more than a boisterous brook, and the moles of Ford and Cutsdean and Taddington speak their Mole with the slow burr of an age gone by. News of their coming travelled ahead of them, and at each of these systems, and many others besides, moles came to greet them, and to invite them to stay a day or two, and share in their food and conversation, and take part in their rituals before the Stone.

Whilst Maple quietly gathered intelligence and support for future resistance to the Newborns, Whillan turned in on himself, as if the moles he was meeting and the values they lived by were things he wished to ponder and assimilate without comment. At this time, to the many who met them, he seemed the weakest and quietest of them all, and on occasion broke free of the little group and spent a day or two by himself, staring over the wide flat tops of the Wolds into the blue distances of moledom beyond, which, perhaps, he was at this time preparing to travel to, as Keeper Husk had suggested he should.

Meanwhile, something deep was happening to Privet as well. Made vulnerable by the revelations of her tale, and keeping quiet through the first part of their journey from Duncton Wood, here in the High Wolds she began to find a new quality of peace and wisdom. It was something those who met her very soon sensed, and when they gathered in the communal chambers of the moles in these systems, it was her words, her tales, her thoughts that others listened to with most attention and respect. Here, they said to themselves, is a true Duncton scribemole; *here* is one who has turned her snout towards the Stone and will not be misled away from it. Here is a mole who carries something of the Stone's Silence in her paws.

However much Privet shook her head at such suggestions, and smiled in her self-deprecating way, reminding them she was not originally of Duncton at all and explaining that she had many doubts in the Stone – just as the great Master Librarian Stour himself had – with each day that passed she seemed to shed those burdens of her past that had so long weighed her down and had made her seem but a grey scholar with something to hide, to become instead a mole others instinctively knew held secrets of the Stone's ways and wisdom.

Now it was that she dared speak again those ritual liturgies she had learned so unhappily at her mother Shire's flanks, saying what a pity it is when dogmatic moles, or those that do not feel love, so often seek to teach great truths without understanding them . . .

'Moles who feel no love, and have only dogma as a friend, had better say nothing, and listen to the silence of their hearts. There they will hear the great Silence of the Stone, if they listen hard enough, and it will show them the portal that leads out into the light from the darkness and confines of the narrow tunnels they are in . . .'

Privet professed, when she said such things, to be speaking of the moles of the Word, but few who heard her had any doubt that the Newborn moles were also in her mind. She left her listeners in no doubt that she preferred their way of life to any the Newborns might offer.

'Here, amongst you, day by day, we moles from Duncton have been privileged to see how moles of the Stone should live – and for a short time to witness and be part of communities of a kind which Duncton itself has somehow ceased to be. Aye, it's true enough! For the best reasons, namely tolerance and letting others live their lives in peace whatever their belief, we have allowed the Newborns to thrive in Duncton, and now they threaten it. Well, if they threaten *our* system, they must threaten many others, and perhaps all moledom itself.

57

'In communities like yours here, and perhaps in many other "lost" communities of moledom – in the Anglian heights perhaps, which the Stone Mole himself visited, in the southern borderlands of Wales, in those unvisited areas north and west of Beechenhill, even in communities nearer at home like those of the Midlands, and eastward in the shadow of the Wen, where the two-foots live – I believe there must be others like you: silent, unknown, yet the preservers of the values that true communities sustain.

'Therefore, never say you are moles of no consequence. With the coming of the Newborns, the day may arrive when moledom will see you as most consequential of all, for on you will rest our last hopes that truth and tolerance will prevail . . . Then you may have to rise up and defend what you have, and show others its true worth.'

Whillan and Maple had left Duncton respecting her, and loving her too perhaps, but now their respect and love changed to a kind of reverence, as if they understood that Privet was becoming a mole who had survived harsh times with her inner spirit intact; a mole who, for a mysterious reason none of them yet knew, had been sent out once more by the Stone itself to face the dangers of moledom, and whom, as best they could, they must protect.

This conversation, during the last of their pauses in the High Wolds, had taken place in the Taddington system, which lies but a short distance from the source of the Windrush. The land beyond continues as gentle, rolling, dry valley and it was up this, the following day, that the Taddington moles accompanied Privet, Whillan and Maple on the last stage of their journey through the Wolds. Northwards was Shenberrow Hill, the highest point of that region, where moles thereabout, on great occasions, congregated from the adjacent systems to praise the Stone and wish each other well.

December had now come, and the weather that had blessed the travellers so long with clear skies, and pale sunny days, seemed holding still, but only just. The leafless trees along the way trembled sometimes, somewhat out of proportion to the light cold breezes, as if they sensed that winter storms were on the way.

There had been no expectation that other moles would meet them from Snowshill, the system that lay in the north-east lee of Shenberrow, and faced across the great flat Vale of Evesham, beyond which Caer Caradoc rose. But as they reached the last slopes of the hill they were surprised to see several moles on top, all of Snowshill, all old, and their greeting was not ready, nor many words forthcoming until one of them recognized one of the Taddington moles.

'Don't tell me you lot have become Newborn! You look glum enough to have done so!'

The Taddington mole shook his head, puzzled, and introduced the three Duncton moles.

'*Librarian* Privet? *Strong* Maple? *Studious* Whillan?' repeated the Snowshill mole as others from his system gathered round the three, peering at them with a mixture of curiosity and dismay.

'There you are!' said another Snowshill mole, 'I *said* these travellers must be the ones the Newborns are on the look-out for. You're for it, you lot are. I'd get away while you can!'

'What's apaw?' asked Maple quickly. 'What Newborns, and what do they want?'

At which invitation, the Snowshill moles were only too eager to talk. It seemed that for many a moleyear the Newborns had not extended their sphere of influence above Broadway, a big system on the communal route east and west, and the same one Chater had predicted the Newborns would use as a base to watch for the Duncton moles' coming. Not content with sending scouts up to Snowshill, perhaps having heard already of the Duncton moles' proximity, they had sent a large missionary force as well.

'Aye, and a persuasive lot they are too!' said one of the Snowshill moles. 'You should see how some of our females have already fallen for their smooth talk of the Stone and the right ways to worship, and now our young follow suit. They've only been with us a few days but we're all that remains of those holding out against them. We just came up here for a bit of old-fashioned praying – not that the Newborns approve of course, since they say praying is best done in a group. Anyway, there's moles down in Broadway awaiting you lot.'

'Do you know their names?' asked Maple.

'Oh yes, they're quite open about information. There's one of your own moles, name of Deputy Master Librarian Snyde. He's there, kicking his paws and getting impatient. But the brother they go in fear of is the one they call Senior Brother Chervil, and he's not best pleased with you for some reason or other. Oh yes, you've got a merry reception awaiting you.'

This exchange might have continued, and any one of the several courses of action that Maple was considering have been followed, had not another couple of Snowshill moles appeared, two females this time, and in something of a hurry.

'They're coming up this way, lads,' they announced.

'Who are?' asked a Snowshill mole.

59

'The whole bloody system, led by the Newborns, to have a pray-in. Didn't like you going off by yourselves so they thought they'd join in and swamp you.' Even as she spoke they heard the sound of moles singing from some way downslope to the north, the male voices somewhat overpowered by the high trills of females and youngsters.

'Stone me,' said one of the Taddington moles, 'I'm clearing out of here fast.'

'And me!' said most of his friends immediately, with apologetic looks towards the Duncton moles.

'I think this is where you're on your own! Unless you want to come with us?'

Privet shook her head. 'I'm afraid our way is to Caradoc, and I think it may now be in the company of Newborn moles.'

'Well, if you don't mind we'll be off now,' said the Taddington leader, casting a fearful look towards where the singing swelled ever louder. 'But you lot,' he looked towards the Snowshill moles, 'are you coming with us?'

They looked hesitant, but then Maple went among them and said, 'You go with them. If you've had the wits to come this far, you'd best be with moles you can trust. Send news of this down to Stow of Bourton who knows my feelings about the Newborns, and I've a feeling that others like you will begin to gather now in the Wolds, and perhaps down about the Bourton system.'

'And you, mole, what of you?' they said to Maple. 'Stay with us; we need a mole like you, others will follow you. You've got a vision of things wider than we have, you and Privet, and Whillan. *Stay* with us . . .'

There was a stir of approval, and a sense of a movement forming as the moles surged nearer each other and waited for Maple's reply. But after a quick look at his two friends he shook his head.

'My task isn't here yet,' he said. 'Whillan and I are to go to Caradoc with Privet to protect her, and that will give us a chance to see what kind of mole this Thripp of Blagrove Slide really is. Maybe our fears are exaggerated; but if not, my paws will be strengthened by knowing something more of my enemy than mere rumour and report. Therefore be patient, stance firm here up in the Wolds, follow the lead of the Bourton moles you know you can trust, and when we can get word to you we will do so.'

The singing downslope was louder still, and it could not be many moments before the first of the approaching moles came into sight.

'Now, be off! And be safeguarded in the Stone!' ordered Maple.

60

'And you mole, and you all!' they replied. 'We've learnt a lot from you, Librarian Privet, and we want to learn more. Come back to us soon and tell us you regret having left us at all! Now . . . where will you go, or are you going to wait for the Newborns to capture you here?'

It was the normally silent Whillan who decided for them. 'Let's avoid them a little longer, for we'll learn something of their intentions in the way they pursue us. We can drop down the wooded western side of the hill and make our way at our leisure towards Evesham. I fancy a day or two more of liberty!'

'Well spoken, mole!' said Maple.

With that, and final waves of farewell, the moles of the Wolds turned quickly south-east and were soon lost across the gentle folds of the ground. While the three Duncton moles, without more ado, turned towards the cover and shadows of the stand of beech trees not far to their west and set off, as the first of the Newborn-led moles came into view. But as they reached the darkness of the trees they were astonished to see a mole, stanced firmly and calmly in their path, with an overly weary expression on his face, as if he had been awaiting them for a long time, and they were late.

'And whatmole are you?' said Maple, eyeing him suspiciously.

'An opportunist whose special skills you are about to find you need,' he replied.

'You're Weeth!' exclaimed Whillan, with certainty.

'My notoriety precedes me,' said Weeth smugly. 'And no doubt they said I talk rather too much?'

'They did,' said Maple heavily.

'They're right, I do ask rather a lot of questions. I am a curious mole.'

'And are you going to delay us by asking a lot of questions now, or can you let us by so we're not seen by the Newborns up on the hill?'

'There is one question I wouldn't mind an answer to, as a matter of fact,' said Weeth, who was a sturdy, compact mole with a ready grin and an easy energetic air.

'What's that?' said Privet.

'It's the question that every Newborn this side of Caer Caradoc has been asking,' said Weeth, 'since they discovered that a delegation had been sent out from Duncton and was on its somewhat obscure way across the Wolds in the form of you three moles.'

'And what's the question?' said Maple, advancing on Weeth and leading the other two into the shadows.

'Where's Master Stour? *That*'s the question. Because if he's not with you, and I see no sign of him, where is he and what's he doing, and why is he doing it?'

Maple seemed about to say something, but with a magisterial dignity Weeth raised a paw to silence him.

'Oh, please don't *answer* me,' said Weeth, with apparent alarm. 'The opportunity lies in *not* answering. You see, it now seems that everymole who is anymole in moledom is intending to turn up at the Convocation of Caradoc except the one mole who makes it all worthwhile for sinister Thripp to have summoned it: the good old Master Librarian Stour himself. Most intriguing, and redolent with opportunity. That's why I sought you out, and have been following your progress for some days past. I am so glad you decided to come the way I thought you should – no doubt to stay clear of the Newborns for a few days longer?'

Whillan nodded, impressed by Weeth's perspicacity.

'I will lead you on,' said Weeth grandly.

'And why should we follow a mole we don't know we can trust?' said Maple, wondering what it was about Weeth that made him likeable.

'Oh, you shouldn't and you can't!' said Weeth, 'and yet you will. I will lead you to Evesham and it will take three days. In that time you can assess me for yourselves. Regard me as an opportunity, a kind of resource to draw on.'

'And what are we to you, Weeth?' said Privet.

'*The* opportunity, the one I have been looking for all my life. The one of the decade, of the age, that's what you are. Three moles from Duncton Wood, coming in all innocence to the Convocation of Caer Caradoc, without a hope of achieving anything at all but your own obscurity and probably your deaths! Amazing. Impressive. Just what I was always led to expect from Duncton moles. When I heard who you were, and what you were, and where you were going, I decided I would tag along, because this was *it*!'

'And if it isn't?' said Maple.

Weeth grinned winningly. 'Ah! Yes! That *is* a possibility. I might, as it were, have backed a pup, or three pups! I might be wrong. But like all opportunists I am also an incurable optimist. If the sense of destiny which your coming inspires in me proves mistaken then life will, I imagine – I confidently hope – offer me another opportunity to make up for my failure with you.'

'We'll have to see, won't we?' said Maple. 'So lead us on, Weeth, and let's find where your destiny leads us.'

'Incredible, inspiring,' muttered Weeth as he turned downslope. 'This mole's decisive, this mole backs hunches, this mole's an opportunist too but doesn't know it. "Maple and Weeth"! Sounds good! Sounds *right*. This *must* be the one, the opportunity of a lifetime!'

Without more ado Weeth turned confidently, and led them amongst the trees towards where the hill dropped even more steeply. Ahead the world seemed to open out, as far below, extending north-west, the Vale of Evesham stretched out. Beyond it a line of hills rose up, and behind them one darker than the others.

'Caradoc,' said Weeth; and it was all he needed to say.

Chapter Six

It seemed to Pumpkin that there was no air to breathe, no sound to
hear, nothing, nothing to grasp on to in his tunnels as he tried to
comprehend what Brother Inquisitor Fetter had said so calmly, so
matter-of-factly, so chillingly.

Drubbins *dead*? But how could that be? He had been alive a few
days ago, before Pumpkin had become ill. But then – when Pumpkin
had left the good-natured old mole he *had* looked as if he was in fear
of his life.

'Frightnehned,' repeated poor Pumpkin now, struggling to make
sense of the confusion in his mind; his throat was so swollen and
painful with his cold that just to speak was agony, and what he did
get out was slurred.

Then, 'Hewgh are *yewhh*?' he asked.

He looked through runny, puffy eyes at the moles who had come
unbidden into his tunnels, and knew only too well who they must be.
The Newborn Inquisitors, that's who. The one in command, chewing
the worm, was Brother Fetter. The other two were Brothers Law and
Barre, the latter the cruellest-looking of the three with tiny eyes like
bloodied talon-points.

Pumpkin felt a stab of fear as his mind suddenly cleared and his
thoughts came out of the fug they had been in to a place where
everything seemed all too plain, all too terrible.

They had asked him about Drubbins, and said he was dead.
They were grouped around him, uncomfortably close, one of
them eating a worm and all of them fixing him with stares such
as he had never seen before. Was this the beginning of the kind
of treatment poor Drubbins had suffered at their paws? Had
they brought him death as well? Had it already begun? And if it
had, what was he to do? He felt scared stiff. But angry too. Yes,
angry!

'Why's Drubbins dead?' he asked.

'"Why's Drubbins dead, *Brother*,"' said the Inquisitor.

Pumpkin looked blank.

64

'You're to call us "Brother", Library Aide Pumpkin. You understand?'

Pumpkin stared, and did understand. If he called them 'Brother' it showed them respect, but took something away from him. It meant they were making him behave as they wanted. Everything, every bit of him, protested at calling them 'Brother'. He didn't like moles who barged into his modest little burrow without a by-your-leave or thank-you; he didn't like being crowded; he didn't like *them* not showing him respect, even if he was merely a library aide and they were . . . whatever they were.

'Yes, Brother,' said Pumpkin as meekly as he could, because he wasn't a fool, and he remembered Master Stour saying that his lot might be hard, and if he must pretend to be what he wasn't the Stone would understand.

'Say it with respect, mole,' said the Brother Inquisitor.

'Got a cold,' said Pumpkin, gulping painfully, 'throat hurts, difficult to say anything.'

'Brother.'

'Brother, Brother.'

'Well? And what have you to say about Elder Drubbins, as he was called here?'

'I—'

'You are about to say you know nothing about Elder Drubbins, but we know you do. We know you talked to him only a few days ago, and he told you that he had suffered somewhat at our paws.'

Pumpkin had been about to deny all knowledge of Drubbins recently, that was true. What was also true was that the Inquisitor was clever and there was no point in telling him lies. He – or rather they – knew things. But what things?

Pumpkin stared on and waited, surprised at the sudden clarity of his thinking, and the fact that his fear had subsided, subdued by his anger. They were here to find something out, probably something they did not know; which meant they could not be sure that *he* knew it. He could pretend to be stupid, as he had done already since they had arrived.

'Well, mole? We're waiting.'

The Brother Inquisitor's eyes flicked for a moment to those of his friends and then back at Pumpkin. Shiny black talons kneaded the ground at his paws.

'Saw Drubbins before I became unwell. He looked ill and scared. He—'

'And now he's dead. Did you kill him?'

Pumpkin had recourse to silence again, but his heart was thumping. Drubbins really *dead*? Good Drubbins, wise Drubbins, best-elder-of-them-all Drubbins.

'How did he die?' asked Pumpkin.

Suddenly the meaner-looking of the other two, Brother Barre, came forward, grabbed Pumpkin, and as the others cried out 'No, Barre! Not yet! Give him . . .' Pumpkin found himself being dragged bodily out of the burrow and up to the surface.

'You're a blasphemous little bastard,' snarled Barre ferociously, 'and I'm going to show you the consequences of your thinking.'

'But—'

'We'll go and see Drubbins and see if reality makes you tell us what happened.'

'Aargh!' gasped Pumpkin, every muscle and bone in his body aching, and his head swirling, as he found himself forcibly taken across the Wood towards the Eastside.

'Where . . . ?'

'To the cross-under, you little turd,' said the Inquisitor.

The cross-under? That was a long long long longhhhh . . . way way away, and Pumpkin's body felt so weak, his paws rolling one after another after another and hurting, the Inquisitor's grip on him painful and the trees swaying by and behind him and he reaching out his paws to hold on, to stop, to try to rest, just for a moment so his eyes could close and free his head from such pain and confusion.

'Rest, Brother Pumpkin, rest . . .'

A great grey sky loomed up from between the trees ahead, and the ground fell away into the Pastures, which went down and down and down to the cross-under, dark and dripping wet and cold. Probably something frightening was huddled and bloody there. Oh! Had poor Drubbins been driven to kill himself? Had he stanced in the path of a roaring owl rather than face the Newborn Inquisitors?

'Rest, mole, no need . . .'

How good the voice of the first Inquisitor sounded, almost like a friend, and his touch, which had replaced that of Barre, instead of being a pulling, savage grip, was support, all gentle, kindly and alluring. He could say yes to a mole like Fetter now. Ah, then, was that how the Inquisitors worked – one nice, another vile?

'Rest . . .' Fetter's voice said hypnotically somewhere above Pumpkin.

Rest . . . and the grassy slopes down below fell away because he did not need to go down them but was allowed to stop, to remain here at the edge of the Wood. Pumpkin felt like crying with relief because there was no need to go to the cross-under, no need to see whatever dark thing was there, no need.

'Well, mole?' It was Brother Fetter again, firm and sure of himself. Pumpkin strove to open his eyes and saw a mole, grey and vile violet in the bright light of day. 'What do you see?'

Pumpkin blinked, looked again and widened in shock at what they saw – Drubbins, dead. His mouth was set open, the teeth worn and stained, the snout violet, like a bruise, and the eyes red, puffy and only half-closed.

'And is it the Elder Drubbins?'

There is a quality of decency that brute malevolence cannot recognize, for if it did it would wither into something weaker, and a little better. A decency that is simply a powerful sense of what is right and what is wrong, which is so ingrained in some moles' hearts that it is as integral as the innermost growth rings in a mature oak tree.

Pumpkin stared at Drubbins' corpse and knew it was wrong, quite wrong that he had to do so like this; wrong, all of it; wrong, these moles. Wrong! He had been breaking down, but now he was made strong once more by the wrongness of what they tried to do to him. He stared at poor Drubbins and saw the marks of taloning to his chest and wondered what it was in moledom that could make trees as beautiful as those that rose up above them all, whose roots curved out and wound along the ground, the bark grey, the lichen shining green, yet could also make a mole die as Drubbins had; and moles like these . . . these nothings, who were seeking to bully and break him too.

That sense of decency arose in good Pumpkin's heart and mind, and tears came to his eyes to see such an elder as Drubbins brought to such an end.

'Well, Brother Pumpkin, and why did you do this?'

'Brother' Pumpkin shook his head slowly and lopsidedly, because he wanted to seem stupid, and frightened, and confused, but what he was doing was quietly and most clearly saying farewell to Drubbins on behalf of Duncton Wood and its community, and commending a mole who had given so much to his fellow moles, to the Silence and everlasting sanctuary of the Stone.

'Did talk to him,' said Pumpkin at last, as pathetically and weakly as he could. He was surprised to feel pity for these moles; pity that they should lead such evil, pointless lives. They could not, they must *never* win their war against the followers of the Stone.

67

'Did he tell you about Stour?' said the Inquisitor. How soft and gentle his voice now, and how eager, too eager.

'Master Librarian Stour,' said Pumpkin, as a librarian's aide would.

'Yes, Brother, Master Stour. Well?'

'Drubbins said he had been frightened when he talked to you. He told me my master had gone to Caradoc and left Sturne in charge . . .'

Pumpkin blathered on, telling things which were true, the kind of things a stupid mole might think Inquisitors would like to hear. He was pleased to notice out of the corner of his downcast, abject eye that the brothers were beginning to look bored, at which point he ended abruptly by saying, 'Don't like Sturne.'

'But as your Acting Master, you will obey him?'

'Must,' intoned Pumpkin.

'And us, for the Stone's well-being in this place?'

'Yes, Brother,' said Pumpkin as eagerly as he could.

But oh dear, oh dear, oh no . . . his attempt at idiocy seemed not to have worked, for Barre came to him then and gripped him once more, saying words that the others did not gainsay: 'I'll take him down to the Marsh End for final education.' Then Pumpkin did feel fear, deep, deep fear, and all began to swirl in darkness once again as he was taken unresisting away from the Wood's bright edge, away from that body, to start downslope towards the misty and dreadful Marsh End where Fieldfare had so nearly been lost to the High Wood for ever.

Then suddenly a different voice spoke out: 'Brothers, I heard you might be here. I would suggest *this* mole stays with us. We have need for skilled Library Aides if the Stone's work in the Library is to be completed by Longest Night.'

Pumpkin knew the voice but in his fright and further confusion at being stopped yet again he could not remember the name. He opened his eyes and found himself staring into the chill regard of Keeper Sturne. There was a look of contempt on Sturne's face.

'Wanth to workh in Library,' said Pumpkin, 'thash all.'

'If you say so, Brother Sturne,' said Barre, almost hurling Pumpkin from his grasp. 'But I don't trust moles like him. Alien spirits can rise again. The snake in the doubting heart is hard to dislodge.'

'I shall watch him with due care,' said Sturne, 'and when his task is done I agree that it will be well if he is educated in Newborn ways.'

'Yesh,' said Pumpkin, relief flowing into him, and feeling that saying something positive might help; 'educaishe me ash mush as yewh ligh.'

'He's ill anyway,' said Sturne. 'Perhaps you can detail one of the Brothers to take him back to his quarters until he is fit to serve our cause in the Library.'

'Yesh, yesh,' said Pumpkin, slumping on the ground before Sturne. Why, despite all, did he feel reassured by Sturne? Just because he had saved him from being taken to the Marsh End, or was it something more?

'Drubbins is dead,' he said, tears pricking at his eyes. But Sturne's eyes stayed clear, and cold, and quite dispassionate.

'Recover yourself quickly, mole, your skills are needed. We will take it as errant and perverse if you do not report for duty very soon.'

'Oh I will, I will, shurr,' said Pumpkin most eagerly, as Sturne firmly led him away.

The next Pumpkin knew was finding himself huddled and confused on the surface back near his burrow, with an image in his mind of Brother Barre stanced over Drubbins' body, his eyes blank, black and cold and Pumpkin thinking that it was *he* who had killed Drubbins, definitely, but Stone was where retribution would be, must be, could only be. Moles must not take punishment of others into their paws, only the Stone could do that. Silence would be *that* mole's hell.

A few days later – Pumpkin never could remember how many – he woke feeling better, and clearer, and knowing he had been taken to the void, and held over it, and had survived, and would survive now, *must* survive.

'I must go to the Library today, and report for duty to Keeper Sturne,' he said to himself.

So he did, but taking it slowly, for his paws and limbs felt very weak, and the distance to the Library seemed very great. He had never in his life felt so alone, so beset by doubt and fear, as in that journey back to work across the surface of the High Wood.

'Stone, help me do what's right because I'm not the strong mole you seem to think I am. I'm just Pumpkin, Library Aide, nothing more at all than that. So if you're going to put hard tasks my way give me support, show me how to be strong.'

How modest was Pumpkin's prayer, how full of humility, how *Pumpkinish*.

'I've been ill, Keeper Sturne,' he said, when he finally dragged himself down into the Library's Main Chamber.

'I can see *that*, mole,' said Sturne, staring at him almost without expression before giving him the briefest of smiles.

Wait a moment, thought Pumpkin to himself. *Almost without*

expression; that was how Sturne looked. Which meant there was *some-thing* in his expression, something good, something hopeful. Now that *was* a strange thing, for that little bit of Sturne's response that was not cold and expressionless was . . . sympathetic. Then insight came to him. 'He's all right,' thought Pumpkin, in utter astonishment. 'Sturne's *all right*. Sturne's *not* Newborn. Sturne's strong, like Stour. Sturne *knows*.'

Such was his relief at this so-welcome discovery that poor Pumpkin, overwrought as he had been by the dreadful events of the days past which had left him feeling so isolated and weak, could not help himself at all, but cried with relief.

'You'll work just half the day, I don't want you damaging texts,' said Sturne coldly. Oh, but how welcome that coldness was to Pumpkin! Yes, yes, yes! He knew Sturne was putting on a show, an incredible, wonderful, brave, courageous show. And for whom? Out of the shadows came Brother Inquisitor Fetter, staring. For *him*, then. For *them*. For all the Newborns in moledom. Sturne was being a true, brave, good Duncton mole, and he, Pumpkin, must do all he could to help. This was the way the Stone was answering his recent and desperate prayer – not giving *him* support, but telling him *he* must give support. Here was surely the greatest task a Duncton library aide could ever be asked to perform! Pumpkin wept all the more, and could only hope that his pathetic tears would be misinterpreted as those of a weak mole, so cowed that he would be obedience itself to any Newborn command.

'Stop crying, mole,' ordered Fetter irritably.

'Yes, Brother,' replied Pumpkin meekly, sniffing back his tears and trying to control his gulps as he turned away to find a task.

'He's surely on the way to being one of us,' he heard the Brother Inquisitor mutter to Sturne.

'Yes,' Sturne replied coldly, 'he'll be one of us, and I am sure we shall be able to trust him to be malleable.'

'"One of us"!' declared Pumpkin to himself. 'I certainly am, and so intend to stay. One of the resistance, that's me!'

He began to weep again with relief and joy to know that out of death and darkness and illness had come this clear answer to his prayer, this light of companionable conspiracy, which now shone bright and showed him the way ahead.

'And where does the way ahead lead in the near future?' he thought to himself, as he stumbled and sniffled his way about his tasks. 'I think I know, I think Keeper Sturne has told me. For did he not say when

70

he rescued me from the Inquisitors over on the Eastside – for rescue that certainly was! – that the tasks here must be completed by Longest Night. Which, if that is so, means that something must be happening in our system then, something to do with the Newborns. Yes, yes! I may not be a strong mole, or a fighting mole, or a mole of action, but I, Pumpkin, library aide, will do what I can to help now, during and after Longest Night!'

So he urged himself on that first day back at his duties, and humble and insignificant though he may have seemed to anymole spying on him, as the Brother Inquisitor certainly was, the Newborns now had in him, as already in Keeper Sturne, a formidable opponent in their very midst.

This sense that something ominous was indeed going to happen across moledom on Longest Night was not confined to Pumpkin's perhaps feverish imagination, but had also taken grip in the consciousness of Chater and Fieldfare in the territory south of Duncton. It seemed that such forces as the Stone had at its command it was mustering in the days of November and December before Longest Night, and among them were the motley group of refugees (or pilgrims, as they called themselves) whom the two Duncton moles had discovered in a state of collapse before the Fyfield Stone. Their leader was Spurling, and the name of his mate, though she looked anything but succulent, rose-tinged and plump, was Peach. Their story, though new to Chater and Fieldfare, would have been depressingly familiar to anymole who knew the Newborns. They, like most of their companions, had been raised in Avebury where Spurling was a library aide and copyist. They had witnessed the rise of Newborn power at first-paw, come to understand the special nature of its evil, and bravely formed the cell of resistance of which Spurling, a reticent and studious mole, had become the leader. They had been betrayed to the Newborns, and evacuated forcibly to Buckland, to isolate them from Avebury moles they might 'taint'; and in Buckland they suffered the rigours of starvation and torture which had reduced them to the state in which Chater and Fieldfare found them.

Then, taking an opportunity for escape which arose when the disease of scalpskin had struck down the Newborns in Buckland and weakened their guards, Spurling had led fourteen moles out, their aim being to reach Duncton Wood for sanctuary, and give warning of the Newborns. By a combination of courage, faith, luck, and Spurling's not inconsiderable talent for cunning retreat when their Newborn

71

pursuers had seemed about to catch up with them, they had reached Fyfield two days before Fieldfare and Chater had heard of their presence. But they had lost over half of their group on the way through illness and capture, and two more of their number seemed close to expiring even as they told their tale.

But with Fieldfare's care, three days' rest, and good food, they were ready to move on before the Newborns heard of their presence in Fyfield. Spurling had much more to say of the Newborn threat and that had been the reason why he had been so bravely trying to get to Duncton – to warn it of the coming dangers. Now Chater advised him that it was best to get the party to a place of safety, where they might rest up more and decide what to do.

'One thing's certain, your original intention of going to Duncton Wood is definitely out,' he said.

'It was Spurling's dream,' said the much-recovered Peach. 'He always said he wanted to see the Duncton Stone before he died! I think part of his strength in leading us all this far was the hope of that!'

Spurling nodded ruefully and said, 'Well, that's not to be for now. Where do you think we should go, Chater?'

'Yes, you're the journeymole, my dear,' said Fieldfare, who on these public occasions was much more supportive of Chater than their affectionate bickering sometimes made her seem among friends, 'so you should know. Somewhere near but safe.'

'And somewhere others can find us if they're of a mind to resist,' added Spurling, 'for there's several here who've joined us on the way – some in Buckland brought from other systems for resisting "education", and some we met on the way to Fyfield.'

'Mmmm,' pondered Chater, 'it's hard, for any of the ordinary systems is likely to be visited by Newborns now, and even more so as they gain in strength, which they will in the molemonths coming if other indications we've had are to be trusted.'

'I've a thought!' said Noakes, one of the younger moles. 'There's a place all moles know which the Newborns fear, because they say it was desecrated in times gone by the grikes when they rampaged south in the name of the Word. I'm talking about Uffington.'

'Uffington! Of course!' said Chater, light coming to his eye as he thought of the community which had once been regarded as the most venerable of the seven Ancient Systems, but which a century before had been overrun by moles of the Word, its scribemoles massacred and great library all but destroyed.

'In fact,' said Noakes confidentially, 'between ourselves, a number of my friends set off to go there. You see, the system where I come from, Gurney, which lies south-east of here, is not that far from Uffington Hill, and when the Newborns first came to educate us a few fled Uffington way believing they might find a place to hide up there. I was too afraid to follow them, but when I saw what the Newborns were really like I tried to escape that way myself, and got to the base of Uffington Hill itself before I was caught, which is how I came to be in Buckland. It was obvious to me that the Newborns did not want or intend to go up to Uffington, and had I succeeded in finding a way past them I'm sure they would not have willingly followed. It might be worth a try!'

The matter was debated at length; some of the moles, including Spurling, were reluctant to set off on another long trek in a different direction to a destination they had no certainty of reaching in safety, and which was further away from Duncton Wood, on which they had set their hearts. But Chater saw the sense of it, and when Fieldfare declared that Uffington was a most holy place, and fitting for moles seeking refuge in a time of strife, the decision was made, and they set off, led by night by Chater and resting up during the day. It was in these long enforced pauses that Chater and Fieldfare heard the rest of Spurling's story, and understood the importance of the information that he had.

Spurling turned out not only to be a good teller of tales, but also a tougher and more resilient mole than his natural modest and quiet way suggested, as well as being one who had mastered the skills of scribing and, even more important, of survival in troubled times. His mate, Peach, was a quiet mole too, and though her health improved and the scalpskin she suffered abated, she remained nervous and fearful, and would not happily leave Spurling's flank for an instant.

Their tale was, perhaps, like many that could have been told in that period of the Newborns' emergence into power, and in many places throughout moledom where the sect that Thripp of Blagrove Slide had inspired had gained a grip. Every word of it confirmed Master Stour's long-held fears of what the Newborns might mean for moledom, and the wisdom that lay behind the plans he had made.

Yet darkly familiar though their story was, one part of it was darker than the rest, and concerned a mole whose fateful importance was realized up until that time perhaps by few moles beyond Avebury itself. As it unfolded it could not but put a growing and fearful regret in the hearts of Chater and Fieldfare that what they were learning had not been known to their friends Privet, Maple and Whillan before they set off for Caer Caradoc. Had it been, they would have realized the terrible danger into which their journey was taking them.

Chater could see no immediate way to remedy that, but could only pray that what he and Fieldfare were learning would better fit him for the task that Stour had given them. It was Spurling who told most of the tale, with Peach sometimes injecting here and there some comment or piece of information which served usually to make yet worse the implications of what they heard.

'Avebury was a grand system to be raised in,' began Spurling, 'and proud of the part it had played in the struggles for the liberty of the followers of the Stone in decades past. I became an aide in the library as a young mole, just as my father had been, and from the first I wished to learn scribing. I confess I had intended to go to Duncton Wood, for its fame under the Master Stour was great, but a certain mole caught my eye and I decided to stay where I was.'

He looked at Peach fondly, as if she were still the comely young female he had first met, and not the thin and ragged thing that clung so weakly now at his flank.

'They were good days and I learnt my scribing well, and though I soon realized I would never be a scholar or anything of that sort, yet I had my part to play in the managing of copying tasks, and making sure that we in Avebury passed out to other systems copies of certain texts unique to our library, just as Master Stour long ago arranged at the Cannock Conclave that moledom's major libraries should do.

'Our elders were a good mix of young and old, males and females, and the grim days when we had been herded away from the Stones we loved – for as you no doubt know, Avebury has a great ring of Stones – by the moles of the Word, seemed long past, never to return.

'Now, from what you have already said you know something of the evil of the Newborns, and knowing them as I now do, I daresay their methods in our system were similar to those you experienced. In short, they create what they call a "cell" of trusted moles, and this expands through the system by a combination of persuasion and threat . . . like a malign cancer.'

Chater nodded his head, for it did sound familiar.

'But the Newborns are a secretive lot, and the only mole among them whose name is generally known is Thripp of Blagrove Slide. You'll have heard of him . . . but let me tell you there's another mole who is his evil shadow, a mole whose name few know, and fewer have actually met – Quail, Senior Brother Quail. Now him I *do* know, for he was originally an Avebury mole, born only a season after myself, and in a burrow not far off.

'Oh indeed, I know Quail!' continued Spurling with a shudder. 'He's the coldest mole I ever met, with habits beyond imagining when he was young. He broke the legs off beetles that he might the more enjoy their struggles before he ate them; he put worms out in the hot sun to suffer as they dried; he caught and blinded dormice and watched them suffer as they died . . . and what is more . . .'

Peach stirred, a look of distress on her face. 'It was never proved,' she whispered, 'and the elders met and examined the matter twice.'

'Hmmph!' said Spurling heavily. 'What Peach is referring to is the fact that he is thought to have killed two pups of a litter of three, just out of curiosity.'

'It wasn't *proved*,' said Peach again.

'Those pups were Peach's siblings. Since she escaped being killed herself only because the culprit was disturbed it is perhaps not surprising she cannot quite remember the horror of that moment. No matter, that was the kind of mole Quail was, and it was only the spiritual, forgiving generosity of the system that prevented him from being punished in some way. As it was, the opposite happened. He was a clever mole, very clever, and quite the best scholar of his day with a special interest in modern history and, if I may say so, a morbid interest in certain leaders of the recent past like Henbane, and Lucerne, whose vile doings need no introduction to Duncton moles. He had, too, a pleasure in perversity. Had it not been for his obvious inability to like other moles he would have become our Master Librarian, and not a mole would have begrudged him the post. But that did not happen, and he grew frustrated and bitter and began to look for another outlet for his diabolic energy, and it was just then that the first Newborn missionary came and caught his interest.

'In those days the Newborns were still based in Blagrove Slide because the exodus (as they grandly call it) to Caer Caradoc had not yet happened. Nor could it have, since it was Quail himself who arranged that exodus! Aye, the moment he heard the Good News of the Right Way towards the Stone (their words, not mine) which the missionaries brought, he was a changed mole, a mole with a purpose, a mole who believed himself to be right and to have a just cause.

'I will not describe the process by which he then began to apply his intelligence and cold cunning to the rise of Newborn power in Avebury, nor dwell on the moles who conveniently disappeared, the undermining of the elders and the corruption of the Master Librarian.

75

But in the short space of a cycle of seasons following Quail's conversion to the Newborn cause, he had effectively built up a group of young ardent moles, nearly all male, who called themselves Newborn, and by the organization and leadership he gave they took over the system in which Peach and I were born. Before we knew what had happened it was too late, and opposition to them resulted only in demotion and trouble for those who tried it. *I* tried it, and was removed from my post of Deputy Copy Master to become a mere Library Aide; Peach tried it and found that the tunnels we had inherited from her father, which we had expanded and improved, were taken from us and given to a Newborn pair.'

'They said it was because we were pupless,' whispered Peach, 'but I was with pup, and would surely have had them if I had not been attacked.'

'Attacked?' said Fieldfare, horrified.

Peach nodded, her eyes filling with tears. 'Nomole ever knew who they were, but I think they were Newborns. I aborted and never got with pup again.'

'Well, of course,' continued Spurling, 'Avebury got too small for the likes of Quail. Other Newborn missionaries had come to visit, and he must have realized that his future lay at Blagrove. Anyway, the day came when he left us, along with a couple of his cronies, and went to Blagrove Slide to make his way with Thripp himself – and make his way he did, as we heard later from other Newborns. He made his way so well that he became indispensable to the Newborn leader and seems to have been the inspiration behind the takeover of Caer Caradoc.

'As you can imagine, knowing Quail as I once did, I have been interested to follow his progress. I confess that the only way I could do that was to finally subscribe to some of the Newborn views, like so many others in our system. It may have been weak – it *was* weak – but at least we survived, and you'd be surprised how easy it is to live a secret life under the rules of such a sect.

'I was useful to the Newborns in the library, and they grew to trust me, and promoted me once more, not guessing that already around me others had begun to gather who wished to resist them but did not know how. We remembered what we had been told of the distant time when the Word overtook Avebury and decided that the best we could do was to resist from within – to live the lie of pretending to be Newborn against the day when we might act. We might have remained unsuspected, but one of our number betrayed us – though fortunately she did not know the names of all of us. But some were tortured, and of these one or two broke down and told all. We do not blame them, we might have done the same.

'You might think that knowing they had been fooled the Newborns would have put us to death, but there is a curious hypocrisy in the way they work. They prefer to kill moles spiritually, to suborn them to their cause through a process called massing.'*

He saw at once from Fieldfare's expression that she knew precisely what a massing was.

'Yes, mole, it is a living death. Many of us, myself included, were taken from our posts and harried mercilessly, and put into a massing, and many died. We survivors were taken to confinement at Buckland, far enough from Avebury for us not to be a danger to the stability of their system. In Buckland, a system first developed by moles of the Word and used by them as a prison, we found others of our kind who had also somehow survived. Peach made her way of her own accord to me—'

'I couldn't live without him, not knowing if he was alive or dead, I had to find him!' said Peach.

Spurling's paw reached out to her and held her close. 'So there we were, and have been these summer years past. But Buckland is a place through which Newborn moles come and go, and we have learnt much of what the Newborns intend this Longest Night coming.'

'What *do* they intend?'

'Thripp has summoned a Convocation in Caradoc.'

'We know this,' said Chater.

'Ah, but do you know why? I'll tell you. Come Longest Night or thereabouts, when most major systems still dissenting from the Newborn way will have sent their most trusted moles to Caradoc, the Newborns will rise up in each of them and take control. In some places they have probably already begun to do so. It will be done in the name of the Stone, and the same censorship of texts that I myself have been involved with for mole years past in Avebury will be conducted in all the systems.

'No doubt too the infamous Brother Inquisitors, who are now under Brother Quail's sole direction, will have done their work, weeding out

---

* See *Duncton Tales*: the subterranean confinement of a group of moles suspected of blasphemy or 'wrong thought' in a chamber dangerously small for them in which many die while others are harangued by Brothers and Sisters about the Newborn way.

moles in whom they smell dissent and, as they would have it, blasphemy. Such moles will be "educated" in right thinking – a little intimidation here, a little massing there. The pups this coming spring will be taken from their rightful parents and taught the cold Newborn way – harsh discipline and no love at all warps a mole for life. Well, that's how it is, that's how it will be.'

Fieldfare and Chater had listened with increasing gloom to this chilling eye-witness account of the emergence of Brother Inquisitor Quail and the takeover of this part of moledom by the Newborns, for it mirrored some of their own experience, and confirmed only too starkly that all suspicions about the Newborns were amply justified.

'It's as grim as we had imagined,' said Chater. 'But, Spurling, when we first found you in Fyfield, or soon afterwards, you gave us to understand you wanted to go to Duncton Wood to warn it. What of? Is there something more you've not yet mentioned – something we haven't guessed?'

'What I've said so far is fact, more or less,' answered Spurling sombrely. 'The rest, I've got to say, is intelligent surmise based on things we've heard, or conclusions we've drawn, and though I can't say for sure these things will happen, it's a fair bet they might. Well, now, I said to myself that Duncton moles have stanced up for others in the past, and the least we could do, privileged (if that's the word!) as we were to be privy to some of Quail's secrets, and having contact with some of the moles like Fetter, and a loathsome mole called Barre, who are his most trusted Inquisitors, was to try to warn your system.'

'Failing that,' said Chater grimly, 'warn *me*, and Fieldfare too, and we'll decide if there's anything we can do about your "surmises".'

'Let me just conclude what I was saying about Quail,' continued Spurling. 'He went through a period of illness in which he nearly died, during which he lost all his fur. He is bald now, and frightening, and since he blamed his sickness on an infection received from a female, he conceived a hatred for all females, and began to exclude them from the Newborn hierarchy, as much as he could. In Avebury his successors – the first he appointed direct, and those following I am sure he had a paw in sending from Blagrove and then Caradoc – were especially brutal towards females.'

'That's when they began killing the female pups,' said Peach suddenly, 'though they denied it. But they *did*, I know they did.'

A cold shiver went through Chater and Fieldfare on hearing this unwelcome confirmation of something they had heard murmurs of before but which, in truth, nomole had wanted to believe.

'Aye, the Newborn sect favours males,' said Spurling matter-of-factly, 'and it's a short pawstep for them to say that is what the Stone decrees, and a short step after *that* to say that females are inferior, and so it goes on and on, until at last moles gain power who so despise and fear females that their birth is sometimes deemed unwanted if there are too many of them, and they are done to death. And not, as you might think, by the Brothers themselves.'

'No,' said Peach, ''tis the mothers that do it, to curry favour for their male pups you see, and with the Stone. So female pups often die, and those that survive occupy a servile role.'

Spurling was silent for a time, perhaps feeling through the shocked reaction of Chater and Fieldfare a reminder of what he had felt more strongly before he became used to what the Newborns' beliefs really entailed. Exposure to evil blunts a mole's senses.

'Our system became the focal point for Newborn activity in the south,' he continued. 'That's how I understand it, anyway. I learnt that moledom had been divided up by Thripp into areas, each of which was to be evangelized from one of the twelve systems.'

'Including Duncton Wood?' said Chater in astonishment.

'Oh, especially Duncton Wood,' said Spurling. 'Very especially Duncton Wood. I understand—'

'You seem to understand a lot,' said Chater with some respect. 'I cannot say that in my travels I was much aware of any of this, only that the Newborns seemed to be establishing themselves everywhere I turned. But they were not very aggressive or dominating.'

'That's where Thripp has been so clever, don't you see?' said Spurling passionately. 'In my opinion what he and his kind are trying to do is no different from what the moles of the Word so nearly succeeded in doing all those years ago, and from which our grandparents rescued us: to take over moledom for their ends. The moles of the Word sought to do it from sheer malevolence and hatred of the Stone, but the Caradocians, as the Newborns like to call themselves, seek to do it for reasons of spiritual power. Judging by what we know, and what moles we have gathered together who feel like us have seen, the end result will be no different.'

'You mentioned Duncton Wood and surmises,' said Chater.

'Yes, I did. I believe Thripp's intention is to make Duncton the centre of his sect, the core of the Newborns in moledom. He began in Blagrove Slide, which is not much of a place, I understand. With Quail's help he moved almost his entire system to Caer Caradoc and took that over, by what means, and with what resulting deaths, I leave to your imagination. No doubt one day a scholar will scribe *that* grim tale, but I for one will not wish to ken it. He moved there because he wanted to occupy one of the historic systems, and Caer Caradoc has always been weak, and ripe for takeover. His movement is given weight by calling itself the Caradocian Order, which sounds a lot better and more authoritative than Blagrovian Order, or merely Newborns.

'But such a mole's ambitions know no bounds, and he has had the treacherous Quail at his right flank to feed him thoughts. As a matter of fact Thripp himself is said to be a mild mole – charismatic in his way, persuasive in his words, but unwise in his choice of Quail as a Senior Brother, and perhaps duped by him. Of course Caradoc is a long way off, and marginal to moledom's history. It suited his purpose to begin with, but as he realized that moledom's systems could be easily taken over by the right combination of organization, intimi- dation and authority, his dreams evolved into a desire to conquer a more important system, or one which would occupy the hearts and imaginations of all moledom. None better than Duncton Wood.

'I tell you, Chater, *that* is his intention, but unlike the moles of the Word, who made their purpose and objective plain, Thripp has kept it secret. I would hazard that nomole but Quail himself knows it for certain.'

'Then how do you know it?' asked Chater reasonably.

'I don't *know* it at all. I offer it as a surmise, as a reasonable predic- tion of what such a mole would wish to do when he has discovered how easy it is to gain power. Stay in peripheral, wormless Caer Cara- doc? No! Go back to Blagrove Slide? Impossible to conceive! But Duncton Wood . . . now there's a system to end up in control of as the achievement of your life! Eh Chater? Fieldfare?'

The two moles stared at him with grave concern. It sounded all too plausible.

'What I do know with rather more certainty is that it is the intention of the Newborns – perhaps without Thripp's direct involvement or knowledge, but through Quail's direction – to take the advantage that the Convocation offers of placing elders and librarians from all the main systems at their mercy: to kill them, or to "disappear" them. Aye, I do not think that when the winter ice and snow has thawed off Caer Caradoc we will see any of the dissenting delegates to that pretence of a Convocation still alive. Nor even dead. They will have . . . gone. And in that time, and it has probably already begun, New- borns in each of those systems from which they came will have taken control.'

'You have evidence?'

'I and others have heard things said at Buckland, which is where Quail has trained his Inquisitors, and often draws fresh blood from.'

The moles stared at each other numbly, contemplating this dark prospect.

'But there is worse,' said Spurling.

Peach nodded and whispered, 'Yes, tell him everything. Tell him what you know.'

'Well?' said Fieldfare, who could never bear secrets, especially awful ones, to be withheld.

A look of extreme distaste passed over the mild and serious face of Spurling.

'We understand that the promise given to the Inquisitors who have, as it were, been trained up for this wholesale takeover of moledom's systems, is that they will be allowed to do what, until now, it has been the secret privilege of the Senior Brothers to do.'

'Which is?' said Chater impatiently.

'To impregnate the females. Oh yes, it has long been known to us in Avebury that the Senior Brothers' perk is the right of intercourse with the females they dominate. The fact is that most of the more trusted Newborn guards are the product of unions between a relatively small number of Senior Brothers, and their victim females, who are called Confessed Sisters. It is part of Thripp's theory of things that moles who believe as he does are right, and the rest wrong; that rightness or wrongness carries with it, or not, as the case may be, the right to mate, to produce young. My last surmise, therefore, is this: next spring a great many females throughout moledom will be carrying the pups of Newborn fathers, and those pups—'

'But this is . . . !' words failed Fieldfare, she was so outraged. In her exasperation she turned to Chater and almost buffeted him as if he were the embodiment of Newborn lust and ill-intent.

'I'm not having it, beloved! This cannot be allowed. We can't stance here doing nothing. What are you thinking of!'

'It's the danger to our friends who've been sent all unknowing by Stour to their deaths in Caer Caradoc that I'm thinking of, dearest,' he said with gritty determination. 'I'm sorry, my love, I'm a journey-mole who until this moment was more or less in retirement, but there's no way I, Chater, journeymole of Duncton, can do nothing about this!'

'Well spoken, Chater!' said Fieldfare, looking round proudly at

81

Peach as if to say that *now* they would see what her mate was made of.

'But . . .' said Chater, 'I sort of swore that I would never leave your flank again, my sweet. And when Chater swears a thing it's sworn!'

'I wouldn't be happy for you to stay at my flank for one moment longer than you should if duty calls, and duty does call, it calls very loudly indeed,' said Fieldfare. 'It's telling you to do something.'

'But what?' said Spurling, somewhat bemused by the volatile turn the conversation between Chater and Fieldfare had taken.

'It's telling me, Spurling, as Fieldfare well knows, to get my arse to Caer Caradoc and warn my friends of what you say might be apaw. I'm a journeymole, and going long distances alone is what I'm trained for and best at. I wouldn't be happy kicking my paws up in Uffington in safety when I could be helping others elsewhere. But Fieldfare – why, that's her sort of thing, isn't it, dear? And I'm not being funny. She's good at keeping the home tunnels clean, so to speak, until the wanderer returns. She's used to it. She'll do it for you all in Uffington like she did it for me in Duncton.'

There was silence, until Spurling said, a little apologetically, 'So, what exactly does that mean?'

'Put plain and simple, it means my Chater is off on a journey. When he goes, how he goes, is his business and he's good at it. But from a lifetime's experience I would guess he'll be gone before this day's ended. Am I right, my precious?'

'You are, my own love.'

'Which also means, and I hope you won't take offence, but on occasions like this time is short and moles like us do not stance on ceremony, that Chater and myself would like to spend a little time together.'

'Alone, you mean?' said Spurling faintly.

'It is normal, yes,' said Chater with a grin.

'Well, then,' said Peach, affecting a lighthearted and nonchalant look, 'we must, that is Spurling and I must, go off now, and as it were attend to things . . .'

But Chater and Fieldfare, lovers at heart as they were, were already bickering and buffeting at each other in their customary way, and chuckling too, as they turned from their friends to share a final tryst, as so often they had in the past, before Chater set off on a long journey.

'Aren't they a bit old for that kind of thing?' said Spurling when they had gone.

'No,' said Peach, a little tartly, 'I don't think *they* are!'

Chater left at dusk, turning back towards the setting sun to retrace his steps and try, as best he could, to reach Caer Caradoc in time to warn his friends, and any other moles who were not Newborn, of the danger they were in.

'Goodbye, my own love,' said Fieldfare.

'I'll send word,' said Chater, giving her a final embrace, 'and it'll be good word, encouraging word.'

'My love,' she whispered; and let him go.

Chapter Seven

Stow and the Bourton moles had been right about Weeth, he *was* over-talkative. At the slightest opportunity he launched off into conversation about anything that came into his head, and it was the kind of talk a mole could not easily ignore since it was quick-witted and interspersed with questions which challenged his interlocutor to show that he was listening – or provoked him to tell Weeth to talk less.

Strangely enough, Privet seemed better able to control Weeth's output than the other two – something about her calmed him down, and she was quite capable of saying that she wished for peace and quiet, and would he please go and talk to somemole else.

It could not be denied, however, that he seemed to know the way across the dull flat vale they had dropped down into – or if he did not, he certainly had a good snout for finding a route that avoided trouble. More than once they came across Newborn patrols and yet were able to proceed unobserved, and on the one occasion they were seen, Weeth was very quick to go forward and greet the Newborns as fellow Brothers in the cause, and hope they would not 'long delay my aged relative, a female, and her dullard sons, who I am guiding to Evesham where they are to serve the Stone.'

Such was Weeth's cheerful confidence, and so low did his companions drop their snouts, that the patrol seemed convinced by Weeth's nonsense and let the party go on without any questioning at all.

'It is a matter, you know, of having an eye for what a particular mole will find pleasure in believing,' explained Weeth without prompting, after this near escape. 'Too many moles think others are persuaded by reason, but as a practising opportunist I can assure you that is not so. Moles act on feelings, inclinations and prejudices, and very rarely on reasons, though of course they like to think they are rational. Therefore, what must we do if we are to get our way, to take our opportunity?'

The three moles gazed at him without a word, very confident that if they said nothing he would answer his own question.

'We must give them a good reason for letting us do what we wish to do, and make them feel good about doing it. Take those moles we have just passed. I could see they were hungry and in no mood for trouble, or hard work. By telling them we are going to Evesham – which is where they would undoubtedly lead us if they took us prisoner, supposing that they could – we give them a reason for not stopping us; by appealing to their good nature by mentioning aged relatives and dullard sons (and what a good job you both did of *that*, Maple and Whillan, eh Privet?) they feel good about not troubling us.'

'Thank you, Weeth,' said Maple. 'Now could we proceed in silence for a time?'

'Silence?' said Weeth suspiciously, as if he felt threatened by the word.

'You talk too much,' said Whillan. 'We three like to go along in silence sometimes when we're travelling.'

'My dear fellow, I am sorry,' said Weeth, grandly apologetic. 'I talk too much, far too much. To tell the truth, I always put my paw in it in the end. What friends I make I lose through jabbering. What friends I have lost are disinclined to accept my apologies for fear that I shall jabber more. There is something about me moles wish to dislike, and having discovered that it is because I am a mole who speaks before he thinks and gets himself into all kinds of unnecessary trouble, *when* I do those things I am forsaken . . .'

By now Whillan was half smiling, and attempting to cover his ears with his paws in an effort to suggest to Weeth that he had said enough to be forgiven. He, Whillan, was not like other moles; he, Whillan, would forgive him – only please stop. But Weeth, carried away with his declaration, and not daring to think, perhaps, that Whillan could be so tolerant, continued.

'But do not forsake me, Whillan, for beneath my infuriating exterior beats a warm heart.'

'Be quiet, Weeth,' said Maple with cheerful authority. 'In fact, shut up, mole.'

Weeth immediately fell silent, and stared at Maple with apparent gratitude on his face. He seemed anything but affronted by Maple's uncharacteristic bluntness. But then he appeared to be about to spoil it all, for he raised one paw and said, 'Sir, may I make an observation before I shut up totally?'

'I daresay you will,' said Maple.

'It is merely to suggest that you and I might work well together. I mean not only now, but after we get to Caradoc. Give me an order and I will loyally carry it out.'

'Then be quiet,' said Maple amiably.

'Be *quiet*?' whispered Weeth. 'Quiet?'

He narrowed his eyes and concentrated on the word as if it had never before occurred to him to contemplate its meaning. Then, like stormclouds across a bright sun, the full implication of Maple's command came to him. His mouth half opened in horror and then closed again in dismay. He looked about desperately for some way out of the impasse into which his own impetuous verbosity had led him, and even turned a couple of quick circles as if looking for somewhere to put himself where he might be allowed to speak. Finding none, he beat the ground with frustration as he tried to sort out the dilemma into which Maple had put him. The tension grew unbearable as the rest of them, unable to think of anything else but Weeth's valiant effort to 'be quiet' and what appeared to be his terminal struggle to cope with it, watched in amazement. Had nomole ever told him to be quiet before? Or, as seemed more likely, had *many* moles told him, but he had forgotten that they had?

Suddenly he calmed down, the stormclouds passed on and revealed the sun in his face once more as he assumed a beatific expression and said in the quietest and gentlest voice possible, 'Quiet as opposed to being noisy, you mean?'

He looked triumphant with himself for having found a legitimate way to carry on talking. But Maple was not having it. He hunched forward towards Weeth in his most menacing manner and said, 'I mean, mole, that if you are to stay with us, if you are to be with us, if you are to *work* with us, we require you to learn how to adopt a low snout, and be silent unless talk is necessary, to be discreet and to remain unintrusive.'

'Unintrusive?' said Weeth immediately in his new calm voice.

Maple nodded.

'Unintrusive?' repeated Weeth to Privet.

'Yes, my dear, I think that is the meaning of what Maple said.'

'Unintrusive like *non*-intrusive, or, as it were, unremarkable, in its absolute and literal sense. Something like that, yes, Whillan?'

'I would try if I were you,' said Whillan as darkly as he could, for he was beginning to realize that Weeth was one of those moles who if given half a chance took a whole one.

'I shall!' declared Weeth with conviction. And there it might have seemed to Maple and Whillan that the conversation had ended, but

Privet knew it had not, and understood that beyond Weeth's ready talk and quick wit was something more, something deeper.

For as Maple led them off again, she heard Weeth whisper to himself, 'I shall try!' and thinking he was not seen she saw as well how he watched after the others with gratitude that in their own way they accepted him, and liked him. As they trekked on in silence she wondered why it was that now he had joined them the party felt complete.

Weeth was as good as his word, and did not speak again all day which, the others were aggrieved to find, was something of a pity, so used had they got to him talking as they went. It was just that he did too much of it. Perhaps in time he would get the balance right.

'Ahem!'

That evening, after their meal, he finally broke his silence and when he did it was with a most startling and alarming statement.

'Ahem! Ahem!'

'Yes, Weeth?' said Maple.

'I suppose, being Duncton moles and all good at scribing, and being clever, and what with one thing like that and another, you do realize that the Caradoc Convocation as summoned by Thripp is not merely a trap, but also a sham?'

They waited in silence for him to go on; out of sheer mischief he did not, but quietly hummed to himself and groomed his paws as if all he had just done was to pass a pleasantry about the weather.

'Go on,' said Maple.

'The Great One wishes me to speak? Is this possible? And can it be that the Duncton trio does not know something Weeth knows? It can! It is! Astounding!'

Privet laughed. 'Come on, my dear, tell us what you know.'

To his credit Maple smiled with something like affection at Weeth who, grinning with delight at this warm response to his mischievousness, came closer to them all in a confidential sort of way, and looked first over one shoulder and then over the other. Then, in a low voice, he said, 'May I preface my remarks by observing that the one thing I was never told about Duncton moles, though it is self-evidently true, is that you have a sense of humour. Weeth likewise. Could it be our saving grace, the one unique quality the Stone appreciates beyond all others, which will, as it were, cause it to bend over backwards to help us? It could, it could!

'Now, to work. First the question of it being a trap. Well, I understand that previous Convocations and Conclaves, such as that summoned to Cannock by your own Master Stour, have always been

87

in the summer years, to allow moles to travel there and back in temperate weather and so be away from their systems for as short a time as possible, and certainly back in time for Longest Night. This Convocation being in December means that will not only be impossible, but moles will likely be marooned in and around Caradoc by ice and snow, at least for the January and early February years, thus making them prey to Newborn persuasions of one kind or another; which, I beg to suggest, might include starvation. Oh no, you don't suppose that Caradoc itself is exactly wormful, do you?'

'Such suspicions had crossed our minds,' said Whillan. 'But what about it being a sham?'

'Well, now, *there* we move on to less certain ground. I have a feeling, supported by mere rumour and surmise and things I've heard, that the real action this Longest Night will not be in Caradoc, but in all the other systems so conveniently vacated by moles such as yourselves who will not be in the one place where they might be most needed – their own homes. In short, having got you out of the way by summoning this Convocation, the Newborns will go in for a quick kill in all the systems where they have cells, which is in all the important ones. Having gained control, they will have plenty of time to change things to their taste, and even get local females aplenty pregnant with Newborn pups, for it to be very hard indeed for the returning delegates from Caradoc to do much about it. Get my drift?'

'We get your drift,' said Maple grimly. These were possibilities Master Stour had himself mentioned, but coming from this mole so far along the way to Caradoc, they seemed more plausible, and infinitely more difficult to deal with. What could three moles of Duncton do in such a situation, even if they found allies among delegates from other systems?

'We could go back now,' said Whillan eventually, but without conviction. For all the dangers involved, their going to Caer Caradoc seemed inevitable. Perhaps that was the genius of Thripp of Blagrove Slide – to have persuaded moles to come to Caradoc, where he had control of them, on his terms.

'Oh, he is a genius,' said Weeth, 'and the difficulty with such moles as him is that they are so *convincing*. Of course they never do their own dirty work – they couldn't sully their paws with *that*.'

'Who does then?' asked Whillan.

'Well . . .' mused Weeth, 'it is a moot point. My belief is that it's the mole who lies behind the Brother Inquisitors that moledom should fear. For what would happen if *he* gained power when Thripp dies?'

88

'Who do you mean?' asked Privet.

'*That* mole is said to be Senior Brother Quail. He is said to have founded the Inquisitorial system, having risen up from the ranks to be the secret and malign power behind Thripp. He has none of Thripp's charisma or popularity, but he's ruthless and most believe he will take power. He's probably behind the changes you've already seen in Duncton Wood.'

'Hmmm!' mused Maple, a worried frown on his face.

'Let me tell you two things about Quail, though you'll welcome neither of them. First, when a mole is formally condemned to death by the Newborns – a most rare occurrence, since they contrive to have moles die informally so they cannot be called a killing sect – he, Quail, likes to be there.'

'Likes to carry out the execution?' said Whillan.

'Probably,' said Weeth with distaste. 'They say his look is enough to kill. And this is the mole in whom Thripp puts all his trust. Some sect! The second thing, which worries me greatly, especially if the first is true, is that the rumours are strong that Quail will be in the vicinity. Quail is coming to Caradoc. Which means that the Newborns may have in mind an exemplary death sentence or two, by way of intimidation and so forth. Nasty. Makes the hairs on my spine stir. In fact, the more I think of it, the straighter they stance! Makes me wonder why I'm not heading *away* from Caradoc as fast as my paws can carry me.'

'And why aren't you?'

'Opportunity, Whillan, opportunity. The same thing that brings *you* here.'

'Me?' said Whillan, rather affronted.

'Oh, well, if you want to be mealy-mouthed about it, please do. I expect scribes like you who can make words do all sorts of things would call it "destiny" or the "Stone's purpose" or something of that sort. Well, Weeth is more direct and calls it opportunity.'

'He's got a point, my dear!' said Privet lightly, reaching a paw to Whillan who, after a moment of struggle with his pride, grinned ruefully at Weeth.

'If ever I have occasion to scribe about *you*, Weeth, and I hope I do when all this is over, I shall remember to call you a mole of opportunity and myself—'

'A mole of destiny?' suggested Weeth.

'. . . The other mole of opportunity!'

They all laughed, but what Weeth had said had about it the air of truth and inevitability, and that changed the light mood in which they had begun their trek across the Vale to one more serious and circumspect.

So as these few days of journeying towards Evesham continued, all three Duncton moles grew to like and appreciate Weeth. Others may have found him annoying in the past, but perhaps it was because they did not come from a system such as Duncton, where moles traditionally make time to talk and share their thoughts, and learn to listen, which is not an easy thing. He certainly had a way with words, and though he might seem sometimes to talk too much, yet each of the other three had to admit that his presence added something cheerful and optimistic to their group, and made the way ahead seem easier.

He gained their confidence, and it was not long before his early presumption in offering himself in the role of aide to Maple did not seem presumptuous at all, but just as it was meant to be. For that was never a role that an individual like Whillan could have borne – his star was lone and distant, and though it had not yet begun to shine and lead him where it must, yet all sensed it would when the time was right; and when it did, Maple might need a new helper and companion. This was the role that Weeth instinctively adopted, and after a few days there was not a mole amongst them who would have denied it him.

Yet though it was Maple he seemed likely to end up serving, both Privet and Whillan found him increasingly good company, and each enjoyed some time with him. It was made easier by his ready curiosity about their lives – lives of mystery as he liked to think, and in that he was right. Not that Whillan was able to enlighten him upon his true origins – the events preceding that tragic day beneath the Duncton cross-under when the Master Stour rescued him from a certain death when he took him from the teats of a dying mother, whose name he never knew. Nor was it likely that he would ever now discover the identity of his father.

This was, in any case, an old tale that Whillan knew well enough, but perhaps Weeth's fresh curiosity stirred in him desire to know more. Perhaps, indeed, it stirred too much, for after he told it him Whillan was silent and desired to be alone for a time.

'Forgive me for making you tell your strange tale but I like to know where moles come from, and who their parents are, *especially* if there's mystery attached to it!' declared Weeth.

'I understand,' said Whillan, 'but it gives me pain to think of it, and what is the point when I cannot hope to find the answer? You should talk to Privet, Weeth, if you must pry into things; she likes you and will keep your over-active curiosity occupied. And anyway, the tale she could tell about herself would make mine sound positively boring in comparison!'

Weeth needed no second bidding, for what a snout for a good tale he had, as if he could sense it out like succulent food that needed to be drawn out of the rich soil of life. A look of ineffable pleasure would cross his face as by probing and questioning he managed to free some new tale from one of the moles in whose company he so willingly found himself.

It was no surprise therefore to Whillan and Maple that he should snout out something of the part of Privet's tale which followed her departure from the Moors so long ago. It is a fact of life that once such secrets as she had told in Duncton Wood permit themselves to be unveiled they are not easily kept out of sight again, and lead on to other revelations. Perhaps because the moles who carry them have a need to tell more, as if in doing so they might discover something more of past lives, past truths, that remain unconsummated and incomplete.

So when, one evening, Privet agreed to tell something of her past, in exchange, as Weeth put it, for the tales *he* had told, Whillan and Maple were content that she should do so, though they thought it well at first to remain inconspicuous, the better to encourage her to talk. So Privet shared an evening stance with Weeth, and when it grew too cold to talk outside, retired with him to a temporary burrow down below and told him the outline of her life before she came to Duncton Wood.

For once he was utterly silent, except when he found it necessary to ask her to elucidate some detail of her story. But Rooster and the Moors, the Charnel Clough and Hilbert's Top – all held him fascinated and amazed, with more questions left than had been answered. But being Weeth, when she was finally done, his response was not quite that of a normal mole.

'Oh wonderful, grand, splendid, to burden *me* with such a tale! And what am I to do with it? How can I be expected to free myself of it when you implant it in my mind like a seedling in fertile soil, to grow and burgeon and produce fruitful questions far beyond the normal experience of a mere wandering mole like me looking for opportunity?' Thank you very much, Privet, I am so pleased that you have found my ready ear. I am happy for you, but your delight is my misery! What am I to do with this incomplete tale living in my mind? How do I rest my weary self-centred head in the burrow at night and find peace when I think of Rooster all confused, and Hamble, noble and strong, and that wicked sister of yours, Lime?

'Do they let me sleep? They do not! *They* never sleep, but go on round the circles of my mind and will not let me rest until they escape to a better world than the one you left them in. What a thoughtful mole you are, Privet, what a comfortable companion! Oh, yes, what pleasant opportunity for rest, contentment, peace and leisure I find here! Show me a cliff and I shall leap over it; take me to a roaring owl way and I shall lie across it; anything is better than to leave so many questions unanswered . . .'

But Privet would hear no more, for the night was very late, the others were long since deep asleep, and contentment was coming to her at least, and drowsiness as well. The more Weeth fulminated in his good-humouredly outraged way, the more she liked him, and the more she felt inclined towards the restful sleep a mole can find if she is sharing a warm burrow with another whom she likes and respects, and knows that despite all his words and plaints and bickering, he means her no harm at all.

'Good night, Weeth,' she whispered at last.

'Oh, wonderful!' said Weeth, all wide awake. 'Sleep well! All of you! Go on! Don't worry about me!'

They did sleep well, and they did not worry about Weeth at all, except when morning came and he was lying in contented sleep among them, almost impossible to waken as on his face was a half-smile, and a half-question, as if when he had finally found rest it was because he knew he was among friends.

And when he awoke it was to discover his companions in no mood to travel on, but rather to dally for a day or two and tell some tales.

'Tales!' said Weeth.

Whillan winked and whispered, 'Your talk with Privet yesterday has put her in the mood to finish what she began. She said before you woke that it was time she told us all that she can remember of her past and Rooster's. She feels she might not get another chance once we meet the Newborns at Evesham.'

'Which is why,' said Privet, drawing them all to her, 'I have decided to tell you my story, such as it is, and if you want to ask questions, please do so. It might help me along a way I haven't dared think about all these long years.'

'Where are you beginning?' asked Maple.

'Where I left off with Weeth last night – the day Rooster and I decided to leave Hilbert's Top and take our chances with the real world beyond . . .'

PART II

Privet's Tale

Chapter Eight

So, their winter sojourn up on Hilbert's Top come to its natural end, Privet and Rooster had set off across the Moors to make contact with molekind once more. They met with only two moles on their journey to Crowden – the lonely survivors of the family Privet and the others had stopped with for a time in Ramsden Clough on their way out to Chieveley Dale.

Turrell, their doughty leader, who had been able to tell Privet something of Rooster, was still alive, though only because one of his adoptive sons, Waythorn, had pulled him clear of a vicious attack by Ratcher moles which had left the others dead.

'Even Myrtle, your mate?' whispered Privet.

'Nay, not her! She had the sense to die during the winter years, and was spared the pity of what happened here. Without Waythorn I don't know what I'd have done!'

'You can come with us now,' said Privet, 'I'm sure Crowden will give you sanctuary, and they'll be glad of some extra paws on their side.'

It was Waythorn who shook his head. 'I'm a country mole,' he said simply, 'and couldn't live in a great big community with moles falling all over each other. I'll look after my father, and when the day comes he goes to the Silence, the Stone will tell me what to do!'

They tarried with Turrell and Waythorn a good long time, sharing stories, enjoying the sense of peace in the isolated clough, lying low while both of them adjusted to other company, and prepared themselves for what Privet especially was beginning to feel might be an ordeal ahead. So it was mid-April when they finally approached Crowden; the lower moorland slopes were sprinkled with flowers, and the two moles' fur was glossy and their eyes were bright with the better air, food and exercise their long journey had brought. They mounted a rise, wended their way through the outcrops at the top of a ridge, and found themselves looking down at Crowden Vale.

'The system lies beyond the lake below,' explained Privet, who felt unaccountable excitement and dread as she surveyed her home system after so long away. 'You can see the Moors stretching up higher beyond it, and over to the east on our left flank as well. It's from there the Ratcher moles usually attack.'

Rooster nodded, looking where she pointed, and noting that here and there at the highest places on the horizons there were still some patches of lingering snow in dark, shadowed, north-facing sites.

'The Weign Stones, where Wort scribed her Testimony, lie beyond the southern horizon,' she went on, pointing ahead. 'And to the west, beyond the furthest point of the lake, the Moors finally end, and moledom really begins. I've never met a mole who's been there, and they say they don't speak our language there, they speak Mole. My grandmother Wort told my mother that one day she should go there to the places I've told you about.'

'Beechenhill,' said Rooster. 'Duncton Wood and other Ancient Systems. Gaunt said it was where delvings were. But "Mole"? What do we speak?'

'Whernish,' she said. 'It's the language the moles of the Word spoke who came from Whern in the north. Wort spoke Mole and only learnt Whernish when she came to the Moors. Her Testimony is scribed in Mole of course, as most texts are.'

'Can you speak Mole?' he said.

'I can scribe it and ken it of course, but speak? Probably.'

'You teach me, like Gaunt taught me delving.'

'If you want,' she said. She was always surprised at how much he wanted to learn, and how willingly. She looked downslope towards Crowden and the feeling of dread returned. 'Now we're here I don't want to go into the system at all! I feel I'll lose you when I do.'

'Been good, our time,' he said.

'I'm afraid,' said Privet.

He chuckled. 'Life *is*. Gaunt said that. Said knowing it was hard made it easier. Wish Glee was here to see. Wish Humlock was here. I miss them. I hope I never have to miss you.'

He turned and stared into her eyes. How she had grown to love his lined and furrowed face, his frown, his heavy, slow-seeming ways which hid a mole so sensitive and so courageous. She looked at his paws and wanted to ask him a favour but dared not.

'Ask!' he commanded, his look warm. 'Can see a hope in your eyes.'

'Will you delve a place for us, a special place?' she said. 'For us. Like you did on Hilbert's Top only . . . well . . .' She faltered into sudden shyness.

'Have begun already,' he muttered, frowning. 'Feel its delving need. A place where we can be . . .'

But he could not find the words either, and his paws delved and dug at the air, and he looked away from her over the distant Moors, shy as herself.

'Better go.'

But even his saying that did not alter the fact that the nearer they got to Crowden the greater her dread became, even when they reached the Crowden defences and she identified herself to an astonished and delighted guard.

'Librarian Privet! We thought you were dead!'

'As you can see, I'm not!'

The guard eyed Rooster with the same dismay Turrell and Waythorn had shown.

'He's grike.'

'He's a delver, and when Hamble and I left we were in search of delvers,' said Privet defensively.

'Well . . .' said the guard, 'you better wait here.'

'But it's my own system!' said Privet sharply, embarrassed on Rooster's account.

'Ratcher's lot are about and we're being careful.' Other guards came, one of whom recognized Privet.

'Well, by the Stone, it *is* Librarian Privet! But who the 'ell's *him*?' he said, staring at the brooding Rooster.

'Rooster's his name and he's grike,' said the guard.

'Going in,' said Rooster impatiently. 'Hungry and cold, and Privet's tired. Understand?'

'You can't just come in here, mate!' said the guard, bridling.

Rooster grinned, almost amiably. 'Can,' he said. And taking Privet firmly by the paw and frowning in a ferocious kind of way he bore down on the guards most peaceably, and with open mouths they let him by.

'You wait here!' said one.

'I'll go and get Hamble himself,' said the other.

'Is he nearby?' asked Privet, her dread replaced by excitement at the prospect of seeing her dearest friend again.

'Where?' said Rooster to the guard. 'Heard of Hamble.'

The two guards looked at each other wearily, and one said as patiently as he could, 'Look, you stay *here*, chum, in the warm. We'll get you food but don't move otherwise Hamble will have our guts. There's a war on. Against *grikes*. You're a grike. *Please*.'

By now others had come, and the news that Privet was back was running through the system like wildfire.

'We'll stay where we are,' said Privet to Rooster firmly. 'You scare them, Rooster. It's because you're so big and so unafraid.'

'Hmmph!' said Rooster, pacing about restlessly as the guards gazed at him in awe, and eased out of his way as best they could. He peered at the defences. He poked his snout into portals and out again. He touched walls, and reached up his huge paws to roofs.

'These moles can't delve,' he said to Privet.

Privet smiled.

'Feel the delving need,' he said, 'like itching. Terrible all this.'

'Keeps the grikes out,' said the first guard, more cheerful now that his reluctant prisoner was staying more or less where he should, and wasn't causing trouble.

'Didn't keep me out,' replied Rooster.

They did not have to wait long before Hamble appeared, and several others with him.

'Privet *here*?' she heard his deep familiar voice saying as he approached down a tunnel. 'My Privet?'

He turned a corner, ducked under a portal, and there he was before her, big and familiar, his face just a little lined, with an expression that changed from disbelief to joy and then to astonishment as he saw Rooster at her flank.

'Privet!' he thundered, as if angry she had been away so long; then coming to her, he took her up in his paws, and held her so close that she almost lost her breath. 'Thank the Stone! Thank the Stone you're safe!'

Tears came to her eyes at the warmth and love in his welcome, and she felt joy that she was back with her oldest friend, and that she had so much that was good to tell him.

'And this mole,' he said, putting her down and turning to Rooster, who was just a shade bigger than him, 'can this be Rooster? They said he was just another grike, but I'll warrant it's Rooster you've brought home!'

The two moles stared at each other, the smile fading on Hamble's face as all Rooster did was frown and look ferocious. The stares continued in silence, and joy began to leave the reunion.

'*Am* Rooster,' said Rooster suddenly, as if deciding Hamble was all right. 'You're Hamble. Privet's friend.'

'Yes,' said Hamble, still uncertain.

There are some moments that go down as essential details in the

98

tales moles tell – not important in themselves, yet, if left out others remind them to put them in if the tale is to be properly told, saying 'Didn't he . . . ?' and 'Wasn't that when . . . ?' This was such a moment, and one not to be omitted.

For Rooster stared a while longer at Hamble and then, with a vigour that the assembled guard mistook for a few moments for violence, he came forward, and reaching out his paws put them about Hamble's not inconsiderable frame and in the same warm gesture that Hamble had shown Privet, he lifted the warrior mole right off the ground.

'Rooster's happy!' declared Rooster. 'You took Privet to Chieveley Dale. I brought her back!'

Hamble laughed deeply, the guards relaxed, and as Hamble's paws touched the ground again he laughed some more, reached out a paw, buffeted Rooster in a friendly way and said, 'You'd better come and tell us your tales. By the Stone, you're welcome, mole. And for seeing Privet back here in safety, a mole I value more than any other, you've instantly become a friend of mine for life! Added to which, it just happens we'll need a delver in the coming days. In fact, Privet, wasn't that why we set off to find Rooster in the first place?'

She nodded, proud of them both, pleased that they seemed so willing to be friends. Yet they seemed already more than that: more like colleagues, moles whose task was the same, and whose joint presence was greater than each of them as individuals. So much so that the chamber seemed barely big enough for them and other moles.

Rooster pointed a paw at the delvings he had appraised earlier and found wanting.

'You need a delver. And I need a home. That's good!'

'It's very good,' beamed Hamble, and he led them both off to Crowden's communal chamber, for talk, and food, and an exchange of news. 'There's moles here of Chieveley Dale who will be more than delighted at your coming, Rooster.'

Rooster's head lifted. 'Charnel moles? Delvers?'

'We got some out in safety, and some had come across the Moors earlier, the ones who alerted us to what was happening in the Dale. But I don't think any of them are delvers in the sense you mean. They're what I'm told you called helpers.'

'No delvers?' said Rooster, snout lowering, hope going. Privet saw the loneliness in his eyes, and felt his pain. Could the Stone be so cruel as to make him the only delver to survive from the Charnel, and therefore the one on whom the responsibility for the continuance of the delving arts must solely rely? Just him? She put a paw tenderly to his flank.

'They'll be waiting for you in the communal chamber,' said Hamble. 'Come!'

When they reached it, a great crowd had gathered, all excited and abuzz. Their chatter fell silent the moment the new arrivals appeared, and at first Privet could see little in the gloom. Rooster went forward a step or two, peering and frowning at the group of moles, perhaps confused to see so many after so long living only with Privet. Then Hamble pointed to a far corner of the chamber from which the Crowden moles fell away to reveal five gaunt, quiet moles. They were stanced still and huddled close together as if for comfort, and all held their snouts low, not wanting to look up, not daring to believe perhaps that a mole they loved and held in awe was come among them again. None there but Privet truly understood the nature of that moment, as the survivors of the Charnel, of the crossing of the Span, of the exodus to Chieveley Dale, and then the escape across the Moors, saw Rooster, the mole whom they already thought to be a Master of the Delve, and the whole reason for their lives, their *meaning*, come amongst them once again.

Rooster stanced still before them, staring, his eyes wide and filling with tears, perhaps for the moles who were not there and who might have been. For Glee, for Humlock, for Samphire, for Drumlin, for Gaunt, and for the Senior Delvers, Prime, Terce, None, Sext and Compline. All lost, surely all dead now. That world was gone, that world was no more, and Privet alone knew she was looking at a remnant of a system gone, a last thing, a grouping that would soon be absorbed and lost for ever.

So Rooster stared, and though he tried to speak, he wept; and his friends and helpers stanced with bowed heads before him.

'Am safe,' he said at last, 'have been lost and am now found.'

The Charnel moles looked up, and if Privet had ever wondered in what regard Rooster was really held she wondered no more. Joy, relief, pleasure; love and awe – all were there, and more. Suddenly the five moles came to him as one, their tears as free as his own as they reached out to touch the mole whose presence would make them believe in life again. So powerful was the effect of this reunion, so full of deep unspoken meanings which others there could feel, even if they could not quite understand them all, that several of the Crowden moles openly cried too. Even Hamble sniffed a bit, and put his paw

100

over Privet's shoulders, and held her close as if to say, 'What they feel for him I feel for you, and always will.'

What he finally said, as the Charnel moles chattered and shared their news, was this: 'I never thought you were anything but safe, Privet. Always thought you were a survivor, and so you are, and so you will be. But by the Stone I'm glad you're safe. And you've come back when you're needed, and when he's needed.'

'He'll delve like you've never seen delving in your life, Hamble. He *is* what they say he is.'

'And do you love him, Privet? Eh? Is he yours?'

She smiled and looked coy.

Rooster turned from the group, his paw over the shoulder of an older mole, as big as himself, with kindly eyes and a caring way about him.

'Why . . .' said Privet breaking free from Hamble and going to them both.

'This is Hume!' said Rooster proudly and with great delight.

Privet could not but reach out her paws to him, and hold him as best she could, and say that she had heard all about him, and how glad she was . . . how glad!

But as she pulled away, another mole nudged her and spoke a greeting from behind, and though the voice had all the vigour and intonation of welcome the others did, expressing pleasure to see her back home, there was a thin sliver of ice right through it that had Privet tensing as she turned.

'Hello, Privet,' said her sister Lime.

Privet looked at her, but as she did, and began to speak a greeting in return, Lime's eyes slid from hers, and travelled slowly round until her gaze settled on Rooster, great Rooster, powerful mole. Lime's eyes filled with the desire for possession, and with lust.

'Well!' she declared, the moment passing as her eyes came back to Privet's, 'this *is* a surprise. But won't you introduce me to your friend?'

And the chamber seemed full of voices Privet could not clearly hear, and laughter she could not quite understand, and the touches of moles she felt she did not know; and the dread increased, bleak black dread, as bit by bit, Rooster began to be stolen from her.

'It became a nightmare,' whispered Privet, shivering as she relived those moments for Whillan, Maple and Weeth. She had somehow crept over to Whillan's flank in this last part of the telling, as if to find warmth and comfort from him. A sad hush had come to them all, sensing as they did that good would not come of Privet's and Rooster's return to Crowden, or not good that mole could easily see. Only pain, for Privet, and for the mole she loved and was losing now to the others almost before their eyes.

Maple tut-tutted now and then, and Whillan frowned a bit, and put a paw on Privet's as if to remind her that requited love *was* possible. Weeth sighed occasionally and shook his head in sympathy, but then nodded as if he had heard such tales before and wondered if much good could come of telling them. Indeed, poor Whillan looked quite drained, his sensitive face filled with the passions of his adoptive mother's story. His eyes were ageing as he understood more of the mole who had raised him, and done the best she could. She had loved, and now, he saw, she was poised to lose.

The position in Crowden was as grim as Hamble had implied. For one thing, the system had suffered losses through murrain, and was weaker than ever before. For another, Red Ratcher had come their way almost before spring was done, to continue his lifelong war against them. Only now his clan seemed stronger, and at his flank stanced moles as big as he, who, they now discovered, were Rooster's brothers from Samphire's earlier litters. Then, too, the defences had become ruinous, and there were no moles who had the arts of yesteryear to build them in the complex subtle way their ancestors had succeeded in attaining.

'We try, but somehow we don't have the skills, or the will, or the way with the soil and rock,' explained Hamble. 'We've seen the problem coming for a generation, but not known what to do to solve it. So now we're vulnerable, and the harder we try to improve the defences the worse and more confused they seem to become. That's why the three of us set off looking for you all that time ago, Rooster.'

But there was something worse, of which the rest was perhaps indicative.

'We lack leadership, and that's the truth of it,' said Hamble frankly.

'But I thought you were the leader now, Hamble,' said Privet.

'Me?' He laughed. 'I'm a warrior, a fighter, the perfect aide for a better leader than me, if one could only be found. Meanwhile I must bully the others here, appoint the guards, and lead such elders as we have. But I'm no match for Ratcher, nor have I the will to fight as he has. I don't say, as I should, "I'll defend Crowden to the last breath in my body", but instead I ask, "Is Crowden worth defending? Isn't there something more to life than *this*?" Eh? *You* understand, Privet, you used to say you wanted to go off and explore moledom.'

'Duncton Wood,' said Rooster. 'She wants to go there.'

'That's *right*, that was the place. So I'm not the right mole to lead others in defence. You're more the kind others will follow, Rooster, but the trouble is you're a delver.'

Since the Charnel moles had come not one of them had agreed to fight alongflank the Crowden moles, explaining that if they had a creed it was for peace. Delving was a peaceful art.

'Rooster's the nearest we have ever had to a Master,' explained Hume, not for the first time, 'and Masters do not hurt others.'

So Hamble understood that Rooster would be unlikely to fight. But at least he began to help with the defences. Even so . . .

''Tis a pity, Rooster, you look more of a fighter than a pacifist to me. You would have been a good leader. Dammit, our youngsters here already follow you about, and I've yet to see a mole threaten you, or even think of it.'

Rooster shrugged and grinned. 'Best way!' he said.

'And when your brothers come back and attack again, which they'll do before long, what do we do then?'

'Delve,' said Rooster. 'Like we've begun. Not fight, I won't.'

It was true that much good had now emerged from his coming. He had directed the other moles to delve according to marks he made, and in a surprisingly short space of time had created a defence of Dark Sound, just as he had at Chieveley Dale – so successfully indeed, that the Crowden moles were afraid of crossing through their own defensive lines, such was the agony of dark confusing sound the delvings emitted.

'Trouble is,' grumbled Hamble, 'your delvings can't tell the difference between friend and foe.'

'Delvings *can*,' said Rooster, 'but I don't make *those* ones here. Not right. Not holy these delvings' purpose, not made for good reason. Right delving for right place.'

'What's better than protecting your own?' asked Hamble.

'Helping your enemy,' said Rooster promptly. 'That was what Gaunt taught me, what Hilbert taught him through his ancient delvings. Help, love, pacify, give. Best, but hard.'

'You'll really never fight?' said Hamble doubtfully, on another occasion when they were alone on one of their tours of the system. Rarely had two moles found it so easy to be friends.

'If I hurt another I lose all for ever. If I kill I am no Master. If I think to kill it's harder to think like a Master of the Delve.'

103

'But you *have* thought like that, eh? You've wanted to hurt a mole?' asked Hamble shrewdly. 'Like Ratcher, for example?'

Rooster nodded uncomfortably. 'Wanted to hurt him.' He was silent for a little and then suddenly blurted out something that seemed to have been worrying him: 'Wanted to hurt Privet.'

'Privet?' repeated Hamble, astonished.

Rooster looked both ashamed and strangely pleading. 'Have *you* ever?' he asked quietly.

'Wanted to hurt Privet? No, never. She's like a sister, she is, I'd defend her to the death. Wouldn't hurt her ever.'

'Or any female?'

'*Hurt* them?' said Hamble puzzled, and not understanding Rooster's meaning, or his sense of shame and confusion about his previously violent feelings of desire for Privet. 'I wouldn't hurt a mole I loved. But you wouldn't, would you?'

'Not hurt a mole I loved, no, no, no,' said Rooster, shamed even more. Hamble didn't understand that by 'hurt' Rooster meant 'make love', which was something that seemed so violent to him, so uncontrollable that he mistook his natural passion for Privet for something it was against the creed of a Master to do. If only Hamble had understood poor Rooster's guilt and agony.

'You're a strange mole,' said Hamble, not knowing how upset Rooster felt to be told that, or how convinced it made him feel he really *was* strange, and wrong in the feelings he had for Privet. How hard it is to listen to another mole, and understand what his words really mean – how often the right moment slips away.

As the time went by and the work of defensive delving took Rooster from her flank, Privet saw how right she was to worry over Lime, for her sister was without shame or scruple in her desire for Rooster. But Privet had the reassurance of Rooster's response to Lime's advances; puzzlement and growing irritation. He did not like Lime, and sensed that she was trouble, and he did not like to see Privet upset. All of which made Privet feel easier, the more so because from the first Rooster shared quarters with her near the Library, and did not dally with the females as other male moles did at that season. Indeed, though she worried still, she felt all was reasonably well, and even put the threat of Lime to one side in favour of worrying, as friends will, at Hamble's failure to find a mate.

'You're too nice a mole!' she counselled him privately. 'Be a bit tougher on them and they'll come seeking you out!'

'Well, you're the wise one, Privet, having found a mate!'

'We haven't mated,' said Privet, 'we're just good friends.'

'Like you and me?' Hamble laughed.

'More than us,' said Privet shyly. 'But we're not ready for that yet. One day—'

'Hmmph!' said Hamble, unconvinced. '*You* may think you're not ready for it, but I've never met a male who wasn't, and nomole would say Rooster isn't male. And you advise *me* about getting a mate! You better practise being more alluring. Get some lessons from Lime, she knows how!'

So the two moles teased and confided in each other as the days continued, and the sense grew that renewed attacks by Ratcher's clan were ever more imminent.

'It's strange, Privet, but since Rooster's come there's been a different feel to Crowden, a new sense of purpose. He says he's a pacifist but I've never met a mole with greater brooding strength, as if he's waiting for an excuse to get angry. I mean—'

'You mustn't let him, Hamble, not ever. He is angry, angry for his past and for what happened to Samphire. Don't let him get angry; I've seen him and I know how violent he could be. He fears his anger and the feeling of wanting to hurt a mole.'

'Aye, he said as much to me, and he said it about . . .'

'About what?'

'No matter,' said Hamble quickly. 'I'll see he doesn't, if I can.'

'It's important, Hamble. He carries a responsibility far greater than anymole really understands. Being a Master of the Delve is a burden almost too much for a single mole to bear. In the past Masters worked in groups and shared their tasks. I think Rooster had formed a group with Glee and Humlock, but he's lost them now, and Hume and the others here aren't quite the same. I don't know why or how, but his two Charnel friends were part of his Mastership, like a support he needed, and now he's lost them he's angry and vulnerable.* I can't give him the support myself for I'm just a scribe. So you must try to save him from himself until he's found some other way of finding support in the delve. The Stone made him, and the Stone will find a way. It will! I pray to it all the time!'

Hamble stared at her. 'Mole, you love him with a passion.'

'I feel he's my whole life.'

---

* See *Duncton Tales*. The albino female Glee, and her blind deaf-mute companion Humlock were left behind to die in the Charnel Clough from which, because of landslips and river torrents, nomole could escape.

'Beware then, Privet, for in these troubled times a mole had best not believe her whole life depends upon another.'

'We're always giving each other advice, you and I,' she said affectionately.

Hamble held her close. 'With you, Privet, I feel closer to myself than with any other mole. I feel it'll always be like that, always. I never thought for one moment you wouldn't come back from Chieveley Dale, and now I'm sure that wherever you are I'll know if you're well or ill, safe or unsafe. *Always*.'

Privet felt warm and loved, and wished she could feel as sure of things as Hamble did. She remembered the difference between his parents, whom she had loved so much, and her cold mother, Shire, and knew that if there was one reason why he felt such assurance, and she could not quite trust that life would treat her well, it lay in the difference in confidence their parenting had given them.

'I know one thing, Hamble: if ever I have young it will be to the example of your parents I shall look for raising them, and to you as well.'

'And to the infamous Eldrene Wort, my dear, for I know of her Testimony and what finding it must have meant for you. She's kin to be proud of.'

'Oh Hamble, why do I feel so uncertain and full of dread? I have felt so from the moment we first came back to Crowden. I do still.'

'Rooster's the mole to take that from you,' said Hamble. 'When he gets round to seeing the treasure he's got he'll make you feel wanted, and more than wanted! He's a bit shy with females, that's all – just like me.'

He laughed, but when he went his way he found himself wondering if dread could be infectious, because he was beginning to feel it rise up in him as well.

106

Chapter Nine

Two days after this the Ratcher clan's offensive began in earnest, and such things as Privet and Hamble had talked about seemed but niceties of living when set against the harsh realities of war.

A careless guard, made bored and complacent by the recent lack of activity, had ventured beyond the defences and was caught at dusk by the grikes. His screams as he was tortured, deliberately in earshot of the defences, cast a pall of dread and loathing over Crowden. This tactic had been used before as a way of luring out Crowden's guards to the rescue, and though from time to time successful attempts had been made, in recent times, with Crowden under the younger leadership of Hamble, the grikes had known how to ambush the rescuers, and take even more prisoners. Therefore it had been generally agreed that rescues would not be attempted, and the agony of the captured mole was perhaps greater because he knew none was likely to come for him. At dawn his screams became quieter, and later he was found deposited near the defences, mercifully close to death, his snout crushed and his eyes blinded.

It was an experience that Privet, who witnessed the maimed mole being brought back to communal chambers near the Library, could scarcely believe, nor ever forget. In years past such behaviour had called forth savage reprisals by the Crowden moles, but by Hamble's time, as he himself said, some sense of resolve or purpose had gone from Crowden, and the grikes' brutal tactics produced the effect of moles wondering why they should struggle on in such a place in the face of such assaults. Why not leave the Moors and find a better and less brutal place to live?

There were skirmishes, and others were wounded, and two more caught – and returned, dying. One with his snout amputated and in such agony that he was put out of his misery; the other with a wound in his chest so wide and deep that the broken ribs protruded from his body, and each breath he tried to take before he died was an agony that Privet, who was amongst those who tended him, felt herself. Then a third mole was treated in the same way, his face half ripped off, his looks gone, his flanks, so strong, so sturdy, shivering with fear and shock.

In all cases these moles whispered the same name before they died: 'Red Ratcher did it; it was Ratcher himself . . . and one called Grear . . .'

Bleakly Rooster heard this, and saw what his father and brother had done, and stared blankly at the wounded, and the dying, and the dead. His breathing quickened, his restless paws grew deadly still, and there he would stay until one of the Charnel moles, usually Hume, took him away and tried to divert his shame, anger and frustration into delving more and better defences.

'Can't do nothing,' Rooster said, 'not nothing at all. But want to want to; WANT TO.'

And when he tried to sleep at night with Privet he was restless and distressed, wanting to go out to the defences, to stare into the dangerous night, to do *something*: to rise up in fury, to attack his kin that brought this agony and death.

'Want to hurt,' he whispered again and again, 'want to. Want to kill him. Grikes only bad because leaders bad. I'm grike and I'm not bad.'

As the days passed, and the siege and attempted incursions all about the system continued, Rooster suffered more and more from doing nothing. While Hamble and other males fought to preserve the system, all he could do was delve – and despite others' praise for what he did, to him it was not enough. So that nowhere was the agony of war, its fears and its rising hatreds, greater than in Rooster's head and heart, and passive paws.

The siege went on, and on, and the Ratcher moles, soon learning that the Dark Sound of the eastern defences was impossible to pass, began to probe Crowden's periphery in places they had not been to before. They were sighted by day, and Hume and Rooster confirmed that the mole who seemed to be in charge and helped do the torturing was Grear, whom they had seen on their escape from the Charnel. But they saw Red Ratcher too, lurking and laughing among his kin, making his violent gestures and shouting obscenely.

They gained intelligence from the prisoners they took that the grikes had come in greater numbers than before, and that under Grear's and Ratcher's more effective leadership some from the southern Moors had been persuaded to join the fray. Crowden was in mortal danger, and grim fear and gloom pervaded its tunnels, despite Hamble's every effort to rally morale.

The Crowden moles, it must be said, stopped short of torturing the grikes they caught, though only because of Hamble's direct intercession. However, there were some things he could not stop, and questions were not asked about what happened to the prisoners once they had given what information they could – nor about the bodies of grikes that drifted grimly in the lake adjacent to the outer defences to the north.

Meanwhile, Rooster could not be hemmed in all the time, and sometimes when things were quiet he went out on the surface, despite the pleas of Hume and Privet, and Hamble himself. He was drawn to where the action was, as bees are lured to the sweetest flower, and there was no shortage of young moles willing to go out and guard him, as if they felt he was special, and almost a leader. Indeed, none could fail to see that morale lifted and moles felt reassured when he showed his snout.

'He's a natural leader, Privet, a warrior greater than any of us,' said Hamble. 'You can see it in his face, you can almost smell it on him. It's no good you, or Hume, or any other moles pretending otherwise. He's made for it.'

'He's a *delver*, never forget that, for on it so much depends,' insisted Privet. 'I'm beginning to wish I'd never brought him here.'

Early summer came across the Moors as April gave way to May, and still the attacks continued, and the grikes dug into positions all about the system. Slow molemonths of attrition, and occasional mistakes by the Crowden moles. One night, after an ill-conceived attack on the Ratcher clan went wrong, they lost part of their defences when the grikes burrowed in from above and destroyed something of what Rooster's skill had made, so that ground was lost, and moles as well.

Then more sights of blood and pain, more sounds of agony that moles could not escape; not even Privet down in her Library, working now to seal up as many of the precious texts as she could in secret burrows, against the day when the system might have to be abandoned, or worse, was overrun. In that, at least, Rooster could work with her, and for a time both sought escape from the agonies above in hard work far below, and many texts were hidden.

But now Lime began to be more bold, as if sensing that Crowden was fragmenting in spirit, and opportunities might exist for . . . play. She became insinuating and clever, whispering things to Rooster when Privet was watching at which he could not but smile, wheedling her feminine attractive way into Rooster's confidence as he, ever more

109

discontented and restless at being unable to help Hamble more, turned his frustration on those he loved.

Lime was seen with him here, accompanying him there, touching, reaching, mouth open and moist pink tongue that showed when she laughed as she cajoled him to come . . .

'Where?'

'Oh Rooster! Anywhere.'

All of this poor Privet saw, and suffered at, trying to tell herself that the turmoil and unreasonable jealousy that surged in her, and had her watching out for him and wondering where he was, and what he was doing, and going to places she would not normally go to see if he and Lime were there, and thinking that if they were not, where were they . . . was uncharitable, before the greater tragedy that was beginning to take Crowden by its throat and destroy it for ever.

Then, suddenly, one afternoon, when Privet was in her Library and blessedly free from jealous fears, all unknown to her Rooster was involved in an affray: nothing much, little more than a brush with grikes down in the defences when he pulled a mole to safety through Dark Sound and faced a talon-thrust towards himself. He did nothing, but the blood of the mole he saved was on him, and he was bruised where he was hit; Lime was quickly in attendance.

'Come, Rooster, they don't like you here,' she purred, and her paw caressed Rooster's back as they went, and Rooster turned and frowned, not at her, but at the evil that was on them all, which he was, as he had said, prevented from trying to stop. A guard saw them go and grinned and thought of certain things that he would like to do with Lime again – for he had done them once. Lime was a mole who liked males.

'Come delve with me,' she purred to Rooster, and for relief perhaps from the violence of the grikes and the pressure of his peers, Rooster went with her.

A mole need be neither old nor especially wise to imagine what occurred, just as that guard had already imagined what *might* occur. A pause in a tunnel, the hot breath of a whisper, a quick caress, and Lime, who knew it all, aroused what Rooster thought was his anger, but she knew was his angry lust.

'Leave me. Want Privet now. Not you.'

'Yes, my dear, then go,' she said, her sliding subtle talons hurting him just enough where they explored and caressed to make him feel more angry still, yet stay for more.

'Not here,' she whispered as his great paws turned on her roughly, 'not *here*, my love.'

'Wasn't going to hurt you,' he said in dismay, as he tried to push her away and she clung on in pretended fear, closer still.

'No,' said Rooster, finding he was holding her.

'Oh yes,' she said, as somewhere out on the edge of the system more screaming was heard as the grikes and Crowden warriors fought again. 'Unless you want to be a real mole and go to that.'

'Can't,' said Rooster.

'Then come with me, my dear, come with me,' and though her paw was ever so gentle in his, its pull was a command, and Rooster was led down one tunnel, and then another, and then a third, to a place all dark and soft and warm which scented good, where a mole did not have to think or speak, but only touch, and explore, as if it were a delving that he made.

'No,' he said one last time, as her paws rose up his body, firm and sure.

'Forget yourself,' she said.

He tried, and found it was not hard. 'Want to hurt you,' he rasped, his paws strong on her, and she curled her body into his, biting and scratching him to make him want to hurt her more.

'Then hurt me, Rooster, if you can,' she gasped, as she felt a strength in him greater by far than of any mole who had ever taken her before. 'Do to me what you want to do.'

'Want to . . . hurt you!' he said again, as she felt his lust begin to mount, and the passion in his suddenly hard delving paws all urgent, potent, living; matching her lust, meeting her need, as she pushed at him, and bit at him and made him so angry that he roared, and turned, and took her to him as she screamed for more and more and more of his hurting, of what he wrongly felt was his destructive force.

'More,' she sighed, stronger than him in that at least, 'more and more.'

'Yes,' said Rooster, and lost in her, he forgot himself.

When Rooster did not appear in their tunnels at dusk, nor later as night deepened and the fighting began again over on the eastern part of the system, Privet worried for him and wondered what she might do. Not for one moment did she think he might be with Lime, being now more concerned with the dreadful difficulties he was having over the fighting and his non-involvement with it. Some time in the night

111

she could no longer bear tossing and turning and fretting, and went off to find him, or news of him.

She got none, or none that was direct. Instead she saw some injured moles near the defences, and heard that earlier there had been more vicious fighting and that Rooster had been seen just before that. There was something shifty in the way she was told this, as if her informant, a guard, knew something more; but more was not forthcoming. Nor did she suspect the real cause of his absence even then, for Hamble came by and it was plain from what he said that the Crowden system was in deeper jeopardy than he and other elders had previously thought.

'Unless we can muster a counter-attack on the Ratcher moles we are going to be driven further and further back into our system, and eventually we will be forced to yield to them,' he said.

But they had long since prepared plans for this eventuality, so used were they to the attacks of grikes, and there was a drill for retreat into inner tunnels and chambers from which it would be hard to flush them out. What was more, if such a retreat should ever happen, and it had only once in the distant past, there was a well-arranged system of escape through deep tunnels which not only evacuated females and pups and older moles up into an adjacent clough, but enabled the defenders to emerge in a position to ambush the incursive grikes from behind, when they would be in tunnels that were unfamiliar to them. This long-standing arrangement gave the Crowden moles their calm confidence, increased these days since Rooster and his delvers had improved the defences of these inner sanctums of retreat and escape.

'I'm not saying it'll come to that later tonight, or tomorrow, Privet, but things are as hard as I remember them, and this mole Grear is working with Red Ratcher now and seems a sight more astute in his management of attacks than Red Ratcher himself. Since you're here, I think you better go back to the inner tunnels and just make sure that everymole's where they should be in case there is an incursion and we have to act quickly. Come to that, what *are* you doing here?'

'Have you seen Rooster?'

'Ah!' Hamble shook his head uneasily. If a guard had told him something he wasn't saying. 'He's not fighting, if that's what you mean. If he was, and giving us the leadership he could, then we wouldn't be in the position we are!' He laughed affectionately. 'He's a mole I admire more as the days go by,' he continued. 'It must be hard for him having moles like me making no bones of the fact that we think he'd be a fine fighter. But don't worry, Privet, I've promised to keep him out of it and I shall, and if I weaken there's always Hume hovering about like a mother watching over a pup. He'd rather die than see Rooster raise a paw to anymole. But dammit, it might be just the thing he needs.'

'So you don't know where he is?'

'I must go, Privet,' said Hamble, and was gone as quickly as he could, but not so fast that Privet did not have time to see the hesitation in his eyes.

She went back to the inner tunnels, checked that all was well, and in the evening she went slowly back to her own chambers, half hoping as she reached them that Rooster would be there. But he was not, so where could he be?

How slowly the time passed as she lay and tossed to and fro, thinking of all the possibilities, turning them over, dismissing them, recalling them, worrying at them, on into the deepest, darkest part of the night when vague possibilities become probabilities, suspicions develop into dark certainties, and a mole's silliest fears seem to change into oncoming nightmares. Suddenly Privet recalled Hamble's hesitation, and the guard's reluctance to talk, and having decided they were withholding something they knew, she quickly convinced herself that she knew what it was, and that its name was Lime.

Lime! Yes! That was undoubtedly it! He was with her *now*.

Privet was wide awake immediately, her heart thumping with the implications; Lime and Rooster, all this time together and out of sight! Had not Hamble *warned* her that somemole, some female, might seek Rooster out and steal him from her? He had not mentioned Lime but then he would not have done; he too had once desired her, and perhaps had his reasons not to name her.

By now, having convinced herself that something was apaw between Lime and Rooster this very night, Privet was up and stanced by the portal of her tunnels wondering what, if anything, she could do.

'But I haven't warned Lime about what Hamble said, of the need to be especially careful, and I must! Now!' That it might have waited until morning did not occur to her, nor that the true reason she wanted to go to Lime's burrow there and then was nothing to do with her sister's safety, and all to do with satisfying herself that her suspicions were untrue. That they might be true did not occur to her, as without more ado she hurried along the communal tunnels and turned into the less familiar ways that led to Lime's burrow. Nightmares live in fearful imagining rather than stark reality. It was simply a matter of satisfying herself that her fears were groundless; then she could go

113

back to her burrow and sleep. Yes . . . it would be for the best.

So on she hurried, ever faster, thinking only of how weak her words would sound on waking Lime at such an hour of the night – or dawn rather, for day was breaking now, and the light from the entrances she passed made the tunnel seem a gloomy, still place. Whilst out on the surface above all was silent, the fighting over for now; *everything* silent, but for the patter of Privet's busy paws, and the thumping of her heart.

She stopped, and nearly turned back, suddenly painfully aware of her true reason for coming here, and feeling it unworthy to have such thoughts. It was almost day, and when she next saw Rooster she could try to break through the embarrassments and barriers, tell him she loved him, reach out to him, and soon, during the coming afternoon and night perhaps, they could retreat to the privacy of their tunnels and . . . make love. As other moles. Hamble had been right – it was time.

Thinking these more cheerful thoughts she turned away, and would have gone back; but just then, coming down the still tunnels, she heard – what? Lime's voice? A nightmare become reality?

It *was* Lime's voice. And what it asked was, 'More . . .'

Silence, rustles, a deep chuckle or perhaps a groan.

'More, my love . . .' said Lime again.

Privet's heart seemed to stop utterly for a moment, but then as she crept forward towards those sounds of love it started such a thumping barrage in her chest that others might almost have heard it beat.

'Want more,' Privet heard Rooster say. Agony, anger, violent thoughts were Privet's now.

Then, 'Yessss . . .' in Lime's voice, and the beginning of a cry of ecstasy, and a strange groaning roar which must be, *was*, Rooster.

Privet crept on, driven by the terrible need to be sure, even though she knew already from the sounds of love alone, on and on until she came to a side tunnel whence the gasping, violent passionate sounds of love came forth. Drawn in by the inexorable need to be sure, to witness, to *see*, she ducked under Lime's portal and went to the entrance of the chamber where they were. Grey the light, loud and violent their gasps, and then, when she went near and stanced boldly and looked, she saw a sight nomole should see; her beloved taking another in his great grasp and giving her all, as she takes all, and taking her all as she in turn gives it, and more.

'More!'

Limbs, fur, snouts, opened mouths, gasps, moans, stressing, slid-

114

ing, insinuating talons that caressed, and held, in forms and shapes that made two bodies one – grotesque and most horrible to the watcher who stood apart.

A nightmare then, fears come alive, jealous thoughts confronted with the naked, savage truth. Then worse still, she saw that the heaving corporeal coupling that she watched, watched her. It had a pair of opening eyes. As Privet froze in horror, part of that writhing thrusting body took shape and meaning; eyes gazed at her, wide, surprised, and then, more terribly still, triumphant.

Privet stared into Lime's eyes, and Lime found perverse pleasure in being seen, as Rooster mounted her and entered her again and roared out his pleasure, not knowing he was watched. Then, worse yet, Lime's eyes flickered with her mounting pleasures, and slowly closed as she yielded up to what Rooster gave her, yet had never given Privet; and Lime turned to him, and ignoring Privet, encouraged him with touch and teeth and writhing limbs.

'More!' she screamed.

Then Privet turned from the hateful, sickening sight, turned blindly away and ran for the dawning light of the surface, to escape from the suffocation of the chambers and tunnels and what she had seen, which was the end for her.

Numb, blind, broken, wild, filled with the hopeless desire to rip what she had seen from mind and memory, where it burned and tormented her, she broke out on to the surface, and floundered eastward, towards where the Ratcher moles were encamped. Perhaps she screamed; perhaps she cried. Whatever sound she made, any watching mole on either side would have heard her, and known of her coming. Indeed, a Crowden guardmole turned to repel what he thought was an assault from behind as Librarian Privet, running wild and maddened, charged upon him along the way that led amongst Rooster's dark delvings and out of the defences and then beyond to the mortal danger of Ratcher's lines.

'You can't!' he cried as she ran past, pushing him with violent strength. 'They're nearby, they've got another of our moles! You *can't*!'

She reached the delvings before he could stop her, and raising her paws to them curled her talons and scored viciously down and then across, making the worst Dark Sound anymole had ever heard, made more dreadful still by her savage laughter, which mocked the sound and chased it into echoes of hatred and betrayal.

'Tell Rooster where I've gone,' she cried out to the guard with a wild laugh, 'you'll find him having Lime,' before running on and out

115

through the last exit, to the exposed ground beyond and the besieging grikes.

They caught her easily enough – indeed, so careless was she, so desperate to escape the pain that Crowden represented for her now, that she welcomed the cautious advance of the first grike that saw her, and minded not his rough handling, and the way he pushed and shoved her into the area in which they had established themselves. She saw crude scrapes, a place where moles had groomed and defecated, and a low peaty bank on which two grikes lay wounded, one grey of snout and near death, the other with a limb that had been broken. All seemed no more than a dream, and she was, so far, quite unafraid. Moles stared at her intrigued, and if she saw lust and amusement in their eyes, she did not care.

'Take me to Red Ratcher,' she said, wincing at the strong hold the grike had on her.

Moles gathered about her; some prodded her lewdly, others stared, cold and malevolent, and all had the rancid smell of ungroomed bodies.

'Take her to Grear,' said a senior-looking mole. 'He'll know what to do with her.'

There were more crude laughs, and comments about how skinny she was, how small, how pointed her snout. If this was a Crowden female no wonder the Crowden males were failing . . .

Perhaps it was only then she began to feel afraid. Anger had carried her this far but now, as she was hustled along, she realized she had come to a place from which she would not escape. She heard a scream, turned a corner, and saw a mole laid out on his back; over him another loomed, raised his taloned paw and then thumped down hard into the tender parts between the mole's pale, soft belly and left hindpaw.

It was a Crowden mole being tortured, screaming and jabbering, as grikes stanced about him, staring and bored, watching as the biggest of them questioned him. Some did not even watch, but ate worms carelessly; one even dozed. She knew even before he turned that the torturer was Grear. She recognized his rough fur with its russet tinge, and the great back, and the power; it might almost have been a slightly smaller version of Rooster she stared at. One last moment of defiance made her stance proud as Grear turned round to look at her, but then she saw his eyes, cold, hard, and pitiless, and she was struck still with fear, and the horror of where she was and what she had done.

Grear stared at her for a moment, turned back to what he was

116

doing, and said to his victim, 'The defences, mole, we want to know what you can tell us and then we might stop.'

The mole was crying now, huddled, bloody, shaking, and trying vainly to protect his softer parts and face and snout from the talons poised over him. Grear ordered another to carry on the vile work and turned back to her.

'Well?' His voice was deep.

'We found this mole—'

'A female?' Light glistened in Grear's eye. He reached a bloody paw to her, played roughly with her face, and then caressed her flanks appraisingly.

'Take her to my father. She's too small for me. Ask him not to kill her for when he's done she'll talk. *Explain* that to him or otherwise he'll do what he usually does with females and kill her in the act.' He hunched forward and down towards her like a shadow from the sky. 'What do you know, mole? Eh?'

'Nothing,' faltered Privet, her mind a blank.

He laughed. 'They all know "nothing" until asked the right way.'

The Crowden mole nearby uttered a heartrending, hopeless cry as he suffered another talon-thrust; it was the cry of one abandoned, even by the Stone, and echoed what Privet was beginning to feel in her heart.

'*He* knew nothing until we asked him the right questions, then the answers started coming,' said Grear calmly. 'Now? He has nothing left but the need to scream and, perhaps, to draw out his fellows from behind their strange defences to seek to rescue him. He is our bait. And you . . .' Grear's eyes narrowed. 'You may be our pleasure. But my father had best have you first, or he'll object.'

He turned away.

'You missed a treat there, Grear!' she heard a mole say ironically as she was led away.

'A small treat,' said Grear, laughing, 'yet . . . strange she should come.'

Numb, numb, numb, Privet's feelings in the time that followed – an endless time of brute sound and mole, of odours and cries, of stares and vile touches, and a world that shook because she could not stop shivering. She slept, she woke to a mole hitting her, she slept again. Then she was dragged to a quieter place, where a vile old mole brooded and stared at her with cruel lust and then turned on her with such savagery that her world began to turn blank and dark.

117

Chapter Ten

Privet regained consciousness to the violent grip of talons at her face. Unable to move, shocked and in pain, she struggled to open her eyes, only to be half blinded by sun. Then the red-eyed face of the vile mole blocked light out as it came close and stared at her.

'What's yer name, mole?'

'Privet.'

His teeth were yellow, and the stench of his fetid breath made her retch; his eyes were the most evil she had ever seen; his face had Rooster's furrows and shadows, and in his fur was that same russet tinge. She had seen Rooster in Grear; now he loomed over her in the form of Red Ratcher.

'Scared?'

She nodded.

He grinned malevolently. 'I would be,' he said. He turned on the two moles who stanced nearby, watching. 'Bugger off.'

She stared immobile and mute and watched his paw, rough and gnarled, reach out even before the others had gone. It grasped her flank, its talons curled painfully into her flesh, it groped and gripped at her and his huge ugly head was near, and his breath hot and vile on her face and clustering in her snout like filth.

'Is this dying?' she asked herself, as he slowly drew her more and more tightly to him, 'is this the dark and fearful way of death?'

She screamed as sudden pain was like a talon in her, hard and piercing, and her eyes filled with tears that felt like blood.

He made a sound of sorts, a filthy guttural baying sound, and his breath and teeth and moist tongue were at her face and then shifting to her back, and she knew he was going to take her then and there, going to hurt her like Rooster hurt Lime only *that* was not hurt, that was . . . The pain again, deep and mortal, pain a mole cannot forget, and then he laughed, and bit her back; his great paws slid down her flanks on either side and his full weight was on her, at her haunches, crushing her, and the pain was pushing deep at her, terrible, and she was drowning in a sea of dark, wild, forbidding agony, screaming as

118

she sank into a humiliation that she had never known a mole could suffer, nor another create.

'NOOOO!' But it was not her voice.

Ratcher's movement over her stopped, and she felt his paws hasten and scrabble from her, and the pain withdrew. She was buffeted aside by a violent blow across her head, and the clouds about her grew darker still; the voice she had heard began shouting and screaming in rage.

'NO!' The tone was deep, angry – and familiar.

She turned, strove to see, then crawled further back into the shadow of a peat hag, expecting that at any moment his paw would take her once again; none touched her, while struggle and raging filled the space about her. As the pain in her haunches lessened her vision cleared; she tried to focus her eyes, succeeded at last, and saw Ratcher, snarling, staring, talons out, his body hunched against a foe far greater than himself.

'No!' she had time to cry in vain as the full horror of the scene became clear to her – a horror greater than the obscene death she had been about to die. She saw Rooster rampant, Rooster with his great paws raised high above Ratcher's head, the talons pointed and ready to strike the life from those red eyes for ever.

'NOOOO!' She cried, knowing it was too late.

The Master of the Delve's delving paw descended, talons out, and before her gaze it seemed to travel so slowly that she saw, or seemed to see, every detail of its strike, and to hear every slow moment of Rooster's blood-lust roar. Ratcher's head shot back as the thrusting talons burst into it, and smashed it; then the bloodied paw rose again and struck down where Ratcher's head was already rent, his eyes already smashed and dead.

'NOOO!' roared Rooster, and his strike went into that vile old body and burst its bag of fleshy fur and blood and bone. Rooster's paws and face and shoulders were turned red with his father's life before he raised the body up and hurled it out across the Moors. Then he reared and turned, and found himself staring at four great grikes who now faced him, amongst them his brother Grear.

In the numbed and silent world from which Privet watched the tragedy unfolding before her, it seemed to her that the outcome of the fight was inevitable, and events moved forward with the same slow unstoppable power of the black storm she and Rooster had once watched crossing the Moors near Hilbert's Top. Perhaps the quartet of huge moles who now advanced upon him did not think quite the

119

same thing, but they must have felt a certain trepidation arising from what had just happened, unknown to Privet, and from the bloody evidence that Rooster had just hurled from him with such power and disgust.

Moments before all had seemed well to Grear, and normal enough – if normal it was that the air around their stronghold was filled with the whimpers of the tortured Crowden guard and the screams of the pathetic female Ratcher was in the act of ravaging; but then, the grikes of Ratcher's clan liked that kind of thing.

Then came warning shouts, and what seemed a rampage of moles, led not by one of the normal Crowden lot, with lighter, smoother fur, but by a mole who looked like one of the Ratcher clan – grike, dark-furred and savage. The posted guards had been taken and killed, and then the second line of defence, and on this charging force had come, more powerful and resolute than any the grikes had ever met.

So sudden was the attack, so total the surprise, that when Rooster grabbed the nearest mole by the throat and said, 'Where is she?' not only did the mole point the way to Red Ratcher without demur, but the others stayed rooted to the spot. The Crowden moles turned on Ratcher's mob, inspired by the power of Rooster's bold example, and began, without more ado, to beat them into submission. Rooster went on regardless of his safety, sensing that he had no time to lose.

He had found his way amongst the peat hags, rounded a corner, and there seen Privet bent and trapped, her back bowed beneath Red Ratcher's vile force as the evil mole began to have his way with her. Nothing could have contained Rooster then – not moles, not training, nor any sense that in terms of his Mastership he was destroying all. Perhaps if the moles concerned had not been Privet and Red Ratcher, if the act he sought to stop had not been so cruelly obscene, he might have held himself back.

The truth was that Rooster launched himself upon his father with awesome might, like a mole who had been held back too long from something he had desired to do all his adult life. So he had gone forward, taken his father's life in a few appalling blows, and stained his heart with the blood of patricide.

Meanwhile, Privet crawled to one side and began to understand what was apaw, whilst Grear and three of his strongest clan-brothers, recovering from the shock of surprise, broke free of the Crowden moles and rushed round to the defence of Ratcher himself.

'Too late,' whispered Rooster, eyeing them. Before the maddened, ruthless sight of him three of the four began to quail. Only Grear

120

himself did not, for he saw his father dead, and the blood fresh upon his murderer's paws, a mole he had seen before, and now recognized.

'Charnel mole,' hissed Grear, raising his not inconsiderable paws to the same level as Rooster's, whilst looking to right and left and inspiring his friends to stand firm. Four against one was surely number enough to take *any* mole.

Privet, the only independent witness of what happened next, felt that her sense that the outcome was inevitable had as much to do with the tragedy implicit in Rooster discovering his taste for violence and so taking a path he could surely never retrace with his delving spirit intact, as with who would win or lose. Her cry of 'No!' was but the whisper of dry grass in the wake of passing storm-winds.

Rooster's eyes narrowed in those fateful moments, his paws gyrated as they did before a delve, his head turned a little to one side as if he were divining the nature of the moles he faced, and then, just as he had on Hilbert's Top when he had decided on the right delve to make, he moved – suddenly, swiftly, powerfully, and with a killing ruthlessness that struck fear in all those near. He hunched forward, lowered his snout, pulled his right paw back and began to power it forward again, talons extended to the full.

Into Grear's chest he struck, so fiercely that the violent expulsion of air from his lungs was heard by everymole there. It was Grear's last breath and it ended with his head shooting back in agony before his mouth filled with blood and phlegm, and his eyes stared for an instant of horror at the sky, and saw no more.

The blow was so powerful that it shook even Rooster's great body, and for a moment his back paws rose from the ground. Then as they touched earth again, and the dead Grear shot back into the advance of one of the others, Rooster powered a left paw-thrust into the face of the next mole along the line that had been advancing upon him.

That mole did not die then, but he did not live for long thereafter, and suddenly all was in disarray and Rooster was triumphant over the moles about him, who retreated into the talons of the Crowden moles who had come from behind.

No words can adequately describe the frightening power of what those moles witnessed, and its effect was the same on Crowden and Ratcher mole alike: all stopped, all stared, all were in utter awe. They had seen come among them a mole of such strength and resolute purpose that before him they could be neither friend nor foe, but followers all.

Then Rooster began to give commands, and took over the position they had assaulted, and changed for ever the face of the endless strife of Ratcher and Crowden mole across the Moors.

We who follow the tale of Duncton Wood and the moles who strive for the peace of the Stone's Silence, and the Light of its wisdom and love, will wish to turn from this dark, fell scene; in disgust perhaps, in shock certainly, in hope always, that despite all the Stone will find a way back to Light and love. Therefore let us turn our snouts to one mole in that savage madness that followed Rooster's turning towards the way of violence he had resisted so long, and follow *him*.

Hamble, good Hamble, strong Hamble, witness to it all, and mole enough to keep his head, he'll be our guide. He realized in those fearful moments that whilst nomole could have kept Rooster from the path of violence of which Lime had been a conduit, but his grim past the true creator, there *was* something *he* might do for good.

Privet lay ravaged and half broken, quite forgotten in the carnage of the fighting that Rooster now led. Hamble went to her, placed a paw at her shoulder, and whispered urgently, 'You come with me. Now. No whimpering, no crying, no questioning. Come. I must get you out of here!'

'Must . . . stop Rooster.'

For a moment she even tried, rising to her paws and reaching out to him, but at her first touch he turned on her with a look of chilling indifference.

'Not you,' he said. It was utter, and final, dismissal.

Yet still she tried . . . and at her second touch he even raised a huge paw at her; then, sensing not the horror of what he did but its irrelevance, he turned from her and moved away.

Again she ran to him, and this time the watching moles thought she would die. He reached down to her, raised her up, and seemed about to hurl her after the dead body of his father. Instead he dropped her at Hamble's paws.

'I do not want to see this mole again,' he growled, turning away a final time.

'Come,' said Hamble gently, leading her away.

So in the confusion of battle and change, one good deed was done, and Privet found a protector and guide away from what, a mole might argue, she herself had caused. Perhaps. For now, judgement is better left aside as we give our support to Hamble, who kept his head and saw the one ray of light that still shone in that Moorish scene. What it meant he did not know, but it was to do with Privet, and with the future, and it was not long going to stay alight in this grim place.

'Come on, mole,' said Hamble urgently, 'I'm taking you far from here.'

'But . . .' cried Privet, her paws scrabbling to keep up with him as he almost dragged her through his own ranks and out of the Ratcher stronghold towards Crowden's defences again, past scenes of murder and fighting, warding off moles with talon-thrusts of his own. But as they reached the first tunnel he suddenly balked at following that way.

'No! No more! You'll not be safe now, not if my guess of what's to come is right. Rooster's made his choice and nomole will change it. But my father promised to get you out of here and away from the Moors, and now I shall fulfil that promise. But after that, Privet, you'll be on your own. And may the Stone help you!'

He turned south towards Shining Clough, the way up on to the Moors that led to the Weign Stones, though Privet had never ventured there. On and on he drove her through the day, on and on into dusk.

'I can't go on,' she whimpered finally.

'Then sleep,' he snarled, hurling her into a temporary scrape. 'And say nothing. What you have done—'

'But I—'

'You had a look of triumph on your face, Privet, when Rooster killed Grear. I saw it. You looked like Lime, you looked like the Eldrene Wort must once have done. You looked like nomole that I ever want to know.'

She stared at him aghast, unable to speak, for she sensed something of the truth of what he said.

'I was confused . . .' she tried to say.

'Shut up, Privet, and sleep. For when you wake I shall continue to take you on until I can be discharged of my responsibility for you.'

'Hamble,' she said, trying to win something of him back to her, 'you're not yourself either. You're not the mole I know—'

'Sleep!' he thundered, buffeting her into weeping dark tears, a hurt huddle of a mole who in the short space of that nightmare night and day had begun to lose all, even dignity.

On, on they went the next day, up and up into the Moors, and on the following day they reached the Weign Stones. Near these Hamble left her crying and went to the Stones and stanced quietly, staring bleakly about.

'The Eldrene Wort scribed her Testimony here,' he said. 'For you! Ha! Some mole you've turned out to be.'

'Rooster went with Lime. He—'

'He craved you, my dear, and all you could make him seem to think was that his desire was to hurt, not love. You know what he said to me before . . . before he charged upon the Ratcher moles? He said, "I didn't know that she wanted me like that. It felt violent, what I did to Lime, but it was like delving, it was another way of being one with her. But it was Privet I loved."'

'Let me go back to him . . .'

Hamble shook his head. 'My dear, all, all has changed. He thinks now he has taken Lime he must have her always. He feels *responsible*.'

'And Lime?'

Hamble laughed aloud. 'She doesn't know what she's done! I'll warrant she's going to find that her night-time of pleasuring with Rooster will turn into a lifetime of discovering she's barely worth a single hair of the mole your timidity let her steal from you. But now he'll not let her go! Oh no, Privet, you'll not be wanted there.'

Poor Privet wept uncontrollably, but Hamble stared at her with little sympathy for a time, until his eyes softened.

'But then,' he muttered, more to himself than her, 'I've got a feeling this was the way it was meant to be. The Stone's in this, all of it. When I saw you where you had crawled away from Ratcher, I saw something beyond all this. I saw a light, a hope, a dream, and Stone help us all but it's dependent on you. That's why I'm taking you out of here.'

'Where to?' she whispered.

'I've no idea, Privet, but when I get there I'll know it well enough. But if you've a prayer to say before the Stones, now's your chance, because we're going on shortly, however tired you may be.'

Privet went to the Stones, and tried to be still and think of what to do. She felt angry, confused, upset, jealous still, and lost; and worse, she felt if she had known differently she would have been able to act more judiciously.

'Did *you* feel like this?' she whispered, directing her thoughts to Wort. 'I feel perhaps you did . . . only more than I do, because your life . . .'

A strange peace began to come to her, and tiredness, and a curious sense of warmth. Through it all she sensed that Hamble loved her, deep enough to care, and wisely enough to see that only time might heal what had happened, and that she was a mole who should go on a journey, just as Wort had done and advised her to do in her Testimony: a long and lonely journey at the end of which, if she had faith, if she was true to herself and the Stone's Silence, those dreams she had had of Rooster, of peace, of pups, of normality, might one day come true.

She turned from the Stones to Hamble, and smiled wanly. 'I love you, Hamble,' she said. 'And I love Rooster!'

'Funny way of showing it,' he grumbled, putting a paw to her. She cried, and he held her for a time.

'Come,' he said, 'I'll see you as far as I can along the way, until I'm sure you're clear of Ratcher's lot, or rather, Rooster's lot, as I have a feeling we may all soon become.'

'He is still a Master of the Delve,' she said, 'whatever he may do, and however far he may seek to run from it.'

'Come on, mole, put it behind you. Let others sort out their own lives while the Stone leads you on yours.'

So on they went for several days, up into Bleaklow Moor, and thence by way of Whillan Clough into the High Peak and fabled Kinder Scout.

'No place for moles!' said Hamble, surveying the awesome, desolate scene.

'You're not going to leave me here!' said Privet, smiling.

'I'll know when,' he said.

On, on to the south, until a dusk came when the bleak heather gave way to pasture, and the air was warm and scented with flowers and hay, and lights shone across the sky, and the horizon was low and blue. They slept, close, and when they woke they saw a sight they had never seen; green grass stretching to greener valleys, distant trees, colours of lower land.

'It's moledom,' whispered Privet in a voice shaky with emotion, and fear of the unknown that lay ahead.

'Aye,' said Hamble, ''tis where I always wanted to go. But this . . .'

'This is where you're going to leave me, isn't it?'

He nodded gravely.

'Come with me, Hamble, you and I have always been friends and understood each other. Please come . . .' She took his paw as if to lead him into the future that stretched below them.

He stanced still and shook his head. 'I must go back into the Moors, my dear. I want to come with you, but my task is there. Rooster's a mole needs others at his flank, to help and perhaps to guide. He has a task, and it is a great one, but others must be with him. I feel . . . close to him. As close to him as to you. And anyway, I've got to watch over Crowden for a time, and the moles who choose to live there, including your sister Lime.'

He looked back upslope towards the dark Moors and a shadow of apprehension crossed his face; Privet's too, as she looked south, at the long, unknown way she must soon begin to travel alone.

'You go for all of us, Privet, *all* of us moles trapped on the Moors. Find a way to lead us out of there, out of our darkness. Seek out moles and places who will take you further on your journey. Travel for me, for Rooster, for Hume, even for Lime. Find a way to tell us what we should do, and where we should go.'

'I'm frightened, Hamble,' Privet said.

'You went out to Chieveley Dale, you were lost, and yet you found a way back. Go now, Privet, seek the task the Stone has set for you, and it will lead you back in some way to us. To me. Even one day to Rooster, who loves you.'

'And to the Master of the Delve?'

'Aye, the light I saw that made me bring you here was strong enough to show the way even to a Master of the Delve.'

'Hold me, Hamble, so close, so tight, that I shall never forget the way you feel, the way you are. Hold me, my dear.'

So there the two friends embraced one last long time, the future and task of one leading northward to the Moors once more; but for the other, southward into moledom, and a new liberty.

'Go,' he whispered.

But she shook her head. 'You go first,' she whispered, 'and don't look back. Look after yourself, Hamble, and see that Lime is protected too. Tell her that I think no ill of her. I hope one day I shall see her or hers again. And guard Rooster, that he may return to me one day, as I to him, safeguarded, and as we were meant to be.'

Then Hamble turned from her, and climbed slowly back up into the Moors, until he was gone and out of sight.

Only then did Privet turn from what had been her life, to face the light of the sun, and to find what liberty moledom held for one who had lost all but faith in the Stone, and the courage to pursue it.

Chapter Eleven

A cold and fractious breeze worried at the vegetation around the little rise where Whillan and the others had settled down to hear Privet's story. She had paused for a time, and then wandered off from them to stare over the Vale of Evesham and gather her thoughts once more. All of them knew that time was running out for this part of their journey; moledom, like the wind, was on the move, and they were moving with it, though to what destination or for what purpose, they did not know.

Returning to them at last, Privet looked uncertainly about as if deciding where to stance down to continue her tale, and then turned to Whillan, and smiled gently.

'You've said hardly a word since dawn,' she whispered, going to him, and reaching out to put her paw upon his. 'I want you near me now as I tell what happened after I left the Moors. Strange, but the time taken up with that was almost as long as all that went before, and yet it seemed to pass in no time at all . . .' She laughed lightly again, looking around at her friends and seeming to sense the new and sombre mood that had come to them since Weeth had revealed his forebodings concerning Quail's intentions at Caer Caradoc.

'You see, when moles suffer as I did, and lose everything, they do not easily recover themselves. Perhaps they never do entirely. For a long time after that I did not feel a part of life at all, but like a fallen leaf in autumn, hurled and swept along by the winds, pausing here, drifting there, with no power to move itself at all. Then rain comes and winter, and the leaf settles in some obscure place, and is lost, breaking down into fragments, until it is no leaf at all.

'That was how I felt in the moleyears of summer and autumn after Hamble left me at the edge of the Moors and I began my long journey into moledom, which in time brought me here with you now, the future no more certain than it has ever been.'

It was to fabled and holy Beechenhill, the system that lies south-west of the Moors in limestone country above the River Dove, and where the Stone Mole gave himself that moledom might be saved, that Privet found her way the following summer.*

She had the advantage in her journeying of being female and harmless, no threat to mole at all. Then, too, it was the summer, when moles turn their minds from raising young and protecting their tunnels, and travel a bit, or are glad to welcome passing wayfarers to their tunnels, and hear their tales. How quiet and subdued the strange thin mole from off the Moors must have seemed, and how strange her Whernish accent, as she struggled to learn to speak Mole better; until then she had only kenned it at Shire's arid flank, and scribed it in those texts she made on Hilbert's Top.

At Beechenhill Privet came under the protection of Master Librarian Cobbett, who, though she discovered the fact and its significance only long afterwards, originally came from Duncton Wood and was the Master Stour's brother. Cobbett was warmer, less orderly, less formidable than Stour, and soon had reason to welcome Privet's arrival, for her ability to scribe and, even more, her knowledge of Whernish, made her a rarity in those far-off parts. Master Librarian Cobbett, battling as he was to establish a library in the furthest north of the systems chosen at the Cannock Conclave as worthy of receiving copies of the great texts, welcomed her as a most useful aide. The more so, perhaps, because despite the importance of Beechenhill as the place to which the Eldrene Wort had harried the Stone Mole, few journeymoles ever ventured up into the obscure hills where the system lay, and few aspiring scholars ever stayed long with the vague, eccentric Cobbett.

Set high among the limestone gorges of the River Dove, the system was quiet and few moles lived there. Its texts were in a sorry way, and it was not long before Privet found she had a useful role. The two got on well, and perhaps Cobbett, whose obsession was collecting tales and preserving them in scribed-down form, found Privet a rich source of Whernish lore.

Certainly, he put her to work on the Whernish texts his Library held, which were in truth its only claim to a specialty. So Privet found a place, and tried through the winter years following to come to terms as best she could with all that she had left and lost. How often she must have gone up to the Stone of Beechenhill, in the shadow of which her grandmother Wort had performed the deed against the

---

* See *Duncton Found*, third volume of the *Duncton Chronicles*, for the story of the Stone Mole.

Stone Mole for which moledom ever after reviled her, and reviles her still, despite her later redemption and Testimony! But there, as Wort had hoped her daughter's daughter might, Privet began to find the peace of the Stone, and know something of its healing Silence.

She herself could later recall little of that time, mainly because of the trauma she suffered after she left Beechenhill. Only the sense that Cobbett watched over her, and led her through a study of texts that educated her in the modern history of mole, kept her balanced and at peace. There was much about the coming of the Seven Stillstones to Duncton Wood, and the coming of the Books, saving only the Book of Silence, whose whereabouts nomole knew. These stories resonated in her heart and helped her see her losses and troubles in perspective.

We do not know for certain how well Cobbett understood the nature and powers of the female scribe who had come so modestly into his little domain, but from all the evidence we may guess that, if only instinctively, he saw that she was rather more than the insignificant Whernish scholar that she seemed. It appears she did not tell him at all of Rooster, of delving, of her journey to Hilbert's Top; nor that the Eldrene Wort was her grandmother, and that her coming to Beechenhill was part of a sense of mission whose nature and purpose she did not yet know. These things were held back from him, and yet Cobbett told her early on that if it was a task she sought, she could do no better than to ponder the last great mystery of modern molish times – the whereabouts of the Book of Silence.

'Of course, my dear, you'll not find it by sitting on your rump. But equally you'll not find it by rushing off and looking for it without pondering the problem first. Right thought *precedes* right action, as right action must be *followed* by right thought. It is an endless gyre of improvement by which moles ascend ever higher towards an understanding of themselves.

'I hesitate to use the word "thought", since thought in too many moles' minds is separated from feeling, which is that vast force of energies of which thought is merely a superficial expression. I used to argue this point with my brother, who was given rather too much to thought in my view, and too little to feeling. I argued too with another who felt the opposite, losing himself in the telling of emotional tales which were all very well and so forth but led, as it seemed to me, nowhere in particular.

'I, as you gather, am somewhere between these two views, which is why I urge you to learn to stance still with your paws firmly on the ground, and *think* before you *do*. Then when you have thought, you should do, for without that the previous thinking is somewhat of a waste.

'Therefore, since you seem a clever and industrious mole scholastically, but one who has no task, why not commit yourself to this small matter, which others seem to have forgotten, concerning the Book of Silence.'

'Where do I begin?' Privet asked.

'Oh, at the Stone of course, both figuratively and literally. Make a habit of going to our Stone – few do, you know, since most find doing nothing rather hard, so you won't often be disturbed. Meditate before the Stone, ponder where the Book might be, and when you're not doing that, ken what you can about recent times, and commit Woodruff's "Duncton Chronicles" to heart. If all that fails, and you need a break, then kindly help me with my Book of Tales.'

This set out Privet's agenda for the long winter years she spent in Beechenhill, years which she now, before Whillan, Maple and Weeth, characterized as 'numb' years, when she was seeking, as Cobbett realized, to define her task, and find ways of following it; a time, too, when she was striving to reconcile herself with parting from the Moors and Rooster for ever.

Yet numb though that time seemed, there were moments of respite, when the cares of the past and concern for the future gave way to enjoyment of the present, and of the rich and fecund landscape in which she found herself, such a contrast to the sterile Moors on which she had so far lived.

'My belief that moledom was a place of beauty was affirmed by all I saw after I left Hamble on the edge of the Moors and entered new territories. Beechenhill itself, which lies in an elevated position above the incised meanders of the Dove above the system of Ashbourne, was a place of natural beauty, whose tunnels had been delved in ancient times amidst light airy soils and the pale limestone, which formed scars high along the valley sides.

'When the snows came, the place seemed almost ethereal, and the sense of light enhanced my slow meditations upon Silence, before the Stone. I felt moments of great joy. Spring came, the ice and snow gave way to the pasture grass beneath, and the trees to which I was so unused began to spring and bud in the valleys below.

'The Stone Mole himself seemed near as I stanced before Beechenhill's Stone, and the Eldrene Wort as well, for whom I asked forgiveness, just as she had asked the mole who kenned her Testimony to do. It was sometime then that I began to feel that the time was coming when I must journey south to Duncton Wood. It was what my mother Shire had been advised to do, but she had never been able to; but now I had the opportunity. To give me impetus and courage there were the stories of Cobbett, and my growing sense that the mystery of the Book of Silence must surely end in Duncton Wood, as so much else had done.'

Privet left Beechenhill in spring, with something of the pilgrim about her. She went alone, in hope and faith that the Stone would see her safeguarded, and with the belief that it would be in Duncton Wood that her true task would begin, as if all else had been a preparation.

'But . . . what I did not go with was any understanding of the ways in which the Stone orders the lives of moles, which is by offering choices they must take with truth and courage; what happens along the way may be very different from what a mole expects, and very hard to accept. I left Beechenhill with Cobbett's blessing, believing that the hardest part of my journey was over, and the rest would be easier.'

'But something more happened, didn't it?' suggested Whillan.

'Something more? Oh, many things,' said Privet vaguely, 'but I remember few of them.'

'You remember one of them all too well, I think,' said Weeth sharply.

'I . . . I certainly had difficult times, yes,' replied Privet in a measured way, 'but nothing that any of you would really be interested in.'

It was suddenly depressingly obvious that Privet did not wish to go on with her tale. She seemed to be reaching something too terrible for her to face, and Whillan looked despairingly at Maple, and neither knew how to break through her block. But Weeth looked at neither of them, staring intently at Privet instead, a puzzled frown on his face as if he could not quite believe his thoughts. Then he seemed to resolve the problem and his face cleared. He nodded and said, 'To us you'll say no more, Privet!'

'To you?' replied Privet, looking puzzled in her turn.

'US. Followers. Friends. Kin. But . . . a Brother Confessor; you might speak to him. Not *might*, you would have to.'

'Have to?' repeated Privet.

'Yes, Sister Privet, or whatever the name was that the Newborns gave you, to your Brother Confessor you must speak the truth.'

'I . . . was called Sister Crowden . . .' began Privet faintly, while

131

Whillan and Maple, making as if to interrupt, were stopped by an imperious wave of Weeth's paw.

'Advance nearer to me, Sister!' he cried out, turning almost savagely on Privet.

'I will, Brother Confessor . . . I will,' she gasped in a strange voice, sounding much younger, as Whillan and Maple looked on in amazement.

'Then do so,' snarled Weeth as if he addressed an erring pup and not the adult female who had revealed so much of herself with such maturity through the hours just past. Whillan looked angry, whilst Maple seemed about to remonstrate with Weeth.

Yet to their surprise Privet meekly moved forward and stanced before him, snout low. She looked afraid, and all the boldness that had carried her forward in her telling of the journey from the Moors to Beechenhill had gone.

'You have transgressed, Sister Crowden! Is it not so?'

'Brother Confessor Weeth—'

'Do not be so familiar as to use my name, mole,' he snarled at her.

'But Brother—'

'Aye mole! Confess to your Brother Confessor. Speak what is in your heart that the Stone may know the truth!'

By now the change in Weeth was as startling as that in Privet. As he grew ever more threatening and imperious, Privet became ever more cowering and abject, until her voice was a faltering, tearful shadow of what it had been but moments before.

'Brother Confessor . . . I . . .'

'You are nothing, mole, nothing before the rituals and majesty of the Stone, nothing but a Confessed Sister who has made vile transgressions of thought against the rules of the Stone, and deserves punishment.'

'But Brother—'

'And who argues even with her Brother Confessor as with others, and has the reprobate thoughts of a mole in whom arrogance and distrust of the Stone's appointed brothers lingers still.'

'No, Brother Confessor . . .' she began to plead.

'Yes, menial Sister, oh yes – I see the sinfulness in your heart, and how your will conspires against the Stone.'

'I did not mean—'

'You have transgressed and you must be punished, as a mole not worthy to have young.'

'But my pups—'

'Your pups are the Stone's pups, mole, not *yours*. Do you think the Stone would have you corrupt ones so young and innocent?'

'You cannot take them!'

Horror was in Privet's voice, and she was shaking. Maple had to put his paw out to prevent Whillan from rushing to her flank, and assaulting Weeth on the way.

'The Stone shall take them from you . . .'

Nothing of Privet's tale they had so far heard compared to the horror and helpless, hopeless sense of betrayal and failure in Privet's sudden scream.

'Noooo!' was the word she sought to say, but it was lost in the power of the loss it tried to express.

'They shall never be returned to you!' cried Weeth.

'They are barely weaned!'

'You have transgressed, you are punished, you are excommunicate of us and all your pups, you are—'

'NOOOO!'

'No . . .' whispered Weeth in a very different voice, as he reached out to Privet, and shaking and crying and beside herself with the memory of loss at which he had so accurately guessed, she went to him and buried her face in his shoulder. 'No, dear Sister, no.'

'How did you know?' she said at last.

'Was I right?'

She nodded. 'I wanted to tell but the nearer I got the more afraid I became to remember.'

'I know, I know,' said Weeth, excitedly looking round at Whillan and Maple. 'I had *heard* what the Brother Confessors of the Newborns do to sisters, but never thought to learn of it directly from a victim. I recognized something in Privet's hesitation and guessed. You must tell us now, Privet. It is best, for we all need to know the truth of the Newborns' evil. I know of no female who has been entrapped in one of their systems and survived to tell her tale.'

'Then how did you know who they were and what the Senior Brother said? You're not . . . ?' She pulled away from him as if she suddenly thought that *he* had been such a Newborn brother.

He smiled wanly and shook his head. 'No, no, not me. But guardmoles talk, nothing is secret for ever. Now, for Stone's sake tell us your tale before you decide not to once more, and I shall tell you how I guessed the way they treated you.'

'Yes,' said Privet meekly, with the ghost of a recovering smile.

*

133

Privet's descent from the White Peak, at the southern end of which Beechenhill lies, to the lower lands due south, was a journey into an accelerating spring. She had learnt enough of travelling to know that at such a time, when moles are mating, and some already pupping, a sensible mole does not cross another's territory without due warning and many courtesies, but chooses routes which are communal, and avoids occupied systems altogether.

Yet there are always enough moles who, through age, circumstance, or inclination, have not pupped and welcome the exchange of news and views a passing traveller brings. Coming as she did from Beechenhill, a system by then more revered than visited, and being an accredited scholar and scribemole, and one on course for Duncton Wood, Privet met with little hostility, and such as she suffered was short-lived.

She enjoyed the freedom from workaday scholarship the journey brought, and the opportunity it gave her to see for herself some of the landscapes and places in which the recent history of moledom, and its war of Word and Stone, had been made. She soon found that her own concern with matters of Silence was beyond the interests of most moles, and perhaps even over their heads, and those who met her were more bluntly curious about springtime matters, in particular why a female in her prime such as herself was not nested down somewhere having young.

Privet learnt much about ordinary living in these molemonths of her journey, and she was content to travel slowly, and share worms and conversation with whatever moles the Stone put in her way; and if, as sometimes happened, the occasional male suggested that perhaps she should settle down and have a few pups, well, she was not unwilling to feel flattered, even if she firmly chose to do nothing about it.

She had not yet recovered from the loss of Rooster and all the horror surrounding her ravaging by Ratcher, and after the numbness she had felt through the winter years at Beechenhill she now had recourse to lightheartedness, as moles with such histories often do. However, balmy spring air, the scent of wild flowers, the busy doings of other mated creatures raising young, are all powerful aphrodisiacs, and inclined to make even the most timid, prudish, and unconfident moles think that they are missing out, and that they might at least fantasize about doing something about it. Privet was never a flirt, but the natural fact is that in spring, given the right circumstances and the right moles, flirtation will always take place, and several times in her journey along the way southward of Beechenhill, Privet enjoyed the thrill of close encounters.

Yet enjoyable though these moments were, they provoked in her an underlying restlessness and dissatisfaction, and unhappy thoughts of Rooster and the pups she had wanted to give him, which she would now surely never have. Mixed with these annoyingly intrusive thoughts were others; jealousy of Lime, and wondering if she and Rooster were still together after the winter years, and if so whether Lime was having pups – *his* pups, pups that should have been hers. Privet was fully aware of the futility of such thoughts but powerless to stop them recurring, and the occasional flirtations she enjoyed – modest things indeed compared to Lime's fulsome goings-on – served only to provoke them more.

So as the days went by, and the air grew warmer, and the number of tunnels with pups she approached increased, her broodiness increased as well, and her physical desires, so normal but so unwelcome. In short, Privet, scholar, scribe and pilgrim, desired to have young, and had no mole by which she might have them, nor did it seem she had any prospect of finding one.

It was at this point in her journey that Privet first heard of the Newborn moles, and of Blagrove Slide. In those days neither the Newborns nor the name of Blagrove Slide carried any threat to followers – they were known only as overly earnest moles observing a system of faith led by the elusive and charismatic Thripp. She heard of a prayer meeting being held at a Stone upon the Harborough Downs and out of curiosity diverted her journey to attend it. The mole conducting it was young, dark, and male, and so were his acolytes. It did not occur to Privet then that most of those at the meeting, which was held at a communal place equidistant from several thriving systems, were female, young and unpupped; and even if it had, it would not have struck her that *she* was in the same category, and that her attention to the prayers and the whole occasion was made much easier by the attractiveness of the youthful, well-spoken males who conducted it.

Mention of being Newborn in the Stone was gently made, without doctrinal cant or pressure, though even at the time Privet felt as a scholar that these moles – 'brothers' they called themselves – were a little over-zealous in their claims of what the Stone might do for mole who gave themselves up to it, and cast off their 'wilfulness and self-pride'. But by then Privet had learnt that her liking of scholastic argument and debate did not go down well, and she felt it best, since

135

the moles seemed harmless enough, to keep her reservations to herself and conceal her identity and abilities. Moles worshipped in many different ways, and anyway, she enjoyed their company.

Most of the congregation dispersed when the prayers were done, but some felt inclined to stay, the more so because the brothers had prepared some food to celebrate the Stone's goodness, and it seemed churlish to refuse it. In fact, six moles stayed, five of them females without attachments or any special need to hurry off anywhere in particular; the remaining mole, a male, was somewhat simple in the head, and Privet noticed that the brothers soon got rid of him. But that was the only doubtful sign she saw.

Naturally the brothers were asked from where they came, and their answer was Blagrove Slide, a system some way to the south to which on the morrow they would be journeying. Their manner was charming yet firm in a reassuring kind of way, and they did not immediately respond to the hints, which one or two of the females ventured, that their system must be well worth visiting. The brothers merely smiled, and contrived to suggest without saying so directly that to visit their system would be a privilege for anymole, and not one given lightly.

'But given to some?'

Privet was ashamed to remember that it was she who asked the question first.

'Given to those who worship the Stone truly, and do not wish to corrupt the minds of the young or the ignorant with false notions of the Stone's meaning and purpose. We are peaceful moles, who suffered much at the paws of moles of the Word in the times of the war on the Stone, and we ask only that moles abide by the true way.'

In retrospect it is easy to see in this answer the dogma of sectarian moles who have a narrow, unyielding interpretation of the Stone's meaning and fellowship, but to moles inexperienced in such matters, as Privet and those with her then were, it seemed a reasonable reply.

The following day, when the brothers had intended to leave for Blagrove, they did not go, but lingered and prayed for guidance, inviting the 'sisters' to join them. It was pleasant, it was companionable, it was flattering to be looked after by such moles. Even so, two of the 'sisters' left, saying there was something they did not like about the brothers – too serious, no fun, too inclined to pray all the time; or something like that, at least. Privet was not one of those who left; she lingered on pleasantly with the others, and after three days the brothers announced that they had received guidance that the three remaining sisters might, perhaps, be 'meant' to go to Blagrove . . . if

136

they wished to, and on certain conditions. Which were – to be obedient especially to the elder brothers' commands and to be prepared to stay for several days, to help in matters of the routine running of the system.

'It all seemed so convincing and so appealing,' said Privet with a sigh so much later, 'and I honestly did not see the harm in it, or in agreeing to the conditions. Nor, as we began to discover that Blagrove was further off than they had said, and that their stops on the way were very brief, did it occur to me to wonder why moles who claimed to be benign should deliberately give us so little time to sleep or even eat . . .'

Chapter Twelve

'We arrived at Blagrove Slide in a state of exhaustion,' continued Privet, 'and it was, I believe, a state deliberately induced in us.'

'But why?' asked Whillan, very puzzled. 'Why would anymole want to do that? Surely, they would have better persuaded you of the justice and wisdom of their beliefs by treating you well.'

'My dear,' said Privet, 'what I am going to describe to you has nothing to do with wisdom or justice, but everything to do with evil, and cunning, made worse because it pretended to be benign. Also, it was carried out by the most dangerous moles of all – those who believe themselves absolutely right, and any that argue with them not only absolutely wrong, but inspired by evil *and therefore not worth arguing with*.'

'Sounds like moles of the Word in former times,' said Maple.

'That is exactly what the Newborns are like,' said Weeth quietly. 'Now, madam, continue your tale as you remember it, and leave out nothing, for I have a feeling that before long each mole here may have to face some of the realities you are about to describe, and it is as well each is prepared.'

Privet nodded, and frowned as she pondered where best to resume.

'You must understand that when I reached Blagrove Slide I had no reason to think that I was entering tunnels out of which I would find it very hard to find a way, and that when I finally did I would be as nearly broken in body and spirit as anymole could be. Nor could I have possibly believed then that when I *did* leave I would have lost something more dear than life itself.'

'Your pups!' whispered Whillan.

'Yes . . . but now you are going to ask what happened in Blagrove, and how the Newborns worked on me to reduce me to the state I have just described. To which I must reply, I do not truly know, for the way they led us there so exhaustingly put us into a state of mental fatigue from which I never escaped, so that my memory of all of it is weak and nightmarish, as if the images I have from that appalling time were of another mole than me.

'The place itself I remember as unremarkable and nondescript, lying at the southern end of the Harborough Downs. It has only one earlier claim to notoriety that I know of: scholars of the war of Word and Stone will remember that it was here that the vile prosecutor of the Word's ways, Drule, committed a mass murder of a quarter of the system's moles. Drule forced the females to choose which of their kin could live, and which die, only half being permitted to live.'

'It is true,' said Maple, 'and if I recall the contemporary accounts, if the females refused to choose then *all* their kin were done to death. This was punishment for resistance made by some of the females against the Word.'

'I did not remember all that history then,' said Privet, 'but perhaps something of those shadows lingered there and affected the surviving moles. Certainly it was an event I heard the Blagrove Newborns recall again and again, as if it were something they could not forget, even so many decades later when all those living at the time were long dead.

'The brothers who brought us to Blagrove apologized for the haste that had left us so fatigued, saying there were celebrations they must take part in and they could not miss them on "pain of punishment". I remember that phrase – I was to hear it often afterwards. I know that we were not the only females brought by brothers into Blagrove and, in fact, some who were there already tried to tell me to escape while I could. I could not understand what they meant, or why they looked so drawn and ill and seemed so anxious that we did not report what they said.

'One of the females I had come with *did* tell the brothers what they had said, and she was much praised – and the pathetic creature who had given us the warning was chastised in front of us and held up before the Stone as a reprobate, and then taken away. I saw her no more, and learnt to bide my words.

'I know that I was never told the names of any of the brothers we met in Blagrove, except of those who first "collected" us – that was the term they used – which later proved false in any case. Newborns are never to be trusted with the truth. However, there were two moles whose names I heard spoken, and they were the names of senior elders, most notable and revered of whom was Thripp. In Duncton, among us traditional Stone followers, he is sometimes referred to as the "sinister" Thripp, but amongst the Newborns he was seen in a very different way. He was revered by all, his name spoken in hushed whispers, and he was held in affection by allmole.

'However, the other mole whose name I heard of was Quail, a chilling elder brother. The first shock when I saw him was that he was not particularly old – not much more than I was. He was at one of the rituals I later attended and I heard him referred to then, though I had already heard of his reputation, as the feared executioner of Thripp's commands, and that is not the wrong way to describe him. He was quite striking – well-built, with bleak eyes and a face whose skin seemed drawn tight about his snout and eyes and mouth, and yet was lined as if it had aged prematurely. His fur was balding and patchy, as if he had some obscure disease. He looked old yet vigorous at the same time. His gaze settled on me just once, and though I looked down meekly I swear I could feel it on me still, like the juice of an acerbic plant upon a cut.

'But moments like that were very rare, and Thripp himself I never met, nor ever saw so far as I was aware. For the most part I remember being set to menial tasks, always in the service of the brothers, female serving male – *always* was that the pattern there. When I asked to be instructed in the worship of the Stone – oh yes, I was soon reduced to asking in those terms – I was chastised and told to wait until they told me I was ready.

'On it went, day after day, with never a moment's rest, which was the secret of their successful conversion of us to their ways – such resistance as we had initially was driven out of us by exhaustion, and by being punished and isolated if we transgressed in any way. Since we were never told what the rules were it was hard not to transgress at times, and so we ended up in fear of thinking or doing almost anything that we were not told to do. My mind got to wandering as I went about my tasks, and I began to speak aloud to myself, for company perhaps, and I reverted to Whernish in what I thought were dreams. I talked to Rooster and called for Hamble, as if one of those moles from my past would come to my aid. Even Cobbett seemed of my "past", as if all former life had drifted far from me, and only the present mattered.

'Now I say I spoke in Whernish, and I think that this indirectly saved my life, for one of the brothers heard of it, and I was summoned to a Senior Brother and asked what it was I spoke. I saw no reason to lie, not realizing that Whernish was perceived as the language of the Word, and speaking it put me in mortal danger. Some instinct prevented me from telling all my tale, and though I spoke of the Moors and Crowden, I never mentioned matters of scribing, or Rooster and delving, or Beechenhill. I knew I was in dire trouble, and had broken

140

some rule of theirs. By then I was anxious to be favoured, for the other females I had come with had long since become Confessed Sisters, and various transgressions had meant that I had been isolated, and felt without friends.

'I have little doubt now that the Senior Brothers watched over us carefully, and knew the state each of us had reached, and when the right moment for conversion to the Newborn way might be. In retrospect, I suppose I was rather slower, or more resistant, than some.

'I said that I feel my Whernish was the saving of me, despite the initial inquisition I suffered for it, and the real fears I felt as a result. For a time I was left alone, but one day I was summoned to meet a Senior Brother and naturally I went with considerable apprehension. Indeed I was crying and shaking, certain that something terrible would happen. The young brother who led me there I had not met or seen before. He was more friendly than some and spoke with an accent I could not identify, nor can I now remember it well enough to say I have ever heard another speak it. It was warm and rolling in its intonation, and he was somewhat similar, except he seemed harassed. He led me through unfamiliar tunnels and eventually I found myself in the presence of the Senior Brother.

'"You are Sister Crowden?" he asked.

'I nodded; naturally, he did not give his name.

'"You stance accused of speaking Whernish, mole. Is this true?"

'"It was the dialect I was raised to," I explained, adding hastily I was of the Stone.

'He waved me into silence and I instantly obeyed. I must confess at once that I felt a certain attraction to the Senior Brother. He was less formidable than some, less accusatory, and he asked his questions in the manner of a scholar, much as some of the moles at Beechenhill might have done. I waited in silence until he spoke again, and when he did I was astounded to hear him ask me a question in Whernish.

'"How came you here?" was what he said. How came you here . . . He spoke it in a measured careful way, and not as a native – perhaps as I myself spoke Mole! Yet to hear it at all moved me deeply, and I burst into tears.

'At this he frowned and turned away, clearly much displeased, and I rather desperately controlled my emotions.

'"Sister Crowden, you do not need to cry. Now, tell me of how you were reared to the Stone."

'I told him gladly, my resistance all but gone as I described the Crowden system, and the grikes and Ratcher's clan, and how we

141

sought to protect ourselves. I described the Weign Stones, and our simple rituals, and much else. Yet every time I came near to talking of Rooster, or delving, or the Eldrene Wort, I found some instinct warned me off, and nor did I tell the true reason I left the Moors – how could I without mentioning Rooster? Nor did I even mention I could scribe – I knew enough to guess that sisters could never do that!

'He listened in silence, his eyes pale and still on me, and I remember feeling fear and fascination at the same time; I sensed that he believed I was holding something back, but did not know what.

'When I had finished he continued to stare at me in a most unnerving way. Then suddenly he said in a sharp voice, "Sister, do you wish to confess anything to me?"

'Confess? I wished to confess that I was lost and lonely, and afraid, afraid even of the world outside; I wished to confess that I needed love, and even as these words tumbled out of me I knew them to be the wrong things to say and felt I was letting slip my chance of "proper" confession and finding the protection of a Senior Brother. But I spoke of "confessing" to feeling desperate.

'He smiled with pity and shook his head and said, "No, Sister, I mean a confession of sins, of transgressions against the Stone."

'"But I have not . . ."

'He suddenly grew cold, so very cold, and disappointed too, so that I felt that if I had sinned it was against *him*.

'I wanted desperately to say something different, to beg his forgiveness and his favour, but he peremptorily turned from me without a word, the first mole who in all that time had shown any care for me, and as he left he turned back and said, "Mole, none of us is without sin. Examine your heart, confess your sin, open your heart to the Stone's mercy." Oh how I wanted to cry out a confession, *any* confession, that he might not leave me alone and lost once more. Eventually the young brother came and led me back to my burrow, and would not answer my pleas to know if I might see the Senior Brother again.

'I wish I could report that I resisted these assaults upon my reason and sense of truth, but I could not, I could not. It all became so confused after this, or much of it. I have lost the sense of that time, but I know that when I saw the Senior Brother again I was so afraid of being dismissed once more that I freely confessed to the first thing that came to my mind. Or rather, the *second* thing, because the first would have been an admission that I had lied by default about Rooster, and delving and the Charnel and all of that. That I *would* not tell. So

I made something up, some trivial sin or other, and I remember thinking that it did not matter what I said, *I* knew it was all trivial and all nonsense, but at least I would have his favour.

'Now, I believe he knew I was making false confession. How often must Senior Brothers have seen weak and desperate sisters like me, eager for their attention and concern, willing to say anything! So why did he not press me harder? Well, I think now that it is the *act* of confession that the Newborn brothers seek most of all, not the nature of what is confessed. Indeed, they may even think it better that we do tell lies in confession. You see, a mole loses something of himself by laying himself so open to another – how much more does he lose if he lies in the name of the Stone? The sorry guilt! Yes, they weaken moles and they twist their minds to make acts of overt subjection, both mental and physical, and confession is the talon-thrust they use into our inmost being.

'It was only later that I came to suspect that each one of us sisters was assigned to a Senior Brother according to his particular suitability to weaken us and mould our minds. The clue to my vulnerability lay in my Whernish, and so they found a Senior Brother who could speak it, and so reach into me. It says much for their skill and subtlety that despite what he later did to me I *still* remember him not as a tormentor, or even corrupter, but as the only mole in that nightmarish place who ever comforted me. Except perhaps for his young assistant brother, who had a kind of gentleness very rare in Blagrove Slide.

'I wish I knew my Senior Brother's name, but of course we sisters were never permitted to call them anything more personal than brothers, though in those shared moments when we were together, we would make up names for our Senior Brothers, and speak in a juvenile pubescent way of how "ours" was better than the others, and how we loved them, and they were surely beginning to love us . . .

'"Mine" – I am sure now he had other sisters than me! – was perhaps two Longest Nights older than me, and intelligent enough to deal with my doubts in the course of the instruction he gave me without imputing to me the sin of transgression simply for having them. It was not long before he persuaded me that the Newborn way to the Stone was the only true way, and led me towards asking if I might become a Confessed Sister.

'He said he was able to accept me as a Confessed Sister on trial but that if I was to be fully accepted then Elder Brother Thripp, or perhaps Quail – he used their names – must grant permission. I was overjoyed at this, and cried myself to sleep with happiness that the Stone had so honoured me. Confession brought certain privileges: better food, better burrows; but also certain responsibilities – attendance at rituals before the Stone to perform minor tasks of preparation, grooming of the Senior Brothers as they prepared themselves for the ceremonies.

'Imagine my thrill at being allowed to groom the Senior Brother whom I now regarded as my protector and guide, and the delight I felt if by the slightest of nods or the smallest of smiles he acknowledged the minor service I did for him.

'But I knew there was a dark side to being a Confessed Sister. For now the slightest transgression – whether a mistake during the rituals, or a complaint, even illness – was enough to earn the Senior Brothers' punishment, though they referred to it always as punishment in the Stone. Punishment was banishment to a state far worse than that initial one from which we had risen with such difficulty, and being forced to do the vilest and most menial of tasks. Some of these penalties were brief, others permanent, and sometimes moles we had known were suddenly seen no more. We Confessed Sisters therefore lived in constant fear of losing our privileges through transgression.

'It was at this time that I was permitted to attend one of the Newborn celebrations before the Stone, a rare privilege, and one which we were only allowed to enjoy at a distance. I was overjoyed to discover that Blagrove had a Stone, tall and thin, thrusting up to the sky, and I could not keep my eyes off it, such were my adoration and faith.

'When I did drag my eyes away from the vibrant surging thing the Blagrove Stone seemed to be it was naturally only to look out for the Senior Brother who had befriended me, who was there taking part in the ritual. I felt very proud to see him stanced prominently among his peers and wished I could have told him so; but of course, I knew that for a female to do such a thing would have meant punishment. In fact a female was chastised at the celebration, and humiliated, but I remember feeling only slightly sorry for her. I wondered what she had done, and felt sure that she deserved what she got, for by now I was convinced that the Senior Brothers were all-wise. Two other sisters were blessed at the ritual because they were with pup and I noticed that one of them had been among those who came with me to Blagrove – she who had reported the mole who had tried to warn us to escape.

'I noticed that "my" Senior Brother conducted that part of the ritual which blessed the sister, and I wondered if he was her Brother Confessor as well! How jealous I felt! The words of the blessing were interesting, for they referred only to male pups, and indeed asked the

144

Stone to grant that the pups the female bore would *all* be male. It did not occur to me to question this, perhaps because I was so exhausted by the work and lack of sleep and the feeling of being cut off from the world that I had lost my ability to question anything.

'Soon after this I was summoned again before my Brother Confessor. He complimented me, and said I had done well at the ritual and that he had good reason to think I was among the chosen. He asked if I desired to serve the Stone and I said I did. He gave me to understand that I could best render service by doing what females are sent by the Stone to do, which is procreation; that was the word he used.

'He spoke simply and well, and his eyes were strangely bright, and I said, provocatively, that I would like to serve, I would like to have pups, but I had no mate. Those were my very words, "I have no mate," and I confess here that I looked coyly at the ground, hoping that *he* would take me. This is all as it was. This was the truth of Blagrove Slide.

'He said that such a thing was a matter for the Elder Senior Brother but if he gave permission and I was deemed to be clean of spirit and body it might be arranged.

'"Elder Senior Brother Thripp or his representative will be gener-ous in his assessment of your desire to serve the Stone," he said. "Of course, this acceptance into the Stone's service carries with it certain privileges; extra food and a comfortable place for the period of your gestation." The way he looked at me, his eyes warm, betrayed his desire. Innocent as I was, abject as I had become, that much I recognized.

'"Would it be with you, Senior Brother, I mean . . . ?" I faltered. I felt shy and brave at the same time, and filled with desire such as I had never felt before. So dependent had I become, and so obedient! I wish I could say I have forgotten all that occurred from that time on, but I have not, not all of it. Some days later I learnt he had been given permission to "know" me, as he put it, and I was overjoyed; but first I had to pass through a period of meditation by the Stone.

'"But I cannot go to the Stone alone!"' I said.

'"No, you cannot, Sister Crowden. I will go with you, and instruct you in the act of abasement before the Stone, and the need to open yourself up to it, to give yourself to it entirely, to . . . to touch and caress it with your faith, with your heart, with your body."

'Oh yes, my Brother Confessor instructed me before the Stone all right! Whispering instructions before it through the night, putting his paw to my shoulder and flank and haunch, that I might be, as he softly

145

put it, in the right position to receive the Stone's Light and power . . . until I found myself urged on and on, and I felt excitement and utter abandon before the Stone's great spirit and his desire that I make the admission of the need to procreate.

'"Yes, yes, yes . . ." I sighed, hoping that what I thought might happen would happen, then, and there, in the night before the Stone of Blagrove Slide.

'"I must know you, Sister, know the truth of you, know the deep of you, know the quick of you!" he cried, and I remember thinking that for the first time he sounded as if he was not quite in control. Oh, the power of that moment, and the passion of what I thought was faith, and the ecstasy as he came closer still and I felt his desire for me, and the sharp unique pain of the moment of knowledge, when he took me that first time and knew me, only me, all of me, before the straight and risen Stone!

'The excitement, as he mounted me and together we ascended heights of ecstatic faith – for the first time I felt him not as a Senior Brother but as a mole, as vulnerable as myself. I heard him gasp, I heard him cry, and I heard him give thanks to the Stone that at last, at last . . .

'And I knew with an absolute certainty that I was the first female he had known. I knew, or felt I knew, that for him, as for me, this was a moment that transcended who and what and where we were. We were any two moles that had ever made love with abandon, each discovering for the first time the excitement of union.

'After that my Senior Brother knew me many times before the Stone and I am not ashamed to say that I more than enjoyed it, it was a kind of ecstasy. But if a confession of anything is needed it is this: I felt a secret triumph that I was doing with him what Rooster had done with Lime. Yes, before the Blagrove Stone I recovered a kind of pride. Yet there was a new understanding too – of what my prudishness and Rooster's innocence and fear of "hurting" had denied us, and why it might be that he had wanted to take Lime, and had enjoyed doing so. My Brother Confessor showed me the way to an understanding of why Rooster had done what he had.

'There was one more thing. When a mole makes love to you, and gives himself to you, he cannot but reveal things he might normally hide – and certainly things a Brother Confessor would wish to hide from a Confessed Sister. I felt in those moments that he was alone as I was, and sensitive, which though it was never in his words, for they were as dogmatic and cast in the Newborn mould as all the rest, was there in his touch, and most of all in those brief moments of ecstasy. I felt I had made him discover something in himself he did not know was there, and in that I felt the Stone, the loving true Stone of Light and Silence devout followers seek to worship, was trying to show him what he otherwise could not see. You might think that what he did was wrong and hypocritical – reducing a female to obedience and then saying it was the Stone's will that he mate with her. It *would* have been wrong, had not something in our love transcended what we were and did. I felt something in him that was wonderful, even great, and that our meeting, and all we did, was meant to be. Each of us had been hurt, and each helped the other to be whole again, or at least to go forward better than we might otherwise have done. Was this my delusion? I thought not then, I think not now.

'I said before that we sisters had talked of love, and I described it as juvenile. Yet after he made love to me – for call it what you will, or what the Newborns wish, that's what it was – I felt love for him: for what he had given me, for that unspoken secret he had revealed. So that when, soon after, I found I was with pup, I felt utter joy. I do not think I have known such intense happiness as that; except perhaps sometimes, Whillan, when you were a pup; and with Rooster, so long ago on Hilbert's Top, when we lay and held each other close, and all the world was as nothing to us – that was deep abiding delight.

'But there in Blagrove Slide . . . the fact that I was making life gave my existence a meaning it had never had before. I could not but feel good about the mole who made that life in me, despite the circumstances in which he did it. But that time of joy was the best of Blagrove Slide for me, for what went before was grim, and what came after was hell. For one thing, I was put in quarters with other pregnant sisters, and far from helping each other through, jealousy was rife between us, added to which was the feeling of being sick and tired which came on us at the beginning. I learnt too that female pups were "disappeared" soon after birth, and some said only the males were given favour and allowed to survive. Even though I had by then become convinced that males *were* better than females, I felt a profound need to seek ways to protect my unborn young – and a deep despair, for there was no way that I could see.

'I have mentioned the young brother before, and he now came to visit me regularly – provoking jealousy in the other sisters, for their Brother Confessors sent nomole at all – to see what my progress was. I asked him hopefully if it was possible for my Brother Confessor to visit me, because it would be a comfort.

147

'"The Brother Confessor does not see females he has made with pup," were his devastating words. Females! Oh, jealousy! I felt it then! "My" Brother Confessor was not mine at all! Yet even as I thought that, I answered it by chastising myself for thinking I might be his only Confessed Sister, and comforting myself that even if I was not, I was surely *special*, because he had seemed to reveal something of himself on those treasured occasions when we had been at the Stone. How easily weak excuses satisfy the meek!

'One of the things I had wished to talk to my Brother Confessor about was the important question of naming my pups, thinking that it might involve him in some way and give me a legitimate reason to share something with him about them. This I was now denied, and lacking his company or any other that was friendly and which I could trust, I did what many a mother does; I whispered to myself the names I thought to use, trying out the sound of them, seeing if they felt right for the pups that were beginning to move with tiny life inside me.

'Being a scribe, it was but a short pawstep from speaking them to scribing them, though I knew well enough that this might be construed as a serious transgression. Sisters did not scribe, and certainly I had never once revealed that I could, not even to *him*. . . So as I grew heavier, and rested more, I would turn to the wall of the little burrow I was by then able to call my own and scribe some of the possible names, and reach out a paw to ken them and repeat them, which gave me pleasure and comfort. I always scored out the scribing when I had done, and even when moles approached down the communal tunnel, so I had no fear of discovery.

'As my time approached I was taken by the young brother to the place of my confinement, which was isolated from all other moles but him, and a wan, mute female who used to come that way to clear out the tunnels and bring fresh litter. I was not allowed on to the surface, though I asked to go many times. The new burrow was more comfortable, and brought me relief from the other females, and the food was better too. Perhaps that made me careless, or perhaps being with pups changes a mole and stops her being as careful as she might be. However it was, I knew by feeling that I carried four pups and that all were active and well, and one day I scribed down the names I wanted to give them in a neat line on the wall. I hoped that all would be male, yet secretly I longed for a female pup, and superstitiously I felt it best to "pretend" I had two of each and so I scribed down names for two of each as well. There they were, living inside me, and scribed down too, and I stared and mused and dreamed of what might be; too long, it seemed, because I fell asleep.

'When I woke I knew even before I opened my eyes that my Brother Confessor was in the chamber, and that I had not scored out the scribing. Even as I reached out to do so I heard him say, "Sister! Leave that!"

'I turned to him with pleading eyes, to beg forgiveness, to ask . . .

'"Whatmole scribed it? Eh? My Brother Assistant, presumably. Brother! Come!"

'Before I could stop him he had gone and summoned his assistant, who appeared meekly at the portal.

'"What is the meaning of that, Brother?" he said, not unkindly.

'I stared in mute fear at my friend, who looked at the names on the wall at which the Brother Confessor pointed, and gaped with blank surprise. He looked at me with his kind eyes and I knew that he understood immediately that it was I who had scribed the names – and I saw astonishment and respect in his face. More than that, I felt a surge of joy that he should so quickly believe that I *could* scribe. It meant that I must have some qualities left that others could respect.

'He turned to the Brother Confessor and smiled and said, "Forgive me, but she would insist on speaking out the names she wants to give her pups and I felt it might be a comfort . . ."

'"It is well enough, if a little indulgent," said my Brother Confessor, turning to ken the names. But even as he did so I sensed that no matter what the reason why the Brother Assistant wished to protect me, and whatever he was protecting me from, if I allowed a lie to live about my pups, even before they were born, I was no true mother in the Stone. That was the moment in Blagrove when I began to find strength to become a mole again.

'To make it worse, my Brother Confessor was repeating the names to himself, playing with the sound and thought of them as I had so often done, and a slight smile was on his face as he whispered them to himself, half turned from me, of course, because it would never do for anymole to see him expressing feelings in that way. Yet I knew what I must do.'

'"Thank you, Brother, for seeking to protect me and my pups from the transgression I may have committed," I said quietly to the assistant, "but I would not be a true mother to them if I allowed their father to be so misled. It was I, Brother Confessor, who scribed their names."

'"You!" he said, astonished.

'I nodded, and so complete was his disbelief and horror – horror that I could claim such a thing, for still I do not think he believed it – that I reached up my paw and scribed before his very eyes my favourite name of all the four, which was "Loosestrife". How I had dreamed of her, a female pup such as I had never been, beautiful, a pup to be proud of, a pup to make a mother feel her life was given meaning by making her.

'He stared in silence, seemingly appalled at what I had done, and affronted too, as if thereby I was no female mole at all, but an alien mutant thing with which he wanted no intercourse lest she infect him with something unspeakable. In that look I saw the face of dogma and rule challenged by a fact which opened wide the hypocrisy and myopia of its thought, and showed it to be the nonsense that it was. In his narrow world females could not scribe; they were not intelligent enough, they were not *able* to.

'"You *scribe*?" he said. Nothing can convey the profound horror and shock in his voice.

'"Yes," I replied. He turned to his Brother Assistant.

'"You did not do this?" he asked.

'The brother could only shake his head. I saw that my confession meant punishment for him. "Leave us, Brother," said my Confessor, turning to me with a look of such savagery that I felt deep fear.

'"What do you scribe?" he asked. "A few names, that sort of thing?" I think he hoped that I had learnt just a few words by rote, and that in some way this might affirm his prejudice that females could not scribe "seriously".

'"I scribe Whernish and I scribe Mole," I said. "I was Librarian at Crowden, as my mother was before me. I—"

'"Enough, mole! It is against the Stone for females to scribe!"

'"It is no such thing," I said, "any more than it is against the Stone for mothers who can scribe to carry your pups!"

'"What did you say?" he thundered, almost shaking with rage. It was the first time I had ever seen him angry and it did not suit him, he was not that kind of mole. The respect he normally warranted came from the power of his personality, not his voice.

'"I said," I shouted back at him, for I was angry too, "that you have one standard for yourself and another for females, and I know of no Stone law that supports that unequal notion!"

'"You dare tell *me* how the Stone's commandments are to be interpreted?" he said a shade more quietly.

'"Moles are equal before the Stone, and it is reasonable therefore to assume they are equal before each other!"

'I was getting more spirited and confident by the moment, and I swear I heard something of my mother Shire's voice in my own! I have said already that I felt a kind of love for my Brother Confessor, though of a different kind than the passion I felt for Rooster. Now, as I watched him frowning and muttering to himself, and then pacing about the cell and glaring at my scribing and then at me, I knew why it might be I loved him, and it was not just because he had made me with pup or woken new feelings in me. No, it was because I saw in those moments of anger and argument that he had heard and understood what I had said. He had *listened*, and listening is a rare gift from one mole to another, and to be greatly valued. It takes effort to listen, and a kind of love; and even more for a mole to keep his mind open to a new idea, and accept the need for change within himself. It takes humility to listen well and such listening is a gift because it imparts to the recipients the feeling that their ideas are heard, and that therefore they are real moles, worthy of attention. It is not only pups who gain confidence when they know they are truly heard, it is all of us!

'So now I sensed my Brother Confessor heard me, and was accepting something of what I said, and for that I felt a renewed surge of love for him. I went to him and he let me touch him with affection – indeed, I saw his eyes half close, and heard him let out a sigh, as if he wished to yield up to the same impulse of acceptance and harmony as I did.

'"Mole," I whispered familiarly, "we are as one before the Stone; can you not feel it to be so?"

'"As one?" he whispered in response. "Would that it were so easy, Sister!"

'"It *is*," I said passionately, my paws gripping his as I tried to turn him that he might look into my eyes. I felt I was in some strange way fighting for the lives of my – of *our* – unborn young. If only I could get him to understand the way I felt.

'I wish I could say now that I saw clearly then how dangerous and destructive the Newborn way was, and would become, but I did not. I was young, confused, carrying pups, and driven by instinct, not reason. It is to my Brother Confessor and not myself that I owe what happened next . . .'

'Except that without your willingness to resist . . .' said Weeth, interrupting her, yet rather sorry that his excited involvement in her tale had made him do so.

'You are right, Weeth. But that is how moles who care for each other carry each other along.'

'But he . . . he . . . !' expostulated Whillan.

'Raped me?' said Privet matter-of-factly. 'Perhaps he did use his position and implicit knowledge of the Stone to seduce me. But I cared not then, and I do not now. I regret not the seduction, but its outcome.'

'So what happened?' said Maple heavily, glowering at the other two as if to warn them against interrupting again.

'My Brother Confessor turned to me, gently took my paw from his as if such affection was improper, and he said, "Sister, supposing two moles, a male and a female, were to meet in some anonymous place, not knowing each other's name, and in the certain knowledge that they would never meet again, then what might they talk about?" He smiled at me then, such a gentle smile.

'"They would speak what was in their hearts," I replied, "and perhaps they might answer each other's questions." I think perhaps my voice faltered when I said this because young though I was, what he was suggesting was plain enough. For the first time, and probably the last, he was opening his heart to me, one mole talking to another with all fears and prejudices cast aside. I sensed that it was most dangerous for him to do so, and therefore courageous – and not only in the sense that his superiors, like the awesome Thripp or malevolent Quail, might find out. It was *personally* courageous – he was willing to risk something of himself.

'I can't remember quite what I said, except that I felt nervous, and pleased that a mole was willing to do this for me. With Hamble I had talked without thinking, the intimate talk of instinctive friends; with Rooster I had touched some deep love and destiny which had proved far beyond our power to understand or control. But with this mole I was faced for the first time in my life with a new equality of mind, a chance to explore a place I had never been, and to which I might never go again.

'"Well then," he said, evidently as nervous as I, "we are two moles, one falsely called Sister Crowden and the other somewhat pompously entitled Brother Confessor. In reality we are anymoles, and I swear, Sister, that what we speak of now shall be a secret to my heart for ever."

'We talked then of whatmoles we were, except that we did not give our names. But of our different faiths we talked, of our backgrounds, of our hopes. Of Rooster I told him, and of the Eldrene Wort; and he told me of his strict upbringing at Blagrove Slide without affection or love of any kind. I understood that I was the first female he had ever been close to – none other had he ever known. Worse! I was an experiment, for he felt that as other brothers had females, so should he. That pups should be the result seemed to have taken him by surprise. In the hierarchical structure of Blagrove Slide he had risen from the lowest ranks to his present seniority, and his mother had made him disciplined, and led him to moles who taught him to scribe, from whom he had learned the Whernish he had spoken to me.

'"Was this what made you choose me as your Confessed Sister?" I asked him.

'He shook his head and explained that the Stone had guided him to me, and he took my speaking Whernish as a sign that he had understood its wishes right. Of that he said no more.

'We talked about our doubts and fears about faith, neither commenting much upon what the other said, but, rather, just letting the other talk. I remember he told me, "I was reared strictly before the Stone, my mother being of low rank in Blagrove, having come to it after a history of vagrancy in her family which dated back many decades to the time of the war of Word on Stone. The only detail she ever told me of that past was that originally her kin came from a place called Mallerstang in the north, of which she had heard good things, and at the mention of which her eyes would soften. Enough of *that*! she would say, those days have gone.* Now we must strive to do right by the Stone, and to show up by our example the errors of others in worship, and establish for ourselves a worthy position in Blagrove Slide, which has admitted us wanderers into its care, and whose concern we must repay.

'"Aye, my mother was determined we should do right, and of her offspring I was the one determined to do most right! One day, before the Blagrove Stone, after prayers and confessions for which my siblings and peers used to mock me, I saw the right way forward! I knew the Newborn way to be the only one, and with my mother's encouragement I followed it earnestly, taking my training from the best and most sincere moles I could find. If discipline was to be imposed, I imposed it most harshly on myself! If a mole needed chastising, I felt his sin as my own! If some offence had been committed and no culprit found, I was the one who offered myself for correction! How mistaken those notions were, and how unpopular I became."

* See *Duncton Found.*

153

'"I would have thought that a mole like Brother Thripp would approve of such sincerity!"

'My Brother Confessor laughed and said that *he* did, *he* certainly did, but they were early days of the Newborns and better ways had to be found if more moles were to follow the Newborn creed.

'He told me: "Spring came, my first, and I fell in love with a mole who felt as sincerely as I did about matters of faith. But my mother warned me against her, saying she was evil, and that my desire for her was a sinful temptation to distract me from the Newborn way. *That* was the destiny I must follow. My mother made me promise as she died that I would never know a female until I had seen the truth of the Stone and known its living Silence. Many were the females I wanted, but always I heard my mother's cold voice warning me against temptation, and reminding me of my promise. How often I wept and felt guilt for my sinful thoughts."

'"And yet you dared take *me*."

'"How nervous I was, how afraid. But the Stone led me to you, or you to me."

'"And your mother, and your promise . . . ?"

'"Her voice faded before what you gave me, and that promise, I saw, was unfairly drawn from me. I feel no guilt in our mating – a mole must be able to throw off the weight of the past to be Newborn."

'"You speak as if your words are those of Thripp himself!"

'He smiled at me and said indeed they were, the Elder Senior Brother surely spoke the truth and there was no harm in quoting him.

'So did we talk, about those things and much that was more personal which I shall never reveal, even if I could remember it all. I recall better the sense I had that this exchange with him would surely never be repeated, and it was all the more precious for that. For much of the time I forgot the pups I was carrying – *his* pups, ours – but towards the end I remembered them or, in their way, they reminded me of themselves.

'"You look afraid," he said to me then, and when I hesitated he added, "remember that tonight, just tonight, we can say the things deepest in our hearts. Fear not, Sister Crowden, none shall ever know what you say tonight."

'"And if Thripp commands you, or Brother Quail? If you are brought to confession, as I presume even Brother Confessors must be!"

'He frowned and said quietly, "Only the Stone shall know the truth. Only the Stone does know the truth." How bleak his look, how heavy his doubts! I thought to myself that if ever a female was to have pups, this was the mole to have them by! Somehow he seemed to show all his heart, and it was like an open wound that would not heal. Again and again I said to myself, "I love this mole, yet I love Rooster more. The one has given me pups, but the other has given me something of his heart for ever. Oh, to love this mole . . . !"

'"Speak your fears," he said.

'"Our pups: what will become of them? The sisters say that only the males may live, to be trained as brothers in the Creed. But the females! Tell me they shall be safe – that you shall see to it."

'"There can be no favour," were his terrible words, and I knew he had begun to retreat from me. Desperate suddenly to save the lives of my unborn pups I pointed at where I had scribed the names I dreamt they might have.

'"Look!" I beseeched him, "and ken their names: Loosestrife, that's my favourite—"

'"No! No you must not *say* their names," he cried out, the names seeming to bring to reality the pups he had made in me.

'"But . . . !" I protested.

'How strange males seem! How much mystery there is for a female in their desires and moods!'

Privet was suddenly smiling again, her eyes alight with a final memory, yet shyness was there too.

'The only way he could think of stopping me saying their names was to grab me, and he did it with a laugh, and despite my protests – feeble and affectionate as they were – he took me one last time, but not in lust, I was too heavy with pup for that! Oh dear, Whillan, am I really telling you, of all moles, these things?'

'You are, madam, or so it seems,' said Weeth, 'and you cannot stop now.' And nor did Privet try.

'Well then, he clasped me to him in a pleasant cumbersome sort of way and we, and I suppose I must include the pups as well, made a kind of love, a welcome and farewell kind during which I remember he said, "You have shown me happiness, mole, a thing I thought would elude me for ever; I see I cannot grasp and hold it, and that I should not try."

'Then we slept in each other's paws, as I had never slept with Rooster, though I had often dreamed of doing so. The sleep of those who have for a time given themselves to each other and, abandoned, let the tide of unconsciousness flow over them, and then ebb away again. When I woke day had come, and he had gone, and I was left alone to wonder what the night had meant, and why it provoked in me thoughts not of fear, nor of consequences to my pups, but of all things, *of all things*, of Silence, and my quest, so long forgotten, after the nature of the Book of Silence. In the stillness and solitude that followed I spoke a prayer for him I have sometimes spoken since: "Stone, guide him, and bring him to thy Light and Silence safe-guarded."

'I said that from this time Blagrove Slide became a hell for me, and so it did. But from that time as well, and the saying of that prayer, which might speak for all moles that wander confused and in darkness, I felt that I was beginning the long trek back to light again; in my own way, I had become finally newborn!'

'Yes, but what mole was he, madam?' asked Weeth, beside himself with curiosity. 'Did you not think to ask him?'

Privet shrugged. 'He was a mole like me who dared make himself open and vulnerable before the Stone. His name would have made no difference to that. But I pray that one day I might meet him again in better circumstances.'

'And if you had the choice,' said Whillan suddenly, 'which would you choose to meet: your Brother Confessor or Rooster?'

Privet stared at him, suddenly still, as if the thought of never meeting either of them had never occurred to her. Then slow tears came to her eyes and rolled down her face and all of them felt how great her loss had been. She would not – would never – answer such a question, because deep in her heart she felt that the Stone could not in its wisdom impose such a choice on any mole. Or could it?

'It is in how a mole faces her suffering that the way towards her discovery of the Book of Silence may lie,' she said, and she smiled at Whillan, sun across a winter landscape, and she could smile because she had been loved. 'I never lost either of those moles, but for a time we have lost sight of one another – they and I, and the moles of moledom too.'

Chapter Thirteen

Privet's pups were born soon after this meeting with her Brother Confessor, and without difficulty. There were four, as she had expected, but her hopes regarding their sex were not quite fulfilled – they were three females and only one male.

'For the first few hours afterwards I lived in helpless fear, expecting moles to come at any moment and take the females from me. But that did not happen, and after some sleep, and some food which the Brother Assistant had earlier laid just beyond my portal, I felt better.

'My time was so taken up with tending to the tiny things, cleaning them and suckling them, that I was lost in my own little world, and my fears receded, almost as if they lay beyond the portal and would not disturb me. The pups grew well, and began to crawl here and there as I suppose pups will, and I grew to love each one and began to see that each was different in some way. One lively and loud, one serious, one small and quiet, whilst the male, though no bigger than his sisters at that stage, was more inquisitive and exploring, and as the days went by more ready to push the others out of his way to reach my teats. But all were mine, and I loved them all.

'I was aware some days later that I was watched one night, and I guessed that it was my Brother Confessor – his Assistant had also dared to poke his snout around the portal once or twice, though he had been so intimidated earlier that he said nothing. But at least he gave me a quiet smile when I thanked him for what he had tried to do, though he answered none of my questions. Still there were no threats, and I began to fall into a dangerous and complacent state, believing that the rumours about females being taken away were untrue, and that somehow my Brother Confessor had taken pity on our pups, if not on me. What was to happen to me afterwards I did not even think about.

'The days passed, and my pups were beginning to take pieces of chewed worm as well as milk, and even, as it seemed to me, to answer to the names I had given them. Their eyes had long since opened,

157

and they gazed on me so brightly, so full of trust, and dabbed at each other with their soft weak paws, and pushed and shoved, and began to play, or frowned as they struggled to climb over each other, and over me . . .'

Privet paused and smiled, and Weeth nodded and sighed, thinking of times of pupping he had heard of. But then shadows came back to Privet's face, and a drawn, defeated look.

'It was after my pups were weaned that they came at night, the moles who took them. Three females, one of whom I knew well – she was that same informer I had met at the beginning of my stay at Blagrove Slide, made senior now. Two held me, and the third took up my pups one by one. I screamed, my pups bleated, the females cursed me in the Stone's name as a reprobate and transgressor, and then they were gone, and I was alone.

'I tried to chase after them but the Brother Assistant came to the portal and blocked my way. My friend had become my foe.

'"You cannot follow where they are going, Sister Crowden," he said, "and it is best you do not try." I screamed and cried and beat him, and hit him, but he held me back, as gently as he could, saying again and again it was for the best, and that I could never understand.

'"They even took the male pup!" I shouted, grasping at some semblance of justice, as if taking the females was all right, but the male . . .

'"They took *him*, especially," said the Brother Assistant. When I demanded to know what he meant he did not reply, as if he had said more than he should. I did not understand his meaning then, and I do not now.

'I turned back from the futility of fighting and arguing and retreated into my own loss; my pain as well, for though the pups were weaned my teats were swelling and taut. I cannot describe the numbing grief I felt as the night continued, so quiet, so normal; my world had been taken from me, and I was powerless to help my pups. That night I journeyed into a darkness and beyond, and saw myself as I was, a trapped mole who had failed her pups and herself. Yet I dared to think again. I dared whisper to myself that there was no Stone!

'Dawn came and I turned to the wall of what I now knew to be my cell, and defiantly I began to scribe the names of all the moles I had ever known, one after another, after another. Wort, Rooster, Hamble, Shire, Lime . . . and when for a moment my memory of moles failed me, I scribed the names of places I had been. I screamed and shouted the words that I scribed down and the Brother Assistant came briefly to watch and then went away again. I did not care.

'By that scribing on the wall of my cell I repossessed my past and brought it to my present. The last words I scribed were the names I had given my four pups, names I held more dear than any I had scribed, names I have never spoken from that day – but for sweet Loosestrife, which I spoke to you just now. Oh, they were the names of life I made and lost.'

Privet stared at her paws, her mouth trembling before she looked up once again.

'By scribing the names of moles I had known and loved I was delving them into existence as Rooster had taught me to, and thereby informing the Stone that they *were*, because they were something of me, and I was alive. My pups *were*, and nomole, no faith had the right to take them from me. I felt that by scribing their names I was protecting them, as also I was protecting those other living moles I loved, like Hamble and Rooster, and even Lime, even her. I felt too that in those moments of scribing I was using almost the last of the strength that had kept me alive so long. It was as if the Stone had allowed me to conserve something of my true self for a final moment of trial and effort, and that there and then that moment was about to be.'

'Will you tell us what all their names were?' asked Whillan. 'It is as if they are part of my past too, the shadow siblings who were with me when you reared me.'

Privet turned, and speaking as if to him alone she said, 'My dear, when you were very young, too young to know what it was I said to you, I used sometimes to speak their names, imagining for a moment you were they. Just for a moment . . . The smallest of the females, the one the least likely to survive, was Brimmel, which is the Whernish name for brambles such as those that grew down by Crowden Lake. I had shared happy times with Hamble there in the autumn, when their shiny leaves turned red. Her two sisters I named Sampion and Loosestrife, and I confess that Loosestrife *was* my favourite, don't ask me why. But she had a way with her, she was the one in whom I put all my dreams and hopes of living life differently and better than I had done, with more courage and more joy.

'Pups are all different, Whillan, even when so young, as one day you will find if the Stone blesses you with them.'

'And the male pup?' asked Whillan.

'I never could find a proper name for him,' she said, 'not a name worth having. I think I was intimidated by the knowledge that of them all he was the only one likely to survive, even if it was as a Newborn brother. I used to call him Mumble, and that was the name I scribed on the wall. He used to mutter and mumble to himself in an endearing kind of way as he pushed and shoved his way about, and perhaps his sturdiness, which contrasted with his sisters, reminded me of Hamble, and so "Mumble" came readily to me.'

'"Mumble,"' repeated Whillan, almost with embarrassment, as if greeting a mole he had heard a great deal of but had never met before. 'And Brimmel, and Sampion, and Loosestrife.'

'Yes, they were my pups,' said Privet steadily, 'and then they were taken for ever from me.'

It seemed that by speaking the names aloud that dawn Privet had allowed her pups to be real once more, however brief and anonymous their lives had been.

'They're good names,' said Maple.

'Are they?' whispered Privet with real delight.

'They are!' said Weeth, his eyes brimming with tears for what might have been.

'Well, well . . .' said Privet, sighing and struggling to control her emotions. 'What happened next? Yes, it was then that *he* came to the portal of my cell, summoned by the Brother Assistant no doubt, and as I turned and faced him I saw his eyes were on my scribing, with the same appalled horror as before.

'"Where are our pups?" I shouted at him, quite hysterical.

'He winced at my use of the word "our" as if he wanted to deny that *we* had a part in them.

'"What is this?"' he said, ignoring my question and advancing on my scribing.

'"They are the names of moles and places that I love," I said, adding as a deliberate provocation, "and if *you* can ken, then you will find the names of our four pups at the end."

'"I can ken," he said sharply, and I understood in that moment that he was a mole to whom pride was important.

'"Then ken," I challenged.

'He hesitated between the ignominy of obeying a suggestion made by a female, even if she was one to whom he had dropped his guard for a time, and appearing a fraud if he did not show he could understand what I had scribed.

'He raised his paws to the wall and following my scribing with his paws. He did it very quickly, like a mole well used to scribing, and

160

he did not go over the same markings twice. He turned to me and to my astonishment repeated what I had scribed name by name, like liturgy he had learned by rote.

'"Hamble, Rooster, Wort . . ." until he reached the last of all that I had scribed, "Loosestrife." Then he went back to Wort.

'"Wort?" he said. "The Eldrene Wort?"

'How I was tempted to tell him who I was, the one thing I had not told, and what that made his pups, but even in my anger I knew it would endanger even the male pup's life. Such progeny as that would not be acceptable to so dogmatic a mole of the Stone. So I remained silent, and a flash of anger crossed his face, and then pity, as brothers often responded when sisters had transgressed. It is a look that turns a sister into something less than mole.

'"The last four names you spoke are the names of our pups," I said at last, "and you have taken them."

'"I have taken nothing. You have given them up to the Stone."

'"You have taken them from me, and their lives are now your responsibility. If you let them die, in body or in spirit, you are nomole of the Stone, for you kill something of yourself."

'"You cannot speak to me, to a Brother Confessor, thus."

'"I am their mother and as I cannot go to them this is the last I can do for them. Before you harm them, Brother Confessor, turn your snout towards the Silence of the Stone and ask for the Stone's guidance. The pups are not yours to mould, as you have moulded moles like me."

'"They are—"

'"They are not yours."

'"Sister Crowden—"

'"My name is *not* Sister Crowden. It is—" and I stopped. I could see the anger mounting in him, but it was well under control, as you would expect from a Senior Brother. Such control is a formidable and frightening thing which the male Newborns no doubt learn from a young age and it gives them strength, and a power to command. As I stared into his eyes I felt my own strength weakening, not yet in spirit, but in body, and I knew that my last reserves were almost gone and that if I had anything left to say that might influence him for the good of our pups I had best say it.

'"Promise me they will all live," I said.

'He hesitated, and I knew the mortal danger some of them at least must be in.

'"The Stone will—"

161

'"Put your talons on the names of our pups I have scribed, and promise."

'He stared at the scribings he had just kenned but did not move. "The male will live to glorify the Stone," he whispered.

'"Promise they *all* shall live," I said, with almost my last strength. "If you do not, Brother Confessor, you are nothing before the Stone – nothing."

'The chamber swayed and darkened about me, and as I tried to hold his gaze, I heard him say softly, "You know, Sister, *I* would not harm a single hair on their bodies."'

'"Promise," I whispered with my last breath, "for our pups are more than us, and one day . . . one day we must go to the Silence. Go not with the shadow of their robbed lives upon your face."

'I remember seeing his paw reach out towards the wall, and his eyes staring at me, and his mouth opening, but nothing more, nothing more. However hard I try I can remember nothing more of him, or of that cell.'

'But later, Privet, later?' said Whillan urgently.

Privet shook her head. 'There was no "later" for me in Blagrove Slide. The next I knew I was on a long, dragging journey through tunnels I had not seen before, being half carried, half pulled by the Brother Assistant. I remember that I cried out to him to stop and let me rest, but he only whispered "Sssh!" and I thought I was being taken to my pups, but I was not. On and on I was led. We rested only once that I recall, if it is a true recollection. We seemed to be in the shadow of a portal, and what I saw there a mole such as I would not be likely to forget, and nor would *you*, Whillan! I saw a library the like of which I had never seen before, nor have since. There were rows and rows of identically made texts, their covers birch-bark, all thin, all neat. The place was well-lit and clean as well. No nooks and crannies, no scholars hunched over ancient texts, nor scribes busy editing new ones: just texts, and not a mole in sight.

'Was it a real library I saw in Blagrove, or a dream of endless obedient brothers and Confessed Sisters, turned into endless texts all made to be the same for ever more, and safe, a place cleaned of transgressions by doctrinal moles? That's what I think I dreamt or saw . . . until it ended, and the darkness came back and the running went on down a tunnel into nightmare, and I awoke on the surface beyond the confines of Blagrove Slide. The Brother Assistant was stanced over me.'

'"Sister," he commanded me, "go far from here and never return or try to, or think of doing so. Go south or east. You must go *now*."

'"My pups—" I began.

'"Sister, speak not of this and all your pups shall find favour with the Stone. Your Brother Confessor wishes it. But speak not of this; go now, and never . . ."

'"All" he had said, and it was enough to send a surge of joy and gratitude through me – the unreasonable gratitude a victim feels who has been given a mite of comfort by her oppressor. But it made me believe that I could turn and go, knowing I had done all I could for my young; they were left with a chance, even if they were in the grip of the Newborn moles.

'I had but one more thing to say to the Brother Assistant, and in saying it I finally found myself again: "Tell the pups their mother's true name!"

'"I know not your name, and I *should* not know it!"

'"It is Privet, tell them *that*, Privet of Crowden. *Tell* them, mole." And with that I left him, and did not look back.

'Instead I trekked off into the last of the summer years, as low as a mole could ever be, to a state of shocked wandering, a kind of living oblivion. Did I meet other moles? Perhaps. Did I enter other systems? Perhaps. Did I pause awhile in lonely places along the way, and watch the seasons advance, and see the autumn come? I think I did. Once or twice I think I came across the Newborns, and when I did I turned from them as I turned from the Brother Assistant that last day at Blagrove Slide, without looking back. I preferred not to even think of them, for to do so was to remind myself that they had taken part of me.

'Sometimes in those long moleyears I wept for moles I had known, and the pups I had lost. Sometimes too I asked myself that question *he* had asked of himself, Why me? What was there between us that was meant to be, and which the Stone made happen? And why, when those questions came, did my mind turn again and again to the nature of Silence, and the search for the Book of Silence? Perhaps the power of the task I had set myself in Beechenhill sustained me, for lost though I was within myself, and numb though my feelings were, beneath it all remained the drive to carry me to Duncton Wood, as if it had always been my destination.

'By November I had reached Rollright, but when I discovered there were Newborns there I turned away again, and wandered on. I was rarely troubled. Whatmole noticed a thin, strange, vague female, who looked middle-aged, and worth nothing at all? Nomole heeded me, and I felt invisible as I journeyed on. Sometimes I whispered as I went, asking myself what Silence was, and where I might find it, and why my snout always brought me back towards Duncton Wood.'

'And did you come to a conclusion about Silence?' asked Weeth.

Privet paused and thought about the question, and when she replied she did so slowly, as if drawing on deep and well-considered thoughts on which she had long pondered. Indeed, to add to the variety of 'Privets' they had witnessed that night, from scholar to mother, from prudish librarian to Newborn lover, there now came forth another – a Privet who had begun to discover the peace of mind that enabled her to speak with authority and grace on matters of the heart and the Stone.

'The question moles should really ask when evil befalls them is not, "Why me?", nor even, "What is the purpose of the Stone in this?" But rather, "What talons of truth and faith has the Stone given me by which, now that I am in darkness, I may proceed back to the light?"'

Weeth allowed a slight smile of acknowledgement to play across his face, a sign that he felt that this was indeed an important question, and more relevant at the present hour than any but he and Privet yet knew.

'Make no mistake. My experience of the Newborns was an experience of evil, yet evil in disguise enough to confuse me, and to leave me wondering if I was in darkness at all. At the time I was not so philosophical or capable of detachment as to ask the crucial question I have raised now. Indeed, until this very moment I never asked the question so clearly of myself before, but I think it is one we must all ask ourselves in the coming times of darkness: "What strengths have we that will aid us in reaching the light again?"

'Remember: the task I had accepted was the pursuit to the very end of the search for the Book of Silence. Perhaps where the wisdom of the Stone most deeply lies is in directing moles into circumstances which force them to ask, and to answer, questions they would otherwise be reluctant to raise. So I was directed to Blagrove Slide.

'We all want an easy life, or hope for one. What I had in Blagrove Slide was an experience so shocking, and so searing, that I would never again believe that life can be easy. Pleasant perhaps, joyous, fulfilling; but never easy. And for many moleyears, until now indeed, I lost all confidence in myself as mole.

'But as I have talked tonight of my long journey, and come at last to the trauma of my time at Blagrove Slide before I ended my travels in Duncton Wood, I have begun a second journey, which is that which has taken me out of the darkness of my life until now into the light of acceptance and love: the love of moles like Fieldfare, and Master Librarian Stour, and Whillan here, and my other friends. I see now, for the first time, that there can be, or can have been, no great Books without such journeys as these, nor any scribing of them unless it be by moles who have made such journeys. I know now that I may still have some way to go along the path which I started on so long ago, and from which I found respite for a time in Duncton Wood.

'And what of my journey to Duncton? It ended a few days before Longest Night when I reached the cross-under on the south-east side, and passed through it on to the Pastures whose slopes lead up to the Wood.

'I looked up and saw the great beech trees, all leafless and tossing in a storm of winter wind, and I came slowly up. There, at the edge of the Wood, I turned and stared back as if to look across the moledom I had journeyed through, and say goodbye to all my former life: to the Moors, to Rooster, to Hamble, to Cobbett, to my pups in Blagrove Slide. If they lived they would be so changed and grown I would no longer recognize them, with only their names scribed on a wall, and for ever in my heart, to record what they once had been before they became Newborn.

'Then I turned into the Wood, and Fieldfare was there to welcome me. And welcome me she did, and led me to a new life, and gave me time to find myself. I joined a system to which I feel I have given but little, so lost have I been in the darkness of forgetting what I was.'

A sudden gust of wind caught the surface where they talked and when it had passed by they knew Privet's tale was done – at least, so much of it that related to the past. The rest had yet to come, and each knew he was now a part of it.

PART III

Into Darkness

Chapter Fourteen

The following day they found themselves approaching a second and larger patrol of Newborn moles and realized that they were now very near to Evesham, and to discovery by the Newborns after so long journeying unobserved.

'This may well be it,' said Weeth. 'One and all, now may be our last chance to retreat.'

'We're going on,' said Maple.

'You're going on,' said Weeth, 'but *I* will not unless you tell me if you accept me as your companion. You've had these days of travel in the Vale to judge me and now you must make up your minds. You've seen me as I am, for better and for worse, and—'

'Mole,' said Maple, 'I speak for all of us when I say we want you with us. We have no choice, but even if we had I'd choose you as a companion on the way!'

Weeth seemed much touched by this, and blinked his eyes as if about to cry, though no tears could be seen at all.

Whillen asked, 'What would you have done if Maple had said no?'

'I would have gone over to the other side, of course,' said Weeth matter-of-factly, 'as Maple knows, that's why he speaks of having no choice. Mind you, I would have regretted betraying you, but a mole must . . .'

'. . . take his opportunities where he can?' suggested Whillan with a smile.

'Young mole, you are learning fast, and I rather think that what you have learnt may be the saving of your life one day, as it has been of mine in the past. The study of opportunity – what a rich, worthwhile field that is! But look, we have been seen. Observe the humourless aspect of the Newborn patrol! See their joyless eyes! Thrill to the sterility of the purpose of their paws!'

It was true enough, the patrol had seen them and shouting to others nearby a good few Newborns were bearing down on them with ominous speed and intent. Weeth kept up his commentary for a little longer before breaking off and turning to his adoptive friends.

'Weeth pledges himself to you and yours. Weeth's years and months and days of non-commitment to anymole but himself are done! Weeth is *yours*.'

'Beware, Weeth,' said Privet gently, as the first Newborn arrived, 'for the Stone may turn what you think of now as opportunity into the very destiny you doubt, and it may ask much of you. Remember, if that happens, that in us you have three friends who will give you loyalty in return.'

'Well!' declared Weeth, unable to say more, and with a sudden brightness to his eyes that certainly *was* tears.

He sniffled a little and without being asked, pushed forward towards the first Newborn. Raising his paw in a benign but imperious way said, 'Hail, Brother in justice, truth and good intent, take us to your leader!'

They were led to the tunnels of Evesham and thence into the company of moles the stench of whose vile sectarian beliefs benumbed the mind. They were first examined by various Brother Inquisitors as if they were fleeing reprobates, and they told truthfully who they were and how they had come, exactly as they had agreed. Ironically, it was Privet who was treated most lightly, almost with indifference, as if her questioners could not believe a female could be of importance, or have anything useful to impart. But her age, obvious reserve, and sharp retorts made even those dogmatic moles realize in the end that she was not the travelling concubine they seemed to think her, but was indeed who she said she was, Privet of Duncton Wood, a scholar and scribe. After that they treated her with a mixture of fear and suspicion, and made life as hard for her as they could.

'Their attitude and interrogation tells us more about the Newborns than they will have learnt from us,' said Whillan when the Inquisitors, accepting their story at last, hurriedly brought them together again in a comfortable communal chamber, and gave them better food.

Of the four of them, only Weeth had been physically abused, for his face had marks and swellings that betrayed he had been buffeted a good deal, but when the others asked him what had happened he shrugged it off, saying that as a Newborn who had reneged on the cause he had got off lightly.

'Worse might be in store for all of us,' he said ominously. 'Attitudes are hardening.'

Soon after this the four found themselves summoned at last into the presence of the mole who had fretted so long to catch up with them, and question them, and assert himself over them once more: Snyde.

'*Acting Master Librarian* Snyde,' he said when they addressed him as Deputy Master, and he smirked at them all, preserving a look of especially condescending disdain for Librarian Privet.

It must be said that the journey from Duncton to Evesham, which had brought a gloss to the fur and a brightness to the eyes of Whillan, Maple and Privet, had done the same for Snyde. But whereas they looked the better for it, he contrived to look the worse, or at least the more unpleasant. The sheen on such fur as his bent and twisted back sustained now contrived only to highlight his untoward deformity, while the shine to his mean snout, and the devouring eagerness of his healthy eyes, served only to reveal what a ruthlessly self-seeking mole he remained.

They had been brought to him in an ante-chamber to Evesham's great communal chamber, wherein, within earshot, some ritual presentation or other was being made.

'I was of course invited,' said Snyde with a quick look in which false modesty vied with overweening pride, 'but on hearing that you had so magnanimously decided to join the delegation here I felt it only fair to brief you.'

'About what?' growled Maple.

Snyde frowned, trying hard to keep his patience, and certainly the large Newborn brothers who had been deputed to act as his bodyguards and retinue did not like the way that the four journey-stained moles regarded him with barely concealed contempt. They stared malevolently at Maple, which made Snyde's sharp unpleasant smile seem all the worse.

'About what? About whom, you mean,' said Snyde. 'You will perhaps be aware that a certain mole, an important mole, has chosen to honour me with his company on this journey to Caer Caradoc. Senior Brother Chervil is here, and will be leading us on towards Ludlow on the morrow.'

'I thought—'

'It matters little what you thought or think, Whillan,' said Snyde contemptuously. 'When you meet him you would be sensible to address the Senior Brother in the Newborn way; that would also be wise and politic. You would also be advised to answer his questions, or those of any Brother Inquisitors he may depute to examine you on certain matters in which he has, I think, a justifiable interest.'

'What matters, Deputy Master?' said Privet calmly.

Snyde allowed a cunning smile to play across his face and then let it lapse into a chilly stare. He seemed to want them to know that he

171

felt they were playing a game with him and he understood it, in which he was nearly right.

'The Master Stour, mole: where is he?' The words came out in a nasal, staccato way which betrayed Snyde's great concern to find the answer.

'We will be glad to inform anymole of that,' said Privet, 'though I fear the truth is something some moles may find distressing.'

'He is dead along the way . . . ?' said Snyde with ill-concealed delight.

'I thought it was Chervil who wished to ask the question,' said Privet.

'It would be wise of you not to play verbal games with me, Librarian Privet,' said Snyde, looking at Whillan menacingly, and making it very plain that he had powers to make life uncomfortable for the mole he perceived as the weakest of the three Duncton moles.

'I will tell Senior Brother Chervil all that he wishes to know, to the best of my ability,' said Privet a little wearily. She had no need of the gentle nudge Maple gave her to indicate the snooping shadow of a mole at a small portal beyond where Snyde squatted, she had seen it already, and assumed that if it was not Chervil who spied, it was one of his Brother Inquisitors.

'We are weary from travel, Acting Master Librarian,' said Privet impatiently, and as much for the spy's ears as Snyde's, 'and if we are to see Senior Brother Chervil let us do so now. If not, let us go and rest.'

'Speak more respectfully to the Acting Master, Sister,' snarled one of the watchful brothers at Snyde's flank, the first open expression of the hostility they had sensed from the beginning in Evesham against Privet because she was female.

'Speak more respectfully yourself,' said Whillan hotly.

Snyde raised a crooked paw and half laughed, in an almost apologetic way, before saying, 'Brothers, you must be patient with these Duncton moles, they are not trained in Newborn ways, and their females are regarded as our equals . . .'

'Tstt!' said one of the brothers with genuine incredulity.

'. . . and perhaps they are, perhaps they are theoretically . . .' He paused, enjoying the dismay produced by his unexpected support of Privet, though he ended it soon enough. '. . . for all moles are born equal before the Stone, and go forward equally into its Silence. It is just that it is ordained that males have rather different tasks than females, whose main and first concern must naturally be the rearing of young through procreation with a male.'

172

' 'Twould be difficult any other way, Brother!' declared Weeth suddenly, winking broadly at the assembled Newborns.

'Is that mole Newborn?' said a voice from the shadows.

'I wasn't born yesterday,' responded the irascible Weeth, turning to the mole and finding himself snout to snout with Chervil.

His riposte was perhaps ill-advised, for hearing it, and seeing at which mole it had been directed, if unknowingly, several brothers moved forward menacingly towards Weeth as if to roughly eject him from the chamber, when Chervil said quietly, 'Leave him be!'

The moment Chervil came fully into the chamber – and he did so from a direction which showed he had not been the spying mole – its atmosphere changed. For one thing, he commanded an awed respect quite different from the authority that Snyde wielded.

He too was trimmer from the journey, but also more powerful-looking, as if he had cast off some shadow that had beset him in Duncton Wood and now saw his objectives clearly. He was, undeniably, a mole with charisma, and had the ability to inspire in those around him, even in Whillan and Maple if not Privet, a certain sense of excitement.

'You must forgive the Acting Master's questioning, Librarian Privet,' he said courteously, nodding his head towards Maple and Whillan, and speaking their names. 'He – I should more fairly say we – have been impatient for your coming. Your late arrival has caused a delay, and we were all of us anxious to take advantage of the fair weather we have had and get to Caradoc. Fortunately, the days are still mild.'

He eyed Privet with considerable respect, as she did him. 'It seems strange, Sister, that we have both had to travel so far to meet, when for so many moleyears past we have resided in the same system. But, well, I preferred to pursue my spiritual studies and meditations in the Marsh End of Duncton Wood, well away from the taunts and temptations of your Library. But of course your reputation precedes you here and I trust you will forgive some of the moles you are likely to meet for their brusqueness, even rudeness perhaps; they are not used to lettered females. Great reforms of the kind for which my . . . the Elder Senior Brother Thripp has been responsible do not proceed all at once; some things must wait, and the radical equality of Duncton Wood is perhaps one of them.'

It was elegantly spoken, and the Duncton moles had the clear impression that though he had not said so directly, perhaps because of the presence of others both in the chamber and close by outside it, he himself was a reforming mole, not entirely set in the old ways, even if his rank and natural authority meant that he represented them.

Having spoken, he paused, eyeing them searchingly and finally letting his gaze settle on Weeth. One of the brothers came and whispered in his ear.

'You are the mole Weeth?' said Chervil.

'I am,' said Weeth with no sign of fear.

'But no longer Newborn.'

'Arguable,' said Weeth. 'I have been trained in Newborn beliefs here and there in a sporadic kind of way, but now I have the honour of being attached to Maple of Duncton here, as a kind of aide or helper.'

'He does not look a mole who needs much help,' said Chervil.

'Nor do you, Senior Brother, if I may say so, but there seem a great many brothers here eager to help *you*.'

There was a flurry of dismay at this rejoinder but Weeth ignored it utterly, and instead smiled and did not let his gaze on Chervil waver, and to his credit Chervil smiled back. But it was the smile of a confident and intelligent mole who appreciated the joke; there was no hint of weakness in it.

'Well, you are now of Brother Snyde's party and since all in it naturally have a safe conduct to Caer Caradoc, I am sure, Weeth, that you will come to no harm along the way from anymole, Newborn or otherwise.' Here he looked heavily at the Newborn guards to make his meaning plain. 'Now, we are interested to know what has happened to the Master Librarian Stour. We had understood from the Keeper Sturne that he was journeying with *you*. I trust that nothing has harmed him on the way?'

The reply Privet gave was the nearest she ever got to a lie, and she was conscious of it, and it was the reason she hesitated. Even though it was a lie by default and what she said was nearer the truth than either Maple or Whillan expected, or Weeth could ever have predicted, she did not like it. But in this company the whole truth might be, as Snyde would have it, impolitic.

'I had imagined that Keeper Sturne would have told you what Master Stour *wished* him to tell you,' said Privet. 'The fact is that to the best of my knowledge Stour is still in Duncton Wood, where he remained when we left. He is in retreat in the Ancient System.'

'In Duncton Wood . . . ?' said Chervil slowly, his intelligent eyes flickering as he rapidly weighed up what that might mean. It was plain

174

he did not doubt that Privet was telling the truth. 'And can you tell us what he is *doing* in the Ancient System? That is, is it not, the system of old tunnels deserted by moles for many decades, which the Duncton Library is adjacent to?'

'In the Ancient System,' spat out Snyde. 'But—'

'That is so,' said Privet ignoring him, and though her voice was quiet it carried increasing assurance, for she felt that the only thing worth speaking now was the truth, and in that moment of confrontation with Chervil she sensed that the real struggle between Stour and Thripp was beginning, and everything before had been a gradual gathering of support and preparation of position.

In speaking to Chervil she felt she was speaking indirectly to Thripp himself. Chervil seemed to understand this too, and there was no trace of disdain or condescension towards her such as they had experienced from the other Newborn moles and Snyde.

'So what is moledom's most venerable librarian doing in those obscure and deserted tunnels when moledom's other respected librarians are all on their way to confer with the Elder Senior Brother in Caradoc?' he asked.

'You could hardly expect him to make the trek to Caradoc and survive,' said Privet, who was proving to be as in control and as commanding as Chervil himself, though in a different way.

'I confess I was surprised when I heard it,' said Chervil, darting a questioning glance at the discomfited Snyde, 'but we could find no trace of the Master Stour, *could* we, Acting Master Snyde?'

Snyde stared through narrowed, hate-filled eyes at Privet. He felt excluded by the dialogue, and perhaps he thought the 'Acting' append-age to his title was now even less deserved than it had been before. Privet was making no friend in Snyde, not for herself or those on her side, but then she had never wished to, and the rising tide of truth and purpose in her would surely see that she never would if it compromised her task.

'The Master Stour charged me, through Deputy Master Snyde,' she continued, 'to inform the Convocation of Caradoc that in his judgement the calling of such a Convocation was mistaken, and the trend of the Newborn sect towards retributive dogma and censorship of contrary views – not to mention texts being called "blasphemous" which are not – is a most dangerous thing, which all moles should resist. As for what he is doing in Duncton, I am empowered to tell you, though I would have preferred to do so through my colleague here,' (she nodded her head towards the fuming Snyde), 'with whom

175

I have not yet had time for a proper talk, but if he permits I will tell you what I know.'

'Does he permit?' said Chervil a little ironically, turning graciously to Snyde, who spat out some word or other to indicate that of course he did.

'Well then?' said Chervil, turning back to Privet.

'As you may infer from what I have said, the Master Stour is somewhat concerned about the future safety of certain of the Duncton Library's more revered and ancient texts, his view being that the role of a librarian is not only the dissemination of knowledge through texts – a task he in particular has advocated and advanced all his life – but their preservation as well. The texts he is most concerned with are the Books of Moledom.'

'There are copies in most libraries, are there not?'

'In all of them but Beechenhill, I think, thanks to him,' said Privet. 'But he is concerned for the originals, believing as he does that there is something special, perhaps sacred, about the texts and the folios they contain which were scribed by the holy moles who originally made the Books themselves.'

'And where is he preserving them from this supposed danger?' asked Chervil quietly. 'He seems to have told you much, Librarian Privet, perhaps he has told you that as well.'

'He did not,' said Privet, 'he is not a fool, Senior Brother Chervil. He would have realized the considerable dangers in our journey to Caradoc, and with all due respect, being dubious about the Newborn sect and their likely treatment of moles with dissenting views, he may have felt it wisest that we did not know, lest the information be forced out of us. Forgive me if I sound cynical – I am.'

'Which being so, Librarian Privet, a mole must admire your courage in coming at all.'

'A mole must stance up for what he believes,' was her quiet reply.

'You mean *she* believes,' said Chervil with a confident and now humourless stare. What Privet had said seemed to have angered him somewhat.

'Oh, do I?' said Privet innocently.

Chervil frowned with displeasure, discomfited by her assurance, which had increased with each moment, and seemed in some subtle way to undermine his authority with the other Newborns there. Then, with a brief and chilly smile, he turned and was gone.

News of this encounter was very soon all around Evesham and since even Newborns permitted themselves a moment of gossip here and

176

there, the question of who got the better of the exchange between Chervil and the female Privet was much debated.

'What they seem to find strange,' said Weeth, who was able to get more out of their 'captors' than anymole else 'is not only that a mole of Privet's rank should be female, but that she should be taken seriously by Chervil. Some see it as a sign of weakness, others as an indication of his cunning in getting information out of moles. There is acrimony in the ranks over the failure to realize Stour was in Duncton, and annoyance with Snyde because he seems not to have known or guessed that Stour might so boldly preserve the originals of the Books of Moledom. You have caused a stir, Privet. And you undermined Snyde's position.'

'I did as the Master Stour would have wished me to do,' she said demurely. 'Perhaps sectarian moles find it dispiriting to discover that they cannot have everything their way.'

'Chervil did not seem *very* dispirited,' said Whillan, 'just annoyed.'

Maple nodded and said, 'Chervil strikes me as a very formidable mole indeed. It is he we should fear most, for he is the one who holds power.'

'Ah! That! Yeees . . .' said Weeth, his face glowing with the pleasure he normally felt when he was about to make a revelation. 'The other piece of information I have gained, which Snyde conveniently forgot to tell us, and which everymole else in Evesham seems to know, is that Chervil is none other than Thripp's own son. I am not sure how long he was in Duncton Wood . . .'

'A full cycle of seasons,' said Privet, 'for he came some time before myself. So twelve moleyears or more.'

'Well, as they tell it, Chervil fell out of favour with his father and was banished, as it were, to Duncton Wood; as *I* interpret it, he was sent to Duncton to prepare the ground for whatever Thripp intends to do. If, as I believe, it is to take over the major systems while the Convocation is taking place, then the fact it was his son he sent to Duncton Wood does suggest what importance he attaches to that particular system. The one thing to remember about Thripp is he does nothing without a reason, nothing at all, obscure though it may be to everymole else. It would be nice to know why he was really sent there.'

'I shall ask Chervil himself,' said Privet calmly, 'if the opportunity arises. We were frank with him, it may be he will be frank with us. For the moment I feel us to be safe – at least until we get to Caer Caradoc. History shows that moles like Chervil and Thripp, who wield power in the name of narrow truths, often have their dirty work done

177

out of sight and out of mind by other moles who, they can claim with paws on hearts, they did not order so to do. Perhaps, to Thripp, such an evil shadow is the mole Quail.'

'And perhaps to Chervil,' said Whillan quietly, 'such a mole may one day be Snyde.'

Maple nodded his head slowly. 'The more I see and the more I hear, the less I like any of it. We are knowingly going into danger, and I do not say we should try to turn back. But the light on the way forward is dimming, and the shadows and obstacles are increasing, and I pray that the Stone will guide us to the moment we can turn our back on these moles and go into open opposition. A mole like me is happier with that.'

'We must go on as the Master Stour bid us do,' said Privet. 'We must go to the very heart of matters, the better to judge how to conduct opposition in the future, if that is what it is to come to. For myself I can only pray that we shall not see another war, but rather be granted by the Stone a peaceful way through to harmony.'

'Aye,' said Maple slowly, 'and not a word of that do I disagree with. But history is against it.'

'History, Maple, is all past. It is here and now where *we* live, and this is *our* chance to make a history for which moles may one day be grateful.' She looked away from him and the others. 'I am afraid for all of us, I pray for all of us, and I believe in all of us.'

Whillan reached out a paw to her in reassurance and at its touch she turned to embrace him. 'My dear,' she whispered, 'whatever may happen, never forget that you are much loved.'

'You're trembling,' he whispered, holding her tight.

'Yes,' she whispered, 'oh yes, I am.'

Chapter Fifteen

For some moles that same long winter was a time of unremitting toil and danger without the relief of good company or any prospect of escape. Such a mole was Pumpkin of Duncton Wood, than whom nomole had a more lonely nor more difficult task in the struggle against the Newborns, unless it be Keeper Sturne, now Acting Master Librarian.

After Pumpkin's discovery in November that Sturne's conversion to the Newborn way was a brilliant but dangerous masquerade, the two had judged it best to see as little of each other as possible. As the days had gone by and winter set in poor Pumpkin had felt his faith tested and his courage in jeopardy as no news or instructions came from anymole as to what he could or should do. 'Wait and see' is easy advice for moles to give who live in comfort and security, but very hard to follow when surrounded by enemies, and in undoubted danger, as Pumpkin was.

To make matters worse he knew that the Inquisitors, and particularly the bullying Brother Barre, disliked him, and would have had him eliminated long since but for Sturne's insistence that he was indispensable to the Library. The trouble now was that time was running out, as the censoring of the Library neared completion and other Newborn aides came to know the nooks and crannies of the re-ordered stacks as well as Pumpkin did.

'It is getting hard to protect you from them, Pumpkin,' whispered Sturne in a snatched moment of privacy. 'The trouble with you is you don't *look* like a Newborn – can't you try harder? You may at least have to submit yourself to some "education".'

'Humph!' exclaimed Pumpkin, 'I'm not Newborn, that's why I don't look like one. I'm very "oldborn" and intend to continue to be! I could volunteer for instruction as some Duncton moles have done.'

He intended this ironically but Sturne, never one to see a joke, took him seriously.

But they were interrupted and with a quick nod followed by a harsh command to Pumpkin to get on with his work Sturne resumed his role as Newborn Acting Master Librarian.

He was right to give his warning, because some days later Pumpkin found himself being harassed by Inquisitor Barre for no better reason than his dislike of the old library aide. Barre called him insubordinate, and a nuisance, and more besides, and for a moment it looked as if he was going to dismiss him altogether from the Library.

'Brother!' piped Pumpkin in what he hoped was a manner at once abject and spiritually purposeful, 'may I seek counsel?'

This surprised Barre and silenced him. He did not know what was coming – nor, in truth, did Pumpkin. But instinct had told him that if he did not do *something*, and fast, something worse than dismissal would very soon be upon him.

'When you and your fellow Inquisitors came to Duncton, Brother Barre, I must confess I was an unhappy mole, uncertain of my true way.'

'Yes, yes,' said Barre impatiently, for he was the muscular rather than spiritual element in Duncton's inquisitorial triad.

'It is true I was given a certain amount of instruction, but my tasks here were many in those early days of your arrival and I was unable to get all the guidance I needed. Now the tasks are less, the Library is ordered and I would like to ask if you believe a mole as old as myself, and not of strong religious inclination, could benefit from instruction, or would it waste your time?'

'Instruction?' muttered Barre impatiently as he frowned with horrible ferocity. He seemed on the brink of ridding himself of Pumpkin for ever.

'Oh yes!' cried out Pumpkin ecstatically, deliberately misinterpreting Barre's question as a suggestion, 'I will receive instruction with glad heart and open mind. Praise the Stone! I knew that the Newborn way was wise and great enough to accept to its bosom even a broken-down old mole like me! But then, when there are moles such as yourself, good Brother . . .'

It is one of moledom's pathetic truths that the more terrible, the more brutal, the more stupid a mole, the more he is susceptible to fawning flattery. Barre put on a token show of resistance, but the fact was the more Pumpkin blathered on in this vein, the more Barre's scowling dislike softened into the self-satisfaction of a powerful mole hearing what he liked to hear. Had Pumpkin said such things to the more intelligent Inquisitors, Brothers Fetter and Law, they would have seen straight through it, but then having done so their response would not have been to brutally eliminate Pumpkin, as Barre's would certainly have been.

180

Since few moles before had been so asinine as to appeal to Barre's non-existent spirituality, Pumpkin got away with it – but only up to a point. For, having diverted Barre's probably murderous intent, he now attracted the Inquisitor's grotesque concern for his spiritual well-being and was forced to listen to a long and inarticulate lecture on the Newborn way, which included gobbets of the Newborn creed, and the significance of the confessional and – so carried away with it all did Barre become – he forced upon Pumpkin one of the most disagreeable experiences of his life, a mutual prayer.

'Great Stone,' said Brother Barre, his oft-bloodied paws on Pumpkin's lowered head, 'he's a sinner, and done grievous wrongs, but give him a chance to try to learn your proper ways. He will confess. He will die to be reborn again. Praise the Stone.'

'Praise be!' bleated poor Pumpkin, wondering if his neck could sustain much longer Barre's over-eager laying-on of paws. 'Where to now? I want to begin! Hear me, Brother, lead me on!'

This outburst, which allowed Pumpkin to break free from Barre's paws, had the unfortunate effect of attracting some of the more effusive and simple-minded of his Newborn fellow library aides to his flanks, sensing confession and redemption. Pumpkin was better known than he imagined as a mole who really had not quite embraced the Newborn way with the expected fervour. Everymole knew that it was only his expertise as an aide, and the special if mysterious trust Master Librarian Sturne placed in him, that had kept him ensconced in his senior position.

Now here he was proclaiming that he was Newborn, through the intercession of Brother Barre no less, and in the Library too! For such constrained and regimented minds as those gathered about him this was excitement, and a highlight, and deserved celebration. Praise be indeed!

Throughout the songs, chants and effusions of appealing little prayers that followed, Pumpkin was all too aware of what was coming, and it made his heart sink with gloom and apprehension. His mood darkened still more when Sturne, drawn to the Main Chamber by the noise of his diverted aides, decided his own best strategy was to take part in the rejoicing in his emotionless way which involved, among other things, grasping his old friend's unwilling paw and saying, 'These are glad tidings, Brother! Aye, gladsome indeed!'

But all good things must end, and when they had, and Sturne and Barre had restored order, Pumpkin found himself sent off down to Barrow Vale in the company of several of the Newborn aides, with no immediate prospect of returning to the Library at all. He could have done with a word of encouragement from Sturne but that had not been possible, though the two had exchanged a brief and meaningful glance which Pumpkin interpreted as, 'Stone help us all if these are the moles who are now in power across moledom!'

Quite why his modest expression of the discovery of being 'new born' should have caused such happiness among the aides Pumpkin could not guess. But since it seemed out of proportion – he was after all but one old and obscure mole in a large system wholly converted to the Newborn way – he thought there might be more to it than met the eye. He had, he thought, noticed a paradoxical sombreness on the faces of one or two of the delighted aides, as if their pleasure in his second conversion was no more genuine than the conversions themselves, and this puzzled him.

Meanwhile he went with apparent good cheer from the Library downslope into the communal tunnel that led eventually to Barrow Vale, accepting with what grace he could manage the joyful inanities and 'Praise be's' of his unwelcome companions. There were even times when their pleasure in his declaration seemed to have intoxicated them, as if they had eaten rather too much of the notorious cloven root of the spear-thistle which wise moles avoid except on hot August afternoons when they have nothing serious to do until nightfall.

'Don't you feel the joy of the Stone in your heart, Brother Pumpkin?' one of them said, stopping him suddenly and fixing him with a smile that Pumpkin presumed had a spiritual dimension.

'Joyful day that a mole discovers it!' cried out Pumpkin fervently.

'Many more to come, Brother, many, many more, now that you have opened up your heart to the true way.'

'Oh, really? Yes, many more I suppose,' he cried out. 'I am so happy to think of them!'

'And we are happy for you, Brother.'

'Oh, galoo galay,' Pumpkin thought to himself, 'how happy am I! Happy day, oh happy time. But Stone . . .' – and here his inner voice took on a grim warning tone quite uncharacteristic of him –, '. . . you had better find a way out of the dilemma in which my continuing and not always whole-hearted service to you seems now to have put me!'

There are too many accounts in moledom's libraries of the kind of Newborn education and indoctrination to which Pumpkin was now subjected for followers of this history to need another now. The harangues, the rote-learning, the massings, the ritual humiliations, the facile thinking and the profound despairs, the slow and steady destruction of all that is individual in a mole . . . these were as much in evidence in Duncton Wood as in other systems at that period. The routines varied a little perhaps – in Duncton 'difficult' moles were isolated in cells down in the cold damp of the Marsh End, prepared specially for the purpose – but all in all it was little different from elsewhere.

How many of those accounts describe how the strongest moles broke down! How many catalogue the despair of moles who knew that the darkness of a harsh doctrine was closing in on them, from which there was no escape, unless it be ill-health, passivity, and, most tragic of all, self-mutilation and death! Yet no system of mind-repression is perfect and here and there across moledom a pawful of moles succeeded, despite their circumstances of desperate isolation and privation, in resisting all pressure and remaining as true to the Stone in the old way as they had ever been. But only in Duncton Wood, only in Barrow Vale indeed, did something happen yet more remarkable than those cases, an achievement so notable that when a mole remembers it and repeats the tale, others are justified in exclaiming with glad hearts and joyful voices, 'Praise be! Praise be for liberty! Praise be for moles of spirit and stout hearts! Praise be for the triumph of humour, common sense, and a faith in what is right over the forces that seek to repress and destroy not just the great things, but the small as well . . .'

And the mole responsible for this unique and special triumph at that dark time of moledom's history? Why, Pumpkin himself, library aide and ordinary mole to end *all* library aides and ordinary moles.

The Barrow Vale into which Pumpkin found himself ushered so eagerly by his earnest friends was very different indeed from the one he remembered from those happy days before the coming of the Newborns. Even more different, he now realized, from the distant days of his youth, when timid and not yet sure of his vocation he lingered in the shadows of the busy place, listening to the talk and laughter of the adults, and replying happily to their friendly enquiries after him, his siblings, and his parents. In those days moles were still happy and secure in their system and shared their excitements and sorrows, memories and hopes, openly and with faith that the Stone would see them right in the end.

Now the laughter had gone, as had the free comings and goings of moles who had no master but the needs of family and friends, and a proper duty to themselves. In those happy days, if the sun was shining out on the surface and a mole felt it imperative to go up and warm his snout in it, well, that was his affair, and off he went! If a mole was getting tired of this or that mole's rendition of a particular tale, he said so truthfully and declared, 'I've had enough of this! My tail's drooping with boredom! No offence, old friend, but you'd do us all a favour if you'd shut up for a bit and we all tucked into some juicy worms! Here's one for you to start with!'

Pumpkin could see at once that such easy frankness in social intercourse had been driven out of Barrow Vale by the Newborns. In its place was an atmosphere of fear and suspicion in which moles scurried here and there without a friendly smile or passing word. A few moles, mainly sleek middle-aged males, stanced about the place looking important, and the others went to and from and between them with every show of deference and humility. Pumpkin recognized several moles he had once known to be cheerful individuals now looking as miserable as fox droppings; worse, he saw beneath the sleek and satisfied lines of the Newborn masters of the place the once awkward and appealing forms of moles who had been happy-go-lucky Duncton youngsters before the Newborns had 'educated' them.

It was not long before Pumpkin was taken into the education system, now infinitely subtler and more organized than that to which he had briefly been exposed when the Inquisitors had first come to Duncton Wood. Then he had spent a couple of days in the company of a tedious young Newborn before being brought back into service as a 'reformed' library aide. Now he was questioned and catechized, and put under the tutelage of one of the sleek moles to whom, routinely, he had to report as he progressed with an education of the vile imposing kind already described.

In fact, Brother Barre's instinct that Pumpkin was by nature insubordinate was correct, if we mean by it that he was preternaturally quite incapable of altering his basic tenets of truth, decency and faith in the face of any threats, pressure, or brute force. Unlike some rebels, however, Pumpkin had the virtues of greater years and inner modesty, and so was prudent and self-effacing and happy to nod his agreement to one thing while thinking another.

This should not be mistaken for simple hypocrisy; it was rather the wise discretion of a modest old mole who had heard (and kenned in texts) a lot of blathering and nonsense in his time and was not inclined to argue. If some mole or other wished to lecture him on the proper way to pray to the Stone, or on the nine tenets of the Newborn way,

let him do so, it would have little effect on what he himself thought –
'unless of course he's right, in which case I'll change my mind,' as he
told himself. But then, as Pumpkin had observed amongst the often
unpleasant and bullying scholars in the Library, moles will use any
means to persuade others they are right, or wrong. Or, put another
way; it's how a mole gets to his destination that reveals the true nature
of a mole, not the destination itself.

Pumpkin, then, was unusually well able to withstand the pressures
of Newborn education, but it was not quite this that was to win him
such admiration in the heart of allmole, but rather something that
arose from a fortuitous meeting some days after his arrival in Barrow
Vale. He had already been puzzled by the seemingly disproportionate
jubilation of the Newborns at his conversion; and now something else
surprised him – the fact that moles seemed to come out of their way
simply to *look* at him. Why he was a curiosity he could not imagine,
and in the hurried and harried Barrow Vale of those days, when moles
were fearful of saying anything to each other lest they be spied on,
reported, and admonished, it was impossible to easily find out.

Several long days after his arrival, and after spending the whole night
and half the day in a mass chanting session interspersed with the
rote-learning of names spoken one by one by a brother – the idea
being to cleanse the mind of wasteful thinking – he returned to the
little cell they had allocated him on the Westside, and found a female
of four Longest Nights waiting for him, all furtive and frightened in
the shadows.

'Brother Pumpkin?' she whispered, coming forward into the light
as he stopped and turned her way.

'Yes, Sister?' he said with that mock good cheer which the brothers
were expected to affect.

'Brother, do you recognize me?'

He stared hard at her, thinking immediately it was some kind of
Newborn trick to catch him out.

'Should I, good Sister?' he said, rather proud of this answer, but
sad that fear and doubt breeds evasion and half-truths. In fact he did
not recognize her.

She said her name was Elynor and told him they had once met in
'easier days'. He had learnt enough to know that this was a coded way
of saying 'in the days before the Newborns came', but a mole could
not be too careful.

He looked dubious and said, 'Well, Sister?'

'Brother Pumpkin, are you truly Newborn?'

185

He hesitated before he replied. She was a well-made mole, with good features and intelligent eyes, though her face betrayed a fatigue and anxiety that made her look older than she was. Whilst it was clear that this was more than a simple question, he could not tell what lay behind it. Nor could he risk enquiring further without undermining his pose as a believer.

'Praise be, good Sister, but I am, for I have seen the light and the only way.'

'The Newborn way?' said Elynor.

'If you have any doubts I fear I am not the brother to discuss them with. Now I am tired—'

'I have no doubts, none at all,' she said hastily. 'I was just, well, glad to hear of your conversion.'

'I am not so famous a mole that others would hear of *my* conversion, Sister, or be interested in it now.'

'Oh, but you are, Brother Pumpkin. You are *very* well known. All over Duncton moles have been speaking your name.'

'Surely, my conversion is not a matter for others' talk!'

'Oh but it is Pumpk—, Brother Pumpkin, it is!'

'Oh dear,' Pumpkin muttered to himself, 'she is trying to tell me something but I don't know what. And I have had my instructions – none but Sturne must know what I am.'

'Well then, Sister,' he said, turning from her, 'I would prefer it if it were not. We are nothing before the Stone.'

Whether or not this last comment was a Newborn sentiment he was not sure; probably not. As he left her he heard her whisper, 'May the blessings of the Stone be on thee always.'

'Well one thing is certain!' he said to himself as he entered his clean, mean little cell, '*She*'s not Newborn – that was the old way of giving a blessing. She'd better watch out for herself, she'd better . . . oh botheration, what *was* it she wanted?'

In the space of a few moments his mood shifted from satisfaction at having maintained his Newborn pose to a feeling of deep dismay at having missed something important. The way she had said 'May the blessings of the Stone . . .' The eagerness with which she claimed so many had heard of him, her final disappointment . . .

'Pumpkin, you have done wrong and must make amends!' he said to himself. 'This mole needed support, not evasion. The pose is not as important as the faith it hides. Come, before it is too late!'

He turned back out of the cell, and thence up on to the surface in the direction he hoped she had gone.

'Oh dear, oh dear,' he muttered as he hurried amongst the trees of the Westside, 'if I don't find her soon I never will.'

But there she was, round a root and across between two trees, and the reason she had not got far was because she was hardly moving at all, so wan and defeated she felt.

'Mole! Mole! It is I, Brother Pumpkin.'

She turned, stared, and a glimmer of hope came to her eyes. At that moment Pumpkin decided to declare himself openly and not prolong the lies. There is a time when a mole must say what he is and risk the consequences, for denial is a kind of self-mutilation from which there is no full recovery.

'Er . . . Elynor . . .' began Pumpkin as he reached her, his eyes warm and his face kind, 'you were good enough to ask if I was Newborn.'

'Yes,' she faltered.

'Well, now, you put me in a quandary, you really did. On the one paw I have my own task to fulfil for which it is better I am Newborn, but on the other it is very plain to me that you are hoping that I am a follower in the old way. I shall tell you at once that I am not Newborn now, never was in the past, nor shall I ever be so.'

Elynor's reaction took Pumpkin by surprise, for she reached out and clasped him to her, crying out through tears and laughter as she did so, 'I knew it, Pumpkin, I *knew* you were not Newborn!'

'There, there!' said Pumpkin, easing her off him as best he could and feeling the embarrassment such gentle unmated old males as he often feel in the face of female warmth. 'You had better explain what all this is about.'

'That's easily done!' she said, taking his paw and leading him to the cover of an oak tree's roots. 'You see, there's quite a number of moles down here in Barrow Vale, and scattered about the system too, maybe up to twenty in all, who've kept their faith so far despite everything they've suffered. Some others have been lost . . .'

She named four moles who had fallen foul of the Inquisitors and had disappeared.

'They take them out into the marshes beyond Marsh End,' she said darkly. 'But that was in the early days when they made examples of a few. As you've seen, most moles have acquiesced.'

'There are always a few who will resist! Especially in a system like Duncton Wood.'

'There are, there are. And in addition to those there are a few in hiding, including some of my own kin. There are moles who don't want to pretend, and young males for whom the Newborns seem to have a perverse predilection. Humph!' Anger was mixed with contempt and disgust. 'Now, you seemed surprised when I said there were many who had heard of your conversion!'

'Well, yes, I am,' said Pumpkin blinking. 'For one thing I am merely a library aide, and for another I have done my very best these last months to adopt a low snout.'

'Let me tell you, "Brother" Pumpkin, that you are very well known indeed. Why, all Duncton knew of Pumpkin, library aide to Master Librarian Stour, long before the Inquisitors showed up. When they did, and the Master Librarian went into retreat again in the Ancient System, and Privet and those others went off on their mission—'

'You seem remarkably well informed, mole.'

'This *is* Duncton Wood; moles with their snout to the ground can put twice two worms together and make four. Of course, when that Sturne took over . . .' and here Pumpkin was greatly relieved to see from her look of dislike that at least Sturne's cover was intact, 'we asked ourselves, "Isn't there anymole in the Library will stance up to them?" There was one of my sons up there, a junior aide called Cluniac.'*

Pumpkin hastily raised a paw to stop her telling him the mole's name – too late. He felt the less he knew the better.

'All I'll say then was that he came down to Barrow Vale one day and says, "There's Library Aide Pumpkin declaring himself Newborn, but if he's Newborn I'm an owl. You can tell he's not by the twinkle in his eyes. The Inquisitors can't, and nor can other Newborns, because they don't have a Duncton sense of humour."'

Pumpkin grinned and said, 'And I thought I was doing so well.'

'You have, you have! But *we* were *sure* you weren't Newborn, and your example over these long months has given us few who have pledged to resist the heart to continue to do so. The Newborns suspected, mind, but you never gave them cause to doubt you for one moment, and you could not be replaced. Though how you could work alongflank such a one as that Sturne I can't imagine.'

'Oh, with difficulty,' said Pumpkin, hoping that in the shadows

---

* This is the same Cluniac whose early exploits as a spy against the Newborns have been eclipsed by his courageous exploration in later, happier years of the lands beyond moledom. See his own account *North of the North, and Other Adventures of a Traveller.*

where they talked the twinkle in his eyes would not be observed. 'A most unpleasant mole, that one!'

'So we believed, or chose to believe, that you alone of the senior workers in the Library were resisting the Newborns, and what heart that gave us. Oh Pumpkin, you can't imagine how good it was to know you were *there*! Without you few of us would have survived this long.'

'Without me?' repeated poor Pumpkin faintly, as she squeezed him tight once again and then let him go all ragged and breathless.

'But then we heard the terrible news you had converted, and then when you came here, it seemed to be so.'

'Well now you know I haven't,' said Pumpkin mildly, 'and nor, as I said before, was I. Ever.'

'That will mean so *much*,' said Elynor.

'But it would not be a good idea if others knew for *certain* that all this Newborn business of mine is a pose,' said Pumpkin. 'I would prefer it if I had to speak to no other mole about it.'

'None but me shall know for certain,' replied Elynor. 'It's enough they think it might be – that will keep them going. But for how long?'

'How many moles feel as you do?'

'Just over twenty, with those in hiding.'

'Well, then we must do what we can for them.'

'Of course, the reason the Newborns were pleased by your conversion was that they suspected you but could not quite prove it. Now they think they've got you.'

'Yes, yes,' said Pumpkin, suddenly uneasy to be out in the open with a mole who, for all he knew, others might suspect was a doubter. 'You must do what you will with what you know. If you think it best to tell them that I remain untainted by Newborn thinking then do so – but I shall deny I ever talked to you, and you should deny it too.'

'Mole,' said Elynor with sudden concern, 'it will get worse, you know, far worse. They have been concentrating on the Library so far, but now that's done they'll be giving us recalcitrant moles their full attention.'

'I know it will be hard. I know others have already died, and many disappeared. Perhaps I shall be among them.'

'If *you* stance strong, Pumpkin, us others will. We'll be there beside you in spirit.'

'Like true Duncton moles!' Pumpkin's eyes were suddenly alight with excitement, for he was beginning to realize that in its eternal wisdom the Stone worked its wonders in the simplest ways, and through ordinary moles surviving extraordinary circumstances with

189

faith. In modern times Duncton moles had never failed to play their part, and in his own small way he would now make sure he did not fail to play his.

'Keep in touch with me then,' he said quietly. 'Only you, mole, none other. I shall deny all others.'

'Then may the Stone be with thee,' said Elynor more quietly still, watching after the grey mild form of Pumpkin, a little stooped now, and a little slow; she thought she had never known a braver nor a truer mole than he.

There now began in Barrow Vale a struggle of spirits which, though it was as powerful and awesome in its way as any war, was silent, secret and unspoken. The Inquisitors Fetter and Law had heard of Barre's apparent success in turning Pumpkin to the Newborn way, but they had their doubts. The curing of souls, especially intelligent ones that have erred almost from birth and been reared to a culture as insubordinate and liberal as Duncton's, is never an easy matter, and it seemed to them unlikely that of all of them Brother Barre should be the one to succeed with Pumpkin. Fetter himself had always believed Pumpkin to be less dim and ingenuous than he made out, if only because as library aides go he was one of the best – and Master Librarian Sturne did not suffer fools for long.

Therefore Fetter instructed that despite his age and protestation of faith Pumpkin's education should be of the most rigorous and ascetic kind. He suspected that the solid core of resistance they had met in Barrow Vale had always focused on one mole, though only now did he think it might be Pumpkin.

'Kill the bugger then,' said Barre.

'Ah now, Brother, we do not want martyrs here. If there is a mite of weakness in him, and if the snake is coiled in his heart, we shall find it.'

In the terrible winter days that followed, when bitter winds gave way to a snout-numbing rain, and that froze into a savage frost, Pumpkin was singled out for the harshest possible treatment. Permitted no sleep, deprived of proper food, he was humiliated again and again in the communal chamber of Barrow Vale as he stumbled over the lines of creed and liturgy he was forced to learn. His paws grew thin, his cheeks grew hollow, his eyes red-rimmed and staring, as day by slow day one Inquisitor after another intimidated and bullied him. He was laughed at and reviled, and more than once his snout was bloodied and he was made to crawl away publicly from the severe talonings and buffets they meted out to him.

190

It was not enough that he proclaimed theirs the true way, for they said the snake of doubt was still hidden in his heart, and that insubordination poisoned the blood that flowed in his veins.

'Admit you are wrong, mole! Admit your hypocrisy! Confess the sins of pride and resistance!'

But though poor Pumpkin was declining in health before their eyes, he never once weakened in his resolve to call the Newborn bluff. The harder they hit him, the louder his declarations of faith in their ways; the greater the humiliations they imposed on him, the more willing he seemed to declare his humility and unimportance before the wise Newborn way; and the more horrible their punishments, the more passionate his protestations that they *must* be right since the Newborn way was *always* right.

But the true insubordination of Pumpkin's brave stance was this: the more he declared the wonders of the Newborn way, the more he demonstrated to those who knew of his masquerade how rotten, and how vile it was; the more he agreed that theirs was the way to liberty of spirit in submission to the Stone, the more he showed the withering narrowness of that kind of faith. Yet more than all of that: the more he confronted their assaults with agreement and acquiescence, the more he gave heart and encouragement to those twenty or so moles in Duncton at that time who stayed fast in their attachment to the old ways of the Stone.

It was a resistance, and a most courageous one, that the Newborn Inquisitors could not easily deal with because it was silent and undeclared, and the more they tried to 'educate' the more they had the sense that they were failing in some indefinable way on which they could not put a talon.

Not that many of the senior Newborns ever understood the problem – Brother Barre, for example, remained convinced for a long time that Pumpkin *was* converted simply because he said so so fervently. But Quail's appointment of Brother Fetter to Duncton Wood had been a wise one – Quail knew his history, and felt it likely that if there was going to be resistance, systems like Duncton and Avebury were likely to spawn it, and therefore sent his very best Inquisitors to these.

'I smell the odour of deceit and mockery in this system,' hissed Fetter late one night, 'and the more these Duncton moles like Brother Pumpkin declare themselves Newborn the less convinced I am. Proof is what we need, and proof is what we shall find, and when we do then the Stone shall demand resolute action.'

'My snout tells me something similar,' said Brother Law, 'and never have I known the snake to be so subtle in his twinings as in this system. We have cleansed the Library, and now we must cleanse the mole, however final we must be.' The way he pronounced 'cleanse' was like talons scratching down the face of a broken flint.

Brother Barre opened his mouth to disagree, and then slowly closed it again, his pig eyes blinking – perhaps, after all, they were right. How disappointed he would be if his judgement of Library Aide Pumpkin had been wrong, as his fellow Inquisitors were beginning to think. But if so, Brother Pumpkin would soon find death a happy release from the pains and tortures of just punishment for having made a fool of him.

Yet, despite these suspicions, the Inquisitors did not act directly on them, perhaps out of respect for Sturne, who had so long protected Pumpkin from their attentions. Instead they decided to allow Pumpkin to return to the Library, thinking no doubt that he might give himself away and confirm their suspicions. At the very least his education had now become counter-productive, and as Sturne had frequently remarked, the Library could ill afford to manage without so valuable an aide.

Not that the Inquisitors could bring themselves to announce Pumpkin's 'release' kindly. Oh no, they had to twist their talons in him one more time. One day, with no warning, he was taken forcibly from Barrow Vale and marched upslope to the Library to 'help' Sturne.

When he arrived it was not easy to separate Pumpkin from his Newborn guards, but even Newborns will weaken if offered a worm and a cosy place to eat it; awed and impressed by Sturne's chilling presence they were happy to yield Pumpkin to his care for a short time. Thus able to talk, the two old friends caught up with each other's news, their low whispers masked by the hissing wind-sounds out of the tunnels of the Ancient System nearby.

'Pumpkin, this cannot go on. You look thin and ill, and your body bears the signs of brusing buffets such as a young mole could not long withstand, let alone an old one.'

'I am beginning to wonder when it will end,' admitted Pumpkin in his mild way. 'The joke is wearing a bit thin.'

'Now listen. Inquisitors Fetter and Law do not believe you are genuine and it is now only a matter of time before that Brother Barre decides to punish you. You really must escape back upslope soon and we'll find somewhere to hide you.'

'Splendid!' muttered Pumpkin, his old spirit of irony and good humour evidently not all gone. 'What a good plan. "Escape upslope" to where I wonder?'

'The Ancient System,' said Sturne matter-of-factly. 'You can hide there as the Master did.'

'Ah!' said Pumpkin, exasperated and annoyed. Sturne did not seem to appreciate that hiding in the Ancient System was not something he relished. 'Sometimes, Sturne, you can be very *difficult*,' said Pumpkin irritably. 'Now you listen to me. Have the Newborns you know, like Brother Barre and the others, betrayed any knowledge of how many moles in Barrow Vale are resisting them?'

Sturne shook his head. His eyes were a little gentler than they had been – Pumpkin was one of the few who had ever treated him like an ordinary mole, and he did not mind being admonished by him. He knew he was stiff and formal and nomole more than he wished to know how to be what he was not.

'But, Pumpkin, I did not mean . . . I mean to say . . . You mean . . . to me . . . I mean a day does not go by . . .'

Pumpkin patted Sturne's paw and said, 'It's all right, I understand! Now . . . what about my question?'

'No, no . . . I have heard nothing about other moles. Are there such?'

'Many! So many, it makes a mole proud to be of Duncton. We are not alone, Sturne. But if you hear they are really in danger you *must* let me know. Only one of them is able to talk to me and her name is Elynor, a most worthy kind of mole, though somewhat physically overt if you know what I mean.'

'I'm not sure I do,' said Sturne, looking somewhat prudish.

'Well, anyway, for all that I recommend her to you and suggest you find a means of informing her son Cluniac who's an aide in the Library in case of likely trouble, and she will inform me.'

'I would much prefer if you would just slip away quietly and save yourself while it is possible,' said Sturne uneasily. 'But failing that I'll send any message I have to. Of course I can't make myself known to this Cluniac, and I don't even know him unless . . . ah yes, a rough-formed mole! I know him! He works in a lowly way about the Library! He would make a better warrior than aide!'

Much more than this they were not able to say. The Newborn guardmoles, their food eaten and afraid they might be judged to be failing in their duty, came busily along looking fierce and officious.

'It's the Brother Inquisitor himself, he's on his way!'

Sturne registered nothing; Pumpkin looked suitably humble.

'All well, Brother Master Librarian?' asked Fetter smoothly, the moment he arrived.

'No, not all well, Brother. The library aide seems to have taken leave of his memory and can't help me at all—'

'That's a pity,' said Fetter, cutting him short. 'You've been pleading to have him back these moleweeks past. Well, now you've got him. We've done with him what we can. His education is as thorough as it's going to be and we wish to waste no more time on him!'

'You mean, he's to return to work in the Library?'

'Exactly,' said Fetter, his eyes glittering with menace and leaving no doubt that neither he nor his fellow Inquisitors had much liking for or faith in Pumpkin, and that if he put a paw wrong it would be the end of him.

Pumpkin tried not to dance around the Library with pleasure, but Sturne succeeded in looking almost displeased.

'But I trust I may be harsh with him, Brother Inquisitor?'

'The harsher the better, I should say,' said Fetter. 'Now, can't you find some task for him, for there's much more important matters for us to discuss.'

'With pleasure,' said Sturne, turning to Pumpkin with the briefest of triumphant glances, and able, for once, to feel completely sincere. 'You had better be very careful indeed, Library Aide Pumpkin, for if you're not I'll withdraw the support I've so long given you!'

'Yes, Acting Master!' said Pumpkin eagerly, understanding perfectly well that this was a very real warning: the Inquisitors had let him come back hoping that he would give himself, and others, away. Well he would not, not ever! 'I will do the best I can, Acting Master, the very best!'

'I don't doubt it,' said Sturne with heavy sarcasm intended for Fetter, as he gave his brave friend a menial task and sent him off to get on with it.

Chapter Sixteen

The day following their interview in Evesham with Chervil, Snyde summoned Privet and the others once more and, accepting with ill grace that Weeth was now of the party, told them that the Newborn guards would shortly be leading them on the long trek to Caer Caradoc.

'It will be hard, for I understand that Senior Brother Chervil now intends to make up for the time your delay has cost us. Longest Night is not so far off when set against the distance we must travel, and I am told the weather may worsen as we climb into the hills of the Welsh borderland.'

Snyde sounded like a mole acting under the restraint of orders to be nice – indeed he looked as if he would have been glad to be rid of the lot of them – and there was little doubt whose orders he was following. He prefaced his next remark with a smile of sorts (which might easily have been mistaken for a wince of pain, for trying to be pleasant caused him great distress), and did his best to straighten himself up a bit, and look like a mole others might respect. He tried even to soften his unpleasant snouty voice.

'I must order you all, including you, Weeth, who for the purposes of the journey and our stay in Caradoc I appoint as library aide, to desist from argument, provocation, or discourtesy towards any of our hosts.'

'Hosts!' exclaimed Maple.

'Aye, hosts they are, Brother Maple. Their ways may be different from Duncton's – and I have spoken to some of them, Librarian Privet, and asked them to tone down their remarks about females. But we must respect their different views, and indeed on my journey with them I have seen nothing untoward in anything they have done, nor received anything but the greatest respect and consideration. I am not, as you know, a travelling kind of mole – the Stone made me fitter for study and scholarship than something so physical and tedious as journeying – but they have shown consideration by the easier routes they have taken, and the rests they have allowed. All this is especially due to Senior Brother Chervil and you will therefore treat him with especial respect . . .'

There was more of this from Snyde then, and in the days following, as they trekked north-west across the Vale towards hills which never seemed to get closer. They quickly discovered that Chervil and several of his Senior Brothers were no longer of their party, having set off earlier; some said he had gone ahead to Caradoc, others that he had business to attend to along the Welsh borderland which must be settled before the Convocation itself. Either way it meant a change of mood among the moles, for Chervil had left in his place as most senior Brother, the Brother Inquisitor Slane, a mole who was impossible to talk to, who surrounded himself with younger brethren, and set a rigid routine of travelling and rest, travelling and rest. The vast plain of the Vale had looked flat when they first saw it from the top of the High Wolds, and beyond it they had fancied they saw Caradoc; but it turned out very different to moles travelling across it. The soils were wetter and the ways less straight than the high, dry routes of the Wolds, and their trek soon turned into a daily slog.

Then, when they reached higher ground at the far side of the Vale, they found that after two days their route again dropped down to another Vale, that of the River Teme, whose flat and winding north-western course was wetter still as it led them slowly up into Wales, with higher territory on either side. It was the kind of ground that after a day or two none of them wanted ever to see again, and there were times when all longed to rise out of the valley to a place with views, and open skies, and earth that gave a paw support, rather than clogging its talons with damp soil and clay.

'The Newborns say that things improve after the Ludlow system,' Weeth was able to tell them, 'after which we turn to higher ground and Caer Caradoc will then not be far off.'

So Ludlow became their goal, and hopes of it kept them going day after day, as weary mole followed weary mole, and each strove to keep up with the one ahead.

During these long days they rarely saw Brother Inquisitor Slane himself, and assumed he travelled ahead or behind with another group of Newborns, perhaps because here and there along the way it was necessary to cross roaring owl ways, and stretches of marshy ground, and smaller groups were safer in such places. But nightly he would appear briefly in their chamber, and stare silently at them for a moment before asking if they had any problems, or wished to make complaints. It seemed he had strict instructions to abide by, to do with ensuring that they were comfortable – as comfortable, that is, as moles could be who were being forced to travel faster than they ever had before. But it needed courage to complain to Slane, and as it was, none of them felt any great need to do so.

Occasionally Snyde was not with them, and when they saw him again he took smug pleasure in explaining that he had travelled that day with Slane, who had wished to share his company for 'purposes of consultation'. Any notion of Snyde sharing intelligence he had gained about the Newborns with his fellow Duncton moles was not entertained at all – Snyde had never consulted any but cronies on his rise through the Duncton Library, and he was not going to start now. He seemed a mole without a single redeeming feature, except, perhaps, the fact that he showed stamina and did not complain of the rigours the speed of their journey imposed on them. In addition to his brief duty visits, they occasionally caught sight of Slane in the evening, particularly if the stopping-place chosen was in a smaller system with little chance of seclusion. On these occasions he nodded politely to them, but it was noticeable that if Privet was among those he had to pass he too betrayed the Newborns' general inclination to be ill-at-ease with females ranked higher than mere mate, or mother.

The expected deterioration in the weather occurred the nearer they approached to Ludlow, and so what they gained in the improvement in the soil as they broke free from the River Teme's floodplain, they lost in the heavy rainstorms that now began. This gloomier weather, with cloud and blustery December winds, slowed them down, and the days were growing shorter too with the inexorable approach of Longest Night. There were few incidents of note, and over the Duncton moles and Weeth there descended a fatalistic sense that for the time being they could do little but trek on, in the hope that the Stone's guidance would come when it was needed. How many more days' travel they had ahead of them the Newborns did not say, and Snyde was unable to get anything more certain than that it would be a 'good few more days yet, but certainly in time for Longest Night'. That might normally have been a comfort, but for Privet and the others the Longest Night approaching now seemed charged with fateful trial and danger for them, and for all moledom.

It was Maple, always sensitive to such things, who first noticed that as the valley narrowed and they drew nearer to Ludlow, some of the Newborn guards were growing restless and irritable, and their discipline began to break down. It was hard to say how it became evident – except that Slane showed his snout about more, and some of the younger, tougher-looking Newborns, who had until then been only at his flank, were now dispersed among the more ordinary brothers as if they expected trouble to erupt.

The brothers themselves were silent about what was apaw, but there was a sudden halt to their progress one afternoon and the Duncton moles were taken underground for their 'protection'; on the surface above there was much hurrying and scurrying, shouted orders and urgent whispered conversations in which Slane himself was involved. This unexplained stoppage went on for some time, until eventually they were allowed up to the surface again, and told they would trek on into the dusk 'to make up for lost time'.

Nothing more was said, but two days later the party veered upslope from the valley of the Teme to where the Ludlow system sits below a promontory called Rockgreen. It was not a place Privet and the others were ever likely to forget, for that night there was much movement about the tunnels they were in, more whispers, more goings-on, until when the daylight came and the Duncton moles emerged they found a system in considerable, almost festive, excitement. Slane's tough minions went about looking pleased with themselves, flexing their talons, and stopping still with studied menace to their stance.

As ever, it was Weeth who wheedled out of a Newborn what was going on, but when he came to his friends to report, his expression was anything but excited and festive.

'There's going to be a strettening,' he said grimly.

It was a word the others had heard before but could not quite place until Privet remembered with horror that it was what the Cuddesdon moles had once done to Chater when he had journeyed to that system, and it had almost been the death of him.

'Yes, that's exactly what it is,' said Weeth, 'and this is just the place to do it. They like a hill to send the victims running down, for then they cannot control their movements quite so well, and the moles they run between have a better hope of making more damaging blows.'

'Who are the victims, and what have they done?' asked Whillan.

'I don't know their names, but I'm told they absconded two days ago, and that was what the fuss was about when we had to stop and go underground. They were caught yesterday and brought back into the system last night and arraigned by Brother Inquisitor Slane at dawn. They will be strettened on the northern slopes of Rockgreen at midday.'

'But what did they abscond for?'

198

'They were trying to get to Bowdler, which lies close by Caradoc. It's where the females are kept, and no doubt they believe their mothers and siblings to be there.'

'Mothers? Siblings?'

'Where do you imagine the mothers and sisters of Newborn male pups go?' said Weeth. 'They may have further uses, and sisters grow to be potential mothers. Thripp is a *planning* kind of mole.'

'We thought they were . . . killed,' said Whillan faintly.

'Oh, did you?' said Weeth. 'Sadly the Senior Brothers are not quite so straightforward as that. They do not like to sully their paws with anything that can be clearly called killing, as you will find out with the strettening when you witness it.'

'Us?' said Maple, outraged.

'The word they like to use in such affairs is exemplary – and examples are no good if they are not witnessed and well kenned by those they are intended to warn against misdemeanour. If Chervil was here he would have the sense to keep you out of the way, but Slane is a different kind of mole, being a Brother Inquisitor pure and simple. You will be expected to attend.'

'And if we do not?'

'You will be made to. I have fortunately only witnessed two strettenings, and at one of them, when a mole refused to watch – he was not Newborn – he too was strettened and did not survive. The mood on these occasions gets unpleasant, or as the Inquisitors say complacently, "over-eager". In short, murderous. You will be ill-advised to object in any way, but there is no rule against closing your eyes – it is only a pity that we cannot close our ears as well.'

'So, Bowdler is a place . . . ?' said Whillan.

'. . . the place, rumour has it, to where mothers and sisters that are judged fit for further use are dispatched after the spring birthings in Caer Caradoc. It would not do to have such disruptive influences too near; at least, not until the male pups have been educated and taught to despise all their female kin. But some moles, it seems, harbour weak notions of seeing their mothers, if only once. Those who have been caught were two such moles.'

There was no time for further explanation because Snyde came bustling in, accompanied by several Newborns, and looking more cheerful and excited than they had ever seen him.

'You may have heard . . . ?'

'We have heard, and we do not wish to go.'

'Oh you must, you *must*,' said Snyde, his twisted head turned

199

eagerly towards Maple, and his moist thin tongue flicking out and in, 'and you will. It is for our good.'

They argued, and Snyde grew angry, but the Newborn guards impatiently cut the talking short, as if eager to get out to see the fun. They ordered them to the surface in such a way that it would have been impossible to refuse without a fight, and fighting against such numbers, on such an occasion, seemed most unwise.

'Our day will come,' said Maple through gritted teeth, as he reluctantly followed the Newborns out into the communal tunnels. Even without their guards they would have had no difficulty finding where the strettening was to be, since the tunnels were abuzz with moles, and the air was alive with that distinct and unpleasant excitement whose only name is blood-lust, born of a situation in which punishment and killing are deemed to be justified. The normal pretences were gone, and allmole was happily off to stance down that long killing route of talon-thrusting moles which the victims of the Newborn punishment must run.

Privet and the others found themselves drawn along with the crowd in a state of numbed disbelief, and after several early attempts to slip away, which the guards prevented, they settled into a blank kind of state as they went up on to the surface, and found themselves following others across the grassy slope. The hill rose high above them, far beyond where anymole went, for the main area of the punishment was lower down, and two lines of moles were already forming downslope, with laughter, ribald comment, and curious jerky taloning into the air as if practising for what was to come. Their voices were ugly, their faces more so, the eyes half smiling, half filled with a hungry desire that seemed almost sexual. Beyond, the day was grey and wintry, the sky covered in high cloud, the grass bent and battered by harsh winds.

'There's only one mite of consolation in all of this, if it helps,' whispered Weeth. 'In less busy times the two culprits might easily have not been punished here, but sent to Wildenhope which lies to the east of Caradoc and is its secret place of interrogation, torture and punishment. Here at least it will all be over quickly. But in Wildenhope . . .' He was able to say no more, but the name of the place hung grimly about them like a menacing storm.

They found themselves approaching a group of senior moles, which broke open and revealed Slane himself. He nodded at Snyde in a half-respectful, half-dutiful way, and darted a glance at Privet, and then at Whillan, Maple and Weeth.

'A punishment is due and we are here to witness it. I trust we can

200

continue with our journey tomorrow without further interruption. I do not expect further dissension among those whose duty is to stance by their vows and our customs.'

'We do not—' began Maple.

'Frankly, I care not what you think, mole. You are, so far as I am concerned, a mere traveller. If I had my way you would have been discarded before now, since the Deputy Master here, and his colleagues, have no need of your protective services.'

He turned dismissively from them and went upslope towards the top end of the line of moles. For their part Privet and the others were led downslope to an area where a good number seemed to be who, like them, were not to take part in the strettening, but had been brought as witnesses to it.

Even so, as the line shifted back and forth, more moles arrived, and the chattering continued, they found themselves uncomfortably close to where the victims must soon pass on their way downslope amongst those who had been told, or ordered, to strike powerfully at them as they went past.

'Each must make his blow,' whispered Weeth to explain what was going on, 'and those Senior Brothers scattered down the way are there to see they do. Each will be inspected afterwards, to see that they have anointed their talons with the victims' blood, for all must bear responsibility for the punishment. It is the Newborns' way.'

There was a sudden hush across the hill as the chattering stopped; moles turned, as if by some collective instinct they knew that shortly the victims must appear. Whillan was filled with horror and dismay at such communal cruelty; Maple with disgust, Weeth with pity, and Privet with the recollection of other violence she had seen, when she was a young mole living on the Moors, the like of which she had hoped never to see again.

There was a collective sigh, then an ugly hum of deep voices, as the waiting moles saw Newborn guards dragging two young males from a tunnel. They were so weak from fear or shock that they had to be supported as they went. They came near enough the Duncton group that their sweating fur, pale snouts and wild desperate eyes could be easily seen. One was gasping uncontrollably, as if each pawstep were a mighty effort; the other was crying silently.

'Be warned,' whispered Weeth, 'you must not try to interfere. If you do nomole can say what the outcome would be, for Newborns in this state cannot be easily controlled, and Slane may not wish to try. Do nothing.'

'Nothing but suffer,' whispered Whillan, his face drawn, his eyes terrible, his snout pale at the unfolding horror of it all.

The prisoners were taken upslope to where the line started and there held out for all to see. There was talk, there were announcements, even a liturgy of sorts, and lastly there was hypocrisy as Slane spoke of 'this last opportunity for the moles to win the Stone's mercy'. That would be, it seemed, if they survived; if they did not it meant that the Stone had not wished them to.

Silence suddenly fell, and stillness, and then a sound such as none of the Duncton moles had ever heard before, an ugly rasping beat across the slopes, a chant.

'Be-gin, be-gin, be-gin . . .'

All but one of the Duncton moles pulled back, wishing to turn away from this terror, this vile face of moledom, as if sensing that even to witness this shame was to be touched with collective guilt – to look was to collaborate. The exception was Snyde, who craned forward as the guards did, his face shining with desire to see what was going to happen, and his moist ugly mouth began to whisper the chant others were now thundering out: 'BE-GIN, BE-GIN, BE-GIN!'

Then they did begin; the murderous chant died away into an ugly gasping shout, and upslope of them the two lines of moles closed in; a scream was heard, as in a surging wave of paws and grunts and eagerness to be among those that made the strike, the first mole began his treacherous descent. The scream came from his companion, held back by Newborn guards and forced to watch the torture of the first as running, stumbling, taloned forward and falling he came downslope, ever nearer where the Duncton moles were gathered just behind the line.

They watched as moles' paws stamped and pressed against the ground to gain a better purchase for the thrust they were preparing to make as the wave of taloning forced the victim down towards them. Sometimes a bloodied paw was seen above the line, or the turn of a half-crushed snout, and a mouth open in agony and gasping blood. Then there he was, frozen in a moment of horror before them, his eyes half torn out, his face and body horribly mutilated, yet living still, and crying out from that agony for help, – help that nomole, no Stone, no thing could give. And the roar, the blood-lust roar of moles degraded by the desire to kill making their thrusts or, the lowest and last remnant now, still fretting to strike their blows into the ragged broken thing that was driven on towards them, near to death.

It went on by, the last struck it in its blood-sodden face, and it

202

collapsed into a final crawl of death, limbs twitching and struggling as if it sought to creep away to a safety it could never find, to a peace which, in life at least, it could never more know.

'Stone, help that mole,' whispered Privet, tears streaming down her face. Whilst beyond her, straining to get free of the guards that he might take a closer look, and hurl his maddened abuse at the broken mole, Snyde pushed, and tore, and slavered in his lust. Obscenely his excitement showed beneath his belly, between his twisted back paws. Never had he known such potent delight.

Then another roar and the chant again, as the second strettening began, and down, down the slopes towards them came that sickening frenzy of moles taloning a companion into senselessness and death. Down, down, as the sweat-streaked twisted back of Snyde, chafing at the restraint he was under, struggled to stay still, and the others watched the slow-motion descent of a second mole they could not help. This one seemed to seek to cry out, gabbled, broken words that started deep and turned to a scream, which ended as it had begun so helplessly so many moleyears before, as but a pup's cry for its mother – a mother it had so briefly known. As Privet watched the cry was silenced most cruelly by a thrust of a taloned paw into the mole's torn and gaping mouth; laughter followed, cruel and filthy and corrupt.

'Why?' whispered Whillan, 'why . . . ?' The victim went on by, slumping through the last moles in the line and into the blessed unconsciousness of death.

But the worst was not over yet, for suddenly one of the Senior Brothers nearby cried out, 'He taloned not!'

'I have blood on my paws! I did!' screamed out one of those who had stanced in the line, and had seemed to strike.

'He taloned himself to make it seem he did! Punish him, moles, in the good Stone's name!'

For a moment the accused mole stanced clear of all those about him, looking desperately around for a way of escape. Since he was facing the Duncton moles, and almost within reach, they saw his face, his wild eyes, his fear; and it was also clear that what the Senior Brother had said was true: he had a talon-thrust in his belly which he must have inflicted upon himself as one of the victims went by, hoping thereby to avoid having to strike a stretten blow. In the midst of evil then, there was still good. But its reward . . . ?

Briefly the mole looked into Maple's eyes, saw his sympathetic horror, and seemed about to appeal to him for help. Too late; the nearest of the Newborns had already raised his paw to strike his

203

erstwhile friend, and with that the blows rained on to him from one side and another so that he seemed to dance in his agony from side to side, back and forward. His fur turned red, and his body began to open, as if breaking from inside. The crowd surged round him, he tried to scream, and then was pushed or carried right in amongst where the Duncton moles stanced so deathly still, and his bloody face thrust into Privet's flank.

As she turned and reached out to him, her paws the only gentle touch offered to him on the slopes that day, Maple stanced forward and with one massive heave pushed the Newborn moles from him. Had he struck they might all have been attacked, but he only pushed, and then when others surged forward once again in anger he grasped the first one and threw him back. A circle of moles formed around him, where he stanced protectively about Privet and the stricken mole.

She whispered to the dying victim, a prayer to the Stone, the gentle Stone in whose name this foul thing had been done, and she reached out and touched his torn face, that the last thing he might remember was what, perhaps, he had never known as an adult – a female's touch. Indeed, perhaps few moles there had seen such gentleness before, for they pushed away and back, not from fear of Maple, and Weeth, who was equally angry, but from Privet's loving-kindness, that gave the lie to their self-righteous pious anger. Whilst behind, Whillan turned away, and might have wept had he not seen the last of the horrors of that dreadful day, a sight more terrible than all that he had so far seen.

For downslope of them, where the victim-moles had finally fallen dead, was Snyde, broken free at last, unnoticed by anymole but Whillan. Bent, twisted, grinning, sadistic, evil of body and of expression, he stanced powerfully over one of the dead moles, as with gasps of perverse joy he struck his now bloodied taloned paws again and again into the dead face. Yet worse Whillan saw, for Snyde stanced in a potent sickening way, his body thrusting as he struck, like a mole whose greatest pleasure was mounting death itself, and his haunches gathered blood to his excited shivering flanks as he thrust into the gaping bloody holes of the dead, and his paws rose towards the sky as he screamed out his climactic filthy ecstasy.

Then the moment was over, seen only by Whillan. Slane appeared, and the Newborns were ordered to disperse; the Duncton moles, utterly disconsolate, were taken from a scene that only Silence itself would finally obliterate from the minds of those who witnessed it; and those who, journeying in times to come, stare across the empty grassy slopes of that hill in memory of moles whose lives, and deaths, were part of a journey westward to Caer Caradoc.

Chapter Seventeen

A long, slow, and subdued line of moles left Ludlow later that day, and not one amongst them was likely to go wandering. What all had witnessed, and all shared, was exemplary enough to prevent *that*.

The cold grey weather continued, and everything made the Duncton moles morose and sad; they had nothing now to look forward to at the end of a journey that seemed to have gone on too long, and whose outcome was so uncertain. Whillan in particular was cast down, appalled by the deaths, and the final obscenity he had witnessed – or was only now beginning to believe he had witnessed, so shocking was the fact of it – of Snyde and his defilement of the corpses of the strettened moles. He travelled a little apart and in silence, answering no questions from his concerned friends, feeling himself too shamed and too tainted even to tell them what he had seen.

Then one afternoon, with Caradoc now but a day or two away, news went among the journeyers that Senior Brother Chervil was back, come to lead the moles into his father's unholy stronghold. Privet had not forgotten her wish to talk to Chervil again, and since the strettening at Ludlow her desire had been increased by a kind of angry despair at the futility and injustice of what had happened. What was a sect worth if it killed moles who disobeyed its rules from a natural desire to see mothers and sisters whose society they should never have been denied in the first place? How could such force be justified? Or such hypocrisy, which pretended that strettening was not a sentence of death at all, and it was the Stone's will if a mole survived it, or did not? These and many other questions and accusations Privet turned in her mind, and wished to put to Chervil, feeling perhaps that once they reached Caer Caradoc it was unlikely she would get a chance, and more than likely she would not see him again to talk to privately, as she might now along the way.

The following dawn she woke with a sudden start, wide awake, as moles sometimes do, with the feeling that if the dawn was a clear one she might enjoy it alone. She had cherished her moments of seclusion on the long trek across the Wolds, but since joining the Newborns there had been no chances for such privacy. In any case they were normally well watched by their 'helpers' and it was hard to get away. However, in this later stage of their journey, and especially since Ludlow, the guards seemed to have understood that they had no intention of fleeing, and had left them more alone. So it was that Privet was able to rise quietly amongst the slumbering bodies of her friends in the communal chamber, and slip up a side tunnel unchallenged and out to the surface above. The dawn was indeed as beautiful as it had felt below ground, with a clear sky, and cold air, and shining dew on the stems of the grass of the sheep pasture where they had stopped.

They had arrived as night fell and so it was only now with the dawn, as she turned and looked about, that Privet saw that the hummocky ground below gave way to a view of a winding valley, filled for the moment with slowly drifting mist. As the sun rose its light caught the mist and turned it silver and shimmery in the dawn, and here and there across it trees rose, like islands out of a gentle sea. Where Privet stanced the sun cast its weak winter rays on the rough ground about her. She moved a little way from the exit, disturbing some rabbits which bobbed upslope and out of sight. She followed them, partly to get a better view, partly to increase the pleasant sense of being alone, of renewing herself. But as she moved round the corner of a little rise of ground, out of shadow and towards the sun once more, she was astonished to see, stanced quite still and with his snout towards the rising sun as he stared down at the still, misty valley, Chervil, all alone.

Her first instinct was to retreat, not from fear of him but because she could see he was taking time alone as she was, and would not wish be disturbed – or observed. But since she was now to one side and still in shadow, and the sun was full on him, she had the advantage, and the chance to look at him in a way she never had before, so she stayed where she was, remembering too that this was perhaps the only opportunity she might have to talk with him alone, and perhaps reach into his Newborn heart in a way that would be impossible with other moles about.

He seemed a different mole out on the surface, stanced quiet, thinking about nomole-knew-what – not so commanding as when others were about; just an ordinary mole born to take an extraordinary role. He was well made, and his paws were set and firm, his fur unmarked by scars. Neat, well ordered, a little too sombre perhaps, as if he had never quite laughed out loud. A mole, it seemed, who knew his mind and accepted his destiny; yet in such a moment as this, when he thought himself unobserved, might there be a brief pause for doubt, and a fleeting wish to be a different, more ordinary mole?

Such were Privet's thoughts, and her hesitation turned to impulsive decision; feeling it wrong to intrude, whatever mole he was, she was about to move quietly away and rejoin her companions when suddenly Chervil turned absently towards her, thinking still of whatever had been behind his silent gaze across the valley. As he did so, and his look caught hers, she saw not a Newborn mole, or one in command, but a younger mole from whose face the dogma and rule of strict belief had lifted. He seemed to see her not as a member of the female gender that he had been taught to despise, but simply as a mole, a female mole, who might tell him something he did not know. Only for a moment did this vulnerable, open and almost longing look remain; then it was replaced by one of extreme dismay at having been seen as he was, and by her of all moles.

'Well?'

How self-possessed he was again, how distant – but what she had seen briefly, the mole behind the Senior Brother, was now part of her knowledge of him, and he could never deny it. The Stone had shown her the way to reach beyond Chervil's facade, and this she knew was as it wished things to be. Better than questions and evasive answers, better than playing with words; she had seen the mole behind the mask of authority, and both of them knew it. Privet stared at him and felt a power over him, and no need to reply to his second puzzled and peremptory, 'Well?'

She smiled beyond the mask, beyond the role he played, and said, 'I have come out to see the dawn rise as you have, mole, as I did sometimes when I was young, when I saw it across the Moors. I disturbed you, as your presence disturbed me, but for a moment stolen from the long trek to Caer Caradoc I will speak to you as mole should speak to mole.'

She was surprised to feel at ease, and to find herself moving towards him and talking as if she had the right to the assumption of intimacy, and that this way of being with a mole – direct, unafraid, yet not assertive – was the only proper way. Had the Stone found her so slow a pupil of life that it was only now, with a Newborn, she could be herself, and (as she guessed) only for this magical dawn moment before full day, when normal reservations to behaviour felt lifted?

He stared in silence at her, and strangely seemed more vulnerable

208

still as he opened his mouth to order her away, or to make some excuse to leave; but he said nothing and made it possible for her to continue.

'As I gazed across that valley moments ago I was wishing I was not making this trek to Caer Caradoc, but was stanced instead in some quiet place with a companionable mole in whose silence I could be at ease. I was thinking of other misty valleys I have seen and how very few are the quiet uncluttered moments in a mole's life. What were you thinking, Chervil, before you saw me here?'

'Of Duncton Wood,' he said after a moment's hesitation, 'to where, as you know, I was sent a cycle of seasons and more ago. I did not want to go; when I left I did not want to leave, least of all in the Deputy Master Snyde's company. I was discovering that I miss your system, Librarian Privet. That was all I was thinking of.'

But Privet knew there was more. 'Mole—' she began.

'Librarian Privet, you should not address me like that, and must not again.'

'But now I will, Chervil, now and for this dawn, I will. Caer Caradoc and all it means cannot be far off. I have a feeling that all our lives will change there, for Thripp, your father, and others close to him have set in motion policies which seek to alter moledom. Perhaps they are already apaw, indeed I am sure they are, but it will not be too late for us to add our wishes to them. As long as there is one mole among the Newborns with the courage to open his heart to real change there will be hope that all may follow. You must not make moles do what their hearts tell them not to. No faith is so true, no dogma so certain, no rule so right that it empowers moles to trespass into others' hearts. You need only look at those who gather around you, the Newborn brothers, and look into their blank eyes, to have to ask if such a way is right.'

'They have free choice.'

'There is no free choice for male pups torn from their siblings and mothers at birth and taught that what is right is what they are told by Senior Brothers, and what is wrong is that they should ever question it. No choice for their female siblings, segregated and forlorn, and if the rumours are true, put in the way of death.

'And speaking of death, Senior Brother Chervil, you will be aware that your Brother Inquisitor Slane permitted the public torture of two moles, and the murder of a third, but a few days ago.'

'It is unfortunate—'

'It *was* unfortunate! For three moles very unfortunate indeed!'

209

'When you have so large a force to command, rule and discipline are necessary. Mistakes will happen.'

'For moles of evil intent, perhaps, and those who wish to impose their will on others. But those whose intentions are honourable, whether one or thousands, the only discipline needed is of the spirit, and the heart and the mind.'

'You do not know of what you speak. But . . . but my father never condoned such excesses as torture, or supported such practices as strettening.'

'Yet his moles—'

'The Newborn faithful today are not his moles, or anymole's. They are the Stone's.'

'The Stone does not condone such discipline.'

'Oh, you are sure of that, are you, Privet?'

'I have kenned the texts, I know the Stone Mole's words, I know the truths in my heart, and in those of the communities in which I have lived.'

'Indeed! And so do I!'

They stared at each other, the sun growing brighter and more beautiful about them, its rays angling across the grass, the valley below all green and blue with distance.

'Librarian Privet, I have never in my life argued with a female before. It is . . . strange.'

'Think of me as a mole, Senior Brother, not a female, and you will find it easier. My heart and mind and spirit are no different from any other mole you might respect.'

A glimmer of a smile passed across his face, and it made him look younger and something nearer to the mole she had caught a brief glimpse of when he first turned and saw her there.

'Your heart and mind and spirit, Librarian Privet, are all rather stronger than in most moles I know! In fact I know only one in whom they combine to be stronger and he—'

'Your father Thripp?'

'The Elder Senior Brother Thripp, yes.' Chervil turned from her and stared across the valley. 'I said I was thinking of Duncton Wood when you caught me stanced here unawares. I was also thinking of my father. He is misunderstood by some and perhaps has not had the time he should have had to see places in moledom others take for granted. He has dedicated his whole life to moledom and wishes only for its improvement, and to advance the work that the Stone Mole began.'

'And you were thinking of this?' She had come a little closer to him, and he to her, and they stood nearly flank to flank, looking not at each other, but at the birth of a new day. There were no shadows where they looked, no dark corners. The world seemed made of light.

'I was thinking of how I will explain to him why I regretted leaving Duncton Wood.'

'Well, mole,' she said, unaware of her unconscious familiarity, 'I regret not having the time or occasion to talk with you in Duncton Wood.'

'Yes,' said Chervil, 'yes, so do I.'

'And does the Elder Senior Brother think that moles can improve on this sunshine the Stone brings?'

'Of course not.'

'And yet the Newborn Sect thinks it can improve on mothers, for they take them away, and sisters, and—'

'The Stone Mole—'

'The Stone Mole gave no sanction to such cruel stupidity!'

'You go too far!'

'I do not go far enough. Can you be sure that if I spoke thus at the Convocation of Caradoc I and my friends would live to tell the tale?' She turned and stared at him.

'No harm will come to you, whatever you may say.'

'Really? Can you promise that?'

'No harm will come to you,' he said frowning, and near to anger.

'You promise it? By the Stone? You have such control over your Brother Inquisitors?'

'No . . . harm . . . will . . . come . . . to . . . you!' Chervil was close to real anger as he said the words.

'And moledom? What of that? And innocence? And truth? And—'

'You go too far, Privet of Duncton, and you malign the genius of my father! He intends no harm to any mole!'

'I would like to see *him* stance there and promise no harm to moledom, as you promise that no harm shall befall us! It's easily said!'

'He . . . my father . . . the Elder Senior Brother could not stance here, nor look at this rising dawn, nor speak as loudly as I have done. I believe my father is dying, as he has been for a long time. Why do you think I was summoned to Caer Caradoc? You think I don't feel the hurt as he does, when moles' excess and over-eagerness threaten his great work? I feel it deeply, as he taught me to.'

Privet stared in astonishment as she heard these words, and saw the troubled lines of conflict on Chervil's face, where duty to the cause

211

struggled with desire for freedom, and the wish for privacy fought with the need to speak to a wider world, such as she now faced him with. She sensed that her moments with him were dying now, her further chances to reach into his heart fading, and perhaps this made her desperate. In his strange exposure there before her, and his confusion, she remembered a mole she had faced out on Hilbert's Top, and learned to love.

'And what did your *mother* teach you, mole?' she said sharply. 'It is a pity she probably never had the chance!'

He seemed to loom over her then and stared at her with hatred, as Rooster had loomed, though *he* had raised his great paws! He had grabbed her! Rooster had almost hurled her out of the tunnels on to the surface of Hilbert's Top, he . . . and she found that she was smiling, and she knew there was fondness and remembered love in her eyes. If her earlier question had shocked him, her laughter, gentle though it was, seemed to confuse him, and then to anger him.

'Forgive me, mole,' she said, 'I am not laughing at you but at myself. I had a memory of a mole I loved who stanced over me as you do now, who looked angry and confused as you do, and who came as near to striking me as perhaps you have just done. Please . . .' Instinctively she reached a paw out to him and touched his, and felt a surge of pity and love, of sympathy and concern, and gratitude as well. 'You have courage, Senior Brother Chervil, as the mole I loved had.'

'Courage?' he whispered, staring at her paw, and not moving his own away as he might have done.

'To dare to listen with an open heart. To allow yourself to feel. To stay and hear what you did not wish to hear. You made me a promise,' she continued with sudden fervour, 'and I shall make one to you, for I feel the Stone's Silence is in our meeting here this dawn and what we have said is not for other moles. I shall speak of this meeting to nomole, neither traditional Stone follower, nor Newborn, not ever, unless you give me permission to.'

They stared at each other in silence, each surprised at this most intimate and unexpected of contracts, yet feeling too that it had somehow been intended.

'Well, then, I must go,' she said, 'and leave you to what is left of the dawn. They say we shall be in Caer Caradoc in a few days.'

'Tomorrow, if the weather stays as fine as this. By dusk today we should see it.'

'I am sorry that your father is ill, Chervil,' she said. She meant sorry for him, not for Thripp whom she did not know, nor had any reason

212

to feel other than hatred for, considering all he had done. Except that hatred was not part of Privet's nature now, if it ever had been. They were silent a few moments more, as if neither wanted to leave the other for fear of the lives, and stresses, they must turn back to.

'He is ill because he feels he has failed,' said Chervil at last, 'and I think he wishes me to take his place. But I am . . . uncertain.'

There, it was said, what he had really been thinking of as dawn came, and as they approached the threshold of Caer Caradoc, where lives would for ever be changed. For Chevil now, between him and Privet, a portal had opened that could not again be closed.

'This is how the Stone wished it,' she said to herself in wonder. Yet their dialogue was not quite done.

'The mole you loved,' he said impulsively, 'what was his name?'

'If you had known that you might not have promised that I would be safe! But . . . his name was Rooster. Rooster of Charnel Clough.'

For a moment Chervil literally swayed, quite incredulous; then suddenly, delightfully, and as unexpectedly, he laughed, the spontaneous laughter of a real mole.

'Well! Of course! I should have known!' he said. 'And that's something I will not mention to another mole, least of all the Elder Senior Brother Thripp of Blagrove Slide! Rooster!'

Privet knew that somehow she had broken through to him, or, more accurately, she had touched some good quality in him that had allowed her to.

He opened his mouth to ask another question, and she knew in advance what it would be. She had been asked it before, many times it seemed, and each time she felt she was coming closer to an answer.

'What is a Master of the Delve, Librarian Privet? It is something that for all their learning the most scholarly of Newborn moles seem unable to explain. Even my father—'

She shook her head, and looked in the direction from which sounds of mole came.

'It would take too long, mole, to tell you now. Ask me again one day and I shall tell you.'

'Is that a promise too?'

She smiled her yes, feeling suddenly that if indeed this mole, stiff as he was, trained in narrow ways as he had been, was to take on the task that Thripp had set himself, moledom could do worse. His mind was still open, still curious. Perhaps, after all, the Stone was wiser than anymole could have guessed. She did not want to go but knew she must. There were sounds of movement nearby, and the growl of

213

guards' voices, and already the face of the Newborn was returning to Senior Brother Chervil.

'Is your father really so ill that he will not live?' She said. 'Or is it . . . ?'

'In the mind?' he whispered, guessing at her thought in his turn. He shook his head. 'The reports say it looks like wasting murrain,' he whispered. 'Few of the Senior Brothers know it because he has stayed hidden away, and why I have told you I do not know. This has been the strangest conversation of my life. But . . . yes, he is ill, and it may be of the mind for all I know. Never was there so sane a mole as he, nor one that suffered so for others.'

'Perhaps too sane?' She said. 'Too logical? Too much a genius, as I have heard him described?'

He permitted himself one last smile and as she turned to go he called after her, 'Perhaps he is!'

'Well?' said Whillan for the hundredth time, 'and what did you talk about, what did he say?'

The others had tried, especially Weeth, who prided himself on being able to extract rather more than most moles wished to give away, until finally they had deputed Whillan to the task, feeling that perhaps to her adopted son she might reveal at least a fragment of her conversation with Chervil. What made it worse, or more frustrating, was that the more they asked, the more she looked benign and pleased with herself, not like a mole nearing Caer Caradoc at all.

'No, my dear, I shall say nothing and my only regret is that Weeth saw me talking to him. Otherwise you would not have badgered me with questions as you have.'

'But—'

'No!'

So there was nothing said, however much there was to say. She had promised Chervil, and found a comfort in the fact. A comfort, and a stimulus to thought as well, in the outrage, frustration, anger, and final silence her reticence on the subject provoked.

'You look as if you're *thinking* something,' said Whillan with exasperation.

'I was, my dear. I was thinking that never in my life until this moment had I appreciated how effective being silent is. It is remarkable what it does to moles when one amongst them will not respond; or rather, I should more accurately say, responds with silence. I shall think about that more as we trek on our weary way.'

214

She was thinking of it still as dusk advanced, and they climbed westward over a ridge and saw, rising before them, the dark, enshadowed south-eastern face of Caer Caradoc: steep, high, once a holy place but now the stronghold of the Newborn sect. They went no further, but were informed that they had nearly reached Bowdler and would stay the night in communal tunnels which served Caradoc and Bowdler, and all ways north and south. Excited as they were, and apprehensive too, they slept the sleep of moles who want to forget the past for a time, and have no wish to ponder the future.

The following day they arose to the grey light of a dull dawn which cast itself across the steep face of Caer Caradoc, whose lower slopes bore patches of dead brown heather, and whose topmost part was edged by a scar of grey rock which angled very slightly up towards its northern end to form the famous Stones of Caradoc.

They journeyed but a short distance further before they dropped down into an extensive network of communal tunnels which Maple immediately saw was part of a defensive system designed to ensure that nomole could easily gain access to Caer Caradoc itself without making his presence known to watcher moles. There was indeed a military air to the place, and much movement of individuals and groups of moles, so that their arrival seemed but one of several, and of no great consequence.

Perhaps moles might have taken more heed of them had Chervil been amongst them, but once more he was nowhere to be seen and must have gone on ahead of them earlier that day, or even the night before. Brother Inquisitor Slane was again in charge, and the Duncton moles and Weeth felt themselves closely watched – being forced to pause together here, eat there, groom somewhere else, and then wait. Other moles unknown to them went back and forth, some, like themselves, travel-stained and weary, possibly delegates from other systems; others seemed more like watchers, or journeymoles bearing news and information. Certainly there was an air of movement and interchange, a sense of preparation and planning towards an imminent event in which moles such as themselves had but a small part to play, and must know their place.

Apprehensive though they were they felt a natural relief to have arrived, and a concomitant frustration when they found they were made to wait for a day and then a night and then into another day again, with no information about what was happening, or news of when they might go up to Caer Caradoc itself. All that was clear was that a great deal was going on about them, and not all of it to the

215

Newborns' liking, and that for the time being they must stay where they were.

Snyde was no use to anymole, for though he was allowed the privilege of going off and meeting Senior Brothers, when he came back he was unwilling to report much of what he had heard beyond the fact that 'matters are complex' and 'it is right that certain rebellious elements are taken and incarcerated until the end of the Convocation lest they disrupt things'.

Whillan himself avoided conversations with Snyde so far as he could, having come to detest the little mole since Ludlow; Maple too, who perhaps guessed something of what had happened, barely concealed his contempt. It was left to Weeth to find out what he could, but even he was unable to get information, and he reported that the Newborns who had formerly talked to him willingly enough had either been moved on, or were suddenly unwilling to say anything at all.

'Something serious is apaw, that's all I know.'

As the hours passed Maple grew increasingly uneasy, and growled that he did not like things one little bit, and that they had made themselves defenceless and vulnerable, and with hindsight should not have allowed themselves to be trapped in tunnels that did not even seem to have a name.

'The sooner we're up on top amongst other delegates to this supposed Convocation the happier I shall be,' he said.

The hours passed by, and the sense of events continuing without them increased until, sometime near dusk of the second day, a Newborn guard they had not seen before appeared. It was at a time when Snyde was out of the chamber.

'Sister Privet?' he called out from the portal, 'will you come with me, please?'

'What for?' said Maple protectively.

'Talks about talks,' said the Newborn brother in a reasonable and reassuring way.

'I'll come along with her then,' said Maple suspiciously.

The Newborn nodded as if to say yes, and then said, 'I quite understand your concern, but it might be more politic if the mole Weeth accompanied her. Which one is he?'

Weeth raised a paw in an exaggerated way. 'That's me,' he said.

'It's all right, Maple,' said Privet. 'If the Stone does not protect me I am sure Weeth will.' Then addressing the brother she asked, 'How long will we be gone?'

216

'As long as it takes,' he replied, moving to one side to let her and Weeth pass by before Maple could raise any further objection.

'But Privet . . .' called Maple after her.

She turned and gazed at him, and then at Whillan, and said, 'I shall come to no harm and nor shall you. The Stone is with us all in this.'

Then Privet was gone, and Weeth after her, and Maple could only look at Whillan and say, 'You know what that sounded like?'

'It sounded like goodbye. But it also sounded as if Privet *knew* she was safe to go with the mole.'

'Which can only mean that Chervil made some kind of promise to her which she could not reveal. I *hope* it means that, because if it doesn't then when Snyde shows his pointed little snout in here again I shall . . .'

Whillan grinned and said, 'If you don't, Maple, I shall do it for you!'

Maple's fears were more than justified. Only a short while after their two friends had been so quietly, and so expertly, separated from them, four large Newborns appeared in their chamber. For one grim moment Maple and Whillan thought their time had come, and squared up to the sudden threat, ready to make a final stance against what seemed their murderers. But they lowered their paws and felt rather silly when one of the guards simply said, 'Time is short and it is better that you come with us now.'

Naturally they protested, asking where Privet was, and Weeth, but the best they could get – and it was plain they were powerless to get more – was the assurance that the Deputy Master Snyde was waiting for them up on Caer Caradoc, and there all would be explained.

'Divide and rule, divide and rule!' growled Maple, going with the guards with great reluctance. 'That's what they're doing! I should have known better.'

'And if you had,' observed Whillan, 'is there anything you would have done differently?'

Maple frowned, and stomped along the tunnel pondering the point.

'Never come in the first place!' was all he could say.

But divide and rule it really seemed to be. For at about the time that Maple and Whillan were being led up towards Caer Caradoc at last, Privet and Weeth found themselves ending what had seemed a long journey through confusing tunnels.

More than once they had asked the Newborn brother where they were going, but his only reply had been, 'To a place of safety.'

'I thought we were to have talks about talks.'

217

'Where you're going, mole, you can talk in safety for as long as you like, and without annoying anymole or causing difficulty until the Convocation's over.'

Soon after this they arrived at a chamber which seemed to be a staging-point. It was wide and echoed with the voices of moles from several directions, and had at least three portals leading off into other tunnels, apart from the one they had come down. By one of them were three hefty Newborn guards of the dimmer sort, who stanced up and looked interested the moment they set eyes on Weeth.

'Ah!' said Weeth in a failing voice, 'not good! I do believe that I am to be confined. Oh dear, oh dear, Maple will be annoyed with me.'

At another portal were moles who, in some ways, were more surprising and intimidating than the guards. For one thing they were female, the first Privet had ever seen in Newborn tunnels, except those servile moles she remembered from Blagrove Slide. For another, their faces were chillsome and stony of expression; they looked like moles out of whom all happiness, all feeling, all life, had long since been sucked.

'That is my destination, I think,' said Privet, reaching a paw to Weeth. 'We had best wish each other luck.'

'Privet, you sound to me like a mole who half expected something like this to happen.'

Privet said nothing.

'You also seem like a mole who is quietly confident.'

'I have been given pause to think,' she said.

'By Chervil?' asked Weeth perspicaciously. She did not reply.

'So,' he continued, 'separated like this, what are we all to do? Tell me that, wise mole of Duncton Wood. And tell it quick, because I feel the heavy grip of the Newborn guards descending.'

'We shall each of us do what you yourself most often advocate, Weeth, though we may not do it quite as well as you. We shall take our opportunities!'

'Ha! There it is again, the Duncton sense of humour! I tell you, Privet, it will be the death of the Newborn sect, a scourge it cannot possibly survive.'

'I hope so,' said Privet with a smile. 'I shall pray that it is, as I shall pray for you. Every day for you, Weeth, for you give us heart!'

'Thank you,' said Weeth graciously and as if it was his due, waving one last time at Privet as each was surrounded by their respective guards and led off to 'a place of safety'.

'Where's *she* being taken?' asked the irrepressible Weeth.

'Where all females round Caradoc have to stay,' was the reply – a reassuring one, as it seemed to Weeth, for it meant she would not be summarily 'disappeared' and, if there was only one such place, it would be the easier to find.

'Ah, the joys of opportunity!' he said cheerfully to himself as the tunnel grew darker and danker, and here and there they passed guards who looked somewhat permanent.

'A place of confinement is simply an opportunity to escape! A place where a mole is kept? An opportunity to think those thoughts he has been too lazy to think before! A place of gloom and doom? An opportunity to—'

But Weeth was not given a chance to say what such a place might offer as he was told to be quiet and was hurried, protesting, along more dank tunnels until ahead, beyond a group of bored-looking guards in a wide well-lit chamber, he saw a narrow way bordered by boulders. Beyond it, gloomily lit by fissures in its high roof, stretched a chamber in which a large group of moles was confined.

'Ah!' said Weeth, 'a cell. Let us, even as we enter in, remember to practise what we preach and look for opportunity.' He glanced quickly around as he was hurried on, to take in what salient features he could of a place through which, he hoped, he might come back in something of a hurry. He was roughly gripped by the paw, and another shoved him firmly at the rump and he found himself struggling and scrabbling through the narrow way until he was clear of it, stancing up, and facing his fellow prisoners.

It was hard to make them out at first in the murky place, but there were a good few; all large, and all staring at him. Weeth grinned, and being a positive mole, advanced towards them; typically, he did not hesitate to choose the largest and ugliest to address first. There is nothing like being bold and resolute in the face of danger.

He stared up at the mole, who regarded him from deep-set eyes in a huge and furrowed head hanging from massive shoulders. Weeth eyed him as cheerfully as he could, taking in his face, his muscular body and his massive, misshapen paws.

'And whatmole are you?' asked Weeth pleasantly.

'Named Rooster,' growled the mole.

Weeth's eyes widened, his heart-rate increased, his breathing grew more rapid.

'Rooster?' he rasped. 'The one from the Moors? *That* Rooster?'

Rooster nodded slowly, staring at the strange, grinning, excitable mole. 'And you?' he asked.

'Me?' said Weeth faintly, '*Me?*'

'You.'

Rooster loomed closer still, like a great rugged rock that threatens to crush a mole. But Weeth had already recovered his composure and his wits.

'I am Weeth, and I want you to know, Rooster, and your friends too, that I have a tingling sensation which tells me that I am the mole you may have been looking for since the Newborns shoved you into this place of temporary confinement.'

A weary smile cracked Rooster's face. 'Go on,' he said.

'Oh! I will, yes, I will,' began Weeth, feeling suddenly that never had the Stone been as obliging to him as this: to put him in so right a place, at so opportune a time.

Chapter Eighteen

Devastated though Fieldfare had been to see Chater set off on a dangerous journey from which there was no promise of a return, she felt that what he did was right, and she must make the best of things, just as she always had. But it was not in Duncton she was left behind this time, but in the middle of a dangerous situation, in which moles looked to her for guidance and support though not for actual leadership – *that* task she willingly left to Spurling, who had the snout for it. But none among their number doubted that it was Fieldfare's spirit and sense of what was right that would keep them going and help them reach safety, as much as Spurling's quieter skills of leadership, and commonsense decision-making about matters of rest, the disposition of their little force, and route-finding.

All of them sensed her deep despair and concern at losing Chater to the greater cause of warning Privet and the others of all that Spurling had told them the Newborns intended, but perhaps only Peach understood something more: that this time Fieldfare felt in her heart that she might never see Chater again.

'It *is* different from our separations before,' confided Fieldfare, 'almost as if the Stone wants to prepare me for the fact that he is gone and I will not see him again. But I feel it was meant to be, and that the Stone gave us this last time of journeying through beautiful places, time to love, to make love, as if it knew I would store them up in my heart against the wintry day when my love would be no more with me. Well, now that day's come, and I'm sad, Peach, I'm terribly sad, because he's gone where I can't help him, or be with him to comfort him. I know he's strong, and I know he's doing what he does best, but it's hard to accept I can't be with him.'

'Yet you can take comfort from knowing that what you've had is more than most moles ever have,' said Peach. 'You've had true love and true companionship, a mole at your flank whom you respect, and who respects you.'

'You understand, Peach, because you've got the same,' said Fieldfare tearfully, 'and I'm glad for you, and grateful a mole like you is here to comfort me, just as Chater would have done.'

The two nodded and smiled at their happy memories, and spoke for some time more upon the subject of love and relationships, agreeing that moles who have never had them don't know what they're missing, and those that do had better not be too complacent, since life can change quite suddenly, and they had better enjoy what they have to the full while they may.

With this and other generalities of love discussed and agreed, Fieldfare felt much better and was ready to turn her mind to the task in paw, in the hope that her fears for Chater were groundless and Peach's belief that he would come back sooner than they expected was right. Other moles needed her now, and it was her task to help Spurling get those who had entrusted their lives to their care up to the sanctuary of Uffington Hill.

The nearer they got to Uffington the more they came to rely on Noakes, who was younger and fitter than most of them, and knew the ground and the likely danger-points. For there were cross-unders beneath certain roaring owl ways, and two-foot ways over rivers and streams which they had to take, where Noakes suspected Newborn spies might lurk, watching for movement to report. Moles seeking dominance like nothing less than freedom of movement in those they wish to dominate.

So whilst Spurling and Fieldfare continued to lead the group in spirit it was the chirpy Noakes who did the route-finding, and had the energy and courage to go forward or back to make what reconnaissance was necessary. If, as happened increasingly as they approached his home system of Gurney, he spied Newborns, he had the common sense not to panic, but to creep back and warn the others to go some other way. Meanwhile Peach saw to it that Fieldfare's abilities in giving comfort and simple healing remedies were put to full use amongst the more feeble of their group, perhaps as much to keep Fieldfare's mind off Chater as to keep her friends going.

All in all, however, their progress was slow, and the good weather which had prevailed before Fieldfare had come to Fyfield had now gone; winter came, and with it the kind of wet and miserable weather which did not much encourage moles, especially old ones, to wander on in search of a home. They continued to travel by night when they could, stopping over during the day unless they were sure that the way ahead was really safe. It was during these long waits for the cover of darkness that Fieldfare found good use for her knowledge of

Duncton Wood and its simple time-proven rituals, for the others asked her to tell them all she knew of the system that to them seemed a dream, or a myth of great days gone by.

Then too she told them the old tales she knew, of the days of Bracken and Rebecca, and Tryfan and beloved Mayweed. The stories of these moles, whose paws at different times had trodden the ways to Uffington, gave comfort to the refugees, and stirred them on so that they saw Uffington more and more as a worthy destination, and one which might give good succour to moles who regarded themselves as pilgrims on a long and difficult trek. Through all of this, as Peach recognized most of all, Fieldfare began to change and take on a new identity – or, more accurately, to shed an old one. She gained confidence in her own worth, she found that moles in general, rather than just the pups and friends she had always liked to look after, had need of her, and not only her physical help. She discovered that special confidence that comes from the discovery that she had things in her mind – wisdom, knowledge, insights, tales – which others wanted to hear.

This state of affairs was somewhat reinforced by the surprising fact that along the way the group was joined by no less than four vagrants – a pair and two single moles – who were refugees from the Newborns like themselves, and were seeking a safe haven. These moles quickly found that though Spurling was the leader, and Peach his mate, it was Fieldfare who increasingly with her warmth, her good nature, her common sense, and her matter-of-fact coping with the many problems that arose, embodied best the spirit of the group, and gave it cohesion and a sense of purposeful mission.

Soon after they had successfully by-passed Gurney, the looming presence of Uffington Hill made itself plain to the south-east. From a distance it was no more than a dark ridge that defined a vale, but closer to, this once most holy of places was seen more clearly for what it was, a steep escarpment of chalk, covered by tough sheep-shorn grass, which rose up to an edge so precipitous and high that a mole had to tilt his head back awkwardly to observe its top. Seeing it at dawn, when the sun rises behind it, not only must a mole bend his head back to fix his gaze properly on its high ridge, but he must squint as well, against the vast brightening sky. But in the evening, when the light comes from the west, Uffington is more easily seen, and the scars that mark the places where the underlying chalk shows through shine out white against the dull winter grass.

The final approach was near to where Noakes had once been caught, and they went most cautiously, slinking in the shadows of the night, keeping low lest the gazes of the roaring owls which are prevalent in those parts should sweep across and show them up as they made their passage over open ground.

Spurling was much concerned about the last part of their trek, the climb up the escarpment itself. Decades before great Tryfan of Duncton had come this way, in the company of a holy mole, and the two had succeeded in making the climb in daytime. But their account, which Fieldfare knew well, spoke of the dangers of rooks and kestrels, which use the rising winds there to prey on creatures like mice and voles that live and burrow among the grass. At night these dangers might be less, though tawny owls could always strike, but such a weak disparate group as they were might easily get separated and lost across the hill, leaving them much exposed if they were overtaken by dawn. Noakes had faced the self-same problem and had chosen to travel in daylight, and blamed his capture on that decision.

In the end Spurling decided on a compromise, which was to set off in late afternoon and gain as much advantage as they could from failing light before they faced the trials of darkness. After that they would have most of the night to climb slowly on, and time enough to ensure that the pace of the group was that of the slower ones, so that all kept close together.

'We'll wait for a day that promises a clear night so that the stars and moon can help us see each other,' decided Spurling finally, and two days later it came.

They started in late afternoon as planned, and to Noakes the biggest danger-point was soon after they started, when they had to cross the roaring owl way that runs along the bottom edge of the scarp, for apart from the dangers of roaring owls he believed it was here that he had been seen by watchers on his previous visit. But they crossed the way safely, and nor was there any challenge later when they started to climb up through the tussocky grass; nor even after that when, with much labour and shortage of breath they ascended still higher into a night of stars and a bright moon, already waxing towards Longest Night.

They had taken a sighting on the upright of a wire fence which stretched tight and barbed across their route, its bottom strand so low that they had to duck under it as they went by. There was the smell of sheep about, though they had seen none, and the barbs of the wires had caught some of the sheep's rough white hairs. Beyond this the grass was shorter, the slope steepened and the going became harder, especially for the old moles who found it difficult even to keep their balance, let alone climb. When they looked back they saw far below them, beyond the fence, the silvery line of the roaring owl way caught in the moon's light, along which, their yellow gazes reaching ahead, roaring owls occasionally passed.

But most of the moles preferred not to look back down at all, but to struggle slowly on up the benighted hill as Spurling and Peach, Noakes and Fieldfare urged them on, that they might reach the prow of Uffington before dawn came, and find a place to hide where the Newborns might leave them well alone.

'Halt! You! Halt there!'

The shouts were male and commanding, and came from some way across the hill. Newborns!

'We could make a dash for it,' said Noakes immediately, realizing that watchers must be posted on these slopes and have seen them.

'Some of us might get away,' said Spurling, 'but some would not.'

'There's more of us than of them, I suspect, so we'll just have to face it out!' said Fieldfare stoutly, thinking to herself that was what Chater would have done. Journeymoles often have to brazen things out, he always used to tell her, so they would do that now.

They did not have to wait long before two Newborn moles appeared out of the darkness slightly below them; big, young, confident. Perhaps they felt so because the group of refugees *had* stopped as ordered, and were clustering uncertainly, as best they could on the difficult sloping ground.

It is often at such moments of crisis that moles discover they have cool heads and strong talons they never dreamed they possessed, and Noakes discovered it now. Realizing that the two Newborns were at a disadvantage so long as they were on the slope below he moved forward towards them and cried out, 'What do you want with us?' so firmly that the Newborns stopped short.

This gave the refugees heart, and they gathered more resolutely together; bright though the moonlight was, the Newborns perhaps could not quite see how frail some of them were. Even so they advanced warily upwards and one of them asked which mole was the leader.

Spurling boldly came forward and said he was, but what business was it of theirs anyway . . . and it was then that the Newborns, perhaps used to such confrontations, rushed up the slope together and grabbed Spurling, saying, 'We're taking him to a Senior Brother down below. If you lot move from here he'll die a painful death.'

225

Even as they said this they began to haul Spurling downslope, hoping no doubt that the group would not react quickly enough to prevent them getting away below towards Newborn reinforcements.

But Noakes, having gained enough time a moment before for the group to form itself, now responded yet more effectively.

'You're not taking him!' he cried, and aimed a powerful kick at the lower of the two Newborns, catching him painfully in the snout. There was a cry and curse, and a moment's teetering struggle before Field-fare, inspired by Noakes' example, leaned forward and herself buffeted the Newborn in the face, pushing him finally off balance and causing him to fall backwards down the slope.

To his credit, the other Newborn kept hold of Spurling and in his turn strove to push him downslope, at which he might have succeeded had not the redoubtable Noakes, by now emboldened by anger, come determinedly forward and sought to wrest Spurling from the New-born's grip. But the mole was young and strong, and vicious too, for he talon-thrust poor Spurling in the stomach and pushed Noakes to one side, so that the brave mole was sent plunging helplessly downslope after the first Newborn.

To the others, watching in horror as this violent confrontation unfolded, the moonlit scene seemed almost unreal, and for a few moments more not one of them moved. But then Spurling let out a cry of pain as the Newborn talon-thrust at him to make him more biddable, and out of the murk below into which Noakes and the first Newborn had disappeared, worse sounds came, of a mole in agony, a mole screaming suddenly into death. Fieldfare and Peach, the protec-tive instinct in them aroused, rushed down to where Spurling was struggling, and threw their talons and their female wrath into the face of the Newborn. At first he almost seemed to laugh, but that only provoked them more, and they lunged at him, and grabbed him, and all four, for Spurling was now fighting as well, began a wild, struggling, shouting, violent descent of the slope as the Newborn, realizing he was out-taloned, tried to get away to his colleague below and re-group.

Pushing, shoving, he succeeded at last in holding them at bay, then turned and fled down the slope – straight into the treacherously sharp barbs of the tight-stretched wires. With a scream of pain he struggled to extricate himself from this unexpected and entangling hazard, pull-ing himself off and back a little way up the slope, unable to go higher, because there the others now stanced still, yet unable to go down until he saw a way through.

It was at this moment of sudden pause that he, Fieldfare and the

226

others who had all tumbled down together saw the reason for the grim sound they had heard earlier. For there, stanced still and staring, was Noakes, and what he stared at was the first Newborn, who had rolled down the slope after Spurling had buffeted him, and fallen violently into the barbs, from which he hung now by his tender snout, emitting a gurgling, suffocating sound of death, as he drowned in the blood that the sharp barbs caused to flow down his snout and into his throat, and on into his lungs.

Panic overtook the second Newborn and in a sudden burst of energy, he turned from the horrors of his dying colleague and the watching moles above, to try once more to find a way under the wire and escape to his friends below. Which he might well have done had not Noakes, seeing his intention, suddenly and most violently lunged at him and taloned him without word or warning straight in his wild fearful eyes. Worse; Noakes followed it with two more talon-thrusts, hard and bloody, so that the bigger mole turned with a gasping cry and fell once more into the barbed wire which had so fatally prevented him fleeing to freedom. This time it was the stretch of higher wire that caught his desperately flailing paws and suddenly he was lifted off the ground, swinging in the night air; then after a final paroxysm of struggle, he was still, and the moonlight caught the swinging of his body, back and forth, back and forth.

Noakes stared horrified at the violence he had committed and the others stared with him at the two dead moles who hung, still and silent now, on either side of him.

'If he had got away downslope,' whispered Noakes, staring at his bloody paws and then in horror and disbelief at the Newborn he had killed, 'he would have told others we were here, and they would have come . . . I did it to stop him. Somemole had to . . .'

Fieldfare was winded and shaken by the buffeting she had suffered, and Peach was exhausted, so it was Spurling who rapidly took charge once more.

'There is nothing we can do for these moles,' he said. 'We will go back upslope and continue to climb up to Uffington Hill, and then we will find a safe place to hide. I do not like violence . . . but we *were* attacked, and but for Noakes and Fieldfare one or more of us might now be in the paws of the Newborns, and the rest uncertain what to do and likely to be taken prisoner before long. As it is we may yet escape undetected, for dead moles tell no tales.'

They turned from the grim moonlit spectacle, returned to their companions, and in silence and with a strange almost ferocious energy climbed on up through the night, so that as they clambered at last over the final gentler slopes, and faced the eastern horizon, they saw that dawn was already beginning to reach its talons to the sky.

Nor did Spurling let them dawdle once the party was all collected, and they had gained their breath. He had already instructed the fitter moles to gather food for the slower ones, and they ate it quickly, from hunger and a desire not to stay where they were for long, and then stanced up once more, ready to leave.

The presence of Newborns so high up made Spurling suspect that Noakes' belief that the Newborns stayed clear of the Hill might not be true any longer, a suspicion confirmed by a quick examination of some of the tunnels they found. In former days, they knew, the system of Uffington had been extensive and most splendidly delved, but most of what they found was ruinous and open to the sky. Here and there the beginnings of ancient arches survived, and a few tunnels stretched away, their roofs still intact. But there was sign and scent of recent unknown and unseen mole about, and with that, and no promise of good cover or ways of escape, it was plain that so large a group as theirs would be conspicuous and it would be unwise to linger.

To the west the escarpment stretched into a ridgeway of lingering darkness, while southward its dip-slope went gently down across fields, amongst hedgerows, to dry valleys in which copses nestled.

But it was to the east that Noakes turned. '*That* way,' he said, 'lies the Blowing Stone, if I'm not mistaken; it has always been a place of sanctuary.'

'Aye!' said several of the moles, who remembered hearing of it in tales of the old days, and whose imaginations, when they were pups, had been stirred by tales of how the strange fissures and contours in its sides caught the wind, and sounded a deep roaring note – once as a warning, twice for guidance, three times for sanctuary.

'Aye, and "seven times and moles shall rise and know their way"!' said one of them, quoting an old legend of those parts.

But the air was still, and there was no chance the Blowing Stone would sound now, not in warning, nor to guide or offer sanctuary.

'We could go along the ridgeway to the place where once the Silent Burrows were . . .' mused Spurling.

'But we're not sure how to find them, or even if they're still there,' said Peach.

But Fieldfare had been staring steadily to the south-east, and watching how the strengthening dawn lit up the graceful curving vales which seemed to invite a mole to follow them.

228

'Seven Barrows is down that way,' she said, 'and according to old Duncton legends that was where good Mayweed, greatest route-finder that ever lived, found his way to Silence. I feel that it is a place where we could go and find safety, and as a Duncton mole I would like to pay homage to my forebear.'

As she spoke she felt a strange, sweet surge of certainty that it was the place to which they must go, and she went a little forward of the group and stared ahead, suddenly excited.

'This is the way Chater would have led us if he were here, for he is a journeymole and always said that Seven Barrows with its mysterious Stones was the place in moledom to which he most wanted to go. Oh, Chater . . .' she whispered, and longed for his affectionate presence, his good humour, his growling impatience with her at times, his love; 'you *want* me to go that way.'

But if he was not there, the Stone seemed to be, for from over the dark high pastures to the east came a haunting note carried on the wind; and then another. Deep and sonorous, mysterious, and if not quite frightening, then enough to awe the troubled moles.

'The Blowing Stone!' whispered Fieldfare. 'That's what that must be. It sounds when . . . when it needs to, when followers need to hear it. In the wind . . .'

'There isn't much wind now!' said Spurling softly.

'No,' said Fieldfare, 'but we may be guided by its sounding. In all the old legends of this place, when the Blowing Stone sounds then moles should be alert. Oh, Spurling, we must go to Seven Barrows. I'm sure of it now . . .'

'Then it's the way we'll go!' said Spurling, going to Fieldfare's flank and nudging her affectionately. 'We'll find sanctuary among the Stones of Seven Barrows, and the time to decide what we should do next.'

So off into the dawn they wearily went, wending their way from the summit of Uffington Hill, and leaving behind its ruined tunnels, forgotten and unvisited ways, and wild historic surface. Only when they were gone did the winter day rise, and what little touch of cold breeze there was turned and wound, swirled and fell, to find its way down the steep slope they had climbed, to linger for a time where barbed wire stretched and two moles dangled dead. Above them two black rooks circled, eyes sharp, beaks eager, before they dived at the carrion, to remove all evidence that violence, of a kind that might soon come across all moledom, had visited that desolate place the night before.

*

229

It was a mob of rooks too, turning and diving at something on the flanks of Rockgreen Hill above Ludlow, which caused Chater to deviate from his route to investigate, and so be caught right near the end of what many have described as one of the swiftest treks any journeymole ever made.

How far he had travelled, and how fast, following after Privet and the others into the Wolds in his desperate effort to catch them before they reached Caer Caradoc, and warn them of what he knew. By the time he reached Bourton he had begun to tire, but there Stow gave him news of his friends, and he in turn reported all that Spurling had told him.

'Tell Maple when you find him,' said Stow, 'that already moles have begun to gather across the Wolds in expectation that they will have to do their duty and stance their ground against the Newborn threat. If he needs us we will not fail him, and if he wishes us to follow him we shall do so!'

Thus encouraged Chater had journeyed on night and day, night and day and night, snatching sleep only briefly here and there. Once he had dropped down into the Vale of Evesham he had gone yet faster, up the valley of the Teme in the pawsteps of his friends, picking up information along the way which told him he was gaining on them rapidly. Then on he had gone, ever faster, fooling two parties of Newborns he encountered, and gaining useful news from them too.

But at Ludlow he had grown tired, and careless, and when he saw the rooks he went over towards where they preyed, thinking that there he might find moles to give him information. He found moles all right, dead ones, the same indeed that had been strettened days before by the Newborns, torn to pieces now and scattered over the field; the remnant of a head sunk in a pool of water, and fur caught in the basal stem of a withered old thistle plant. It was there he was caught, there questioned, and might have been killed had he not been forced back on to the tale he had always planned to tell if all else failed.

'I'm part of the Duncton delegation to Caer Caradoc,' he said, rightly suspecting that no Newborn would dare harm him if that were true, not then anyway.

A Brother Inquisitor was found, one going that day Caer Caradoc way, and his story seeming at least plausible, Chater was taken along by Newborn guards, once more at a fast pace since the Brother was anxious to get to Caradoc before Longest Night. The only part of his story that was not believed was how recently he claimed to have left the area of Uffington – 'not possible,' he was told, 'nomole could travel that far that fast.' When they neared Caer Caradoc Chater was detained as his friends had been before him, without explanation or interrogation. That was, it seemed, the Inquisitors' way – detention and uncertainly soften up a mole.

At last a Newborn came who said, 'You're to come with me.'

'Where to?'

'Ours is not to reason why,' said the guard, going on ahead of him, and though Chater was not one to follow another meekly and without questioning, it was hard not to in a tunnel when two were prodding him along from behind with sharp talons.

'Just asked,' said Chater, thinking to himself that this was beginning to have the feel of as bad a situation as any he had got himself into in all his long days as a journeymole. Just then he felt, inexplicably yet powerfully, the presence of Fieldfare with him, urging him on, giving him support, praying for him, and he followed on down the dark tunnels with the Newborn guards determined that to the end he would try to do his duty to his friends, and to his faith.

'At least I've told Stow of Bourton what I know,' he consoled himself, 'but by the Stone I would have liked an opportunity to warn Privet, Maple and Whillan . . .'

The tunnels seemed suddenly dark indeed.

It is reasonable to think from such evidence as we have that it was on that same day, at that same time, that Fieldfare found herself alone out on the surface of Seven Barrows, staring over the rough grass towards the Stones that rise so mysteriously there. The weeks had passed since her escape with Spurling, Peach and the others up Uffington Hill, and without further incident they had made their way to Seven Barrows, and found it safe, quite free of Newborn mole.

What was more there had been a few more vagrants about who had joined their number, and they had formed a little community, and in their rough and ready way, under Spurling's sensible guidance, created a system of simple interlocking tunnels and places for watchers to stance unnoticed by any alien moles that came nearby, such that only a force of mole, deliberately looking for them, would have found them out.

They had decided to over-winter where they were, and then, when spring came and travelling was safe once more, to send out a few of their number – Noakes early on volunteered to be one of them – to go and find out what was apaw in the vales below Uffington Hill, and

231

if they might yet dare venture back to Duncton Wood. It was a dream of all of them to go there, and one that would sustain them well through the hard winter years.

Meanwhile they shared their lives and memories, and, almost without realizing it, after the stress of moleyears under the paws of the Newborns, they could allow the special Silence of Seven Barrows to seep into their hearts, and shine out as a new-found peace from their wrinkled, care-worn eyes, as such a light *should* begin to shine, in the days and hours immediately before holy Longest Night.

Amongst their number Fieldfare had become quietly pre-eminent. Like the maternal mole she had always been, she was the one who knew how to care for those who needed attention; the old, the ailing, those who had lost moles they loved in spirit or in body to the Newborns and now had time to discover that there were great empty, lonely, spaces in their hearts. To these moles loving Fieldfare gave help and succour, and in truth, by doing so, as Longest Night approached she found a way to escape the aching void she felt in her heart for the mole she loved, and missed more and more.

Sometimes she came up on to the surface to be alone, to stare at the Stones that rose in the distance, among which, like all the others in their group, she never quite dared to roam. Chater himself had often told her the tale of how they were uncountable – 'a mole sees six, yet history says there are seven there, and when two moles seek to show which ones *they* saw it always seems to be a different six . . .' – and how these were Stones best stared at from a distance, for wraiths of old moles roamed there, bringing whispers of the past, and dreams of what might have been. 'Moles only go among the Stones of Seven Barrows to die,' Chater had once warned her. Well, she had no intention of going there now!

'What might have been, Chater!' she whispered aloud, her eyes shining in this pretence of talking to him. 'I miss you so much my dear, and I know that you miss me . . .' There for a time she could have in imagination what she might have had in reality, and experience what might have been, and she could shed those tears that she had always concealed from other moles, even her beloved Chater. She had mothered so many for so long that she did not even realize that the tears were for herself, a reminder that she *too* might, just once in a while, need to be cared for by somemole else. Cosseted, nurtured, attended to, pampered without reserve. Just briefly, only for a time – but sometimes!

But on the afternoon of the eve of Longest Night just such a mood suddenly gave way to something darker, and a feeling of terrible foreboding came over her. Quite unable to account for it, and feeling increasingly restless and ill at ease, Fieldfare went up to the surface to be alone for a time. Perhaps fresh air would do her good, perhaps she could stare across the stonefields of Seven Barrows and find comfort, as so often before, in the stones themselves.

The foreboding deepened, and to try to escape it she stared at the Stones and even ventured a little towards them, to try as she had before to see if there were really seven; but there were not. Just six, some near, some far, one off to one side, another to the other side, but further away, except that surely *that* one had not been there before?

'Six!' she declared finally after the third recount, smiling to herself for doing something she knew Chater would have done, and thinking fondly of how they would have fallen to arguing about which six there were, beloved, my dear, my dearest . . . my love. Oh my dear, you need me, I know you need me now . . .

Through her sudden desperate tears she saw that far across the fields beyond the last Stone rooks flocked, no more than black specks in the wintry sky. Fieldfare watched them with a sudden clutching fear, which left her breathless, in pain, and almost beside herself.

Chater needed her, not sometime, but *now*.

She tried to call out to him, to reach him, and invoked the Stone's help, at first vaguely in a general plea, but then more specifically. He needed her now, he was calling her name, and she must find a way to reach him. She looked at the Stones in the distance and in a low, intense voice, quite unlike her normal speech, she prayed to them to help her reach him.

'Now, now, now . . .'

She might have continued this strange and hopeless-seeming prayer, but that she heard a shout from some way behind, and one of the elderly watchers waved a paw and came hurrying.

'Glad *you*'re here, Fieldfare,' he gasped, all of a dither, 'there's moles approaching from the north-east.'

'Newborn?' she said quietly, calming him down. But her own heart was not calm: *Chater needed her.*

'Could be moles seeking sanctuary with us,' said the old watcher hopefully.

'Did they see you when you came running to me?'

It had been agreed that in such circumstances watchers must not show themselves.

'They might have, they gave a wave, they . . . seemed all right. I didn't think . . .'

'It's all right. Now listen, I'll go to them and draw them away from here. But you go quickly and warn the others.'

'But what if . . . ?'

'If they saw you, my dear, they'll come searching if somemole doesn't go to them. If they're Newborn, well, I'm sure it will be all right. The Stone will guide me.'

'Fieldfare, I'm frightened, I—'

'Go on, mole, you'll be safe if you go back now. Go, now . . .'

So she sent him on his way to safety, and without a thought for herself and with Chater's need pushed to the back of her mind, turned towards the north-east, climbed a rise, and saw their approach. They were big, and male, and Newborn, and too near to escape from for long.

'You, mole! YOU!' one of them shouted as he sighted her and broke into a run.

She ducked away back out of sight to gain just a moment's time, and then turned in a direction opposite to Seven Barrows and all her friends, towards the Stones.

'Oh, Chater my dear, it's I who need *you* now,' she thought, as the danger of her situation came to her and she tried her best to run.

'Too old, too plump, too . . .' and even at such a moment, with the rough grass tumbling up towards her and catching at her paws, and the sounds of the two moles reaching the rise above her and shouting, even now she managed a wry smile.

'I *told* you I was too plump, beloved, and that I ought to lose some weight, and how right I was! Oh dear, Chater, is it going to end like this with you so far away and needing me, and me so far away and needing you?'

'Mole! You there! Stop now!'

Their shouts were nearer, and so aggressive that she nearly stopped obediently. She half turned as she ran, stumbled as she reached flat ground, and saw them a little way above her: big, strong, angry.

'It'll be all the worse for you when we catch you, mole!' The voice was harsh, mocking, vindictive.

But then suddenly, and not for the first time that day, the Blowing Stone sounded, not as loudly as Fieldfare had grown used to, but loud enough to frighten the Newborns who were afraid of such things. The guardmole hesitated and, taking her opportunity, Fieldfare pushed herself on towards the first of the stones, recovering herself as her paws crunched on to what the moles called the stonefields, where the grass thinned and old fragments and shards of flint and hard chalk lay across the ground. Even on a dark day splinters of crystalline rock glinted and glistened across those fields. It was here that the Stillstones, which complemented the Books of Moledom, had been found.

But such thoughts were far from Fieldfare's mind now as she felt her chest tighten, and her breath begin to grow short and desperate, her limbs heavier by the moment. The moles were almost on her now, their paws crunching over the stones, their panting powerful and angry, and ahead the first of the Stones seemed to now recede from her.

'Oh Chater, I can't reach the Stone, I can't go on, I . . .'

'Beloved, you never give up when you're being chased, never!' she had often heard him say when he described the adventures of a journey, and the dangers. 'You'd be surprised how often something turns up just when you're giving up all hope. No, no, never give up!'

'But I can't, Chater, I just . . .'

'Mole! Stop right there!' a Newborn roared from behind her, and she felt his talons clutching at her left flank and ripping her skin, as gasping, breathless, tired, and near defeat, she tried to run a few more steps, two more, one more . . .

'Got you! Bitch!'

The mole's paws held her, tumbled her, and then the two of them were over her, angry, breathing heavily, mocking.

'Runs fast for a fat mole!'

'Would have been better if she hadn't run at all!'

She stanced up and faced them. She looked to her right and saw the Stone. It was so near, so near.

One Newborn followed her glance and then looked quickly away, frowning and angry.

'Get away from there! Go back this way!'

She did not move, eyeing them warily as she realized with surprise that they were afraid of the Stone. Of course, Newborns were!

'Don't try it, mole!' said the other, reaching out towards her.

'Chater!' she called out, as if he could hear. Oh, she needed him now, for the Newborns had her and they were moving round to block her from running to the Stone's sanctuary.

'Plump Madam! Boldness is needed!'

Plump Madam?

She looked around in surprise. There was nomole here but these two, waiting for her to move and eyeing the Stone uneasily. Plump Madam? Whatmole spoke like that?

'Humbleness, who knows something about finding routes, suggests you concentrate on the task in paw! Be bold I say, be brave!'

She looked around wildly and then she saw him by the Stone, in its shadows, grinning in a friendly way, his fur patchy.

'Yes, yes, fair one, Fieldfare! It is I, invoked. I, summoned up. I, lingering in shadows, sliding in and out of Silence, by this Stone.'

'Mole,' growled one of the Newborns, coming no closer, his voice betraying his unease about the holy place they were in, 'you better come with us now, or else.'

'He sounds unsure of himself!' thought Fieldfare in amazement. How could anymole be frightened of the Stone? Even if, in its shadows, moving, grinning, disappearing, speaking, a mole so familiar to her, so much loved by her, whose name she could just now not remember, was beckoning her.

'Fat Fieldfare, be bold, and come to me. I cannot come to thee! Come, come, come . . .'

Then Fieldfare felt the fragments of the stones at her paws, and saw the light of the day upon the Stone, and knew that if she turned towards it, it would shine upon her face and guide her, help her be brave, teach her to be bold.

'Mole!' cried the Newborn, his voice strangely desperate.

But she ignored him, and with the light full upon her, and the grinning, patchy, marvellous mole dancing with glee in the shadows and beckoning, she advanced towards the Stone.

The Newborns shrank away from her, their faces full of fear as if she was contaminated, which she supposed she was – by the Stone, and her own faith in it, and . . . well, by the mole who seemed to be summoning her to his phantom flank.

'That's right, plumpness, fat one, comely Fieldfare, you show them! Or, as moles of the younger generation might put it, "Go for it, fattie!"'

Well, why not! If faith and the Stone's Silence were the only reality, life was an illusion and she could go right through it! And Fieldfare did, boldly, and bravely, right up to the Newborns, her eyes proud and fierce and full of a pity for them which they did not seem to wish to see.

'Madam,' said her guide in the shadows, 'what a worthy one you are! Me? Humble Mayweed! Dead as dead can be! But invoked to be your guide amongst these Stones. For a moment I thought, "Chater's beloved isn't going to make it!" but you proved humbleness wrong, which is not the first time, he is sure. Nor the last.'*

Behind her Fieldfare was dimly aware that the Newborns were retreating, shouting to each other, frightened, puzzled, and wondering where she was for she had been there, right there before their snouts.

'I'm here!' she wanted to say, 'here among the Stones.'

'Follow, Madam, for he needs your love. Me, I'm just here to see you get there. Follow!'

Yes, yes, yes she would, now, in among the shadows of the Stones whose deeps and darks, whose greys and pale shinings held the magic light of Longest Night which was so near, and here so powerful and full of joy.

'Follow, don't dally!' Mayweed called, and she smiled and followed him, or rather the shadows amongst the Stones where he seemed to run, for she had trusted the Stone, and for a time it would keep her safe.

Much later, as night fell, Noakes, disconsolate, trailed his weary way back from Uffington, and almost all the moles of Seven Barrows, led by Spurling, waited for his coming. Fieldfare had saved them all by leading the Newborns away from their tunnels, but when they went out looking for her she was nowhere to be seen.

'Let me go back towards where the Newborns were seen coming from,' the bold young Noakes had insisted. 'I'll be quicker alone, and safer too!'

Spurling let him go. They could not just let Fieldfare be taken, yet they could not risk other lives.

So Noakes had gone, and they had waited, all the joy and good spirit arising from the preparations for Longest Night on the morrow gone. Fieldfare taken! The very heart of their community had been ripped out.

Noakes knew what he was about and ran and searched across the ground, using the rises to advantage, looking ahead and hoping to catch sight of the Newborns and Fieldfare. On and on, tirelessly he ran that afternoon, knowing that time was of the essence. If he found them he might be able to help, even get her free. Why, he would give himself up to them if they would let her go! He would!

Then he had seen them, two of them. Arguing in loud voices,

* Mayweed was the great route-finder of the *Duncton Chronicles*, and much loved by all who knew him.

237

trailing along, angry, half-frightened of where they were. And Noakes crept after them, listened, and knew that Fieldfare had escaped in among the Stones. She was safe . . . or was she?

So he ran back, fearful for her, only reaching the stonefields again as dusk deepened towards the night. He had stared across the Stones, and even ventured in among them calling her name.

'It was no good, Spurling, I couldn't hear or see a thing. But she's definitely not with the Newborns, that's good news at least.'

'We could try to find her,' said Spurling, distressed beyond words.

Noakes shook his head. 'Not now, but I'll get some of the young moles organized for the morning. We'll keep a watch and call out for her through the night. If she's among the Stones she'll be safe. Come the dawn we'll find her, Spurling, we will!'

He wished he could believe it. He wished that when he had stared among the Stones on his return they had not seemed so silent, so forbidding, so ungiving. He wished he had more faith.

'Aye, mole, that'll be for the best,' said Spurling. 'But I might join you later, when I've settled the community to some semblance of rest. Longest Night's coming, the seasons are turning, and there's hope for us all in that . . .'

Chapter Nineteen

When Weeth was taken out of Privet's sight and into custody by the silent Newborn guardmoles, she wondered why she felt no fear on his behalf, or on her own. Even when the grim-faced female Newborns put their paws roughly to her flanks and hurried her through the entrance by which they had been stancing guard, and then down and away from all further contact with her friends, she felt no trepidation.

Instead a certain calm came to her, and it was a feeling she recognized and could turn to, as if it were an acquaintance she had travelled with for a long time past but had not yet had the chance to get to know better. Now she felt that they were at the beginning of a long journey they were to make together, and she would do well to become more familiar with . . . it?

She smiled at her hesitation, for she had almost thought of 'calm' as a fellow mole, but then, when she considered further, and reflected on the many emotions that had stirred her since she had first begun her tale in the privacy of Fieldfare's burrows in Duncton Wood, feelings *were* like fellow travellers – bit by bit, for better and for worse, a mole should make an effort to get to know them. Otherwise they remain dark shadows she is afraid of and life's journey is diminished by the simple fear of facing them.

This calm she now felt had to do with a growing sense that all this rushing about, all these cold-eyed Newborn moles, all this *striving*, were of no great importance at all.

'Is it fatalism I feel?' she mused, doing her best to keep up with the sister in front, and to comply with the insistent pushing of those at her flanks, and behind. 'No, no, it is more *generous* than that! Why, I don't feel badly about these moles at all . . .'

'Hurry, Sister! Stop dawdling!' said the mole at her left flank, who had mean, chilly eyes.

'. . . I almost feel affection for them!' she concluded, amazed at the discovery. 'They're so trapped in themselves, so unfree, and that's why they're pushing and shoving at me!'

There was a sharp jab in her rump which brought tears of shock and pain to her eyes.

'Get *on*, mole!' said the one behind.

Privet stopped suddenly, and the one behind bumped into her, while those at her flanks looked outraged and pulled at her to continue.

'Why?' said Privet quietly. 'Why harry me, and hurt me? Is moledom really going to change if we arrive wherever we're going a few moments later than we would otherwise have done?'

'The Senior Brother said we must do it quick.'

'Do what quick?' said Privet, feeling calmer still, and thinking that the most they could do was jab her more and the hurt would only be short-lived. This talking, this looking into the eyes of these moles, this breaking through to who they were was much more important than a little pain. She had done it with Chervil, she could do it with them.

She was jabbed again, this time by the one in front who had hurried on, not realizing at first that her charge had stopped, and had now been forced to return. She looked outraged and puzzled, and a little nervous.

'Come *on!*' she said, grabbing Privet.

'It's because you want to get me away from my friends as soon as you can, isn't it?'

'We don't know about *that*,' said the mole, her anger lessening before Privet's calm. 'The Senior Brother said we must get you into Bowdler just as quick as we can.'

'What's your name?' asked Privet; the feeling of affection for these poor driven sisters had returned to her, and with it the memory of how when she herself was entrapped in Blagrove Slide she had been grateful when moles used her name. 'I'll come without complaint if you tell me your names.'

She had turned in the direction she had been going to look squarely at the first mole, and the ones behind tried pushing her and hitting her in their efforts to get her moving, so hard indeed that she slewed to one side, and winced with pain even as she stared into the eyes of the mole she was addressing.

'Stop that!' this mole said, 'leave her be. Please come, because otherwise we'll get into trouble.'

Privet saw that it was so and yet still she asked, 'Just tell me your name.' She sensed that if she could only reach through to one of them, she might reach through to all.

'All right then . . . my name's . . .'

'Your real name,' said Privet resolutely, 'the one you had before you became a sister. The one your mother gave you.'

A look of dismay came to the mole's eyes, and those behind fell back uneasily.

'Not allowed to use those names,' said one of them.

'No, mustn't,' said the one in front, almost desperately.

'I won't move if you don't tell me,' said Privet, 'and then the Senior Brother will definitely not be pleased.'

A look of conflict came over their faces, and it was of the especially painful sort suffered by those unused to making decisions for themselves because they normally only take orders from others. Privet had confronted them with the need to decide, and hit them where it hurt most, because a name is a mole's identity and they had, perhaps, gone a very long way towards losing theirs.

But not all the way.

'Oh, well, if we must,' said the first mole. 'I'm Plumb, that's my name.'

'Thistle,' said another.

'Because she's spiky!' said a third, with a grin. 'I'm Heron.'

'That's a funny name,' said Privet, liking her.

'And you're Privet,' said Heron.

'Yes,' said Privet, turning to the fourth mole, the only one who had not given her name. She was a little younger than the other three, and shy-looking.

'Well?' said Privet.

'Mustn't,' said the mole, really frightened. She was the most junior of them all, and her voice had the soft accent of the Welsh borderland.

'No . . .' said Privet judiciously, understanding that she had gone far enough, but knowing too that of all the four moles the one who had not given her name was the one who most wanted to.

'Well, now I know most of you, anyway,' said Privet, 'I'll come along with you. What are they going to do with me?'

'Confine you for the duration of the Convocation,' said Plumb, gratefully turning back along the tunnel as they all set off once more.

'And we've heard that a very important mole indeed is going to come to talk to you,' said Heron. Her voice was awed.

'Thripp?' said Privet.

There was a gasp from Thistle. 'You must never call him just by his name like that,' she said. 'He's Elder Senior Brother Thripp. Anyway, it's not him who wants you, unfortunately. *He's* all right, really. No, it's Senior Brother Inquisitor Quail who wants to see you.'

At the mere mention of Quail's name a shiver ran through the sisters, and they seemed distressed and increased their pace.

'Why me?' said Privet; wishing to keep good faith with her promise not to hinder them further she was hurrying with them, rather surprised to find that her long journey from Duncton Wood must have made her fitter by far than these confined, trapped sisters, who were huffing and puffing as they went.

'D . . . don't kn . . . know,' puffed Plumb over her shoulder.

'With *him*,' panted Heron confidentially in little more than a whisper, 'there's only two reasons for asking to see a particular sister: for information or for *that*.'

'That?' repeated Privet. The pace had slowed a little, and now they were merely going fast. The long tunnel, which had various side-turns along the way but in general headed southwards, if Privet's sense of direction was correct, now dipped down. Since the surface was still only a short way above, and the soil was darker and more moist than before, she deduced they were going down into a shallow valley and that their journey would end near water. From the complete lack of tree roots, and what she remembered of the surface when they first arrived, and the scent of livestock, she also guessed they had been travelling beneath pasture grounds. Now the soil held evidence of dead tree roots, the livestock scents had gone, and she guessed they were near a wood.

From Heron's silence, and her coy but knowing look, Privet guessed that '*that*' with Quail meant mating, which was, she remembered well enough, a thing Senior Brothers were privileged to do with the captive sisters.

'If it isn't mating,' she said matter-of-factly, and to Heron's embarrassment, 'and frankly in my case I doubt if it would be, then it must be information. I have found that Newborn males find it rather hard to believe that a female can scribe.'

Plumb came to a sudden stop, so sudden that Privet bumped into her, and the other sisters tumbled to a halt as well, all telling her at once she must not even think such words as scribing, let alone say them, because it was a blasphemy.

'But,' said Privet cheerfully, 'it's perfectly true, there's no reason why a female should not scribe. Why, I myself—'

Heron, Plumb and Thistle nearly fell over each other to stop her saying more – 'Please, Sister Privet, *don't*, we're almost there and in no time a brother will come and . . . you *mustn't* blaspheme' – but it was not their terror of the brothers that stopped her, but the look in the eyes of the fourth mole, the one so far unnamed.

'Why,' thought Privet to herself with sudden conviction, 'she *knows* females can scribe, she knows more than she's letting on, just as I did when I lived in Blagrove Slide. Poor mole, she's frightened for her life. Poor thing.'

Whether or not the mole guessed what Privet was thinking was impossible to say, but she looked down as if collecting her wits, and then up, and in a voice louder than the others said, 'Sister, you must never say things like that. Everymole knows females can't scribe or do anything needing skill. Only brothers can, and merely thinking it will get you into trouble and you'll deserve it. No wonder Senior Brother Inquisitor Quail wants to see you!'

This quietened them all down, and somewhat chastened they trekked the last stage of their journey in silence until they came to a large portal at which squatted a hugely fat male with a round, soft face.

'You're late and you're in trouble, Sisters four,' he declared in a curious squeaky voice, adding as he eyed Privet with vindictive distaste, 'and *you* are the cause. Take her to the guest burrows and one of you stay with her so she doesn't wander. The Senior Brother Inquisitor is coming before too long and oops-a-daisy it won't be a pretty thing if he knows of your tardiness, no!'

'We'll bring you some worms, Senior Brother Squelch,' said Heron.

'Lots!' said Plumb.

'And lots!' declared Thistle, hurrying Privet past. These promises were made in a half jocular, half puppish kind of way, which left the mole Squelch giggling like a female, though his eyes remained cold, lingering on Privet and the fourth of the sisters as he whispered darkly, and then repeated in a squeaky half-scream, 'Two of a kind! Two of a kind! Squelch sees with his all-seeing eye, Squelch scents with his all-scenting snout, Squelch tastes with his all-licking tongue – ha ha ha!'

Then, as they scurried by, doing their best to avoid his groping attempts to caress them, he flicked out his tongue, which was very long, and played it about in an obscene way, laughing and panting and making something of a dint in Privet's new-discovered calm.

She had gone cold, the more so because the four sisters who had accompanied her had, in a way, become more themselves, more ordinary, and she sensed that not far below the surface was normality, and humour, and even warmth; which contrasted with the corrupted, tainted and perverted evil that she had sensed – almost scented – about the mole Squelch, and the system of things he must represent.

243

'We've talked to you too much, Sister Privet,' said Heron, suddenly cold, and the others went chilly too; 'please don't report us.'

They went through some more tunnels, unnaturally clean and sterile, and then past another plump male mole, who might have been Squelch's brother, though he did not have the special vile energy that Squelch exuded. He blinked and nodded as they went by and called after them in a raspy voice, 'Put her in the end one.'

The 'end one' turned out to be the last of several empty cells, with no way in or out but by one portal, and too deep down in the earth to easily burrow out of through the hard, dry sub-soil above. Clearly the 'guests' – though she seemed to be the only one – were put in a sterile part of the system, and under the watchful eye of unfit and unpleasant males.

'One of us has got to stay with her,' said Heron unenthusiastically. There was a general air of reluctance to volunteer and finally Plumb turned to the unnamed mole and said, '*You* do it for now, and we'll relieve you tomorrow.'

'Don't want to,' said the mole. 'She's a sinner and corrupt. Don't like her.'

'Do it now and it'll be over the sooner,' said Thistle with a weary sigh, apparently used to the over-virtuous attitudes of this particular sister.

'Good luck with the Senior Brother Inquisitor!' said Plumb, and with that last heartfelt wish the three moles were gone, their duty done, and Privet was left alone with the righteous female.

'Yet, is she so righteous?' mused Privet to herself, eyeing her in a friendly way. 'I somehow think not.'

'What is your name?' asked Privet.

'Sister Hope,' intoned the mole without expression.

'Your real name, like Plumb and Thistle and Heron are real names. The one before—'

'They should not have given their former names; I could report them.'

'But they know you won't.'

The mole shook her head non-committally and said, 'I'll get your food. You are permitted two worms in the morning and two in the evening. We do not indulge ourselves here.'

'What is your name, mole?' asked Privet once more, her voice warm and friendly, and filled with the real sympathy she felt before a mole she knew was suffering in her silence, and wanted so much to talk. 'You can scribe, can't you, or you know something of it?'

The mole stared back at her, plainly upset and uncertain.

'Mustn't . . . even talk,' she whispered, and was gone.

Privet watched after her, wondering how she might reach out to her and make her talk. Scribing! It seemed a long time since *she* had done that. So much had changed, so much been shed, and now there was this growing sense of rightness and certainty in herself that things would be well, things *were* well, if moles but knew it and learned to forget the worries they made for themselves.

'But it's not so simple as that!' Privet thought, chiding herself for expecting all moles to be as she was. 'So what can a mole like me do? I don't want to fight like Rooster decided to so long ago, or command others as Maple wishes to and most certainly will. I don't need to go on long journeys as Whillan surely must, or to find "opportunities" at every turn as Weeth seeks to do, and will! No, I'm more like Stour now, wanting only to be quiet and to find Silence, and to see moles live contentedly without interfering with each other so much. So what do I do to help? Can I do *anything*?'

Privet was surprised to discover herself stanced down with her eyes almost closed, and going through these thoughts as clearly as she remembered ever having thought before. No rushing, no panic, no running hither and thither in her mind, and that companion calm, which had been but an acquaintance hours before, now felt a true friend, and one who was rapidly gaining in importance amongst all the feelings she had.

'The word that springs to mind is "exemplary",' she said to herself, remembering the word the Newborns had used to justify the cruel punishment of the young moles who had run away to come . . . 'Why, to come *here* to Bowdler of all places, where I've been brought. Those two moles were killed for doing what I'm made to do. How strange, how fickle, how upsetting the Stone's will can be! But *exemplary*, now why do I think that? Because it is the only thing a mole can ever do to really influence others; be an example, to show them a way of being or doing. Well, then, Privet, what can *you* show anymole?'

As she arrived at this important point of her thinking, and began to address a question that she would ponder for some time yet, she heard the sound of the mole approaching once more, and turned her thoughts back to the problem of reaching through her fears. It seemed important that she did, for calm though *she* felt, others were in danger and much was happening, and the greater the number of moles who could free themselves, if only a little, from the thrall of the Newborns, the more likely was it that the Newborns would not be able to change moledom the way they so fatally wished.

On a sudden impulse Privet went to a shadowed corner of the cell and scribed quickly on the earthen floor, stanced back, and was staring at it when Sister 'Hope' came in bearing not two worms but three, which she placed near some nesting material. Privet did not move, but pointed instead at her scribing. The mole hurried over in alarm, stared down, reached her right paw out and ran it over the scribing as if to ken it, and looked more troubled still.

'Please, you mustn't do that,' she said.

'Can you ken it?' asked Privet.

'I . . . not very well.'

'It says, "If you know your name, scribe it". Well, mole, *do* you? *Can* you?'

'Scribe it . . . ?' faltered the mole, her right paw fretting at the floor. She slowly reached out and scribed her name, then stanced back in alarm at what she had done, staring at it as if thinking that now she could not go back to what she had been before.

Privet quickly ran her paw over the scribing and turned back to the mole with a smile and said, 'So, "Sister Hope", your real name is Madoc?'

'Madoc,' repeated the mole, nodding vigorously and allowing herself the slightest of grins when she said the name, 'is the name I was given at birth, and the name they said in the Midsummer ritual, and the name they took from me because it wasn't suitable to keep it.'

'Why ever not?' asked Privet.

'You see, to be truly Newborn a mole must be given a new name; then she knows she must cast off the old ways and take on the new.'

Privet eyed her, unsure whether Madoc believed in what she said or not. That she was unhappy was plain, but a mole may be unhappy in her faith for a time and still feel that what she follows is true.

'*Are* you Newborn?'

'It's very hard,' said Madoc, 'and gets harder, to believe something is true when they do things so wrong. But I think being Newborn is right, it's just other moles don't behave as they should.'

'Other moles don't behave as they should?' repeated Privet carefully. She had no wish to impose her own ideas on Madoc.

'I don't think so. They hide things. They close their eyes to things. Like scribing: I know females can scribe because my mother could – she learnt it from her father who was a scribe here in Caer Caradoc before the Newborns came. My mother secretly taught me to scribe

246

my name before I went with the Senior Brother. She said, "I'm teaching you this, my dear, because it will remind you of two things – the mole you are, and the mole you could be again." My mother didn't like the Newborns and didn't like them calling me "Hope".'

Privet smiled softly and said, 'Well, I can understand that. I wouldn't want a pup of mine called something different; certainly not "Hope", which is a strange kind of name, though maybe there are moles for whom it might be appropriate.'

'What kind of moles?' said Madoc seriously. At least, she seemed serious about it, though there came to her eyes a tiny hint of a smile.

'That's how her mother looked,' thought Privet to herself with sudden insight. 'Her father a scribemole, and her mother a learning, humorous kind of mole, and it's all in *this* mole's face, despite the fear and doubt the Newborns have put into her. That's like moledom too, full of things that have become hidden for a time because of the fear the Newborn dogma instils, but beneath the surface . . .'

'You're a very intelligent mole,' said Madoc gravely. 'I could see it in your eyes and in the way you refused to be hurried. It was reassuring to me because I'm intelligent too, more than some of the Senior Brothers.'

'You are?' said Privet, rapidly warming to Madoc.

She nodded and said, 'Have you had pups?'

Privet hesitated only a moment before she said she had. She realized a mole cannot expect forthrightness from another if she is not honest herself.

'What were their names?'

'Their real names?' said Privet, playing for time, though only because even now, and even having repeated the names to Whillan and the others, she found it hard to think of them, let alone say them, without wanting to cry. There are some losses a mole never fully recovers from.

'There were four of them, three females and a male: Brimmel, Loosestrife, Sampion and Mumble.'

Madoc pondered this information for a moment with a slight frown and then her brow cleared as if she had worked something out.

'You liked Loosestrife best of all—' she began.

'You're right, mole,' interrupted Privet with pleasure.

'Your voice gave you away, you spoke the name differently. And the other thing I was going to say was that you were once like me, weren't you?'

'Like you?'

'In a Newborn system. A sister. It's obvious. You wouldn't have asked if I meant their real names when I asked what they were called. You have escaped, haven't you?'

Privet studied her closely for a time and said finally, 'Madoc, you are *definitely* an intelligent mole. I have a feeling that the Stone wishes us to talk.'

'I have a feeling,' said Madoc quickly, and with another of her secret mischievous grins, 'that we have already begun to do so.'

'Well, then, my dear, we shall continue while we can.'

'What with?'

'With a lot of questions which I think I need to ask, and which you need to answer, because I have a feeling there is not so much time left.'

'No, there isn't,' said Madoc, 'because Longest Night is tomorrow, and that's when it's all going to happen, isn't it? That's why they wanted you out of the way down here with us females.'

'Is it?'

'Is that the first question?'

'Of many, my dear,' said Privet stancing down, feeling suddenly quite sure that she might be 'out of the way', but she was in the right place, at the right time, with the right mole, and that if she was going to find an answer to the question she had asked herself about how she might do something 'exemplary' it might well be here that she would find a clue to what it was.

Chapter Twenty

But there were moles other than Privet who had the feeling that same dull afternoon that questions they had so long been asking might soon be answered – though perhaps not in a way, or a place, of their choosing.

After a long and impatient wait in the chamber where they had been isolated, Whillan and Maple had been forced against all their instincts and wishes out to the surface, and from there up the steep side of Caer Caradoc, utterly impotent against the power of their escort of six guards. Naturally they protested at Privet's and Weeth's absence and demanded to know where they were, and why the promise to return them had not been kept, but it got them nowhere.

It is hard to demand anything for long of moles who do not reply, but stare all stony-eyed and say, with a faith and conviction that subordinates intelligence, that 'it's for everymole's own good' and 'for the best'.

'What's for everymole's good? Should we not be free to judge what's best for *us*?'

But their protests waned the higher they climbed, and they resolved to stay resolute and together, and do what they could when they reached the top of Caradoc itself. So angry and concerned were they on their friends' behalf that they had no time to think about what might have concerned most others, and should perhaps have most concerned them: their own safety among such tough expressionless moles as those that forced them on.

Yet even Whillan and Maple, brave as they were turning out to be, and unconcerned with personal safety, could not but think the Stone was giving them due warning of real danger on the top when, a little way before they reached it, black rooks gyred along Caradoc's steep south-eastern edge, their wings ragged, their grey beaks sharp as they opened to emit rasping calls. Then, at the top itself, which mole should be waiting in the shadow of a rock, with a flocking of flapping rooks all about making such a din they could not hear his first words of hypocritical greeting, but Snyde himself.

The flattish summit of Caer Caradoc stretched beyond him, roughly rectangular, the other longer side straight ahead. Nothing but sky was visible beyond it, adding greatly to the sense that here at Caradoc they were on top of moledom itself. To the left flank, or south, the ground dropped away slightly, covered in tussocky grass, while to the right, or north, it rose up to end in an impressive cluster of Stones, russet in colour and stolid of form; the place to which a mole's eye was most naturally drawn.

'Ah, so good to see you,' smirked Snyde.

'Where's Privet, mole?' demanded Maple immediately, looming over him so fiercely that the Newborn guards put out paws to restrain him.

'Ah, yes. It was decided, that is to say that Senior Brother Chervil felt it best, that she would be safest away from here during the Convocation.'

'Why?'

'She *is* a female. Tempers may rise during the coming debates and most moles here do not expect or think it right that females should participate. They get emotional. They can't think straight.'

'You didn't warn us of this,' said Whillan. 'And you know it to be untrue of Privet.'

'My dear mole,' said Snyde, doing his best to sound avuncular, 'I did not know this would be the decision. I am but one delegate among many.'

'Where is she?'

'I understand she is safe,' said Snyde slowly. He plainly did not know where she was, and yet he tried to say the word 'safe' with reassuring conviction. 'Senior Brother Chervil himself told me that and I think it is true.' Strangely, he sounded disappointed, so perhaps it *was* true.

'And Weeth?'

Snyde's eyes hardened still more. 'As a disaffected Newborn he is not welcome on Caer Caradoc, and in any case he is not an official part of any delegation.'

'He is with me,' said Maple.

'You!' said Snyde, his eyes contemptuous. 'You are not part of Duncton's delegation. *You* are a mere protector of moles, Maple. I do not wish to seem disrespectful, but your role is somewhat limited and, now we have arrived, redundant. Nevertheless, I felt it only courteous to arrange for you to be allowed up here with us in these coming days of deliberation, though clearly your role will be merely that of an observer.

But, well, since a number of other systems have much larger delegations than our own – a matter that Master Stour could have taken my advice on if he had bothered to consult me . . .' He paused, clearly expecting a look of acknowledgement or even a word of thanks from the infuriated Maple, whose experience on the journey of late had been one of increasing frustration. Maple only stared stonily at him, so Snyde turned to Whillan and fixed him with his smug, weaselly gaze.

'You, mole, may take Privet's place and, if I give permission, you may perhaps say a word or two,' he said, turning away so dismissively that Maple, for one, would have forgiven Whillan if he had seized the jumped-up little scholar by the snout and unceremoniously hurled him over the steepest side of Caer Caradoc. To Whillan's credit, however, he barely showed displeasure on his face, though his eyes narrowed dangerously as he nodded his understanding of what Snyde had said.

'I will only speak if you suggest it, Deputy Master,' he said.

'And Weeth?' said Maple, 'where is he?'

'Where he should be,' said Snyde, 'with other potential trouble-makers in a cell, from which he will not be released until the Convocation is finished and dispersing. And before you raise the matter, Maple, I have complete assurances that he will be safe, though why I should have felt it necessary to petition on behalf of a mole who is not of Duncton I cannot think. Now, follow me, for we have been assigned to quarters and are to be briefed by one of the Senior Brother Inquisitors before long.'

With this, Snyde led them off, accompanied by some of the New-born guards, passing by other groups similar to themselves who were hurrying to and fro on the surface before dropping down into entrances, as they now did, to the great airy, arched tunnels underneath. Here pawsteps echoed everywhere, and there was the muted muttering of voices in tunnel and chamber, at corner and turn, in ante-chamber and side tunnel, talking and whispering and falling silent meaningfully as others went by, as moles do in the days and hours before a great Convocation begins.

'Oh, and do not try to wander,' said Snyde with forced casualness, and a tight smile. 'The Elder Senior Brother Thripp has given instructions that nomole is to leave once they have arrived.'

'And what moles will enforce that?' asked Whillan as innocently as he could, and casting a glance at Maple.

'Senior Brother Inquisitor Quail's minions and guards, I expect,' said Snyde, 'but that need not worry us, need it?'

'Of course not, Deputy Master,' said Maple heavily, his eyes already assessing the route they were taking, and pondering future options for escape.

As they followed on after Snyde they heard the cawing of rooks out in the sky above the surface, and at one of the entrances they passed, Whillan drew Maple's attention to a high and noisy flocking of rooks above the hill. They flew about in fractious and fretful excitement, and kept diving at each other as if they had seen a vision of bloody carrion across Caer Caradoc, and were already squabbling over which was to take up the first morsel of the coming carnage.

Their passage over Caer Caradoc and through some of its tunnels told them a good deal about the arrangement of the hilltop system, and eventually brought them to a communal chamber busy with moles from whom they soon learnt a great deal more.

There was not a female in sight, and earlier impressions they had gained of the Newborn society being male-dominated, which Privet's account of Blagrove Slide had suggested, were now amply confirmed. Whillan and Maple had lost track of the various ranks of the Newborns – the brothers, the Inquisitors, the senior Brothers, the minions, not to mention the delegates – but it was obvious enough that there were moles of all these ranks present, huddled in whispering cabals in corners, or going purposefully about the adjacent tunnels in ones and twos. There was a general air of final preparation, and occasionally the normal chilly reserve of the Newborns was broken by some rushing or panic-stricken mole who, it seemed, had discovered some problem or other which he was trying to put right before the morrow.

Here and there Whillan saw dusty, travel-stained moles, and from this and their more relaxed and frankly curious manner, compared to the neat and generally expressionless Newborns, it was easy enough to make out which were delegates from afar like themselves.

These moles kept together, and though it was unfortunately true that Snyde attracted a lot of attention – partly from his curious and twisted appearance, but also because he had the dutiful attentions of one or two Newborn brothers – it was a group of dark, large, rough-looking moles who drew the most glances for a time. Though they seemed to try to talk in whispers, yet their voices were deep and growly, and their laughs rasping yet melodious.

'Siabod moles, it seems,' whispered Maple, after he had managed to have a brief conversation with another visitor nearby where they had stopped. 'We must make ourselves known to them. The Siabod system was friendly to Duncton in the old days.'

'Mandrake came from there,' whispered Whillan, invoking the name of the fearsome Siabod mole the resistance to whose tyranny in Duncton more than a century before, many historians claim, marks the true beginning of the emergence of modern Duncton as a force for good in moledom.

Maple nodded, and they stanced together making out what they could of the confusing busy-ness about them as they waited for Snyde to find out from the Newborn officials where they were to have quarters.

Their wait continued, and as evening advanced more moles arrived, and they found that provided they did not attempt to reach the surface they were permitted a degree of freedom to wander about and talk to others, though not the Siabod moles, who had gone off for a time. They were able to piece together the expected arrangements for the Convocation the next day, and found consolation and some reassurance in the fact that amongst the visitors were a good few like themselves, who were not of the Newborn persuasion at all. Many expressed the same fears of the outcome of the Convocation, and gave reports of minor repressions in their systems as the Newborns had gradually gained support in recent moleyears – usually among the females and moles in less wormful areas – until they had ascendancy. In only a few cases had there been physical repression, though most moles had heard, if only indirectly, of the harshness of the exemplary punishments meted out to those who having committed themselves to the Newborn way, had strayed from their vows or the rigours of the routine rituals.

Snyde returned and took them the short distance to their quarters, which turned out to be a recently-delved chamber accommodating four – themselves and a Newborn guard. If that was not enough to serve as a way of watching over them, their chamber was separated from those of other visitors by tunnels and chambers occupied by Newborns.

'I think we should not take this as a sign they are spying on us in any way,' said Snyde in all apparent seriousness, 'but rather as an expression of the Newborn wish that strangers such as yourselves (I think they accept *me* as an equal they can respect) may gain by fraternizing with them in these few days of harmony and intercourse. Now, if you don't mind, I believe that Senior Brother Quail himself wishes to see a number of us more senior delegates, and to give us a task.'

'"Harmony and intercourse"!' repeated Whillan ironically when Snyde was out of the way again. 'That's a laugh. I wonder what his task can be, and whether he'll take advantage of the opportunity to report us as blasphemers to Quail himself.'

'Well, while he's gone I suggest we get off our rumps and find out what we can from other moles in the main communal chambers,' said Maple.

They decided to separate and talk with as many different moles as they could before meeting up again later to find out what each had discovered.

It turned out that the air was thick with rumour and surmise, but enough different sources, including a few Newborns who proved open to conversation, agreed on a few basics for the two Duncton moles to be able to work out what was likely to happen officially, and unofficially, in the next few days.

The Convocation itself was to be held in a great chamber some way from the Stones, which had been specially delved for the occasion. It was to start in the middle of the following morning and its first day would end with celebrations for Longest Night. Thripp would be formally declaring it open and though the matters to be discussed remained unclear, it seemed they had to do with the ordering of moledom's major and minor libraries, and the Newborns' desire to rationalize the existing texts in them so that all moles, wherever they might be, would have the same opportunity for study and education. At the same time, there would be some public confessions made, presumably by moles who wanted to set an example to others of piety, or show remorse for sins committed.

'If there's an opportunity to speak out against the Newborn ways I'll take it,' said Whillan, 'especially in my . . . Privet's absence, because she would certainly have said her piece, with or without Snyde's permission.'

'We'll see how things go before you open your mouth, Whillan!' responded Maple. 'Having an open and free debate may be their way of finding out which moles to get rid of first!'

'Certainly things are not as they seem to be,' said Whillan. 'Did you hear what some are saying about Thripp?'

'Being ill? And Quail taking more and more power?'

Both moles had heard more or less the same story, and one confirmed already, though they did not know it, by what Chervil had privately told Privet concerning Thripp's state of health.

Whether or not it had been secret then, it was general knowledge now that Thripp had suffered a mysterious ailment which had left him weak for molemonths past, though with his mind alert. For personal assistance he now relied on a few loyal old moles, who had no doubt been his aides for many years; but for matters of moledom, and the development of the Caradocian Order, as the Newborn brethren were formally known, it seemed that a power struggle had developed between himself and Quail for control of the group of twelve Senior Brothers.

It seemed that originally Quail had simply been one of these twelve, and the Inquisitors had reported directly to Thripp himself. But he had of necessity delegated this taxing task to one of the twelve, and had chosen Quail, who had succeeded over recent moleyears in placing moles loyal to himself in the main Senior Brother positions. At the same time, Inquisitors had been able to point the talon of sin and guilt for breaking vows at one after another of the Senior Brothers most loyal to Thripp, and having ousted these individuals Quail got his own Inquisitors appointed, the most senior of whom was a sadistic disciplinarian called Skua.

This much seemed certain, and moles were in little doubt that the long struggle between Thripp and Quail was now coming to a head.

'What's remarkable,' reported Whillan, 'is that Thripp has kept power for so long, but I'm told he's a mole of considerable charm and charisma, and ordinary Newborns revere and adore him, and almost worship the ground he stances on. Because of that Quail has never yet dared try to oust him openly, but the talk is that he might attempt it at this Convocation.'

'But wasn't it Thripp who summoned it in the first place?'

'Aye, it was,' said Whillan. 'And I heard from a Cannock mole that he did so precisely because it was the only way left to him to regain control over the direction the Caradocian Order was taking. Originally *that* was what the discussion was going to be about, but, as we've heard, now it's all about libraries, censorship and so on, which though important avoid the real issue, which is whatmole is to control the Newborns in the future – Thripp or Quail.'

'Aye, I heard something similar,' said Maple. 'Because the twelve Senior Brothers are now under Quail's control they've succeeded in changing the agenda and made the Convocation meaningless as a place of discussion . . .'

'. . . and meanwhile, if Weeth is to be believed, which I think he is, Quail's representatives are taking control of all the main libraries and a lot of the lesser ones right now – just as Master Stour predicted. While it's true that what's discussed here is of secondary importance I'll wager that Quail will want an outcome that favours censorship of non-Newborn-approved texts so that when all this is over he can claim that his Inquisitors have been given the right to continue to impose their control.' Whillan paused and looked about the busy chamber. 'I could do with some fresh air, Maple. I feel this place is tainted.'

Maple shook his head and stayed where he was. 'We shall do nothing to draw attention to ourselves. I have no idea what the two of us can do, separated from friends, not knowing which moles about here to trust, and with Newborn guards at every turn, but I'll tell you the strangest thing: I've never felt more certain that there must be something we *can* do. The Stone has brought us here for a purpose, and if we can get out of Caradoc alive than we'll be in a better position to help defend liberty of worship of the Stone because we were here.

'But we've seen how ruthless the Newborns can be when Quail has his way – and I wouldn't be so certain of Thripp either. No, we stance tight, listen well, and say nothing – and though I know you want to speak up in Privet's absence for the things she believes and would defend, we'll go very cautiously indeed and discuss things before we do them – as Chater would have said.'

Chater! They stanced in silence for a time after mention of his name, thinking of him and the other friends they had left behind, or from whom they had recently become separated, and, in their own way invoking the Stone's protection for them as Longest Night approached.

'Did you talk to the Siabod moles?' asked Whillan, breaking the long silence.

'Yes, I meant to say I did, some of them at least. At first they were only cautiously friendly, and like us seemed to be waiting to see how things work out. But when they heard you and I were from Duncton, and definitely not Newborn, they were more forthcoming – so far as Siabod moles can be. They're a proud lot, and fierce.'

'They always were according to the texts,' said Whillan.

'Well anyway, it was plain that they don't trust the Newborns in Caradoc any more than we do, and their leader is a mole who knows all about the history of the great battles led by Gareg in the old days of the war of Word and Stone. His name is Ystwelyn, and I'd like to make contact with him if I can.'

But Maple did not succeed in doing so before Snyde reappeared, looking excited and pleased with himself.

'I have been given a task, and one we must consider most important,' he declared. 'There is to be a great account scribed of this historic Convocation and as Master Librarian-elect of Duncton Wood they have given to me the honour of co-ordinating and editing it, with a number of scribemoles to work under me. I regret that it has been decided you, Whillan, will not be one of them, for this is an honour that should be spread throughout all the systems represented here. I have already met some of the scribes who will be my subordinates.'

'You have not chosen them yourself then?' said Whillan, trying not to sound greatly relieved he was not to be involved.

'No time for that. But they are all good scribes, I am told.'

'And good little Newborns too no doubt,' growled Maple.

Snyde attempted to smile, but his eyes were like the shining points of talons. 'I can tolerate only so many such remarks, mole. You would be ill-advised to make any more this night.'

'This night?' said Maple sharply, aware from a sudden retreat in Snyde's look that he had given something away he should not have done.

'Any night,' said Snyde hastily.

'But you said *this* night,' said Whillan.

Snyde looked at them both with ill-concealed dislike. 'Matters are well and equitably organized here,' he said evasively. 'Now I have work to do, and moles to see, so I suggest for your own good you cause no more trouble.'

'We have caused none so far,' said Maple coldly.

'Well then . . . that's good, isn't it?' said Snyde, twisting his dark way from them and signalling the two Newborns to go with him. He stopped only once to look back briefly before he was gone into the crowd, and his expression was not of hatred but of triumph.

'I have the feeling that he knows something we don't and it is to our disadvantage,' said Maple.

'And that whatever it is it may have its beginning this night!'

'*This* night we shall be on our guard, and keep a very low snout indeed.' Maple grinned and waved suddenly at some moles across the busy chamber, and Whillan saw that he had caught the friendly eye of the Siabod moles, who nodded grimly at them as if to say that they too were aware that there was danger about.

'That's the mole Arvon,' said Maple, pointing to a small dark mole who might almost have been from a different system, he looked so much less impressive than the others.

Whillan and Maple moved nearer each other and almost together one said and the other agreed, 'We'll find a place to make ourselves scarce; there must be somewhere to go where nomole will easily find us, *this* night.'

*

257

'*This* night?' whispered Privet in shocked alarm, her earlier calm quite deserting her.

Madoc nodded bleakly.

'They are to be *killed*?'

Madoc nodded again.

'Then, mole, we must warn them.'

'Yes, we must,' said Madoc.

Through the previous evening she had enlightened Privet considerably about the true depth of the corruption and evil of the Newborns, and had shown an admirable ability to describe and analyse matters that many moles would have found too shocking to contemplate. What was more, she had shown from an account of her own actions since she had been brought into the Newborn fold against her will, great courage and resource which Privet, having herself been captive for a time at Blagrove Slide, was in a good position to judge. Now morning had come and Privet realized that time had run out and they must attempt to take action themselves, at whatever risk to their own lives.

'I was hoping you would say that, Privet,' Madoc said, 'and especially since I told you all I knew. I feel relieved, but your reaction has also made me see even more clearly how wrong it all is.'

'So, we agree we must escape from here and try to get up into Caer Caradoc itself?'

Madoc nodded. 'That's probably where the male delegates have all been taken by now, so that the ones whose faces don't fit can be dealt with tonight. Now I think I know a way of escaping. You see . . .'

But there was the sound of moles approaching, the echo of voices, and a most frightening chill to the air.

'Oh Privet,' said Madoc in despair, 'it may be too late.'

The voices came nearer and the two females scampered to the portal and poked their snouts into the tunnel.

'They're coming from both directions,' said Madoc. 'It *is* too late.'

They retreated back into the chamber, their escape cut off; the pawsteps drew nearer and a mole laughed too loud outside, a mole they knew, a most filthy and corrupt mole.

'She's in this cell,' they heard Squelch say.

'Alone?' said the coldest voice imaginable.

'With Sister Hope.'

'Do I know her?'

'You may have known her!' said Squelch, laughing in an obscene way.

As Privet and Madoc waited in silence, and the moles' shadows cast themselves at their portal, Privet turned to her new friend, whose flank was shivering with apprehension, and whispered, 'It may be late, my dear, but to a Duncton mole it is never *too* late, *never*. Remember that in the time ahead.'

Madoc nodded her understanding, and felt reassured as the fat snout of Squelch, and his deep-set eyes, showed themselves.

'Lackaday!' he said with a simper, 'you have a visitor, a most important visitor. Stance up and shut up.'

'Yes, sir,' said 'Sister Hope'.

Squelch came into the chamber and stanced to one side to let the next mole through, while several guards assembled outside.

Quail came in and stanced firmly before them. He was of solid build and exuded health and power, and his eyes were dark and penetrating. He had one feature that made him most remarkable, and most frightening. His head, which was large and round, was quite devoid of fur, as was much of his body. It was blue-pink, shiny, strange. It appeared smooth and unlined until any expression passed across it at which point a thousand tiny wrinkles formed and made a mole realize that there was something dead, something rotten, about the smooth skin.

'I am the Senior Brother Inquisitor Quail,' he said tersely. 'Which one of you is known as Privet of Duncton Wood?'

'I am,' said Privet, holding his gaze steadily with her own.

'Well, and so you are the mole Privet who once lived for a time in Blagrove Slide? Who eschewed the Newborn way, and who comes now to Caer Caradoc and back into our power?'

Privet said nothing.

'There are few moles of whom it can be said that I am interested to meet them,' said Quail, 'but you are one of them.'

Privet still said nothing.

'You once knew Rooster, I believe?'

'Did I?' said Privet.

A hard smile made Quail's face repellent. 'It is about that friendship that I wish to talk to you. If you tell me what I wish to know about that mole, who has caused us a good deal of trouble, I will permit you to return unharmed to Duncton Wood. If you do not you will be . . . you will regret it.'

His eyes grew so cold that seeing them a mole had no doubt that whatever might happen to Privet would be terrible. Yet to her now that calm returned, and she was not afraid.

'I will tell you, as I will tell anymole, all that I can so long as doing so is compatible with my beliefs in the Stone.'

'Long words those, Squelch,' said Quail, unexpectedly turning to the fat mole, 'what do you make of them?'

'Short words, long words, they all sound the same to me when they turn into screams,' said Squelch, grinning cryptically. Beads of oily sweat trickled in his face-fur. The evil that had come into the chamber was palpable. 'Don't trust her, she's clever.'

'She is a mere female,' said Quail.

'She is more than that,' sighed Squelch, a tremor passing through his unhealthy flesh.

But still Privet felt calm, staring at Quail in some puzzlement, for his eyes were not only cold – they held signs of curiosity too.

'Why?' thought Privet astonished. 'Why should he be curious about me? And how does he know I was at Blagrove Slide?' For a moment the horrific thought crossed her mind that others had told him; which could only mean her friends, and that they had been tortured.

'You are thinking hard, I see,' said Quail, his eyes almost transfixing her with their power and insight. 'You are wondering how I knew you were at Blagrove Slide.'

'I am,' she acknowledged.

'*This* mole told me,' said Quail softly, taking delight in being able to surprise her.

He stanced to one side and nodded to Squelch, who in turn signalled to one of the moles outside, who, somewhat tentatively it seemed, entered the chamber. He was little older than Privet herself, and though clearly Newborn, was mild in appearance and looked harassed, like a mole who has too many cares. His eyes were kinder than Quail's, indeed along with regret their look carried sympathy, and a certain respect as well.

'But . . .' whispered Privet in astonishment, finding herself staring into the eyes of a mole she had never thought to see again.

Quail looked from one to another and said, 'Of course, as a Confessed Sister in Blagrove Slide you would never have known his name. Nor, come to that, should Sister Hope know it now, but she is of little consequence. Yes, the good Brother here has told me something about you, Privet of Duncton Wood, or rather of Crowden, as you once were.'

But throughout this sardonic and teasing statement Privet had eyes only for the mole who had entered the chamber, and who, she felt sure even as she gazed into his eyes, wished to protect her now, just as he had tried to protect her from the wrath of the Senior Brother whose young aide he had been so many moleyears ago.

'Meet Brother Rolt!' said Quail.

'Brother Rolt!' she said, and against all Newborn tradition, all convention, she went to him and embraced him, at which he backed off hastily, blinking in his embarrassment, his snout turning quite pink.

'I wish that you had not come back,' he said. 'You have caused us much difficulty, much dismay.'

'Come, we shall talk in another place than this,' said Quail authoritatively, 'but not right now. Today I have other things to do, and preparations to make. I just wanted to see this mole who knows Rooster so well. I will talk to her a little later in my own tunnels.'

'May Sister Hope accompany me?' asked Privet, as meekly as she could manage.

'Is she safe, Squelch?' asked Quail, already half out of the portal.

'Sister Hope is most safe,' said Squelch, 'aren't you, my dear?'

'If I can help bring this unbeliever to exemplary justice,' intoned Madoc in a voice very different from the one she had been using to Privet earlier, 'I shall be most glad.'

'Then come along as well, mole!'

'Be ready, be most ready,' whispered Privet to Madoc as she followed Quail out of the cell.

But for what? And when? And where?

But before and behind them the Newborns went and there was no further time to ask questions, or to answer them. Only to be aware that evil stalked their way, and if they were to avoid it they must be ready not to talk but to act.

'All is never lost to a Duncton mole,' whispered Madoc to herself again and again as she followed Privet, and for the first time in her life she understood that being of Duncton was not something of place, but of spirit, and though her flanks shook with nerves and her mouth was dry, she was as determined as a mole could be to try to find something of that legendary and courageous spirit in the hours of trial ahead.

'Oh, I *will* be ready,' she wanted to cry out, as she whispered her thanks to the Stone that her long loneliness was over, and that a mole called Privet, like no other she had ever met or dreamed of meeting, had come so strangely into her life here and now as if to seek her help.

While behind them both, his face furrowed with worried thought,

261

came Brother Rolt. As he looked past Sister Hope to the thin flanks of Privet, there was, in his eyes as well, the distant glimmer of the light of rediscovered hope.

Chapter Twenty-One

The promise of coming opportunity is a song a mole can sing only so long before others tire of it, as Weeth discovered after a day of captivity.

'. . . and so I say, opportunity always presents itself when you least expect it; it *will* come, and, moles, we must be ready for it!' he confidently declared a final time to the intimidating bunch of moles he found himself in the company of, down in the securest and most escape-proof of the cells that the Brother Inquisitors had commanded be delved near Caer Caradoc in their thorough preparations for the Convocation.

This declaration of his had come after he had made an earnest but unsuccessful attempt to make the mole Rooster and the other hulking and battle-hardened moles around him talk. After his initial (and delighted) astonishment at discovering that he had been confined with no less a mole than Rooster himself – the famous Rooster, the Rooster of the different-sized paws, the Rooster who (he had deduced) had once had a more than passing acquaintance with that interesting and delightful female of Duncton, Librarian Privet – he was disappointed to find that to a mole they fell into a deep and malevolent silence, some staring at him, but most, like Rooster, turning their backs on him.

'Is it that I smell?' he had asked. 'Is it the way I have groomed my fur – you prefer something rougher perhaps, something more in keeping with yourselves? No, it is not that. Could it be . . .'

Ah! A thought occurred to him, a thought that posed a problem.

'Could it be they think I am a Newborn spy?' he mused. 'It could be! It is!'

Weeth skirted cautiously around Rooster until he was able to peer into his frowning face.

'I'm not a spy, if that's what you think. I am . . .' But he paused, thinking some more. Rooster's eyes had opened somewhat and were staring at him more intently than might be thought necessary, almost as if the great mole was silently trying to tell him something.

'Strange behaviour in this mole,' he thought, before whispering conspiratorially, 'Would I be right in surmising that you think there is a spy in our midst who might be listening to all I say? Ah! Highly likely. I should have thought of it. That must mean that not all of these moles are of your party, as it were. Some were here when you arrived, or were brought here afterwards. You appear a somewhat uncommunicative mole, Rooster, but if you do not wish to speak at least nod your head to indicate that Weeth, that's me, is on the right track.'

As he had whispered this, another mole, almost as formidable, had come over and joined them, and Rooster stanced a little aside for him.

'I'll tell you one thing,' Weeth continued, since neither of *them* spoke, 'you need a lot of courage to stance here as I am doing and whisper to you two the way you look. Dear me, your looks do not encourage a mole to speak, but as you may have noticed I am not easily discouraged!' He grinned cheerfully. 'I'm annoying to some moles,' he added.

Rooster spoke at last: 'Yes,' he said.

'About me, or about there being spies in our midst?' rejoined Weeth immediately, hoping to see the fire of conversation burst forth from this tiny spark.

'Both,' said Rooster.

'She said you were monosyllabic, and you are,' said Weeth most cunningly. 'Words come out of you like blood out of a stone. She said.'

'Who said?' asked Rooster, just as Weeth hoped he would.

'Privet,' said Weeth so quietly that only a mole who knew the name would have recognized it. So quiet indeed that Rooster and the other mole hunched forward as if they had not quite heard and certainly could not believe, and their eyes were even more intense than before.

'Did you say *Privet*?' whispered the other mole.

Weeth nodded, pleased with himself. He was, he felt, establishing his credentials. 'Now, let me guess!' he said, frowning in an exaggerated way, and touching his talons to his brow. 'Let me *think*. You must be Hamble! Yes? Am I right? Let me out of my misery.'

Hamble grinned. 'That's right, and you had better tell us what you know about Privet or you'll not move far from here again.'

'Well!' said Weeth, sounding mock-shocked. 'Intimidation, and from a mole who is said to fight for the old ways of the Stone! Not the thing at all, I would have thought. But stap my vitals, there's things I want to talk to you about. Yet your eyes are stern, your faces suspicious, and words do not come readily, even allowing for the fact that

264

you are taciturn moles. Why, if I met me in these circumstances I would be all over myself with questions, and looking for opportunities. But no, you hold back, and I think it is because you think I am a Newborn spy.'

'Yes,' growled Rooster.

'There's an easy way to find out if a mole is Newborn: ask him to do something Newborns are constitutionally incapable of, namely, cursing their beloved Thripp. They find that really hard, though I dare say there are a few who have been trained by Quail himself to say such things.'

'Go on,' said Hamble.

'Well, for example, it ought to be patently obvious, even to untutored eyes such as your own – I use the word relative to myself only and not in general judgement of you, but you must understand I am well-trained in spotting Newborn spies since until recently I was one myself – that mole over there,' (here Weeth pointed a talon at a harmless-looking mole stanced quietly in one corner), 'is in fact Newborn, poor idiot. He has been put in here amongst you to pick up what tidbits he can, but I hope your reluctance to talk to me indicates that you have identified him, and the fact that there is at least one other like him in our midst. Namely, *him.*' Here, Weeth pointed out another mole, very different from the first, being large, affable, and at that moment in conversation with some of the moles who appeared to be of Rooster's captured party.

'Ah, I see you don't believe me. Unloved and unrespected Weeth is used to it, and it saddens him. But there we are. So . . . how to tell a Newborn spy? Go and ask him to repeat "Thripp is a blasphemous shit" or words to that effect. Try it.'

Rooster looked wearily at Hamble, and Hamble turned and went to the first mole, loomed over him, and asked him to repeat precisely what Weeth had said. After a few moment of discussion Hamble came back.

'He wouldn't.'

'Try the other one, do,' said Weeth.

By now the gist of Weeth's efforts was being understood and the second mole he had pointed out, having found his attempt to sidle up towards the narrow portal out of the cell blocked by the very moles he had been talking to, was confronted by the same proposal.

'Thripp,' he began falteringly, the use of the name without the title sticking in his throat, 'Thr . . . is . . . he is . . . Thri . . .'

'Well mole, what is he?' asked Hamble.

'Long live the Elder Senior Brother Thripp,' cried out the mole suddenly and with considerable courage, raising his talons as best he could against the blasphemous moles he had sought to infiltrate.

Several pairs of hefty paws grabbed hold of him, some by the head but more at the rump, and propelled him without further ceremony towards the cell's portal where two guards, hearing the commotion, suddenly loomed, talons raised.

'Moles,' cried out Hamble, 'this is one of your kind and we don't want him in here. Take him, before some of my less civilized friends lose patience.' The spy was thrown bodily through the portal. The others turned their attentions next to the smaller of the two who, and again with impressive courage, had cast off his look of abject inconsequentiality and raised his paws to the mighty foes about him.

''Op it!' said one of Rooster's moles benignly, and not without respect. The mole did.

In the silence that followed Weeth turned his gaze on the far recesses of the chamber and said, 'Any more spies about? Speak now or for ever hold your peace!' He grinned into the shadows before muttering to the silent Rooster, 'They normally come in threes, you see.'

For a moment more nomole moved, but then one detached himself from the group he was with and said, 'You are all cursed, you are evil, you will be judged wanting before the Stone!' And, as boldly as he could, he too headed for the portal, and the safe welcome of the guards beyond.

'Leaves *you*,' said Rooster, moving at last as he loomed hugely over Weeth, whose grin faltered into a kind of brief falsetto laugh.

'Me? Yes, me *and* you,' he said.

'Are you Newborn?' said Rooster, reaching out the bigger of his paws, grasping Weeth by the neck and raising him slowly off the ground until his eyes nearly popped out of his head.

'You said "Privet",' said Rooster fiercely. 'Know "Hamble". Know *me*. Whatmole are you if not spying like others?'

Weeth felt himself released, and tumbled towards the ground, his throat rasping and stars spinning somewhere overhead; he knew, or rather *felt*, what he must do and opportunity be damned. He had never felt more certain of anything in his life.

Though he landed clumsily the energy of thought and the desire for action were in him, and gave him strength to spring back to almost his normal confident self; hoarse though his voice was, and painful his eyes, he thrust his snout without demur up towards Rooster's and eyed him angrily.

'Privet didn't need proof,' he said. '*She* knew a good mole when she met one. Violence does not bring out the best in a mole, and it does not bring out the best in me . . .'

Weeth did not, could not, notice that Hamble had retreated a little, and in his worn lined face was a look not quite of respect or trust so much as hope and conviction, as if he saw in Weeth a new direction, a new possibility – even, dare he say it, a new opportunity.

'. . . and I do not appreciate being raised off my paws by anymole and made to look a fool – least of all by . . .'

And here, having regained his poise, he paused to give what he was about to say the greatest possible impact.

'. . . least of all by Rooster of the Charnel, son of Samphire, one-time friend of Glee and Humlock, a mole who lived on Hilbert's Top with Privet (a mole I would have thought would not have spent five minutes with one who grabs others by the throat and humiliates them), and scourge of the Newborns in the north; *least of all* by a Master of the Delve.'

If Weeth had calculated that this title was the one thing that Rooster could not bear others to use, that his friends avoided and his enemies did not repeat to his face if they wished to stay alive, he was right; if, too, he had guessed in his acute intelligent way that it was the quickest way to reach through the brooding taciturnity of the Charnel mole to the heart beyond, he was right in that as well, though the consequences he could not have predicted.

For Rooster reared up from where he stanced, his rough russet fur angrily catching what little light there was, and his brute, furrowed snout flaring as his mouth opened and his eyes seemed to flame red and angry, and he raised his paws over Weeth's head.

But Weeth went resolutely on down the dangerous tunnel into which he had so suddenly and boldly entered, and daring to point a paw at Rooster he said, 'You want to know about Privet? You want to know about her life since she left you? You want to know about the Newborn threat and what may happen here, this very night perhaps, in Caer Caradoc? Then you must trust me, *believe* me. But by the Stone, I ask myself why I should trust *you*. A Master of the Delve who dares threaten a mole with violence? What horror is this? Well, mole, I shall be silent on those things about which I know you wish me to speak until you decide for yourself whether or not I am a spy for the cursed Newborns. And how will you decide? Let me tell you . . .'

To the astonishment of the moles watching Weeth dared turn his back on the huge and smouldering Rooster and go to the far side of the chamber where some light cast itself on the rough hard wall. To this he raised a paw and in a swift untidy motion sketched out a scribing of a kind. It was not much, yet it had a certain form, and to Weeth it had meaning.

'I may not be able to scribe much,' he said, turning toward Rooster once more, 'but I can scribe my name. There it is. *You*'re a trained Master of the Delve, so they say, so ken it as a Master would, and pronounce as Privet did without recourse to stratagems and tricks what kind of mole I may be.'

There was stunned silence at this, and Weeth stanced to one side to let Rooster go forward to the wall. But Rooster did not move. He lowered his paws, staring confusedly at Weeth in strange fear and incomprehension.

'Can't,' he said at last, looking round wildly. 'Haven't ever since. *Can't.*'

There was a lost pup in that cry, a desolate soul, terrible loneliness of spirit; the mood in the chamber changed to one of despair, sympathy, and pity to see a mole exposed so publicly to something all there must have known, as Weeth did, he had for so long been afraid to face.

It was Hamble who moved, good Hamble who had known and loved Privet so well when they were young, and whose scarred and worn body now testified that he had stanced flank to flank with Rooster through these long years of fugitive desolation as truly as the truest friend.

He put a paw to Rooster's shoulder, and his head close to Rooster's lowered snout, and said, 'It's a fair thing this mole has asked and if you can't ken the scribing for yourself, ken it for me, for I would like to hear something of Privet's life if this mole can tell it. And he's not going to talk until you do.'

Rooster looked up at the scribing, and then at Weeth. 'Tell what you know. Can't ken the scribing. But trust you without.'

For a moment it seemed that Weeth, having made his point, would be satisfied with that, and he even opened his mouth to speak, and began to smile as if to say, 'Another time, ken it another time.' But then he saw an appeal in Hamble's eyes, and sensed a need in these moles that Rooster still led, and he shook his head and said, 'You were a Master once, so just for a moment be a Master once again. My scribing is a simple thing which will tell you more than all the protestations of my innocence of spying ever could.'

268

Cornered, Rooster stared and shook his head and his paws fretted. 'Is Privet happy?' he said at last.

Weeth was silent.

'Privet safe?' whispered poor Rooster.

Weeth stanced down calmly and sighed.

'Need to know,' said Rooster desperately.

'You know what to do,' said Weeth.

Then Rooster, moving like an aged, ailing mole, each paw reluctant, and his breathing heavy and almost painful, moved slowly towards the wall. When he reached it he stared at the scribing, almost as if scenting it.

'Can't,' he said, hopeful that he might not have to even at the end.

'Must,' said Weeth, 'and will.'

Rooster raised a paw, the same he had used to pick up Weeth, and so slowly it was painful to see he brought it across the scribing. As he touched it his breathing eased and his head cocked to one side as if, somewhere from afar, he had heard a sound he recognized, but did not expect to hear. Indeed he half looked round somewhere into the high recesses of the chamber and others followed his wild gaze and peered fearfully into the shadows. But there was nothing, or nothing to see at least. But as he touched Weeth's scribing a slight sound came, distant and gentle, perhaps no more than a trick of surface wind, but *something*, and it was good and sweet, and it was not captive at all.

He turned back with more resolution to the scribing and most gently, and with the utmost concentration, followed its form across the wall, not once but twice, with one paw and then the other. As he did so the sound across the chamber seemed to swell just a little, and there came to his stance, to his whole body, a kind of peace, as of a mole who has journeyed far, and lost much, but who now has caught a glimpse across the hills of a place that he once called home and might yet reach again.

For a moment more Rooster leaned against the wall, both paws on Weeth's scribing, and his body shook in what, judging from the soft puppish sound he made, was surely a sob. Then he drew back and lowered first one paw and then the other and turned to Weeth. There was the dark and glittering course of a tear down his face-fur.

'This mole's not bad, mole's good,' he said. 'Loving mole. Mole's all right.'

Weeth stared into Rooster's eyes and for the first time he saw the mole that Privet had loved, and he understood why these other moles had followed him so far, and why Hamble of Crowden, surely a leader, had allowed himself to be led so long. Within this great strange body, this near-monstrosity of a mole, whose eyes were askew, whose paws were gross, Weeth sensed the gentlest soul he had ever known.

'Privet,' said Rooster simply. 'Have missed her all my life. Will tell me now?'

'Yes,' said Weeth, his voice shaking with emotion, 'I will tell you all I can.'

So he did, to the best of his ability; all that morning, as Rooster and Hamble and their colleagues clustered about him, he told them what he himself had been told on the way from the High Wolds to Caradoc. That done, he explained that Privet, Maple, Whillan and the others were close at paw and likely to be in increasing danger as the time passed towards Longest Night.

Their circumstances, and the reason for their coming to Caer Caradoc, he very soon explained, then spent more time, as Rooster wished him to, on matters to do with Privet, and those parts of her tale that he had been told during the journey. Again and again Rooster asked if Privet was 'happy' and 'content', and had she mentioned him and matters relating to him and, if she had, what she had said. Weeth had no hesitation in enlightening him as best he could, and soon found his slightest recollection of incidents along the route from the High Wolds, such as they were, and things she had said – for which his memory was as good as his respect was great – had Rooster and Hamble utterly absorbed.

But one matter in which Rooster was not in the slightest bit interested, and indeed frowned and turned away when it was mentioned, was that of Privet's rearing of Whillan. When Weeth first mentioned him Rooster assumed that Whillan was Privet's natural pup, and his jealousy was obvious, but even when it was explained that he was merely raised by her, having been adopted, his disgruntlement continued, for like all moles that harbour romantic love for some mole they have not seen since they were young, he could not bear to think that she might have loved, or been loved by, another, even if it be a foster pup.

Weeth's task was made yet harder on this point because of the knowledge he had gained from Privet herself concerning her bearing of pups in Blagrove Slide to a Newborn, but this his natural tact and good sense prevented him from mentioning at all. Seeing Rooster's response now he was glad he had been reticent, and said little more of Whillan either after that.

Of matters to do with the Newborns it was plain that Rooster and the others were as well informed as Weeth himself, and their information concurred with his that the situation had reached a critical pass and if moles wished to be involved in the forming of a freer moledom, and one that did not give the heavy dogmatic paw of the Newborns total power, they had best not be confined in a deep, dark chamber. All that he said served to engender in Rooster a great restlessness and concern, and when Weeth reached the end of his tale and told how he and Privet had been parted only shortly before he had been led down to the cell Rooster was nearly beside himself with anxiety to get out and help her.

Not that Weeth was fool enough to think that they had not already considered every possible way of escape, and found that there seemed to be none. But to Weeth 'seemed' was the operative word, holding as it did the promise that there might, just might, be a way of escape they had missed if a mole could but find it.

His tale done, and with a promise from Rooster and Hamble that they would reciprocate with a telling of their tale since Privet had left the Moors, Weeth took a turn about the chamber to see if escape was really as impossible as his new friends said. He found the walls solid and impossible to burrow, and the portal cleverly designed such that its bottom part was so narrow that only one mole at a time could pass through, and that with difficulty. The walls sloped outward above paw height to accommodate a mole's body, and had been cleverly devised to make it possible for a single guard to control access; with two or three talon-thrusts he could immobilize any mole trying to pass through, and so block the passage of any behind him.

'That's certainly the only escape route,' Weeth agreed after making his inspection, 'but it's not unlike the design of a portal in a cell I was once thrown into for a time in a system over near the Wolds. I pondered long and hard about that and a couple of possibilities did occur to me, though . . .' His voice faded as his thoughts and gaze drifted back to the portal. 'I really wanted to hear your tale, but let me just have another look . . . do moles ever go in and out, for grooming perhaps? And how do they provide you with food?'

'We are allowed out singly for a short time to the chamber beyond and thence to the surface if necessary, and we've all thought of trying to escape that way,' explained Hamble. 'But we are very heavily guarded and there is little chance of it – and what is more an attempt to escape is dealt with harshly. We have been told that one who tried, not one of our own, died. Sometimes moles are summoned out for

271

questioning or some other purpose, or sent in to join our number –
more in, perhaps because they're getting vagrant moles like yourself
who might cause trouble out of the way before the Convocation starts.
Food is brought to the portal and pushed in. What ideas for escape
did you have during your previous captivity?'

Weeth smiled enigmatically and said nothing, going back to the
portal for a time and watching the company of guardmoles beyond, at
least two of whom were always on duty at the far end of the portal.
During that time one mole was brought into the chamber and Weeth
intently watched as he was led to the portal and shoved through it.

'See an opportunity?' asked one of the Rooster moles ironically,
when he came back.

'Yes, but one which depends on the mole coming in, a certain kind
of mole,' replied Weeth. 'But that is outside our control. Nevertheless
I shall watch and continue to think. Meanwhile, you were going to tell
me how you came to be incarcerated here, right from the beginning.'

Which they did throughout the afternoon, stopping only when
Weeth, with a polite nod, turned from them to observe the comings
and goings at the portal until, bit by bit, his expression suggested that
he might possibly have devised a plan.

But when they asked what it was he only said, 'No, no, not yet, not
yet! Continue – your tale is so interesting and you appear to be so
near the end.'

Chapter Twenty-Two

The sense of foreboding that Chater had begun to feel on his arrival as a captive so near to Caer Caradoc naturally deepened as he found himself being led away into grim tunnels on the afternoon before Longest Night, and was not helped at all by the sharp and sudden sense that far off, somewhere near Uffington, his beloved Fieldfare was thinking of him. He had never in his life been the kind of mole subject to strange fancies, nor one who gave much credence to premonitions or those inexplicable communions between moles who love each other but have been forced far apart by their tasks in the Stone. But the feeling that Fieldfare was nearby in spirit – so near, indeed, that he half expected to meet her round the next corner of the grim tunnel he was being forced down – would not go away, and added considerably to his belief that something extraordinary and final was apaw, and that it would be part of his task to confront it.

Nor could he shake off the feeling, so uncharacteristic of so optimistic yet cautious a mole, whose life as a journeymole had taken him through so many scrapes, that this time events were running faster than he could control, and that the final turn in his life had come and that the Stone, much as it sought to protect its devoted followers, must sometimes ask a mole as part of his task to make a supreme sacrifice.

'It's given me a lot in my time, and its constant protection,' he muttered to himself as he went along, 'and now it's asking for my help as if it knows there's no other mole hereabout who can serve it as well as I! What it wants me to do I cannot imagine. But I would have liked to see my Fieldfare again, not only because I love her, but because my last words to her when I parted from her near Uffington were that she'd hear from me before long.'

He paused briefly in the tunnel, causing the Newborn guards behind him to talon him in the rump to start him moving again. But in that brief moment of time he had space to stare ahead, and he realized that though he was alone and afraid he was also a lucky mole, for he had been much loved all his rough life by the best mole he had ever known.

'Blow it!' he said resolutely to himself, summoning up all his courage and resolve and trying to rid himself of his imaginings, 'I'm not going to let a bunch of Newborns get *me* down. Fieldfare, my sweet, if you're putting in a word for me to the Stone, because you sense I'm in trouble, you keep on doing it, because your Chater needs all the help you can get him.'

Muttering such thoughts and prayers to himself Chater continued his grim passage through the tunnels, the sweat of strain and apprehension darkening the fur about his neck as he tried to put boldness into his paws, and to stay alert, for whatever it was that the Stone was going to ask him to do it was going to be soon, very soon.

'But not soon enough!' he whispered to himself a little later, when the guards came to a stop as they crossed another communal tunnel and ran into a hurrying search party of Newborns.

'Stay here awhile so you don't cause confusion while the search for her continues,' he heard one in the patrol command.

'What's going on?' asked Chater.

A talon-thrust in the face was the only reply from his guards, but he heard one of the patrol say, as they left, 'Bloody Duncton moles. Should have killed the bitch while we could.'

Chater reacted to this with a mixture of excitement and concern. If the mole was of Duncton and she was female, then, by the Stone, whatmole else could it be but Privet herself? Which made Chater almost inclined to try to escape there and then, except that he had too much sense not to bide his time, and wait for a better opportunity.

'Come on,' said the guards at last after a long delay, 'we're not hanging about here any longer. Let's get you down there now where you can't cause us any more trouble.'

'Where?' asked Chater.

'Move on and shut up!'

So he did, but alert now, and encouraged by his sense of Fieldfare's distant prayers, and the welcome news that a Duncton mole had escaped and was causing the Newborns trouble – just as Duncton moles traditionally caused trouble for those who sought to take away others' liberty.

'*I'll* be causing you lot trouble too before long, given half a chance,' said Chater, as he was led on down the tunnel to his fate.

*

274

The tale Weeth heard, mainly from Hamble, of the wanderings of Rooster and the others was indeed interesting, as many a mole has discovered who has kenned any of the histories of the times, or any of the several biographies of Rooster that have since been scribed.

After the death of Red Ratcher, Rooster had had little difficulty in so cowing the other Ratcher moles, including several who must have been his brothers or half-brothers, that in a matter of hours the situation of conflict across the Moors between the grike-dominated Ratcher moles and the moles of Crowden had changed. Confrontation had given way to co-operation, and though there were to be several more summer moleyears of difficulty, as different factions of the Ratcher moles tried to regain control over their brethren, Rooster's power to inspire and lead was so great that they soon weakened and faded away.*

Before autumn he had been able to return in a kind of triumph to the Reapside of Charnel Clough, going there in the hope that he might find a way to cross into the Charnel itself once more and be reunited with the moles he had been forced to leave behind. But the Span was gone irrecoverably, and though they journeyed up and down the side of the gorge, and even back out of the Clough altogether and over the Tops to try to climb down by way of the Creeds, the Charnel was unreachable. A mole would either drown in the Reap in the attempt, or tumble to his death down the huge cliffs which, from above, seemed impassable to mole. He went back for one last try, thinking that at the upper end of the Reapside, near the Creeds themselves, where the river flowed out from the head of the valley and waterfalls tumbled down from the heights above, a mole might get across – but only with luck, not judgement, and by leaping from slippery boulder to boulder, between which treacherous white water raced, and above which the ravens cawed in the spray, and hopped out for the carrion of drowned moles, dashed by the rushing water against the rocks and washed up dead somewhere down the gorge.

Several of the moles would not venture near the place, and in the end only Hamble would go with Rooster to make the attempt. Yet notwithstanding the dangers and insanity of trying such a thing,

* The most exhaustive account of these times is certainly that by Scammell, entitled *The Master Rooster's Middle Years: Trial or Triumph?* Whillan of Duncton's fascinating *Out of Charnel Clough* is perhaps the most insightful account of Rooster's early life, and is regarded as a classic by moles interested in the story of the recovery for moledom of the lost delving arts.

Rooster was so desperate to reach the other side and find out if his friends Humlock and Glee were still alive, that he certainly would have tried beyond even his strength, endurance and limits had not Hamble hauled him back.

'Finally, it was all I could do to get him to leave the Charnel,' Hamble quietly told Weeth later on when Rooster was talking to another mole, 'for after our failure to cross the Reap he just wanted to stance and stare through the skeins and mists of water at where, moleyears before, he had been forced to leave his dearest friends behind. He felt angry with life and with himself, guilty perhaps, and roared out his grief and pain. To this day, Weeth, he has not recovered from losing those two friends of his, and I believe that their loss lies at the root of his abandonment of the delving arts. Until you contrived to make him ken your scribing as a delver would, I swear I have never seen him apply the arts I know he still commands and probably longs to practise.'

'He never delves at all?' asked Weeth in astonishment.

'He'll delve a burrow like any other mole when he's travelling, and a defensive line as well if need be, and they'll be better than most could delve – swifter, sweeter of sound, better of lie – but they're only workaday and modest things compared to what we all know he could do if he wished. I would say that we have followed and supported him, in the hope that one day he may fulfil his promise as a Master of the Delve. My heart felt joy when you forced him to ken your scribing. There is hope still.'

'There is always hope, *always*,' said Weeth.

'You are a positive mole, Weeth, a remarkable mole.'

'Yes, I think so too!' said Weeth, which made good Hamble laugh aloud.

'I noticed in *your* telling you were reticent about this mole Whillan.'

'Rooster seemed put out that Privet should have reared him,' said Weeth.

'I was glad to hear she had had a mole to love. Her puphood was not good, and she was a timid mole, without the confidence of love. After she came off the Moors with Rooster all had changed, all seemed bright. She was as happy as I ever knew her, despite the pressure we were under in Crowden from the grikes.'

'But her sister, Lime . . .' began Weeth, who remembered *that* part of Privet's account especially well, for it was the only time that she had ever looked bitter.

'Ah, Lime,' said Hamble sadly, and, as it seemed to Weeth, with rather more sympathy than he would have expected, 'you know of her then? She did much wrong, but she suffered much for it too, more perhaps than anymole ever should. In the end Lime gained my respect and proved to me that anymole can grow, can develop, even if, as in her case, it ended in tragedy.'

Weeth might have heard more then, but Rooster came back, and the tale resumed from the Charnel, and Lime's trial and triumph and final tragedy duly unfolded as but part of his greater story.

After Rooster had lingered several more miserable days in the Charnel, staring bleakly across the impassable Reap and becoming inconsolable, his friends finally succeeded in leading him back out on to the Moors, where for a long time they wandered, bringing peace to the places where Red Ratcher and others like him had brought anarchy for so long. Throughout this time Rooster stayed silent and depressed, a wild, desolate mole, whose mood and character well complemented the Moors, which were now his free domain.

At his flank he had Lime, who had stolen him from Privet, and ousted her. He now took her as his own, jealous in his protection of her, passionate in his attentions, and yet – and this was plain enough to Weeth as he heard the tale – Rooster held on to her from duty as much as passion, and in his love was the bitter fruit of the knowledge that through her intervention he seemed to have lost Privet and his true vocation for ever.

The two tried to have pups, and had they done so, then perhaps the nature of Rooster's love would have changed, deepened and grown, and in the rearing of his offspring he might have found the outlet that his denial of delving robbed him of. But they did not, or could not, and so their love was but physical passion, and swung from argument to reunion, from recrimination to reconciliation, from passionate but temporary interest, to passionate and recriminatory boredom.

'Only give me pups!' she would scream in her worst moments of anger. 'But you cannot, Rooster, and you are not true mole. Give me pups or I will take another mole to me for them!'

Then he would strike her, and she would strike him back, and they would rage and weep, and shout and cry across the Moors their wild and fruitless love, or love-hate, the embodied expression of that great pack of moles that Rooster now led, but whom only quiet Hamble, faithful, trusting deeply in the Stone, and with an abiding belief in Rooster's ultimate destiny as a Master of the Delve, kept loyal.

They centred their activity for a time on Crowden, but since Red

Ratcher's death Rooster did not like the place and they moved their centre to the Weign Stones up in the Moors. There, in their own wild ways, they were followers of the Stone, and when females joined their little society they formed a community which, even if it was mixed and rough, was better and more benign than any the Moors had known for decades past. Rooster was its strange and troubled spirit, Hamble its firm and generous organizer: two moles who successfully acted as one, and trusted and respected each other as only true friends can.

But in truth it was Hamble who held the group together, not as the stronger of the two but as the more stable and approachable. Whilst Rooster's moods swung this way and that, not helped (as it seemed to Hamble) by the passions and rages of his relationship with Lime, Hamble was always there – friend to both moles, friend to all. His life was his friend's, sacrificed to some vision of Rooster that seemed all hopeless and laid waste and which had come originally perhaps from Privet. He took no mate, no private companionship, and existed for nothing but the greater good of the moles that stayed with Rooster, and believed there was something in him still.

There they might have remained had not a group of Newborn missionaries, looking for pastures new, made the mistake – the fatal mistake – of venturing up into the Moors to visit the Weign Stones in late February as the snows thawed, seeking to convert anymole who lived there. How could they know they were *Rooster's* moles?

'It was as if they gave a focus to all that anger and guilt and sense of failure that Rooster felt,' Hamble explained to Weeth. 'He has, you see, a way of responding to moles that is instinctual, and has little to do with reason. Perhaps it is because he *is* a delver, and feels things far more strongly than he is able to think them. I do not say he is always right – in the matter of Lime I think he was finally very wrong – but we who are his friends know that usually he is right, and so we follow him.'

When the Newborn missionaries came, Rooster's response to them was rough and ready. He felt them to be corrupt, and perhaps saw more clearly than others could, not simply the facile and arrogant nature of their beliefs, but more than that, the deep corruption of spirit of the system from which they had emerged. He personally drove them off the Moors for a whole night and day, roaring and savage in his threats, yet those like Hamble who followed laughing in his wake, noticed he was careful not to hurt them beyond a mild buffeting.

But at the end, when they threatened him as a blasphemer and a

278

'grike' he should not perhaps have hurled them bodily downslope off the last part of the Moors. They ended up shocked, badly bruised, strained, but worst of all with a pride sufficiently hurt that they took back to the Senior Brothers false stories of violence they had suffered from 'moles of the Word'.

Had the Newborns left it at that, moledom might have heard no more about it, and Rooster and Hamble and their friends have stayed on the Moors and not strayed to the lower, greener and more wormful valleys to the west and south. But at the hint, false though it was, that there were still moles of the Word on the Moors, the Newborns sent out a punitive crusade of missionaries from Blagrove Slide and began a campaign of retribution for the imagined hurts the first four had suffered, in which isolated and harmless moles died, pups were taken, females left ravaged and alone. These were moles in small systems far from Rooster's protection, for at first they attacked only on the north-eastern fringes of the Moors. But emboldened by early success the Newborns made an incursion up the valley of the River Crowden and at Crowden itself, inhabited by then by a small number of unassuming moles, they subjected all they found to vile massacres as moles of the Word. Then all across the Moors a new fear went, and its victims turned to Rooster, who had saved them from Red Ratcher, to rid them of the curse of the Newborn moles.

So began the grim struggle through early March between Rooster and the Newborns, the first in which the Newborns found a foe worthy of the name; moles who fought back, and who rejected the Newborn sectarian faith not with words but with talons, asking nothing but that they be left in peace. This brief and bloody war on the Moors only ended when, after seeking to avoid a confrontation by retreat, which was against his nature, and attempts at negotiation led by the more conciliatory Hamble, Rooster was driven at last to stance his ground and lead his friends against the Newborns in the grim Battle of the Weign Stones.

Between them, Rooster and Hamble brilliantly routed the New-borns and killed a good many, the rest fleeing off the Moors back to the lowlands once more. But this time, sensing that it would not end there, Rooster led his band in pursuit and so began the bloody odyssey through eastern moledom to seek to end for ever the war the New-borns had begun. It was a local war that attracted the worst elements of the Newborns, including it is said the Brother Quail, not yet as powerful as he became, who here developed the bloody and cruel punishments and tortures which he later applied more sparingly through his Brother Inquisitors, and so gained power far beyond any authority vested in him by the Newborn creed.

Meanwhile, Rooster and the others were adjusting to the nature of the lowland territory they had invaded. It is hard for ordinary moles, reared to such things, to imagine the impact that the lowland vales of wormful plenty, of blossom, of warmer winds and clear waters of brooks and streams had on moles reared only to the bleak wormless wilderness of the Moors. To the taciturn Rooster, uniquely sensitive to form and shape, texture and sound, this was a kind of paradise. But it was one marred by the continued and to him inexplicable assaults of the Newborns, who harried them wherever they went, and never seemed to give up. 'Teaching the Newborns a lesson', which was all the 'strategy' that Rooster and Hamble then really had, was proving far more difficult than they had thought.

But what made matters infinitely worse for Rooster was that it was there in the beautiful lowlands that he had his worst, most violent, and final argument with Lime. She had been as taken as he was by the gentleness of the landscapes they found themselves in, and her desire to have pups increased; she wanted to settle down, and be done with all fighting against the Newborns, and against Rooster.

'She simply wanted pups, like any female,' whispered Hamble to Weeth, expanding on a part of the tale that Rooster refused to talk about. 'And then, tragically as it turned out, she *got* with pup.'

'Why tragic?' asked Weeth in surprise.

'Because she fatally chose to tell Rooster, for reasons of argument or vindictiveness, that they were not *his* pups. I have never in my life seen him so angry – which is, of course, just what Lime wanted. After that she could not get him to believe they *were* his, and I myself had to pull him off her or else I swear she would have been killed. First his father, then the mole he got with pup!'

'Can you be sure they were his?' said Weeth.

'I am sure,' said Hamble sadly. 'She loved him as passionately as Privet had done, as all moles do. She taunted, she made foolish claims, but she would never have gone with another mole, *never!*'

'I believe you, Hamble, I believe you!' said Weeth, surprised at his passion about the matter after so many moleyears. 'What happened to her?'

'A female changes when she is with pup, and for the first time in her life Lime had others to think of but herself. I think, too, she saw in the lowland vales a gentleness and beauty that showed her a new way of living. She grew disgusted by the violence of the struggle with the Newborns, and with the mole she felt that Rooster had become. Then too she envied her sister Privet, you know, and often talked wistfully of the journey I had led Privet to the start of, to Beechenhill and, as she imagined – and as has been proved right by your account – to Duncton Wood.

'One day at the beginning of April, after her last argument with Rooster, she simply slipped away. For all the searches that we made, and the roaring and rage that Rooster showed, we did not find her, and she did not come back. I have known other moles of our group do the same, I have been tempted to do it myself – to slip away, to change a name, to become anonymous. Well, that is what Lime did.'

Weeth looked searchingly at Hamble, a clever mole experienced in subtleties studying a simple warrior whose nature was not devious or clever, only loyal, and honest, and good.

'You know more about it than you're saying,' said Weeth.

Hamble was silent for a long time. Moles came and went. Across the chamber Rooster stirred and stared and frowned, and dozed. Afternoon came. Weeth waited patiently, and watched Hamble's face.

'Aye,' sighed Hamble at last, 'I know something. I said she confided in me sometimes, and so she did. She talked to me the day before she left. "I've changed, Hamble," says she. "The fight's gone from me. These pups *are* Rooster's, but by the Stone I don't want him to raise them, to influence them as Red Ratcher influenced him. I don't want their lives to be fugitive and violent like his and mine have been. I want something better for them than we have had, or we can give."

'That's what she said and next day she was gone. Slipped away to anonymity to raise those pups, the pups of a Master of the Delve, where he would never be able to see them, or touch them.'

'At the beginning of April, you say?' said Weeth, with a strange look in his eye and a wondering tone to his voice, and a glance about the chamber, from Hamble to Rooster, and from Rooster to the darkest shadows.

'Aye, that's when she went. We saw no more of her, and I wasn't going to tell Rooster all I knew. In a way I agreed with her – best let her have her pups where none knew who their father was, and would never know. I have often thought of her, and prayed to the Stone that she had her way.'

'At the beginning of April,' mused Weeth again.

'Aye, what of it?'

''Tis nothing,' said Weeth hastily, though clearly it was. 'But Rooster, what did he feel about it all?'

'Remorse. Loss. Grief. He went into a kind of mourning. His life was blighted and I think that if he had not had about him moles who loved him he would have gone mad. Indeed, he did go mad for a time, and it was then that we turned away from the conflict with the Newborns and travelled north until we found ourselves in blessed Beechenhill. High, well made, a place of legend and holiness to us Moorish moles, a place of sanctuary. There were but a few moles there, and the remnants of a library, and the Newborns left us well alone – glad to be rid of us no doubt.

'All through those summer years Rooster tried to find himself. I think he tried to begin delving again, but the spirit had gone from him and he felt cursed. One after another he had lost moles he loved – Glee and Humlock, Samphire, Privet, the Charnel moles like Hume who did not long survive the journey from the Moors, and finally Lime, and with her, as he came to realize, his own pups, the pups he would never know.

'Rooster feels things deeper than most moles I know, and has the courage to turn towards his dark feelings and face them in the desert that he has made in his heart. Had he allowed himself to do what his paws longed to do, which was to delve, I believe he might have put all his shame and guilt and anger – misplaced though it mostly was – out of himself and into delvings. But he believed he had broken the vows against violence he had made as a delver in the Charnel, and had no right to do the one thing that might have given him release from the dark torments of remorse. Of all his friends only I was left, and these few companions here. How could I leave him, unhappy though I was, and lonely too? Do you think I did not want a mate? Do you think I felt happy to have as my task the tending of a half-mad Master of the Delve?'

'But you loved him,' said Weeth quietly, his eyes glancing to Rooster once more, all dark, and rough, and fearsome, and most courageously alone.

'Yes, I loved him,' said Hamble, his voice dropping to a whisper. 'But Stone knows that through the years I have also longed for a different life. I wanted female company, a true companion to share my tunnels, aye, and to raise our young. But what females would share a life with a fool who before all else puts a vision that the mole he follows and helps is a Master of the Delve? None that I ever met! Yes, I loved him, and love him still, just as Privet loved him. But I have also warned him long since that fighting and death is not to be our way any more. Of that I was tired, and that was surely not his

282

proper way. I was the only one left he trusted, or respected, and I felt that gave me the responsibility to nurture as best I could this mystery that was – that is – his continuing burden, the delving arts. Since Beechenhill he has known that I will not tolerate killing in the way we killed the Newborns during our war with them, justified though most of it seemed at the time. Defend himself if he must, but if ever I see him kill another mole when there's a better way to achieve his end then he's lost the truest friend he'll ever have.

'There must be another way than killing, though *I* cannot tell you what it is. If a mole threatens me with death, or my kin or my friends, then I would kill to save myself or them. But not Rooster's way, which is passionate and violent, and sometimes unnecessary. No, not that way.'

'So how come you are here in Caradoc, and imprisoned?'

'Ah, yes,' growled Hamble, 'this was against our better judgement. But emissaries came from the Newborns, claiming to be from Thripp himself indeed, suggesting that the librarians in Beechenhill – a timid couple of elderly moles – might venture here as delegates. I suggested that we ourselves might come if we were given safe passage, and though Rooster was reluctant, well, I persuaded him. But when we came close to Caradoc we were led *here* on some pretext or another.'

'You were fooled,' observed Weeth quietly.

'Aye, even moles of the Moors can be fooled,' said Hamble. 'They have told us little, but that our lives might be in danger if we venture up on to Caer Caradoc itself, because of the Newborns we killed those moleyears ago up in the Moors. We could have put up a struggle, I suppose, but as I've said, I wanted things more peaceable. Now—'

'Now,' said Weeth, 'I would say you – we – are in considerable danger. Oh yes, I scent Newborn treachery here. We'll have to get out, and this night if we can.'

'You said there is a way . . .'

'I did! But it all depends on the right mole coming. But of that I am quietly confident, since I have begun to think in recent days that the Stone is in all of this, more deeply than a pragmatic mole like me would normally concede. As a matter of fact, in one particular regard your tale rather confirms it.'

'Which is?'

'Ah, no, I prefer to remain silent upon *that*. It is but a faint and unconfirmed possibility, and as such I had best keep it to myself.'

'What is?'

283

But Weeth would say no more, turning back instead to the possibility of escape. 'Now, listen. There's likely to be only one way and one chance of getting out of here, and you had better face the fact, Hamble, that moles may die in the attempt. But if we stance here long enough we'll die anyway. This is what I suggest you do, and you had better first find a mole resolute enough to be agreeable to doing something most unpleasant and risky and—'

'*I'll* do it if it will help get us safely out of here,' said Hamble stoutly.

'You had better wait and hear what it is,' said Weeth with a grin.

And when Hamble had, he was still resolved to be the volunteer, though once he had told Rooster the plan, and those others with them had fully understood what their roles might be, not a mole there including Rooster himself but volunteered for the 'unpleasant' task that Weeth had warned Hamble must be done. But in the end, as often before in such matters, Hamble had his way. One by one, with feigned casualness, the moles assembled near the portal, Hamble nearest of all but for Weeth himself, who having conceived the plan now positioned himself where he could see out into the chamber beyond, ready to take the slim chance he was looking for if it should offer itself, and signal to the others to act as he had told them to.

Early evening had come, dusk was settling in, and the moles did their best to laugh and banter as they had before. One persuaded their captors to let him out and up to the surface to groom, and he was able to confirm the number and disposition of the guards, who most ominously were now more numerous than before, and looking grim indeed.

'All the more reason to take the opportunity when it comes,' commented Weeth.

'You're very sure of yourself,' said Hamble. 'I can see why you say you annoy other moles.'

'That is the lot of the confident opportunist . . . but silence! To my post! A mole comes!'

It was the kind of chance Weeth was evidently hoping for, another mole being brought into the cell. But watching carefully as he was, and poised though Hamble and the others were to play their parts, Weeth gave no signal and the mole, an old vagrant who had stumbled across a Newborn patrol near Caradoc and been hauled in, had little to offer in the way of help or information. Except that 'there's a lot of bloody guards about!'

The waiting went on and dusk gathered towards darkness; Rooster dozed again, though the flicking of his tail showed he was alert, but

284

others grew impatient and had to be admonished by Hamble, who stanced quiet and still, ready to act as Weeth had told him to if the moment came.

Then, some time later, when most were beginning to give up hope, sounds of movement came from beyond the portal, and then low-voiced argument. The waiting moles saw Weeth stance up and venture almost into the portal, stare out, and grow tense. He turned and signalled quickly to Hamble, and the great mole came closer, paws fretting on the ground. Rooster's eyes opened as if he heard the mounting commotion beyond the portal through the earth itself.

'I said a mole would come who would help us out and he has!' whispered Weeth gleefully to Hamble. 'Wait and watch. The moment I lower my left paw do as I have told you to. Only then. Not before and not afterwards, just—'

Weeth suddenly stopped talking and all the moles heard a rough, determined voice speaking loudly in protest from the chamber beyond. 'If you think I'm going through that portal, chum, you're mistaken.'

'I warn you one last time, mole, you do not argue here, you obey!' snarled the commanding voice of a Newborn guard.

'Yes! You certainly do!' cried out Weeth loudly through the portal, his left paw rising behind him as he did his best to peer through to the tussle beyond. Then calling out sharply and very clearly he continued, 'If you value your life, mole, and wish to help others, you will do exactly as I say.'

There was sudden and utter silence, just as Weeth had calculated there would be following his unexpected intervention. But he delayed only a moment before he spoke again, this time with chilling clarity.

'Talon the mole in front of you. NOW, mole, if you want to live this night through!'

As Weeth sent out this bold and brutal command he dropped his left paw rapidly and stanced back to one side. Hamble surged powerfully to his paws and ran straight at the portal, but not, as might have been expected, with a view to clambering through its impossibly narrow lower part, but to dive straight into it, front paws outstretched as he fell with a thump and gasp the length of the portal, his body squeezing into the awkward lower space, his head down. His broad rough back provided a surface across which Rooster himself, with a roar and lunge, immediately came charging, his great paws going over his friend's broad back unconfined by slanting walls and with space enough now to move swiftly and unencumbered. With a deep and

285

terrifying roar Rooster was through, and charging down the hapless guard who one moment had been in command of things and the next, having been taloned by the new prisoner who had just arrived, was now picked up and hurled back over the prisoner's head by the grike mole whose reputation for violence and unpredictability was there and then made still more legendary.

Sturdy Chater, who had rounded the final corner of the long series of tunnels he had been brought down through that afternoon and evening, had been absolutely ready to take action, though its nature and direction he did not guess until that astonishing moment when a grinning mole had appeared at the portal at the far end of the guards' chamber and commanded him to strike the guard ahead, and strike 'NOW!' Chater had not hesitated for one moment, and indeed even had Weeth not so commanded him he had intended to strike some-mole anyway and make a bid to escape, for the sight of so difficult a portal into the chamber told him that his last moments of liberty were upon him, and if he was going to try anything he had best get on with it.

So he had struck, and so had the most awesome and astonishing spectacle he had ever witnessed begun, as a great mole, whose name he did not then know, came flying into the portal, lay down, and an even greater one, as wild and frightening as any creature he had ever seen, followed through, picked up the taloned guard, hurled him back over Chater's head and knocked the guards behind him flying.

Realizing that the sooner he got out of the way of the portal the better, leaving space for the others who were already charging through, Chater moved his back to a wall and raised his talons, and soon found he was fighting the Newborn guards alongside moles who were as large and fierce as any he had ever seen.

Indeed, their assault on the Newborns was ferocious and initially unstoppable, so that as new contingents of guards came charging down the tunnels leading into the chamber to see what the commotion was, they found themselves driven back by a storm of fierce talons and angry moles. Chater found himself outpaced by his new-found colleagues, and took as his task the defence of their right flank against any attack that might come down a smaller tunnel that came in on that side.

It was not long, only moments perhaps, before the chamber was filled with the screams of wounded and dying moles and the grunts of fighting ones, and Chater's initial exhilaration at so suddenly finding

286

his wish to escape seemingly fulfilled was replaced by the growing awareness that their victory might be short-lived, for despite making swift progress beyond the chamber they might still be trapped, with their escape to the surface hindered by the narrow tunnels through which they would have to fight their way. Chater knew enough about such situations to know that moles would die, and bloodily, and escape be thwarted if, having gained the initial surprise and impetus they lost it, whilst beyond and above them their captors re-grouped and consolidated their superior forces round the exits.

He turned from the tunnel entrance he was guarding to try to assess the situation, and saw that the first and biggest of the escaping moles was already beginning to fight his way powerfully into a huge side tunnel which, evidently, went up to the surface and which he seemed familiar with. Meanwhile the tunnel Chater had entered by lay at the end of the chamber and on its left side, and another mole like him was guarding it.

'That's the way to go!' cried out Chater, for no sooner had he seen the general situation than he realized that the tunnel he had come through ought to be the one they were trying to escape by, since there had been no moles in it when he came through, and not far down it widened considerably which made it easier for numbers to advance. Even better, some distance up it were several ways out to the surface and the Newborns could not hope to guard them all.

But his cry was not heard, and he was unable to try again because at that moment a Newborn appeared at the lesser tunnel he was guarding, and tried to lunge at him. Once more Chater did not hesitate, but dodged the blow and followed it swiftly with a powerful thrust at his attacker's snout. There was a soft squelch as his talons plunged into the target, and then a scraping rasp as he made contact with bone and teeth. With his other paw he followed up the thrust and the mole staggered back screaming, and slumped to one side, effectively blocking the tunnel with his writhing body.

'Mole, give us a paw!' a deep voice gasped behind him, and Chater turned back and saw that it was the mole who had so bravely allowed his body to be used to fill the base of the portal, now struggling to extricate himself from the narrow confines other paws had pressed him into, so that he might join his talons to the fray.

Chater immediately went to his aid, and with a mighty heave and shove and a final tug released the mole so suddenly that he himself nearly fell over.

He in his turn righted Chater and said, 'My name's Hamble; and yours?'

'Chater!' declared Chater, his mind racing with the strange sense of destiny he felt as he heard the mole speak his name, and knew at once that this surely was Hamble of Crowden, *Privet's* Hamble.

He might indeed have said something had not a face popped in between them both and said, 'Introducing Weeth to one, and as a reminder to the other! Hello! And goodbye too, if we're not careful!' Weeth's gaze travelled swiftly beyond them to the awesome sight of the moles of the Moors fighting alongflank Rooster and after only a moment's pause he continued, 'Mole, were you trying to tell us something before Hamble called for your help?'

'There's a better way out by the tunnels I came down,' said Chater quickly, 'and as the exits lie a good way back I reckon the Newborns may not have thought to position moles there yet; but we'd best be quick if we're to take advantage of it.'

'Hamble, you're the only one with strength enough to point Rooster in a new direction,' said Weeth.

Hamble had no need to be told again, and as he rushed forward, and battled his way among his friends to Rooster's flank to redirect him Chater whispered in awe, 'Rooster? *The* Rooster? *Privet's* Rooster?'

'The same, friend!' said Weeth with a smile. 'And did I hear the name Chater, *Privet's* Chater?'

'You did.'

'Destiny walks in our shadows,' said Weeth grandly, 'and we have things to talk of . . .'

But Hamble had already turned back and was signalling Chater forward to act as guide to the tunnels down which he had come, a task he willingly and bravely began, taloning his way past two guardmoles and leaving them for others to finish off as he led Rooster and the others quickly out of the chamber. Hamble and others fought off the guards who had been at their front, but now found themselves in the rear as their quarry turned and ran swiftly out of sight.

Perhaps nomole will ever be able to describe the extraordinary running battle that now took place as Rooster, guided by Chater, led his moles to freedom through that labyrinthine set of tunnels that the Newborns had delved in the vale to the south-east of Caer Caradoc.

Of the horror of that night there are accounts enough, and false though Stone followers may regard the Newborn sect's methods and beliefs, none would deny that they were courageous and persistent in their pursuit of the moles who had escaped. But quite which moles died where, or by whose talons, is now impossible to say, except that all who were witnesses to the chase avow that Rooster was like a mole possessed by some dark and vengeful spirit of the night, and again and again, and again, when the Newborn guards seemed certain at last to block their way and recapture them, he summoned up the energy to charge forward one more time, and rout those at the forefront of the attack against him.

They finally reached the fresh air of the surface only after night had come, and even then had to fight their way through a cluster of guards who had been warned that they might go that particular way. By then Rooster had lost three of his friends, and the Newborns many more, and blood and the weariness that comes with killing and maiming others was on them.

It was then, in the short lull between killing one of the guards who had sought to prevent their escape from the exit and maiming another, as two more ran off into the night, before others appeared to carry on the fight, that Rooster committed that controversial act which some moles have said no true Master of the Delve should have done. He grasped one of the stricken guards in his bloodstained paw and almost incoherent with rage and the excitement of battle and escape, he thundered, 'Privet? Where is she? Tell now, mole!'

The guard was raised up into the air, just as Weeth had been earlier that day, and as he refused to speak Rooster continued to roar incoherently at him and shook him so violently that Hamble was forced to stop what seemed little short of torture. Perhaps it was, or perhaps the maimed mole was already close to death, nomole can ever know. But he could only stare at Rooster, and mouth some words made inaudible by the blood that frothed at the corners of his gaping mouth, before he died, and Rooster let him fall to the ground.

'No more!' roared Hamble, buffeting his old friend, 'no more killing now! It is enough, and I warned you what I would do if you ever went too far again! No more of this, we'll climb Caradoc . . .'

Then with shouts and curses more Newborn guards approached, led by none other than Senior Brother Quail himself, and the Moors group, as if wishing to abide by what Hamble had said, turned and fled into the night, to begin the great climb up Caer Caradoc. A night like that in Caradoc at that season can grow deep and dark indeed if the clouds burgeon and the moon goes in. At that crucial moment the moon darkened and the stars faded, and Rooster and the others were able to make good their escape, if escape it was that was leading them up Caer Caradoc itself.

So much confusion, so many doubts of what moles wanted that night, and why they acted as they did. As Rooster led the charge up the great hill Hamble found himself disinclined to follow, and at his flank Chater stayed too and Weeth, all well aware that Newborns were coming. But each alike had been made to pause before the violent and terrible death of the mole Rooster had raised up and then let fall, and now they did not want to follow him. As one they turned north into the shadows along Caer Caradoc's edge, three running moles, not one of them wanting to raise their paws in violence for Rooster, for the Stone, for themselves, nor for anymole. Not that night, at any rate.

Above them they heard their friends climbing into the darkness, pursued by the Newborns; but these sounds died away, and about them a silence slowly fell. But one last moment of horror came, strange, memorable, and scribed down by the one of those three good moles who survived to tell the tale.

For as they ran on, up out of the ground in front reared a Newborn mole. Who he was, what he was, or why he was there none knows. But out of the darkness he appeared and raised his paws in self-defence and then, well trained perhaps, or thinking his hour had come, he thrust hard and blindly at the one nearest to him.

It was Chater who took the violent blow, straight into his chest, though at the time it seemed no more than a mild buffet. In the spirit of the three moles' new pacificity, the Newborn was simply pushed aside, not taloned or hurt at all. They ran on for a time, Chater doing no more than clasping his chest at some pain he felt and swearing in the way for which Fieldfare had so often admonished him.

On, on they ran, not from fear, but from a common desire to escape from those tunnels and fields of death to a more peaceful world they hoped might come with the dawn, which would herald the coming of Longest Night, and the seasons' turn to a better world, and better ways, away from the violence they had witnessed, of which they had been a reluctant part.

'Moles,' whispered Chater, stumbling suddenly as his face twisted into mortal pain, 'I cannot go with you further. That mole hurt me, I cannot . . .'

Then Weeth stopped and held him at one flank, with great Hamble at the other, and they shook their heads and said they would not go on without the mole whose arrival, and whose resolution, had given them all another chance of liberty.

'Then help me on,' said Chater, leaning on them, 'and maybe if I

290

can rest for just a little somewhere safe I'll recover my breath.'

But the night stayed cruel, for the sounds of pursuit began behind them, the now-familiar shouts of Newborn guards. No doubt the one who had struck Chater had given the alarm, and had noted the direction in which they had fled.

'Lead him on,' said Weeth to Hamble, stopping suddenly. 'Go on. I'll lead these Newborns another way and find you a little later. Go *on.*'

As he turned back so bravely to mislead the Newborns they heard him stop and call after them, 'But I forgot to tell you about Rooster! There's something about him, about it all. Something I should have told you. Hamble . . . it's Rooster . . .'

But the shouts grew louder, and Weeth's voice faded, as Hamble, his strong paw about Chater, drew him on into the night, to find a place where a journeymole who had served his time and done his duty bravely and well, might now find peace, and rest, and the need to journey on no more.

Chapter Twenty-Three

If Maple and Whillan, high up on the top of Caer Caradoc, had thought they could easily escape into obscurity amidst the busy and over-watched tunnels to which they had been confined that night of death and dark treachery preceding the beginning of the Convocation, they were much mistaken.

But they tried. Sometime in the evening, when things quietened down after the tunnels reached a crescendo of frenetic rush in late afternoon, they set off separately for their quarters, and on the way, in a place they had pre-arranged, met up and slipped away, as they thought, quite undetected.

Snyde at least had not seen them, that much was certain, for he was busily engaged in talking to various scribemoles who had been deputed to him, and to whom he was assigning tasks of recordkeeping. To Whillan it seemed increasingly more likely that Snyde had been given a task by the Newborns simply to shut him up and keep him busy; if this was the Newborns' hope, they underestimated Snyde. But no matter, at least it took his attention away from them.

The two Duncton moles met up and took off, doing their best to look like busy moles entrusted with a task and on their way to do it; they went down one tunnel and then another, keeping nearby the busier parts until they were far from the huge communal chamber in which they had spent much of the day and back towards the Eastside of the hill where they had first come down.

Near there they found a small unoccupied chamber and stayed awhile in it, listening as moles went back and forth, relieved that no great hue and cry had followed them.

'We're benefiting from the general confusion,' said Maple with some satisfaction, and in a sense he was right, for nomole but one had noticed their disappearance. 'Probably the Newborn guards think we've retired to our quarters, and so long as Snyde stays away from them sorting out his stupid task, then there's no reason for anymole to discover we've gone. And when they do, what can they do? Just stance back and wait, for I'll warrant they've got guards about the ways off Caradoc who they'll rely on to pick up wanderers like us who try to leave.'

During a lull they sneaked out of their refuge, and moved on down to yet obscurer tunnels, and found another small chamber, really no more than an underground scrape, to hide in. There they waited, letting night fall deeper, and wishing that the stars and moon were not so bright out on the surface, or those parts of it which they could glimpse from the only entrance near where they were hiding, up which they occasionally poked their snouts and peered about.

'Dangerous to go out or try going further in this gloom – best to lie low here,' said Maple. 'It may not be very heroic, but whatmole can be heroic when he's no idea what's apaw or where he is? My instinct tells me the best thing is just to lie low and stay unnoticed.'

So they stayed where they were, confident that none had seen them or could possibly know where to look.

'We might as well settle down till daylight,' said Whillan sleepily. 'Whatmole's going to come barging in here now?' He looked complacently about the nondescript chamber, and peered out through its ill-made portal to the side tunnel, or rather side-side tunnel, off which it had been delved.

It was perhaps midnight when Maple roused Whillan and whispered urgently, 'For Stone's sake, listen!'

It was the grunting sounds of struggle and strife, and swearing voices, then one scream followed by another, suddenly smothered. There was silence for a short time, then commands for moles to move, and the sound of another struggle, short and desperate, and the grunts of pain, as of a mole talon-thrust into silence.

Maple went to the portal, peered carefully out and then scented the air. 'It's heavy with fear,' he said quietly.

Suddenly there were more cries, the sound of running paws on the surface above, the desperate rasping breath of a mole trying to escape. Then the thud of heavier paws and above their heads a cry of 'No!' as a mole fought for his life against heavier opposition, and lost.

Then the dragging of a body, the sound fading once more, and guardmoles saying, 'That was a bugger, that one!' Murder was apaw.

'We should do something,' said Whillan, impetuously moving forward towards the portal.

But Maple's paw restrained him and he shook his head. 'A mole does not start a fight against enemies whose disposition he does not know, on ground with which he is unfamiliar. We have come here to

293

survive, Whillan, that we may be fit to fulfil the Stone's task when we know what it is. Our time to help others will come soon enough.'

There was another cry in the night, further away this time, and off to the west, and more sounds of continuing struggle.

'Aye, we stay exactly where we are!' said Maple grimly.

Whillan nodded and lowered his snout as if to try to blot out the sound of whatever murder, or hurt, or evil was being done that night in the tunnels everywhere about them. He did not doubt that what Maple said was right, but that did not stop him feeling the guilt and frustration of a sensitive mole who fears that terrible things are apaw and he is powerless to stop them. The sounds went on, and on, and did not fade or cease before Whillan's eyes grew drowsy and he slept once more, only to be woken yet again by Maple.

'Mole's coming, just one by himself by the sound of it.'

'Maybe he needs our help,' said Whillan hopefully.

All was enshadowed and quiet, and by the hesitant sound of his paws and slow progress it seemed that the mole was not at all sure of himself. But sniffing about he was, and his approach towards where they lay hidden had an erratic but inexorable quality. Had he sounded more determined, and had he been more than one, Maple might have been inclined to make a dash for it, or suggest they stance up ready to defend themselves. But it seemed best to stay absolutely still and do nothing in the hope that he would go on by their chamber, and, perhaps, even by-pass the tunnel it was in.

But no, he came on slowly through the dark, still hesitant, until they could hear his breathing, which sounded shallow and nervous and was punctuated by mutters such as 'Here perhaps? No . . . then just down here . . .'

Until at last a short, bewhiskered snout appeared at the portal near which they hid and a voice said, 'I can scent mole, big mole, two moles, *Duncton* moles. Yes?'

For a time that seemed eternal Maple and Whillan stayed just where they were, not breathing, utterly still, hoping the mole would go away, too frightened to try to flush them out more than he had already. But then he said, 'I know you're there. At least I think I know and so I better come in and prove I'm right.'

'All right, mole, what is it you want?' said Maple heavily out of the darkness. He was careful not to sound aggressive, for this was probably some doddery Newborn guard and they might still escape his attentions by claiming they had become lost and then, on the way back, giving him the slip.

'Ah!' said the mole with satisfaction. 'I thought there were moles here. You are the two Duncton moles?'

'We are,' said Whillan.

'Maple and Whillan, one big, one average.'

'That's us,' said Maple, coming out where he could be seen.

'Well, you did the right thing tonight – skulking off out of the way. You're to come with me. I waited until the best time.'

'What do you mean you *waited*?'

'I followed you, more or less,' said the mole, who was elderly, and certainly doddery. 'You did the sensible thing and found a place to stance down for the night out of harm's way. I missed your last move, and then I got stuck while all that . . . that vileness . . . went on, which was why I had to search for you. Harm's the word *this* night! There's been bloody murder all about. Half the visitors if not more are dead, and the rest made malleable.'

Rather disconcertingly he let forth a little laugh, as old moles some-times do who have lived long enough to feel free to laugh at things others don't need to understand.

'Half . . . ?' began Whillan.

'If not more. The ones they could not rely on. There'll be other survivors than you no doubt, but not many. But I suppose you have a lot of questions and all that sort of thing, and though I quite under-stand I am somewhat tired myself and this is not the moment. I'm an archivist, not a guard or active kind of mole. But duty calls and I have been sent. I didn't want to get caught up in *any*thing! Nomole expects archivists to *do* anything much, and how right they are. Anyway, please come with me.'

'Where to?' said Whillan quietly, taking over the task of interroga-tion from Maple, who had less patience for such things. The mole felt all right to him.

'You're the Whillan one, are you?' said the mole with a sigh.

'The Whillan one' nodded.

'Well, it's Privet. The Elder Senior Brother—'

'What about Privet?' asked Whillan as firmly and calmly as he could. 'Which brother?'

'He wants you to be ready to receive her, as it were. He thinks it would be better if you were together.'

'But—'

'*Please* don't vex me with questions!' said the old mole testily. 'This really is not my sort of thing, but he can't trust just anymole these days. Follow me and say nothing, and if I appear to say strange things

295

to any Newborn guards we come across kindly refrain from the Duncton habit of questioning. He simply feels that you had best be in the
right place at the right time. Now . . .'

Whillan turned to Maple and they looked questioningly at each
other.

'Where are we going?' asked Maple, always cautious.

'To the Stones,' said the mole. 'It is unfortunately a bright night
now: but all the better to light up evil with, eh?' He let out one of his
little laughs again, and without further words hobbled away into the
tunnels, turning suddenly northward with them both following closely
behind. If he was up to no good, or intended them harm, reflected
Whillan, then the Newborns must be busy indeed this night if this
vague, weak old mole was all they could spare.

'How far?' asked Whillan.

'So far, so good,' said the mole, who perhaps had not heard the
question. Adding before they had time to make sense of what he
had said something which made even less sense, but gave a certain
solemnity to the occasion: 'For some.' And then that laugh again as
he added yet another afterthought: 'There's a long way to go for *you*,
I should think.'

Then they were off again, as silent and unnoticed as shadows down a
rough-hewn tunnel, stancing still when they heard moles nearby, turning quickly left or right to avoid trouble ahead, and then slipping up
into the grass on the surface when there was no other way to go.

'Look!' whispered Maple, pointing in the direction they were going.
But it was not the two guardmoles who stanced in the shadows ahead
that impressed Whillan, but the great solid shapes of the Stones of
Caradoc beyond them, their right sides catching the moonlight, their
left silhouetted against the starry sky, and the rising hummocky
ground in between (up which he knew in times gone by one of the
great battles of Moledom's history had been fought), now all dappled
with light and strangeness, and empty of mole.

The guardmoles appeared to be looking that way and hesitating, as
if they wanted to go further but were afraid. Then they moved off to
the left, and went underground and the way was clear for the old mole
to lead Whillan and Maple on.

'You're to hide up here,' he said reaching the Stones, 'because
Quail's moles are afraid of the Stones. *That* much is sacred at least.
I'm a bit afraid of them myself, but Duncton moles like you won't be.'

'The Stone doesn't harm moles,' whispered Whillan somewhat
fiercely, 'but a little awe doesn't hurt.'

'As Privet would say!' said Maple, eyeing the great Stones with something like awe himself.

'Quite so,' said the mole, glancing at the Stones uneasily. 'Now, follow me this way . . .' He veered right among a cluster of smaller Stones and then wound his way between much bigger ones, their bases lost in black shadow where the moon's light did not reach.

Ahead, beyond where the Stones' line ended, they saw the grass at Caer Caradoc's north-eastern edge, silver in the moonlight and shivering with the wind which whined above them. The mole pulled them to the very edge and they stanced alongflank him and peered over what appeared a vertical drop into black nothingness which, as their eyes grew accustomed to the strange light, they saw was really a steep inhospitable slope with pits and falls, hummocks and fissures; here and there, where the slope was not too severe, the husky remnants of bracken jittered in the night wind.

But that was not all: 'Look!' whispered Whillan in horror, pointing off to the right. They saw that what had seemed black shadows down the slope were the still forms of murdered moles, one on his back with his taloned paws curled up into the night air, and the moon's light on his snout.

'Bloody murder,' whispered the old mole. 'Quail's doing. Only visitors so far: but moles like me will be lucky to survive the coming days.'

'Who are you, mole?'

The old mole turned to Whillan and said, 'Who was I, you mean? I was once one of the twelve Master Brothers, as Thripp called us in the days when we had great dreams and he was definitely first among equals. None of those twelve is a Master now, and the position of Master Brother, with all its concomitants of learning, charity, leadership and, one might hope, of wisdom, has been eliminated by the Inquisitors, led by Quail. The hierarchy is dominated now by the Senior Brothers, of whom Thripp is Elder. And only the Elder Senior Brother remains stanced between Quail and the final turning of dreams to nightmares. Warned him, I did, when he made Quail a Master. "Never trust a prematurely bald mole," said I. I'll tell you this, moles of Duncton, if they get me I'll be relieved to go. That things should come to such a pass!'

'You said we were to wait for Privet,' said Maple, bringing the mole back to the present.

'She'll come up this way, hopefully. That's the plan, anyway.' He let out another thin laugh, and peered dubiously downslope and added cryptically, 'That's Brother Rolt for you! Always hopeful that it would turn out in the end! Always hopeful. Convinced that the Elder Senior Brother Thripp had a grand strategy that would transform our broken dreams back into spiritual triumph. Some hope, I would say. You have come too late, and there are too few of you. But we must keep the faith to the end, however bitter it may be. Oh, but it's gone all wrong, all so wrong. Dreams is all it was. *You*'ll be lucky to get out of this alive.' Then his voice changed from the despair and helplessness he obviously felt to a matter-of-fact lack of involvement: 'You're to stay here and wait and Brother Rolt will—'

He stopped quite suddenly as the soft sound of scurrying mole came to them from back beyond the Stones; he turned away from the steep drop, darted back the way they had come, peered into the clearing around which the Stones of Caradoc form a semi-circle, and turned back to the two moles. His face was transformed by a look of fierce and passionate concern, and it was evidently not for them.

'You're to stay here!' he said.

With a half-sigh, half-sob, he went out from the protection of the Stones and turned to the right just out of sight. It was as if he had quite suddenly lost all interest in them before the call of something infinitely more important and consuming.

Maple, disinclined to call attention to himself, stayed where he was, but Whillan's curiosity got the better of him and he crept forward among the Stones so that he could peer out unseen from their shadows to see what was apaw. Perhaps it was because he was tired, and because they had suffered two stressful days followed by this fugitive night, but what Whillan then saw had about it a dreamlike muted quality, in which a mole experiences absolutely what he sees, and his emotions are engaged by something beyond all he has ever known, and to which, as yet, he can put no name.

For there, where the old mole had gone, before one of the biggest Stones at the far end of the highest part of Caer Caradoc, he saw that a mole had come, accompanied by two others who were bent over him as if to assist him with their strength to a place of homage before the Stone. Their guide joined the strange group, talked for a moment to the mole about whom they were clustered, and then he and the other two retreated a little, leaving the one they were helping alone before the Stones.

If they were old, this one seemed ancient in the moonlight, or more than ancient. He seemed to have lived beyond age or infirmity and moved into a physical state which was all his own, and for which 'age' or 'infirmity' or even 'death' were words too muted and too weak to express the impression that he made.

He was alive, that much Whillan could tell from the slight movement of his shaking head. His paws, though pale and wraithlike, appeared able to support his ghost of a body, if only just. The moon's shining pallor seemed to find affinity with his frail and woefully thin body, for it made it seem almost white.

If Whillan had been looking for evil that night he did not find it here; nor blood-thirstiness, nor aggrandizement, nor any sense of worldly power and mal-intent. For from that ill and shaking mole, whose head now slowly rose so that he might gaze up at the Stones, came only a sense of awesome and ruthless spiritual purpose. Never in his life, not even with the Master Stour, had Whillan felt himself to be in the presence of a mole to whom all others were subordinate. The power of his presence was so great that it seemed almost indecent to spy on him as he began what was, quite evidently, a time of prayer and contemplation, for which the looming presence of the great Stones of Caradoc seemed entirely appropriate.

'What is it?' whispered Maple from behind, for the line of shadows and positions of the Stones were such that if he had tried to go round Whillan to get a clear view he would have had to go out into the light.

'It's a mole,' was Whillan's inadequate reply.

Maple's paw eased Whillan back so that he too might take a look, and when he had done so he retreated into the deeper shadows, looked at Whillan and said, almost with wonder, 'You know what-mole I think *that* is? I think that is the Elder Senior Brother Thripp.'

As Maple spoke the title Whillan realized that he did so with respect, and that a mole they had referred to throughout their long journey dismissively as 'Thripp' demanded now that they entirely re-think their ideas of him.

'He is not the kind of mole I expected,' said Whillan.

'Aye, it must be Thripp,' muttered Maple after taking a second look. He was as awed as Whillan by what he saw.

For a few moments neither mole moved, but then when more whispered liturgy and prayer came from the clearing, Whillan crept back to his former vantage-point. He was reminded of how in Privet's tale, Rooster had first caught sight of his delving Mentor, Gaunt, and seen a mole ravaged by disease and approaching death. But Thripp (and Thripp it surely was, for the rumours said he was a mole stricken by a wasting disease) did not look ill so much as like a mole whose body had been wasted by life, leaving a spirit and mind to inhabit a thin shaking thing that was barely a body at all.

But here was the remarkable thing: appalling though the impression of his body's frailty was, a mole felt most a sense of his mental strength and spiritual purpose. Thripp seemed, indeed, like a mole who by a slow and painful process had been stripped of all but that, and the effect was made the greater by the self-evident loyalty and love shown by the three moles who attended him and who now stanced back in the shadows watching respectfully. For each shaking move Thripp made, each turn of his head, each muttered prayer, was accompanied by movements in sympathy by his companions.

For Thripp's part, he behaved as if they were not there, pausing as he wished, lowering his head, sometimes turning a little as if to stare at this or that among the Stones. His words were indistinct, but it was Whillan's impression that not all he said was prayer, nor even to the Stone. He seemed also to be thinking out aloud, and using the Stones there as a mole might use others to have a conversation with about an issue that greatly concerned him which he could not resolve alone. It was almost as if, having failed to find living moles to counsel him, he had turned to the Stones for guidance.

As Whillan watched he noticed two more things. One was the curious fact that it was hard to distinguish Thripp's face, for though it turned sometimes into moonlight it seemed enshadowed, an impression greatly increased by the fact that his eyes were deep-set and hard to make out. Secondly, and more remarkably, was the fact that the presence of Thripp was such that he seemed to have the power to slow down time, and bring a calm about the place in which he stanced. Until now, for Whillan and Maple, the night had been one of rush and stress, but here before the Stones, Thripp changed all that.

As Whillan was pondering this point, and wondering why it might be so, Thripp turned slowly away from the Stone in his direction and appeared, suddenly, to be gazing straight at him, to his considerable alarm. Whillan could only stance quite still and hope that he was not seen among the shadows; but if he was not, then what was it at which Thripp seemed to be staring?

Face-on he was a bigger mole than Whillan had first thought, or the outline of his head and shoulders showed that he must once have been of good size. Whillan dared hardly breathe, as peering more closely at where he stanced, Thripp slowly raised his head so that the moonlight was shining on his face, and into his deep-set eyes.

It was then, for the first time, that Thripp came fully alive to him, and he saw a quality in his eyes so powerful, so alluring, that he understood in an instant why so many moles had followed Thripp to Caradoc, and why a new generation had accepted his teachings concerning the Stone; and why, despite the rising challenge of the younger Quail, he must still hold power.

They were not the eyes of a cold sectarian mole such as Whillan and Maple had been taught by all they had heard that he must be. His eyes were pale and clear, as of a mole who had once seen a vision so potent and magical that nothing else could ever matter to him. It was a vision of order, and of love; a view of moledom in which moles abided by the Stone's ways and willingly lived out their lives in its long shadow.

But Whillan saw more than that. There was, too, the hint of ruthlessness, of a belief in his vision that would have no patience with others who did not, or could not, share his view. Yes, there was impatience that others could not see the vision as clearly as he had. All this Whillan saw and absorbed, and understood in that breathless moment when Thripp gazed on him but did not see him. In the moments after he saw something more, for the moon's cold light caught well the way that time, and bitter experience, had etched into Thripp's face a slow dispiriting understanding that his vision was not going to be realized, and that something else was happening, something beyond his control which frightened and concerned him.

'It's about that he was praying to the Stone,' said Whillan to himself, astonished at his own calmness and clarity of thinking at such a moment. 'He wants to change things, he's determined to change things and he won't yield up finally to his infirmity until he has!' Whillan had no doubt that his insights were correct.

Thripp turned back to the Stone, and then raised a paw and whispered a name, bringing to his flank the old mole who had earlier acted as guide to Whillan and Maple. The two whispered for a time and then the old mole stanced back, stared to where Whillan thought himself hidden and then hurried over to him.

'Oh dear,' he whispered irritably, 'I did tell you to lie low. The Elder Senior Brother saw you there and wondered which mole you were. You are the Whillan one, are you not?'

Whillan nodded, his heart thumping in his chest.

'Well come along then, come along, now the Elder Senior Brother's seen you, he wants to talk to you.'

But before he led Whillan into the clearing he emitted one of his laughs and followed it with a most strange aside: 'He's always looking

301

for a mole he can never find, you see, one who can treat him equally. A mole like him craves ordinariness but can never have it, nor find others who are ever in anything but awe of him. They say he found one once, but that was all lost. All lost to him, and yet still he searches. Perhaps you are that mole. Ha! Well, well, mole, so he must spend time with you before he's disappointed once again!'

Nervously, and feeling foolish for having been discovered, Whillan went out into the light of the clearing and made his way towards Thripp. Behind him, he heard Maple move forward and knew he would watch over him lest any trick or attack be attempted, though in his heart the younger mole knew none would be. Time was standing still, all was calm, and he had never felt so safe in all his life as in the presence of this strange inspired mole, and the circle of the Stones of Caradoc.

Uncertain what to say, Whillan said nothing, but stanced respectfully still facing Thripp, who gazed steadily at him in an enquiring and sympathetic way.

After what seemed a very long silence he said quietly, 'A long time ago I had a dream about Duncton Wood. I dreamt it was the place to which I must lead the others. It was the place where the long and troubled history of modern moledom, which has been about redis-covering the Silence of the Stone, began, and would end, and a new beginning be made.'

There was about the way Thripp was speaking a strange, almost inspired directness, which gave Whillan the sense that he was being taken into the confidence of a great mole and being spoken to of great things. Even more did Whillan understand why others had followed Thripp so long.

'My dream or vision of Duncton came at a time when I was begin-ning to learn that a mole cannot order and control the spiritual hearts of other moles as I, Thripp of Blagrove Slide, had thought I could. Already attacks were being made on the system I had established, and certain moles, wiser than I in the ways of evil and manipulation, were gaining power. This you must know. It is common knowledge.

'I decided to send my son Chervil to your system, as much for his own protection from moles like Brother Quail as for him to learn something of the place to which I believed I must finally go. I under-stand that he lived in what you Duncton moles call the Marsh End.'

'Yes, he did,' said Whillan.

'He has told me much of your ways and system of faith and though, unfortunately, he was too well reared by me in the Caradocian Order's

302

ways – Brother Quail was his mentor for a time – to admit to the possibility that there may be better ways of doing things, yet I detect in his recent report to me of Duncton that he is beginning to see things about Duncton's way which he likes.'

For the first time a glimmer of a smile passed across Thripp's face. Whillan could scarcely believe what he was hearing, not only because of the sense of confidentiality that grew with each moment, but because here was the mole who more than any other had created the infamous Caradocian Order actually suggesting there might be alternatives to its sectarian view of things. But thinking is one thing, feeling another, and despite all reason, all logic to the contrary, Whillan could not help being drawn to this extraordinary mole, and felt himself giving up something to him as he spoke on.

'Now, I understand your mother is Privet.'

'Adoptive mother,' said Whillan.

For an instant Thripp said nothing, but only stared, perhaps to analyse Whillan's prompt correction, and to tell himself, rightly, that this was something the Duncton mole was still sensitive about.

'Privet appears to be a remarkable mole,' said Thripp.

'Yes,' said Whillan, suddenly cautious and protective. Thripp stared into his eyes and Whillan looked away, eager to find something to talk about, *anything* which might fill the gap between him and the New-born leader.

'Tell me,' said Thripp at last, 'how would you describe the "Duncton" way.'

This was something Whillan felt he could talk about, and he willingly began to do so, surprised at his own eagerness as he told Thripp about his home system. There was pride and passion in his words, and it was part of Thripp's power with moles that he gave them the sense that they had not only his full attention, but full understanding and sympathy. So Whillan talked, and talked a long time, until he discovered at the end there was longing in his words, a longing to return home.

'But not yet?' prompted Thripp.

'No, no,' said Whillan, speaking now as if to an old friend, 'I must travel a bit more, and see something of moledom. That's what Keeper Husk, the mole I mentioned earlier, told me I must do and I will, I will.'

'Your journey began a good time ago, I think,' said Thripp, 'and it brings you here tonight to talk as we have done. Indeed, Caer Caradoc, this night and tomorrow, which is Longest Night, is a place of many meetings. Here is a confusion from which will come a new

303

clarity. Here is evil and light. Here the dark progress of a mole with a vision born in Blagrove Slide turns towards light, as the seasons turn on Longest Night. When you are old you will be able to say to your young kin, "I was there, I talked with Thripp and he with me. He trusted me with his confidence."'

Whillan stared at the moonlit mole, wondering at the glistening that he seemed to see in the leader's deep-set eyes. Wondering too at how Thripp spoke words like 'journey' and 'talk', investing them with qualities of length and depth far beyond what they could surely have. Or *could* they?

'Tell them, Whillan of Duncton, that I saw the need for change, and in a meeting with a young mole of Duncton Wood, I began to see the means by which it might be achieved. Tell them what you *think* you saw, and one day you may *know* what you saw.

'But tell me . . .' and his eyes softened, his voice grew gentle, he looked suddenly alert, '. . . how is . . . tell me of Privet.'

'Privet?' repeated Whillan, rather surprised. Had he not already spoken of her in what he had so freely said?

'Privet,' said Thripp, 'your adoptive mother. Is she the great scholar and traveller moles say she is?'

'I'm not sure,' faltered Whillan, who knew her best as the mole who had raised him, and saw her mainly in that light. 'She is a scribemole before all else. Before even being a mother . . . or adoptive mother rather. I expect she'll scribe of these times one day.'

'You are sure she will survive,' said Thripp quietly – it was a statement, but Whillan, nervous perhaps, inexperienced as yet, not fully aware what Thripp had really said to him, and was trying to convey, took it as a question.

'Of course she will!' he said fiercely.

'She will if moles hear her,' said Thripp gently, reaching out a thin paw to touch Whillan, and still him. 'There are those who would give up the world to have been reared by that mole, as you were. The Stone was in your coming to Duncton as you did. It will be in your return.'

But even before Thripp turned from him to signal to the old mole to come over to them, and the interview was over, Whillan was asking himself exactly what he had 'seen', and why he had the feeling that Thripp had seen a great deal more than he had, and knew much of the present and the future that he was not disclosing. At the same time, to add to Whillan's confusion, he recognized that in what Thripp had said was the arrogance of a mole who had enjoyed power and felt he had lost it; but beyond that, and this was a final attraction in the mole, was the fact that despite everything, despite his illness, Thripp was still struggling towards a right way, and seeking to cast off a wrong one.

'Of course,' said Thripp, suddenly turning back to Whillan, and interrupting his thoughts, 'it all depends now on Chervil. We must hope that others see the light. My days of influence are nearly over, if not already entirely so. The mole who once led much of moledom with his ideas can now count his true followers on the talons of one paw.' He ruefully indicated the three old moles who attended him. 'If Chervil goes the way Brother Quail wishes him to, then it has been in vain. If he turns the new reformed way, then there is a kind of hope. It is, in the end, about Silence. But where will we find that? I have failed to lead moles to it, so what mole can? I have been praying this night that such a mole will come forward.'

Whillan was reminded of the old guide's comment about Thripp always searching for a mole who might treat him normally and unaccountably felt that in his heart Thripp hoped these two different moles, if they ever existed, might be one.

Thripp was staring at him in that penetrating way again as if he could read his thoughts.

'Sometimes we meet moles too soon,' he said, 'and do not know what it is we let go on by. Remember that and be warned, Whillan: I have lost moles I did not even know I loved, and I would give anything to have them again at my flank that I might tell them that I loved them. Be warned, be watchful, lest such regrets come one day to you.'

Thripp looked suddenly weary, and the shaking that he had displayed when they had first seen him returned; his friends came to him, and tended him prefatory to helping him to some underground place where he might rest, and await the beginning of the Convocation.

'Do as my colleagues tell you, Whillan,' commanded Thripp finally, before he was led away. 'And when you travel on, as you will, remember that it is the journey into moles' hearts that matters more than the journey to strange or memorable places. Seek out moles' hearts and listen to them, and you'll not have regrets. And, mole . . .' Thripp waved a paw to call Whillan to him again, and with a glance he directed his helpers to retreat for a moment longer. 'When you have no other place to go, when all seems bleak and dark, when despair descends, then, mole, there is somewhere you might go . . .'

Thripp's eyes lightened again, and that simple and wonderful smile returned briefly to his face.

'Where?' asked Whillan almost desperately. He felt he had never wanted a question answered so much in his life.

'Oh, yes, I want to say its name. But . . . it has taken me these long years to learn that I cannot make another see the visions that I see. They have their own, and a mole cannot direct them as he wishes. But for you there is a place . . . remember me when all seems lost, remember my paw on yours. Pray to the Stone, trust it, and it will tell you where to go, and what to find; it will teach you what to do. Your journey to that place began so long ago – before I, or Privet, or any other mole, even guessed there might one day be a need for a mole to make it. You'll get there, you'll find comfort beyond the darkness . . .' Thripp withdrew his paw, and retreated again to the shadows and was gone.

'Will I?' said Whillan, himself returning to the shadows on the other side of the clearing.

The old mole came over to him looking fretful. 'That was far too long, far too long. But if he is interested in a mole he gives them time. For some reason he was interested in you. I can't imagine why, but there we are. Genius has its own way. Now, you and your friend had best wait patiently *well* out of sight – and pray.'

'You said Privet will come this way?' said Maple, glancing doubtfully towards the steep slope beyond the Stones.

'Brother Rolt will do the best he can, yes. But nothing is certain, nothing. And Chervil has proved so difficult, even intractable! He was not like that as a pup, nor ever before he went to Duncton. That place disturbs a mole.'

'This place disturbs me,' said Maple.

'Well, we have no time for that,' said the mole impatiently. 'There are more important matters apaw this night. Yes, there certainly are.'

With that, and enough left frustratingly unsaid for a single night, the so-far anonymous mole turned back to the Stones, and was lost among their shadows, presumably to support what now seemed the failing life and cause of Elder Senior Brother Thripp.

While Whillan mused on the final and strangest impression that Thripp had made on him, which was that the Elder Senior Brother had given him advice which was not only wise and good, but was appropriate as well, such as only a mole who is close kin can give.

'What is it, mole?' whispered Maple later, who knew him so well.

'I feel,' said Whillan quietly, 'for the first time in my life, as if I have spoken to a mole who was my own father.'

Chapter Twenty-Four

The calm that had come to Privet when she had first been taken into captivity in Bowdler by the sisters, and which had been replaced somewhat by understandable fears and concerns at the appearance first of Brother Quail, and then from out of her distant past of Brother Rolt, returned once more when Quail's attendants had taken her and Madoc to a different chamber, and told them to wait. A guard was posted at the entrance, and there were others lurking about. 'Sister Hope' was instructed to stay with her, and call out for help should it be needed. Quail went off in one direction, Brother Rolt another, and they were told nothing of what was to happen to them.

While Privet took the opportunity to be still, eyes half closed, Madoc was up and about and all of a flibbert for wondering and fearing what was going to happen. But Privet felt that most such worries had long since been dragged from her and sometime recently, very recently indeed, she had begun to let the last ones go. Her calm therefore was deep and comforting, and gave her space to feel for poor Madoc, who could not be expected to be other than she was, which was very worried indeed.

'The Stone is with us, my dear, and will see us right and I . . . I am sure it will do so before long,' was the best Privet could say.

She had been about to add that she felt she was preparing herself for some major change or event, but since she did not know what it was, or could possibly be, the thought would have been lost on Madoc, and have served to confuse her still further.

'How come you know Brother Rolt?' asked Madoc a little later, a fact which had enormously impressed her. Never in her life had she seen a sister embrace a Senior Brother. Relations, mating, that was a different thing, but a loving gesture, well! It added to the wonder of everything that had happened since she had met Privet, and made her even more determined to stay close by her, and follow her in all she did, wherever it might lead.

'He helped me once in Blagrove Slide,' replied Privet, 'and I believe he will help me again.' But more than that she would not say, retiring into her thoughts in a way Madoc found disconcerting, and she herself simply surprising. From where had this sudden talent for being quiet come? She had no idea.

Rolt came to them not long after this, nodding to the guard outside and telling him that for the moment he was not needed.

'Brother Quail instructed me specifically to stay, Senior Brother,' said the guard.

Rolt shrugged. 'Do so by all means, Brother, but with me here, and Sister Hope, I doubt that our prisoner will try anything, or if she does, that she will get far. So, if you want a comfort break on what might be a long night I suggest you take it.'

'If you say so, Senior Brother, I will!' said the guard gratefully. 'I won't be long.'

Rolt watched after him to see which way he went and the moment he was out of earshot he turned to Privet and said, 'If you stay here you will not survive the night.'

'Senior Brother Chervil personally promised me safe passage.'

'Hmmph!' said Rolt, turning to Madoc and eyeing her warily as if to ask if she could be trusted. If Privet had doubts about Rolt at all they were dispelled by that gesture.

'Have you come to help me as you did once before?' said Privet.

'She is safe?' said Rolt, still cautious. He was clearly under great strain.

'She is,' said Privet.

'Then that's one less complication. But we have little time, Sister . . . I mean Privet. If I may call you that now. It has been so long, hasn't it, and we're all older?'

Why Privet felt touched he should nearly use the title she had borne in Blagrove Slide she was not sure – perhaps because it meant he remembered those days.

'There is much I want to know, that I *need* to know,' said Privet. 'You are well, Brother Rolt. But others . . . I would like to know, just something.'

They both knew she was referring to her pups, whose lives she had begged for and been refused.

'And my Brother Confessor . . .'

'Yes, yes my dear, of course you want to know what happened to him. They are all well enough, what I know of them, and I want to tell you more, for the time for secrecy is gone, but this is not the moment. Later . . . later perhaps.' He said it with little conviction, as if he felt that there was no future, or none of which they could hope to be part. 'Now listen, it seems that two moles at least wish that you escape from captivity this night. One is none other than Senior Brother Chervil who sent me here, for he has not forgotten his promise, and though he is not against Brother Quail, perhaps even for him now and *against* his father the Elder Senior Brother, yet he made a promise he wishes to fulfil – if the Stone allows him to. At least, so he says . . .'

'And the second mole?'

'Quail,' said Brother Rolt shortly. 'Not that he wishes you to escape for long – just long enough for Newborn guards to be justified in hunting you down and killing you. Brother Quail feels that certain moles are best out of the way this night.'

A look of horror had come to Madoc's eyes, but into Privet's there came a philosophic resignation, as if this were the kind of evil nonsense of which she was getting very weary indeed.

'In fact,' continued Brother Rolt, 'my "friend" Quail has sent me here now to aid and abet your escape – no doubt in his tortuous and unpleasant mind he is thinking that if I do then there will be good cause to eliminate me as well. All very labyrinthine, isn't it?'

'It's tiresome,' said Privet.

'Well now, what's to do? I'll tell you. You do escape, now, but you go by a longer way I will take you on, which Quail will not have been expecting, and when you reach the surface you will make for a destination which is the very last to which search parties will be sent: the Stones of Caer Caradoc. It is a steep climb, even a dangerous one, but we cannot change topography.'

The sound of returning pawsteps came to them, and with a final appealing look, and the comment that 'Much depends on it! Follow me!' he set off with both of them close behind.

Although Privet lost all sense of direction whilst they stayed under-ground, for the route was tortuous and took them past occupied cham-bers, down narrow tunnels, and across great communal ways, when they finally surfaced into clear cold night she saw immediately where she was. For there, rising into moonlit nothingness with stars bright beyond, was the eastern face of Caer Caradoc.

'You know where the Stones rise?' said Rolt to Madoc.

'Yes, Senior Brother!'

'Go on then, go on. Hopefully moles will be waiting for you up there.'

'Which moles?' asked Privet.

'Oh, you know, Maple and Whillan. Whatmole else?'

'Weeth,' she replied. 'Where's he?'

'I have no idea. I can't know or do everything, though sometimes it feels as if the moles about me from the Elder Senior Brother down expect it!'

'Brother Rolt . . .' Privet tried again to have him tell her something of the past that she had lost, and he must know about.

'Later. my dear, *later*. We'll talk about all that when we have more time.'

'And when will that be? *Now* is the only time moles truly have.'

'Go on up there, go *on*!' ordered Rolt. 'Save philosophy for *there*, and *him*, it can be the only hope they have.' He turned from them with a gesture that seemed to express the despair of a drowning mole, and dropped back into the Newborn tunnels and out of sight.

Privet stared forward, up into the dark, while Madoc peered to right and left, and then behind them, and listened, and looked fearful and eager to move.

'We had better do as he says,' she said, attempting to get Privet to move.

'We will, but I see no need for speed. I heard nothing behind us – and anyway, it's what lies ahead that should concern you, Madoc.'

'I don't want to be discovered now we've escaped.'

'I feel as if I have been running all my life,' said Privet, 'and I don't like it. In fact I have stopped it. I will not hurry, and if I did I would not get up that great hill without having to rest so long on the way that I might as well not have hurried in the first place.'

'Whether we hurry or not, can't we *go*?' pleaded Madoc.

Privet sighed, and frowned, and then touched her new friend affectionately in the night.

'Come on then, my dear.'

'Who are Whillan and Maple?' asked Madoc as they went.

'You told me so many things and I told you nothing, did I? Well, then . . .' and as they began the long ascent through rough grass, and amidst the worn remnants of rafts of summer bracken, pausing now and then as Privet wished, staring about a little, and looking up at the stars and rising moon, Madoc heard something of Duncton's tale, and of the journey to Caradoc that Privet had made with Maple and Whillan, and latterly with Weeth.

Their progress was slow, and they lost time at one point when, during a pause, they heard moles shouting and rushing about some way below them and they stayed still. During this halt, far above, too far to make out clearly, they heard a faint cry, which might have been a scream, and soon after a scatter of small rocks spattered down across their path.

'I have a feeling,' said Privet, 'which is very comforting, that wherever we go, whatever we do, we will not be harmed this night. I feel as if I am not really here at all.' There was wonder in her voice, and curious cheer, potent enough to calm Madoc somewhat, and cause her to hurry Privet rather less than she had been.

A short while later, as if to prove Privet's feeling right, they turned a dark corner on the climb, clambered around a protrusion of rock, and found themselves face to face with two dozing Newborn guards.

'Stone the crows!' exclaimed one of them when he saw them. 'Damn me. Females! Not tonight if you don't mind, not *this* night. Scarper. Bugger off. Get lost. And not up there!' And with a kick to Madoc's well-formed rump he sent her and Privet back down the way they had come.

'Why didn't he didn't arraign us?' asked Madoc in wonder, when they had gone back downslope a little and out of sight.

'I should imagine it is because he is used to being "visited",' said Privet. 'We chose a bad night for love.'

'Love! You mean they thought we . . . and females below come . . . *here*?'

'There's more goes on here than you know, Madoc, more certainly than you knew to tell me, most of it harmless enough I dare say. Moles are good at scenting out the worst, as you have been; less good at scenting what is better.'

'Well!' declared Madoc, not knowing what to make of this, or quite how she felt about being taken for a 'comfort' to a male guard in the midst of such danger; she did not know what to make of the progress of the night so far, at all. 'What do we do now?'

'Go round the guards and continue our climb up Caer Caradoc, which begins to feel to me like a climb through the stages of life itself,' said Privet, more for her own benefit than for Madoc's; still restless and apprehensive, she was already slipping off their path and contouring the slope northwards.

This second escape of the evening, their first upon the slopes, seemed far enough behind them when they finally found a spot to point their snouts upslope once more and begin to climb. In that time they had heard more rushing and shouting across the flatter ground below them, and guessed that some of it at least must be moles out searching for them. It seemed that Rolt had been right about nomole thinking that they would climb Caer Caradoc, though if the guards

311

were used to females coming up to them (and this presumably was something a more innocent mole, like Brother Rolt no doubt, might not have known about) others might have guessed they could come this way. Other business was perhaps apaw, and fully engaging Brother Quail's Inquisitors and patrols.

No sooner had Privet shared these thoughts with Madoc, and they had succeeded in climbing back to the level they had reached before the guards packed them off downslope, they heard the sounds of mole coming up the slope some way behind them, though further across the hill.

'Time to pause again?' said Privet ironically. Madoc grinned, nodded and stanced quietly down – the Duncton mole's calm was affecting her as well. As they waited and listened the ground about them lightened as the clouds across the stars thinned and shifted, and revealed a clear night sky and the moon.

They heard the approaching moles, and peering southward downslope they saw several great moles labouring upslope and doing their best to be silent, but not succeeding very well.

'They're going straight to where the guards are,' whispered Madoc. 'They must be a party out looking for us.'

She lowered her snout fearfully into the short grass, and then, still feeling exposed, slunk back in among some nearby bracken. But Privet stayed where she could watch, until the force of moles dropped out of sight into a slight fold in the ground, up about where the guards had been.

The guards' confident challenge came soon after, loud and clear, demanding to know whatmole was about, and why, all in the name of the Order of Caradoc!

To Privet's surprise there was no reply, and after a short pause the challenge came forth again, this time more menacing. Some instinct of natural preservation in Privet, that had nothing to do with the idea of being 'invisible' and being especially safe that night, caused her to draw back in amongst the bracken where Madoc already hid. As she did so there was a third challenge, this time sounding rather desperate, and broken off halfway through into an ugly grunt of pain and surprise, followed by a shout, perhaps from the second of the guards, and a savage, attacking roar.

Then there was fighting, fierce and evidently frantic, and a voice, a rough wild voice, cried 'That one!'

There was a scream of pain, and the sounds of struggle grew louder, close at paw, then nearer still.

312

'They're coming here,' whispered Madoc urgently. 'What shall we do?'

What shall we do? Privet found herself staring up through the bracken and on up the silvery slope of Caer Caradoc towards where she knew the Stones must be. All her life, she and moles about her had constantly been asking what must they do, what must they do, and then, before they really found the answer, striving to do it . . .

Privet felt her calm, her friend as she now thought of it, return: nearer, more powerful about her, everything to her.

'We let things be,' she whispered quietly. 'This night it is all we will do, all we must do, let things be.'

The struggling moles were suddenly almost on them, the scent of their angry fear preceding their rolling bodies and wild thrusting paws. One broke free, and reared up for a moment, and Privet and Madoc could see it was one of the Newborn guards who had earlier turned them back; he fled across their sight and crashed his way down the slope and away, blood shining black on his flank in the moonlight.

The other, the one who had spoken to them in so jovial and friendly a way, almost fell out of the darkness on to them, his breathing fast and desperate as three great moles followed him, fierce and terrible, buffeting, pushing, trying to gain a hold to finish him off. He broke free and turned as his friend had done to try to get away but tripped and fell forward, his paws crashing about the clump of bracken where the two females hid, before his body thumped down painfully upslope on the grass beyond.

With a great roar a mole moved out of the mêlée and placed a massive paw on the fallen mole's chest to hold him down before raising his other paw preparatory to striking a killing blow. The light of moon and stars shone on his face with horrid clarity. His brows were furrowed, his eyes angry, his mouth open, his face all shadows and light.

Madoc saw him, and screamed.

The mole beneath him raised a futile paw to protect himself.

And then Privet spoke.

Calm? Aye, she was calm. At peace? She seemed as peaceful as a lake in a still winter's dawn. But never, ever, had she in all her dream thought to meet her love again in a nightmare such as this.

'Rooster,' she said, her voice quiet, her eyes still, her heart so sad to see the mole she once loved come to such bloody murder, no better than the Newborns. 'Rooster, you cannot. This you must not do.'

He turned slightly and stared down at her with eyes that seemed those of a mole who had long since lost himself. Yet he knew her. He

313

stanced back as if afraid, his raised paw falling to his flank, and that which held the Newborn to the ground easing, seeming almost gentle now.

'Oh, Rooster,' she said again, and all was still. He was reared up in the light; she stanced amidst the dry bracken. The Newborn, suddenly free, turned, rose, stared, and ran – all no doubt in but a moment of time, but there, then, it seemed like all time had slowed, and faded away as he fled. Then time returned.

'Rooster,' she had said, but in a voice that was more than mole. It was as if the earth itself had finally spoken to him, or the night sky. Behind him, his companions, grike and mole alike, large and wild, desperate and ready to fight anything, swayed, pushed, shushed and were still as well.

'He let him go,' whispered one. 'He let the Newborn bastard get away!'

Rooster turned to him slowly, his stare silencing him, and then the great mole looked at Privet again, his head bent and fretting in the night, seeing her, and the moonstruck slopes of Caer Caradoc, and the starlit sky rising behind; his mouth opened to speak, but at first he could not find the words.

'Didn't,' he said at last. 'Didn't kill him.'

It was cold comfort, and how long they looked into each other's eyes nomole can be quite sure. Even Madoc, the only witness who left a record of that moment, did not know herself. Longer, she thought, than moles might think.

Nor can we know what Privet or Rooster thought at this ominous and potent first meeting after so many years; except that Madoc believed that each felt that here and now was not the time to say more than had been said: 'Rooster,' and 'Didn't'. Nor had he killed the mole, who was free to tell the tale in better days, in better places, to moles who could never quite believe a word he said.

At last the moment passed and Rooster turned from Privet as if he wished her away from there, stared malevolently at those who followed him and roared, 'Only two females. Mean no harm. Won't tell. We go.'

'Hamble's not with us,' said one of the moles. 'We've lost him.'

'He left,' said Rooster, 'going now!' And off across the slope they went, contouring on as Privet and Madoc had intended to, all suddenly gone. Madoc's record shows that Privet said one more thing before she too moved, not after him, but straight up the slope towards the Stones.

She said quietly, 'If Rooster had killed that mole, he would have killed me, he would have killed us all. Madoc, my dear, stay close, be strong; the way to the Stone will be so hard. It will be so many years before we reach it.' Then, Madoc says, she wept the tears of a mole who has come to the edge of the void, stared over, and seen the darkness as it might have been.

Madoc stayed close, and supportive, understanding in those moments of insight that the journey she was making up the slope was very different from that of her companion. For Privet this was no journey of escape, but a casting-off, a preparation, a night of dying, and Madoc sensed that she was needed.

'It was then my own fear left me,' she scribed later, 'for I felt as a mother feels when she accompanies a pup into a dark place of which it is afraid. The mother too might feel fear, but she cannot let it frighten her away, and does not, but finds courage for the pup's sake. So I found courage for Privet's sake, because I realized that the journey she had begun long, long before I knew her, was fearful indeed, and made my concerns of Newborns, or steep slopes, or great blundering grikes, seem nothing much at all . . . Her needs that night gave me courage to continue at her flank.'

For a time at least they made progress, though it was slow. Rooster was long gone, the crashing and then rustling of him and his small group fading off around the slope as they continued up it. Then the night deepened and became heavy with the sense of movement above and below, to right and to left, and of fearful moles. There were cries of command, cries of pain, cries of heartbreak, and the callings of moles one to another as one lost another, or a group became separated from one of its members and there was no time to go in search, no time at all.

The sky stayed generally clear and bright; the moon rose higher, the stars glittered and sparkled, and all moledom stretched out below them into a distant darkness, across which here and there the gazes of a few roaring owls went, yellow in the silver night. The air grew cold and still.

Twice so far the two moles had crossed the paths of others who had for one reason or another gone on by. The feeling that this gave them, to which Privet had given the Word 'invisible', increased now as they came across other parties. At one place further up the slope, a troop of silent dejected moles, some wounded about the head and shoulders, came stumbling past them, led by a Newborn, flanked by two more, and followed up by a fourth. They seemed to be going down into

315

captivity and though Privet and Madoc made scant effort to hide themselves, they saw them not, but simply went by like ghosts in the night, unseeing, silent, all appearing doomed to play a part from which they could not escape.

This was the first of several such groups coming down from Caer Caradoc above, and the third and largest group came so close that the two females might have been trodden on and crushed into the rough rocky slope had they not backed off and lain low. Even then they seemed not to be seen.

It was at this enforced halt that Madoc remembered Privet turning to her and saying, 'It is all true, Madoc, what happens when moles turn from the Stone. Now talk to me.'

For a time then Privet lowered her snout, her eyes open; with Madoc whispering at her side, she stared unseeing into the night, listening to Madoc telling of Bowdler and the Newborn way with females that Madoc had told her about earlier.

'They did these things, all these things? They do them still?'

'It is common knowledge.'

'Brother Squelch, Brother Quail the Inquisitor. All of them . . . Tell me all you know,' said Privet quietly; and Madoc did.

'But not Brother Rolt?' whispered Privet towards the end, near despair.

'He's a kind mole, he's not one of them. We see little of him, and the old Master Brothers as they were called. No, they're not part of it.'

Privet stared at nothing as Madoc spoke, and fretted impatiently when Madoc stopped talking and tried to move them on, not wishing to stir until she heard it all. Historians may well speculate why it was that Privet seemed increasingly to wish – to need – to pause and think, even to live through, matters which even now are too obscene, too disturbing, for ordinary moles to contemplate.

Yet so she appears to have done. It is enough only to hint at these things that a mole may know that Privet did not shrink from unpalatable truths, and may understand that through the long time of her ascent of Caer Caradoc she was perhaps making a passage through many things that she might come nearer to a vision of the Stone's Light and Silence.

Let us be plain, but mercifully brief. What Madoc had told her was simply this: the relationship between Confessed Sisters and Senior Brothers that Privet herself had witnessed and experienced at Blagrove Slide had become corrupted at Caer Caradoc, and the evil mole who sanctioned the corruption, who created it, was Brother Quail.

The mating of Senior Brothers with sisters as Privet had known it was not all bad – she herself had experienced ecstasies and pleasures she had not known before, or since, flawed and ruined though they were by the stealing of her young, and the possibility that her female pups had been killed. That possibility, however, seemed less, from what Rolt had said. At least, there was hope for some. But with Quail's ascendancy the corruption of the selected males became possible and perhaps inevitable, corruption and control of mind through body, and certain of the Senior Brother Inquisitors had preferences and skills that way. Even this might be tolerated, almost. But what was certainly obscene and evil was the fate of those poor male pups who through weakness of intellect or natural timidity failed to pass the tests of education and achievement which the Senior Brothers and Inquisitors set for them.

For Brother Quail desired that only the best male pups be recruited to his hierarchy of Inquisitors, which meant that as he gained power all others were, by definition, second-best, and therefore, in the twisted minds and logic of those Quail gathered about himself, no longer mole, and therefore to be used and abused as seemed best.

Many became the Newborn guards already spread so widely across moledom – cold, efficient in their way, willingly subordinate to the Inquisitors and Senior Brothers, punitive in their attitude to any of their own kind who, showing a spark of individuality perhaps, trans-gressed their own harsh vows and rules. From such moles came the strettenings.

This much Privet may well already have guessed, though Madoc confirmed it. What she had not known, and her new friend made incontrovertible, was what happened to those pathetic male pups, often weak, very vulnerable, who failed even to have potential as Newborn guards.

Of these Squelch was not only the disgusting prototype but the arch-abuser, and it was common knowledge who he was: Quail's own son. But worse: he was neither male nor female, but both, as indicated by his high voice, his untoward obesity, his corrupted caresses of anymole unfortunate enough to come into his power.

Hushed, whispered, shaming even to utter, was the account Madoc gave Privet of how Squelch came to be made what he was when Quail vented his rage filthily on him when he realized he would never be a 'proper' brother. Or so moles said. Aye, moles had best avert their

317

gaze, or move on past this moment in our tale if they are squeamish, or too innocent, too trusting, to accept that what mole will do to mole at times beggars belief. In his anger, in his rage, in the humiliation he felt the pup Squelch's slowness imposed on him, Quail ravaged his own son, and in whatever moments of evil ecstasy he thereby found, he bit him deep enough to leave the scars that his subsequent obesity made seem mere folds in flesh and fur. By the time the youngster's screams were done he could be, he would be, normal no more.

It was then, said Madoc, that for the first time Squelch did what he did supremely well – he sang. He sang his grief and shame, and to that sad theme his singing often returned, especially after he had vented his urges on some poor young mole, as Quail had on him. Then he sang so well, so beautifully, that moles wept to hear him.

So Squelch survived, and incredibly he was if anything yet closer to his father, yet more eager to please him. He grew, he fattened; his falsetto singing was perfect, but his drives were strange, cruel, terrible. Whether from remorse, or a need to find an outlet for his own wilder fantasies, Brother Quail began to yield to his son's importunate demands for, yes, young, vulnerable pups, male or female, who like him were not going to be Inquisitors, nor grow to be Newborn guards.

Nor did many of them ever have the chance once Squelch had had his way with them, and played with them, and corrupted them until, growing bored, eager for a new plaything – which his father would most willingly provide – he ended their puphood, and in some cases their maleness, for ever. The screams that marked that vile rite of passage into neuterdom Madoc herself heard more than once.

So there was a third kind of mole, called the 'suborns' in the slang of Bowdler. They spoke strangely, were slow and fat, and generally cruel; but where the sisters were concerned they were very safe indeed, and an errant Newborn guard might well watch out, for the fate worse than death that he might suffer, worse than any strettening, was that Brother Quail might yield to Squelch's persistent but mercifully rarely satisfied plea, that a guard's punishment might be that he be 'given' to the suborns . . .

There! That was the heart and root of Quail's corruption of Caradoc, the known secret, the matter which, Madoc informed Privet, the Elder Senior Brother, by then already strangely ailing, did not at first know about; and when he did it was too late to act.

It was Privet's wish to contemplate these unpleasant realities during the pause in their journey of ascent, and no doubt they shocked her. But, if Thripp had discovered these things, no wonder he sent his son

Chervil to the safe haven of Duncton Wood; no wonder too, as Madoc believed, he had been seeking out some way of ridding the Caradocian Order of the monster that had taken effective power over it.

These things Privet pondered, along with others which had to do, as Madoc rightly guessed, with her long journey to Caradoc, which began, she now saw, before even her own birth, in moledom's modern history.

'Madoc,' whispered Privet sometime in that night, 'I want to tell you about a mole you may barely have heard of, the Eldrene Wort.'

'I know her,' said Madoc. 'She persecuted the Stone Mole, she—'

'She did. But she did more. She found the Stone's forgiveness. I want to tell you a little about that because . . . because I think *that*'s where my journey began. She was my grandmother and she scribed a Testimony and, oh Madoc, I want to tell somemole now . . .'

'Tell me, then,' said Madoc.

The night wore on with memory and movement, chance and change. But at the end of Privet's telling of Wort and how she sought a way to communion with an unborn mole – who Privet thought must be herself – they heard more screams, and the thumping down of what they were sure were bodies amongst the rocky outcrops across the slopes above.

'Not ready yet,' whispered Privet finally. 'I am without my grandmother's final courage and unable to go higher now. No more, no more . . .'

She spoke like a mole dreaming, and when Madoc, thinking to help, put a paw to hers, she pushed her away with unexpected strength.

'Must go the way Rooster did, down, down, not ready for Caradoc yet. Not quite.' And she did, with poor Madoc utterly confused, looking up now and then as they went down and thinking that if they had to climb up that way once more she would be unable to.

'Please, Privet, I won't have the strength of courage to come this way again—'

'Sssh!' said the now-strange Privet, 'and be still.'

They crouched down again for no reason Madoc could see or hear and Privet said, 'I heard a mole calling me, I'm sure I did.'

Was it then that Brother Quail came by? Just above them, almost within touching distance, in almost total silence, his bald head a smaller version of the moon that made it shine, his eyes dark slits, his snout sensual, leading ten Newborn guards the way Rooster had gone. What made the sight of him, and them, so terrifying was that they were all running in the same deadly swift and silent way that told the watching moles their purpose was pursuit and capture, their intention to kill the moles they found.

Worse came at the end of this venomous procession: Chervil! His fur glossier and more abundant than the others', his profile somehow cleaner, his presence brooding, and as he ran quick little bursts of breath came from him. Then they were gone, off into the night of menace and murder; a night darker now, for the moon had begun to set. No sooner were they gone than Privet stanced up and began to go on downslope with Madoc following and protesting as they went.

'I thought we were going up, not down. Up there. To the Stones. We're just wandering about.'

Privet looked at her, her eyes seeming cold in the moonlight. 'I heard a mole,' she said.

'They've just gone by. Brother Quail. *Them*. They've come and they've gone. We're invisible, as you said. Nomole seems to see us.'

'This mole will,' said Privet. 'Anyway, I haven't the courage to follow the vision I saw.' She glanced fearfully behind them up the slope. 'Another mole will do that, must do it.'

'But Whillan and Maple are waiting. Brother Rolt said so.'

'Let them wait,' said Privet harshly. 'I am not the mole they need yet, and another calls me . . .'

She turned and ran downslope, down and down, turning one way then another as if she knew where she was going, far ahead.

'Privet!' screamed out Madoc, so that her scream joined the others of the night.

'Here!' cried out Privet, 'here!' Then, more softly, 'Here . . .'

As Madoc caught up with her she saw Privet had come to a little nook of a place, guarded on one side by a boulder that in times long past must have rolled down the great slope from the very Stones which had been their goal, and might be still. In its shelter were two moles, both large males, one holding the other, who was injured in the chest. Chater and Hamble. Such old friends, in need of her now. Oh, yes, it was all beginning now, her journey towards aloneness.

'I'm here, Chater,' Privet was whispering, 'I've come.'

'Had to come,' said Chater, pain creasing his face. 'Bad things, evil things.'

Privet's gaze lifted from him to Hamble and as their eyes met each knew nothing had changed. It was but yesterday, but moments before, they had parted all those moleyears ago. The Stone had set their paths to meet again here, when time began.

'I'll hold him now, Hamble,' she said softly, and she reached out her paws and took Chater's head in them, and bent to whisper to him and tried to still him as bit by bit he did the first thing a journeymole does when he has reached his objective – he told the things he was sent to tell. All he had learnt he told, of the murders already come, of the treachery due on Longest Night, which was the next day.

'They're going to kill moles come Longest Night, they're taking over Duncton Wood, the one to watch out for is called Quail . . .'

A jumble of things he told her, some of which she knew, some of which she had guessed, some of which were too mumbled to understand, until his breathing eased and he slept, and nearby Madoc slept as well. Then Privet and Hamble talked, and told those things each had only partly heard, or not heard but guessed; and some things they had not even guessed. Of Rooster's wanderings, of Beechenhill, of the coming to Caer Caradoc and imprisonment, and of Weeth – how delighted Privet was to hear the part that good mole had played in the escape – and finally of Chater and his courageous response to Weeth's command to strike a Newborn guard. It was for that the Stone had sent him, surely it was that.

They shared so much that night, as Chater lay asleep, beyond any help they could give but comfort, until at the end Privet said to Hamble, 'There's one thing, one mole, you've barely mentioned, and that's Lime. What happened to her?'

Hamble shifted uneasily and explained that he had thought she would not want to hear that, just as Rooster had not wanted to hear much about Privet's raising of Whillan because it made him jealous to think of her so close to another mole.

'I'm not Rooster. So come on, Hamble, tell me the truth – it's the only thing worth knowing in the end.'

So he told her all that had happened and how Lime had finally quietly disappeared. At the end all Privet said was, 'At the beginning of April, she left then? How strange.'

'Dammit,' said Hamble, 'why's it strange? Weeth said the same thing. What's so strange?'

'Did he say that too? He's a *clever* mole is Weeth. But look, the dawn's coming and that means that the day of Longest Night has begun,' she said, changing the subject. 'And somehow or other, we're still all alive. Madoc, get some worms! Hamble, have a sleep and when you've rested you can take Chater over from me so I can rest.'

'We can't stay here!' said Madoc.

'I shall stay with Chater as long as he needs me to,' said Privet quietly. 'Just as Fieldfare would if she were here.'

321

Chater stirred at the mention of his beloved's name, and whispered, 'Here?'

'Near in spirit, I am sure, my love,' said Privet, holding him closer still.

'You're too thin,' said Chater drowsily, 'and I'm getting cold. But the pain's gone.'

'I'll put on some weight,' said Privet.

'You'll have no trouble finding a mole if you do,' said Chater. He chuckled softly and whispered Fieldfare's name, and from the corner of his eyes two tears trickled down.

'Love her,' he said.

'I know, I know how much.'

'She'd be glad it's you who's here now,' he said, 'holding me. Thinks the world of you does Fieldfare.'

'Look,' whispered Privet, and held Chater's head so that he could see how the dawn of a new day was lightening the eastern sky.

'Want to see Longest Night in,' said Chater, 'want to see its first stars. Be close to Fieldfare then because that's what she'll be doing, looking at the self-same stars. I'll hang on till then.'

They looked on at the eastern sky while behind them all, unseen but by the fearful Madoc, the great scarred eastern face of Caer Caradoc caught the first rays of a bloody sun as the last day before Longest Night, when the seasons turn, began.

Chapter Twenty-Five

That same dawn Duncton Wood was beset by a cold mist such as Fieldfare could see in the vales, and Pumpkin poked a reluctant snout out into it from the main portal of his tunnels, retreated inside and wondered how he would pass the day. The mist outside was more or less a fog, and he could barely see the outline of even the nearest treetrunk.

The operative word being 'day' – for the Newborns had made plain that all moles in the system were expected to report at the Stone at dusk and take part in a ritual celebration.

'Ritual celebration indeed!' muttered Pumpkin irritably to himself, wondering which of his modest tunnels was most likely to yield a worm or two on a day like this. 'Mole don't need ritual celebrations on Longest Night. If they have any sense they have a good time anyway. Dear me, dear oh dear, what a miserable day it is! What a sad prospect! What am I to do?'

What he did a moment later was to start up in alarm, frown, widen his eyes, peer at his talons in some faint hope they might appear large and formidable, and finally settle down once more with a resolute expression enhanced by slitty eyes.

For he had heard a sound. Of mole definitely, and of mole up to no good. Nomole who is up to any good creeps about Duncton Wood at this dawn of dawns, especially in such a mist!

'Shall I challenge them or shan't I? I shall! Yes, definitely! Better than doing nothing. And if my hour has come, then this mole for one will be satisfied. I am fed up with life, fed up with solitariness, fed up with pretending to be Newborn when I am anything but, fed up with being an undercover agent for the forces of good when it's as plain as these feeble talons on my paw that the Newborns have total and complete and utter control of Duncton Wood. Yes, I shall challenge, fight feebly and die thankfully!'

With that he advanced timidly to his portal once more, pushed out as small a portion of his snout as possible to allow him to see something of the mist – he found it had grown even thicker, and he could not even see the nearest tree – and cried out, 'Halt! Who goes there? Speak your name clearly and lie prone!'

His cry, bold as it was, echoed about in a dull kind of way, and then seemed almost to fade so much that it might never have been. Pumpkin look relieved that no giant mole appeared, and had just begun to turn back below when to his alarm he heard a voice answer ambiguously, 'Where?'

'There you are, mole!' cried Pumpkin, his thin greying fur rising, his snout flaring, his eyes going slitty once more. 'Don't dare move! I can see you.'

'*Where?*' said the voice, which sounded exasperated. 'Where are *you?*'

'I may tell you that, or I may not. Whatmole are you, and whither are you bound?'

'Whatmole am I? Whither am I bound?' repeated the voice from out of the mist. 'Dammit, Pumpkin, you can be very annoying if you try. I am a lost mole. I am bound for your burrow.'

'Ah, but what is your name?' said Pumpkin, who by now was dancing from one back paw to another at his portal and stabbing at the thick mist, and making it swirl, as he practised making killing talon-thrusts, first with the right paw and then with the left.

'I am Keeper Sturne, you fool, that's who I am. I've been floundering about looking for you since before dawn.'

'You should have said so then, and I would have come to find you!' declared Pumpkin triumphantly.

'Keep talking, Pumpkin, and I'll come and find *you.*' This time there *was* menace in Sturne's voice.

'I will, I will,' said Pumpkin, and he did, about this and that, until Keeper Sturne came lumbering out of the mist, his fur wet through with condensation, his snout muddy, his paws full of clammy leaf-litter, his expression furious.

'Get me food and show me where I can drink,' he ordered the moment he had arrived.

'What have you come for?' said Pumpkin.

'You're needed.'

'What for? I refuse to do work for the Newborns on the morning of Longest Night. Some things are still sacred. Anyway, it's foggy. I won't come.'

'Not work for the Newborns, mole; not even for me.'

Sturne shook his fur, wiped his snout, cleaned his paws and looked into Pumpkin's eyes.

'Not even for you?' said Pumpkin faintly. His heart had begun to thump painfully and he was beginning to feel timid again. He had an unpleasant premonition as to whom he might have to work for and he did not like it.

'The day's come,' said Sturne resolutely, 'when we can be ourselves. I'm not saying that after today we won't have to revert to pretending to be Newborn – that's what we *are* doing isn't it? I mean, you're *not* Newborn, are you Pumpkin?'

'I'm not if you're not,' said Pumpkin.

'I'm not, mole. Never was. Not my way. You know that.'

'I'm not either,' said Pumpkin with a grin. 'You only fooled me for a time. I was a happy mole, Sturne, when I realized you were fooling them.'

'A happy mole, Pumpkin?' said Sturne, frowning in his formal, ungiving way. He spoke the word 'happy' as if it were alien to him. 'You were always a "happy" mole. I envy you.'

'I don't envy *you*,' said Pumpkin honestly. 'But . . .'

'Yes, mole?' said Sturne, not looking at Pumpkin.

'Well, if this visit of yours means you're going to spend Longest Night with me, and celebrate like we used to when we were younger all those moleyears ago . . . before, well, before you were successful in the Library, and all of that – if that's what it means, then you will make me a *very* happy mole, and maybe something of my happiness will rub on to you, Sturne, since it seems to me that you don't have much capacity for it.'

'I always appreciated our Longest Nights,' said Sturne stiffly. 'A mole shouldn't be alone at this special time. I . . . well, let's just say I . . .'

'What, Sturne? Say it. It won't hurt.'

'Well,' said Sturne gruffly, 'it's just that I appreciate it, that's all. I mean you wanting me to come here. I mean, you know . . .'

'I'm not sure I do,' said Pumpkin, who knew perfectly well.

'My Longest Nights, sharing a tale or two with you, have been the happiest times of my life,' said Sturne suddenly and very quickly. But before Pumpkin could respond – and he was thinking that a quick hug might be appropriate at this unexpected breakthrough of feeling in Sturne – the severe mole continued quickly, 'But *that's* not why I've come. We have a task apaw, and the fog will aid us.'

'What task?'

'A mole has asked for our help. He's asked for *your* help, Pumpkin.'

'My help?' said Pumpkin, feeling faint again. 'What mole?'

'The Master Stour needs our help, mole. Needs us today. Needs us *now*.'

'The Master Stour?' said Pumpkin, barely able to catch his breath he was in such a flummox. 'I need to eat a worm or two to get my strength!'

'We both do,' said Sturne. 'Then we'll go.'

'Where?' said poor Pumpkin, yet more faintly. Indeed, he had stanced down in a frail heap and was clutching his thin stomach to calm himself down.

'Into the Ancient System, of course.'

'Oh dear,' said Pumpkin, putting a paw over his face as if to block out reality. 'Oh dear, no. What help can I be *there*? I would die there! I'm half dead just thinking about it.'

'The Master Stour thinks, and I quote, "Pumpkin will be all the help in the world".'

'I thought he might be dead,' said Pumpkin, and there was a hint of disappointment in his voice. 'Are you *sure* he's not?'

'Let's get some worms, let's eat them, and then let's find out if he is or isn't, shall we, Pumpkin?'

'Er, yes, yes, Sturne, let's do that,' said Pumpkin with a forlorn sigh. 'I was just wondering what I might find to do today. Now I know! What fun! Visiting the Ancient System! Tra-la-la! Oh dear me.'

'Food, Pumpkin.'

'Be happy, Sturne,' said Pumpkin heavily, going off to find some worms, and hoping it would take him a very long time indeed.

Over their food Sturne tersely revealed to Pumpkin the remarkable story of his secret support of the Master Stour in the Ancient System since the departure of the others to points south and west, and his retreat in the face of the inevitable takeover of the Library by the Newborns.

Sturne, it turned out, had known all along what Stour's grand plan was, for the Master had taken him into his confidence, and he had been the mole who sealed up the Master's cell above the Main Chamber after Privet and the others had departed, and before the Newborns assumed control.

'I could not risk telling you then, Pumpkin, because I was afraid that if the Inquisitors interrogated you or me, or both of us, one of us would implicate the other. If it was just me, well, perhaps I could succeed in not telling them of Stour's whereabouts.'

'Well, I guessed something like this was apaw and I must say I was relieved because I felt lonely,' declared Pumpkin. 'I could not believe that you of all moles would go the Newborn way!'

A modest look of gratification came to Sturne's serious face.

'Now, when the Master went into retreat he gave me certain instructions which I have followed faithfully. Regarding the texts – I have succeeded in saving a good number, though sometimes I think the Inquisitors were near to guessing what I was about. But some serious losses have been sustained which will need to be rectified one day. Of course, the Master himself secreted away many original texts in the Ancient System, along with the six Holy Books of Moledom, which I believe you yourself saw and handled just before his retreat began.'

'Terrible things!' said Pumpkin. 'Confuses a mole to touch them, breaks him to try to handle them. A great mole like the Master has the character to do it, but a simple aide like me, well, I'm not up to it.'

Sturne allowed a smile to play briefly about his mouth. 'No, no, well, each to his task, mole, each to his task. Now, regarding the Master himself, I have been in the habit of leaving food for him at certain entrances into the Ancient System, when I have been able to rid myself of the attentions of the three Inquisitors. The Master has been in the habit of taking it and leaving a quick scribing as to the next location. In this I have been greatly helped by the records left behind by the great Mayweed, who, as you know, was Moledom's greatest route-finder, and at one time of his life took it upon himself to explore and describe the Ancient System.'

'I always *thought* he had left such records behind,' said Pumpkin, suddenly excited. Nothing thrilled him more than history local to Duncton Wood.

'Gradually, the instructions have indicated places nearer and nearer the Stone,' continued Sturne, 'and I assume that the Master's great and difficult work of carrying the six Books to the Stone is the reason for that. In short, as best he has been able, under cover of the Ancient System he has taken these great works to their final resting-place.'

'You mean beneath the Stone itself, beyond the Chamber of Roots?' said Pumpkin, his voice quiet, awed at mention of this most mysterious and dangerous of places, which lies beneath the ground around and about the Stone Clearing in the High Wood.

'Aye,' said Sturne. 'I think – I believe – he has succeeded in getting all the Books very near that place, and wished to get them through the Chamber before Longest Night.'

'You said "wished" in the past tense, as if he now has no choice in the matter,' said Pumpkin, much concerned. For fearful though he was of anything to do with the Ancient System, Sturne's solid and exemplary courage had stirred in him the desire to help as best he could, and he did not wish to hear that at the final moment the Master had been unable to continue.

'"Wished" is a past participle,' said Sturne impatiently, 'so it would be in the past tense, wouldn't it! Well, anyway, three days ago I finally found one of the Master's scribings telling me to leave what food I could near the Chamber of Roots itself, which I duly did. The food has not been touched since, there is no sign of mole, and Longest Night is on us. Now, I must make an appearance before the Stone at dusk for the Newborn ritual which you will have been told about,' and here Pumpkin nodded, 'but we cannot be sure when we go to the Chamber of Roots what we will find, or what task we must perform. I was reluctant to involve you, Pumpkin, but you are now the only mole I can trust, and I know how highly the Master regards you. I cannot fail to appear at dusk for fear of giving away the fact that I am not Newborn at all, but perhaps one of us will still be needed near the Chamber and you can stay on and fulfil whatever task remains, and you will not be missed.'

'Ah! Yes!' said Pumpkin non-committally. It was just the kind of nightmare situation he had feared earlier on. Worse, in fact. However . . . 'I will not let you or the Master down!' he declared boldly.

'I'm sure you won't, Pumpkin,' said Sturne.

'When are we going to go to the Chamber of Roots?' Pumpkin grinned madly, unable to believe he had asked such a question.

'Now,' said Sturne, 'now we have eaten and are fit for any task.'

'We're not waiting for the fog to clear?'

Sturne shook his head and stanced up.

'Well, can't we just hang on while I tidy the place a bit? I like to leave things orderly, you know.'

Sturne shook his head again and began to climb up towards the portal.

'You don't think later might be better than sooner?' Pumpkin called up after him.

'No, I don't,' said Sturne. 'Now is the time.'

'"Now is the time"!' muttered Pumpkin, looking wildly round his snug chamber and modest tunnels. 'Goodbye home! Goodbye peace! Know that I, Pumpkin, Library Aide, was happy here. Farewell!'

Then, raising his snout as best he could, and puffing out his greying, puny chest, Pumpkin set forth from his portal and into the mist after

Sturne, wishing he knew how heroes felt, for knowing that might have helped. But then practicalities took over and, observing that Sturne was having trouble finding the way, Pumpkin caught up with him and said magnanimously, 'Let me show you, friend, for we're on my patch now.'

'Does your patch extend as far as the Ancient System?' growled Sturne.

'It'll have to if we're to get there, won't it?' said Pumpkin, with the lunatic good cheer of a mole who has finally leapt into the void and, though he has no idea what is rushing up at him from below, knows he can do nothing more to protect himself from it.

He got them there without difficulty, huffing and puffing misty breath back into the thick mist as they straggled at last into the Stone Clearing; peering carefully forward, and with extended paws, they finally groped their way to the darkly looming Stone itself.

'Well now,' said Pumpkin, 'what next?'

'Follow me,' said Sturne, who had got his bearings once again. He turned round the back of the Stone, left the Clearing and went in among the trees of the High Wood, whose trunks rose grey and strange into white nothingness, and came at last to an errant surface root from one of the bigger trees around the Clearing, and followed it deep into the wood.

'Here's the place,' said Sturne.

He delved aside some twigs and leaves and before Pumpkin could say, 'Library Aide!' he had shoved the smaller mole down the hole, and followed him into the echoing, mysterious space beneath.

'Be glad there's no wind about, Pumpkin,' whispered Sturne, his voice echoing back eerily from the tunnel ahead, 'for the wind-sound down here is like nothing I've ever heard. Even so . . .'

Even so indeed. For far off down the tunnels they could hear the awesome and strange sounds of the Ancient System – whispers and the pattering of pawsteps, faded cries and distant callings, such as any Library Aide in Duncton's Library has heard on a winter's night at the ends of some of the more dusty and forgotten tunnels, but never quite grows used to, and *certainly* never ventures near.

'The Chamber of Roots is not that far, so follow me, and don't worry if you hear pawsteps following you, it's the sound of your own, only multiplied!'

It was as well he had been warned, for however quietly he tried to put his paws down it seemed to Pumpkin that an army of moles was just at his rear. Most disconcertingly these phantoms did not stop when he and Sturne halted but, as it were, marched by and disappeared down the tunnel ahead of them.

'You never quite get used to it, but familiarity helps,' said Sturne.

They went on a short way further, turned a corner or two, passed through a portal, and Pumpkin found himself in the ante-chamber that surrounds the Chamber of Roots itself, famed in Duncton's legends and fables but so rarely visited in recent times.

Seven portals open into the Chamber from this circular antechamber, each leading in among a maze of roots which not only fall from the roof to the floor, but intertwine themselves at angles, in twists and bends and folds upon each other; some massive and thick, others no more than slim tendrils in which the green juice of life flows between tree above and soil below.

This colour, this pale luminescent green, seems to tint the air of the place, and casts itself all about the roots, which, even on the stillest of still days – and this was a stillish day – contrive to move and twist, to rasp and sometimes suddenly jerk, so that to the green 'mood' of the place, strange sounds are added, whining, cutting, rasping, mewling and groaning deeply, as if telling of life's mysterious and inexorable process of birth and death and birth again. Occasionally the roots move and part and a mole can see in among them towards the centre of the Chamber, where, it was said, the base of the Stone plunges down into the soil. To this holiest of holy places few moles had ever ventured, and fewer still had returned alive. Down there the Seven Stillstones were returned, each to await the coming of its complementary Holy Book whose heart or essence it represented.*

Pumpkin stared in alarm through one of the seven portals into the Chamber of Roots, and then wandered on round the antechamber to the next, and the next after that, and the prospect of going through them seemed more terrifying each time.

So he circled round the Chamber of Roots uneasily, jumping at the sudden sounds, marvelling how sometimes at one portal or another the roots seemed to shift and open up a way down which a mole might venture, if he was inspired – or insane.

'The base of the Stone lies through there, doesn't it?' he asked rhetorically. 'That's where great moles of the past took each of the Seven Stillstones. Into there Bracken went, didn't he? All the great moles. Boswell, *he* went there.'

* The tale of the Stillstones and their return to Duncton Wood is told in *Duncton Found.*

330

Sturne nodded. 'Great Tryfan too,' he said.

'And now the Master Stour, he's got to go in there,' said Pumpkin. 'He's got to take the Six Books, hasn't he? And it's here that when the Book of Silence, the Seventh and the Last Book, is found, that a great mole must bring it.' His eyes were wide with the vision of so awesome a thing, and he gulped and gasped to think that he, Pumpkin, was stanced so near such a holy place.

'Aye,' breathed Sturne, 'it'll be brought here and taken in. Then will all be put to rights, and the Stone's Light and Silence safe for all time, for moles to seek out as they will, and strive to know as best they may. We must pray that Privet finds its whereabouts, for that is what her quest is for.'

A spatter of sound came from beyond an ancient portal, older certainly than that by which they had entered the ante-chamber. It had been brilliantly delved, such that its sides made use of two jags of black shiny flint, softened only by the gentle curve of the arch that linked them.

'The Chamber of Dark Sound is through there,' breathed Sturne. 'It's the way we'll have to go.'

'We?' squeaked Pumpkin, horrified. *Here* was bad enough, but *there*, through that dark portal into the place allmole who had ever kenned the Duncton Chronicles knew perfectly well only very special moles dared venture. In there was disaster, confusion, and a death caused by one's own pawsteps and fearful breathing being reflected back as Dark Sound, which expressed the evils and flaws in even the best mole's nature. *There* a mole made his own Dark Sound and died from it. *There* he, Pumpkin, would certainly not venture. Here was far enough.

He glanced away from the portal, back around the ante-chamber, and then into the Chamber of Roots with its peaceful green translucent light; among the high hanging roots, thick and gnarled stems intermeshed with the tendrils of fresh growth, and the whiter roots of a different age ran and then broke free and hung; there he saw a thing staring, merely in passing at first, and his eyes wandered to something else. Then his memory put its shapes and shadows into form and he realized *what* he had seen.

'Sturne!' he said, grasping his friend almost frantically. 'Look there!'

They looked and saw that set into the roots, growing there like a living thing, though surely dead, was what seemed to be the face of a mole; snout, teeth, eyes and all.

'It is . . . mole,' whispered Pumpkin, shaken to his core.

'It is a skull,' said Sturne, barely less disturbed himself.

It *was* a skull, round which the roots had grown and surged so that the eyes were living root-bark, and the tongue the russet of some lichen growth, and the teeth – the teeth were real. As, horror-struck, they followed this form further into the tangle of growth beyond, they saw thrusting out of young tendrils the mole's skeletal paw, and talons, distended and twisted, turned and fully extended; still horribly identifiable, the ribs curved up behind, supported by the growth of which they appeared a part. The vertebrae seemed twisted into a spasm of living arboreal pain, and further off still was a single back paw, talons black and pointed. It was a mole who had ventured into the Chamber and become trapped and killed by the shifting roots, and now acted as a warning to others.

Behind them, a spatter of sound again, hinting at a shift in the wind out on the surface. The Chamber of Roots trembled and was still, and they saw here and there in its depths evidence of other moles caught in decades or centuries past by the shifting roots among which they must have vainly struggled. The roots trembled, there was a sudden rasping shift, something seem to break, and all began to move easily.

Pumpkin pointed a paw mutely at the skeletal form of the ingrown mole, and as they stared at it, the roots that held it swayed and rose and as they did so the mole's bones moved and turned; the spine twisted, the head arced back as if in a scream, the paws seemed frantic for a moment, and then all was gone into the shadows of the be-rooted heights of the Chamber, and could be seen no more. Pumpkin's fur almost stood on end and he let out a little bleat of dismay.

'Be not afraid, Pumpkin,' whispered a voice behind him – a voice that made him very afraid indeed – 'these remnants of lost moles are all that remains of those who tried to enter the Chamber of Roots and desecrate it in years gone by. They are nothing now but a warning to those of us with too much vanity perhaps, or who venture where they have no task.'

A paw touched Pumpkin's and he slowly turned and found himself face to face with Master Stour once again. Thin and wizened now, aged far beyond the span of time that had passed since Pumpkin had left him when he went into retreat, fur pale and thin and dusty, eyes all wrinkled, Stour stanced, staring, smiling, peaceful.

'Master,' whispered Keeper Sturne.

'Good Master Stour,' said Pumpkin, tears in his eyes as he lowered his snout in obeisance to the mole whose Library had been his life's work.

'I am glad you came, Pumpkin, you of all moles! The last moments of my task have come but I cannot do what I must without your help. Nor without yours, faithful Sturne. Listen, my good and worthy friends, my body is even weaker, even frailer than it seems. You see a mole who has survived far beyond his years and whose body would crumble to dust if it were not for his mind. Well, I am near my time of rest and Silence. I have traversed whole worlds alone here in the Ancient System, and with the Stone's help I have brought to the portal of the Chamber of Dark Sound the Six Books. Now I shall take them to their final resting-place through the Chamber of Roots at the base of the Stone itself, where, if all we have learnt is true, I shall find the Seven Stillstones. Six at least can be redeemed. Such is my task and you must help me, Sturne, and you, Pumpkin, by bringing the Books one by one to me here.'

He spoke clearly and slowly; his eyes had grown pale and rheumy, and when he blinked the lids moved only slowly, and his body trembled, and sometimes he seemed to wince with pain.

'It is Longest Night?'

'It is approaching, Master,' said Sturne. 'Outside we have done all you asked of us, but we have no news of Privet or the others. No news yet . . .'

Stour shook his head, and waved a paw dismissively. 'No, no, Sturne, tell me not. I am dead to that world now, though I care for it. I pointed a few moles in the right direction, didn't I?'

'Yes, Master Stour, oh yes you did!' said Pumpkin eagerly. Stour nodded vaguely. 'It seems that was a long time ago, so long ago. Maple, he was strong and will do what he must, I know. And Drubbins . . .'

'Master, Drubbins died.'

'Yes, yes, he died,' he said indifferently, as if he had known it would happen. 'Fieldfare, she can be relied on, and Chater, the best journeymole I ever knew. Whillan, a mole I feel I failed and yet, in my time here, I have learnt that great moles are beyond others' failure and success. He *is* a great mole you know, that Whillan; he will come through. We did not understand. And Privet. Care for her, Pumpkin, care for that mole. Her journey is the hardest of them all. Pray for her this Longest Night, for as I end my task she will begin hers. Oh, she will. Care for her, mole, care for her beyond care. The world beyond . . . what a strange hurt thing it has been.'

He fell into silence, almost into sleep indeed, but roused himself suddenly to reach out and grab Sturne's paw with something of his

333

former vigour, and said, 'Go, mole, go to the portal and bring whatever Book you first find there.'

As Sturne went Stour peered after him and said with a smile, 'Book of Healing, Book of Fighting, Book of something or other, that's what he'll find. *I* had to carry them all this way. Not easy. Wouldn't have started if I'd realized. Well, well, we've got 'em here now and all I've got to do is get 'em in there! Eh, Pumpkin?'

'Yes, Master,' said Pumpkin.

'Well, it won't be easy.'

'It won't, Master.'

'Pumpkin, you are the best Library Aide in moledom, remember that, won't you?'

Pumpkin grinned feebly. 'I'll try, Master.'

'Don't try, *do*,' said Stour, frowning. He stared with some severity the way that Sturne had gone, evidently impatient for his return. Sturne reappeared, carrying one of the Books, which though not large, seemed to weigh him down mightily. Sweat was streaming off his back, and his breathing was coming in gasps.

'That's why I needed two of you,' said Stour drily.

Sturne placed the Book on the ground in front of Stour and the ancient Master peered at it and then reached a paw to touch it.

'Book of Suffering,' he said dismissively, 'wrong one. Might as well do this in the right order. Pumpkin, off you go and get another Book, there's a good mole.'

Pumpkin duly did so, peering nervously round the dark portal beyond which, but a few paces on, was a jumble of Books. He darted in, grabbed the nearest, and was well on his way out again when a great rumbling sound of pawsteps charged him down and he found himself flat on the ground, the Book slipping from his grasp.

'Will have to try harder,' he muttered, hauling himself up and taking the Book up again with much greater difficulty, for it seemed to slip and slide in his paws. As he grunted with the exertion of trying to hold it and take it out towards the portal, his gasps and groans and pawsteps all echoed and re-echoed and rumbled and roared about his head, confusing him.

Moments later he blundered out of the portal and found himself almost collapsing towards Stour, before whom he gladly let go of the Book, just as Sturne had done.

'Hmmph!' said Stour, barely glancing at it. 'The Book of Darkness. Sturne? Can you do better?'

'What am I to seek, Master?'

'Well, the Book of Silence would do nicely, but I happen to know it's not there. Never was. Might never be. So the first Book will do . . .'

So it went on, one after another, time after time, until between them Sturne and Pumpkin, with increasing difficulty and distress, had managed to bring forth the Six Books and place them down to Stour's satisfaction. He, for his part, had appeared to grow more lighthearted as this work continued, onerous and exhausting though it was for the other two. It would scarcely be an exaggeration to say that he was dancing about from one paw to another towards the end, when the last of the Books ('Ah, at last we have it, better late than never: the Book of Earth!') finally arrived. Meanwhile, poor Pumpkin, who had portered it, collapsed from the effort and took some time to come round.

The Master Stour, now cool, calm, and collected, smiled benignly, his thin wrinkly skin, like crushed and dusty birch-bark, crinkling into a thousand creases around his eyes and mouth. He touched the Book of Earth with his paw, but gently, for its covers and folios were the most ancient of all the Books, all dry and grey with time.

'Earth is first to go in, then Suffering, then Fighting, then Darkness. After that, if I survive them all and still come out alive, there's Healing – too late for me! – and finally Light.'

'Er, Master,' enquired Pumpkin, 'what happens if you don't "survive"?'

'You two will have to take whatever Books remain into their final resting-place so that they cannot be desecrated by false mole, whether Newborn or otherwise.'

'Us, Master?' said Sturne, glancing at Pumpkin uneasily and then towards the Chamber of Roots.

Stour nodded indifferently. He looked at the Books, then at the nearest of the seven entrances into the Chamber of Roots, then at his paws. He was suddenly sombre.

'What's the weather like outside?' he asked. 'Still quiet? It affects the roots you see, and my chances.'

Pumpkin was only too happy to go and find out. A moment's escape from the Books and the threat that Sturne or even himself might have to set paw into the Chamber, was more than welcome. He ran back down the way Sturne had first brought him, climbed up to the surface, and peered out. The scene had changed little. A shade lighter perhaps, but the mist was still thick and the trees rose up as they had before, grey, looming for a time, and then thinning into the white nothingness.

Except, oh dear, except now the mist was moving, shifting, swirling slowly among the trees, growing thicker for a moment and then thinner once more. It was a subtle thing, almost unnoticeable at first, but then when Pumpkin did see it, it felt as if the Wood was subject to massive movement, the mist being still and the great trees advancing eastward through it.

'Westward,' whispered Pumpkin to himself, 'it's moving before a westerly wind.'

Then, from the direction of the Stone Clearing, he heard a muted call.

'Brother!'

Then, 'Over here! Here, Brother, near the Stone.'

Without pausing to try to see or hear anything more, Pumpkin ran back down below, his pawsteps echoing loudly ahead of him, scurried through the tunnels back to Stour and Sturne and told them what he had seen and heard.

'Well, then, the wind of change is coming from the west,' said Stour, 'but the air is stillish for now. But only stillish. Now each of these Books must be taken in by a different entrance, just as, I have no doubt, their complementary Stillstones were in decades past. Pray for me.'

He said this last softly and quickly, and the moment he had done so he took up the Book of Earth, without any apparent difficulty, and carried it straight into the nearest of the entrances and went in amongst the labyrinth of roots. As he did so he touched one, which vibrated and whined above him, and set off others, so that there was a whisper of sound and a tremor of movement and one of those sudden shifts within the place in which all the roots seemed to move momentarily at once, with the result that their patterns and forms were changed. In that moment Stour disappeared, any view of him blocked now by the shifting, trembling roots among which he wended his way to the innermost holiest place in moledom.

Time passed, the sounds of movement and moles somewhere above were heard, and Pumpkin and Sturne looked at each other, and the precious Books they now guarded, with concern.

'He will come back, won't he, Sturne?' said Pumpkin.

Not being a mole to mouth platitudes, Sturne said nothing, but pursed his mouth and frowned, and stared stolidly at the texts, and then uneasily upwards towards where the Newborns went back and forth, making their preparations for Longest Night.

Then, just as they were beginning to think that they had seen the last of Stour, he reappeared, but not at the entrance by which he had entered. His snout poked out from another portal; he eyed them and said, 'Here! Help me! Phew!'

They went to him, supported him, and pulled him clear of the roots.

'Better get on. It's the turn of the Book of Suffering. Ah yes . . .'

He went to the Books, took another up rather too quickly, staggered back off balance and nearly went flying.

'Master!' said Sturne.

'Master of nothing!' declared Stour. 'Not even myself. This is going to be a long day into Longest Night!' Then, puffing and panting with the Book, he went back to the entrance by which he had come out and went in among the roots again, and was gone as mysteriously as before.

But this time for longer, and he emerged, again at a different entrance, very tired, and looking as if he had suffered a rough passage to and from the base of the Stone. In his absence Pumpkin had gone off and found some food, and this they persuaded the Master Stour to take. He was lost in his own thoughts as he ate it, muttering unintelligibly to himself, staring round in a frowny way at the Books occasionally, and then towards the dark portal into the Chamber of Dark Sound.

'Scribed a journal,' he said suddenly. 'Left something for you, Sturne, so you will know what it was like in here all that time alone. Not good for a mole. Needed all the strength I had, and have none left. Good that I knew you were there, for you are a worthy mole, and will be my successor. None worthier. Go and find my journal when you are ready, it will be the making of you. It's safe in the Chamber of Dark Sound. Now . . .'

Then the old Master Librarian was up once more, and lifting the Book of Fighting, with which Sturne had had great difficulty when he had gone to collect it. But Stour took it up as if it were light as a feather, and tottery though he was, made his way without difficulty to another entrance, for another journey into the Chamber of Roots.

So the day passed on, and when they checked up above as they sometimes did they saw that the day was still cold, the mist remained thick and was still swirling its slow way westward through the High Wood and beyond.

By the time the ante-chamber began to darken towards dusk, and Sturne to fret that he must depart for the surface lest the Newborns miss him, and his secret support of the traditional followers of the Stone be discovered, the Master Stour had succeeded in transporting

337

only five of the six Books to their final place with the Stillstones beyond the Chamber of Roots.

Of what he had seen or experienced there he had said not a single word, but both moles had noticed that when he had emerged after taking in the fifth Book, the Book of Healing, he was very tired and slow, and barely able to talk at all. A mood of resignation, even lethargy, had come over him, and despite prompting from Sturne, now so anxious to assume his duties on the surface, Stour only shook his head, and kept his snout low, unwilling even to look at the Book of Light, which was his final task.

'Master,' whispered Pumpkin, going close to him, 'Keeper Sturne will have to go soon and that'll only leave me here with you and this sort of thing really needs a more important kind of mole than me! If I could fulfil the Keeper's task by the Stone with all those wretched Newborns I would, I really would, but I'm just Pumpkin and they'd laugh. So you must try and take the Book while he's here so that when you've finished, we can . . . well, then we can . . . you see . . .'

'What then, eh mole?' said Stour, looking up bleakly at Pumpkin.

Pumpkin could only stare and look desperately about the place, for he did not know 'What then'. He felt only fear, and an impending loss that seemed echoed by the bleak look in the Master's eyes. But he knew he was afraid to be left all alone down here, waiting for the Master to come back again, with the sounds of the Ancient System, and that dark portal beyond which ghostly moles seemed to lurk. Oh dear . . .

'Keeper Sturne . . .' whispered Stour, turning painfully to him. 'You must go. Library Aide Pumpkin has served me well in the past, and he will serve me well now, despite his timidity and fears. He is a stronger mole than he thinks he is. I could wish for no better mole present here when I decide to take up that Book – which I have no wish at all to take up – and venture for a final time into the Chamber of Roots. Therefore go now, Sturne . . .'

'Master, I do not wish to leave you.'

'But I wish it, mole, I wish it,' said Stour wearily. 'My strength is fading quickly now and I have none left to argue with you, or persuade you. I am sure that your task in the Stone dictates that you go up to the surface, and take part in whatever celebrations of Longest Night the Newborns intend to have, so that you are not missed. Leave us, mole. We are protected by the Stone. Leave us now.'

Pumpkin, discreet and tactful mole that he was, moved a little way off so that Sturne and Stour, who had worked together so many moleyears, might say a few words of Longest Night together, and perhaps words of farewell too, for though none of them had said as much, the truth was that Sturne and Pumpkin felt it possible, as perhaps Stour did as well, that he would not return from the Chamber of Roots once he entered it again with the sixth Book.

The two moles touched paws; Stour smiled, Sturne looked most troubled, and then he turned away, patted poor Pumpkin briefly on the shoulder and was gone down the tunnel by which they had entered, his pawsteps fading away. Immediately he had left, a sense of relief seemed to come to Stour, who signalled Pumpkin over to him.

'The Keeper has served me faithfully, just as you have,' he said. 'Yet I sometimes feel I failed him. He is not a mole who ever smiled easily, nor seemed to know the meaning of happiness.'

'No, Master,' said Pumpkin with feeling.

'See to it, will you, Pumpkin? When I am long gone, and the Book of Silence is come to ground, and all this business is sorted out . . .' (here he waved a paw about as if to indicate the Newborns, the lost Book and the crisis in moledom all in one go) . . . 'as it will be I am sure, if you moles have courage and keep your snouts pointed in the right direction – show Keeper Sturne what happiness is. Will you do that for me?'

'I'll try, Master. I had thought of it already.'

'Of course you had, Pumpkin, I didn't really need to mention it. But . . . well, I'm nervous, you know. I don't know what I'm going to find. I . . . don't . . . kn . . .'

To Pumpkin's alarm and dismay Stour let out a choking cry, pathetic in its weakness, and tears filled his downcast eyes, and coursed down his dry, wrinkled face.

'Master,' said Pumpkin, not sure whether to put his paws round the old mole or not, and finally deciding that he would. 'Master, I don't know why I feel afraid of so many things when you have done so much no other mole could do. It has been the great honour and privilege of my life to serve you. When I was afraid up there of the Newborns, these moleyears of autumn past, it was your example that gave me courage. If you cry tears now, just as I have, well, it only shows what courage you really have.'

Stour nodded, and his weak paw patted Pumpkin's flank gratefully, and he sniffled a bit before he eventually said, 'I better take the Book now. But I want you to promise me something because it will keep me going, so to speak, to know that you have.'

'If I can do it I will, Master Librarian,' said Pumpkin.

'Good, good.'

With new-found vigour, of which it was plain there was not much, Stour stanced up and went to the sixth Book. He took it up and said, 'Wait for me, mole, will you promise to do that?'

'Is that all, Master?'

'It will keep me alive,' said Stour; 'knowing a mole I trust and like is waiting here will bring me back and I want to pray before the Stone one last time. Things to say, things you must do . . . wait for me!' With that he was gone into the sixth of the seven entrances of the Chamber of Roots. Pumpkin, fearful of the sounds about him, and the sudden muted Newborn chant of celebration coming from the surface above, stanced down as calmly as he could and began to wait.

Chapter Twenty-Six

'Pumpkin! Pumpkin! *Mole!*'

A distant voice woke Pumpkin from the deepest of dreamy sleeps, in which moles had chanted by the Stone, night had gathered and advanced, crowds had collected and then dispersed, and a whole Longest Night had been, and now was almost gone.

'Yes?' called out the library aide nervously into the gloom, trying to orientate himself.

'I need your help . . .'

The voice was Stour's and Pumpkin was instantly awake, realizing that Longest Night was almost over and a new dawn was coming over moledom, even if the sky up on the surface was still dark. Now his Master Librarian needed him.

'What can he have been doing for so long?' Pumpkin asked himself, as a diversion from the awful fact that if the Master was where he thought he was then he was still in the Chamber of Roots and needed help getting out.

'*Which means I'll have to go in there myself and give him a paw,*' muttered Pumpkin to himself in a miserable way. Aides get all the worst tasks and in a long career this was the worst of all, Pumpkin thought.

He heard a scurrying and heaving, and headed for the nearest portal into the Chamber, which was the seventh, and peering in he called out, 'Here I am! Where are you?'

Oh, but he saw Stour at once, and all his fears fled as he saw how old the Master looked now, and how terribly frail; half fallen in his effort to get out from among the confusion of roots, he clutched on to what support he could, his thin fur seeming a strange luminous green, like ancient lichen, in the sub-dawn light that filtered in from above.

'Master!' Pumpkin cried out in horror, rushing in amongst the roots without a further thought for himself.

'Almost gone,' muttered Stour grumpily, reaching out a shaking paw to Pumpkin, 'almost lost my strength. Help me out of here, mole,

341

for I've completed my task and can do no more. The six Books are safe, all safe now . . .'

'Master, Master Stour!' cried Pumpkin in dismay, for Stour was sobbing, a raspy, dry kind of sob as of a mole who has no tears left. It might have been with relief.

Together the two moles escaped the last few paces from the Chamber of Roots and Stour said, 'It was knowing you were there, Pumpkin, knowing you would wait and not desert me or be afraid. That's what kept me going.'

'I was asleep, Master,' said Pumpkin honestly, 'and Longest Night is almost over. As for being afraid, well I was, you see, and I am. This place makes me very much afraid.'

'Yet you stayed.'

'I wouldn't leave *you*, Master Librarian, never. Never will.'

'But I think I must leave you now, mole,' said Stour gently. 'Help me to the surface and to the Stone. Help me this final time. But something I forgot to say. Should have told Sturne . . . My journal in . . . in . . .'

'In the Chamber of Dark Sound,' said Pumpkin. 'I was here when you told him.'

'Yes, yes. For Whillan, there's a text for him with it. To tell him what his mother said. To tell him . . .'

'You mean Privet?'

'No, mole, I mean his *mother*. Tell Sturne to give it him unkenned. It is for his eyes only.'

'I will, master.'

'Now, we must go to the surface.'

'I better see if there are any Newborns about.'

'There's nomole about that will hurt us,' said Stour with complete certainty. 'There's just the Stone waiting, as it waits for all of us. Now, I think I can manage this last bit by myself . . . I certainly want to try . . . I . . . yes, yes, that's right . . . that's right . . .'

And with only an occasional paw from Pumpkin to keep him steady, Stour climbed the last short distance out of the tunnel and up into the High Wood, and from there across the surface to the Stone Clearing.

'Now . . .' he said, and he turned to Pumpkin with a look of relief and joy: 'I was so afraid I would not see the Stone again. So afraid . . .' He sobbed a little once more, shook his head, grinned in a strange rueful way, reached out a paw and patted Pumpkin's and with a firm step went towards the Stone.

'Here I found my faith and my destiny,' he said. 'Here I saw the

342

path I must take. Here, this coming dawn, I shall know the seasons have turned again and that my task is done. Here my faith has found its resolution and others will lead the followers on.'

'Shall I try to find Sturne?' said Pumpkin, suddenly nervous as he realized the drift Stour's words were taking.

'He's near enough, Pumpkin, and anyway it's you I need, you I must talk to. Not that words mean much now. You'll know what to do.' He settled on the surface before the Stone.

'Me?' said poor Pumpkin uneasily.

'When the Book of Silence comes, you'll know how it should be served.'

'But Master, you're not . . . there isn't . . .'

Stour smiled, suddenly much weaker: 'I am, and there will be a Book of Silence. It *is* coming, Pumpkin, or trying to come, and the circle of Books beneath the Stone awaits its coming. Privet, she will find where the Book is, she will bring it back to Duncton Wood. But you, Pumpkin—'

'But I don't know anything much, Master, and you mustn't vex yourself thinking I do. Sturne's the one, he knows about such things. I had really better go and get him.'

But there was no more time. Stour's breathing had slowed and deepened, and though he smiled still, his eyes were beginning to fade, and Pumpkin knew he could not leave him, not now. But then, harshly, the silence of the Clearing was broken.

'You there! Disperse and go back to your burrows. The proper rituals are over!'

Pumpkin turned and saw three Newborn guardmoles approaching purposefully across the Clearing. His heart thumped in his chest, but he tried to look as bold as he could, and considered what he could do. His Master was dying, and that was a fact. As his aide it was Pumpkin's task to see that he did so with dignity and in peace – not harried and worried by these great bullies.

The Newborns paused and stared, quite unable to make sense of the scene. One of them knew Pumpkin, but none recognized the elderly mole who lay weakly on the ground ignoring them, as he reached a frail paw out towards the Stone. Their hesitation gave Pumpkin a moment longer to think what to do. He saw that behind them, at the edge of the Clearing, was another Newborn who had under his brutal custody three moles. All young, and, realized Pumpkin, moles who had come to try to celebrate Longest Night in the old way. Good for them! It gave him courage to see it.

343

'We are doing no harm!' Pumpkin cried out, playing for time. One of the young moles started up, recognizing Pumpkin by his voice alone, for the dawn was still so murky that it was hard to see each other plainly across the Clearing.

'Why, that's Cluniac who works in the Library,' said Pumpkin to himself. Yes, of course . . . the Stone would protect them, it would, if only . . .

'Mole,' said one of the Newborns, still unwilling to come any nearer to the Stone they feared so much, 'come here at once.'

'Cluniac!' cried out Pumpkin. 'Listen to me! I have the Master Stour with me, for he has come out of retreat at last to say his final prayers before the Stone. Run now, mole, run as you never have before. Find whatmoles – anymole – brave enough to come back to the Stone Clearing to give him support. Quick mole, now!'

It was well said, and the youngster understood at once what he must do. He turned and buffeted at the Newborn watching over him, and, responding to the situation, the others did the same. The guardmole roared with anger and annoyance and tried to hold on to his youthful charges, but first one and then another struggled out of his grasp and were gone, off through the trees, one after another.

'You go to the Eastside! You to the Westside! I'll take Barrow Vale!' Pumpkin heard Cluniac command his comrades. Oh yes, the Duncton spirit was not dead yet!

The Newborns looked at each other in alarm, and began to argue.

'What did you let them escape for?'

'Well, you're no better, messing about—'

'I don't like this one little bit!'

Pumpkin suddenly felt calm. The Newborns were afraid of coming too close to the Stone, and anyway, he felt its Light and Silence about him.

'Master . . .' he whispered as he took the Master Librarian's frail body in his paws and held him with love: 'Master Stour, don't leave us, you are so much loved. Moles are going to come now. *Duncton* is going to come.'

'Don't let them hurt the guardmoles,' whispered Stour, 'they'll not harm us. One day you'll truly know the Silence, Pumpkin, and you'll not be afraid.'

'Oh Master,' sobbed Pumpkin, his tears upon Stour's old head as moledom's greatest Librarian began to whisper his prayers to the Stone that rose above them.

344

While behind them, awed, uncertain, afraid and angry, the four guardmoles discussed in low voices what to do.

'If that's the Stour I think it is, the Brother Inquisitors will want to know, so I'll go and report to them,' said one of them, dashing off.

As Stour prayed, Pumpkin turned and faced the remaining three resolutely. If they were going to do anything to his Master, they would have to do it to him first. His worst fears were soon confirmed.

'Let's kill the buggers and have done with it,' said the biggest and most brutal of the three, who was only prevented from coming forward and doing the deed by the restraining paws of the other two, who seemed less certain of themselves.

'Best to wait. Best to let Brother Fetter decide.'

'Oh aye? And let half Duncton reach here first and spirit these two blasphemers away?'

'That one's not going anywhere!' said the third, pointing a talon at Stour. 'He's just a pile of skin and bones. He'd die the moment you touched him.'

'Let's do the bastard then!' said the murderous one. 'Let's just bloody do it!'

Again, the two more nervous guardmoles had to restrain their fulminating friend, but this time they did it with less vigour, and it was plain to Pumpkin that they would not curb him much longer. Meanwhile, Stour was lapsing into long silences, and his breathing was becoming laboured, and from time to time he reached out a paw to Pumpkin for comfort and reassurance.

'It's all right, Master, our friends will soon come,' he whispered, unwilling to take his eyes off the guards and stance down to Stour lest at his doing so they finally lost all restraint.

As the situation grew increasingly tense dawn began to flood the Clearing with light, the shadows faded, and the grey roots of the beech trees and the russet carpet of fallen leaves began to gain colour. There was no sun, but even without it the Clearing seemed filled with light, which made the dark fur of the Newborns, and their anger, all the more striking in contrast to the light, and the peace around them.

'Right! I'm waiting no longer!' roared out the belligerent guardmole suddenly, pushing his colleagues aside and advancing on Pumpkin.

'I'll have you for a start, you little hypocrite!' he said, buffeting Pumpkin so hard in the face that the aide fell back, his snout bloody. 'You're that mole helps Keeper Sturne in the Library. Just you wait until he hears what you get up to when his back is turned!'

Brave Pumpkin came forward once more, despite the shock and

pain he felt, protesting on Stour's behalf, pointing out that the Master Librarian was ill, and that the Stone Clearing was a place of sanctuary and always had been.

'Nomole should be hurt here!' said Pumpkin.

'Well, it's not a sanctuary to me!' said the guardmole, shoving Pumpkin back violently against the Stone and bending down to grab at Stour. But whatever he was about to do, he never did, for one of the other guardmoles gave a warning shout; he turned, and saw, growing ever larger by the moment, a gathering crowd of moles.

Most were old, most were breathing heavily from running, but all looked fierce and formidable. Individually there might not be much to them – no more indeed than to a mole like Pumpkin – but together, and increasing in numbers, there was something frightening about them. Worse, from the point of view of the three Newborns, the advancing dawn threw a light upon their faces that seemed to gather in their eyes, so that they looked more formidable still.

'You can try to hurt that mole if you like, mate, but I'm getting out of here,' said one of the Newborns, trying to run to one side. But the High Wood was filling with moles, from the Eastside and the Westside, and up from Barrow Vale, and they were advancing with menacing purpose.

'The Master Librarian's over there . . .'

'He's with Library Aide Pumpkin, near the Stone . . .'

And the guardmoles found themselves overwhelmed by moles whose interest was only to watch over a mole who had been their Master Librarian for so many decades, and to whose flank they had now been summoned for support and help.

'He's dying . . .' one whispered.

'Look how thin he is!' said another; and the guardmoles found themselves part of that crowd, taken over by it, helpless within it, and witness alongflank it to Stour's last moments.

Pumpkin turned to Stour and held him as best he could, listening to the difficult breathing, helping him say his final words of prayers he had spoken for so many years.

'Guide him into thy Silence, Stone, for he has served thee with all his heart, with his mind, with all his body,' said Pumpkin at the end, a prayer echoed by many in the great hushed crowd that gathered now about the Stone.

'Guide him, Stone . . .' moles whispered.

'Show him thy Light . . .'

'Give him thy peace . . .'

346

Then Pumpkin's head bowed closer to Stour's, and his paw reached out to touch his beloved Master. Then, quietly, breathing was no more, his body still, and his spirit gone into the Silence of the Stone.

How long did Pumpkin weep at his Master's flank? Nomole can say. But others reached their paws to him at last, and utterly ignoring the Newborns who had gathered and yet had dared not interfere with the mourning of so many moles, disobedient though they were, they led him away to safety.

The guardmoles watched in furious silence; Brother Inquisitors Fetter and Law let their cold eyes glance from face to face so that they might remember which moles to punish, beginning no doubt with Library Aide Pumpkin. Then, as suddenly as it had filled, the Clearing emptied, leaving only the body, now needed no more, of moledom's greatest Librarian.

'Give them two days, maybe three,' hissed Fetter, 'and then we'll eliminate the perpetrators of this . . . this obscene blasphemy. His colleague Brother Inquisitor Barre advanced across the Clearing, reached out an insolent paw to Stour, and contemptuously turned his body over.

'So this . . . this thing . . . was Stour? He tricked us! And others must have known. Moles will pay for the success of your "retreat"!' said Barre. He raised a paw to strike Stour's dead face and then dropped it. 'I can't be bothered,' he said for the benefit of the guardmoles watching. The truth was that even in death Stour's features were noble and intelligent; and anyway, his eyes, which stared, seemed alive, so full were they of the strange Light of that awesome place.

'Aye,' whispered Barre to Fetter, 'moles will die for this!'

Behind them, unseen, Acting Master Librarian Sturne slipped away, so grief-stricken that he knew that he could not have maintained his pretence of being Newborn in those moments of loss. Instead he wandered for a time through the High Wood, as many others did, saying nothing, grieving, knowing that the seasons had indeed turned, and brought change. With Stour's passing, Duncton would never be the same. And now, from what Fetter had said, many Duncton moles were in greater danger than ever before.

Morning advanced and Sturne remembered Pumpkin. He hurried through the High Wood, making sure that nomole saw him, and made his way to Pumpkin's tunnels. He found him there as he thought he would, staring into nothing, his eyes red, and his face-fur wet with tears. But there were no tears in Sturne's forbidding eyes, no tears upon his tired, etched face.

347

'But there is a grief in my heart, Pumpkin, such as I never thought I could feel. There is grief to lose so great a Master . . .'

'. . . and so great a friend,' faltered Pumpkin.

'I wish,' said Sturne very quietly, 'that I could weep as you do.'

'They're not just tears of grief,' said Pumpkin sombrely, 'but tears of joy as well. Those mixed kind are the best of all, and one day you'll find it in your heart to weep some, you see if you don't.'

'Joy at such a moment?' wondered Sturne.

'Yes,' said Pumpkin, 'for he fulfilled his task. Joy, too, that we knew him; joy that he cared for so many and for us; joy that we shared in his task and that so great a mole as he trusted you and me. These are the comforts I find as I mourn the loss of such a mole in the days and years ahead.'

Sturne looked at Pumpkin; he was secretly so very proud to call him a friend, and there was admiration and a kind of love in his eyes – though he did not let Pumpkin see it.

'He began what we must finish,' said Pumpkin. 'It is our task now. The Book of Silence is coming . . . he said that not long before he died.'

'Yes . . .' said Sturne, who was thinking he had said rather more than that, more perhaps than Pumpkin quite realized.

Suddenly, and impulsively, Pumpkin turned to Sturne and throwing his paws round him sobbed on his shoulder, so that, undemonstrative though Sturne was, the Acting Master Librarian could do nothing but support his friend while he wept. Which he did for quite a long time until his sobs quietened and then unexpectedly turned into something like a chuckle.

'You will one day,' said Pumpkin breaking free, and not in the slightest bit embarrassed by his outburst of emotion.

'What?' said Sturne, scowling.

'Weep,' said Pumpkin. 'Do you good!'

'The Master's gone back to where he wanted to be,' whispered Sturne, and if he did not quite weep then his voice broke a little, as without thinking he reached out a paw to Pumpkin for comfort. 'Let's pray for him together a while longer in silence.'

'Yes,' nodded Pumpkin, who had already said his goodbyes but understood that Sturne was slower off the mark where matters of the emotions were concerned; 'and then I'm sure the Master won't mind if we eat a worm or two in his memory!'

Pumpkin was indeed starving and after such a night of fear and effort, and such a dawn of emotion and grief, he could not but believe that sorrow and fond memory, and hunger and good food, might be worthy – and welcome – companions.

But the morning's trials were not yet over. Their silence was broken by shouts and crashings through the Wood above.

'That aide lives hereabout,' a rough voice called.

'Over *here*, I'll warrant,' said another, right above their heads.

'Sturne,' said Pumpkin with sudden realization of the danger they were in, 'you must say you've come to arrest me! It's the only way they'll not suspect you now!'

'But . . . but . . .' said Sturne, appalled, yet even as he uttered his whispered protestations the noise of Newborns above grew louder and he knew that Pumpkin was right.

'No, I'll not come, I've done nothing wrong!' Pumpkin began to shout hysterically. 'I won't. A mole's free to do what he likes before the Stone! I won't!'

And Sturne, realizing what he must do, grabbed poor Pumpkin roughly, and pulled him bodily out of the tunnel and delivered him to the very paws of Fetter and Barre.

'And not a moment too soon!' said Sturne angrily. 'He would have escaped if I had not come here immediately I heard.'

'Your promptness does you credit, Brother!' said Fetter, his cold eyes on Pumpkin. 'The others we'll arraign in two or three days – they'll not get far, even if they try. Meanwhile, we have questions to ask this mole, not least to do with how it comes about that Stour survived so long. Somemole or moles must have helped him.'

'Aye,' said Sturne angrily, 'and I think I know who did!'

'Well, well,' said Fetter, 'we'll find out soon enough once Brother Barre begins to ask Aide Pumpkin a few questions, down in the privacy of the Marsh End.'

Barre smiled cruelly. Sturne stared, his mind racing to think of a way of helping Pumpkin.

Pumpkin stared at them all as boldly as he could. His Master had just died, and he had never in his life felt so afraid, and so alone. Willing paws grabbed him, and hustled him off downslope.

'It seems your trust in that mole was misplaced, Brother Sturne,' said Fetter. 'Or did you suspect him?'

'Never,' said Sturne with an appearance of absolute conviction, 'did I ever suspect that mole of treachery!'

'Well, well,' said Fetter, 'we all make mistakes. It may help you come to terms with things if you accompany me now to witness the way we Newborns eliminate "mistakes" like that mole Pumpkin.'

'With pleasure,' said Sturne evenly, casting his eyes up through the leafless trees as if to find comfort, or inspiration; for now they were going to need one, or the other.

PART IV

Caer Caradoc

Chapter Twenty-Seven

There was, finally, nothing simple or easy about Chater's slow decline into a gasping, wretched death, during the day that preceded that Longest Night. Nothing romantic, and certainly nothing that showed that the nature of a mole's death reflects the nature of his life. For that good, sturdy, much-loved mole, who had served Duncton so well so long, and had received his death-blow in the course of duty to others, surely deserved to be loved and comforted at the end by Fieldfare, the one mole whose name he constantly called, and who could not be there.

In his last hours, from midday to later afternoon when the air began to chill, and the sky to darken, Privet and Hamble tended him as best they could, while Madoc, who had seen violent death, but not the slow dying of a friend in the paws of another, saw to their needs of food, and watched out for Newborns.

What made his weakening so difficult to accept or comprehend was that his wounds seemed so slight – barely more than the punctures in a mole's skin when he has had a brush with a dry bramble stem. But he had bled internally, and slowly, and strong though he was, and much though he had to live for, the life ebbed painfully out of him; his breathing became thick and troubled, and he gasped for air and held on to the paws of Privet and Hamble as if to assure himself he was not alone as he died.

Until, at the last, when he began to grow still, and his limbs cold, and the strife in his body seemed to ease, he could only stare at Privet and say nothing, a stare that was all he could use to cling on to life; a stare that brought tears Privet could not hide.

'Oh, Chater,' she whispered, 'my dear friend.'

But his last movements, his last struggle with words, were for Hamble.

'Go,' he said, 'go . . .' And he raised his right paw and sought to point south-eastward, Duncton way.

'Go to Fieldfare?' whispered Hamble. 'Is that what you want me to do, mole, to tell her?'

Then Chater smiled, a smile of tears and love and last goodbye, and his paw grasped Hamble's as he whispered, 'Yessss . . .' His eyes, still half open, dimmed, the light suddenly gone from them as he breathed his last.

'This mole saved my life,' said Hamble, 'and that of Rooster and the others. This mole—'.

'This mole was my friend,' said Privet, not letting go of him.

Then they talked, as if unwilling to let Chater go, one an old friend, the other a new one, their words soft and subdued; they talked as if Chater still lived, telling of their own lives, of their journeys, of all they had known and seen in the long years since Hamble had guided Privet off the Moors. Oh yes, Chater might just have been a mole who was listening in.

Until there came a moment when it was right to let Chater go, and lay his head on the rough grass and acknowledge that he was there no more, but gone ahead of them to the Stone's Silence, his paw outstretched still towards distant Duncton Wood where until these last few molemonths his love had always been, the beginning and the ending of all his journeys. Now . . .

'Go to Duncton Wood, Hamble,' said Privet finally. 'Its moles will have need of the leadership you can give.'

'But what of Rooster? Without him I am nothing. His great destiny is not fulfilled.'

Privet smiled. 'I saw him on the slopes, and he saw me. All these years I have longed to see him, to love him again, but when I saw him he was not the mole I first knew. He was still the violent thing you helped me flee from. But the real Rooster is there inside, the Rooster I saw and loved on Hilbert's Top. The mole I love is there still.'

Hamble nodded. 'He is, and I know it, but I can't go alongflank him again and fight with paws that I no longer want to redden with other moles' blood. It is not the way.'

'Go to Duncton Wood, Hamble.'

'And you, my dear, whose friendship I have missed as if it were part of me? What will you do? How can I leave you now?'

'My task is up there on Caer Caradoc now. Last night I fled from it and came and found a mole I loved, and lost him. Today . . . today I will go up to Caer Caradoc and the Stone will show me a way forward. Losing, setting aside, giving up . . . the Stone is telling me what I must do. Go to Duncton, Hamble, it needs a mole like you.'

'What can you do alone on Caer Caradoc?'

'Tell them,' said Privet, ignoring his question. 'Show them. Let them know your heart. The time has come for moledom to fall still once more. Each of us must find our own way now. Go to Duncton . . .'

Hamble was still for a time, head low, and then he turned and looked at where Chater lay to one side, his fur, his face, his snout already stiff and different, and not him at all. Only his last gesture remained, a paw, a talon, pointing the way for Hamble.

'He wanted you to go to Fieldfare and tell her how he died, and where, and why,' said Privet. 'He would want that, and so would she.'

'She's not in Duncton Wood, he told me.'

'Go to Duncton, Hamble. She'll come home.'

'How can you know that? The Newborns . . .'

She stanced up and looked into his eyes, and then beyond him to where so far away her beloved adoptive system waited for them all.

'I'll *tell* her to come.'

'How?' he persisted.

She smiled and shrugged. 'I don't yet know, but the Stone has been inside me with growing calm and Silence for some time now, pointing a way for me just as Chater pointed a way for you. As you find it hard to simply go, so do I. In truth, my dear, we are both afraid to do the simplest thing. Go Hamble, let me see you go.'

'It is not so easy—'

'It is, oh it, is. That's it, you see, so simple. We *do* it.'

'We do it,' repeated Hamble slowly, stancing up and shaking himself as if after a long night's sleep. 'And you say you'll find a way to make Fieldfare come?'

Privet said, almost in wonder at the flow of her own words, 'I will. I don't know how yet, though the knowing's near now, so near . . . Oh Hamble, go, and show me how simple it can be!'

She sounded suddenly passionate and young and he stanced up to her, embraced her roughly, held her close, and said, 'As when we left Crowden so easily to find Rooster, that's how simple it can be. I'll go just like that!'

Then a smile as easy as sun on ripe corn broke across Hamble's rough face and like a mole who had struggled to find a route for decades past and suddenly sees it before his snout, he stared south-eastward and said, 'I'm off. You come home when you're ready, mole, and Madoc, you take care of her. And Rooster . . . ?'

'We'll show him the way, Hamble, all of us. By what we do. The Masters of the Delve used to come when moles were ready for them, and left when there was no more for them to do. Now a Master is among us again, but we have not shown him we are ready. Now we must start. Go, Hamble!'

'Gone!' he said, turning away with a chuckle.

Without further ado, not even a wave, he *was* gone, the way Chater had pointed, alone across the fields, as simple as simply doing it.

'As simple as simply doing it,' whispered Privet after him, watching the rough back of her oldest and dearest friend disappear on a journey she too would have liked to make, for it would have allowed her to turn her back on Caer Caradoc and all its confusions, dogma, lost ways, and treacheries.

'But I cannot,' she said when he could be seen no more, turning at last towards Caer Caradoc again, which looked dark against the lighter western sky beyond now that the day's brief sun had fled.

'Now I am ready,' she said to Madoc. 'You wish to come with me, don't you?'

'It's what I feel is right,' replied Madoc, 'and what I feel the Stone wants. My task lies with you.'

'Whatever happens?'

'I think so,' said Madoc, uncertain of herself.

'Stay close, my dear. Your presence will comfort me. Come, let us climb Caradoc before Longest Night really begins. Let us head straight for the Stones. Come now!'

Then they too were gone from the place where Chater had died, and where he was no more, leaving his body there in the solitude of the morning, for the winter rooks to find.

'Come!' said Privet again, partly to encourage herself as they reached steeper slopes once more, 'the Stones and the future wait for us!'

Whillan and Maple also waited for Privet up by the Stones, though with a hope that had dimmed somewhat as night had passed and morning come again. But they had stayed where they were, discovering soon enough that good fortune, and the guidance of Thripp's friend, had them well placed to observe the surface movements of the Newborns and yet remain undetected. None, bar two of those they had already seen with Thripp, approached the Stones at all, and it seemed that what they had heard was true, the Newborns were in superstitious dread of the Stones. Theirs was a faith based on fear and punishment, and the comfort that Duncton moles felt near and around such Stones was alien to them.

But safe though the two moles were, they were not at all content, partly because whilst they could study the Newborn activity, and guessed that the Convocation was about to begin during the morning of Longest Night, when suddenly few moles were about and all was still, yet it was only surmise; added to which was the continued absence of Privet.

This latter concern was not eased at all when, at midday, their guide was seen to approach the Stones in the company of another Senior Brother, one they had not seen before, and both slipped suddenly through to where the Duncton moles kept their long watch. Their original guide now introduced himself as Brother Arum, and the mole he had brought to meet them was Brother Rolt, who expressed surprise and dismay that Privet had not shown her snout up the slope already.

'I left her myself at the foot of the slope last night,' he said uneasily.

'Well, she's not come and I'm inclined to head downslope to see if we can find her,' said Maple.

'I wouldn't do *that* if I were you,' said Brother Rolt. 'Here you are forgotten, and possibly useful, down there you may be discovered and, as many others have been since yesterday, "disappeared". Not that there is much disappearance involved in the death of *those* moles,' he added, pointing at the moles who had fallen to their deaths the night before, and whose bodies were now all too visible.

'What moles were they?' said Whillan.

'Siabod moles,' said Brother Rolt. 'All killed by Brother Quail's Inquisitors.'

'What good is Privet going to be able to do up here if she ever gets here?' demanded Whillan. 'It's far too dangerous!'

Brother Rolt sighed. 'I wish I knew. But the Elder Senior Brother seems to think—'

'He's not exactly done well in the past, has he?' said Whillan bitterly. 'Now he's suggesting Privet comes into danger.'

'Ah no, that is not quite true. Privet has a mind of her own and will not come unless she wishes to. Perhaps that's why . . . but it is necessary that she meets him.'

'Why?'

'It is time,' said Rolt mysteriously. 'It was time long ago.'

'Did you tell her moles would be waiting for her?'

'I may have mentioned it, yes,' said Rolt.

'Then she'll come if she's able to,' said Whillan despondently. 'She would not want to let us down. But it's all so pointless.'

357

'Yes, it does rather seem so,' said Rolt unexpectedly. 'Yet if you knew the Elder Senior Brother—'

'We met him,' said Whillan. 'I talked to him.'

'Then you know,' said Brother Rolt.

'I know what?' said Whillan.

Rolt looked at him with frank curiosity. 'So you were the mole raised by Privet?'

'Yes, I was. What of it?'

'A rare privilege, I should say. But you were not her own?'

'No,' said Whillan shortly. 'What *do* we do if Privet comes upslope to us here?'

'Well if she does, she'll not be alone,' said Rolt after an uncomfortable pause, 'there's a mole called Madoc with her. And if they do then I suggest you pray, and hope that the Stone will put an idea into Privet's head, for we're short of them. The Elder Senior Brother is quite silent on the subject, merely insistent that she comes. Part of a vision he has had.'

'Another one!' exclaimed Whillan impatiently.

'What of Chervil?' asked Maple to change the subject.

Rolt shook his head with distaste. 'I had such hopes for him, but . . . he is Quail's mole now. And Quail needs him, for many younger moles in the Order, and those who live far from here and serve us at a distance, will abide only by the Elder Senior Brother Thripp's authority, or that of his rightful son and heir. That, I may say, is not his wish, but moles will be moles and revel in hierarchy. Chervil therefore has power to stance between Quail and the complete destruction of his father's great ideals for harmony and shared worship and obedience to the Stone's will.'

'Duncton's free and easy way would have been better,' said Maple gruffly. 'As in the past.'

'Ideas do not stand still,' said Rolt, 'and if they do they usually die. Moledom may yet have cause to be grateful for the Caradocian Order, and to the Elder Senior Brother. Meanwhile you will be safe, and we will hope that Privet will come and that the Stone will guide us well this Longest Night. The Convocation has begun already, in its heavy and close-ordered way.'

'Is Deputy Master Librarian Snyde playing his part?' asked Whillan with an ironic smile.

'Ah, yes. Is he?' Rolt turned questioningly to the old mole.

'That Snyde!' said Brother Arum. 'He wanted *me* to be a scribe and was not impressed by my claims to be an archivist. "You've got a

358

scribing paw, what's wrong with you?" says he. Well, I got out of that. But I must say he's an insidious kind of mole, and like such moles is well-organized. There'll not be a word spoken at this Convocation which is not faithfully and accurately recorded, and copied, and kept for evermore in some text or folio or collection somewhere here and never kenned again by anymole!'

As they were nodding their heads in agreement with this their attention was drawn back to the edge of Caradoc by an upflight of black rooks from below – the same, no doubt, that had been harrying the corpses of the fallen moles.

'It's them, I think!' exclaimed Whillan, pointing to two moles who were labouring up the slopes below, straight towards the Stones. From above, it must be said, their ascent looked steeper and more dangerous than it really was, and Whillan and the others watched their progress with some alarm.

But to Privet, and Madoc, it was the welcome end to a long slog which, at times, had seemed interminable. Whether they were observed or not by alien moles they now neither knew nor much cared – Privet's calm and Madoc's anger at all they had seen had brought them beyond fear, at least for now. They climbed the last short stretch, paw by aching paw, breath by laboured breath, between outcrops of rock, over short grass, round a clump of thistle, on and up, looking only ahead and above them, to where the Stones loomed ever nearer.

Up and up, higher and higher, so steep now that neither of them wanted to look behind them, clinging on to the loose vegetation, veering left to avoid a buttress of rock, shielding their snouts against a sudden flurry of cold and dusty wind, until . . .

'Is that you? *Privet?*' called a familiar voice from above.

They paused and looked up and saw the forms of two moles staring down.

'Whillan?' said Privet in a whisper.

'Praise the Stone!' And down climbed Maple beside her, putting a paw to her rump and pushing her up the last short steep part of the climb to where Whillan's eager paws reached down and hauled her, at last, to the safety of the Stones.

'Another coming up, Whillan,' called out Maple.

And Madoc was on her way, grateful for the strong paws of the great Duncton mole, the first male, as far as she could remember, who had given her a helping paw.

But the first truly friendly male's face she saw, and that of a mole her own age, was Whillan's, as with a smile of welcome and a look of

359

curiosity, he reached his paws down and pulled her up alongside Privet.

'I'm Whillan,' he said briefly, before turning away to Privet.

'My name's Madoc,' she said in reply, but it was Maple's great paw that patted her shoulder in a friendly welcoming way, for Whillan had gone to Privet to see if she was all right. She was more than that – for at the sight of Brother Rolt she was overjoyed, though Brother Arum had made himself scarce the moment they arrived, muttering about females being 'inappropriate'.

No matter, there were other things to think about, and talk about as well. Privet had not been able to talk properly to Rolt before, but now she took her opportunity to ask about those days in Blagrove Slide and what had happened to . . .

'Dead,' said Rolt, sighing, 'your Brother Confessor of those times is dead. But your pups, Privet, I was able to protect them at least and though one died young the other three . . .'

Privet lowered her snout and closed her eyes, thinking of those days and wishing life and circumstances had been different.

'Tell it me briefly for now,' she said, 'for I'll want to ask so much. But my pups, the ones that lived . . . ?'

'The three remaining ones were safe, mole, when last I heard, but ignorant of who their mother is. They are adults now!'

'Their father . . . ?'

Rolt sighed again, uneasily. 'Some things are better left alone. He was not the mole you thought he was, not at all. Love him as he was, mole; at another time, in another place I'll tell you more, with the Stone's help, but for now you'll be hungry.'

It was true, and Maple and Whillan had long since gathered what few thin worms they could find against the arrival of Privet, for they guessed she would be hungry. She and Madoc munched busily, and then stanced down to recover themselves from the long climb. When they had done so, Privet told them as succinctly as she could all that had happened to her since they had been separated by the Newborn guards. Sad and sombre were their expressions when she told them of Chater's death and its circumstances. She did not hide the horror of his end but Whillan observed that at least she had been there, and the mole Hamble, and Chater's beloved Fieldfare would be pleased at that if the Stone and circumstance contrived that she should hear of it.

'Hamble *will* get to Duncton Wood, Whillan, I'm sure of it,' said Privet. 'There was something certain about that at least. But now you must tell me how you come to be here in Caer Caradoc, safely ensconced among the Stones.'

Whillan reported what had happened, and gave what interpretation he could of the events of the preceding night, and emphasized the extreme danger they must all be in. But that done, he spent much time describing to Privet in terms of some wonder his meeting with Thripp, concluding with the same remark he had made to Maple – that talking with the Elder Senior Brother felt like talking to his own father.

'I felt he *knew* me,' said Whillan, 'I felt he understood.'

Privet smiled and nodded and said, 'I am not entirely surprised, my dear, though the idea that you *are* his son seems a little far-fetched to say the least of it – though more astonishing things have happened in moledom's history! But, seriously, history shows that great spiritual leaders (and whether right or wrong, there's no doubt now that Thripp *is* a successful spiritual leader) have the gift of making those they talk to feel wanted, loved, listened to, even needed and at home. I have no doubt that Thripp has made many moles feel as you do – his appeal is precisely that he makes each feel that he alone evokes that special, warm response.'

Whillan looked a little crestfallen and Privet patted him sympathetically and said, 'My dear, I'm not much of a substitute, but it does seem that for now I'm all you've got.'

She stared at him intently – a look which he missed, though Maple did not – and seemed about to say something more, something comforting even; but she thought better of it, turning instead to look around at the nearby Stones.

The moment passed, and Whillan and Maple showed her and Madoc how the land lay, and where the Convocation was being held. The sloping flat top of Caer Caradoc looked deserted, and its surface was darkly mottled with shadow as the sun began to set.

'Longest Night is beginning,' said Whillan. 'What mole could have guessed we would be here of all places to see it in!' He looked at Madoc, whose part Privet had not stinted in praising, and said, 'Thank you for staying with her.'

Madoc shook her head: 'My life changed the moment she made me tell her my true name. I have tasted freedom with her, and want never to taste anything else again!'

'What is it, Privet?' said Maple as the two younger moles talked, for the scribemole had hunched forward suddenly as she stared at the fading light in the west.

361

'It's beginning,' she said, her voice trembling, 'it's beginning now.'

'What is, mole?' asked Rolt urgently. Whillan and the others had fallen quiet, hardly daring to breathe.

'Longest Night. *This* night. Change. What we must do. It's near, and I . . . I . . . Listen Maple, and listen well. You must not stay here, not you. I know . . .'

He had begun to protest and she put a paw to his to calm him.

'I know your task has been to protect us, but you cannot do more now. There are going to be savage times soon, most dangerous times, for ruthless though Quail may have been there will be moles who will stance up and resist what he has done and wishes to do.'

'Stow of Bourton for one!' said Maple.

'But they must not!' said Privet passionately.

'But Privet—'

'No mole, they must not, not in the old way. There is another way, a better way, the only way. You must go to them. Start in the High Wolds, for you are known and trusted there. Lead them in a new way towards peace and silence. Teach them the things we have learnt in Duncton.'

'We have been defeated in Duncton without a fight, and have undone what all our forebears did!' said Maple bitterly.

'No, my dear, we have not. We will attend the Convocation and something will come of it to guide us on, and lead others too. I know it, and feel it!'

Brother Arum came hurrying back with another of the allies of Thripp, a middle-aged mole called Boden. These two and Rolt quickly conferred, then Rolt turned back to Privet.

'You've got to come, but it'll only just be in time. The Convocation is beginning. The Brothers have been spoken to, they've been ritualized, Quail is there, Chervil is brooding, Thripp is watching from the shadows with his few friends gathered round him, so come now with me and let us salvage what we can from all of this!'

The day had grown no lighter, and high above the surrounding countryside as they were, they had the feeling that if they were any longer a part of anything, it was the grey wintry sky above. The dull grass fretted in the cold wind, and such protection as the dark Stones offered was forlorn and bleak. So that as Brother Rolt now indicated to them to follow him, and after a short and silent journey downslope they went below ground, they felt a kind of grim relief to be facing at last the dangers that had loomed so long.

They had not journeyed long down the tunnel before they turned off

362

in a westerly direction, through passages that were large and echoing, making silent progress difficult. Here and there the dry and wormless earth was interrupted by juts of the same sandstone as composed the Caradoc Stones; below ground it was lighter in effect, for the facets of the sand particles glistened in the gloom. The sound they made might have worried them more had not the tunnels carried a general hum of activity, distant but quite noticeable. This was loudest from the downslope tunnels that they passed, and once they even heard a snatch of the rhythmic chant of male voices.

'Good, good!' exclaimed Brother Rolt.

'That means they're pre-occupied,' said Boden with some satis-faction.

It was only when they finally took a downslope tunnel that Rolt began to betray any real concern for their safety.

'If we meet anymole, say nothing. Leave the talking to me. We almost certainly will meet some, but they won't be expecting deceit or treachery today!'

Downslope they went, the sounds ahead becoming steadily more distinct; they heard chants, and talk, deep voices and sudden trailings away, as of a gathering crowd of moles assembling in anticipation of the start of a long-awaited ritual.

More than once they saw somemole hurrying out of a side tunnel ahead of them and then turning downslope, the way they were head-ing. Another time an elderly mole appeared suddenly down-tunnel of them, but as Whillan did his best to look inconspicuous, and Maple readied himself for a dispute, or even a fight, Rolt waved a paw, and the mole said, 'Ah, good, you found them! Better late than never, Brother Rolt, better late than never! You know it's to the left . . .'

Rolt confirmed he did and they hurried on. The walls of the tunnel had until recently been only earth, but now the sandstone appeared again on the left-paw side, forming an impressive and seemingly impregnable wall.

Just as Whillan was thinking that if they *did* get spotted they would have nowhere to escape to and hide, they heard a deep chanting behind them, and the inexorable marching of paws. Rolt turned and stopped them and they pressed themselves as best they could into the hard wall as eight brothers, marching steadily and chanting in time to their own steps, came down the tunnel from behind.

'Lower your snouts and mutter respectfully,' said Arum, suddenly decisive, and they did so, the Duncton moles following the lead set by the others. Whillan did not, or could not, work out what it was the moles were chanting, or what its significance might be. As they went past the mole at the rear of the column called back to them, 'Find your places quickly, Brothers, for this day of days we brook no delays!'

Rolt followed on after him, but slowly so that soon the column and its powerful chanting went out of sight and hearing. Soon after this Rolt stopped once more and with a quick look up and down the tunnel pointed a talon at a cleft in the wall, barely more than a fissure.

'Boden, you take the lead and I'll follow behind. The rest of you keep close together as it's dark in places and easy to get lost.'

For a mole as large as Maple it was a tight squeeze but he managed, following after Privet whom he insisted on keeping within sight. The tunnel was not really a tunnel at all but rather a natural rift in the rock. It was not the kind of route liked by moles conscious of their safety, for they could not turn in it, and quickly escape. A force of two moles – one ahead and one behind – would have kept them all trapped without difficulty. But they pressed on, heaving and panting where fallen rock fragments presented obstacles, until with a pull from the front and a helping shove from behind they reached a spot where the fissure widened into a tunnel once more, a damp one too, for water dribbled in fits and starts down its centre; evidently, on wet days, it served as a temporary drain.

'Not a good place to be if it rained,' muttered Maple, ever the mole to be aware of the dangers of routes from which there were no quick escapes. But with Maple around others always felt safer, and knew that if a crisis arose he would know how to deal with it.

Rolt gathered them together and told them that quiet was essential, and careful movements.

'We're soon going to be at a vantage-point from which you will be able to watch the Convocation more or less without being seen – but the emphasis is on the more or less . . . so be careful.'

The tunnels they were in were some of the most peculiar the Duncton moles had ever seen, being no more than cracks and fissures between solid rock which followed the rocks' grain and fault lines, and ran straight in one direction and then angled abruptly in another, their gloomy overhanging walls towering above. The sound of the gathering nearby was as changeable as the direction they followed, being loud at one moment, soft and sibilant the next, and sometimes fading away altogether. Their route was evidently seldom used, as the soft wet sand underpaw had few prints in it, and little scent of mole.

Rolt slowed, looking back once more to indicate the need for extreme caution, and led them round another sharp corner, and what they saw took their breath away. Stretching out beneath them was one of the largest chambers any of them had ever seen, and it was filled with what at first seemed a confusion of moles – some chanting, some silent, some hurrying busily about, and other just stanced down and staring around as bemused perhaps as the Duncton moles.

The chamber was a great deal lighter than the tunnel through which they had come, and the high arched gallery in which they now silently took rest. The cavern's roof was pitted and fissured in places with the roots of vegetation trailing down or twining about the moist rock, pale green and sinewy. Here and there the reddish-black roots of bracken and broom hung, and just off to their right a mass of them ran down the wall and disappeared into the floor below, a living column amongst the subterranean rock.

It took them some time to work out how the mass of Newborn moles below were organized, but when a hush began to fall and moles seemed to find their places and stop moving about, all became clear. There was a raised area off to their left and towards this most of the moles faced. Behind this platform, which they realized was the focus of attention and the scene for the coming activity, some twelve to fifteen important-looking moles ranged themselves, most having a hint of grey fur, and experience scribed on their faces, all self-confident and formidable. Indeed, the closer a mole looked at them, the more so they seemed.

'Inquisitors,' whispered Boden to Whillan and Maple, frowning in disapproval.

'Don't let them see you, my dear,' said Arum to Madoc, towards whom, since Rolt had intervened by the Stones, he had been showing protective concern, to which she responded with smiles and nods which made the austere old mole's snout turn pink with pleasure.

'They're settling down now,' whispered Rolt, 'and soon there'll be liturgical chants intended to prepare the participants for what's to come. The Elder Senior Brother had originally intended to make the formal proceedings very simple, and concentrate on discussions and debate, perhaps in smaller groups, but since Brother Quail took matters over things have changed.'

'Won't be much debate!' said Arum.

'Nor any discussion at all!' declared Boden a little too loudly, but a stare from Rolt silenced him.

'There'll be a lot of chanting, some of the Inquisitors will no doubt speak and Quail will harangue the gathering in his belligerent and unpleasantly powerful way. Not until this evening will Brother Thripp come forward, but by then it may be too late for his words to have any effect. In his younger days he could have matched Quail at such a meeting at this, but the mood has changed; the younger Newborns don't want to hear about a way to the Stone's Silence. No, they're interested in shedding spiritual blood in the name of the true way by eliminating any obstacles in their path. May the Stone help any-mole who puts a paw wrong here today, for they'll be looking for victims.'

Rolt's voice dropped as the hush in the great chamber deepened, but for an expectant shuffling of paws and the occasional cough. As the moles below waited some stared up from the empty dais facing them to the enshadowed galleries above and the watching moles suddenly felt very vulnerable, and moved not a single hair lest their movement be seen and their dark forms made out.

For what seemed a long time but was probably only a few moments the hush deepened into complete silence of the kind that held all moles in its thrall, fearful that they would be the one to break it. Then in a firm clear voice one of the Inquisitors, whom Boden explained was Skua, the Chief Inquisitor, intoned these words:

> *'Almighty Stone,*
> *At this holy Convocation,*
> *Accept our entreaties,*
> *Direct our lives to thy commandments,*
> *Elevate our hearts,*
> *Purify our bodies,*
> *Rectify our thoughts,*
> *Cleanse our base desires,*
> *Heart and body,*
> *Mind and spirit,*
> *Thought and desire.*
>
> *Reprieve us wholly,*
> *At this holy Convocation,*
> *Almighty Stone.'*

This was no sooner spoken than a deep chanting of the kind they had witnessed earlier came forth from the rear of the chamber. Peering that way, they could see columns of moles emerging from tunnels at the back, and on the far side – and nearside too no doubt, but that

366

was below their line of vision. Their paws moved in time with their song, whose words none of them could at first make out.

Not that Whillan was trying to, for he was so suddenly and inexplicably overwhelmed by the power of the chant and the spectacle unfolding beneath him. What songs he had heard in Duncton Wood, what few rituals he had witnessed, were nothing compared to the mounting force of the singing below them. The columns moved slowly and methodically through the assembled moles, meeting and massing in the centre, their voices deep and harmonious. The very roof of the chamber seemed to shake at their power, the very walls to tremble.

Then, unexpected again, the other moles, those assembled, let out a strange, brief, haunting sigh, and thumped their right paws on the ground in front of them; then they were silent as the chant continued, the deep voices joined now by the higher falsetto singing of a solitary voice whose source the Duncton moles could not at first locate. The image and feeling the chant had at first evoked was of a marching forward, ever more urgently, with ever greater resolution. But it was a marching of moles without faces or personality – a body in which the individual was subsumed and lost within the mass in the name of a common purpose.

But now the new voice came, strange and haunting, male yet not male in its falsetto soaring, nor in the sense of vulnerability and loss it conveyed to those who heard it. At first the Duncton moles, least of all Whillan, who was the most immediately and profoundly affected by the extraordinary chants coming from the moles below, could not understand how so gentle a single voice could be allowed to run counter to the basic chant, and they wondered if it could be a protest of some kind. Perhaps some individual who had evaded detection by the Newborns, and now sang his defiant counterpoint to their ruthless and dogmatic chant.

It was Madoc who saw the singer first, pointing him out to Privet and then to Rolt and his colleagues (who nodded without taking their eyes off the astonishing scene). Privet turned to Whillan and Maple, who asked who the mole was.

'Squelch!' whispered Madoc, eyes wide in fear as she uttered his loathsome name, but filled with bewilderment as well, for the song he sang in counterpoint to the deep chanting was beautiful, haunting, and profoundly sad. She took Whillan's paw and directed his gaze across the chamber to a mole who was stanced clear of the others near one of the Inquisitors.

367

'That's Squelch, the son of Brother Quail,' she said again. 'He sings as no other mole any of us has ever heard sing, but often it's over his victims . . .'

Yet foul as he was, there was no denying how moving the mole's strange song was. Perhaps all the more so for the sight of him, since he was obscenely fat, with folds of furry flesh at neck and haunch, and great flabby paws poking out from beneath his body, like stubby growths. His head was round and bare, turned up towards the roof with eyes shut, as he sang for some life he had lost, or could not have, and wept.

What Whillan found most disturbing about Squelch's lament was that in the midst of the inexorable advance of the Newborn chant there was room for so powerful a contradiction to it, *and nomole minded.* It was surely no simple dogmatic bullying that could produce such subtlety, the like of which he had never experienced in Duncton Wood's simple, homely rituals.

'What does it mean?' Whillan asked Brother Rolt, 'not just the words, but all of it?'

Rolt stared briefly at him and said, 'It means that going forth to fight the fight of faith is not easy, and demands sacrifice. It was the Elder Senior Brother Thripp who made these songs, and he who first encouraged Squelch to sing. He said it might . . . bring him nearer the Silence.' Rolt threw a look of distaste at Squelch but Whillan did not notice it for he was thinking, '*Thripp*? Made this chant and composed this song?' And he was filled with respect and awe. The Convocation had not started as he had imagined it might, and he was beginning to think it would not continue, or even end, in any way he could predict. Thripp had not been what Whillan expected, and now the Newborn ritual was not either, and he felt his world was under an attack he might not be able to resist.

Squelch's song ended as suddenly as it began and his snout levelled; sniffing and dabbing at his tears with a forepaw, he stared about him, grinning strangely. His sorrow seemed forgotten and only vileness remained in its place.

As the chanting muted down preparatory to its climax, Brother Rolt whispered to them all, 'I must leave you now to join my master. The next time you see me it will be a little later today down there. Arum and Boden will see that you don't stray, and perhaps can find you food . . . ? There will be much chanting as the day progresses, and eventually after various other speeches and harangues and some confessions, Brother Quail will speak. Listen carefully – very carefully

– to what he says, and do not be overwhelmed by how he says it. It is the "what" we must fear, for all he has so far said he would do, he has done.

'Watch and listen too, to Brother Chervil. His intervention may be needed and his father was speaking to him about that when I left at dawn, but Chervil was unwilling. We cannot rely on him for he seems more dogmatic after so long away and he may have less use than we think. As for the Elder Senior Brother, I have advised him against speaking; it will be a great strain on him in his present state. But he will do as he is guided and may perhaps be unable to resist the Convocation if by popular acclaim it asks him to speak. Now, I must leave. Be careful, do not let yourself be seen.'

'Will we see you later?' asked Privet. 'And Brother Thripp, I would like to meet him so that I may know for myself what kind of mole he really is.'

'Perhaps . . .' said Brother Rolt distractedly. 'Be careful, listen well, and whatever may happen do not show yourselves.'

The gallery they were in was filling once more with the echoes of the Newborns' rhythmic chant, which swelled louder and louder until it was thunderous about them, and it almost seemed that in hurrying away Rolt was seeking to escape from it.

The chanters had now all pushed forward to surround the front of the dais. Squelch seemed to be singing and weeping once more, though the chant was too loud now to distinguish his individual voice; then, with one final almighty shout, the singing ended.

There was no more than a moment's pause before the Chief Inquisitor who had so briefly begun the proceedings earlier moved forward, raised a paw and pointing a black and shining talon towards the gathering, said, 'Almighty Stone, thrust your talons of piercing Light into the heart of the sinners among us. Cleanse and purify our number lest our holy gathering be tainted and befouled by doubters and hypocrites. If there are any here, let them stance forth, that they may be forgiven by acclamation here and now; let them cry out their shame, let them weep for their sickness and find forgiveness and acceptance beneath the talons of inquisition and redemption.'

In the silence that followed the watching Duncton moles found their own hearts thumping as there came over them a strange impulse to declare themselves sinners and miscreants. A feeling which, however absurd, only increased when the other Inquisitors came forward a little, all dark and severe of expression, and raised their talons to jab and point all over the chamber, as they spoke a guttural command

369

whose words only became clear when the first among them suddenly screamed, 'If you have sinned . . . if you have doubted . . . confess before your peers . . . CONFESS!'

To Whillan's astonishment there was movement among the Newborns – he no longer glorified them with the name 'delegates' – and several moles came slowly down to the dais. One seemed dazed, another terrified, and all trembled. They began, in the hubbub that ensued, to scream out confessions of some kind, of some misdemeanour of act or thought they had committed. The Inquisitors placed their paws hard on the confessing moles' bodies and as they cried out for the Stone to 'accept the sinners', they stabbed and scored them with their talons. As blood began to flow, Skua the Chief Inquisitor invited them to exculpate each other's sins by stabbing at each other. There was chanting, muttering, and the chamber echoed with the ritual sound of suffering and redemption before the confessing moles were allowed to return to their original places.

Then, the most terrifying moment yet, Skua said quietly, 'If there are no more willing to come forward may the Stone pursue those who seek to hide their shame and sin from its awesome Light. They shall be known, and their punishment will be by the slow talon, and a life after death without the Stone. Take this warning . . .'

There was a scream and one last mole came forward to confess, fearing perhaps that the lurid light of shame was so bright upon his face that it would be seen and he be revealed for what he was.

His torturing over – he was dealt with more savagely than the others – he tottered back to his place, weeping loudly. The time of confession was complete but the feeling of relief that followed was not allowed much space before Skua lunged his talons forward once more and declared, 'Watch, listen and be on thy guard. The viper is in thy midst. The canker turns in the crab-apple of thy heart. The snake of doubt and wrongful action is twisting and turning at the paws of the innocent and good. If you see it, declare it, that together we may destroy . . .'

He paused, and so hypnotic were his words that the gathering repeated the word 'Destroy' in a ghastly whisper round the great chamber.

'. . . and destroy again . . .' Skua's talon moved slowly right and left, back and forth, even down and then up towards where Whillan, Privet and the others stared down watching this unfolding drama. It was a frightening thing for a mole to find himself staring at the Chief Inquisitor's talon and into his fierce black eyes, and Whillan felt trickles of sweat coursing down his flanks as for one horrible moment he thought they had been seen.

But then Skua, transported it seemed by his mood of warning and threat of punishment, turned sharply towards the main gathering, leaned forward and pointing his talon towards some moles to the centre-left, hissed, 'There!'

'There, Brother?' cried out his fellow Inquisitors, beetling their brows and leaning towards where Skua pointed.

'There!' thundered Skua, leaping off the dais in his eagerness to root out whatever evil he had seen, and rushing in amongst the crowd until he stanced over a trembling Newborn, his sharp black talon pointing straight into the mole's terrified eyes.

The gathering began to mutter and hum in a most foul and murderous way – the kind of mob sound the Duncton moles had heard before the strettening at Ludlow on their way to Caer Caradoc. But the sound was replaced by a collective gasp of alarm as Brother Skua wheeled round suddenly, pointed to another part of the chamber, and cried out, as if on a private journey of discovery whose successive stages were causing him increasing agony, 'or *there!*'

As the other Inquisitors back on the dais swung their talons towards the new point of corruption, Skua raced through the gathering, pushing moles to right and left to reach the place – and the mole – before it fled his talon. The victim this time was a large and robust male, but before Brother Skua's inquisitorial gaze he broke down, saying, 'No, Brother, I have not sinned, my heart is pure. The snake entwined my paws and rode upon my back but I cast it off. Brothers,' and here he turned to the gathering in general, 'I cast it off.'

'Then where is it, Brother?' asked Skua with terrible intensity, 'where is that snake? If you would be pure, point out the mole wherein the snake resides now.'

'Ah!' breathed Privet when they heard this grim development. 'So I was right. This is a rule of fear, the rule of tyrant and dictator.'

'It was not always like this,' whispered Arum, evidently in distress. 'Not under the Elder Senior Brother Thripp – in our young days our meetings were never like *this*.'

'But Brother Thripp started it?'

'No, Sister, it was never thus,' said Boden, almost pathetic in his shame at what was going on below and his desire to dissociate his master Thripp from all of it.

'Monsters grow from good intentions if they are not founded on the liberty of the Stone's Silence,' said Privet.

371

Once more a hush had fallen below them as Skua awaited a reply to his terrible question. To the credit of the second mole at whom he had pointed the talon of doubt, he did not immediately turn to the nearest mole to say that that was where the snake resided, thus shifting attention and blame away from himself. Rather he wavered, looking about with tears in his eyes and saying in an agony of doubt, 'I don't know, I'm not sure, I am pure of the snake, and my brothers are pure . . .'

'*He* is not pure!' The voice came from the back of the gathering, and it was thin, snoutish, and accusatory. It was the voice of a mole well-used to finding blame in others, and knowing exactly the right time to declare it.

'Which Brother has seen the snake?' whispered Skua, stancing up and peering over the heads of others to see which mole had spoken.

'I accuse!' said the voice again and with a sudden movement of moles the speaker emerged from the mass at the back, while at his flank others held or pointed at yet another accused mole, who struggled to get free as he protested his outraged innocence.

'The snake resides in him and has devoured his heart and spewed it out as filth and doubt. He is corrupt. He is no brother to the gathering here.'

As Skua rushed to this new place of shame the accuser came quite clear of the others. He was small, he was twisted, and his back was as crooked as his cruel and malicious smile.

'It's Snyde,' growled Maple, 'our own dear Snyde. Trust him to get involved in this kind of thing.'

The accused mole struggled and shouted until at a command from Skua he fell suddenly silent. Skua and Snyde conversed in short sharp tones, jabbing pointed talons at the accused. Four heavy Newborns came to his flanks and led him down through the gathering towards the dais. His journey must have been terrifying, because not only did the gathering begin to chant 'Snake amidst us', whose sibilant sound in so many varied voices was like an icy wind through the branches of a dead tree, but on the dais the Inquisitors waited for him with their mean snouts and cold eyes.

While behind him the Chief Inquisitor followed, crying out, 'See where the snake lurked, in our very midst. He shall be judged in the Stone's Light, and if he be guilty, punished.'

'I wouldn't have thought guilt came into it,' muttered Whillan.

372

'It has happened that a mole is acquitted,' said Boden. 'But before this day is out some poor mole or other will be found guilty and punished.'

'Why else do you think they come?' said Arum cynically.

Chapter Twenty-Eight

Maple knew Privet well enough to believe that she would not change her mind about leaving the Convocation before she had learnt what she could from it. Had Snyde shown immediate signs of having seen them, Maple might have been more determined to get Privet and the others to safety, but he had not, and there was still surely much to learn in Caer Caradoc.

But what he could do he now did, which was to take Boden as guide and safeguard while he explored the complex of tunnels in the rocks into which they had made their way, looking for escape routes and places of possible danger. He found that by taking a narrow and awkward route, involving some tight squeezes and strenuous climbing, it was possible to emerge on the surface virtually on the steep west edge of Caradoc from where, he already knew, escape would be easier than anywhere else. He knew this from his studies of the military texts relating to the classic campaign led by Gareg of Merthyr against the forces of the Word a century before, of which Caer Caradoc had been the centre. Indeed he knew Gareg's *Strategy and Attack* almost by heart, as well as his much obscurer text *On Ending Wars* which that excellent library aide Pumpkin had informed him was scribed in old age.

When Maple found himself out on the deserted surface, with Boden keeping watch, he took the opportunity of getting to know the lie of the land. Escape was certainly possible down the steep west face of Caradoc, and if his memory served him, Gareg and Caradoc in their day had found a track which brought them right up behind the Stones at the northern end of the hill. Maple saw no reason for not using it to go down by if need be. While he was at it, he could not resist looking about the high wild surface of the hill to identify places Gareg and another fighter of those days, Haulke, had mentioned in their texts, nor could he help feeling the tragedy and sorrow that war, successful or not, brings to allmole in its wake. Looking across the pitted surface and rough winter grass of the high hilltop where he knew so many brave moles had died successfully defending the Stone against the Word, he could hear their cries more loudly and see their blood more brightly than when he first kenned accounts of the battle in the safety of Duncton's Library. Deserted now, the place seemed too small and ordinary to have been the scene of so much tragedy and triumph.

'May their spirits be with us this night and coming dawn if we have need of them,' he whispered, 'and may you guide me, Stone, to protect the good moles in my charge as best I may.'

But now the darkness was beginning to descend upon them again as in the great chamber down below the Newborns began to gather to themselves the evil forces of hatred of others' freedom, and dogmatic faith in their right to judge them.

Maple had never led a single mole in battle, nor, even, had he had many personal fights, for he had always had an inner strength and authority that matched his outward size and agility and deterred others from attacking him. Yet he knew himself to be a warrior, and felt in his paws the itch to lead, and a faith that he had strength and courage of mind, and the decisiveness that military leaders needed, to bring others through to safety and triumph.

But Maple had more: he had doubts as well – doubts about the value of mere military victory if it was not followed by something more lasting. As he stared balefully across the hilltop, and Boden moved about, and peered down into the tunnels, to check they were unseen, he understood why it might be that Gareg of Merthyr had scribed the text *on Ending Wars* in his old age. Maple wished now he could remember more of it.

As he thought these things Boden came hurrying up to him and said, 'Moles coming, and if I'm not mistaken it is the Elder Senior Brother Thripp himself, and Brother Rolt!' Lost in a world of thought, Maple stared impassively at the approach of Thripp, and felt no special surprise when the leader of the Newborns, leaving Rolt with Boden, approached him alone. Thripp came to him, his stare as bright and deep as it had been when he had talked to Whillan early that morning by the Stones.

'I am told you travelled with the moles Privet and Whillan to give them protection'.

'And learn of moledom,' replied Maple.

'And what have you learnt?'

'To have doubts,' said Maple. 'I had thought to lead moles in any war that was necessary . . .'

'On Newborns?'

375

'On enemies of the Stone.'

Thripp nodded slowly, and stared across the killing ground Maple had been contemplating with such sadness only moments before. He turned and looked hard at Maple, who as he returned the gaze had the disconcerting feeling that this was a mole who knew him better than he knew himself.

'Mole, you were born to lead others for a time, and it may be that your hardest task is to learn when to stop. Simply stop. It has taken me a lifetime, and many mistakes which have affected too many lives, to even learn to ask myself about stopping, let alone to do it. I still think I have things to do, and moles to influence, but true greatness of spirit lies simply in knowing when to do nothing. Moledom will need you, for you have seen something of the monster to which I, Thripp of Blagrove Slide, gave birth. For my Caradocian Order *is* a monster now. You may see today its dark turn beyond adolescence into narrow-minded, self-centred adulthood. Moledom will need you, Maple, and moles will want you to help guide moledom to a better way; and then? Moledom will need you no more. Turn gracefully at that moment, as I cannot, towards the task of peace.'

'Stour, Master Librarian of Duncton Wood, believes the same,' said Maple.

'Ah!' said Thripp, 'Yes. Truth is ever the same, whichever side a mole seems to be on.'

Maple did not know what to think except that he could not understand how so much that seemed bad had come from a mole who made those who met him feel good, and safe. But then . . .

'What of Chervil?' said Maple impulsively.

'Trust him,' said Thripp with sudden vehemence. 'Whatever may happen in the struggle ahead, trust him. Through my son I saw the light of the new liberty, though I am discovering it too late. But what I made badly he may re-make well. Trust him Maple, help him. He is our future peace.'

Maple thought of the dark and powerful mole that was Chervil, who had seemed to see everything with cold eyes, and wondered what peace could come from such a mole. Yet Privet, too, had seemed to have some faith in him.

'Can't you stop all this?' asked Maple simply.

Thripp smiled sadly. 'I shall try, you shall see me try in the mole-months ahead, but a mole cannot stop a storm by holding up his paw against the wind. He can only try to change its direction, and that I am already seeking to do. So trust Chervil, and trust yourself – though such advice to moles from Duncton is perhaps misplaced.' He seemed to hesitate for a moment before asking, 'This mole Privet, Whillan's adoptive mother. Was she born of Duncton?'

Maple shook his head absently and replied, 'No, no, she's from Bleaklow in the north.'

'Ah, yes . . .' said Thripp in a strange, peaceful way. 'She is a remarkable female.'

'She is a remarkable *mole*,' said Maple, not liking the Newborn's differentiation between the sexes.

Thripp smiled once more, warmly this time. 'That may be, but I *meant* female. Now I must leave you; Brother Rolt and I have matters to decide. Oh . . . and if you are thinking that this may be the way to effect an escape from Caer Caradoc you are probably right. Are you aware of Gareg's text?'

Maple looked surprised and nodded.

'Yes,' said Thripp mysteriously, 'it's what brought me here in the first place. Let us hope it helps fair-minded and just moles escape to fulfil their tasks of the Stone!'

He left, and soon after Maple called Boden over to him and they went below ground once more, through the twisting rocky tunnels, and back to the darkness of the Convocation.

By the time Maple returned to the others the Convocation had broken up into smaller groups, some of whom left the chamber, while the others, taking advantage of the greater space they now had, spread themselves apart from each other and submitted to individual haranguing by one or other of the Inquisitors.

Skua himself, ever energetic, went from one group to another, listening, peering, probing and sometimes whispering in the ears of his fellow Inquisitors, the better to consult or advise them, or even perhaps, admonish. All the time Snyde, who seemed now to have attached himself to Skua, followed on in his wake like some abject apprentice to a lord of dark intent.

'So long as we can see where he is I'll be the happier,' said Whillan.

The activity in the chamber produced a lot of noise of a low-level kind, punctuated occasionally by a sudden grunting shout as some piece of information or morsel of Newborn thought forced itself into the minds of the pilgrims below.

Meanwhile, as a bleak reminder of what happens to those on whose heart the snake of doubt has fed, the mole Snyde had exposed was now slumped in the corner of the chamber near the dais with no other mole but the fat Squelch, who was chewing his messy way through a fleshy lobworm, watching him.

Maple reported what he had seen, and also something of his meeting and conversation with Thripp, and he took the opportunity of the lull in the proceedings to quietly show the others the way to the escape route he had found in case they needed to get to it quickly later on. All of them were glad of the break and though they did not risk going out on to the surface when others might be about as well, they thrust their snouts out into the grey winter air, and felt relief to be away from the pressure of the Newborns.

'It's the chanting I can't get over,' said Whillan to Madoc, 'we've nothing like that in Duncton Wood. It was so powerful, so moving – and I admit I enjoyed it.'

'They always do it,' replied Madoc. 'I used to hear them practising.'

'And Squelch? Did he practise?'

'He is their inspiration. His voice is perfection. They say he sings when he mutilates young moles put into his power. They say all sorts of things about him.'

The two moles looked at each other, each glad to find one of their own age to talk to, each wanting to know so much about the world the other had come from.

'I *like* Privet,' said Madoc. 'She's the most brave and wonderful mole I've ever met. It must be so . . . satisfying to have a mother like her.'

'It must be!' laughed Whillan. 'But she's not my mother really. She adopted me when I was a pup.'

'Why? What happened to your mother?'

Even before the question was out of her mouth Madoc saw the shadow cross Whillan's face and realized it had been in his eyes all the time. She felt regret for asking, as well as sympathy and helplessness, and wished she could have taken the question back again. She recognized the shadow because it was her own.

'She died giving birth to me,' said Whillan shortly, 'just as she reached Duncton Wood. She must have been going there for sanctuary. Of course I can't remember her, and Master Librarian Stour, who found me, never knew her name. He knew *something*, but not that.'

'Oh,' said Madoc quietly. She fell silent, evidently upset.

'What were your parents like?' asked Whillan. There was terrible longing in his voice.

'I only remember a little bit because the Newborns separated us. I

378

don't remember my father at all. We've got something in common, Whillan.'

'Yes,' he said quietly. 'I don't know who my father was either.'

Boden called out that he had found food for them and Whillan, asking Madoc to stay where she was, went to get some for them both. He turned, he felt nervous, his heart thumped, he even looked back to see if Madoc was where he had left her and nearly fell over his paws with embarrassment when she caught him doing so. He fumbled at the food, took it up clumsily, and turned back again.

'Thank you,' said Madoc politely. The two stanced down in silence eating, both wanting to speak but neither able to think of anything to say. The silence grew almost unbearable before Madoc said, 'You're lucky, then, to have had a mole like Privet as an adoptive mother.'

'That's what others say,' said Whillan, more sharply than he intended. He laughed – his laughter all strange and not like his own at all. 'She was all right. She's very clever. She sees lots of things I never do.'

He was silent again, and Madoc stole a glance at him occasionally and saw him frowning, and the shadows of loss in his eyes.

Suddenly he looked straight at her and said almost savagely, 'I'd like to get away from all this. I'd like to see moledom and just travel by myself. I'd like to get away from Privet and all Duncton moles.'

He stared hard at her after he had spoken, his face slowly relaxing, breathing heavily after the effort of this unexpected confession.

'Oh!' said Madoc in some surprise and secret dismay, for even as she had begun to dare hope that here was a male mole she could like, and perhaps more than like, it seemed he wanted to be up and off on a journey all by himself which might take, well, Stone knew how long. 'That's nice,' she added weakly, 'but you'll be *needed*. I'm sure you will.' This last was offered as a kind of reassurance to him, and to herself as well.

'Yes,' he said gloomily, 'I might be.'

But then, still flushed with the relief of getting a long-held feeling of constraint out in the open, he added with a delightful grin of the spontaneous kind Newborn moles whom Madoc knew never gave, 'I'm glad you're here. It's nice to talk.'

'Yes,' said Madoc, filled with a sudden and unaccountable desire to touch him which she did not yield to. 'It's *very* nice.'

They allowed themselves a smile into each other's eyes, and talked inconsequentially for some time more, only responding at last to Maple's third summons to hurry back, for the Convocation seemed about to start again.

Whatever thoughts and nascent passions Whillan and Madoc had discovered in each other – and a mole should not think that the eager seed of love will find even such unpromising soil as that of the Convocation of Caer Caradoc, infertile – they were very soon subsumed by the burgeoning events of the afternoon's Convocation. As the moles returned to their places, and the chamber filled out and quietened down, the distant singing of falsetto voices was heard, mixed with that of young male moles. Squelch had disappeared, and a large strong-looking henchmole had taken his place to watch over the abject accused – the only mole there, it seemed, who had not benefited from the break in proceedings. He languished miserably, snout turned to the wall, and all the more noticeable because from the roof nearest to him came more light than elsewhere, and since its whiteness had a hint of pale green from the roots through which it filtered, the glow was almost luridly luminescent.

The singing had a certain rhythm to it, but its main effect was to lift the spirits and make even doubters like the Duncton moles think a little more brightly of the future. This time the singers entered from the side of the chamber, led by four young moles, followed by some older ones, the owners of the falsetto voices. These were led by Squelch, who only just managed to keep up with the young ones in front, though their pace was slow.

The Duncton moles were among the last to see them enter since they came into the chamber immediately below their vantage-point, but they could see the response of the watching delegates, who peered eagerly towards the singers, and then at six other moles processing behind.

Skua and two other Inquisitors were already on the dais and they now stanced up, which was the signal for every mole in the chamber to do the same. Simultaneously the bass voices of the original chanters joined those of Squelch's singers and the chamber was suddenly tumultuous with formidable and soaring sound. All eyes were fixed on the procession and moles muttered and whispered to each other concerning those who now came into view. The singing ended quite suddenly and the final part of the procession entered in a quiet that steadily deepened into a reverential silence.

Without Arum and Boden there to comment the Duncton moles could have made no sense at all of the proceedings. 'That's Brother Quail,' whispered Boden, pointing down at the bald head, back and rear of a mole much bigger and stronger-looking than most of the others. He moved leisurely, looking to right and left, and Whillan noticed that few moles willingly met his gaze.

'And that's Brother Rolt,' said Arum, and it was as well he did for from a high angle the good Brother looked thinner and greyer.

'And is *that* the Elder Senior Brother Thripp?' enquired Privet, peering down at the mole who came at Rolt's flank. How thin he looked, how different from Quail in his gait. The one bold and belligerent, the other moving with slow grace. From the position they were in it was quite impossible to see his face.

'Yes,' breathed Arum, 'that is the Elder Senior Brother. Look!'

But he had no need to point out the extraordinary change that overcame the nearest moles as Thripp went by. Whereas with Quail they had been afraid, with Thripp they were open and frank in their stares, and deeply respectful. Some even went so far as to reach out to him, which he seemed to acknowledge with a nod. Those further back pressed forward to get a better view as an excited buzz went through the chamber, seeming to say, 'He's here! That's him!'

'He was a fine-looking mole before illness ravaged him,' muttered Boden sadly.

'Aye, he was,' said Arum, 'full of fire, full of energy and faith. When he was young . . .'

'You remember him when he was young?' said Privet surprised. Despite her scholarly background, and kenning of history, she had fallen into the trap of thinking of Thripp as 'coming from nowhere'. But moles do not emerge into moledom fully formed – they are made by other moles and circumstances, and perhaps the changes that Thripp had recognized the need for in himself came from parts of his past only now coming to the fore. Parts, no doubt, others had recognized before he himself – the parts, indeed, which kept moles like Arum, Boden and Rolt loyal to him, and which inspired adoration and trust in the hearts of so many of the Newborns down below.

Privet looked down on the mole she had come so far to see, hear, and possibly to meet, and was moved by the last feeling she had expected: compassion. He had once had the courage and resolve to do what few can do, to stance up with faith and declare his beliefs of the Stone, and persuade others to follow him. He had created a sect and that sect had grown into a monster.

'And why?' whispered Privet looking down at Thripp. 'Because others let him, and nomole had the like courage and resolve to stance in his way and persuade him to take another way. Except . . . Rooster.'

Her eyes softened at the memory of the Rooster she had known

381

and loved – loved still. When she had seen him blundering across the slopes of Caer Caradoc the night before, as wild and angry and confused as he had ever been, she had felt disappointment, and anger in return. Now where was he? Caught again? Wandering off?

'Oh dear,' Privet whispered to herself, 'we moles become so lost and so confused when we waver from the disciplines and the mystery of the Silence of the Stone. Why does the Stone give us such liberty to lose ourselves? Well, I know why . . . I know. It is because in the finding of our way back again to the Silence we lost when we were born is the discovery of true liberty of spirit, which is the positive act of choice, and of commitment.'

As Whillan and Madoc had earlier been so lost in their thoughts they did not hear others call them, so deeply was Privet now absorbed in hers. She ignored Arum's attempts at further conversation, and when Whillan tried to speak to her she waved him into silence and continued to stare absently down at the slow rituals in the chamber.

The memory of Rooster had brought softness to her eyes; now the memory of the Newborn mole she had briefly known at Blagrove Slide, and who had been the father of her lost cubs, brought tears. So . . . Rolt had said he was dead.

'Dead,' she whispered. 'Oh why I am weeping, Stone? I have barely thought of him since those days. He was nothing to me, and he was of a corrupt system that sought to turn me into a Confessed Sister. Oh Stone . . .' For through that mole, who had been forced on her, had taken her, and held her, she had known the thrill of ecstasy and passion, all the more intense for being secret, unexpected, stolen out of the bonds of captivity and restraint. The sweet passive power of her life, whose very existence she had denied even to herself until that night on the way to Evesham Wood when Weeth made her talk of it. It was now as dear and sweet in memory as it had been so briefly in life.

Tears trickled down her face, and Whillan came to her and simply touched her without words. She looked at him briefly, grateful for his silence, and saw what he did not see, which was Madoc glancing shyly at them both; even in that glance, timid and tender, hopeful yet not daring to hope, wise Privet saw much more.

'Is it because of what Rolt said about that mole you knew once, the Newborn?' asked Whillan.

'You heard?' sighed Privet.

Whillan nodded.

'Yes,' she whispered. 'I didn't think that a mole who gave me such a memory could die.'

'But maybe Rolt will know what happened to your young.'

'He may, and I would like to know. You don't mind, Whillan?'

'If you found them still alive? I don't think so,' said Whillan honestly, 'but it would be strange.'

'They were told my name,' said Privet, 'but would they want . . . ?'

'To know you? They would be *proud*,' said Whillan.

'Yes. But then . . .' and suddenly she shook with weeping once again, and cried out; Maple turned round and frowned, and Whillan shushed her.

'What is it?' asked Whillan again, exasperation beginning to show through.

'Rooster,' said Privet, '*he* was the one I really loved. He *is* the one.'

'Rooster,' repeated Whillan blankly. He could not keep up with the rush of Privet's emotions.

'He is the great force of my life, you see, and the Newborn at Blagrove Slide was just a season.' Privet grinned suddenly and added, coyly, 'Well, something like that. You would like Rooster, Whillan. You would, I'm sure.'

Poor Whillan, doing his best to comfort Privet; he looked round helplessly at Madoc and his eyes expressed his bewilderment: 'She's smiling now, even laughing' they seemed to say. Madoc came over and Whillan left her to complete the job he had begun. As she did so and her paw went out to Privet's, he could not but think that Madoc was the gentlest, kindest, most endearing female he had ever met.

The moles in the procession into the chamber had long since made their way to allotted places, Squelch having guided his singers to his original position, which he had now assumed. Thripp had stanced down on the near side of the chamber almost beneath them and unfortunately was barely visible. But Brother Quail at least could be clearly seen, for he was on the opposite side and nearly facing them.

He was a powerful and charismatic version of his fat, strange son. His paws were large and well-made, his flanks and back fleshy yet dangerously muscular, and his head as extraordinary as the Duncton moles had heard: large, round and bald, pink-grey and shining. His eyes were intelligent and clear, his snout handsome, his demeanour friendly yet awesomely personable, wise yet authoritarian, concerned yet impatient. He was a mole it was impossible for others to keep their eyes off once he was in the chamber, as if nothing of import would happen until he *made* it happen. And yet . . .

There was the smaller, quieter, Thripp, whose face they could not see, yet whose effect was as powerfully benign as Quail's was disturbing. And between them was a tension that began, as dusk advanced to night, to dominate the proceedings absolutely. They had been warned several times that it was here that the future course of the Newborns would be decided, and for all Quail's devastating takeover of the Convocation, and control of the proceedings, there was still a sense that somehow or other Thripp would find the power to countermand all Quail had done.

'There's Chervil!' said Maple, who had been looking out for him for some time. 'Over there.'

Thripp's son was stanced on the far side of the chamber near the back, as darkly impenetrable as ever. Once he was seen he was not to be missed, for like his father, and like Quail in a quite different way, he had the charisma that attracted moles' gazes to him. Though he was a little separate from the main body he was not alone, for either side of him, and behind as well, were three very tough-looking moles indeed. Two were younger than he, but it was the older one, who was on his right flank, who looked the toughest of all. His fur was short and grizzled and his face was lined with experience; his eyes looked this way and that all the time, alert and ready.

'It's Feldspar,' whispered Arum.

'A good sign,' said Boden.

'What, the older mole at Chervil's right flank?'

'Aye,' said Boden, 'and two of his sons. The one behind is Fallow and that large one on the left flank – aye, that one – he's Tarn. Brother Chervil has found himself some henchmoles.'

'Henchmoles and not guards?' said Maple doubtfully.

'Well . . .' began Boden, 'that is a possibility, I suppose. We're not sure of Feldspar. He used to be the Elder Senior Brother's bodyguard years ago and I doubt there's a more experienced fighter among the Newborns. But Brother Quail lured him across for duties concerning the Inquisitors, who certainly needed protection on some of their earlier journeys. It seems that Brother Quail has appointed him to watch over Brother Chervil.'

'But you think he and his sons may be obedient to Chervil?'

'Hard to ken. Feldspar gives little away and is not one, and never has been, to involve himself in matters of religion and faith. He regards himself as a fighter, not a brother.'

Maple looked at Feldspar with some interest, for he looked the kind of no-nonsense mole he liked. Anymole who succeeded in surviving with Brother Quail while refusing to be a 'brother' must be a survivor indeed, and one who knew his own mind. As for his two sons, Maple saw they were about his own age, and what was more unusual, his own size as well.

As for Chervil, now Maple was witness to his powerful and brooding presence he realized he was as much an important part of the pattern of power in the chamber as Thripp and Quail – indeed his presence completed it. More and more Maple was glad that they were here at the Convocation, for he was beginning to feel a pattern of rivalry and change in the Newborns which opponents to them must surely understand and exploit if they were to challenge them, and properly defend the liberty of followers of the Stone.

'So now they're all finally in place,' said Privet ironically, 'and all we can do is to wait and see what the turning-point between them is going to be, and who is best prepared to meet it. So far, apart from that poor mole who has been singled out and now awaits his punishment, we have not seen much!'

'I think we've seen a lot,' said Whillan, 'and I can't imagine what's going to happen now. The atmosphere in the chamber is getting heavier by the moment, as if a storm is building up which will break before Longest Night is out.'

The singing and chanting had stopped and after a period of quiet, expectant chatter, and whispering counsel among the moles on the dais, a hush had fallen; Skua, the sleek Chief Inquisitor, came forward. He bowed to Quail and then to Thripp in a brief impersonal way, lowered his snout, and began to speak. Unlike the solemn and sometimes tedious commonplaces of routine liturgy his voice was vigorous and his words challenging:

> *'Brothers in the Stone,*
> *Awake, listen and respond!'*

The gathering was utterly silent for a moment before with one powerful voice it replied:

> *'With the Stone's help,*
> *We shall.*
> *In the Stone's name,*
> *We will.*
> *For the Stone's sake,*
> *We must.'*

Then Skua continued, his speech quick and his voice deep and compelling:

> 'Oh Stone,
> Who has warned us of what
> Thou wilt require of those
> To whom thy grace is given,
> Help us.
> Make us strive together this holy day,
> Make us work together this holy night,
> Renew our zeal to act as one.
> Oh Stone,
> Save us from the consuming snake,
> Protect us from the cankers of doubt,
> Put into us your avenging power,
> Help us.'

The response was unexpected, for while the whole gathering began with the words 'Oh Stone' some continued with the following three lines, others with the next three, and a final third with the last three, until all finished simultaneously by repeating 'Oh Stone!' and then a loud 'Help *us*!'

The hissing echoes of '*us*' had not faded before a mole near Skua thrust his head forward towards the gathering and said:

'Brethren, it is decreed that when we are gathered in one place we shall together declare our faith aloud, that all may know in what we believe, and to what tenets our lives are made dedicate; therefore let one among you, to whom the spirit comes, rise up and state the beginning of our creed that others may remember that though we speak these words in public and together, their meaning is at its greatest when they are spoken in the silence of our hearts. May one speak now, and all follow.'

The silence was brief but impressive, and then, somewhere in the midst of the gathering, a young mole rose and spoke these words:

'*I believe in Stone the Maker Almighty, Creator of Silence and faith . . .*'

then the rest spoke the Newborn Creed:

> '*I believe in Stone the Maker Almighty,*
> *Creator of Silence and faith:*
> *And in Beechen of the Stone our maker,*
> *Who was conceived of the Light immaculate,*

Born of the Holy Stone,
Suffered at the talons of the Word,
And was snouted, dead, and lost;
He descended into darkness,
But rose again, up into the Light,
And is stanced now in the Silence
Of the Stone, to know us and to judge.
I believe in his holy power,
In the venging of his talons,
In the savage thrust of death.
I believe in the resurrection
Of the faithful,
And the eternal damnation
Of the faithless.
I believe in Stone the Maker Almighty,
Creator of faith,
Creator of the Silence.
All this I believe.'

Whillan listened to this statement of faith with fascinated horror, and reasonable though most of the words were of themselves he was as aware as the others of the menace in them, of the threat of eternal damnation to unbelievers, and of the terrible earnest tone in which the brethren spoke.

As for the invocation of Beechen, and the story of his vile death at the paws of the Eldrene Wort acting in the name of the Stone, he was surprised, and curious. He had often wondered why the Stone followers of Duncton had not made more of Beechen and his teachings of peace and non-violence, and understood why a creed such as this might invoke his name. But so aggressively? So judgementally? Surely this – all this – was not the Stone's proper way, nor did it express Beechen's vision of how moles should worship together. Yet it was impressive, and there was something to be learned from it.

As silence fell, the leader of the litany did not let thoughts wander, or allow the mounting sense of passion and purpose to dissipate. The purpose of the Convocation, it seemed, was to lead the participants on a journey whose beginning would be with the season's turning this Longest Night, but whose ending would be far from Caer Caradoc in the months and years ahead, and would be Newborn, and absolute. A tide of history was beginning to flow before the very eyes of the Duncton moles, of a colour and in a direction they did not like but were beginning to wonder how they could stem, or re-direct.

Now Brother Skua raised a paw and cried out; 'Oh let thy mouths be filled with praise!'

And the others replied, 'That we may sing of thy glory this Longest Night.'

Then the next part of the statement and response came, and the next, and the one after that as the leader spoke faster and more vehemently and the gathering grew more and more frenzied and eager in its responses.

> Oh let my mouth be filled with thy praise,
>> *That we may sing of thy glory this Longest Night.*
> Turn thy gaze, Stone, from my sins,
>> *And put out all our misdeeds.*
> Cleanse my heart of the snake and the filth of doubt,
>> *Renew right spirit within us.*
> Cast me not away from thy Silence,
>> *Nor take thy light from our dark lives.*
> Give me the benefit of thy close help,
>> *And preserve us from the wicked and profane.*
> Strengthen my paws for thy just work,
>> *Deliver thy enemies to us, Stone.*
> Weaken not my heart to the sinner,
>> *But give our talons thy power to punish.*
> Save me,
>> *Kill the snake.*
> Forgive me,
>> *Punish the hypocrite.*
> Love me,
>> *Destroy our enemies.*

Thus did this extraordinary litany of personal statement counterpointed by general response end: brutally. From their aggressive looks, their wild breathing, their physical restlessness, it was all too plain that rather than talk about it any longer, the gathering wished now to actually kill the 'snake'.

'It is plain to you all, I suppose, what the snake *is*?' said Privet quietly.

'Anyone who disagrees with the Newborns,' said Maple.

'And the darkness that drives these moles and their leaders,' added Whillan.

'Yes,' whispered Privet, frowning. 'I am afraid now of what we are going to see. That poor mole . . .'

They knew the one she meant: the unnamed accused whom Snyde had put the talon on and who, as the day had gone by, had grown progressively more pathetic and abject.

A foul odour of retribution was in the air and the victim upon whom to inflict it was already available, waiting only for some mole to point a talon at him, and there was no doubt at all who that prosecutor would be: the Chief Inquisitor, Skua. Not that one glance, nor one hair of his sleek thin fur, nor one twitch of his sharp snout, betrayed his intent, which made him and the atmosphere all the more threatening.

Adding to the formidable build-up was the continuing silence of both Thripp and Quail, who stanced still on either side of the dais, Quail, at least, expressionless. The Duncton moles would have liked a better view of Thripp, but if anything he was even harder to see now, for Rolt and others clustered about him and the most the secret watchers could observe without betraying themselves was his flank. At some point he would no doubt address the Convocation, but the longer he delayed doing so the tenser things would become, and the greater the sense of conflict between Thripp and Quail would grow in the dark imagings of the delegates' minds, and make a confrontation ever more inevitable.

Any thought that the Duncton moles had – or any other genuine delegates still surviving among the mass of moles below – that a Convocation meant debate and discussion, had surely now disappeared. Nomole but a mad one would have stanced up in this chamber and spoken anything that ran counter to the mood of self-righteous crusade that was beginning to develop, unless it be one indifferent to his own fate.

Subtly, the chamber's light faded, a reminder that the Longest Night meant the Shortest Day, and it was an extra spur towards the grim act of retribution for sin that the gathering collectively needed before the coming revels of the Night itself could begin.

Now it was the turn of another anonymous mole, one of Skua's Inquisitors, to come forward and announce the beginning of a period of public confession that would precede an address 'by the moles who have pointed their talons towards the future that we must make on behalf of the Stone' – which could mean both Thripp and Quail, and even Brother Chervil, perhaps.

Without more ado Inquisitors and other senior-looking moles went separately amidst the delegates and were soon surrounded by moles eager to make their sins and failings known to one and all. But with so many declaring themselves at once the chamber was filled with general hubbub, and it was only when there were momentary lulls that the Duncton moles could hear any of the liturgy at all, and then it was fragmentary.

They heard the confessor say, 'The Stone be in thy heart . . . confess . . . in the name of the Light . . . Holy . . .'

And they understood parts of the ritual response, 'I confess . . . sinned exceedingly . . . fault . . . fault . . . fault . . . I accuse myself . . .'

Not much perhaps but enough to gather from the words and the mortification evident in the faltering voices that these were moles beset indeed by things done and left undone. How dark the afternoon seemed, how dreadful the hurriedly whispered guilt of mole, how silent the Duncton moles before this display of secret shame.

Occasionally some fragment of a wrong confessed drifted up to them, 'vanity . . . sought to hurt . . . felt desire . . . asleep when waking I should have been . . .'

'Asleep when waking I should have been . . .' repeated Privet with a smile. 'What thinking and feeling mole is there alive who should not confess to that great sin? I know I have been guilty of that for too long.'

Mysteriously, and impressively, the light in the chamber seemed to grow a little more bright as the clamour of confession died away at last and a final few moles declared themselves. As the confessors began to shift back to the dais the final words of the individual ritual were heard from somewhere across the chamber, '. . . forgive thee all thy sins, and kill that snake within thee, and bring thee to everlasting Silence.'

The gathering settled once again and Skua ominously turned his back on the moles to face his own Inquisitors and said, 'Are there any whose confessions reveal a sin so bad, or a wrong so deep, that the forgiveness of the gathering as one is called for?'

The silence was sudden and deep, and once more apprehension filled the chamber as all eyes watched the Inquisitors to see if they would point out a mole for more public scrutiny.

'Yes,' whispered one of the more elderly Inquisitors contemptuously, 'there is one who confessed to wrongful torture of a junior member of our brethren, one who confessed to that.'

'Let him come forth,' said Skua quietly, turning to face the gathering again, his eyes scanning them, for he, like all others but the Inquisitor who had spoken, did not know who the guilty mole was.

There was a stir, and a retreat among the moles across the chamber

390

opposite the Duncton moles, at the back, very near to where Chervil stanced so still and silently. A mole glanced up with faltering paws and trembling snout, his eyes wide with fear and his mouth half opening as if he were seeking words with which to defend himself but could not find any. He seemed rooted to the spot.

'Brother Chervil, bring him forward please.' It was Quail, breaking his long silence, and his voice was deep and reasonable, yet loaded with dreadful menace.

'Brother Chervil . . .' This time the menace was more noticeable. It was plain that Chervil wanted no part of this game of confession and punishment, nor welcomed the clear implication that by doing Quail's bidding he was at his command.

Chervil glowered at the moles to right and left, Feldspar nodded briefly, and the two of them came forward to lead the sinner to the front.

'Brother Chervil by himself, I think,' purred Quail, his eyes fixed impassively on the guilty mole, 'I hardly think the confessand is going to seek escape, or that you, Brother Chervil are liable to be . . . well, hurt by him.' He grinned evilly and there was a sycophantic titter about the chamber.

Chervil frowned, nodded to Feldspar to resume his place, and led the hapless mole slowly to the front, himself somehow made to seem demeaned and tainted by the sorry ritual.

But worse was to follow. Only at the last moment, when Chervil and what now seemed his prisoner reached the dais, did Quail raise a paw to stop them both and say with considerable force: 'Has he not confessed in good faith, and were not the words of forgiveness uttered by the good Inquisitor?'

'They were,' said Skua through gritted teeth.

Quail turned and faced the gathering with an encouraging smile. Such was his personality that as one they cried out. 'They were . . . he was forgiven . . . forgive him now!'

'Well then, you see, Brother Chervil, he must be left to go in peace.'

The confessand literally fell over himself in his gratitude and eagerness to get back to safety at the back of the chamber, and Chervil too tried to return, but this Quail would not have.

'Oh, now we have need of thee,' he said, still with the smile, but with menace, and now with contempt as well.

'Yes,' said Skua, 'there is still the accused.' He pointed at last to the mole who had been waiting in such agony for so long.

'Yesss . . .' sighed the gathering with satisfaction, 'arraign him now,

391

for the snake entwined his heart and he must be tried and punished.'

'If guilty,' said Quail benignly, 'if guilty, Brethren! For judge not too soon, lest you yield to the snake of doubt and lies and are arraigned.'

'No, master . . .' chorused the moles in reply, their whispers, which were at first a jumble of sound, transmuted suddenly into the ugly chant, 'Arraign him! Arraign him! Arraign him!'

As the cry went up, Squelch, perhaps at a signal from Quail, rose up ponderously and approaching the accused, took him by the paw and led him forward, snout low, gasping, eyes hopeless, to the front of the dais near to where Chervil reluctantly waited.

'Should we?' said Quail. Then more powerfully, 'Must we, Brother Chervil?'

'Kill the bugger!' some mole shouted at the back.

'Aye, he's guilty so let's show him the Stone's judgement,' cried another.

Chervil turned to look at them and they fell silent before his cold and powerful gaze; while at the rear Feldspar and the others with him had moved a little closer, though whether the better to protect him, or to prevent him doing something he should not, was hard to say.

Chervil turned back to Quail and said carefully, 'Brothers, he should be judged according to the laws of blasphemy and sin.'

'Judge him! Arraign him!' shouted out the excited gathering impatiently.

'Judge him, Brother Chervil?' said Quail, heaving himself up for the first time and coming to the accused, on whose shoulder he placed a paw in an avuncular way, as if he was the mole's protector from the crowd. 'Judge a brother on Longest Night? And perhaps punish him?'

Chervil said nothing – *could* say nothing – and the crowd fell uneasily silent. For the first time a look of faint yet distinct hope came to the stricken eyes of the accused, while nearby, frowning and concerned, the crooked form of Snyde sought what narrow shadows it could find to hide among. Forgiveness was not his intent, but nor was a wish to be the one who pointed the talon of accusation at a mole forgiven.

'Forgiveness is indeed a blessing,' said Skua icily, 'on such a night as this.'

'Yet we must not shirk our duty, not now, not ever,' said Quail suddenly. 'As I'm sure Elder Senior Brother Thripp would agree?'

Thripp said nothing from the shadows, hardly visible.

Quail seemed to be growing in size and confidence by the moment, almost, indeed, revelling in the power he had and which inexorably he was imposing.

'Yes, we must even tonight punish where punishment is due.'

'Oh yes,' sighed the gathering.

'Because I know a mole . . .'

'Oh,' whispered the gathering pleasurably. A punishment was coming, was imminent. Their waiting was nearly over.

'I know a mole who has sinned, in whom the snake has lived for many a long year, a mole who may confess here and now . . .'

'What mole, Master?' hissed the assembly.

'A mole alongflank whom *this* mole's transgressions' – here he thrust forward the hapless accused – 'are as nothing, but brief shadows in a place of light.'

Quail pulled the accused to him, so close that their snouts were almost touching, and he caressed the mole's shoulder almost intimately.

'Are you confessed before the Stone?'

'Yes, Master!' said the mole, his snout glistening with fear.

'Are you free of the snake?'

'Yes, Master,' he sobbed.

'Cleansed?'

'Purified, Master.'

'Empty of guilt?'

'Freed, Master.'

'Ready for the absolution of penance?'

'Yes, Master,' sighed the mole uneasily.

'Ready for the pain which shall not defile the Silence with a cry?'

'Yes, Master,' said the mole, looking doubtfully at Squelch, who at some hidden signal from his father or Skua had lumbered across to take his place behind the accused.

'Command it, Master,' sighed the gathering, leaning forward and staring with horrid fascination at the great taloned paw which Squelch had raised slowly over the rear part of the accused's back during these final questions.

For final they undoubtedly were – something was going to happen.

'If he cries out, if he screams, if he makes any sound at all, he will be judged unclean and killed,' whispered Boden. 'Very few survive.'

'What, would you stop us?' whispered Quail accusingly to Chervil, who by a glance perhaps, or some slight movement, had indicated horror, or disapproval of what was happening. Chervil said nothing.

'For ours is the punishment of the Stone, the just judgement of the Light, the pain in the Silence that makes clean and purifies!'

393

With that, Quail stepped back and nodded briefly to Squelch, who without more ado drove his talons down on to the spine of the accused. The blow was hard enough to set Squelch's flesh juddering, and he let forth an unearthly gasp as he struck. But moments later this was lost in the collective gasp of pain that came from the gathering; which was just as well, for it drowned out the cries of sympathy and shame from Madoc, Privet and the others. But this was not the worst.

The shrieked response was followed by a grim silence as all watched the stricken mole and his reaction to what at the least was a painful blow, and might easily have been a mortal one. Perhaps if he had screamed or cried out initially it was not heard against the general sound, but now, as Squelch moved back from him, his talons bloody at his flank, the wounded mole seemed to shiver briefly, and then opened his eyes to stare out at a world which was not one which any other mole in that chamber could see. A place of talons and darkness, of agony, in which the only relief was a cry, long and loud, of pain. His mouth opened to emit that cry, all leaned forward to hear it come, Squelch raised his talons once more in excited expectation of a command to kill; but with an effort of will that took that mole far beyond the evil and corrupt Newborn world in which life had trapped him, he screamed silently. No sound, no cry of agony, could have been more loud, nor more memorable, than that silent scream that no mole heard. Its suppression at the command of Brother Quail, and in the name of that perverse sect and its unwholesome ideas, before a gathering of willing moles not one of whom stanced up and condemned it, said more about what the Newborns had become than any sound ever could, or a million words.

If the mole had cried out and been killed many would no doubt have been satisfied. But this way, with pain conquered in the name of the Newborn interpretation of the Stone's requirement, Quail could afford to look smug and satisfied. And, too, to turn and stare insolently at Thripp.

The accused sighed long and deep, his haunches striped where blood dripped down; he pulled himself forward, half turned and had not Chervil stepped out and caught him he would have collapsed to the ground. But there he was, still mute, and forgiven.

'But there is another?' whispered Skua, looking not at Quail but at the gathering.

'Oh, yes,' said Quail, his look still smug and self-satisfied. It was all going so well, and he was in command, and nomole but he knew quite what was going to happen next. Nor was he going to pause and let others – Thripp perhaps – take the initiative; not that it would have been easy with the gathering, having now tasted the pleasures of forgiveness and blood, wanting more, and something terminal perhaps before the festivities of Longest Night began.

Quail signalled to the rear of the chamber where there was an entrance that had been guarded throughout the proceedings by four impassive henchmoles.

'Let him be brought before us,' said Quail, and an excited chatter passed among the gathering as moles turned to catch a glimpse of the third and final accused of the afternoon.

When he came, half supported by his guards, his size and appearance brought all chatter to a halt. Huge he was, his snout twisted and angry, his great face furrowed deep with creases and scars and his strange wild eyes glancing here and there, half dazed, dulled, and seeking to interpret what was happening to him. Quail opened out his two front paws in a hypocritical gesture of welcome – indeed, he even smiled, and his bald head shone with pleasure and delight as all asked whatmole it was.

But a terrible gasp from Privet indicated that she knew the mole, and all too well.

'It's Rooster,' she whispered, horror struck. 'My Rooster . . .'

'Brother, have you come to make confession?'

'Have,' mumbled Rooster.

'Then the Stone be in thy heart and in thy mouth, that thou mayst truly and humbly confess thy sins before this gathering of thy brothers in the Stone, in the name of the Stone and its Light and its eternal Silence.'

There was a long pause while Rooster steadied himself and seemed to try to speak. Quail frowned and at his flank Skua hissed, 'Has he not been prepared?'

'He has, Chief Inquisitor,' faltered one of the guards, and turning to the mole he jabbed a talon in his flank and whispered audibly enough for others to hear, 'you know what to say, you bastard, so say it.'

Rooster raised his head, looked at Quail, peered round in a lumbering, lopsided way to right and left and said slowly, as if thinking of each word and only able to get it out when he believed it, 'I confess to Stone Almighty, before the whole company of blessed brothers, and to thee, Quail . . .'

'Brother Quail will do,' purred Quail.

'. . . and to thee, Brother Quail, that I have sinned exceedingly in thought, word and deed; through my fault, my own fault, my own grievous fault. Especially I accuse myself that I have . . . I have . . .'

But the words he had evidently been forced to learn by the guards had ended and he was on his own at the edge of the void of confession, not knowing how to continue. His great snout bowed, his flanks heaved with stress and strain, and his paws, huge and misshapen, tore at the ground as he glanced sideways as if looking for help or for escape.

Above him, masterful and so dangerously benign, Quail smiled a little and contrived to look compassionate.

'What is your name, Brother? Begin with that. A name is a good beginning to sincere confession.'

'Am Rooster,' said Rooster, 'am that mole.'

A sign of recognition and excitement passed through the chamber.

'Oh my dear,' whispered Privet, unseen but so near, 'oh my love, what have they done to you?' And she might have cried out, and made him know she was there had not Whillan held her tight, and Madoc too.

While to Maple's face, unseen by the others, had come the bold and resolute look of one born to lead, who now sensed his moment for decision and action had arrived, and he must think, and analyse, and plan, for a chance had come, and it must be grasped and used.

'You must not speak or draw attention to us here,' Maple commanded Privet. 'Whatever happens you must not. In this turn of events we have a chance and I begin to see some light.'

'But Maple—'

'Trust me now, Privet. Surprise will be everything.'

Below them the gathering had whispered and muttered to itself when Rooster spoke his name, perhaps as those who knew it explained to others that this mole had long been an enemy of the Newborns. The snake was in *his* heart, all right, and nothing he might say once he had finished his pathetic confession would rob them of their just reward, his punishment and death.

'Yes,' said Quail subduing them, 'this is Rooster, whom some blasphemously claim to be not *a* Master of the Delve but *the* Master.'

'Nooo!' cried out Rooster. 'Am nothing now, nothing any more.'

'No?' whispered Quail, 'then will you confess?'

'Will,' faltered Rooster, his voice breaking into slow and terrible sobs which echoed deeply round the chamber; 'have journeyed far, have known all darkness, am ready to confess; am ready now.'

Chapter Twenty-Nine

All across moledom, as the afternoon darkened towards Longest Night, moles were making their preparations for the celebrations to come. Some, in obscure systems whose names appear nowhere on the rolls of history, did so in the quiet old way, with faith for the future, without regret for the past, their devotions untouched, it seemed, by the ravage of dispute.

Others, including those in all the seven Ancient Systems whose name allmole knows, did so under the thrall of Newborn ways, the simple and easy rituals of the followers displaced now by dogma and close organization. All fun and love of the occasion lost to dutiful ritual and the fear of doing things the brothers would deem wrong. Here and there, even in the midst of Newborn rules and sanctions, a few followers bravely persisted in their own secret celebrations, old moles teaching the young traditional prayers and incantations to the seasons' turn, praying that their harmless faith might find a way to survive and live on.

In this history of the coming of the Book of Silence we too may pause as Longest Night approaches, and share the company of three different moles whose thoughts that afternoon dwelt upon Caer Caradoc, and the Duncton moles in danger there.

The first, and the nearest, was Weeth, who, since he had been separated from Hamble, had not been idle. He was not a mole who minded being cast upon his own resources – indeed, until he had met Maple and the others his whole life had been self-centredly dedicated to fending for himself. Meeting Maple, listening to Privet, talking to Whillan, Weeth had caught a glimpse of a different life, one dedicated to the Stone and the good of mole. Being practical he had seen at once that to pursue this noble dream he must attach himself to a mole who was going places, and he had no doubt, none at all, that that mole was Maple.

So when he had separated from Hamble and the injured Chater to lead the pursuing Newborns off the scent, his first thought was this:

'Once I've got rid of this lot where do I find Maple so that I can help him? He may well need me!'

It must be said that nomole could have been more surprised than Weeth himself that such altruistic thoughts should have entered his head as he ducked and weaved his way through the undergrowth in the lee of Caer Caradoc, making noise enough to be sure that he was followed. He knew well that but a short time before, in such dangerous circumstances as these, one taste of liberty and he would have been off and away from danger as fast as he could go, without a moment's thought for anymole, however much they might have needed his help.

'But no! A committed mole am I!' said Weeth to himself as he huddled painfully into a clump of spiky spear-thistles and watched the Newborns flounder by and out of sight. 'Now what must a mole do? What was I taught when I was young? Why, that a mole must take his opportunities where he can. Therefore Weeth, accept that this sudden and unexpected turn of events – namely that I am here, at liberty, within reach of Caer Caradoc and *no mole knows where I am* – offers the opportunity of . . . surprise! That's it! I can appear where I will without anymole expecting it and thus achieve maximum effect.

'Do I retrace my steps and seek to find Hamble and Chater? Or do I go to see what assistance I can be to Maple? The latter, I think. Therein is my commitment. I must not spread myself too wide, there is not enough of me. A paw here, a snout there and a flank across the way is not what I call commitment, and is unlikely to be of real help to anymole. It is the whole body or nothing, and so, Maple, Weeth is at your command!'

At this point in his monologue, Weeth had spoken aloud, and he now raised his head as if expecting a response from Maple himself. When none came Weeth continued, 'So! I must scribe my own orders! I must use my initiative! I must attempt to rejoin my commander and render what assistance I can. But, where? How? And when?'

The day was already well advanced and Weeth had pondered long and hard before deciding where he must go: 'Caer Caradoc! If Maple has been able to he will have gone there and I can join him. If he is unable, well, he will wish me to go and make what observations I can and report back. Therefore Caer Caradoc it is!'

He set off without delay and reached the eastern lower slopes of Caer Caradoc without difficulty, though with some danger, for there were patrols about and moles scurrying here, there and everywhere. But dodging these, Weeth had reached the climb up to Caradoc itself safe and unseen.

He ate a little, rested, and then began the ascent. He could see the rough dark shapes of the Stones high up to his right, and the easier, flatter top of the hill above and to the left, and, since he found evidence of mole routes that way opted for the rough, unrouted way to the right beneath the Stones, just as Privet and Madoc had done earlier.

Privet had seen and heard some of the violence of the night before, and now, in the cold light of day, Weeth saw the results of it. Rooks circled and flapped where the bodies lay, paws twisted and turned and dead mouths wide open to the winter sky. Some were by themselves, others together in black huddles, all still and strange, for so close were they entwined that it seemed some of the corpses had three front paws and some two heads.

Weeth had seen death before and its presence here only served to increase his resolve to find Maple. To his surprise, there seemed no living mole about at all and so he took time to examine the dead to see how they had died. It did not take him long to conclude from the lightness of the talon wounds on many of them, and the signs of bruising and crushing on their bodies, that they had been thrown, or pushed, over the sheer rock face above, and tumbled to their deaths on the scree beneath before rolling downslope to where he found them. That such a killing of moles should be done so openly, and the evidence left for anymole to find, suggested that the Newborn murderers felt they had little to fear. Rooks swooped down, their eyes black, their claws grappling, their harsh cawing wild across the slopes. Weeth stared and knew he would not forget.

He decided to contour the hill and strive to ascend on the north side, and set off once more. But the ground grew rougher and steeper and as he rounded the curve of the hill and saw its northern face he gasped. It was steep and forbidding and at its highest point rocks outcropped in vertical buttresses, all unscalable. Time had passed and he felt tired so he descended to gentler slopes to rest and eat of the scrawny worms he found beneath loose rocks that had fallen from the heights above.

Then as he retraced his route at a lower level he came across a sight more terrible in its special way than that he had seen earlier: a dead mole he recognized as one of Rooster's friends, savagely wounded about the head. But the blood on the grass and rocks about the place showed that he had not died easily, and had dragged himself to his final resting-place.

'Weeth is getting nowhere but into despondency,' he muttered to himself. 'Weeth must decide . . .'

But the decision was made for him. Just as he was leaving the dead mole he heard the sound of struggle and fighting some way along the route he was retracing, and creeping silently along to see what was apaw, he witnessed the tail end of a fight. The victors were six tough Newborn moles; the vanquished a single bleeding mole, Rooster: roaring and struggling, but beaten half unconscious into submission. Weeth came to the scene in time to hear one of the Newborns say, 'Thank the Stone we found him or it would have been *us* who'd have to atone. Brother Skua's instructions are to take him up above.'

'He'll never make it!' said one of the others.

'We'll make him make it,' said the leader grimly. 'He'll be needed to make a confession to the brothers before he gets himself back down the slope again.'

'He'll come down a bloody sight faster than he'll be going up!' one of them said laughing.

'Come on then . . .'

'Will,' said Rooster, heaving one of them off him, 'Will come!'

'This is called opportunity,' said Weeth to himself from the shadows, 'for Maple may be at the end of the route Rooster is now upon, and *there* I believe will be things to do. Opportunity is all a matter of the point of view; one mole may say "Rooster, there you go!" and another "Maple, here I come!" and the strange thing is we are both, Stone willing, going to the same place.'

Weeth turned his eyes upslope towards the top of Caer Caradoc, fixed it with a sharp good-humoured gaze and, watching after where the Newborns led Rooster, quietly followed them in the shadows behind, to take what opportunity came his way.

As the first hint of dusk darkened the eastern sky that same Longest Night Fieldfare sniffled and snuffled in the shadows of the Stones of Seven Barrows far to the south, and woke. She could not be sure, but it was the haunting note of the Blowing Stone that had woken her, and she lay with her eyes closed for a moment longer, wondering if it had been warning her, or offering inspiration. Then she remembered the events that had led to her being among the Stones. She knew she had been chased by two Newborns; she knew, or thought she knew, that she had been helped by a mole who spoke and looked like the fabled Mayweed, great route-finder at the time of the war of Word and Stone.

He could not be alive, of course, but, well . . . it was the time of Longest Night, this was where Mayweed had gone to the Silence, and whatmole was she to doubt that in some form or another he had come to help her? That was the kind of mole the tales said he was!

With a sudden hard conviction, Fieldfare felt certain that her Chater was dead. She had sensed it coming for several days past and the day before had felt his slow decline into Silence as if it were her own, as she had wandered out among the Stones of that mysterious place and ended up being chased in amongst them. She knew well the legend of the Barrows, and of how it was that while any normal mole could count six Stones there, some were graced to discover a seventh, taller than the others no doubt, and a place of discovery and peace.

Unable to think of any other way of diverting the Newborns she had run out across the stonefields beyond the Barrows. She had hoped, perhaps, not only to save her friends and her own life, but also in some vague despairing way that if she could find the seventh Stone she would be able to reach out to her Chater one last time, and touching him, know that he was safe in the Silence and merely waiting for her. Moles like he and she should not be apart for long.

She felt his death now and wept before the Stone where she found herself. Then she wandered a little, remembering past and happier times, weeping for her love and wanting so much to touch him once more, just once. Strong Chater, irascible Chater, journeymole Chater, who she had always believed would come back but who now never would. And yet she felt he would want to let her know, to send his love to her. He loved her so much he would not want her to be alone.

'My sweet love, you're coming home to me, aren't you?' she whispered, but as the tears fell from her cheeks to the great Stone against which she now rested her head, she knew in her heart that he was not, not really.

'But *here*, my love, you could come here, for a journeymole might linger for a time about these Stones, and say farewell to the moledom and the mole he has loved. Mightn't you, my dear?'

Later, much later perhaps, she continued her thought in a way younger moles might not have understood, being unfamiliar with the stories and legends of modern history on which a Duncton mole like Fieldfare had been reared.

'Mayweed did! He lingered here! He came and found the one *he*

402

loved and lost to the Silence, as I've lost you. He did, loved one! So *you* could!'

She counted the Stones hopefully in the half-light, but she could make out no more than six spread out across the Pastures west of Seven Barrows.

So she grieved, content to be alone in such a place, and touching the Stones as if each touch was a happy memory of Chater to which she now said farewell. Sometimes she smiled, and sometimes wept through that dusktime of memories.

'Longest Night will soon begin and I must return to the others,' she had whispered sometime earlier on. 'The Newborns will surely have gone and it'll be safe to return. Anyway, Spurling and the rest will have been out searching for me . . . There's work to be done, for they seem to think the tales and legends I tell of Duncton Wood are worth scribing down. Just fancy that, Chater my dear, your Fieldfare with her name on a text. Fancy!'

But she lingered on, unwilling to say a final goodbye and turn back to the future, and so the first shadows of dusk had touched the sky.

'Fieldfare! Fieldfare, are you there?'

It was young Noakes at the far distant edge of the stonefields, calling for her.

'Fieldfare!'

She rose at last to go, sniffing and wiping away a final tear.

'Comely Fieldfare!'

But neither the voice nor the turn of phrase sounded like Noakes' now.

'Lachrymose mole!'

Nor was it far off, but nearby, among the shadows. She turned, awed by the sudden light that seemed among the Stones, yet not fearful.

'What mole is it, and whither are you bound?' she whispered in the shadows, not daring to look up.

'It's not whither I am bound that matters, says this modest mole, for he may lay claim to having got here; no, Portly One, it is you who should ask whither she is bound.'

'"Lachrymose mole" – "this modest mole"? – "Portly One"? Why, there's only one mole in all moledom's history who ever spoke like that,' she said.

'And modest Mayweed is his name!'

'But Mayweed, you're . . .' she said, still not looking up, though the light was brighter now, and his presence nearer.

'Dead? Finished? Done for? Totally and utterly gone? In a manner of speaking, in a mortal sense, this is true. But this is Longest Night, the time of the seasons' turning, and you, clever and well-fleshed as you are, have chosen to stance right at the very place where the seventh Stone stands. Therefore, we may if we choose come out of the Silence for a time and say a brief hello!'

Mayweed *here*? Now? A dead mole come alive? So, what she had imagined the afternoon before about a mole helping her was true. Still Fieldfare dared not look up, but stared instead at her front paws and wiggled her talons about to see if they were real. They moved and she seemed as normal, except for the awesome light that shone upon her fur and gave it a silvery look. But Mayweed? Why, he *did* speak just like the storytellers of her youth *said* he spoke – as indeed *she* made him speak when she told tales of his route-finding exploits and of his friendship with Tryfan, Spindle and the other great moles of those days (of which he was himself one of the greatest).

'Pondering Plumpness,' he continued, 'tell me, of what you think!'

'I was thinking—'

'Madam, you can raise your eyes and look at me, I will not flee. I will not leave you as I left you yesterday, but then, fair Fieldfare, I had a journey to make and a mole to find who had been calling for you. Now, raise your eyes.'

Slowly she did so, and there, in the lee of a great Stone, he stanced once more as he had the day before – thin, with patchy fur, and eyes more mischievously alive than any she had ever seen. As for the light, it was an aura about him, and round the Stone as well.

'Plumpness was pondering on what?'

'Chater, my beloved.'

'Yes,' said Mayweed, his eyes sympathetic, 'he has found the Silence now, or nearly so. A mole dies and must then journey for a time. Sometimes he needs a guide and it seems I am Chater's. He knew you needed help, you know, and so I brought him to you in a kind of way. I had to leave you for a time to go and get him and guide him here.'

'Is he here now?'

Again Fieldfare looked at her paws and prodded at the dry grass to see if she was awake; she seemed to be, except that beyond the circle of the light there was a kind of dimness, as if nothing existed but the here and now.

'If madam will do me the honour, modest and humble though I am, of taking my paw – yes, thus, with dignity becoming to our age and sorry status – I will show you . . .'

She did so and did not even flinch when he led her towards the Stone he had been near and then (as it seemed) into it.

'So, flummoxed Fieldfare, here we are, and you can see your Chater one more time as I lead him on to where he was always journeying, which is the Silence.'

She dared to look in the direction he pointed and saw the dark and stolid form of Chater, looking not at her but forward, towards a Light nomole can ever describe in words. She saw he had been hurt in the chest, but knew that he was in pain no more.

'My dear . . .' she said, for he looked so alone, 'My love . . .' But he did not, could not, look at her.

'I must go to him, Fieldfare, for he hears your love's call and knows it comes from the Silence. Your beloved voice leads him on, not back. It is his final comfort.'

'But I am *here*, Mayweed,' she whispered desperately.

'The love you two made was born of true Silence, Mistress Field-fare, and one day you will return to it. Out of the Silence we were born, into the Silence we will return.'

'Mayweed, can I . . . can I come with you now to be with him?'

Mayweed turned to her, and his eyes were the Light itself, and his voice the Silence as he slowly shook his head and said, 'Madam, you have still a task to do and moledom needs you: and clever Chater knew it. His task was done: he told moles what he needed to, and he helped save Rooster's life that moledom would not lose its Master of the Delve before his work was complete. Nor is your task yet quite over. Therefore, turn back now of your own choice, turn back and do what you must. The time on the mortal world outside the Seventh Stone will seem but brief before you come back once more and journey into Silence. Chater will await you.'

'Care for him, Mayweed.'

'I shall, and he shall watch over you. Fulsome Fieldfare, go back to the life you are not yet ready to leave.'

'And be bold?' She even dared to smile when she said this, for they were Mayweed's words, a long time before, to another mole in this same place. Or so the story went.

'Be bold indeed, Fieldfare – bold and comely!'

With that he turned, or seemed to turn, to Chater and together the two moles went slowly into the Stone's Light.

'Bold and comely!' Fieldfare found herself whispering aloud, and with a smile, as the light about her faded and she found herself out by the Stone where she had been stanced before Mayweed came. It looked like any other Stone.

Any other Stone? She reached out and touched it, and then, suddenly alert, slowly circled round and counted all the other Stones, one, two, three . . . and there were seven. There were!

'Fieldfare!' It was Noakes, calling to her still, from so far away.

Such light as was left was fading with each moment, and the winter breeze was fretting in the grass.

'Longest Night is come,' whispered Fieldfare, feeling tired and content. 'Now I never need to worry about my Chater again and one day, when the Stone wills it, I shall join him. Meanwhile I have a task to find, which, I suppose, I must fulfil – and in a bold but comely way!'

'Fieldfare!'

'Yes,' she called, turning from the Stones at last, 'I'm ready now.'

Out of the dark she came, slowly and gracefully, as the loyal and determined Noakes, the first to go searching for her the day before, and now the last to seek for her before giving up, called one last time.

'Fieldfare?'

'Yes,' she said again, coming ever closer to him; he was unable to believe what he saw – that she was alive, and unhurt, and . . .

'I have been to see my beloved, my Chater,' she said, her eyes alight with love, and sadness, and relief that all was done as it should have been. Nomole so loved as he, so good, so true, should go to the Silence all alone.

'But he wasn't alone, you see my dear, he had me to say farewell; and Mayweed, he was there to guide him on into the Light.'

'They thought you had been taken,' said Noakes with tears of relief coming to his eyes, 'even Spurling thought so. But I knew . . .'

The two moles held each other, both in tears; one because his prayers had been answered and Fieldfare was safe and well again, and the other for knowing that her love had been blessed with a final farewell in the Stone's Light.

They sniffled, and they snuffled, and they talked as moles do who have shared something secret, and Noakes asked, 'What was Mayweed really like? I mean . . .'

'He was like the tales they tell of him, rather thin, rather patchy, and with a toothy grin and a grand way of talking.'

'Fieldfare,' said Noakes, 'we better go down to Seven Barrows.

406

There's a lot of very unhappy moles there, quite unable to celebrate because they think you're dead. Well you're not, and you better go and show them so. But, Fieldfare?'

'Yes, mole,' she said, feeling suddenly very tired.

'Well, I'm just an adventuring kind of mole I suppose, and I never thought about the future until these hours I've spent watching the Stones for signs of you.'

'You could have come among them, my love. You might have found me sooner.'

Noakes shook his head. 'No, that didn't feel right, though I thought about it. And anyway, I knew you'd be safe if you were out there among the Stones. But the future . . . it didn't seem possible to have one without you. I never wanted to see anymole alive so much as you!'

Fieldfare held him close in a warm and motherly way. 'Mole,' she said, 'I don't think anymole has ever said such a nice thing to me on Longest Night, not ever before. And do you know . . . ?'

Noakes shook his head. His face-fur was wet with tears, his eyes wide, and he looked even younger than his years.

'Well, I think if you *hadn't* called me, I might not have been able to come back. I didn't want to, I wanted to stay with Chater, and to go on with him into the Silence. But you called and Mayweed said that perhaps I ought to go back.'

They were silent a little longer as above them, one by one, stars came out. Then together they turned towards Seven Barrows, whose curving shadows loomed ahead in the darkness, and a watcher saw them.

'Halt! Whatmole goes there?'

'Noakes!' called Noakes, 'and a friend!'

'A good friend!' called out Fieldfare.

'What do you mean "a good friend"?' replied the watcher dubiously, coming a little closer. 'Why it's . . . but bless me you're . . . by the Stone, I do believe . . . no, no it can't be!'

'But it is!' cried Noakes triumphantly.

'It's me, Fieldfare,' said Fieldfare, and she had never felt so glad to be alive.

'Fieldfare alive!' cried the watcher, deserting his post, and rushing about hither and thither, calling out for Spurling, for anymole to come and see because it was a blessing it was, a wonder, a Longest Night miracle.

'Fieldfare's alive and safe and well?' cried out another, and moles

407

came running, and shouting, and laughing, and the celebrations for Longest Night began.

Although Hamble's departure from Privet after Chater's death had been impulsive, and a response to her persuasions that he might find a new task and a new direction in distant Duncton Wood, as the day had worn on he had felt increasingly right about what he was doing.

The years of journeying and struggle had begun to wear him down, and he had reached a point where he felt there was no more he could usefully do for Rooster. He had not lost one bit of his faith that Rooster was a great mole, a Master of the Delve, but he had come at last to the conclusion that he had lost his way – his friends could help him no more.

He knew the depth of Rooster's suffering, and felt it now all the more for having, so briefly, met Privet again. For on her face was a look of growing peace and self-discovery, and in her voice an acceptance of life and changing circumstance that so far was not Rooster's.

'I can't bear his burden for him, and do him no favours trying to,' said Hamble to himself as he crossed the moist fields of pasture and ploughed land that lie eastward of Caer Caradoc.

Occasionally he turned back and looked at the great hill receding, his discomfort and guilt at not being at Rooster's right paw to help giving way to unexpected feelings of relief to be free from it all. At liberty to go where he liked at what pace he chose; at liberty to talk to moles if he felt inclined or to nomole at all if that's how the mood took him.

But that was in the future – for now he was in Newborn territory and must watch where he went, and avoid the obvious routes where patrols might be. Of those, and how to evade them, he had learnt much in recent moleyears – indeed there were few moles as experienced as he in predicting the Newborns' tactics and strategies.

'Though they did catch us on our approach to Caer Caradoc,' he admitted to himself ruefully. He frowned and paused, thinking for the briefest of moments that if Rooster was in trouble he would need a friend. And there was only him who understood, who knew the depth of confusion and suffering in the Delver's mind.

'Only me? No, no, there's Privet as well. She said she would continue to watch over him, and by the Stone I believe she'll do a better job than me!'

Then, content to let others continue with a task he had begun long ago but now left behind, Hamble surveyed the land ahead and chose

408

a route which looked safe, and would put as much distance as possible between him and Caer Caradoc in the shortest space of time.

Next day, long before the sky dulled towards dusk, Hamble felt a tiredness coming upon him such as he could not remember feeling so heavily before. His limbs could hardly move his paws, his mind began to wander and his eyes closed towards sleep even as he moved along. This was no physical tiredness, but rather the fatigue of one who has finally given up a struggle he has continued far too long.

'I'd better find a secure place before I drop down where I am,' said Hamble to himself, as he yawned, and shook his head and rubbed his eyes to keep awake. He wandered on a little more, turned from the path he had found towards a small stand of ash trees at the end of a hedge line, almost under some barbed wire and the remnants of a fallen fence, checked that there were no signs of moles or other tracks, and delved himself a temporary burrow deep enough that he could sleep underground and safe, but for his snout which prudently poked up into the winter air.

'This'll do,' he sighed contentedly, snuggling down and back, 'nomole will find me here. Today brings the first Longest Night of my life that I'll be all alone . . . yes, this'll do . . .'

And great Hamble, good dependable Hamble, old friend of Privet and Rooster, fell asleep, just as the afternoon darkened towards Longest Night, and safely beyond the vales across which he had come, the light on Caer Caradoc's eastern face began to fade.

Chapter Thirty

'Through my fault, my own fault, my own grievous fault,' Rooster had said, and he now stanced before Brother Quail, Chief Inquisitor Skua and the others to confess his sins.

But broken though he seemed – his sobs had stopped and now his brute head moved wildly from side to side as if trying to fend off his anguish – his towering presence dominated the chamber. There was a sense of danger and unpredictability about him which perhaps was what put the wary glitter into Quail's otherwise smug and confident eyes.

It was this very unpredictability that now hung over the Convocation which had given Maple the idea – the hope – that matters might not continue in the smooth and contrived way that Quail had so far successfully arranged, by which Chervil had been controlled and humiliated, and Thripp brushed aside and made impotent. With a mole like Rooster about, however helpless he seemed at the moment, things could happen of which quick-witted moles might take advantage.

So Maple had suddenly become very alert indeed, and his eyes began continuously to scan the chamber below to spot anything at all which might have to be considered if he was to make the move that he was already considering.

'What are you thinking?' whispered Whillan, who if he had to help was satisfied that Madoc would watch over Privet and see that she did nothing foolish, for her distress on seeing Rooster had changed to a kind of blank numbness.

'I am thinking,' said Maple slowly, 'that from the expression on his face our friend Chervil is thinking the same kind of thought as I am, and also, that it is significant that sometime in the hubbub of Rooster's arrival Feldspar and the other guards have moved a good deal closer to him as if they expect something to happen. We'll just have to wait and see, and be ready to act.

'I'll tell you this, Whillan, that whatever else happens somemole's going to be sacrificed to the Newborn need for retribution this Longest

Night and I am going to see that it's not one of our own, or Rooster, if I possibly can. And it looks like Chervil's going to see that it's not himself. As for Thripp, well, nomole can guess what's in his mind!'

Thripp was still barely visible below them, the only mole there it seemed who had not moved or spoken. His presence was felt not by what he did or did not do, but because many others looked over to him expectantly from time to time, as if the question about him was not *whether* he might do and say something, but *when*.

But all this was unspoken, and for now it was Rooster who held their attention as Quail coaxed him into confession.

'We await your leisure, mole,' said Quail.

Rooster stopped moving his head, peered up at him and said, 'Have been ready since that day the world went dark.'

'"That day the world went dark"', hissed Skua, coming forward and nodding to Brother Quail that he would take over now. 'When was that, Rooster of Charnel Clough?'

'Long time, long ago. I used these paws . . .' He raised one of his front paws and then rearing up he showed the other, turning hugely round that everymole might see. 'These paws and these talons. Different. Always were. Different . . .'

'Mole!' said Skua, for Rooster seemed to be wandering, but there was no stopping him. He turned his back on Skua and spoke directly to the Convocation. Those immediately before him – or rather beneath him – might well look intimidated. Rooster was not a mole that made others who did not understand him feel safe.

'Ugly, these paws. Big. Did wrong and defiled them.'

'When?' said Skua more softly, trying to regain control. Rooster turned round and glared at him, almost snout to snout.

'When,' he said blankly. 'At Crowden, did wrong, killed with them. Killed . . .' He faltered into a silent confused world of his own, far more frightening to him than the stolid and apprehensive silence of the moles listening to him.

'You have killed since, have you not?' tried Skua once again, but Rooster ignored him altogether, and remained silent for some time before picking up his thought where he had left it.

'. . . I killed Red Ratcher, and killed everymole in that. Killed me, killed her. But can't kill, can't never kill.'

'But you did, Rooster,' said Skua quickly, sensing the confessand was feeling a guilt that could be played upon.

'Yesss . . . YES!' roared Rooster, 'killed him in darkness.'

411

There was silence once more, which Skua broke in the hope of luring his victim back to confession.

'Darkness,' he repeated, 'it was night when you . . .' Like a good confidant he had long since discovered that moles said most whose words were repeated back to them.

'Night in my head. The peat moor was not dark – the sky was not dark. But her cries were fading into dark and I saw Ratcher's body on hers. I took this paw, and this one, and I broke my vow and killed him.'

'What vow?' asked Skua quickly.

'Delving vow. Ancient. Delvers do not kill.'

'But *you* killed, Rooster, you offended the Stone.'

'I hurt all Stones, I hurt all moles, I saw him hurting her and I hurt him.'

'What mole was he hurting, mole? Tell us what mole it was . . .'

This was not Skua's voice but an old one, a little frail, and gentle. Mole looked at mole and nodded. The Elder Senior Brother had spoken at last. 'What mole?' was the question, and Rooster would answer, for Thripp himself had asked.

'No, no, no,' said Rooster. 'Never speak her name. Her name not mine to speak.'

Above this strange grim scene, unseen, Whillan turned and stared at Maple, who nodded briefly in Privet's direction. Privet was staring down below; her eyes were filled with tears, her mouth open yet silent, as if she wished to speak but knew she must not.

'He's talking about Privet, isn't he?' whispered Whillan.

Maple nodded and said, 'It's the tale she told us on the journey here, about how she had to leave the Moors after Rooster killed Red Ratcher.'

'She blames herself for it.'

'And *he* blames himself by the sound of things.'

'We can't let this go on,' said Whillan urgently.

'No, we can't. Look, Whillan, the time for action's coming and I want to get Rooster out of here. He's a mole the Newborns fear, maybe because he's the only one who's ever stanced up to them. All the more reason to get him out.'

'It's very risky,' said Whillan; 'can't we get Privet and the others out first and then come back?'

Maple nodded appreciatively at the young mole's pluck. 'We could if we could get Privet to leave, but that might be difficult now she's seen her Rooster in the grip of the Newborn Inquisitors. There's not

412

much doubt about what Skua and Quail will want to do when they have his confession, and that might be soon.'

'But Chervil might slow things down – he doesn't look too happy with what's going on. Have you any idea how to get Rooster out?'

'Not much of one, and it may hardly be worth the risk, but my instinct tells me we've got a better chance than might at first appear. More than that, if we get away with it then the Newborns will have been hit hard, right where they least expect it. If others heard that, they'd know they're vulnerable. It makes sense to try. If you could lead Privet and Madoc out to the west side by the way I showed you and get them to hide on the steep western slope you could come back and help me free Rooster. They're not expecting any trouble up here on Caer Caradoc, and certainly not in the chamber itself – except from Rooster himself perhaps. So we have the advantage of surprise.'

All this was said in a low and hurried whisper. When Maple was sure Whillan understood he went over to Privet, signalled to the others to listen in, and briefly told them what he wanted them to do.

'But I can't leave Rooster here among them,' said Privet.

'Whillan will talk to you about that,' said Maple judiciously. 'For my part I must go exploring again and see if I can get safely to one of the chamber entrances below us, and find a way to lead Rooster out to safety; that will confuse the Newborns enough to make them think we're escaping by any route but the steep west side. But whatever else you do, Privet, and whatever Rooster says or does, do not shout out to him . . .' He paused, frowning and thinking as the light of an idea crossed his face; 'At least, not yet!'

With that he was gone, and all the others could do was watch Rooster's continuing confession, as Whillan sought ways to persuade Privet that if circumstances seemed right the best thing she might do was leave.

Below them, despite Skua's best efforts Rooster had not yet mentioned Privet's name as the mole for whom he had killed, and about whom he evidently felt such deep distress. But still he talked in his wild and wandering way, a mole who wanted to be free of the darkness that haunted him, but whom life and circumstances had placed in the worst possible place to do so, and before moles who were likely to be not in the least receptive or sympathetic. They were looking for weakness and failure, but what Rooster needed was a release from the past, and the love and support of moles dear to him who might lead him to a better future. Of these only Privet perhaps might have known how to reach out her paws to him and make him feel safe and good, and in any other circumstances but these she might have done so.

'Never wanted killing, not first, not since. Was trained to other things. Good things. Felt the delving need. Not satisfying it. It eats my heart away.'

He raised his paws – the same paws that had not only killed, but (as Privet knew better than anymole alive) had once delved most beautifully and with great love and wisdom – and peered at the walls of the chamber. His eyes softened and looked hopeful and though it was but momentarily Privet was not the only one who saw it, and understood.

'Mole, if it's easier for you to tell us what's in your heart you can delve it here and now,' said Thripp, moving a little closer to the centre of the dais, with Brother Rolt at his flank. Privet looked down appreciatively at his back and again wished she could see his face and eyes so she could the better assess what kind of mole he was. She was surprised that like others there she felt an instinctive warmth and sympathy towards him.

Rooster turned towards Thripp, and his heart was still.

'The Stone honours delving,' said Thripp. 'It was once the greatest of arts, taking precedence even over scrivening and scribing.'

'Is still, does now,' said Rooster in a calm voice. 'But I can't, now nor never. Broke the vow.'

'What vow is that?' asked Thripp, waving Skua into silence when he tried to interrupt. Quail glowered, not liking Thripp's involvement, nor the way his voice and seeming sympathy seemed to quieten Rooster, and turn the Convocation's goodwill towards him.

'Old vow. Made to Gaunt. Gaunt taught me, he was Mentor and said the centuries' guarding of the delving art ended with me.'

'Why with you, Rooster of Charnel Clough?'

'Must go forth as Master, must do right. Must show moledom. Was my task.'

'Show us . . .' said Thripp seductively.

Again Rooster looked appraisingly at the walls and floor of the chamber, and his paws fretted and moved restlessly in the air so that the watching moles could feel his need to express himself through delving as if it were their own.

'Can't,' said Rooster, 'afraid. Can't never. *Must never.*'

But how desperate was his need, and how his very desperation and frustration explained the conflicts that seemed to plague him.

'Perhaps the Stone will not mind . . .'

Perhaps so, and perhaps given time Thripp might have persuaded

414

Rooster to delve there and then, had not Quail, uneasy with his diminishing control, reared himself up and said harshly, 'Do as the Elder Brother says you must, for the snake is in your heart and you must bring the evil up and out before us now.'

'Can't,' said Rooster, faltering and upset once more.

'Do it, sinner!' ordered Quail, his voice suddenly vicious. Whatever bloom of hope and trust Thripp had succeeded in bringing to life withered and died before this unnecessary harshness, just as, no doubt, Quail had hoped. Yet Rooster continued to be capable of surprises. He turned on Quail and said with brutal honesty, 'Would be a bad delving with you here, and others. Darkness of the moles in this chamber would make my delving be dark, and would frighten you. Need peace, need love, for delving to be good and pure like the Stone. So can't.'

'And the vow?' said Chervil, who was stancing closest to Rooster throughout all this. 'The vow the mole Gaunt made you make; can a confession not make you free of it?'

'You,' said Rooster compliantly. 'Felt you from the first. *You* should leave.'

'Moles,' said Skua, addressing the gathering generally, 'this mole is wasting our time with his wandering and the things he says, this mole—'

'Am *confessing*,' roared Rooster, thrusting his snout at the increasingly hapless Skua. 'Like a journey in dark it is confusing, like delving for something unanswered. You talk, he talks, all talk: none listen and I am alone. None hear and I cry. None know, but I know. Darkness in mind, for I have done wrong and only moles who could help are gone. Knew moles could help but all gone and Rooster's alone. Rooster's in darkness. Rooster cannot see . . .'

His anguish was so genuine and palpable that it was impossible for moles to do anything before it but stay silent, or weep as Privet did; and Squelch. Oh yes, fat Squelch was weeping now and very quietly crooning some new lament.

'He knows,' said Rooster, pointing at Squelch without looking at him, 'he is in darkness. He has sinned. His singing is like my delving need – but he *can* sing, I can't delve. Can never. Never will now. All friends gone . . .'

'Mole!' began Quail and Skua simultaneously, no doubt to admonish Rooster for what they in their narrow-mindedness understood to be an attack on Squelch.

But like a rising surge of floodwater in what had been a dried-up watercourse Rooster was now rising to his theme, far beyond their power to control. His voice was loud and full of pain, his gestures clumsy yet fearsome and his eyes wide and compelling in the sudden stares that transfixed one mole after another, the whole effect making all feel that they were somehow to blame for the sins, supposed or otherwise, that beset the great mole.

'All friends of my life died. All kin, all gone. All, all, all made to go by me. Samphire my mother who bore me, she's gone. To her I was beautiful. To her I was worth saving. To her I was worth living in the Charnel for. Stone forgive me. She did not know my ugliness!

'Gaunt my mentor, he suffered pain to teach me. His paws were diseased, his body hurting, but he used them to teach me. Stone forgive me.

'Humlock, in silent darkness, he knew me, he was part of me, my delving born of his acceptance. Humlock I left to die. Glee was only mole like a sister I knew, white-furred like snow and eyes that saw like Samphire's the beauty that lies beyond these misshapen paws, and behind this furrowed face. Left her to die. Stone, Almighty Stone, forgive me. Hear my confession now.'

'Yes, yes,' sang Squelch softly, tears streaming down his face. 'Stone hear him.' And against Rooster's anguish, Squelch's voice was the lament of a wild wind through leafless hawthorn alone in a winter's waste.

'Is more, more and bad. Mole found me up there where I was alone, where Hilbert was, on the Top. Came out of my tears and found me. She did. Found Rooster and not afraid. Found me.'

There was still an innocent wonder in Rooster's voice at this sweet memory, and had they seen Privet's tears and mute anguish for the suffering of a mole she loved, no mole would have doubted who had done the finding.

'Found me and taught me, like my Mentor taught . . .'

'Oh no my dear, you taught me as you are teaching those who hear you now,' whispered Privet helplessly.

'. . . taught me to delve a different way. Like Gaunt said, life would teach me more than he ever could. He showed me how, not why or when. We lived together up on Hilbert's Top and I knew joy. Rooster knew joy. Life taught me new delving ways, and she was life to me. Was all.'

'Was she the one you killed for?' said Thripp from the now enshadowed dais; and even Quail did not interrupt. He had retreated and Privet and the others could not now see him at all.

416

Rooster nodded massively, eyes imploring others to understand. 'Was the one. She was my life and from what she gave me and would always give me, all my delving would be, all, all was hers. She could hear beyond the Dark Sound of my delving. To her I was not ugly.' He bowed his head. 'But I wronged. Wronged her, wronged us. Did wrong to the Stone in that.'

'You wronged,' insinuated Skua, with the relish of a mole who after a long hunt has found a very large and tasty worm indeed.

'Not wrong, but wrong,' said Rooster wrinkling his brow at a confusion he still felt. 'Didn't feel wrong what Lime did. When she did. How she did.'

Skua's eyes glistened with pleasure and zeal and his snout rose quivering as, carried on the air, he found the heady scent of base desire.

'Fornication,' he whispered almost silently, turning to share his discovery with Quail.

'With Lime it was good. Only one was Lime. Was right . . . but wrong. Destroyed her love for me.'

'Lime's?' whispered Quail.

'No, no, no,' roared Rooster, angry at Quail's misunderstanding. 'You're dark as deep tunnels. You're where things die. You're . . .'

As a collective gasp of dismay at this sudden attack on Quail went through the gathering Thripp cut it short.

'Then who's the mole you love, mole? Speak the name you dared not speak before.'

'Privet's,' said Rooster at last. 'Hers was the love I broke. Confused her. Red Ratcher found her. My father, who took Samphire and made me. Dark, dark was Ratcher, like *him*.'

Nomole need ask any more who *he* was! Quail!

'He was taking her. Like disease across a young mole's face; like odour in a place of flowers; like death all filthy on life. Ratcher was the slash of Dark Sound across a perfect delve. So I killed him and broke all vows. A Master must not kill; a delver cannot kill. A delver makes, a delver creates, a delver brings to life the sound of life, of happiness, of all. A delver *cannot* kill. So, I was delver no more. I hurt Privet and destroyed our love that was all we had: me to delve and she to scribe. Killed Ratcher with these paws and killed myself and Privet who was more than myself.'

'Privet of the Moors,' whispered Thripp's voice.

Rooster glared at all the moles about as if defying them to speak. His chest heaved with the effort of memory and confession and he

417

muttered incoherently to himself, his head swaying from side to side as it had at the beginning.

A few moments before this Maple had returned. Now he gathered Whillan and the others about Privet and said urgently, 'It's possible to get right below here to the entrance to the chamber. The Newborn guards are all listening to Rooster, and preparing to have their fun with him once Skua has had his say. I was seen but nomole said a thing. Maybe they think I'm Newborn. Now listen. Privet, will you go with Whillan when he decides the moment's right? That could be very soon.'

She nodded bleakly and asked, 'But can you get Rooster out?'

'I shall try. There's going to be confusion and that will be our chance. We can take advantage of the obvious dissension between Thripp and Quail. Then there's Squelch and his singing, and Chervil and his doubts. Not to mention Feldspar and his sons. Well, if an opportunity for escape doesn't come from that lot none other will.'

The moles nodded grimly.

'But we're going to be chased, so the further Privet and Madoc can get downslope once you've got them on the west side the better.' He turned to Arum and Boden. 'Do you know what lies downslope of there?'

'Only by hearsay,' said Arum. 'But we can't leave Caradoc ourselves, the Elder Senior Brother will have need of us; but perhaps we could go a little way downslope with the two females and wait behind on the route to show you which way they went.'

Maple nodded his agreement. 'Now I shall go below. Choose your moment well, Whillan – though it would be better if it were now.'

'No,' whispered Privet, 'let me watch him just a moment more.'

At which Maple left them again, to see how best he might rescue Rooster, while the others turned to look down into the chamber for what might be the final time. The light had steadily lessened so that the narrow tunnels behind them, amongst whose sharp bends and fissured ways Maple's pawsteps receded, were in the deepest gloom.

For long moments now, after his declaration of guilt and loss regarding Privet, Rooster had said nothing, but seemed to wrestle so terribly with some remaining thing he wished to say that all who watched him said no word. Then without warning, like sudden thunder, he roared it out.

'But there is *more.*'

His voice broke into a half-sob, and he nodded in agreement with himself, thinking perhaps that none other there knew enough to understand.

'More. Worse. End. So when guards found me didn't care. Came to confession, didn't I? Came to be free. Will be free?'

He turned once more to the Inquisitors on the dais behind him, and specifically to Chief Inquisitor Skua.

'Will I?' he asked.

This seemed to take Skua by surprise; considerably discomfited, he narrowed his eyes, frowned, and finally said carefully, 'That is for your judges to decide.'

A look of despair came to Rooster's face. 'Thought confession meant freedom. Will I be forgiven? Will I *ever* be forgiven?' How desperate his cry was, how hopeless his expression as he raised his misshapen paws and bent his head, and scored his talons over his face until he drew blood. 'But there is more,' he said pitifully.

'You shall be forgiven,' whispered Thripp, and a sigh went through the gathering.

'For ever and always?'

'For now.'

'Not harmed and hurt more?'

'Not by Newborn mole.'

'But there is more.'

'If you speak true and of all that is in your heart,' said Thripp quietly, to Quail's and Skua's ill-concealed rage, 'the Stone may have mercy on you, forgive your sins, and bring you to everlasting Silence.'

'Two moles stayed by me. Two moles good to me. One was Lime, only mole I knew. Only mole I mated with. Only one. But no love, not like with mole I lost. But when one mole mates with another and there's no love there's still something. Didn't know that until I drove her from me. Didn't know and nomole told. Stone forgive me for hurt.

'And Hamble. He was last. He warned. He said, "Rooster, you must kill no more. Rooster, you are Master of the Delve, you must not kill. Rooster, if you kill more I will leave you".'

Rooster looked at Thripp and said from the depth of all his confusion and despair, 'I kill my friends. I kill all things. Sin is in me. Lime . . .'

'And what of her, mole?' said Thripp gently.

'She was with pup when she left. Our pups. Unborn, unformed. Just as well with me as father.' He roared with an unbalanced laughter that was tinged with the deepest sadness. 'I would have liked to know what I made. Know what I could have delved because I can feel it and see it all. Would have been good. But my pups – wanted to see, wanted to know, but I drove Lime away, I . . .'

But for a moment neither Whillan nor Privet heard him because as Rooster spoke of Lime, Whillan, eyes searching the chamber for the kind of opportunity Maple hoped they would find, saw something he could scarcely believe.

'It's Weeth! There! Among those moles by the entrance on the far side near Squelch. Weeth!'

Indeed it was, but not a Weeth they knew. He had, somehow or other, inveigled his way amongst a group of pious and contrite-looking Newborns, and on his face was a look of even greater piety and contrition than on theirs. At the same time, typical Weeth, his eyes were all over the place.

'Looking for opportunity,' breathed Whillan, with admiration for the bold mole, and delight too, for his presence raised their hopes that rescue and escape might really be possible. 'But had he seen Maple?' They could only hope.

'So then only Hamble stayed with me,' Rooster continued. 'In all my darkness only him to touch and hold so I would not die in my own Dark Sound. He alone was my Light. Yesterday I killed again and he left. He was gone. And he . . . the guards said he was dead. Killed not by these paws, but dead because of what I am become. So killed by me. So nothing left and nomole and Rooster's in darkness and the Stone cannot hear. Rooster's alone because he sinned. Rooster's near death because he could not find the way and lost all moles who could have shown him. All are gone. Stone forgive me, for this is my confession spoken true. Mole Thripp there says forgiveness can be. Forgive me. Mole Thripp says nomole shall harm me. No, Stone, can't be harmed more. Mole Thripp says forgiveness with thee, Stone, in your Light which I cannot see, in your Silence which I cannot hear; Stone, forgive this mole . . .'

But poor Rooster could not continue. He had said what he had wanted to say for so many years, and those moles who heard him and still had open hearts could surely not doubt that the Stone did hear, and somehow would help.

'Sooo . . . Brethren,' hissed Skua, his moment come, and grasping it before Thripp could take it from him and turn it to something weak like forgiveness or love. No, no, that could not be tonight. The mole had killed and killed again, had fornicated and not repented, had insulted every senior mole present, and the snake in him must be destroyed.

'So what are we to do? Can the snake in this mole be drawn out, or is he in too deep for that?'

'Too deep,' sighed the watching moles, taking Skua's lead.

'Too deep,' moaned Squelch in falsetto song, 'and death the only cure.'

'No, mole,' began Thripp, trying to stem the mounting, murderous flood of judgement, 'no . . .' But his voice was too weak.

'Death will be his liberty!' said Quail with studied sadness, his sharp talons flexing behind Rooster's back.

'For the snake must die for ever,' began the chanters from all over the chamber, and none could surely doubt, as the heartbeat of the chant began to swell, that once it found full force nomole would stop before the passions that had been held in check so long found expression in a killing punishment on this great, rough, brutish mole who had made his incoherent confession and must suffer now the Stone's judgement.

Rooster himself sensed what was coming for he raised his head from his dark despair, crying, 'Stone forgive me . . .' Yet he did not move. He seemed about to say something more above the rising chant when another voice was heard, powerful enough to be louder than Rooster's and audible to all above the chant.

'Listen now how the snake seems to vomit its filth from out of his mouth, but do not hear! Hear the sound of sin, but do not listen!' It was the voice of one of the ordinary brethren. 'Let not this vile mole seduce us along with his black confession!' that same voice cried, maddened and enraged. 'I shall take him forth from here while our brothers make their holy judgement in the Stone!'

The voice was pious, fervent and compelling, but to moles with ears to hear it had a faint but welcome ironic ring.

The voice was Weeth's.

And no sooner said than done. Before anymole could react to his words, except to think that this was a spontaneous outburst from one of the delegates, of the kind officially welcomed, Weeth broke free of the group he was with and boldly headed for Rooster. In fact his action was only clearly seen by those moles in front and on the dais and already some, Skua among them, were signalling to guards to discreetly stop the zealot making his way towards the confessand Rooster.

They might have succeeded had not Privet after so long restraining herself in the face of Rooster's desperate call for help, which is what she recognized his 'confession' to be, finally decided to intervene. She did not mindlessly call out to Rooster as Maple had expected and as

421

he now hoped she would. She had a better way by far of reaching out to the mole she loved, to touch his heart and rescue him from the void into which he had thrown himself. She did something whose meaning was exclusive to herself and Rooster alone, but which had the effect of calling the attention of the whole Convocation to the place where she and the others had so far remained successfully in hiding.

She reached up her right paw to the high side-wall of the gallery, extended her talons and calmly made a vertical scribing, from roof to floor. At first the sound was no more than scratching but as the scribing took form, increasingly massive in shape and powerful in effect even in the half-light, it gathered volume, enlarged by the echoing nature of the place; loud, thunderous and dark, it brought the chanting below to a halt, and quelled all interest in Rooster and Weeth's approach. As Privet bent lower to her task she seemed to gain strength and passion, and let out gasps and sharp cries at the effort needed to make the scribing on the soft sandstone wall.

Not only was the sound dark, but frightening as well. It scattered the moles below and all turned their gaze up towards the gallery, including even the moles ordered by Quail to intercept Weeth. Seeing which, Weeth naturally took his opportunity, and reached Rooster's flank as the sound of Privet's scribing, rebounding on itself and its own echoes, reached its most awesome point.

Rooster had turned as the others had, not in shock or fear, but in recognition. Indeed as Weeth reached up a paw to touch him and attract his attention the great mole was instinctively starting towards the sound.

'Rooster!' whispered Weeth urgently, and though Rooster did not look down at him, at least he paused.

'You've got to come with me, now. There is no time. This is your only opportunity.' Weeth had indeed seen Maple earlier, and his action now was the result of an instinctive understanding between them, aided by some subtle nods and signals.

But a new sound came now from the gallery above them, lighter and more pure, and like the first it increased in volume as the moments went by.

'It's Privet,' muttered Rooster in blank astonishment. Then, acknowledging Weeth, perhaps simply because he was the nearest mole with whom to share his delight, he reached down his paw and buffeted the mole of opportunity in the chest. 'That's Privet. Now listen.'

'*You* listen,' said Weeth, looking round for inspiration and finding

422

it in Rooster's eyes. 'Privet is alive and needs you. So come *on*.'

'Won't forgive, not like Stone.'

'She's forgiven,' said Weeth, trying once more to steer him over to Maple.

All this had taken but moments, and now in the gallery above them Whillan saw Privet complete her extraordinary scribing. Just two words – two names. 'Rooster' for the first and 'Privet' for the second.

'It's the same as I did on Hilbert's Top, when Rooster said it was like a delving. I *told* you,' said Privet calmly, looking over her shoulder at the sea of upturned faces below, not at all surprised at the dramatic effect her action was having.

'There was Silence between our names, you see my dear, and if he can hear it again now he'll know what to do.'

'He must go with Weeth,' said Whillan almost desperately, 'but he's not moving.'

Privet smiled, reached up her left paw to the Rooster scribing and her right to her own and with one swift movement scribed them both simultaneously. The result was like nothing Whillan had ever heard or imagined, it was not so much loud as powerful, not so much unbearable as simply overwhelming, and he instinctively did what most of the moles below did, which was to cover his ears and lower his snout to protect himself from a sound that taloned itself into his very heart.

'Yes!' said Rooster below them, grabbing Weeth by the paw and hauling him upright, for he had covered his ears and closed his eyes as well. 'That's Privet! Take me!'

As the sounds still echoed about them and slowly began to fade, and all the gathering seemed dazed and confused, Weeth began to push Rooster the short distance towards the entrance where Maple waited. As he did so he felt a paw and heard a commanding voice behind him. 'Mole! Stop!'

Weeth turned faster than Rooster and saw the dark hostile eyes of Chervil on him, and Quail upon the dais gesticulating. There were but moments left. With a quick shove at Chervil, who though he was a stocky mole fell back and knocked off balance a guard who was approaching, Rooster and Weeth were away. Rooster buffeted aside two more moles, and they were out of the chamber into the cooler air of a tunnel, pushed forward by brave Maple who said, 'Quick, straight ahead and stop when I shout.'

Above them, no less speedily, Whillan had ushered Privet and the others out of the gallery – though Privet did not leave until she was satisfied Rooster was gone. As the last to leave the gallery Whillan could not himself resist one final gesture, which was to sweep his right paw down Rooster's name. How astonishing it felt to him! How different to a normal scribing! 'Is this a delving?' he thought as he turned to follow the others into the gloom of the narrowing tunnels, and the dark and confused sound filled the gallery and chamber once more. 'Is this really how a delver feels?' It was most strange, and most awesome, like a sublime irritation on his paw. 'Is this the delving need,' whispered Whillan, 'or just how Rooster really feels, as Privet knows him?'

Then the noise of the delving was overtaken by shouts of anger, and calls of command, and all about them was the thunder of the running paws of guards, seeking, searching, hunting.

'Up here!' came the cry.

'Down there!'

'They must not escape!'

Whillan caught up with the others, and all of them ran for their lives.

By the time Whillan had successfully guided his party through the tunnels, up and out on to the surface and down over the edge of Caer Caradoc's west side, darkness had fallen. It was a night of moving cloud and chill air, but with enough light from occasional stars and the half-hidden moon for them to see each other.

Their journey had been hard and at times fraught, for naturally there were moles searching about, and twice they had to lie in what side tunnels they could find, as patrols went by. Arum fell badly at one point but had recovered enough to travel on with them rather than stay behind so as not to delay them.

'You'll need me to stay on the route in case the others are not sure which way you have gone, as Maple suggested.'

Whillan had not for a moment doubted that Maple and the others would escape safely, and had half hoped that they might have reached the west side before his own party. If so they could all have set off downslope from Caradoc immediately, which would have given them a much better chance of getting clear away. But there was no sign of Maple, and Whillan did not hesitate to get Privet and Madoc, with the two older moles, off and away downslope. There was a brisk breeze blowing up into their faces which meant that both sound and scent might give them away to moles above. The lower they got the better.

Whillan had already decided not to attempt to return to the chamber to give Maple help as he had suggested, for by the time he did he would have no idea where to find the fleeing moles. No, what he would do would be to see the others well on the way, travelling down until the little path they had found split and Arum was safely posted to await the others and guide them on. This done, he said a brief farewell and retraced his steps up the hill.

Once there he snouted about to be sure that Maple had not already come and was in hiding waiting, and then settled himself down in a rocky spot from which he could see and hear all that might come that way without himself being seen.

Several times he heard moles nearby, and later a lot of commotion on the far east side, which he hoped came from moles mistakenly thinking that was the way the escape had been made.

But then, coming more silently than he expected, he saw the murky shapes of two large moles and a smaller one emerge from the same tunnel he and the others had used earlier. He approached cautiously, and when he was quite sure it was Maple, Rooster and Weeth, he whispered, 'Over here!'

They needed no second call, and greatly alert and still unseen, Whillan guided them to the point on the hill's edge where the path started and led them down and away from Caer Caradoc.

They made contact successfully with Arum and Boden, leaving those brave old supporters of Thripp to return upslope to the chaos and confusion left behind and, if necessary, to mislead any pursuers. There was no time for anything but the briefest farewell before they went on downslope the way Boden indicated and came at last to Privet and Madoc. Perhaps Whillan expected something more of the reunion of Privet and Rooster but it was neither the place nor the circumstances for effusive greetings.

'Heard you,' said Rooster with characteristic brevity. Privet only laughed and touched him in a gentle, familiar way to which Whillan responded with, of all things, a pang of possessive jealousy which took him by surprise.

'We'll talk later, all of us,' said Privet. 'Now, Maple, you're in charge, so you had better get us to a place of safety.'

'Since it's Longest Night nomole will expect us to travel far, and I daresay the Newborns will delay their full pursuit of us until the night's rituals are done. They'll start early, hoping to catch up with us. Therefore we will travel hard and fast tonight and tomorrow and not rest until we are satisfied we have found a place in which we can safely hide.'

Nomole disagreed, and with Maple in front and Whillan and Weeth taking up the rear, the party set off downslope once more. When they reached the bottom of the steep hillside Maple found a route that went north and south.

'We'll go north,' he said, 'for that's not the way they'll expect us to go.'

So north they went, and not one of them looked back.

PART V

Duncton Rising

Chapter Thirty-One

They travelled north along a river valley for a full two nights and a day with only the briefest of stops for food and sleep. Maple might have stopped earlier, but the area they passed through was well-populated and with so large a party it proved impossible to avoid other moles.

Some hid from them, a few accosted them and asked whither they were bound, but most simply stared blankly and did not encourage conversation.

'This looks like Newborn country to me,' observed Whillan. 'You can be sure that news of our passing this way will get back soon enough to anymole out looking for us.'

'But with Longest Night just passed, and the Convocation on, perhaps they expect to see strangers about,' said Weeth.

'Maybe,' replied Maple dubiously. 'But the time's come now to find an obscurer route where none will see us, or if they do we can hope they are less likely to be under the Newborn influence.'

'And we do need to stop for a time,' added Privet quietly, 'Rooster needs to rest.'

Rooster had said barely a word since leaving Caer Caradoc. He trekked with them unsteadily and with quite evident effort, but would not respond to word or touch. He simply stared ahead, or at the ground, or peered in a fretful way at his great paws. Only when Privet was near him did he seem at peace, and only alongflank her would he sleep.

'He's tired and shocked,' said Privet, 'and he needs a time of peace.'

But Whillan was not so sure. Indeed he was unhappy with the way matters stood, disliking Privet's familiarity with Rooster, and feeling there was an untamed menace about him which might easily bring disaster to them all. Whillan felt there was truth in something he had said during his confession – that he was a mole who brought trouble to others.

To add to Whillan's discomfort was the galling fact that Madoc seemed to show an inordinate concern for Rooster, helping Privet find food for him, and giving up what resting space she found if it seemed to make it easier for him. These and other little kindnesses Whillan felt to be unnecessary, even indulgent, to a mole whose injuries, whether physical or mental, were surely largely self-inflicted.

'You seem almost *angry* about it all,' commented Weeth, who was the only mole to whom Whillan felt able to express himself.

'Well, I know he's been through a bad time . . .'

'Yes, he has.'

'And he might have been hurt . . .'

'It would seem so.'

'But Privet and Madoc are overdoing it, aren't they?'

'If you think so,' said Weeth annoyingly.

'Well, what do *you* think?' demanded Whillan, exasperated.

'Ah! Me!' said Weeth. 'I think you're possibly fed up. Maybe that's it.'

'With what?'

Weeth shrugged. 'You may be in the wrong place at the wrong time. Or, come to think of it, in the right place at the wrong time.' Weeth laughed, pleased with this ambiguity. But Whillan saw nothing to laugh about.

Nor was Madoc more accommodating, and there seemed nothing left of that brief intimacy they had shared – as Whillan believed – during the break in the Convocation. Now she seemed to have eyes only for Privet and Rooster, and to answer Whillan's few questions and attempts at conversation with a kind of cool aloofness he could not make sense of. It was all very difficult and beginning to cause Whillan to dislike Rooster very much indeed.

As dawn rose on their second morning out from Caer Caradoc Maple went ahead a little, and snouted at the air to left and right, while the others groomed and ate, and tried to rest. The valley had widened and the ground was undulating with signs of higher terrain to their left, the east, but nothing much on their right flank.

'But that's the way we'll go,' Maple decided. 'Moles can easily disappear in a place with few features and fewer paths. What's more, we've not been seen by mole since yesterday at dusk, so it will not be easy to trace us. I know you are all tired, but with luck and the Stone's guidance we may by tonight or tomorrow at the latest find some anonymous place where we can hide up for a time.'

This prospect was enough to put new energy into their steps and they turned up off the valley plain to drier pasture fields and headed north-east in single file. The gentle rise was deceptive, and it was not long before the valley and its river was spread out below them to their left, and beyond it they could see the high rising ground of the Welsh Marches . . .

'. . . Which leads a mole in time to fabled Siabod, if he goes west far enough,' said Maple later, during a rest period. 'In Gareg's account of the wars against the Word he describes how on a clear day the snowy heights of Siabod itself may be seen from Caradoc.'

Whillan stared in imagination at this distant prospect and breathed in the winter air, his heart suddenly lighter. Travel, that's what he must do, as Stour and Thripp had said, and as he himself had suggested to Madoc when they had talked at Caradoc. Aye, travel away from the constraints and pressures of other moles. It made a mole feel good to dream of it, even if duty and present tasks would surely always prevent it.

They journeyed on, feeling freer and safer by the moment as they went on over rolling ground, and the valley and with it all sense of Caer Caradoc disappeared behind them.

That night Maple allowed them to have a long sleep for the first time since leaving, though each of them but Rooster had to take a turn keeping watch. They all found it hard keeping their eyes open, but the nearest they came to danger was the sound of an owl giving a quick night call, and the short sharp bark of a fox.

By dawn all were rested and Maple felt it prudent to move on once again, the more so because the weather was showing signs of becoming colder and calmer. If frost came finding food would be harder as the worms burrowed deeper underground.

'We'll need a safe haven for a few days,' said Madoc, 'so that Rooster can recover more and we can get some proper rest. All this travelling and broken sleep is not good for a mole!'

'That's exactly what I'm looking for, Madoc!' said Maple appreciatively, his great paw on hers for a moment before they led the others off. 'Now, come on, we've not had time to talk. Tell me something about your life as a Newborn female.'

They chattered on, laughing occasionally, all of which, and the familiarity that preceded it, Whillan noted with annoyance and dismay, for despite his moody silences of the last three days he felt in some disconcerting way that Madoc, while not exactly *his* friend, had less cause to be Maple's.

'But anyway, it doesn't matter!' he told himself, kicking at the ground disagreeably and not looking ahead to where Maple and Madoc went along together oblivious of his jealousy, 'because as soon as I can I'm going to leave them all and set off on my own. After all, nomole here needs me! Once Privet and Rooster are somewhere safe I'll have fulfilled my task. Weeth will go with Maple to get involved in assisting in the fight against the Newborns, and as for Madoc, she might stay with Privet or even go with Maple. Anyway, it's no concern of mine, thank the Stone!'

With such hollow words of self-comfort as these (and many more), and thoughts of places he might visit like Siabod, or Beechenhill where the Stone Mole died, or even fabled Whern in the north, Whillan contrived to pass the morning without speaking to them at all. And yet . . . as the day wore on his jealousy gave way to something more: a restlessness, a sense of being ill at ease, as if something was happening which he could not fully understand. It was like an irritation on the flank which a mole cannot quite locate, nor get rid of; or some half-forgotten task reminding him that it needs to be done and done *now*!

In mid-afternoon they came to a point where the route offered them two alternatives – one was to the west, and up a steep slope into a great wood which rose above them, not unlike the prospect of Duncton Wood from the south-east; the other was directly north, and looked as if it undulated for a while and then might go downslope again.

They all gathered around Maple while he pondered which way to go.

'We'll go west,' he said finally, 'because while it may be a harder route for tired moles to take, it also seems less likely others will follow us that way.'

He set off and all the others followed him but Whillan, who had turned suddenly to the north and was snouting at the air.

'Come on, mole!' called out Maple.

But Whillan did not move, seeming almost transfixed to the ground, and so still that he looked odd.

'What's wrong, my dear?' called Privet, who knew him best of all.

'North,' he whispered, half turning to her for a moment, his face full of concern. 'We must go north. I feel a need to.'

The others looked mildly irritated, and Weeth seemed bored. Only Rooster appeared to really listen to the worry in Whillan's voice, and raising his paw to the others to still and quieten them, he moved a little way towards Whillan.

'What need?' he growled. Whillan turned again, and looked at

432

Rooster with real concern on his face, his animosity and jealousy not showing at all.

'Don't know,' he said, almost to himself. 'Like . . . like a nagging kind of thing. Like . . . *I don't know.*'

'Need,' said Rooster, coming closer still to Whillan; 'I know.'

The others were utterly quiet, watching the strange sight of two moles they had all sensed were distanced from each other suddenly involved in a dialogue that was almost private, almost in a language all its own.

Whillan stared north again, searching the sky and the land, increasingly restless, his front paws fretting. Rooster loomed behind him, rough, patient, warm, understanding.

'You don't know!' Whillan cried out impulsively, wheeling round on him. 'You can't!'

'Do,' said Rooster unperturbed. 'You feel need. Don't know what from. Don't know why. Something forgotten trying to find its way back again.'

'Yes,' said Whillan subsiding, and nodding his head, 'like that.'

'What to think? What do we do?' asked Rooster, scratching his head.

'Go north,' said Whillan. 'It will make the need feel easier . . . but I don't know why.'

'North!' declared Rooster, turning back to the others. 'North is best 'cos Whillan knows.'

Maple sighed and shook his head.

'I'm not going to argue with anymole about it!' he said cheerfully. 'If you two think north is right, then let's go north. We'll find somewhere to lose ourselves quick enough.'

But Whillan, having cast a quick and grateful glance at Rooster, was already up and off along the northward path, still restless, still snouting out ahead in search of he knew not what, with the others having now to follow his lead.

'It's getting colder by the moment!' said Madoc sometime later, eyeing the clear chill sky above them with concern. Anymole could tell that a spell of very cold weather was on the way, and that by the following morning, exposed ground such as they were crossing now would be too hard to tunnel for shelter and food.

But none of them needed a second telling. Whillan's earlier pace had scarcely slackened, but now with a new urgency he led them off once more, turning north by ways which went across pastureland and past occasional ploughed fields. The air grew still and colder, the

433

bright clear sky turned pale blue, and the only movement they saw was the occasional flapping of rooks on distant hedges and trees. Then Whillan slowed and let Maple take the lead again, almost as if he wanted to conserve his energies for another push later. He went back among the others, and all sensed something subtle had changed between him and Rooster, some unstated understanding been found.

Not until late in the afternoon, when the first ominous signs of white frost crystals appeared in some of the rutted earth they passed, did Maple see at last a possible safe haven – not that the others could see it at all.

But their route had taken them alongside a ploughed field which curved away to west and north, its furrows deep and its clods of earth great; not an easy place for mole to cross.

'You see that clump of trees beyond it all?' said Maple. The others nodded, mostly thinking that they were so tired they could happily stop right where they were. 'Well if you've got the energy . . .'

'We haven't,' said Weeth, 'but no doubt you'll convince us we need to find it.'

Maple grinned. 'It's just that Haulke, in his text on war, describes how a party of wounded Stone followers evaded imminent capture by crossing a ploughed field nomole would have expected them to cross. Well we can do the same now, and if a freeze does come down a few trees will give us just the shelter from the cold we need.'

He glanced at Whillan, to confirm it as the way he wanted to go too, and Whillan nodded briefly. Yes, yes, this was the way, it surely was.

To moles as tired as the party had become the rough ridges and furrows of the ploughed field were a grim prospect, but the promise of final shelter, and security, was an attractive one, and to continue over such nondescript country in the hope of finding something better had little appeal. So off they set, clambering over the clods of earth and helping each other on. They began by heading straight for the coppice of trees, but climbing up and down the steep furrows was so exhausting that they took the easier line along a furrow to get as near the trees as they could before crossing the ridges again.

They made slow progress and the only bit of comfort they found was when Rooster, who had not said another word since his support for Whillan's choice of route, stanced up when they were halfway to the wood and feeling they would never get there and said, 'Good place. Safe place. Like it, Privet!'

So on they went until with darkness all but on them, and the leafless trees turned to black silhouettes against the icy sky in which stars were already shining above on the far horizon as they reached the wood's edge. Whillan and Madoc scurried about seeking worms beneath the turned-up clods of earth on the ploughed land, while Maple and Weeth investigated the ground just inside the trees and found the soil beneath the old leaves and twigs soft enough to burrow. They quickly made some temporary burrows for the night, thinking that in the morning they could explore a bit. Provided the coppice was uninhabited by mole, they would be able to establish a proper system of tunnels in which they could stay in comfort for as long as they felt it necessary.

'It's wormful enough!' said Madoc, pointing at the worms she and Whillan had found.

'And it's off any route Newborns are likely to follow!' added Weeth.

'Well then,' said Maple, 'I suggest we eat and sleep, and when dawn comes everymole can go to sleep again if they want because we're going to rest. Except . . . it will be well if we maintain watches as we have done – not that I believe we will be followed at night over *that* field, but we don't know what's beyond the wood, and whether moles might be about.'

'Weeth, you can take first watch; Privet . . .' and so, quietly authoritative and sensible as ever, Maple organized them for the night and, their duties agreed, they settled down in a weary way to eat their food and crawl off thankfully to the burrows Maple and Weeth had prepared.

Before they did so Rooster said something strange, and Whillan responded with something stranger still.

'Six of us,' said Rooster a little gloomily.

'We'll need another for the Seven Stancing,' said Whillan, surprised at his own words.

Privet stared at them both, and at the dark sky, and sniffed at the air.

'I feel restless,' she said.

And suddenly they all did.

But the real restlessness came on them subtly, after they had munched their worms. Maple had again told all but the watcher to sleep and one by one they should have done, with a last glance about the benighted wood and at the starry sky beyond, and with a final stretch and yawn. How tempting a burrow would surely be, how companionable its close warm silence, broken only occasionally by a sniffle, or a scratch, or a snore.

But that strange night was only just beginning and it would be most accurate to say that one by one they failed to sleep. Whillan and Madoc went below to the communal burrow, hoping to find rest for a time, but lay in silence, not speaking to each other. Madoc tried to sleep, for she was very tired and her watch was much later – but she lay restless, her mind active, her eyes on the jagged round of sky she could see above her where she lay.

'Whillan . . .' she softly whispered. She had enjoyed searching out food with him, the first time they had done anything together since Caer Caradoc, since when, judging by his silence and ignoring of her, she had decided that he did not like her. Well, he could not possibly if he behaved like that! But this evening, why, he had been almost friendly, and once his paw had touched hers.

She liked Whillan, more than any mole she had ever known! Except for Privet – but that was different. She liked the way he looked, which was more interesting than the Newborn males she had known; she liked the way he frowned sometimes when he spoke; she liked the way he talked quickly and nervously – not to her, but to Weeth and Maple; she liked the way he showed no fear of the Newborns.

'I even like the way he got exasperated with Privet when she was being emotional in Caer Caradoc at the Convocation and passed her on to me to comfort!' said the sleepless Madoc to herself, liking the fact that she had been entrusted by one to care for the other, however briefly. 'But what don't I like about him?'

It was the way his eyes sometimes seemed to seek out the more distant prospect along the way, especially when the talk concerned moledom as a whole, or some distant part of it. It was plain that he really did want to travel, just as he said he would when they had talked briefly together in Caradoc. Well then, perhaps she could find a way of persuading him to stay . . .

Whillan, for all his general and inexplicable unease earlier in the day, had become acutely aware of Madoc's presence near him when they had been collecting the food, and later when they had all settled down together to eat it. His distress at whatever it was that nagged at him, gave way now to his consciousness of her, which grew more acute by the minute.

He tried now to work out if she was asleep or not. Her breathing was regular, and disconcertingly alluring to listen to, but occasionally her paws and body shifted. He stared up at the stars beyond the portal wishing he dared do what he most wanted to, which was to move nearer to her, right next to her, to *touch* her.

Up above he heard Maple laugh, and moles move, and his mind raced with disappointment at the prospect of others joining them and spoiling these moments.

'Madoc,' he wanted to whisper, 'I like you more than anymole I have ever met. Madoc, I want to talk to you. Madoc, I would like to feel your fur and flank against mine.'

So easy to say things silently, so hard even to start in reality. What *does* a mole say? Could he say anything now? If she was asleep she wouldn't hear, wouldn't know, so it wouldn't matter. 'Madoc, I'd like to be near you!' That would do. It would make him feel better just to say it. But . . . supposing she was awake? Well, he couldn't say it then. It was *difficult*.

'Whillan?' it was Maple from above. 'The others are restless and there's the brightest moon we've ever seen come out. Do you want—?'

Whillan yawned loudly and said, 'No thank you, I'm really tired, I mean—'

'And Madoc?'

'She's asleep, I think,' said Whillan hopefully.

'We'll not be far . . .' and Maple's voice and pawsteps faded away.

It was Madoc who broke the silence that followed, a silence in which poor Whillan felt his heart might burst from its thumping, and his chest explode from the way he felt himself holding his breath – why, he did not know.

'I'm not asleep,' said Madoc.

'Oh,' said Whillan, unsure what to do or say. 'I'm quite tired.'

'Oh,' said Madoc, disappointment in her voice.

'Does she want to talk?' Whillan asked himself in the dark, his heart still beating too hard and fast, and the sense of a missed opportunity looming near. What would Weeth have said?

'I'm not *that* tired,' Whillan said, suddenly inspired by Weeth.

'I'm restless,' said Madoc, her body rustling in the dark.

'I think I am too,' said Whillan, easing his body nearer to hers.

'Whillan?'

He realized she was nearer than he thought – *and moving closer*.

'Um, yes?' He moved too. And more.

'Are you really . . . I mean you said . . . well, um, Whillan . . .'

'It's, well, they said the moon . . . Madoc.'

They started back from each other when they first touched, the

437

disintegration of their thoughts well expressed by the reduction of their words to nothing but each other's names, and the discovery of that huge world of acceptance and warmth that exists for any two moles who dare reach out and find it in each other, when need and circumstance, and a moment's courage, permit them to.

Acceptance and . . . ? Love? Too soon for that word for two such moles, great though their need for it might then have been. It was enough that they touched, and held, and began the incoherent chatter of mutual discovery that is all the talk necessary to fulfil their new-found needs for now. But if the stars that shone through the leafless branches of the trees out on the surface did so more brightly after they touched, and if the light that came from those self-same stars and the moon grew brighter in their burrow, and shone in their eyes, let nomole be surprised.

Young love below, self-centred and blinded to all but itself – but none the worse, nor less real, for that. While up on the surface was old rediscovered love, there for others to see and stare at. For when night fell the moon had grown bright indeed, and it had been Privet who had said, when the younger ones had gone below, 'We'll keep you company for a time, Weeth, and you, Maple, for this is as beautiful a night as I remember in many a moleyear and I'll not sleep without a time for thoughts of the hard days we have been through.'

Then turning to Rooster, Privet had said, 'Will you come with us my dear, to the edge of the wood?'

'Will,' said Rooster, who had become more good-humoured and communicative by his standards ever since they had first seen the wood. 'Good place, *safe* place, we have come to.'

'That's more words than you've said in all the days past,' said Weeth cheerfully.

'Had nothing to say,' said Rooster, 'now may have. Whillan feels a need he does not understand. Is afraid of it, but I feel it and you feel it, Privet. Yes?'

'Yes,' she confessed, 'I do. It worries me.'

'Worries all of us.'

'Why did you need to say there were only six of us?'

'Like Whillan said: need one more. Hard night coming. Like storm building. Like terrible storm.'

Together the four moles felt their way slowly and silently to the edge of the wood – their quietness as much to do with the respect and reverence they felt for the way the rising moon caught the trees in its clear cold light, as to any fear of being detected. They settled down, the air so still and cold that the silvery trees above them were utterly silent but for the occasional creak of ancient branch, or nearby fall of withered leaf or tiny twig which had survived the autumn winds only to tumble in this time of holy quiet.

For holy it seemed to become, as the moon rose higher, and every battered remnant of grass, or torn bramble, and ploughed clod of earth in the field they had crossed and over which they now gazed was caught by moonlight, and slowly gaining a covering of frost. While further away they could see almost more clearly than by day the dark rise of the wooded hill up which, had they so chosen, their route might have taken them.

The air was very cold, and now the leaf-litter in the grass where they had stanced down was stiff and crackly with frost. Their breath was white in the night, and the stars bright, clear and innumerable as far as eyes could see.

It was the kind of night which a mole contemplates in silence for a time, especially if after travelling far and doing much that is difficult and dangerous, he has found a safe haven. Having done that, and collected his thoughts, and if the company is of like mind, it was also a night to talk of memories and things that matter, and wish well of old friends who are far away.

'I wonder,' said Privet quietly when the moment felt right to talk, 'what Fieldfare is doing tonight, and where she is?'

'Aye,' whispered Maple sadly, thinking of Chater. Then, quite suddenly he knew what she was doing, as if she was there at his flank. 'She's watching the sky. She's wondering like us. She's . . . restless.'

'I think she may know she will not see him again,' said Privet, not fully aware of how strange Maple now felt. 'Those two knew each other as a right paw knows its left.'

'Don't know Fieldfare,' said Rooster, contemplating his own misshapen paws, 'and don't know if left knows right! Doubt it! But know tonight we can't sleep yet. Nor mustn't.'

There was such rueful good humour in the way he spoke, staring quizzically at them in the moonlight, that the others could not but smile.

'Would you like us to tell you about Fieldfare and Chater?' asked Privet.

'No,' said Rooster, 'tell about Duncton. There, it is. There tonight we'll send our thoughts. Now. Must.'

He looked up and around at Privet and gazed into her eyes, worried, determined.

439

Watching them, Weeth, and perhaps Maple too, realized how shy he was with her, and how tender she with him. But more than that, Weeth saw they had a mutual trust as palpable and strong as a tree's greatest root. This was no great surprise to him, for he had guessed as much from what he had heard before about Privet and Rooster's past history. But to Maple the surprise lay in seeing Privet with another male in this way, for he had only known her mateless; but here she was, her voice tender, her severe face softened by an inner contentment, her manner easy.

If only he himself did not feel restless and uneasy. First Whillan, then Rooster, then Privet, if he kenned her right, now he himself.

'Weeth,' he whispered while the other two talked softly for a time to each other, 'if it doesn't seem a strange question, how do you feel tonight?'

Weeth looked at him, the light of the night sky on his face, which was serious and unsmiling.

'How do I feel? I've been asking myself that question since the afternoon, since Whillan went strange. Well, I'll tell you: I feel terrified tonight, that's how I feel. Something isn't right.'

'No,' said Maple.

The other two had fallen silent, and they now came closer.

'Not right,' said Rooster, echoing Weeth's words.

'Maple,' said Privet suddenly, 'go and get Whillan and Madoc now. Go and get them quickly.'

'Why, mole, what is it?' asked Maple, stancing up.

'Whillan will know, he must know. We all feel something's wrong but he felt it most of all. Get him, my dear.'

Maple was soon back. 'They're on their way,' he said, his grin indicating that he had disturbed their tryst. But . . . 'Whillan was half expecting it, I think. It just needed somemole to remind him.'

Moments later Whillan and Madoc came hurrying to join them.

'What is it?' they asked, a little shy.

'We're not sure,' said Privet, 'but something's wrong, somewhere.'

Whillan peered up into the starry sky, he stared at the silvery leaves on the branches above their heads, he looked around at his friends, and then reached a paw momentarily to Madoc's. He took one step and then another beyond the edge of the wood and into the open, turning a little so that he faced south-east.

The air was bitterly cold now, and deathly still.

'It's Duncton Wood,' he whispered. 'It's not still there, not peaceful at all! It needs us; Duncton needs all of us. It needs us *now!*'

Chapter Thirty-Two

It was the third evening after Pumpkin had been so savagely hauled off to the Marsh End by the Newborn guards, and it was the grimmest of Sturne's life. He waited now in that shadowed and cursed place that lies beyond the trees a little to the north-east of the Marsh End. The night was already cold and foul, and promised to grow worse, for dusk had settled on a livid blizzard sky, and the winds cut through a mole's fur and chilled his heart.

'All the better for what I must do!' said Sturne through gritted teeth, trying to encourage himself. 'All to the good!'

He crouched invisible among the rotting weeds and freezing wet of the Marsh itself, trying his best to keep clear of the oozy puddles of water all about. Yet there was worse than that. For scattered around him were pathetic humps and unrecognizable remains of moles 'made eliminate' by the Newborns, some by order of the Brother Inquisitors no doubt, others not. This was the Newborns' killing ground and here on a hunch, a guess, and a prayer, Sturne had come in a last bid to save the life of his first, his oldest and his only friend, library aide Pumpkin.

Somewhere behind him the roaring owl way ran, with its rumbles and roars, and its occasional yellow gazes of the owls, and the reds of their disappearing tails. Sometimes a gaze cut over his head and the dank pasture's humps and hollows loomed in the lurid light for a few moments, before it swept on. Beyond the Pasture the Wood's edge rose black and ragged against the sky, shifting a little in the erratic and violent wind.

'He should be there by now,' whispered Sturne to himself, 'I pray that he is there.'

'He' was the young follower Cluniac, and that night he was a most frightened mole, his teeth chattering with apprehension and fear as much as from the cold. He was not a Marsh End mole, and its unfamiliar shapes and sounds by night, quite apart from its evil reputation since the Newborns had come, unnerved him. Yet here he was, and wondering why, and what it was he was going to have to do as he stared out across the Pasture at the evil Marsh.

Earlier that day, as the afternoon darkened suddenly and cooled towards the blizzard storms that lingered in the sky above them, waiting to descend, he had been in the Library, trying to fulfil what tasks he was set. But his mind, like those of most moles who had been involved in the extraordinary scenes by the Stone on Longest Night, was upon the life, and imminent death, of Pumpkin, aide and hero.

The mole who had served the Master Stour to the end, and so given up his life to the Newborns, was to die tonight. He had been dragged down the communal tunnels into Barrow Vale, and there beaten and as good as tortured in front of moles like Cluniac and his mother Elynor, who were forced to watch. How weak and hurt he had looked, how unlike a hero! Yet he took his punishment nobly, staring into the eyes of his tormentors as long as he could, blood coming from his snout, one eye swelling, but always trying to rise again.

It had been the most terrible thing Cluniac had ever seen; he had never hated a mole until he had been made to watch Brother Inquisitor Barre raise his talons to Pumpkin and begin the 'punishment'. No doubt it was meant to intimidate the followers watching, though it only made most of them more angry, and even more determined to resist; but it was useless to try to intervene, for guardmoles had been drafted in from their posts on the periphery of the Wood and down by the cross-under expressly for the purpose of preventing further revolt. Then Pumpkin was taken away, and the moles told to go to their own burrows and not leave them on pain of death.

The next day, morning and evening, it was the same: Pumpkin dragged up from the cells in the Marsh End, tormented, abused, hurt, yet not so much that he would not be fit enough to suffer again on the morrow . . . and the followers forced to watch, and then retire.

The day after that Cluniac avoided the morning spectacle by dint of going off to the Library to work earlier than was his custom. He saw that once he was past the guardmoles about Barrow Vale there were fewer than usual along the higher tunnels, and the Library was almost deserted. Except for Keeper Sturne, in his usual foul mood, and other aides who, like Cluniac, had the idea of coming early.

Then, sometime in the afternoon, somemole, and Cluniac did not know who, had placed a brief and startling text amongst the folios where he was working. How, or when, he had no idea.

'Cluniac,' it kenned, 'if you valew the lives of those followers who have faith in the Stone, reddy them for escape this evening. Speak to nomol. Alert all you can and all you trust. Then wait amongst the trees by the far corner of the Marsh End, and have faith. Pumpkin may come. Save him. Save the others. Save yrself.'

Cluniac stared at this strange missive with doubt and suspicion. The tortured, spindly scribing he did not recognize at all, and it was obviously by the paw of an ill-trained scribe for it was ill-spelt, and ill-placed on the bark. 'Speak to nomol . . .' it said, but that was precisely what Cluniac did as soon as he could escape the Library without causing suspicion, and return downslope to Barrow Vale.

He showed the scribbled bark to his mother Elynor, who could not ken at all.

'Repeat it again,' she said, and he did. 'Well?' she asked.

'It's a trick,' said Cluniac.

Elynor placed her paw on the bark and bid Cluniac put his paw to hers.

'Close your eyes, mole, forget your fears, and have courage to believe what you feel. Well?'

'I feel . . . it tells the truth.'

'Aye,' concurred Elynor, nodding her head slowly, 'so do I. If the Newborns had identified you as the mole who alerted us all on Longest Night do you think they would have let you roam free since? Or entrusted you with this?'

He shook his head. On Longest Night the Newborn guard had rounded him up, but he had later escaped when Pumpkin ordered him to run for help, before the guardmole had a chance to ask his name.

'No, you'd already be in the Marsh End cells with poor Pumpkin. And by the by, Pumpkin wasn't brought up to Barrow Vale this evening, which does suggest they're going to kill him tonight. But whatever mole sent you this knows he can trust you, which means he's more likely to be a follower, or a follower's friend, than anything else. Well then, we must act on it. But so far as the others are concerned we know what to do, don't we?'

Cluniac nodded, his eyes wide, his breathing tight, but determined to do what he must.

'Mole, your father would have been proud of you. You're still young for all this, but when the Stone calls us to its aid we must answer its call, whatever age we are. Now listen, the plans Drubbins and I made molemonths ago before he was killed must now be acted on.'

So they had gone about the tunnels adjacent to Barrow Vale, Elynor as far as the Westside, and Cluniac to the Eastside, whispering to

443

moles they knew: 'This night; it is to be this night! Prepare, be careful, and get to the right place in time!'

Then, that dangerous work done, Cluniac had taken advantage of some guardmole bullying in Barrow Vale to slip away like a shadow in the dusk to make his way down to the edge of the Marsh End trees, and wait. He was worried for himself, for his mother who had become unofficial leader of the secret followers since the murder of Drubbins in November, and for those brave moles, mainly elderly, who he knew would do their best to muster as had long been arranged, and seek to flee the murderous talons of the Newborns in one last bid to escape the punishment and death that now, it seemed, was inevitable.

Another yellow gaze from the distant roaring owls broke across the sky, and swept over the Marsh and the Pasture in front of Cluniac. Behind him he heard various sounds and knew moles were coming. He shrank down deeper into the dank leaf-litter where he hid. He heard voices, harsh commands, swearing, and four moles came right past him to break clear of the Wood and go out on to the Pasture.

A roaring owl gaze swept over them, and briefly and starkly, Cluniac saw Brother Inquisitor Barre leading the group, two large Newborns behind him supporting a third mole between them: Pumpkin.

'Hurry up, you blaspheming bastard,' one of them growled at Pumpkin, "'cos we're getting cold. We want to get rid of you as fast as we can.'

'Shut up,' said Barre ahead of them. 'I can't see for hearing you talk.'

From Pumpkin there came not a sound.

'They *are* going to kill him!' thought Cluniac desperately, and to his credit he gave serious consideration to trying to charge the whole lot of them and getting Pumpkin to safety.

'The Shtone's guided me all my life,' said Pumpkin suddenly, though with a slurry voice, 'and it w . . . will guide me now.' He sounded a weak but purposeful mole, not easily broken.

'There's no bloody Stone where you're going, chum,' said one of the guardmoles.

'Nor any "Shtone" either,' said the other mockingly, which provoked Barre and the other one to break into cruel laughter. Another yellow gaze briefly lit up the scene; finding his line to the Marsh's edge, Barre led the others on as Cluniac watched in utter misery, a chill of fear and horror rising along his spine.

'I must wait, I must hope, I must pray,' he whispered, but no words of prayer came to him.

Yet, beyond his vision, and all unknown to him, Sturne mouthed words in the reeds and muck where he lay shivering. He had seen the coming of Barre, and hoped it would be Pumpkin they were leading here. If it was not . . . but it must be!

For that morning Brother Inquisitor Fetter had confided that 'this evening the mole Pumpkin will be executed for crimes against the Stone; and the miscreants who infect Barrow Vale shall be finally punished.'

It was what had decided Sturne to act, after two nights and days of personal agony since Pumpkin had been hauled away, and his public punishment had begun. What to do? Sturne had had no idea, knowing that almost anything he did would probably not save Pumpkin's life, and would reveal to the Brother Inquisitors that he himself had been deceiving them. It seemed a dilemma impossible to resolve.

Then, that same day, Sturne had been waylaid by the mole Elynor, an old friend of Drubbins, and certainly a follower. Bravely, risking her life for all she knew, given that Sturne was known to have switched to Newborn ways, she had tried to invoke in him loyalties to Duncton.

'For the Stone's sake, sir, if you have any pity in your heart, try to put a word in for Pumpkin,' she had said, and more; all of it as brave, as true, as inspiring, as any words he had ever heard mole speak.

But after all of it, unable to give himself away, he had had to shake his head and say, 'Mole, the most I'll say is this: these are hard times for us all. You're under stress, you're not yourself, and so for the memory of Drubbins, a worthy but misguided mole but one who was your friend, I'll forget you spoke to me. Justice must be done! Moles who deserve it must be punished.'

'My, but you're a hard, cruel mole, Keeper Sturne!' she had cried at him. 'Your words wither a mole's heart, and I care nothing for your discretion. If I can't raise my voice for a mole as good and true and loyal as Library Aide Pumpkin then what is the liberty that our ancestors fought for in this very wood a century ago? Damn your smugness! Drubbins had more good in him, more kindness, than you can even begin to think about!'

When she had gone Sturne muttered to himself, 'Like mother, like son! Aye, the Stone spoke to me through her. There may be a way, there may be a way . . .'

Hopeful for the first time in days he had gone back to the Library, his mind racing with ideas.

'"Your words wither a mole's heart" she said,' he muttered to himself. 'Well, so they may do, so they can do. There's a way, but where's the text to be found? Eh? And how . . . ?'

He had scribed the missive for Cluniac to find, disguising his paw as best he could to preserve his cover. Then he had searched through such texts on ancient liturgy as the Inquisitors had allowed to be preserved in the Library and found even as dusk deepened the brief passage he wanted.

It was in an obscure and rarely used part of the Library, near the tunnels of the Ancient System itself. He heard the roar of alien wind-sound and knew the weather to be worsening. The Ancient System was angry, its Dark Sound rising, its mood threatening.

'Like mine!' said Sturne aloud, finally taking down the text he had sought. 'Oh yes, like mine! And here it is, here's what I need.'

He opened the text wider, ran his right paw over it and turned a page, and he peered long and hard, kenning as quickly as he could.

'Yes . . .' he whispered fiercely, 'oh yes . . . the ancient liturgy of Exorcism. Ha! This will make them fear the wrath of the Stone. This will make them show the whites of their eyes!'

Sturne sounded positively cheerful for a moment – until he started kenning the text aloud, and his voice carried up into the dim reaches of the deep-delved heights of the chamber above him, and down the dark forgotten ways of the tunnels that led into the Ancient System itself. He sounded savage and cruel.

'Vengeful Stone,' he kenned, 'the evil Snake of possession entwines this mole's heart! Thrust thy talon fiercely into it, wound it, and rip it out from its nest! Aye . . .'

Sturne paused, blinked and frowned and speaking in a very different voice said, 'Of course, there may be more than one of them. I must remember to say "These moles" rather than "This mole" if that is the case. Now where had I got to . . . ?'

Then he continued as before, except that his voice was louder, and he even raised a paw in declamatory style to help himself along. 'Fasten thy wrath upon this evil spirit that mocks thy good, and destroys thy harmony! Seek its nestlings where they creep and crawl, rot them, break them, make their skin peel and their eyes bulge and their—Humph!' exclaimed Sturne, interrupting himself again, 'this is just a little extreme. I'm sure there was something more . . . more coldly savage. That's what I want. Ah! Aaah! Yessss . . . the terrifying liturgy of Commination, which expresses the Stone's anger against sinners. This'll make their talons drop off and their snouts droop!'

He had found what he wanted, and the sibilant hiss of his final and

446

gratified 'yessss . . . !' wound away and grew fat and horrid in the dark tunnels about him as he kenned in silence the Commination he would use that very night.

'This very night! Here and now! Yes, yes, I must try to remember,' Sturne muttered to himself as, repeating the words he had learnt for what felt like the thousandth time, he saw the moles come out of the wood and cross the Pastures, straight towards where he lay.

'Oh Pumpkin,' he whispered as a yellow gaze caught the limping, wan form of his friend between the guards as he was brought to meet his end. To be killed, to be hurled in here among these reeds, to be left to rot, forgotten in this Stone-forsaken place – except that it was not Stone-forsaken. Sturne was there, nervous no more, his just anger mounting, the words he had learnt needing no more rehearsal, for they were ready now, ready and waiting for these murderous foul-minded moles of an evil sect.

Sturne watched, angry but in complete possession of himself, waiting for the right moment. He glanced briefly beyond them to the wood's edge and could only hope that Cluniac would be ready and waiting there. He knew he himself could not be seen, for being a disciplined and thorough mole he had stanced roughly where he expected the Newborns to come and stared towards the reeds where he now crouched. He had watched, he had seen how the shadows looked all the more dark and impenetrable for the ever-changing lights of the roaring owl way east of them, and he had worked out precisely what to do. He had guessed that they would not kill Pumpkin until they reached the edge of the reeds – otherwise they would have had to carry his body across the Pasture. Yes, yes, that was what they would do, wait until they were right up to the very edge.

Yet it took nerve to wait, since he could see them more and more clearly and they appeared to be looking straight at him. He could only stare, be still, and prepare himself. Timing was of the essence. Too early, and they would have time to recover themselves, and his bluff might be called, and he and Pumpkin both lost. Too late, and Pumpkin might have suffered the fatal blow. He presumed that that was how they killed moles – a few swift blows to the head and snout, and . . .

'Wait here!' He heard the familiar and unwelcome voice of Brother Barre. 'I'll find a good spot.' Barre approached yet nearer, splashing about, swearing, peering at the ground, until, a little to Sturne's left, he declared, 'This'll do. Bring him here.'

The voice was a growl, almost dispassionate. Sturne watched as the two guardmoles, who now seemed huge beside Pumpkin, almost carried him to where Barre stanced impatiently.

'Come on, come on, we have other sinners to chastise tonight! And females to enjoy!'

The cold about the Marsh was bitter, the dark deep, the lights of the roaring owls sinister and strange; Sturne, so near to the real sinners of the night he could almost touch them, felt ice in his heart. 'Other sinners to chastise tonight' Barre had said, and 'females to enjoy'. Aye, tonight was the night of rapine, bloody talons, tonight . . .

'Are you going to bother with the intercession, sir,' said one of the guards,' or shall we just do it?'

'Oh–Stone–we–commend–to–thy–everlasting–mercy–our–most– miserable–miscreant–Pumpkin,' said Barre, the words spoken so quickly and meaninglessly that they melded into each other. 'Now do it!'

'May the Shtone forgive you!' cried out Pumpkin.

'Fuck forgiveness!' said the other guard, and with one violent movement he and his colleague grabbed Pumpkin, raised him off his paws and upended him snout first into the murky black ooze at their paws before Sturne could guess what they were doing.

Not a taloning, but a drowning in mud: silent, but for the victim's desperate splashing, and cruel. Everymole's nightmare.

There was a distant roar behind them across the Marsh, and the yellow gaze of a roaring owl swept its slow way round, nearer and nearer to where they stanced, and Sturne knew the moment had come; now or never.

As the gaze of light shone finally from directly behind him he rose out of the reeds and in a deep and powerful voice, with one paw raised as he pointed his talons at Barre, he began the terrible liturgy of the Commination, the ancient statement made by Holy Moles which expresses the Stone's anger and judgement against extreme sinners who have gone beyond normal redemption: '*Brethren, seeing that here stance three moles that are accursed in that they do err and go astray from the commandments of the Stone, let the talons of thy spirit stab them; let the talons of thy mind pierce them; let the talons of thy wrathful love destroy them!*

'*It is a fearful thing to witness such wickedness as these cursed moles, and in particular this Brother Inquisitor Barre, do practise here, and now, before us. Aye, brethren, fearful though it is yet we must pierce and stab and destroy the Snakes of evil that entwine them,* and have made them internally foul and beyond the forgiveness of living mole . . .'

His voice was a most fearful thing indeed, and stanced above them (as he seemed) and speaking out of the darkness of the Marsh and the light of the gazes of the roaring owls, a mole might have thought that he was the voice of many brethren gathered and advancing there. To add to the effect he trod his paws ominously into the plashy ooze about him so that it sounded as if many moles were advancing.

Certainly the two Newborn guards seemed to think so, for they let go of Pumpkin, who rose out of the mud and water spluttering and gasping, and fell back on to drier land, leaving Barre alone. He, it must be said, was not as immediately impressed by Sturne as his minions in murder, but mention of his name by this mole that seemed (and sounded) more than ordinary mole shook him. Then as Sturne's words of the Commination continued like some rapidly advancing storm of thunder and lightning across the sky, Barre too fell back.

It helped that the night was bitter and increasingly turbulent and that rushes of wind rattled and shook the reeds, making the black form of Sturne seem all the more substantial.

Thou art accursed in the Stone for that the Snakes are in thy bodies, feeding upon thy pride, thy spiritual sloth, thy indulgence and unpurged by any true faith, or love, or charity. Therefore . . .'

And by now Sturne was a terrifying sight, the very image of the Stone's wrath, so that Pumpkin, now nearest him, was himself terrified, staring up at his friend and not recognizing him at all. Indeed, he had never much liked the Marsh End, though he had always dismissed stories of the fell spirits and dark phantoms that lurked thereabout as mere fancy. But not any more, never again, definitely not!

Sturne advanced upon the mute and transfixed Pumpkin and putting one paw about his shoulders turned him to face his would-be murderers, while with the other he thrust his talon towards the three hapless Newborns, and Barre in particular.

'This good Brother Pumpkin is forgiven his sins, but you are cursed in yours. Be gone! Be gone lest the wrath of the Stone visit you here and now in this place made accursed by your own pride and blasphemies. Be . . .'

Sturne was about to utter a third, and, he hoped, last 'Be gone', but was thinking that if they did not go they might very soon guess who he was, and what he was about. The two guards seemed very ready indeed to be gone, and were looking fearfully at each other

449

and at Barre as if to encourage the Brother Inquisitor to give them permission to flee.

But even as Sturne uttered the word 'Be . . .' he sensed that something more than declamation was now needed, and he wished he knew what it was. Perhaps he sent an intercessionary prayer to the Stone on his own behalf, perhaps Pumpkin did the same; however it was, the fillip that was needed to turn Barre's irresolution into outright fear and panicky flight came just when it was needed.

For suddenly there came from behind the Newborns, and not far behind, a most piercing and terrifying scream, so that Sturne's 'Be gone' was, as it were, emphasized as if by some power greater even than the terrifying thing he himself had become.

The scream was loud, potent, deep, and infinitely sinister – and it was one that the resourceful young Cluniac had often utilized to good effect against his siblings on a dark night.

'No!' cried one of the guardmoles, and it was the only word all three of them said: 'No!'

And they were off along the Pasture, away from the Accusing Brother of the Marsh, and to avoid the fearful thing that shrieked and screamed from out of the Wood itself; away, away as fast as their paws could carry them, and none faster, none more afraid, none more stumblingly, terrifyingly panic-stricken than Brother Barre himself.

Meanwhile, nearly murdered, now frightened out of his wits, Pumpkin felt inclined to sag down into the wet ground, and cover his eyes and ears with his paws.

'Pumpkin!' cried out Sturne, still thoroughly carried away by the role he was playing, and the power of a liturgy he had half invented. 'Flee now to the wood!'

'Er . . . *there?*' panted Pumpkin, still not recognizing Sturne, but not wishing to go rushing off to where unearthly screams came from.

'Here!' called out Cluniac. 'Quick!'

'I mean . . .' muttered Pumpkin, confused, afraid, shocked, and wondering what else could happen that night.

But Sturne was in charge and knew what he must do.

'Be gone!' he said, now sounding like some avuncular Holy Mole speaking to an errant Brother at fabled Uffington.

'Well . . .' said Pumpkin, at last beginning to move.

'Come *on!*' shouted Cluniac. The sudden scream having worked, Cluniac now wanted to get away as soon as possible.

Pumpkin did manage to take a few steps back on to the Pasture, but he paused yet again, and turning, said, 'But whatmole are you?'

450

A roaring owl gaze swept their way; Sturne turned a little into it, his face bearing an uncharacteristic smile. 'I am your friend, your good friend. Now be gone, lest Cluniac comes forth and discovers who I am.'

'Sturne . . .' said Pumpkin softly, understanding everything, and imagining in a flash how all of it had been – Sturne's worry, Sturne's determination, and Sturne's solution. At that moment Pumpkin's affection for his oldest companion turned to abiding love: never could a mole have a truer friend than he. Pumpkin felt his limbs begin to tremble, he felt the cold thrust of the wind, he felt his whole body tired and broken, and he knew that if he did not go now, he never would be gone!

'Sturne,' he said affectionately, 'you fooled even me!'

'Fooled myself!' said Sturne wryly. 'Now, go with Cluniac and he will know where to take you. Head for the Stone and from there enter the Ancient System by the tunnel that leads from the Chamber of Roots, which you already know. It is the only hope for you all. Now, I too must go,' and Sturne retreated back into the Marsh, and where he had been only reeds fretted and freezing water splashed.

Pumpkin ran and staggered and stumbled upslope to Cluniac, who reached out a paw from the cover of the wood and guided him quickly and with barely a word in among the trees, and away.

While across the Pastures where the moles had been murdered the first harsh streaks of blizzard snow came down and raced over the grass, and lost themselves in the killing ground that was the Marsh.

Chapter Thirty-Three

Snow of a different kind fell at the coppice where Privet and the others had gathered hushed and worried at the trees' edge. Light, tiny flecks from out of the still night air, and but momentarily.

'It's going to be a bitter night,' observed Weeth, eyeing the branches of the trees above them, which now stirred occasionally, and uneasily. 'But if a wind gets up there'll be a blizzard yet.'

'Duncton's troubled,' whispered Whillan, who had said little since his first declaration that his home system was in need. 'We must be able to help, somehow.'

'What to do? We must wait,' said Rooster. 'Stone knows.'

'Stone does know,' exclaimed Weeth ironically, 'even if I don't. This place is strange, but what you moles are saying is stranger still.'

'Not strange,' said Rooster.

'Waiting,' whispered Whillan.

Rooster nodded and said, 'Yes. Stone is waiting here. We wait, it decides.'

'Decides what?' asked Weeth, exasperated, and looking at Maple for some support. The moonlight touched Maple's face and he shrugged as if to say, 'Don't ask me! Leave it to them!'

Weeth sighed and settled down for what looked like a long wait for something nomole could name.

'Was Longest Night, the night you took me from Caer Caradoc. Wasn't it!' said Rooster suddenly, turning to Maple.

'For some,' said Maple grimly.

'All the spring years, all the summer years, all the autumn years I thought of that Longest Night. I looked towards it thinking, "Rooster will try to be free by then. Of darkness. Of need. Rooster will not run more. Rooster will be free." Never thought I would be needed on Longest Night. But now not sure.'

He was silent, the deep furrows on his face like rockfalls down a snowy void in the moonlight, and his eyes rugged impenetrable caverns of darkness. Maple and Weeth exchanged a glance, and Privet moved closer to him. It was clear he wanted to talk.

452

'But not to be. Newborns' journey to Caradoc was journey into new darkness. Caught and put into captivity. My friends, because of me. What friends? Most dead. All gone. Hamble, Hamble.'

'He's *safe*, Rooster, I told you that. He wanted no more violence so he is going to Duncton Wood. It has always been a sanctuary for moles like us who have lost their home burrow and cannot return. It was for me. It will be for him. It could be for you.'

'But Longest Night! You lost that because of me. It went by and we never knew. That day I confessed to all those moles, but did they hear? Now is second chance.'

'*We* heard,' said Weeth with a grin. This kind of talk made more sense to him.

'You're good, you are,' said Rooster, laughing suddenly and buffeting Weeth in a rough way.

'You did confess, my dear, and many more moles heard you than you might think. I was not the only one to hear your . . . despair.'

'It is that,' said Rooster. 'Confusion, like when you're searching for the right delving line but cannot find it, or hear it. Only in your mind. There it's beautiful, there it's clear, there it's everything. Then your paw tries to find it and cannot and makes something less, and something dies. In you. In here!' He thumped his huge chest and looked disappointed in himself.

'But what's it feel like when you get the delving right?' asked Maple. They all looked at Rooster with interest, and he stared at the ghostly ground, and then ran the talons of his right paw into the grass.

'Haven't delved for long time and said I never would again. But now, tonight, here, may have to. The need's growing all the time. Whillan feels it. All may need us.'

'But you remember how to delve?' said Weeth.

Rooster nodded and said slowly, his face softening a little, 'Once travelling with Hamble I woke at dawn. Went out. On a valley side looking down at the river that was there the evening before but was gone now, the water, the banks, the pasture, gone beneath a layer of mist. There was sun and in the distance there were trees. Thought, "I'm glad I've left the Moors, glad to see this, glad to be alive to know this beauty." Then out of the mist, slowly, came the wings of a heron flap-flapping up towards me. Grey wings out of white, slow but sure, power out of strength. Out of that white nothing it came beneath which was the river I could not see but knew was there, and the grass I journeyed across the day before, and all the earth, which was lost that morning. Up and out came the heron, its great wings stirring the mist and then rising into sun, and then it was clear into the day and going forward, going on, certain, sure, a flight from a nothing I knew existed to a future I had to believe was there. That is what a delving is, that is what it feels like when it's true. Only the Stone could make it be, for delving begins and ends in the Stone's Silence, which begins in the past, is in the now, and will be in the future. And tonight. Whillan?'

Whillan looked at him expectantly.

'Tonight you must obey. Know you don't like me. Know you don't like love of Privet and me. Know anger when I see it. But tonight moledom's more important than you or me. Tonight you obey. Understand?'

'But to do what?' asked Whillan.

Rooster shrugged. 'Don't know. Delve, probably.'

'I can't delve,' said Whillan, 'but I can scribe!'

Rooster laughed. 'Oh yes, you *can* delve. Good that you don't know how, will do it better. First time can delve out of innocence. After that it's difficult. You must obey. Tell him, Privet.'

'I think he understands, Rooster.'

Rooster growled, frowned and fell silent, but the others did not speak for it was plain enough he wanted to say more.

'That was spring I saw the heron. And that was the day I started to look forward to Longest Night, praying to the Stone to bring me to it free of what I was in, which was darkness. But was not to be. We were escaping on Longest Night. Didn't pause for thought or prayer. The Longest Night when all would change went past without a thought. Stone did not hear my prayer.'

'Didn't it, my love?' said Privet, reaching her paw without embarrassment to his.

'She knew me before,' said Rooster. 'Privet saw me delve when I could. Do you remember those days, long, long ago?'

Privet nodded but could say nothing.

'She came to Hilbert's Top, and that was the Stone's answer to my prayer too. The Stone *does* answer prayers but a mole cannot say when or where or how. He must wait. He must go into the darkness where no answers are. He must wait. I prayed for her up on Hilbert's Top and she came. Like I prayed for Longest Night but the Stone did not answer. I have sinned. Now the Stone begins to answer. It says it needs me to delve, but I need another. Whillan will help.'

'Are you so sure you'll delve again, and tonight?' whispered Privet.

'Longest Night was a time of *missing*. But with you there was

454

Longest Night. Up on Hilbert's Top before darkness of my killing Ratcher, before that. Do you remember what we did, Privet?'

'You held me all night my love, so close.'

'You remember?'

'I remember everything.'

'We were happy then. But now . . .'

'I'm here. And Longest Night . . .'

'I remember it like yesterday. Cannot forget, not ever.'

'It can be again.'

He shook his great head and said, 'A mole can't delve today what he didn't delve yesterday.'

Privet said, 'Not the same, no, but maybe better! Look at the trees behind us! Look at the stars above! Look at moledom stretching away beyond us in the moonlight. If we had been here on Longest Night what would we have seen? Not as much as now!'

'Some,' growled Rooster unconvinced. 'Would have seen you, Privet!' He grinned.

'Not so clearly,' responded Privet, laughing.

'Sshh . . .' said Maple softly.

'Yes . . .' whispered Weeth, turning round sharply and peering into the wood. 'Sshh . . . it seems to be . . .'

'Mole,' said Rooster.

'Yes,' said Whillan with sudden eagerness, 'it sounds like mole. Need . . . we need . . .'

'The seventh you said,' said Rooster, 'yes?'

Whillan nodded though he did not quite know why. But he felt suddenly relieved and wondered why Weeth and Maple looked so concerned. Couldn't they tell what they could hear heralded completion, not danger? And if they could not, how could he? He looked at Madoc in wonder and she came closer.

'What is it, my love?' she asked.

'Don't know,' said Whillan. 'Something. Something important's beginning. Here and now.'

'You sound like Rooster!' she whispered with a giggle. Whillan nodded seriously, unsurprised. He felt something like him too. He wondered where his anger had gone.

The sounds, which had faded for a few moments, were suddenly louder and they all turned towards them. What they heard were snatches of a song, and a cheerful one too. The voice, though cracked, was tuneful, and it was getting nearer.

'Humph!' said Maple, irritated to have their evening disturbed, but not overly concerned. This did not seem like a patrol of Newborns advancing to attack.

'There's probably an isolated community here,' he whispered, 'though why they are out singing on a night like this Stone knows. Not much point all of us hiding. Privet, you and Rooster had best keep out of sight.'

Rooster laughed and shook his head. 'Said it was a good place and it is. One mole won't harm us.'

'Might be more.'

'Not moving,' said Rooster firmly. 'Stopped running when we got here.' Privet nodded her agreement and Maple sighed and began to wish he had a force of disciplined moles to command, not these individualists.

The voice fell silent and they heard the rustle of undergrowth as the mole – if there were more than one they were very quiet – moved from inside the wood to its edge, some way south of them. Then there was complete silence for a time and then the muttering of the voice before it broke into what was evidently the same song again, and began moving steadily nearer. The words were now quite clear, the melody lively and rhythmic; the voice now quite obviously that of a mature male.

> *Followers awake, salute this happy night,*
> *Wherein the seasons' turn does turn again!*
> *Rise to adore the mystery of the Stone,*
> *Which waits now to hear your voice join mine.*
> *Hark to its call, sing out our song,*
> *For now is the glorious time of Longest Night.*
>
> *Followers awake, salute . . .'*

As this last repetition began the singer finally came into view, and since, for no obvious reason, he was moving backwards, he naturally did not see the six moles looming in the moonlight. He simply continued for a line or two more, and while singing he beat the ground with one or other of his front paws: '. . . this happy night, (bang!), Wherein the seasons' (bang!) turn does turn again (bang bang!).'

At this natural break he paused, glanced behind him to see where he was going, and found himself peering first at Maple's paws, then at his chest, and then up into his eyes. The mole froze, looked away, shook his head as if he did not believe what he had seen, and repeating the last words he had sung simply as speech he said, 'Does turn again

456

– was that a mole I saw? A large mole? Let us turn like the seasons and look.'

He slowly turned once more and looked first at Maple, then one by one at the others, his eyes growing ever wider in astonishment as he did so, though otherwise he appeared absolutely calm.

Finally, just as Maple was about to greet him, he said with considerable aplomb, 'Tell me, do you wish to be within or without?'

They stared at him blankly.

'Within what?' asked Privet.

'The stomp,' said the mole.

'The stomp?' repeated Maple and Weeth with one breath.

'Oh . . . ,' began Privet, her expression and voice conveying dawning understanding, 'so that's what you're doing. Stomping.'

'Well yes, of course,' said the mole. 'Sensible moles like me do not normally go backwards through a wood at night singing an unfamiliar song and stomping the ground with their paws. One must, however, maintain the traditions. Evidently, madam, *you* at least are aware of them.'

'You're stomping the bounds,' said Privet with some excitement. 'I have only heard of the custom from my kenning of Rhymes and Tales – but I thought it was a north-eastern tradition.'

'So it may have been, so it may!' said the mole, who spoke in a quick, light voice, which matched the way his eyes danced here and there among them. He was thin of fur and body but sprightly enough, his face being lined and full of expression, mainly benign. He had seen perhaps four Longest Nights through, or five with the one just past, but he was young of mind and spirit.

'Would one of you enlighten us?' said Weeth.

'Well,' said Privet, 'I had thought stomping the bounds was a tradition of Longest Night, but—'

'That's right, it is,' said the mole. 'To demarcate a mole's territory prior to joining with the community and celebrating Longest Night.'

'But tonight is not Longest Night,' said Weeth.

'I know that,' said the mole testily, 'it was three nights ago. But since the weather was poorly, and I felt ill, and there was no mole about to know, I had an amicable talk with the Stone and decided to delay matters for a few days until I felt better. I cannot say I feel perfect now, indeed I feel somewhat restless and uneasy.'

To his surprise several of them nodded vehemently.

'Ah! You seem to know what I mean! It's not just me then. A very strange night this, cold and getting colder and I should be aburrow,

457

but I can't sleep a wink. I thought I might divert myself somewhat from my unease by singing the stomping song and getting on with things. Naturally I had not expected to meet moles *here*, but life never ceases to amaze me. It is usually we who are dull, not life. But we do not generally start talking in earnest until after this part of the evening is done. I assume from the fact that you talk civilly and do not talon me into the ground and then act the inquisitor that you are not Newborns? So . . . I have asked you if you wish to be within or without. If without, then I stomp *that* side of you and go on my way. If within, I stomp on the far side of you and on we go together, singing the song, bashing the ground with our paws and generally getting into the spirit of things whilst we complete the tour of the system's bounds and all head back to the centre.'

'The custom died out in most places as bigger communities formed and the bounds grew too large,' said Privet in her old, scholarly way. Being "within" means we are within the bounds of the Stone.'

'Is there a Stone here?' asked Whillan.

'Well, now, that's an interesting question to which there is no clear answer,' replied the mole. 'There is a Stone, in a manner of speaking, and the erudite madam here is quite right: I am stomping to define its boundary of influence. However, the Stone itself is something of a disappointment, as you will soon see if you join me. Enough of talk. There is as much difference between talking about customs and doing them as between night and day . . . Now, are you . . . ?'

'Within!' declared Maple, 'Eh, Rooster?'

'Within!' said Rooster, giving the ground a mighty thump.

'Within!' said Whillan with unfeigned pleasure and relief. Whatever it was they must do, he felt this would get them nearer to it.

'That's settled then,' said their host, 'off we go! We had got to, "Rise to adore . . ."'

With that, and much muttering and laughter as they struggled to get into the rhythm of the thing, the four moles followed their new-found leader backwards in the stomp. 'Rise to adore (bang!) the mystery of the Stone (bang! thump!), Which waits now to hear (bang!) your voice join mine (bang!). Hark to its call (bang! thump! bang!), sing out . . .'

As they set off, quickly getting into the routine of the stomp, the moon rose higher still, but from the eastern horizon clouds began to loom, while above them a rough wind worried at the trees. But soon all reservations and concerns were cast aside. It was a dance of movement, of song, of merriment and of laughter, and the fact there were

458

no more moles to be within or without mattered not one bit, for here all the good feelings of moledom were suddenly free to flow.

'Don't know what we were all so worried about earlier!' exclaimed Maple.

'No!' agreed Privet breathlessly.

Madoc laughed, Weeth danced a circle all by himself, and even Whillan seemed to be beginning to forget his strange apprehension.

But not Rooster: he danced well enough, he lumbered about, but his eyes were everywhere as he looked among the trees with apprehension, and his frown grew deeper.

Nomole can say how many times they sang the stomping song, certainly not the moles who sang it that starry night; nor how many times they beat the ground to mark out their shared territory and (as Privet later maintained) to liberate the good spirits of the earth that they might celebrate the seasons' turn.

One thing only was certain, and that was the name of the mole who led them. For at some point during the dance one of them asked his name and he replied most solemnly (before tumbling, or being tumbled, headlong over Madoc):

'Hobsley is my name, and this coppice is . . .'

He was going to say what he was only able to say later, namely that the coppice had only been his home since the autumn just past, and that nomole-else lived there, and they were his first visitors.

'This coppice must be Hobsley's Coppice, then!' declared Whillan, looking about them all, at the moonlight among the trees which shone also in Madoc's eyes, and thinking he had rarely – no, *never* – seen anything as beautiful. 'And I'm Whillan, and this is Madoc, and this . . .'

And so as they neared the end of their dance, and Hobsley led them back to where he had begun, which was on the far western side of the little wood, they exchanged names, and wove them into the banging and the rhythm of their song.

Until at last, paw to paw, they circled to a stop among some ancient oaks whose roots were rimy with frost.

'Well now,' said the breathless Hobsley, still holding the paws of the moles on either side of him so that the others all continued to do the same, 'let's see if I can remember all your names. Well, Madoc to my left, I know yours, and yours as well, Whillan. Then Maple, and Privet, and Rooster, who could forget your name? And finally on my right is . . . Weeth!'

459

There was a general shout of congratulation at this feat of memory.

'Which means, if I am not mistaken, that there are seven of us altogether, which makes us . . .' and here his voice dropped a little and became more serious, more reverential, '. . . seven. Seven in all. Which means . . . Well, I believe Privet here can tell you what it means.'

'It makes us a Seven Stancing,' she said, 'and means our meeting and communion tonight is blessed.'

'I would be grateful, madam,' said Hobsley courteously, now very solemn indeed, 'if you could say a prayer appropriate to the occasion. I am sure you can think of one.'

'There is a prayer moles say on Longest Night,' she said, 'and I am beginning to think that the Stone has given us back three lost days that we may celebrate tonight together.'

'Say it,' said Rooster. 'Make Longest Night be here and now!'

'That's right,' said Weeth.

'Seems very apposite to me,' said Hobsley.

'And . . . us,' said Whillan, daring to speak for Madoc too, whose paw he held tightly in his own.

'Well then . . .'

But before she could begin Hobsley said, 'This spot is where I spend the daylight hours, for I like the shelter of the oaks and the view westward towards the setting sun. Most suitable for an old mole whose days are numbered. But there is a place nearby which I feel I should show you if we are to speak the ancient liturgy of Longest Night. It is but a few paces, in among these trees . . .'

'Where Stone is,' said Rooster, and even as he said it the mood changed utterly; wind rushed in the trees above, and the first spots of sleety snow drove in among them. It was not that the song and dance had been displaced, so much as that they had faded before a sudden and more urgent need of community. The chatter quietened, the laughter died, and they followed Hobsley into moonlight and shadows, past dark crannies of woodland floor, round the huge contortion of an oak tree's surface roots, to what, by the night's starry moonstruck light, at first appeared to be part of a fallen treetrunk, now overgrown with moss and black ivy, whose leaves were white with frost. Or perhaps it was the stump of an old tree, as Weeth suggested, until he saw how it extended massively along the wood's floor.

Hobsley nodded his head. 'Aye, I thought as much myself at first, and that was by daylight. But don't you notice something about this place, different from where we were just now?' He looked up at the massive trunks all about them, and his voice echoed up among them, and out to the stars. 'One day I looked more closely at that fallen "tree", and you know what? It's a Stone, that's what it is, a fallen Stone.'

It was Rooster who spoke first, his voice but a rough whisper.

'It's a delved place, this. A holy place.'

One by one they went to the strangely overgrown Stone, parting the foliage, peering into its shadows, and staring about behind them as Hobsley had done, as if half expecting to see other moles, or their spirits, nearby.

Only Rooster did not touch the Stone, but he was not idle. He peered here, and snouted there, his paws touched and buffeted at trees in the shadows about them, and too at their roots and the soil itself, until at last he came back to the Stone. He seemed somehow bigger before it, and strangely in command.

'What's beneath?' he asked Hobsley.

'Haven't looked. Haven't thought to; perhaps it wouldn't be right if I did. This is a holy kind of place, as you say, and the soil's best left undisturbed.'

Rooster stared at him and blinked. He reached out a paw as the others had done and pushed his huge talons through the pale frosty foliage to the surface of the Stone beneath. It was like a healer examining a sick mole.

'This Stone is waiting,' he muttered. 'There's delving beneath and around, deep delving. Long time fallen. Long time waiting. Rooster feels it. Place of need. Rooster knows. Privet, you say that prayer now, bring light to this dark place, say it now.'

He spoke more powerfully and when she hesitated his voice was a sudden command: '*Say* it, can't you feel the need? Longest Night has not been celebrated here for centuries past, so that's its need. A mole found this place, alone. Delved here, alone. Knew one day a Seven Stancing would be here. Us! Now! Tonight! Listen! This place was delved for tonight.'

He held up a paw and all of them were still, his command to Privet temporarily forgotten. He seemed to hear something, but they did not; and yet so strong was his presence now, and so unpredictable his actions that not one of them moved or spoke.

He looked around at them enquiringly and said, 'Hear? *Now*? No?'

'Yes!' whispered Whillan, 'I can hear something, I can . . .' His face expressed wonder and awe.

'No time, no time, need is now, tonight.'

461

'Duncton,' said Whillan matter-of-factly. 'It does need us, I know it does.'

'Maple?' said Privet. 'Do you feel or hear anything? You're the only other mole here who was born at Duncton.'

Maple said, 'I feel uneasy, nothing more than that. I wouldn't know it was Duncton. I mean—'

'It *is*,' said Whillan, as if others doubted him. 'Rooster understands. Must act, mustn't we Rooster?'

'Was waiting for you to say it,' said Rooster. 'Can now, and will!'

Suddenly, and violently, he drove his front paws into the foliage covering the Stone and began to rip it away. It was like watching a great warrior delving up a mole that is helplessly buried and needs rescuing. Up flew bits of black ivy, dead leaves, moss, and whole stems and roots of plants that had begun to grow on and around the Stone. His assault was fast and furious and it was not long before he moved back and pointed to part of the Stone's face, wet and shiny in the night and smelling of humus and the sap of broken plants. Across the surface he had revealed a thin strong root curving its light-restricting way up from one side and down the other, and this success-fully resisted his efforts to move it.

'Listen now,' he said, moving forward and thwacking the Stone mightily with his paw. 'Hear it?'

And they did, like the rumble of thunder beneath them, like the running of great moles among the trees, ancient sound, echoing and feeding back into the vast chasm of time whence Rooster had briefly freed it.

The moles responded very differently to this performance by Roos-ter. Maple was simply astonished; Weeth intrigued; Privet calm; Hobsley dancing about with excitement; Madoc overawed; and Whillan . . . Whillan was touched deeply by the sound Rooster had resurrected. He recognized it as akin to the sounds he had sometimes heard from some of the tunnels of Duncton Wood's Ancient System, but this sound moved him as a mole's call for help from across a valley would move others; and when it had gone, and been unanswered, would leave them restless and concerned.

'Now, Privet, say the words,' said Rooster.

Privet gathered them about the small part of the Stone Rooster had cleared, joined their paws, and said this prayer:

> 'Eternal Stone,
> Who makes this most holy night

When seasons turn,
Bring us with thee
Out of the darkness of our life's winters
To the light of thy spring.
Let us see thy radiance
And hear thy silent call.

Eternal Stone,
Be with us this most holy night
And teach us to renew our love
Of friends, of kin, of life;
Lead us out of the darkness
Into thy eternal Light.
Eternal Stone,
Be with us now.'

The prayer released them all and at its end they sighed, and whispered, and Hobsley said, 'Haven't heard that spoken properly since my first Longest Night. If I remember right there's a few more prayers . . .'

'Not many!' said Privet with a smile. 'Where we come from moles are relaxed about such things.'

'There's no time for chatter!' said Whillan suddenly, turning on Privet and the others.

'What must do? You decide!' said Rooster.

'Must . . . must . . .' Whillan said, or tried to say.

'What my dear?' asked Privet, coming closer. Indeed all of them came closer but for Rooster, who had backed away to stance down near a tree and was watching, his eyes black voids, his expression excited.

'Delve,' said Whillan faintly. 'But I don't know why.'

'Yes, yes, yes!' roared Rooster, rearing up. 'Privet, you stay by Stone, here. Not there, do not go there, dangerous there. Here only with the others. Pray. Pray. And pray again.'

'For what?' she asked.

'Duncton. And we, Whillan, what'll we do? You know, mole, you know well. You know all of it, deep, deep, deep inside. Beginning now to find it.'

'Delve,' said Whillan again. 'It's all I know.'

'For what?'

Whillan shook his head. 'Don't know that; don't know . . .'

'You do,' said Rooster. It was a command.

463

'The fallen Stone,' said Whillan. 'There, somewhere there. Where sounds come from.'

Rooster came close to him, took his paw, and held it to the Stone. 'Not fallen,' he said gently, 'not fallen at all. Waiting, waiting since a Master of the Delve came in times long, long past. *This Stone has yet to rise.*' He sounded as awed as they all looked, and muttered to himself, 'Ancient delving skill that. Very hard. That's why I'll need help. But Whillan, remember to obey all. Yes?'

Whillan turned to him, nodded, and asked, 'What must we do?'

'Said before, you did: delve. They pray, we delve, and together we make a Seven Stancing in the cold night, through to the cold dawn. Ancient and modern, here and far, in earth and on surface, old season and new; all, all, all turning. Stone will rise. Moles who need help will be helped. Listen!'

All of them heard it now, the distant rumble and chatter and echo of time from beneath the Stone. Calling them – no, urging them . . .

'Come, mole,' said Rooster, 'will show you. You must help. Even Master can't do this alone.'

They were suddenly gone into the shadows, first to where Rooster had stanced before and then beyond.

He called back to Privet: 'Us delving below, you praying above, Privet, mole. Stone to Stone across the ages. Stone to Stone across the country. Mole to mole, now and now, and now again. Begin.'

As Privet began to pray, and those remaining with her touched paws and circled in the spot Rooster had indicated, he thrust his paws into the ground with a grunt, and began to delve. Deeper and deeper until he was gone, calling Whillan to follow him into tunnels and delved sound nomole had known since they were first made.

Whillan found himself staring down an echoing, whispering tunnel, lit with a filtering of moonlight.

Rooster put his paw on Whillan's shoulder in the darkness. 'Master made this place long, long ago. Now a Master is back again with work to do. Come and help me, mole, with the raising of a Stone.'

Chapter Thirty-Four

There are few molish traditions more recently nor now more widely established than that which moles generally call Night of Rising, which comes three days after Longest Night. It is a time of thanksgiving and hope, when the secular jollities and celebrations of Longest Night finally give way to to a time of contemplation and prayer. Now the community has dispersed once more to face the trials of winter, and in smaller groups of family and friends, or even by themselves, moles take time to forsake the warmth and comfort of their tunnels and go to the surface and petition the Stone on behalf of all those who that night, and in the coming winter years, may through no fault of their own be in need of special support, and comfort, and faith.

'Yes, Stone,' a mole on Night of Rising might be inclined to say, 'I have had my tribulations and my difficulties, but here I am, in my system, near the entrance to my tunnels, safe, secure and in good community. Therefore on this special night I pray for those in peril, those who are not secure, those beset by danger and difficulty, and ask that in whatever way you can you let them know they are in my thoughts.'

Such a caring mole might well conclude his simple prayers of Rising like this: 'Stone, you alone can judge to where my prayers should be directed. Send them there, let them be a comfort and support to those who need them. And Stone, bless the moles of Duncton Wood!'

Oh yes, one thing is certain on Night of Rising – all prayers end with the blessing to the Duncton moles, for it was with them and their need, and their great bravery not so long ago, one third night after Longest Night itself, that the first Night of Rising came to be.

More is known about that particular night than about most nights. For historians are given to researching and scribing down the details, however obscure, of days and nights and periods of significance to moledom. Such has been the fate of the first Night of Rising which occurred that night when Pumpkin was so nearly murdered at the

Marsh End and when Privet, Whillan, Rooster and the others in Hobsley's Coppice sensed that their help was needed in Duncton Wood, and with the Stone's guidance, found a way to give it.

Yet, before we journey on through that unforgettable night in the company of these groups of moles, we may pause briefly to remember others who, the historians have shown, were strangely aware that same night that Duncton was in peril, and its moles in mortal danger, and that they needed the help that prayer and benediction can give, from however far off.

In fabled Beechenhill, for example, despite the dangers of being discovered by the Newborns who by then had occupied their system and library, three followers went to the Stone and prayed, driven by a need they felt but could not then understand.

Similarly, at the Fyfield Stone, the vagrant mole, Tonner, reported feeling that he must go at once and touch the Stone and whisper Duncton's name.

'I did so throughout that night, though it was a foul one with blizzard winds driving freezing snow into my eyes and under my belly,' he is recorded as saying.* Tonner was one of many moles who felt the need to actually touch a Stone that night and to keep on doing so right through to dawn. But, as everymole knows, the most striking example of it was at Seven Barrows. A mole might have thought that the community there had experienced enough excitement for the season, with Fieldfare's disappearance and recovery, but it too played its part on the first Night of Rising.

Uffington Hill, on whose gentler southern flanks Seven Barrows lies, is so much higher than the vale it dominates that in the winter years the weather is harsher up there, and snow falls earlier and lies longer. That December was no exception, and the ill-tempered weather of the Night of Rising brought heavier and more violent blizzards across Uffington than elsewhere in southern moledom. The winds that heralded the snow had begun a day or two earlier, so that the community of Seven Barrows had grown used to the sounding of the Blowing Stone, which lies just east of Uffington.

That particular night the soundings were, as Fieldfare observed to Spurling, 'becoming steadily more insistent. Why, traditionally the Blowing Stone is only ever meant to have sounded seven times once, but I swear it has sounded a lot more than that tonight.'

* Quoted in both standard works on the subject: Bannock of Avebury's popular *Rising Tales*; and Bunnicle II's reference text *The First Night of Rising*.

Spurling nodded and said, 'Yes, but not regularly, as in the tales of former times. Even so . . .'

'Even so, we should pay heed to it!' said Fieldfare. She had fully recovered from her experience among the Stones before Longest Night and now seemed full of energy and purpose. 'I think we should go up on to the surface despite the weather and just, well . . . listen. Be. Pray, perhaps.'

Most agreed with her, and up to the surface many of the Seven Barrow moles went, huddling together in the lee of the barrows themselves for warmth, and company. The deep haunting note of the Blowing Stone as it was caught by wind sounded over them quite frequently, and as the evening gave way to night ever more so, and more erratically, like some mole caught and lost in deep caverns who calls and calls more urgently for help, and his voice echoes and re-echoes ever more loudly.

It was Noakes who suggested that perhaps one or two of them might venture across the stonefields to the nearest Stones because 'touching one seems the right thing to do tonight'. They debated it this way and that, as was their wont with Spurling as leader, and finally decided all of them would go. So they did, watching over each other, across the wild stonefields to the first great Stone, and then to the second which rose nearby, gathering, touching, and praying into that strange forbidding night when moles all over moledom sensed the need to help; though whatmoles needed them, and where, they did not yet know. And still the Blowing Stone sounded, and still it grew more insistent, and the wind gathered strength, and the night grew dark and dangerous.

Yes, a historian could cite many examples such as these to show how so many followers were affected that terrible night of trial. He might well conclude, before returning again to Duncton Wood and the plight of Pumpkin and his fellow followers, with a reference to the evidence from Caer Caradoc. For even there, whose windswept Stones were so high, so wild to the wind, so bitter cold, that it was dangerous to venture out – even there two moles came out to help. Perhaps *especially* there. *And here alone across all moledom that night, Duncton's supporters were not Stone followers.*

It was the Elder Senior Brother Thripp, assisted by Rolt, who battled his way out to the Stones, and stared fiercely into driving snow, which beat into his thin, lined face.

'Forgive me, Master, but now we're here what do we do except

467

freeze to death?' shouted Rolt into Thripp's ear, the wind's howl being so loud.

'Wait,' rasped Thripp.

'Humph!' muttered Rolt, pulling himself round into the shelter of one of the Stones as wind and sleet rushed by. It seemed to him that whatever it was Thripp was watching out for he could not hope to see it.

'Wait for what?' said Rolt at last, reaching a paw out to support the Elder Senior Brother, and pull him in to shelter as well for a time. Thripp's shoulder and flank were covered in icy sleet.

'For something you'll never forget, mole,' said Thripp purposefully, submitting to Rolt's ministrations as he wiped the freezing wet off him.

Rolt stared out at the other Stones, and the livid night sky beyond the driving sleet.

'Nomole else will be out on a night like this,' he said. 'It's bad for you, Elder Senior Brother, it'll do you no good.'

'You may be right about it being bad for me, that's true. But nomole else? You're wrong for once, Rolt, very wrong,' said Thripp, battling his way out into the sleet again, and snouting this way and that. He peered round the Stone and back at Rolt again. 'She'll be out tonight, Privet will. And the mole Rooster, he'll be out. Oh, and many more. The seasons have turned and the Book of Silence wants to begin its long journey home. This test had to come, and allmole is part of that; allmole must help, but thus far it is only the followers who understand. Wait, Rolt, and watch. Tonight we moles struggle for our destiny.'

Rolt sighed, thumped himself to keep warm, and watched over his Master with affection. Tonight, as on all the nights and days he had served Thripp since he was a young brother in training, there was nowhere else he wished to be.

'Touch the Stone, Rolt!' cried out Thripp suddenly, venturing out further into the open, and lowering his head against the wind. 'Touch it, mole!'

Rolt did, and what he felt and sensed beneath his paw, and saw in light about the Stones, made him begin to understand why Thripp had said that this was a night he would not forget.

'Touch!' screamed Thripp over the wind as he stanced up against the wild spirit of the night, and turned his snout south-eastwards, towards distant Duncton Wood, and muttered its name to himself, as if he was beginning to understand that an enemy might be a friend.

*

468

But whatever power it was that seemed that night to be drawing the thoughts of so many across moledom towards Duncton Wood, there was not much evidence of it yet in Duncton itself. All poor Pumpkin could think of was how to stay upright on his paws as he was rushed along an obscure night-fraught path by young Cluniac, a mole he was beginning to dislike intensely. All this 'Please hurry up' and 'Watch that root!' and 'We're never going to make it if you stop for breath!' was not doing Pumpkin's heart any good at all.

'I am being as quick as I can, young mole,' he puffed at one point, as Cluniac heaved him to his paws again after yet another tumble, 'but it's . . . not easy in this dark, following a path I've never been on and aware that moles hereabout might well have another go at killing me! Drowning isn't very nice, I can tell you.'

'Please, sir, stop talking and put your best paw forward!'

'Best paw forward indeed!' muttered Pumpkin to himself. 'I'm not a pup in need of homilies and encouragement, I'm . . . I'm . . .'

Well, he knew what he was: he was alive, and he was a lucky mole. This night Sturne had proved himself a friend beyond compare, and this brave, young, and marginally irritating mole was no doubt risking his life for him as well. No, no, Pumpkin said to himself, I'm not really annoyed at all.

Thwack!

'B . . . b . . . botheration!' exclaimed Pumpkin as a stem of bramble bashed him in the eye. 'How much further?'

'Not far,' whispered Cluniac, pausing for a moment as he too caught his breath. 'We're clear of the Marsh End now where I was most worried about getting caught, and now we're heading up to the Eastside.'

'To escape, you mean?'

Cluniac nodded wearily.

'No, no, I forbid it!' cried Pumpkin, despite his aches and pains and weariness. 'Others will be in danger once Brother Inquisitor Fetter discovers I have escaped. We must do what we can to alert them, we must!'

To Cluniac's astonishment Pumpkin clearly meant what he said, and began to snout about towards the west, no doubt in an effort to find a path towards Barrow Vale. For a moment the youngster was so amazed that he did nothing but watch the library aide. Until Longest Night just past he had always thought of him as a stubborn old mole with nothing much about him at all. He had said as much to his mother Elynor, who had rounded on him fiercely and said,

469

'Pumpkin? He's one of the finest there is, and don't you ever think otherwise. It's moles like him preserve our liberty, as they always have. You think it's been easy for him pretending to be Newborn, and working up there in the Library for that treacherous, cruel mole Sturne? No, don't you underestimate the power of a traditional Duncton mole once he's riled. Oh yes, Pumpkin's a mole in a million all right, and we older moles know it.'

Now, as Cluniac watched the old mole forget all about his fears and hurts in an effort to go to the aid of others, he knew it too; and knew as well that what he had done this evening had been the best thing he had ever done. To save such a mole, to assist him . . .

'Sir! It's been taken care of! You've no need to worry, it's not just us who are escaping.'

Quickly he told Pumpkin what had happened – about the missive he had received, and how he had gone down to the Marsh End while the secret followers gathered themselves to escape up to the Stone according to a plan pre-arranged by Drubbins and Elynor before the former's death.

'There's others led by my mother Elynor on the Westside and they'll be waiting for us. We're to join a few older moles here on the Eastside, and then all go on together to Elynor, though they may have gone ahead by now. We didn't know how long it would take to rescue you, you see, sir.'

'Onwards and forwards and upwards then!' cried out Pumpkin with renewed spirit. He knew well enough whatmole must have sent the missive to Cluniac – Sturne, of course. His resourcefulness knew no bounds!

'Before it,' said Pumpkin to himself, 'what are my puny aches and pains? What are my fears? As nothing!'

Then, seeing that Cluniac appeared to be slowing, Pumpkin urged him on: 'Hurry, mole! Don't dawdle! No time for pauses!'

'Yes, sir!' puffed Cluniac, thinking that for the first time in his life he was beginning to see what this Duncton spirit old moles rabbited on about really was. Well, if an old library aide like Pumpkin could display it after all he had been through, he was not going to let the system down!

So it was, that a short time later, the two moles chased up a final slope, rushed round a tree root and found . . . nothing.

'They've gone on!' said Cluniac with some concern and disappointment. 'Gone on across the system to where Elynor will be. I thought one of them at least might wait.'

470

'No matter,' declared Pumpkin, who felt disappointed too and wondered how he would keep on going. 'At least we're on more familiar territory. On we go!'

The wind was stronger now, though they were deep enough in the wood for its full force to be taken by the leafless branches above their heads. But sleet was scudding between the dark treetrunks in a most unpleasant way.

'I'll take tunnels where I can!' said Cluniac, his spirit revived by Pumpkin's.

They ran on through the night, pausing only twice more; once because Pumpkin thought he saw guardmoles lurking, and the second time because they heard the growl of alien voices in a nearby tunnel.

They diverted on to the surface, for the first time thankful for the noise of the rising wind which masked their pawsteps. On they went, across-slope to the west until at last they neared the meeting-point. Up a slope, past a timid watcher, and they were falling exhausted among a cluster of wan and frightened moles who had been waiting for them with increasing trepidation since darkness had fallen.

'Cluniac!' said the doughty Elynor, 'I knew you'd be all right. And you Pumpkin, battered but not bowed!'

'Correct, madam,' said Pumpkin, at whose name the moles about them let out a ragged cheer.

He had been feeling more tired yet more excited with each step he and Cluniac had taken since the Eastside but now he only dimly knew the way, for much had changed since he was young. Above them the night was wild and bitter, the wind hurling the debris of soil, humus and sleet down at tunnel entrances, while where roots of trees broke into tunnels they heaved and stressed dangerously, seeming positively alive.

The light was livid and strange, as it often is when wild winds blow through a wintry snowbound wood. In some places there was absolute darkness, but mostly it was shadows and light, and the sense that anything might move, and all spelt danger.

To Pumpkin's surprise the followers Elynor had gathered were out on the surface of the wood – huddled in the twisted protection afforded by the roots of an ancient oak across which one of its branches had fallen long ago. There were fourteen or so moles huddled there in all, with two posted as lookouts. On the last part of the journey to reach them, which was on the surface, Pumpkin had found himself battered by sudden violent assaults of wind, which hurled sleet into his eyes and made easy balanced progress quite impossible.

471

'We had better set off immediately!' said Elynor the moment Pumpkin and Cluniac arrived. 'You can tell us about your journey later. The others were disturbed and so they came on, with a couple of moles taking another route in an effort to divert the Newborn guardmole who nearly found the group. I pray they may join us later.'

'Did you get the two you mentioned?' asked Cluniac.

Elynor nodded in the direction of the others and Pumpkin saw two very old moles, both of whom he vaguely remembered, though he had long since forgotten their names. They were a pair, both frail but with the female looking a little stronger and doing her very best to protect her mate from the cold winds. His flanks shivered pathetically and he looked frightened and despairing. Instinctively Pumpkin went nearer, and the rest of the huddling group raised their heads against the elements to look at him, some hopeful, some weary, all trusting.

'He's come . . . he's here!' Pumpkin heard them whispering to one another. Why, some had been too old or infirm to see that he and Cluniac had arrived.

He was surprised at how old most of them were, contact with Elynor before having given him the impression that the rebel followers would all be younger. The very few youngsters among them Pumpkin did not recognize, and he guessed that these were ones who had gone into hiding when the Newborns came, fearing that otherwise they would be taken for special training, or something worse.

'Bless you, sir!' cried out one of the older ones.

'Aye, bless you for what you've done,' came the cry.

While one or two of the very old ones who could not see or hear too well grew confused, asking, 'Eh? What is it? Who's there?' at which others explained and reassured them.

'You had better say a few words!' said Elynor, to Pumpkin's dismay. The only words he felt inclined to say were that this was not what he had expected, and the chances of getting such a group up to the safety of the High Wood in such conditions quickly were not good. His own escape had been a miracle, and the chances of surviving this night at all . . .

'Er, well, it's good to see you all,' he said, to shouts of 'Speak up, sir!' and 'What's he say?'

Pumpkin decided to make it short and sharp. 'We've got a long trek ahead of us,' he cried out, the wind snatching the words from his mouth, 'but if we stick together, and don't think of anything but getting there, we'll all make it. We're going first to the Stone in the High Wood . . .'

472

'The Stone! The Stone!' repeated several of the moles, delight and hope in their eyes. Since the Newborns had taken power the only time they had been to the Stone Clearing was on Longest Night, for rituals they did not like, and then to witness Stour's death. Now they were going for a different reason, and if their faith seemed to Pumpkin a little hopeless, well, it was all they had.

'So if you get tired, if you begin to doubt, think of the Stone. It's what's kept *me* going these hard molemonths past, and it'll keep *you* going now and guide you to safety!'

'Well said, mole!' cried out one or two of the fitter, older ones.

Pumpkin felt suddenly he wanted to say just a little more. 'Friends,' he continued, 'fellow followers of the old ways, I want you to know that Master Librarian Stour warned for a long time that such dark days as these would come. He never liked or trusted the Newborns, but there was no easy way to stop them, and even if we in this system were inclined to violence, which we are not, he did not believe in it. What he *did* have faith in was that when the need came there would be moles in Duncton who would have the courage to stance forth, put their trust in the Stone, and face their enemies, not with talons of hatred and violence, but with the powers of love, and faith, and peace.

'I know that nothing gave him greater solace in the moment of his death on Longest Night than the fact that many of you were able to come and be with him! Tonight we are fleeing for our lives to the Stone's sanctuary, but there will be a tomorrow when we can turn to face the darkness, when it will fade into light once more and we can return to our homes, and the simple way we wish to live. So turn your snouts towards the Stone, and continue to believe in it.'

'Well said!' came the cry again, and there was another cheer, this one a little less ragged than the first.

'It would be best if you younger moles take up the flanks and rear of the party,' said Elynor. 'Cluniac, who you all know, will go back and forth making sure we don't lose touch with each other.'

There were muttered explanations in the shadows as these instructions were passed on to the less able, and then, without more ado, and greatly inspired by Pumpkin's words, the moles broke out of their shelter in an orderly way to begin the long trek upslope.

So far as so violent and harassing a wind could be said to have a direction, it was against them. Had it been wholly from the east they might have trekked along the very edge of the Pastures in the lee of the wood itself, which would have made the journey easy, and the route-finding straightforward, but it was not, as they discovered when they tried it. The wind, laden with stinging hail and sleet, blasted down the Pastures straight at them, forcing them back into the shelter of the trees. But there the contrary wind swung viciously round roots, shot down from the roaring, swaying darkness above them, and constantly did its best to dishearten them.

Nor had they recourse to the tunnels of the Westside below them, for those mainly ran east to west, and the only communal tunnel that ran upslope from Barrow Vale to the Stone was known to be patrolled by the suspicious Newborns – which was why so few had dared venture up to the Stone in recent times. So they were forced to take a surface route in conditions which, in ordinary circumstances, nomole would have attempted, least of all an infirm one. As for such a party as Pumpkin now found himself leading in company with Elynor, well, only fear of the Newborns behind them, and faith in what they would find ahead, kept them going.

But progress was painfully slow, and became slower still as, the night advancing, one after another of the party faltered and needed attention, obliging all to stop. It soon became clear to Pumpkin and Elynor that they were not going to get to the Stone much before dawn.

'We can't risk lying low through the day,' said Pumpkin, during one of the halts, 'and nor does it seem wise for the fitter among us to go on ahead – I know little about such matters, but dividing up a party does not seem a sensible procedure. Anyway, *I'm* not leaving moles behind who cannot fend for themselves!'

The words cheered up the ailing moles about him, and fortified by the rest, and further encouraged by being told that the Stone was not *much* further, on they went, helping each other around and over obstacles, whispering prayers, and finally lapsing into silent, dogged plodding in which their only ambition was to get one paw in front of another, and for the wind to cease its relentless onslaught into their eyes and snouts.

The worm-rich part of Duncton moles call the Westside ends where the ground steepens towards the High Wood into an area of fewer trees and patchy undergrowth called the Slopes. It was a place Pumpkin knew very well, for his own modest tunnels lay at the upper part of the Slopes very near where the High Wood proper begins. In certain wind conditions, and these obtained that voracious winter night, the Slopes were filled with an awesome roaring sound, like storm waves driven on to a treacherous shore. Even the pluckiest mole was inclined to feel intimidated by this terrifying noise, though it was caused by nothing more sinister than the wind catching the highest branches of the great and ancient beech trees of the High Wood itself.

This roaring came upon them now, and it was all Pumpkin could do to be heard above it, and persuade his weak and faltering group of moles not to worry and press on.

'It's nothing – nothing at all. This is the final part of our trek and if we can only make it before dawn . . .'

But that now seemed unlikely, because for every mole that remained fit and strong, there was one and a half who needed help and encouragement as they struggled slowly upslope from root to root, from bramble to windswept trunk. The sky above had lost the dark of deepest night, and began now to take on the earliest hues of dawn: streaky greys, glowering mauves and sudden voids of blackness once again.

'Come on!' cried out Pumpkin, suddenly afraid that the Newborns had already discovered their disappearance, made some quick deductions, and sent guardmoles upslope to find out what they could. 'Keep on going, for we've not *so* far to go!'

'How far?' asked somemole desperately, for the slope ahead was steep, and the dawning light made it look endless, with no Stone in prospect at all.

'Not *too* far!' responded poor Pumpkin, wondering how much longer he could keep them going.

'You can do it, every one of you!' cried out Elynor, who like Pumpkin sensed the group was close to giving up, or at least going to ground until it had recovered sufficient strength to continue.

'Yes!' said bold young Cluniac, 'Come on, all—'

But he did not quite finish before a cry of alarm from one of the other youngsters brought the party to a sudden halt.

'Look!' warned the mole, pointing ahead of them through the grey light to where two confident-looking Newborn guardmoles stanced solidly in their way.

Pumpkin and Elynor went boldly forward without a moment's hesitation, while Cluniac instinctively marshalled the others behind them in some kind of defensive position.

'And where are you going?' one of the guardmoles demanded.

'To the Stone!' said Pumpkin as fiercely as he could – and it *was* fierce, because he had not come so far to be turned back at the last moment.

475

'You're not going further,' said the other guardmole, raising his voice against the roaring of the Wood.

'Oh really!' said Elynor, as angry as Pumpkin, but secretly as alarmed.

'That's right,' said the first guardmole, his eyes dark and ruthless in the way Newborns manage so well. It was the ruthlessness a mole has when he thinks he is in the right. Like the other he came forward, and Pumpkin could sense his party, even Elynor, begin to falter. It would need little more now to undermine their resolve and he knew there was not much he could do or say. Indeed, a wave of tiredness and despair was coming over him as he felt even himself weakening before the Newborns' assurance. So, they must have realized some moles had fled, and sent out patrols, just as he had feared. He heard whispering behind him as some of the older ones asked what was apaw, and others tried to explain.

But then the second of the guards, perhaps less experienced and not quite seeing that the moles were rapidly weakening, said in what he hoped was a commanding way, 'The Stone does not wish you to go further! Return downslope to the safety of your burrows.'

'The Stone does not wish?' cried out one of the oldest moles there, quivering with rage. 'And whatmole are *you* to judge what the Stone may wish or not, eh? You tell me that!'

'Aye,' chorused several more, pressing forward until they all crowded round Pumpkin and Elynor.

'A young whipper-snapper like *you* telling *us* what the Stone thinks!' continued the redoubtable mole. 'Get out of my way or grey though my fur is I'll *push* you out of the way. Nomole tells us where to worship, and we in Duncton are fed up with all you so-called Newborns.'

'Or *when* to worship, come to that!' shouted another.

'Aye, well said! Clear off you two!'

'Go on, get lost!'

And as the little group found its courage and its voice once more, Pumpkin raised his front paws and most boldly pushed the Newborns out of the way. If there was a moment in that night when Pumpkin sensed that the Duncton spirit was beginning to rise from the darkness into which the Newborns had cast it down, that was it.

'There'll be more guards here soon,' said the first of the Newborns, grudgingly retreating to let the group past.

'They're coming already,' said the second with evident satisfaction.

'Go on, keep on moving!' urged Cluniac suddenly from the rear.

476

There was something in his voice that made Pumpkin steal a glance back downslope. There, to his horror, he saw three Newborn guards coming rapidly towards them, and he knew that their chances of escape to freedom were diminishing by the moment. And yet, the Stone Clearing was not so far upslope now if they could only just . . .

'Keep on going!' commanded Pumpkin, 'and keep together. Look neither to the right nor left, and ignore the Newborns. Go . . . for the Stone is with us, and will guide us and see us safeguarded!' Such was the certainty and faith in his voice that everymole there was carried on rapidly, upward and forwards among the great trees of the High Wood.

'I'm going to the rear to be with Cluniac,' Pumpkin whispered to Elynor, 'so you must keep them together, and moving.' He dropped back, saw that the Newborns were not far behind now, fell in with Cluniac and together the two brave moles pushed and shoved the party from behind, knowing if they once stopped it would be the end.

The Newborns lost no time in closing in on the hurrying group, reaching Pumpkin and Cluniac first and telling them to halt. One or two went so far as to reach out a restraining paw to the moles, but none dared yet physically stop them. As they entered among the great trees of the High Wood, the light of dawn advanced to reveal a troubled, windswept scene, and a path littered with broken twigs and branches, and patches of sleety snow. A strange, nearly silent tussle developed between the two groups; the followers hurried on, panic in their breasts but anger and faith in their hearts, while the Newborns pressed ever closer, trying to detach first one mole, then another, from the group.

'Keep close!' urged the more able moles, 'look ahead! Don't answer them . . .'

'It will be all the better for you if you stop now,' said one Newborn, his voice gentler than before.

'Where do you think you'll get to anyway?' asked another belligerently, shoving at Elynor.

Ignoring him, and pressing even closer to her friends, she said, 'The Stone's getting nearer, can't you feel it?'

She spoke almost as if they were static, holding off the forces of evil, while the Stone was rushing to their rescue, and there was a sense in which this was indeed true, and is always true. The Stone and its Silence wait but for a mole to open his heart, and then its grace comes rushing in with the power of flood-water through a gap in a river-bank that has held fast too long.

Then, only moments later, there was a lightening amongst the trees ahead which signalled the Stone Clearing itself where the trees encircle the Stone at, as one scribemole has aptly put it, 'a respectful distance'.

There was only one problem – a Newborn, and a large one, stanced athwart their path, his paws raised and his talons extended. For a terrible moment Pumpkin thought it was Brother Barre himself, but as they approached he saw it was not. Even so, with Newborns at their flanks and this extra one ahead their plight had worsened once again.

But the party had gained a volition of its own and ancient though some of its members were they continued their flight straight at the mole; not aggressively so much as inevitably, as if there was nowhere else for them to go and they would certainly not be stopping. Not that Pumpkin now had any great expectation of this heroic charge, for though he had plenty of faith he could not see how even the Stone, in its infinite wisdom, could find any escape for them here. They would reach the Stone Clearing, and then what? Be scattered on through the High Wood to be chased, harried and assaulted by the Newborns? Or simply put their rumps to the Stone and make a last fight of it as others had in past times, usually at the cost of their lives. No, Pumpkin could not see . . .

Except, as they neared the solitary mole, Pumpkin did see something, or rather somemole. There, off the path, obscured by roots and the wind-pulled stalks of dog's mercury, was the very last mole he expected to see: Sturne. His expression seemed one of entreaty, or possibly warning. For a moment Pumpkin faltered, thinking that Sturne had taken this terrible risk of discovery because there was an ambush ahead of which he had forewarning.

But then Sturne mouthed something and waved his paws about urgently, which Pumpkin interpreted as meaning, 'Whatever you do, don't stop. Go on! The Stone will provide!' Then he retreated into the undergrowth, and was gone.

'Humph!' thought Pumpkin, '*that* promise has been offered us all night.'

But there was nothing more for it but to be bold and face it out, and as the mole ahead stanced his ground, and the party began to slow, Pumpkin once more urged them on, raising his paws and shouting with a certain mild ferocity – which was the most fearsome he could be. The others followed him, and the mole ahead lost his resolution and moved to one side.

As they burst into the Clearing the Stone at least was easy to make out, since it seemed to have gathered to itself such light as there was, and the great tree behind it swayed and shook in an intimidating, powerful way.

'To the Stone!' cried Pumpkin, pausing to shepherd his charges past him. It was only then, as he turned to follow them, that he was able to take in the disturbing scene which their sudden arrival had interrupted.

There were four Newborns already in the Clearing which, with the one they had passed on the path, and the five who had been pursuing them, made ten in all. All strong, all young, all determined, and all, presumably, trained in the arts of intimidation and fighting, not to mention killing.

Even as Pumpkin surveyed the grim scene, other Newborns arrived, among them Brother Inquisitor Fetter himself, and a furious-looking Barre, while already at the Stone was a huddle of five or six moles, all tired and abject, self-evidently a few followers who lived in isolation; Elynor's warnings of the need to escape that night must have reached them, it seemed.

Their story was not hard to guess. The Newborns had intercepted them, found out about the 'escape' and brought them on up here to await the arrival of the others. It seemed certain too that a Newborn or two had gone down to Barrow Vale to report this blasphemy – as no doubt it would be perceived – and even now reinforcements would be on the way. All for naught then! And yet there had been that cryptic look on Sturne's face; had it been a warning after all?

'Oh dear!' thought Pumpkin as he joined his friends and felt the fight going out of them as the Newborns now massed opposite them in the Clearing. 'Oh dear!'

To fight or not to fight? That was the unpleasant question Pumpkin pondered as his new friends gathered pathetically about him and he realized that though their numbers were greater for the moment, they would not be so for long, and they stood little chance of success. Even if fighting was their way, which it was not, what injuries would it mean? What deaths?

Yet how affecting were the mute pleas of the old moles who now reached out to him! They had given of their last strength this night in their brave trek to the Stone through savage blizzard winds, not to harm others but simply to protect their right to live and worship as they wished. They had wanted to march to freedom and all they had found was this grim dawn of failure and despair.

479

If it had been just a little before that Pumpkin had first sensed Duncton's spirit rising to its own defence, it was only now that he felt something more: there were other followers out and about that night, at that very moment, all across moledom, and they were urging Pumpkin and his friends to have courage, and faith, and purpose.

'Yes!' said Pumpkin to himself, looking at the moles who now clustered about Elynor, Cluniac and himself so pitifully as the Newborns began a slow advance, 'yes, I am certain of it. We are not alone tonight.'

Then he cried aloud his private thoughts: 'We are not alone, moles, others stance with us, here and now. Aye, my good friends, my fellow followers, all across moledom this night are those who hear our call for help, and stance now with us, and touch the Stone with paw, with faith, with hope and add their courage to our own, who are beset and endangered by evil!'

One or two of the Newborns laughed at these words, but the followers with Pumpkin did not. There was something new in the library aide's voice, something so potent that many of them instinctively looked round and up at the Stone as if in some way it might confirm his words. They were not disappointed. It rose into the dawning light, and against the strange racing sky, and seemed to express the very spirit of what he said. Some of them touched it, others reached their paws to him, and all found their strength and faith renewed, as he himself seemed to have been renewed.

They could not know that even as these surges of confidence came to him, so too did doubts, and he groaned silently to himself, 'But Stone, I'm only a library aide, I really don't know *what* to do . . .'

A gust of wind shook the trees around them, and drove down into the Clearing scattered leaves and snow on the ground that separated the followers round the Stone from the Newborns.

'Brothers, and Brother Barre in particular!' Pumpkin found himself crying out boldly, though from where he found the words he had no idea, 'these other moles are harmless. Take me, for I am the reprobate and sinner here. Take me and let the others go!'

Brave Pumpkin – no! Heroic Pumpkin! – now advanced out from the Stone to face the Newborns alone. How thin his old body seemed in that winter dawn, how weak his paws, how grey and patchy his fur.

He did not see that behind him Cluniac and Elynor had gathered to their flanks the only two or three other moles there capable of fighting, and were about to rush out to his side. Nor did he see what

480

the Newborns saw, that the light about the Stone grew brighter, and the Stone itself appeared ever more formidable, as if to say, 'These good moles are in my care and sanctuary now, touch them at your peril!'

Many of the Newborns, including Fetter himself, seemed aware of this strange threat in the air about the Stone, but Brother Inquisitor Barre, never a sensitive mole, was not. He saw only a puny mole who had escaped him once, and once was too much – now he had a chance to make amends by killing him.

At Barre's flanks were the two moles who had been with him earlier down in the Marsh End, and whose paws had thrust Pumpkin into the water to drown. Their fears seemed to have gone and, encouraged no doubt by the presence of a growing number of Newborns behind them, they advanced with Barre towards Pumpkin.

All Barre saw now was an old mole coming towards him, and he sensed that with a single talon-thrust into his face he could destroy completely the little resistance these blaspheming Duncton moles were about to put up. His instructions had been to kill the mole Pumpkin, and now he would do so. If killing one would make the rest biddable he would do it and anyway . . . Barre smiled grimly. It had long since been decided that not one of these pathetic, blaspheming followers was going to survive the night. Not one. How fitting that the library aide would be the first; but all made themselves guilty by simply being there.

As Barre began to raise his right paw to deliver a killing thrust Pumpkin's fear went quite away, and was replaced by regret. For though he might have seen ruthless determination in Barre himself, he saw in the eyes of the Newborns beyond him genuine awe at the sight of the Stone.

'If *only* I was a fighter!' was Pumpkin's final regretful thought as he raised his own right paw in peace and said the prayer that seemed to suit the moment best, the prayer of peaceful moles.

'Stone, deliver us from evil! Help us in our hour of darkness. Bring us out of the night of this evil spirit into the dawning light of thy good day!'

'Aye,' whispered those he had sought to protect, 'Stone deliver us now and in the moment of our darkness.'

In that moment of darkness two of the followers behind Pumpkin found their destiny. They were the old pair whom Elynor had per-suaded to escape with them; they had seemed hardly aware of them-selves, let alone of the events around them. Yet now, led by the

481

ancient and doddering male, the two of them broke forth from the group, muttering and shaking their heads.

'No,' said the male almost gently, certainly sorrowfully, 'you must not strike the mole who leads us. Cannot you see he means you no harm? Can you not sense the Stone's Light and Silence all about us? Good mole . . .'

The raised paw of Barre came crashing down out of the night and struck the old mole in the face. As Barre sought to withdraw his talons and blood began to flow upon the Clearing's floor one of the guardmoles next to Barre struck a second blow into the mole.

'No!' cried Pumpkin, but faintly, for this was bloody murder before his eyes; this was the worst thing he had ever seen. 'You cannot; you must not!'

'Oh, yes we can!' cried Barre, his rage risen, his two friends excited, their three bodies moving together like one evil, killing thing as sleet and leaves and blood seemed to swirl about them.

Even as the female reached her dying mate, but before she had time to reach out to him and tend him, and show she was at his flank, Barre and his creatures struck her down too. Their talons thrust sickeningly into her, the scene made more dreadful still by their killing grunts and cries of pleasure at the evil that they did.

But worse followed, even as behind them Fetter cried out to them to stop, Pumpkin raised a paw in protest at their vileness, and somemole among those followers by the Stone screamed out in shame and pity for all who witnessed this depravity.

For Barre, brutalized by power and the cruelty of his life, carried forward by his own violence, driven now by the rage that Pumpkin's escape had engendered, reached down his great paws to the limp form of the female, lying dead across her dying mate, and raised it up and cried in a voice more terrible than any of those present had ever heard, 'For thee, great Stone, we make this just sacrifice.'

But there was worse yet, for thinking that Fetter and the others must approve these evil and obscene acts, and no doubt believing them to be the prelude to the massacre of the secret followers the guardmoles had anticipated since their insubordination on Longest Night, one of Barre's minions reached down and took up the body of the male. It moved; it bled; it was alive.

'And this as well, Stone, this sacrifice for thee!'

And then he dropped the body, raised his bloodied paws, and he and his friend taloned death finally into that weak, frail, brave mole; and they laughed.

The silence that followed was a void as deep as time, and in it rose and melded, swirled and scattered, a thousand, a hundred thousand evil things. It was a void before which all in the Stone Clearing now faltered, slipping and sliding down towards it as the darkness of revenge and hatred, loathing and abhorrence began to overtake their minds. Yet in the midst of all of that, as followers and Newborns teetered on the brink to which an evil act had brought them, one alone stanced fast.

From where such inner goodness flows, nomole knows. From where such love, in the face of evil? From where compassion, when all compassion is lost? From where forgiveness?

Pumpkin saw true evil; he heard true blasphemy; he knew, because he saw the depth of the void to which Barre's act had brought him. But he raised his clear mild gaze from it and stared for one terrible moment into Barre's black eyes.

Then he turned his back on Barre, and looked up at the Stone, unafraid. He cried out his simple prayer for all of them, follower and Newborn alike, fearless and full of faith that it would be answered.

> 'Good Stone,
> Deliver us.
> Send us thy grace,
> For we are but ordinary moles,
> Without grace unless you grant it us,
> Without deliverance unless you bring it us,
> Without love but in your Light and Silence.'

As Pumpkin spoke, with all the pity and compassion and love that was in his simple heart alive in every word, he slowly raised his paws towards the Stone, and to the dawning light of a new day that rose through the wild winds of winter beyond it; and he cried out again:

> Good Stone,
> Deliver us!

Chapter Thirty-Five

The downland of Uffington Hill at Seven Barrows was overwhelmed that dawn by the urgent sounding of the Blowing Stone, as Fieldfare and the others held each other's paws and touched the Stone, and sent the power of their thoughts into the sky.

'Now is the time,' whispered Fieldfare, '*now.*'

The blizzard winds had abated only slightly, and as the dawn light came they saw that the downs about them were white with snow.

'Duncton it is that needs us!' Fieldfare had cried out earlier, and none had doubted it. So it was to Duncton now that their prayers for intercession and deliverance went.

Far, far to the north, where the snow had been thicker, and the ice more bitter, three brave followers still stanced by the Stone of Beechenhill. Dawn was a hard rising that morning, but with prayer and faith it came, and though the name Duncton did not come to their mouths, their prayers seemed southward-bound, to moles whom the Stone's touch told them needed help.

> '*Good Stone,*
> *Deliver them!*'

At Fyfield, the vagrant mole Tonner sensed that his long vigil was reaching its climax, and though he felt half frozen with cold he would not have deserted the Stone for one moment. He knew it was nearby Duncton that needed help, and such prayer as he had, though he was not a praying mole, he offered up: '*Stone, deliver them!*'

While at Caer Caradoc, in the open space amidst the Stones, Thripp seemed close to death, so bitter had been the winds, so determined had been his stance all night. Yet there he had stayed, muttering prayers, staring bleakly into the night until it became dawn, and raising paws as if to try to beat back the elements – perhaps very life itself – that had threatened all moledom that long and dreadful night.

'Master, Master, you cannot do more,' Rolt cried, deserting the

Stone he had been commanded to touch, and going to Thripp's aid.

Thripp shivered and shook, his eyes half closed as he slipped in and out of consciousness, yet still he whispered, 'Stone, help them. Help them, Stone . . .'

Then, as dawn light came and tinged the sleety snow grey-mauve, Rolt led the Elder Senior Brother unresisting to the shelter of the nearest Stone.

'Touch my paw to it, mole, for I have not strength,' whispered Thripp, 'and pray for Duncton Wood.'

Which Rolt did, huddling his body to Thripp's in an effort to warm him, and knowing wonder and awe once more as he felt the Stone's grace and power come into Thripp, and realizing that in this night of prayer and invocation for others, his Master might have found a way to live anew.

'Help us help them . . .' whispered Rolt, one paw round Thripp's weak shoulders, and the other upon the Stone.

At so many other places followers sent out their prayers. But it was with Rooster and Privet that the most ancient of ritual affirmations of the power of life found its expression once more on that first Night of Rising.

Beneath the Stone that Hobsley had led the moles to earlier in the night, Rooster and Whillan delved; above it Privet led the others in meditation and prayers, but as the night went by all of them knew that time was running out.

'The Stone guides, the Stone teaches, but it cannot make moles do. They alone make themselves do that!' Privet said at one point, when the others were flagging. 'Now, think and think again of Duncton, urge the moles there to have strength, ask the Stone to send its power to the followers there, and especially . . . yes, especially to Pumpkin, library aide, brave mole, survivor.'

Oh no, Privet had no doubt that it was around that good mole that tonight's events were circling, for again and again the Stone brought his name to her mind. She knew him, she loved him, and the Stone kept putting an image of him before her: bold, brave, beset but determined.

'Stone, help him to help the others, for I know he'll do his very best. But he'll be full of doubts, so guide him, let him know we are praying for him, guide him . . .'

Weeth, Maple, Madoc and Hobsley joined their prayers to hers, and when she grew tired one or other of them took over from her. All were inspired by the roarings and callings that surrounded the Stone

485

which lay along the ground, its great mass shifting sometimes as the wind about them gathered strength, and the tree roots heaved and stressed in the earth.

Sometimes Privet gave a thought to Rooster and Whillan, unseen, no doubt endangered by the stressing roots about them, but she trusted Rooster. Here he was becoming Master of the Delve once more. This new beginning might make his travails worthwhile. Here the old and the new were one, and if the seasons were turning a little late, well, let it be so. It was the Stone's work he was delving.

Then, as the winds now drove thicker and thicker sleet in among the trees and straight at the praying moles, as if to dislodge them from their stations, Weeth leapt back and cried out, 'Look, moles, look!'

He pointed at the Stone he had been touching with the others, and then one by one they each saw what he had felt: the Stone was moving. Juddering, shaking, heaving in the dawn, and the ground at one end of it, where Rooster had said they must not stance, was shifting, slipping, sinking away.

'Rooster!' screamed Privet. 'Whillan!'

And well she might, well she might.

For down the tunnels about the Stone Whillan and Rooster had found a huge delved chamber, filled with light, and violent disruptive sound. There they had gone, and as Rooster touched the delvings over the walls, Whillan waited for instruction.

'Touch nothing, mole!' Rooster had roared above the noise. 'Only do as I tell you!' But with the sense of danger and doubt so palpable in the air Whillan needed no second telling.

He had watched as Rooster ran his great paws in the shadows and deeps of the delvings, which echoed and shrieked to his touch; he had covered his ears at the sound, and his eyes had watered with its pain.

'Aye,' said Rooster, who went hither and thither in the dark, snouting at roots, touching indentations, feeling the buried part of the Stone which hung above them, and listening to the whining and groaning of the roots that encircled it.

'Aye, this is the Master's work. Born of a lifetime of suffering and love. Born out of darkness to reveal the light. He knew. He knew. Feel this, mole. And this!'

Again and again he summoned Whillan to him, insisting that Whillan felt the delving deeply.

'You learn, mole. You remember. You'll know.'

Then Rooster had been almost silent and still for a time as if listening, when the only word he said was, 'Waiting!'

486

Waiting.

To the occasional sound of the prayers above they waited, into the night, into the darkest delved sound, frightened, wanting to run, the great Stone poised above them.

'Be ready,' growled Rooster. 'Time coming. Need growing. Stone nearly ready.'

But that had been a long time before.

Now dawn was coming, the chamber was lightening, and danger seemed ever more imminent. For above his head Whillan could see that the soil about the Stone was crumbling as the roots entwining it heaved and stressed; at last the Stone did what it had so long threatened, and began to move.

'Not you, you stay!' commanded Rooster.

But . . . There were no buts, and Whillan stared in horror at the massive shifting Stone above his head, and at Rooster at the far end of the chamber.

'Won't fall,' said Rooster grimly, 'but can kill. Root'll hold it if we help.' He pointed at the mass of roots at the Stone's central part which now whined and flexed from the huge winds above.

'What are we waiting for?' Whillan dared ask.

Rooster shrugged. 'Don't know,' he said. 'My first time too. Difference between Master and assistant is that one is trained, the other not. Being not might help. Being trained might help. Don't know!' He grinned, and Whillan felt strangely comforted. They waited.

Now and then snatches of the prayers Privet was speaking were carried down to them: 'Aid . . . forgive . . . help . . . courage . . . love . . .'

Then, quite suddenly, silence. Utter and complete. Rooster frowned, puzzled. Whillan stared at the Stone, which was still, though at a slight angle. All sound was gone – no wind, nothing. Just a few particles of soil and gravel falling from the roof adjacent to the Stone.

> 'Good Stone,
> Deliver them!'

It was Privet's voice, quite clear now, powerful, a plea, a demand, a cry for help, and as it faded the wind-sound began to come back, suddenly rapid, faster and faster, ever faster, and the chamber began to seem to break, and turn, and be destroyed by noise.

'Now, mole, now!' cried Rooster to Whillan, as out on the surface, the eye of the storm having come and now gone, the winds redoubled, and the trees all about the Stone began to creak and whine with the strain.

'Now!' cried Privet, reaching her paws to the others to pull them clear of the Stone.

'Now delve, Whillan, delve!' roared Rooster, pointing at a place where roots heaved down from above on one side of the chamber, while he delved at the other.

'Here?' cried Whillan.

'Delve where your paws tell you!' cried Rooster, and Whillan did, as if delving for his life. To free the roots, to clear the soil, to make way for the shifting Stone which rocked down, up, and down some more, and up again, more and more, closer and closer, almost crushing him, the roar of sound no different in his ears than the savage sight of soil and rock bursting asunder all about him, and all over Rooster it seemed, who stanced as powerful as rock, and root, and Stone, and delved that it might rise.

'Now!' roared Rooster.

'Now,' whispered Whillan through debris and flying fragments.

'Now!' cried Privet as she stanced clear with her friends and they watched as the wind drove blizzard snow hard and ever harder against the Stone which tried and struggled and strove to rise against it. Up, and down; up higher and driven down again, until, resolute, unstoppable, majestic, the Stone rose from the soil, bursting the roots that still held it, throwing debris to right and left, a Stone rising, rising to the sky; rising for all time. *Now* . . .

'Now!' called out Pumpkin into the heart of the High Wood of Duncton, turning back to face Barre and the other Newborns as the Stone seemed to shudder at his plea, and its Light to become the colour of the driven sky.

'Now you will not take us. Now we are not afraid. Now we take our rightful liberty!'

Then, as the Newborns stared dumbstruck, their paws immovable on the ground, Pumpkin turned once more and pointing to the shadows beyond the Stone said calmly to Elynor, 'Lead them there, you will find the way. For these few moments they'll not dare harm us!'

One by one the followers slipped away where he indicated, whilst he turned back yet one more time to out-stare the Newborns, his clear eyes the colour of the Stone, his stance, his body, his spirit a challenge to anymole not to move, not to interfere with the Stone's good work.

Until at last one by one they were gone beyond the Stone and found, as Pumpkin thought they would, the entrance down into the tunnels that led to the Chamber of Roots, ready cleared and prepared by Sturne himself.

Then Cluniac came to him and whispered, 'Sir, they're all below but us now. Come, sir, come while you can.'

Barre opened his mouth, Barre stared at his paw, Barre frowned at the Stone; Barre moved.

'Come along Pumpkin, sir, they're . . . they're going to start again.'

Pumpkin nodded, and half smiled, and turned his back to Barre again, and went quickly to the Stone and touched it.

'Now,' he said at last, 'am I ready to commit myself to the sanctuary of the Ancient System.'

But even as he moved the wild winds drove wet leaves and snow against the Stone's face, and Barre roared, 'Take him! Take that mole!'

Cluniac hurried Pumpkin behind the Stone, thrust him down the short way towards where the portal into the tunnel had been revealed.

'No!' cried Pumpkin, 'you go first!' and he shoved Cluniac through the entrance and down out of sight. Only then did he call out, 'Keeper Sturne! For Stone's sake escape while you can!' for he guessed whichmole had cleared the entrance and made it easy for the old moles to enter. Whatmole else but Sturne and himself knew the place so well?

Then Sturne appeared out of the shadows. 'Go on!' he ordered Pumpkin.

'But they're coming, Sturne, they're coming now!'

Sturne assumed his grimmest and most formidable expression and said, 'As Acting Master of the Library I order you, Library Aide Pumpkin, to go down into the Ancient System and help those refugees to escape. Go, mole! Be gone!'

As mole, Pumpkin would have refused, but as an aide he could not, and he understood why Sturne had to order him.

'Mole,' he said, reaching out, 'you'll be discovered, you'll be identified.'

Sturne replied, 'Perhaps, but I may slow them, and have the satisfaction of knowing I did the best I could: be gone, so I can cover up your tracks.'

Pumpkin ducked into the entrance and joined Cluniac below, and they ran for their lives down the tunnels after the other followers.

On the surface above Sturne did not even try to cover the entrance, for he knew he had no time. There was a crash of undergrowth from the direction of the Stone, and Barre and his two minions were upon him.

'You are accursed,' Sturne began to say, thinking only to slow them.

Barre knew the stance; he knew the voice. He had heard it earlier that night in the Marsh End.

'You!' he cried, his rage almost beyond control.

'Yes, me,' said Sturne.

Then, as other Newborns came racing in, but before they saw what-mole he was, Sturne turned and went down into the portal, and to the tunnel below.

He paused, waiting for Barre and his friends to follow so that he might divert them a little while longer, and Privet and the others get clean away. What matter that he was identified? The followers were safe in the Ancient System, safe for a time: he could do nothing more now but add just a little to their chances.

Yet perhaps, after all, it had not just been for Pumpkin and the followers that the rest of moledom had been praying, but for Sturne as well. Perhaps, too, when he had played at looking like the wrath of the Stone down in the Marsh End, he had invoked something more than images.

Barre chased after him, his outrage on fire once more as he discovered that he had not only been fooled by the puny mole Pumpkin, but by Sturne as well. He swore words of blood and damnation, and he and his two friends dropped down into the tunnel and set off in pursuit after the Librarian.

Sturne knew he had little time left, but at least he might still delay things, so he went as fast as he could, round the ante-chamber that encircles the Chamber of Roots, past portal after portal that led into the Chamber itself.

He did not need to look inside to know what he would see: with such winds, at such a dawn, the roots were a terrible sight. Threshing, twisting, clashing and pulling, they formed a shifting chamber of certain death for any mole who ventured in among them.

'No, no,' thought Sturne, 'that way cannot be. I must slow a little lest I bring Barre to the only other portal out of here into the Chamber of Dark Sound wherein Pumpkin and the others must already be.'

He slowed and glanced back and saw that there was little time left. He would soon be caught, and when he was he had little doubt what his fate would be. Barre's eyes were puffed and red with anger, and his voice rasping and foul in its belligerence.

'Bastard mole! Blasphemer! Liar! I will personally . . .'

Sturne passed the fifth portal, then the sixth, and he saw ahead the seventh to his left, and to his right that dark jagged way through which Pumpkin and the others had fled. Here he must make a last stand, and do his best to give his friends extra time; unless, of course, the Stone chose to punish Barre with Dark Sound, which would be a fitting end for such a mole.

'Pumpkin and the followers should be all right,' he said to himself, as he turned round finally to face his end. 'The Dark Sound will surely not harm them this night of nights. Has not the Stone given them its protection?'

He watched dispassionately as Barre paused in front of him, staring suspiciously about as if he expected an ambush. His friends reached him and together the three began a slow advance. Sturne felt fear. He felt cold. He felt sad. He had saved Pumpkin from death this night, only to engender his own. So this was how it was to be.

Yet something odd was in the air – subtle, strange. He frowned and considered, as Barre came ever nearer, his great ugly paws raised, their talons at the ready.

Sturne looked to the right and saw nothing; to the left and saw nothing. To the left again, for something was odd, something . . .

Sturne stared through the seventh portal in disbelief. The Chamber of Roots was quietening, all sound dying; Silence was coming, and a Light suffused what had been chaos before. Even as he watched, and Barre came nearer, Sturne saw the pattern of roots beyond the portal shift silently, and open into a clear way through.

'Oh!' he sighed, thinking he had never seen anything so peaceful, 'oh yes . . .'

And as Barre reached out to him, and the other two shouted at him, he slipped from their grasp and went through the portal into the Chamber of Roots.

'Don't follow,' he said gently, for whatever else they were, they were moles, and this was not for them.

'Don't follow?' roared Barre mockingly. 'We're going to catch you, mole, and put you to a painful death.'

The roots trembled about Sturne as he ran lightly among them, following the path they opened for him, shifting first one way and then another, huge and massive all about.

'Don't follow, my arse!' cried out one of the guardmoles.

'No!' said Sturne, turning to warn them.

He saw that the route behind him was still clear; Barre entered, his friends following him, despite Sturne's further warning cries. Sturne

491

saw through the roots to right and left a mounting and a shifting, an angry wave of stressing and forcing, as sound came back to the chamber, and danger, and anger – he saw the Stone's wrath made plain.

'Go back!' he warned one final time.

'No!' shouted Barre, reaching out a paw to haul back one of the guards who had seen what was coming from either side, had understood the danger and was trying to retreat, 'no . . . !'

Then the dark roots took them before Sturne's eyes, swift and most terrible. The fleeing guardmole first, torn from Barre's grasp by a tangle of roots, turned sideways, pushed forward and down as he began to scream with pain.

Then the second, upended, mouth open, eyes wide with fear, snout twisted and torn from his head by roots that seemed alive with rage.

'No!' prayed Sturne, for nomole should suffer thus, whatever they have done.

While Barre, who had turned to his guardmoles, was as yet untouched, he saw them torn and crushed to death before his eyes. He turned towards Sturne once more, his mouth opening into a plea, his paw reaching forward as a pup who knows he has done wrong might reach up to his mother – and then the first root took him. Suddenly he was dragged sideways, turning, roaring in shock and pain as a second grew taut and struck him back again. Then, worse than anything yet, three roots closed on him, their massive forms almost gentle as he strove to struggle free of them, but they held him tight. Then as wind-sound roared through the chamber they took him up vertically, twisted him, turned him, held him, and slowly began to squeeze.

Every detail of that slow death Sturne saw, his cries to the Stone to save the Brother Inquisitor unheeded. How long did he feel the crush of roots about his chest and head? Too long. How long did he know the extremity of pain? Too long. How long was Barre conscious? For too long.

His mouth was forced into a stretching grin, his head began to go squat, his eyes bulged and blinked obscenely, his tongue pushed out, his paws grew fat with his own blood before the roots cast him down and he lay screaming on the riven floor, blood and muck pouring from his snout. Then, mercilessly, he was taken up once more as the roots began to make him of their own. And where he had been blood ran down, and was lost in the shifting soil.

Nor was that all. As Sturne stared up into the dark roof of the

Chamber of Roots, in the shadows there, in the deeps, he saw the lost eyes of a mole; he saw them stare, and heard a voice squeak out its hopeless plea for mercy from an agony for which the only cure would be death, and terribly, so terribly, he saw that thing which Barre had become. Caught, half crushed, immobile, misshapen by the roots, teeth splaying out, tongue half bitten off, his belly split and gaping, guts spilling, yet living long enough to know what the roots had made him, and to become insane.

Much later as it seemed to Sturne that crushed creature which had once been Barre laughed the unfunniest laugh Sturne ever heard; the roots shifted once again, and there came the final scream into death of a mole lost to his own cursed self.

How long Sturne stayed where he slumped down then, bereft at what he saw, he did not know. The roots shifted and vibrated about him. Then they opened once more, but not to let him out, rather to urge him on. Peace was come, and Silence of a kind, and renewing Light.

He followed the way the roots made for him, and reached the inner part of the chamber. He saw the great vertical thrust of the Stone above him, he saw ancient, quieter roots across the ground; peace came over him, and he knew he had nearly reached the inner sanctum of the Stone.

Summoned to go forward, he went, slowly and falteringly and filled with awe. The roof seemed cavernous above him, the Stone's base enormous, and he felt tiny by comparison. Light glimmered ahead, shadows were without darkness, colours were gentle and changing and without name. He clambered over roots, he ducked under rocky overhangs, he reached out a paw to pull himself forward and then, turning a corner, he knew what he would see.

They were there in their circle, the seven Stillstones, and the six Books so far found. There in their places to form the circle of harmony which is moledom's gift from the Stone itself. There for him to see.

'You are worthy, mole,' the Silence seemed to say, 'worthy to be Stour's successor. He entrusted you with a task you have fulfilled and now you are the worthy Master of the Library in his place. Sturne . . .'

And the roots shifted, and the Stone, and he heard his name called from out of the Silence.

'Now your own last task begins, Master Librarian. To wait and to watch, to guide and to protect, for now is the Book of Silence being made ready to come to ground.'

493

Light was on his face and on his paws, the holy Light of Silence. He saw where the one place empty of a Book remained, before it a single stone, not large, but shimmering.

'The Stillstone of Silence,' he whispered, knowing well its tale. 'I will strive to fulfil all you ask of me,' he whispered, and he reached out his paw and put it near the place where one day the Book might be.

Darkness, heaviness, danger, and terrible fear were his for a moment.

'I will do my best,' he said, withdrawing his paw.

'It is all we ever ask,' the Silence whispered. 'Now sleep, mole, sleep, and be at peace, for your friends are safe now, where they will not be found.'

'Sleep,' whispered Pumpkin later, 'all I want is sleep, but—'

'But nothing, mole,' said Elynor, holding him. 'We're safe now, nomole will find us here, and the Stone watches over us in this place to which you led us. So sleep, mole.'

Deep in the Ancient System, in tunnels whose ways they could not easily retrace, and whose sound was now as gentle as a mother's song, Pumpkin and his friends found sanctuary.

'Sleep,' Elynor said, and her eyes closed, and Cluniac's, and all those who had dared to travel with them slept as well.

'Mustn't . . .' whispered Pumpkin; but he did, deeply. The sleep of the just and the brave.

Sleep might have been that dawn's name amongst the many moles who had answered Pumpkin's plea for help. At Fyfield, Tonner slept out in the snow as if he were in the deepest, warmest, safest nest. The Stone watched over him.

At Beechenhill three moles slept, their vigil over, their tired limbs just carrying them to shelter, their minds at peace.

On Caer Caradoc Rolt fell asleep even as he led Thripp to the safety of the tunnels, and the winds above him began to ease.

'Sleep, mole,' said Thripp, sighing, 'for your night's work is well done. But now I must think.' Perhaps so, but for now he too slept.

While north of them, at Hobsley's Coppice, seven moles stared up at the risen Stone. All were tired, but now their delvings and their prayers were done. Moledom was ready for the winter years, and those in peril were surely safe for now.

'Come,' said Hobsley, 'there's a chamber big enough for all of us. We'll sleep, and then, well, whatmole knows . . . ?'

He led his weary guests from the Stone, through the trees which fretted still with the winds that had rushed by and all but gone, and showed them the chamber where they could rest. Down they went, eyes already closing, down towards slumber, one after the other, until only Rooster and Privet were left awake, while Weeth, troubled by the night's events, it seemed, lingered outside.

'Haven't talked much since I found you again,' said Rooster.

'Haven't talked at all, my love.'

'Talked to Whillan! I delved with him! He's got the delving touch. Can sound a delving once he's been shown.'

'You didn't tell him?'

'Did. Some. Not all. Such knowledge proved too much for me. He'll find out.'

'Rooster, what didn't you tell him?'

Rooster was silent, and Privet suddenly concerned.

'What do you know about him you haven't said? It's more than his delving skill, isn't it?'

'Can't say. Won't . . .' But Rooster said no more.

A deep listening silence followed, and then the whisper of winter wind. Old thoughts that must be allowed a space to die . . . and new thoughts, new insights.

'My Sister Lime . . . and the way you loved her,' said Privet at last.

'Yes . . .'

'Tell me everything, tell me now, here in the dark.'

'Will,' said Rooster. 'Want to. She was with pup. Mine. My own. All lost now, all gone.'

She felt his tears as he felt hers. New insights . . . something she had begun to . . . to *know*. But had *he* seen it yet?

She glanced across the chamber to where Whillan lay, his paws about Madoc, both deep asleep. Did Rooster . . . ?

'Privet,' a voice whispered from the darkness near the entrance to the chamber. 'Privet . . .'

It was Weeth.

'What is it, mole?' said Rooster, stirring reluctantly.

'I would talk with Privet, mole. Just for a moment . . .'

Rooster sighed, reluctant to break the moment of intimacy with Privet, and perhaps wondering what could be so important after so much had happened and all moles wanted to do was rest, and sleep.

'It will take but a moment . . .'

Privet went to Weeth, already guessing what it might be he wanted to say. No, *knowing* what it was. The two of them whispered, both looked at Rooster, both looked beyond him to Whillan, and Rooster rose uneasily.

'What? What do you know?' he asked.

Privet came to him, and Weeth as well. 'It's Whillan, Rooster,' said Privet.

'Yes?'

'You've heard how he came to Duncton Wood?'

'Something.'

'A female came in April, she gave birth to pups at the very entrance to the system. Master Stour found them but only one survived.'

'Yes,' said Rooster. He was suddenly very still, and his eyes shone strangely.

'I believe that female . . .' began Privet.

'It's only a surmise,' offered Weeth.

'That female was almost certainly my sister Lime,' whispered Privet. 'I thought it before, and often wondered why moles said Whillan looked a little like me . . .'

'And he delves,' said Rooster softly, 'like he was born to it. If he's Lime's . . .'

'He's yours, my dear,' said Privet.

'Mine,' rasped Rooster, turning almost wildly towards where Whillan lay. 'My . . .'

Silent, transfixed, Privet and Weeth watched as Rooster went to Whillan's flank. He stared down at him, huge, shadowed, mouth open, as he reached out one of his paws to touch what he thought he had lost for ever.

Madoc shifted and Whillan stirred, and whispered, 'What is it . . . ?' Perhaps he saw the shadow of Rooster's gentle paw across his face, for he opened his eyes and drowsily repeated, 'What is it . . . ?'

'Is nothing,' said Rooster in a broken voice, 'is nothing, mole. Sleep . . .'

Whillan smiled, turned to Madoc, tightened his grip on her and whispered, 'It's nothing then,' and slept.

'Is nothing and is everything,' said Rooster gently, and his voice was a father's who sees for the first time his first-born pup.

Weeth reached a paw to Privet's and squeezing it smiled at her and then was gone to other shadows, to leave them alone, and to find sleep himself.

Privet watched Rooster but did not move. The great mole stared at his son in disbelief, doubting it still, yet knowing it was true in his innermost being; as a delver he knew it, and it felt as certain as a true line delved.

At last he turned back to Privet and she saw a new look in his face and eyes, as of a mole who has found his way once more. How long his dark journey had been, how hard.

'Privet . . .' was all he needed to say before he held her, and she him, and there was no need more for talk now.

Sleep became theirs as well, and talk would wait as they knew peace in each other's paws again, and out on the surface above them, and far beyond, the winter advanced across moledom and snow began to turn to ice.

While across moledom too, the Stones rose towards the sky, silent, watchful; at all of them the seasons had turned, and the light of a new season was rising upon them. At the Stone of Beechenhill, and the ring of Stones at Rollright, light; at the Stone of Fyfield, and the Stones of Siabod and of Avebury, and of Caer Caradoc, light.

At the newest Stone, which had risen into the dawn of Hobsley's Coppice, and at the most ancient Stone of all, which rises amidst the high trees of Duncton Wood, light and peace.

There too the winter wind whispers of brave moles and true; and of a Book of Silence for which allmole has waited these centuries past, and for whose coming new hope has risen.

EPILOGUE

So, mole, Pumpkin sought the Stone's help, and with a little assistance from friends he knew (and some he didn't) he found it.

Now you want me to continue without a pause at all. You look around this Stone Clearing of ours as if you hope to find the rest of our tale hiding under the fallen trees, or lurking over there among the roots of that great beech.

You're out of luck, which is a pity, for if only leaves and roots and tunnels and trees could talk, what tales would we moles hear! You must make do with me, and now I'm sleepy and night is drawing in. I'm not like the moles of our inspiring tale of Duncton Rising who seem able to stay awake till dawn. No, no, I'm a little more traditional.

But don't worry, we've not followed Pumpkin the long way on his journey only to abandon him in the lost and forgotten tunnels of the Ancient System! Nor have we forsaken those other moles like Privet and Rooster, who still have much to do if they are to find the Book of Silence, and bring it home to Duncton Wood.

No, no, mole, you've still some scribing down to do if you're to discover the truth of their brave lives, for isn't that your task? I tell, you scribe!

Thripp? Yes, I'll tell of him as well.

And Quail, and Skua, and the vile Squelch, and Fetter, and all other moles of ill-intent and misguided thoughts. As I have said before, you don't find light without shadow, you can't have warmth without some cold.

Talking of which, the sun declines, and so do I, and a worm or two would now not be amiss. That's your task too, to find me food! Mine? To make my way to where I'll be comfortable, to think, and to remember those times of which I tell, and will return to on the morrow. Before then, sleep . . .

But if the moon rises bright tonight, as I think it will, and your mind is too active for you to sleep, then by all means come back up here to the Stone and stance in silence near it. It may speak to you for all I know, it may even whisper your name. Who can say? Not I!

But of our tale, well . . . it would not surprise me one little bit if all things end as they began, here, by the Duncton Stone.

William Horwood

DUNCTON STONE

VOLUME THREE OF
THE BOOK OF SILENCE

As Pumpkin, library aide extraordinary, leads the followers against the Newborns into retreat in Duncton Wood, all Moledom awaits the coming of the lost Book of Silence.

But Elder Senior Brother Thripp has been displaced by the loathsome Brother Inquisitor Quail and the cruel Skua, and the sectarian Newborns are in the ascendancy. The only hope seems to lie with the scholar and scribemole Privet, with her lost love Rooster, Master of the Delve, and with the Duncton warrior Maple. When they are separated once more and Privet disappears, all hope for Moledom and for the return of the Book of Silence seems lost for ever.

Yet always the Light and Silence of Duncton's fabled Stone beckons, offering hope to all moles with the courage to confront their faith, and a final chance to discover the truth of the Book of Silence.

Duncton Stone is the last tale of moles whose task is the discovery of truth, but whose hope is only that one day they may return home safeguarded.

DUNCTON STONE
will be available in hardback from
HarperCollins*Publishers*
in Spring 1993

PUBLISHER'S NOTE

Since *Duncton Wood* was first published in 1980, William Horwood has received thousands of letters from readers asking about the conception and writing of what has become a fantasy classic. Readers who would like more details of his work should write to William Horwood at P.O. Box 446, Oxford, OX1 2SS.